LAKE SPARK

The Complete Collection Volume 2

EVEY LYON

THE LAKE SPARK WORLD

CONTENTS

WAITING TO SCORE

WAITING TO SCORE

AUTHOR'S NOTE

Welcome to Lake Spark during the off-season! This is a spin-off series of Lake Spark. **You do not need to have read the Lake Spark series to enjoy the off-season series.** Will you get a special feeling from the cameos if your read the Lake Spark series? Absolutely.

Whereas Lake Spark focused on neighbors and various sports, this series focuses on a new group of next-generation characters, new faces, and only hockey.

Waiting to Score takes place where Worth the Wait ended—six years in the future from the previous series. Violet first appeared in Worth the Wait as Ford's little sister, and she is now the one to fall in love in an unconventional and lighthearted way in Waiting to Score.

1

DECLAN

Loosening the collar of my crisp white shirt is priority number one as soon as I get out of this arena.

But the tie around my neck is a reminder of many things.

For one, professional hockey players wear suits to show respect for the game, and during my time as the captain of the Chicago Spinners, I was most certainly no exception. But those days are over, and now I need to focus on a new way to occupy my time, and it just so happens that today required a tie.

The paperwork still needs to be finalized, but, nonetheless, a proud smirk wants to escape me as I walk through the Chicago arena's empty halls. Hockey will always be in my blood, which is why when the ink dries, I'll be the new owner of the Spinners.

I'm sure there will be opinions, there always are. Like when most people assumed that Declan Dash's parents bought a position for their son on a professional hockey team, but I proved them wrong with every winning goal until I held the title of Captain. And now I have the ultimate F-you to all the naysayers.

The perfect timing was presented to me when the former owner sadly, unexpectedly passed at the end of last season, which led to a quick sale. With my retirement status looming and contract ending, I put in a highball offer on impulse, thanks to the cashflow of my hockey career, family money, and an app investment from years ago.

Now I'm striding through a hallway as the man on top.

"Declan," I hear a familiar voice call out my name.

Turning back, I'm greeted by the legend himself, Ford Spears, in jeans and a T-shirt. I was lucky to have him be my mentor during my early years on the Spinners before he retired. I consider him a friend; we have dinner together every few weeks or so.

"Hey!" I greet him with a side hug, as two men who have high-caliber sportsmanship and friendship would.

"One step closer?" He raises a brow at me.

I try to control my grin. "Maybe," I say, playing it cool. Rumors run rampant, but I'm under agreement not to discuss my latest career move until everything is officially announced. Truth be told, the former owner was neither great nor bad at his role, but fate seemed to step in to give the team a change. That's what I'm going to bring to the table.

"Either way, don't forget that you promised to help with the summer camp this year." He gives me a pointed look.

I beam, holding my hands up in surrender. "I would never forget. It's for a good cause." When Ford retired a few years ago, he moved to Lake Spark to run a sports complex. His training facility includes teaching skill development for players and summer camps for kids that every one of our teammates, present and past, volunteers at for a few days. I just skipped the last few years due to other commitments, so I owe him a week for sure.

"What brings you to the city?" I wonder.

"Just met with the marketing department about arranging a charity event later in the year out in Lake Spark. Plus, I need to pick up some supplies for the wifey. She's decided that baby number three gets a space-themed nursery to try and see if we will actually have a son who doesn't enjoy hockey." Ford smiles proudly as he swipes his hand—his wedding ring visibly shining—across his stubbled jaw.

"There you are!" A woman's voice breaks our conversation, and we both look to our side.

Well, my day just got better.

Ford's younger sister, Violet, saunters over, and her striking looks have my eyes instantly committed to staring at her more than I should.

Her sparkly blue eyes greet me with a glimmer of curiosity, which is highlighted by the dark hair framing her face. Her expression appears neutral to me, and it's throwing me for a loop wondering what she thinks of my presence.

"Violet saved my ass by joining me in Chicago to handle the shopping and promised to meet me here," Ford explains. Lake Spark is a small town about two hours from here if traffic isn't a pain, and the last I heard, Violet moved there to be close to her brother.

She quickly interjects and nudges her brother's arm. "Because you owe me lunch before I bid you farewell and meet my friend for our concert tonight." Violet clears her throat and turns her attention to me again. "Hey, Dec, long time no see."

Nobody calls me that. Nor do I seem to care in this moment. She can call me whatever she wants, and I'll answer either way.

"I think that's the point. Your brother has a strict rule that no hockey player should go within a five-mile radius of you, not even just to say hi," I joke, but we all know that it's true.

I'd be lying if I said I didn't find Violet attractive, but Ford always made it clear that hockey players shouldn't go near her, which made sense since she was in college when he played, and not every man on our team had noble intentions.

Including me.

But I've been respectable to her through the years when I've seen her around, always a gentleman, except for the occasional flirty remark to test the waters for the very unrespectable fantasies in my head.

"Excuse me for watching out for my little sister, as any big brother would. Only guys who bring their A-game and honorable intentions will do," Ford states, while Violet just rolls her eyes.

I glance at my watch, knowing that as much as I would like to figure out if Violet is wearing black lingerie underneath her pink dress, I have things to do and places to be.

"I guess Ford is aiming for the big-brother-of-the-year award. Anyhow, I need to run, but we'll catch up soon." I offer my hand to Ford for one of our team shakes.

"For sure," he promises.

My eyes land on Violet again, whose lashes flutter as she offers me a half-smile, and I still can't pinpoint why her eyes on me feel heavy, yet playful. It's a thought I should probably ignore.

Even when I walk away and notice that she's watching me leave.

———

FINALLY, this damn tie can go. The rest of my suit stays.

"Are you ready for tonight?" My childhood friend Brent gives me a devilish grin as he greets me in his front hall, mirroring my dress code, with his hair slicked back. A subtle sound of electric house music plays in the background.

This is one of *those* parties that involve a bowl with names to pick.

The invite list is carefully vetted, and everyone here knows they will be leaving with someone.

It's not that I do this on a weekly or even monthly basis, but this isn't my first.

Sometimes, you just need to indulge in a wild night.

"This is exactly what I need today," I admit.

I undo the top button of my shirt, relieved I ditched the tie during the elevator ride.

Brent pats my shoulder, indicating to follow. "Come on, we need to get you something strong to drink before a night of debauchery."

I walk through the penthouse, taking in the familiar surroundings. Floor-to-ceiling windows offer exquisite views of Chicago at night, with little specks of light scattered in the foggy night air outside, as we are so high up in the building.

Making our way down the hall into the kitchen, I trail behind Brent to the island counter where he instantly begins to pour a fresh glass of Scotch, while my eyes scan the room. Everyone is dressed to affect, because impressions count.

Brent has a strict protocol for choosing guests, and he can be brutal with his criticism too. Nobody here would call themselves committed in a relationship with someone, and they purely enjoy the thrill of this setup.

He hands me my drink with a smirk, and his eyes narrow in on me.

"Thanks," I say. Taking a sip, the burn hits my tongue just right, but my eyes do a double take back to Brent who seems to have intel he's holding onto. "Something you want to share?"

"In a few minutes we will get this show going." Brent gives me an assuring nod, but his look is indescribable. "Did you see who just walked into the kitchen?"

I didn't take much notice of faces when I came in, since a drink felt like the priority.

I turn around and notice a pair of legs that I missed in my assessment of the scene. A pair of legs that has me invested to explore further, which is why my sight draws a line up from her black stiletto heels, along her defined smooth legs, to her pink dress. It's different than before, better. This magnificent journey of exploration ends when my eyes land on her lush lips stained with dark pink lipstick.

But her cute mouth isn't the only thing familiar. It's her blue eyes that hit a button somewhere inside of me, just as they did earlier today. Those curious eyes that wander the room, taking in her surroundings.

She's standing there, patiently waiting, like a doe lost in the forest.

And I'm the big bad wolf.

She is the last person I would ever expect to see here.

Violet Spears.

●2

DECLAN

I pause with my lips on the rim of my glass.

"I know, I'm surprised too," Brent mentions, glancing over his shoulder in Violet's direction.

I can't tear my eyes away from her. "How the hell did she end up here?" My voice is half-edged and half... well, intrigued, far too much.

"Her brother would go through the roof."

My eyes whip to Brent's. "Again. Why is she here?" Now my voice is clipped.

"Violet knows Charlotte, and you know I can't say no to Charlotte when she requests an extra invite."

I rub a hand across my jaw from his explanation. "Thank fuck for the NDAs that we all sign." I'm not even joking.

This woman, oblivious to my gaze, is completely off-limits.

But since I'm no longer her brother's off-limits hockey player friend and everything stays between these walls, then I have no problem looking a little longer at her, trying to comprehend how in the world she wound up standing before me twice today.

She's a bad idea, but I'm the selfish guy who ignores potential alarms when the parameters allow… as in the rules of this party preventing anyone from finding out.

Lucky me, the parameters allow.

Violet's eyes catch with mine and blaze in recognition. She looks away quickly but then back to me, as there is no escape.

She's been caught, and I've been caught.

My interest is far too piqued, because she doesn't strike me as someone who would come to these types of parties, and my guess is that this is her first.

"Knew you would love the guest list," Brent speaks low before I move.

I'm too confident of a guy to pretend to ignore this coincidence of being at the same party, which is why I stride my way toward Violet, with her eyes now glued on me as I approach her.

Planting my feet next to her, standing side by side, I notice the way her breath catches and her body flinches in my presence.

"Violet," I greet her firmly, with a sinister laugh brewing in the back of my throat.

"Declan." She returns the tone but doesn't look at me.

"I thought you had a concert tonight. This is the last place I would have guessed to run into you."

"A little white lie. I doubt my brother would enjoy the specifics of what I'm doing tonight. Charlotte is a friend of mine; we went to college together." I've never hooked up with Charlotte, but Brent loves to. Apparently, Charlotte is wild, and she's married to her job in marketing and detests relationships as much as Brent.

My eyes roam the room to see if anyone takes notice of us, which they don't.

"Brent and I have known one another for years. You do know that nobody leaves this party alone, right?" I tell her, and it doesn't surprise me that it comes out almost as a dare, because I've thought about bending her over a few times through the years, in various ways.

She turns her body to me and gives me, I swear, a seductive smirk. "I do know that." She pauses for a second while her demeanor turns relaxed. "How are you, Declan? I didn't get to ask earlier. It was your last season of hockey. All good?" Her tone is purely genuine, soft, and it's refreshing because nobody ever asks me like they truly care.

I half-smile. "We're at a sex party, and you're asking me how I am?"

"Why not?" She shrugs.

"Your brother wouldn't be thrilled if he found out you were standing before me."

Her smirk turns humorous. "Considering you telling him would immediately reveal what you get up to in your free time, then I severely doubt he'll find out. Besides, nobody wants to talk to their friend about their little sister's sex life. Not to mention the contract we all signed," she challenges with a cocked brow.

I like her bite. "True. But *why* are you here?"

"Why are *you* here?" she counters.

I have no qualms revealing the truth. "I'm a man with needs who enjoys a beautiful woman. I don't do relationships and don't go for the puck bunny bullshit; I have a little more class than that."

Violet scoffs a laugh. "Wow, that's some honesty."

I have to quirk my lips and squint an eye to study her. "You've done this before?"

She crosses her arms over her chest, which doesn't help this situation, as it draws my eyes to her pert cleavage, and she taps her arms with her dark pink nails. "There is a first for everything." I admire her candor and the hint of assurance in her voice. "Everyone is allowed to live a little. There are many things in life that scare me, and this little rendezvous of an evening is not one of them."

"What does scare you then?"

She side-eyes me. "Birds. Freaking hate them."

I chuckle. "Any bird in particular or all birds?"

"All. I just have a complete trauma thanks to Hitchcock."

"Fair enough. I hate maple syrup, if it's any comparison."

She snorts an adorable laugh. "Doesn't your family own Grizzly Dash, that maple syrup company?"

"That and a bunch of hotels. But maple syrup is… sticky and too sweet."

"Many delicious things in life are sticky and sweet… it's natural." Her tone is floaty and seeping with innuendo.

"I like your philosophy." And her dirty mind.

Her head lolls to the side slightly. "What *really* scares you?"

I have to rile her as my mouth curves up. "That you'll end up with me tonight."

She glances at me with her wistful eyes. "The odds of that are slim."

"Want to bet on it?" I challenge.

She lets a chortle escape her edible mouth. "Not really, no."

I step closer to her, eager to touch her arm and feel her skin that looks silky. Leaning in, I whisper, "That's a shame, it could be fun." I let my lips gently graze her cheek, desperately wanting a little nibble before I step away.

Her breath changes as she straightens her back; she's affected, which was my goal, so I take another step back to create space, admiring the goosebumps spreading down her arms, and I enjoy my victorious smirk that I'm now entitled to take.

Our eyes hold, but we are interrupted by the sound of a glass clinking.

Brent is standing on his coffee table, tapping a drink glass with a fork. "Ladies and gentlemen, shall we get started?" He grins.

The small crowd gathers around him, and my eyes remain laser-focused on the prize I know I want.

———

WE GET to the final two couples, and the four of us stand in a square, as if fate has already paired us off. Brent next to Charlotte, and Violet near me.

Violet's eyes darken as her eyes shift to mine. I'm not sure if Brent picks up on this or if he heard me once mention how it would be good to screw Violet into oblivion to get what I need out of my system, but Brent gives me a confident look.

"Well, ladies, last draw." Brent smiles at Charlotte and Violet. Charlotte is all game, even nudges Violet's arm in excitement, but Violet looks nervous as she nibbles her bottom lip.

Odds are completely in my favor.

Brent slowly pulls the paper up to reveal his name. Then he looks between all of us as he draws a paper up from the other glass bowl, moving inch by inch to draw this out, making me nervous that he'll pull the wrong name, because random my ass, I'm counting on luck.

"And the name is… Charlotte." He displays the paper.

Relief hits me. Looks like he gets his wish, and I'm not complaining either.

I immediately turn to my prize who parts her mouth gently, hoods her eyes, and then opens them in slight disbelief. She can't seem to look at me as she breathes a long inhale.

As Charlotte and Brent leave with their hands interlaced, eager as can be, I soak in our newfound silence as I pull the last two papers, one from each bowl, with our names on them.

I step into Violet's space. "Well, look at that. You and me." I'm smug, and she focuses on our names scribbled on the paper with a droll smile gracing her luscious lips.

As I move closer to her, it causes her to stand taller. "Rules are rules, Violet," I taunt her with a breathy whisper into her ear, and I feel her tremble in my presence. She smells like fresh-cut flowers, and it tingles my nose, and for a split second, I'm not sure what the play is for this game book.

She stares directly into my eyes, and anticipation is already flowing to my dick.

"You and me, it seems," she whispers huskily then swallows, before she surprises me by yanking my arm to drag me with her toward the hall, with her heels clicking at a fast pace.

Brent is worth millions, so it is only fitting that his place has exactly five bedrooms, along with an office that I'm sure someone is using without care for a lack of a bed. I mean, there is a nice leather sofa in there.

We're already alone in the hall, as most head straight into what they came for. I grab Violet's wrist to stop her and swiftly spin her until she's pressed against the wall, with my hand fitting perfectly against her hip. She's warm to the touch, and her whimper from the element of surprise sends a promising surge through me.

But I gotta be virtuous for one sec.

"This is where I throw you over my shoulder and get you the fuck out of here, out of respect for your brother," I grit out because I hate throwing in a yellow card right now.

"No!" she is quick to reply, nearly panicked.

"Ah, so you do want to be here and with me?"

A sly, sexy-as-fuck smirk takes form on her mouth, a confidence that feels new. "What if I say I'm not complaining?"

"Consent. I need to hear you say it." I'm direct, but damn, my voice swelters with heat.

"Yes. I'm here and with you, apparently." She escapes my hold and reaches out with her fingers to touch my chest under the sides of my suit jacket.

I tilt my head slightly to the side. "Did you know I was going to be here?" This coincidence has me slightly in disbelief.

She shakes her head and chides, "Rules are rules." Of course, none of us knew exactly who would be here until we arrived. Her fingers are playing with my buttons, and I hope she breaks every single damn one of them tonight.

"Vi, a woman like you should be getting wined and dined by some lawyer who plans on buying you a house in the suburbs."

She laughs nervously. "A woman like me deserves to explore… things. And I doubt I would find this opportunity in Lake Spark."

I'm not going to question her more; it's not in me to knock down someone's sexual confidence, which she clearly has.

Her brother would kill me. But I don't seem to care about that at this moment.

Especially when I feel Violet's body warmth mingle with mine and notice when she steps closer, inviting me to snap and ravish her.

"Not here, sweetheart, let's go," I inform her, grabbing her arm and dragging her with me.

"What, why?" she protests.

I don't answer, instead continuing our journey to the front door. I see the line of purses on the side table, and I indicate for Violet to grab hers.

When we go into the hall near the elevator, I pin her against the wall, this time pressing my body against her middle that makes her jolt and let out a gasp.

"I know this is your first time doing something like this, and by all means, I can take you into Brent's guest room. But at some point, you will have to face everyone when you leave, and as much as I appreciate the idea of them knowing how much you enjoyed having my cock inside of you all night, I'm going to show one ounce of respect for our delicate dynamic tonight."

I'm direct as I trace her mouth with my finger. Her hot breath hits my flesh, making me slightly delirious, imagining her mouth spreading heat down my chest until she goes lower where I like it the most.

Her bottom lip falls, her eyes near pleading, and I'm doing my damnedest not to slam my mouth onto hers.

Not yet, anyhow.

"My place is up one floor, has a better view too. The rules apply for the night. You and I will be more comfortable there," I clarify.

"What if I say that takes away from the experience?" she dares. "Isn't the whole point that maybe I get a glimpse or hear someone else and vice versa?"

Nuh-uh, I draw a line at the idea of anyone spying on her. Something inside of me doesn't like that thought. She's mine for tonight, only mine.

I huff a chuckle. "You're a bit wilder than I anticipated. Kind of had you pegged for being vanilla, an on-your-back-in-bed kind of girl."

Her mouth falls open in humorous offense. "You may just be a piece of work."

Stepping between her legs, my hand lands on her inner thigh, causing her to gasp. Slowly, I trail my fingers up her bare skin until I feel the heat of her soaked panties that I run my thumb along, her body writhing against my touch as her breath catches.

"Which apparently you love." Fuck, I feel like I may crawl out of my skin if I can't dip a finger inside of her stat.

That hint of flowers on her skin occupies my brain. *I bet she tastes like rose water*, that's what comes to my mind. My tongue will discover soon enough.

Because lucky for me, tonight is about pure pleasure with the unexpected surprise that is my friend's little sister.

3

VIOLET

The first time I decide to try something outside of my norm, and my brother's ridiculously handsome friend has to be the guy whose name is pulled out of a bowl?

There are *most definitely* worse things in life. I'm just not used to this kind of luck.

Just watching Declan swagger into his penthouse has me ready to tear his clothes off.

A voice somewhere, no clue where, probably inside my head, that I choose to ignore reminds me that this guy is the poster of everything my brother has warned me against, and friends would roll their eyes too, knowing that he's trouble.

Following Declan into his living room, I see the place has expensive leather furniture and fancy art on the walls. I don't take much notice, as I enjoy watching him throw his suit jacket to the sofa without a care that it will wrinkle. Declan's sandy brown hair is combed back, screaming for me to run my fingers through it, and it looks soft to play with. Just like his lips that currently display a wry smile, while his piercing blue eyes seem to be assessing me.

Because rules are rules, and we are one another's prize.

This brings me back to the thought that I have no complaints that this is how the night ended up.

My heart is pounding from anticipation. I was prepared for sex with a stranger, not a man I see at my brother's yearly holiday party.

A man who just took a calculated step in my direction.

Gulp.

"Last chance for an out," he says as he begins to undo the cufflinks at his wrists, preparing himself for whatever ideas he has in his head.

"I'm still here." I sound confident, but my stomach just flipped.

Remember why you are here.

Reaching behind my back, I find the zipper on my carefully chosen dress, and with one tug of my fingers, I slowly pull down. My thoughts go through my reasoning as the zip comes undone, tooth by tooth.

I'm single, life is merely a routine lately, and the pool of men in Lake Spark is lacking. I miss sex. Like, a lot. When Charlotte mentioned her plans, I was intrigued and turned on. I'm not against trying new things. A perfect escape from the ordinary.

I carefully studied the list of rules, and I signed on the dotted line with no hesitation, which I have no regret over.

Relief and nerves twist inside of me. Not going to lie, the idea of sex with a stranger you just met was daunting, and I wasn't sure it was for me, and luckily, I went in knowing there was always an out, as the rules value your choice. But Declan deleted the random-man factor and brought familiar to the table. Maybe too familiar, because I'm far too excited that it's him.

I'm a complete beginner at this kind of thing, but Declan's look informs me that this whole setup is ordinary for him. He seems willing to guide me.

My spine straightens when his finger presses firmly against my lips, indicating that I shouldn't speak, only listen.

"I'm not going to sugarcoat this. Tonight is slightly out of the usual for me, in terms of my knowing you a little more than I probably should, considering what I'm about to do to you." He tips his head gently to the side and a scoff escapes his mouth. "Why on earth would a party like this interest you, Violet?"

I'm not afraid nor shy of this man, maybe slightly in awe. Which doesn't make sense either, because I'm used to hockey players, so starstruck isn't me. If I had to pinpoint it, it's his confidence in this situation, probably because I'm about to match it, and I'm not used to that. Not many guys can handle me.

Feeling bold, I dart the tip of my tongue between my lips to touch his finger, a mere poke, causing Declan's eyes to blaze in surprise as he attempts to anticipate my next move.

I wrap my lips around his finger to suck, with one long stroke of my tongue, ensuring my eyes stay fixed with his, before I pop my lips off. "Stop questioning me, because I'm not making assumptions of why you do this, and trust me, I could make plenty." My voice feels heavy with a yearning for us to move faster.

He chuckles under his breath, shifting his focus to his watch that he begins to undo. "Fine. I'll just assume you are living a mundane small-town life and needed a thrill. You decided to play this game and got damn fortunate by ending up with me." He holds his watch up before clasping his hand around it to place it in his pocket.

"You just assume that then."

Truth be told, he nailed his theory. I love Lake Spark. I moved there to be closer to my brother and his growing family. Despite living in Ford's shadow, I hold no resentment, and he's key to my life. Not to mention, there was a perfect little store on Main Street that was calling my name.

"You're not the type of woman to be fucked by a stranger." Declan begins to unbutton his shirt.

I shimmy my dress down my body. "Do I even want to know what type of woman you think that is?" I step out of my dress in front of this man as if this is a normal occurrence.

He discards his shirt to the side, not even blinking an eye as he examines me in my black bra-and-panty set. "You smell like expensive roses, not perfume, but natural. You don't need to put in the effort with your looks, and your smile is sweet. You're the woman that some guy will bring home to meet his parents, which means you should never settle for someone who doesn't give you conversation and effort."

My eyes widen at his explanation. I should be flattered.

Dragging my hair to one side, I turn to offer him the clasp of my bra. "I do smell of expensive roses, because I own a flower shop." I tremble slightly when he takes his time to unhook the strap, the back of his finger sliding along my skin, lingering and causing a ripple in my body, including my nipples that now peak.

"That's what you do?"

"You never talk about me with Ford?"

"It rings a bell now from what your brother has mentioned, but I don't make a habit of taking interest in a woman that I can't fuck, to be honest."

I have to smile to myself. I never knew he was so candid.

"But now you can have me," I state the obvious.

Purposely, I wait to turn and face him, instead sliding the straps of my bra off my shoulders to toss the garment to the floor.

"I'm happy you highlight that. I would hate to be the boyfriend who can't impress you with flowers since you own the flower shop," he says metaphorically.

I chuckle softly. "Just means he has to be creative to catch my attention."

I should feel vulnerable right now, but it's only the opposite. I'm empowered by confidence brought on by undeniable attraction.

His warm hands land on the curves of my shoulders, and I feel him step closer behind me, our body heat becoming one.

"He shouldn't need to be creative, unless he is compensating for something. Lucky for me, you're single and here. Tonight, you have my full attention," he whispers against the shell of my ear.

My clit pulses from anticipation, while I clench my thighs to gather stability.

"Oh gee, only tonight," I tease.

Declan's hands fall to my hips, and he grips them. "Maybe you had my attention a little before too, which is why I already have ideas of exactly how I want to play with you." He guides me by the waist to turn me around.

I try to suppress my smile because it's a boost knowing someone has noticed you. I'm a confident person, but that doesn't make a compliment worth any less.

Facing him, his gaze dips low, as I'm completely topless, and a smirk twists on the corners of his mouth.

"No going back," he warns as his eyes graze back up to my mouth.

"I'll survive." My tone is flippant.

"This is probably a bad idea." He rubs his thumb along my bottom lip.

I take hold of his hands to guide them to my chest. "Good thing it's only one night then." The feeling of his palms molding my round breasts sparks electricity between us.

His smirk grows. "I like your mindset."

"I'm only here to appease you," I joke with a light tone.

"You deserve a gentleman, and maybe I'll be that at some point tonight, but right now, I need to do this." His fingers pluck a nipple while his eyes stay pinned to mine. "Have you thought about having me inside you before?"

"Your ego needs a boost?" I cock my head to the side, with his hands still on my breasts. He won't give me what I want until I answer. "Once or twice," I admit.

"Good girl, honesty is key for tonight." He begins to trace his lips along my jawline. "In that spirit, you'll tell me when you've had enough, because I intend to go a few rounds, making you come with my fingers, mouth, and cock. Hopefully, you feel in a giving mood too."

Have mercy on me, this is exactly what I was imagining.

"I think I can be persuaded," I say breathlessly.

"Good. I need to watch you touch yourself, because I want to study the way you like it so my tongue can show you how to do it better."

A new wave of heat runs through me with the realization that his cockiness is apparently something that I like.

In a flash, he moves his hands. I feel at a loss until he instantly cups my face to slam his mouth onto mine, stealing my breath and driving me wild. His one hand threads through my hair then yanks slightly to tilt head in a better angle, a clear position for him to consume my lips.

He's firm, then tender, to downright greedy. I have no chance to explore because his tongue is already flirting with mine because Declan is a step ahead of me.

I loop my arms around his neck, enjoying his kiss that turns messy.

This is just a little fun, except judging by the feel of his cock pressed against my middle, then he isn't little at all.

Thank you, heaven, for finally allowing me to win something.

He hoists me up, my legs instantly wrapping around his waist, while our mouths don't part as he walks us to the couch.

I gasp, as I'm startled by the way we fall together perfectly against the cushions. With his body over mine, my hands begin to wander down his abs, attempting to reach his belt, but he's quick to pin my wrists above my head.

I'm a version of myself that I don't quite recognize… and I love it.

We're all allowed to have wild nights.

A one-of-a-kind sort of night.

Even if they end with a morning after and an empty bed with a note in place of a warm body next to you.

4

DECLAN

This is my test.

The last time I saw Ford was a few hours before his sister became my dirty little secret.

Now? We're alone and sitting at Catch 22 in Lake Spark. The restaurant on the water overlooks a few docks with boats and is an easy walk from Main Street. This town is busy as hell during the summer months, which is why this restaurant is bustling with people. We're at a table for two outside on the deck, with late-morning sun shining down on us.

Yep, just the two of us.

I'm one soft drink order in and I've already pictured Violet straddling me while my dick pistoled my way up into her, causing us to moan in sync.

A wave of guilt hits me because I left before she woke up.

I haven't seen or spoken to her since.

That's my doing.

"This week you're going to meet with my staff at the rink?" Ford asks.

I shake the memories out of my head and focus on the hockey king sitting in front of me. Sunglasses cover his eyes, but his brown hair doesn't show any signs of age. Then again, he's only thirty-six.

"Every day, I'll train with the kiddos in the morning or afternoon and have my meetings in between. Will that be okay for you?"

Ford nods with a grin. "Of course, anything you want. You're the one bringing my old team to Lake Spark."

I take a sip of my iced tea, relieved that the world now knows my new career title. "One of the perks of becoming owner of a hockey team is that I get to make decisions. I think it's good that the Spinners will move their training and practices to Lake Spark next season; it'll bring more focus. Where they train now is already 45 minutes outside of the city, so Lake Spark isn't much farther in retrospect. Plus, the existing building needs a total refurbishment, and the last owner passed before the team was able to renew the contract. This could be the start of transitioning everything," I explain.

Ford looks at me, impressed. "You've really thought this through. Then again, people forget that you're more than a pretty boy who can shoot a puck."

I grin at his comment. "Story of my life. Everyone assumes something about me, yet all I do is prove them wrong."

"I always liked that about you."

"It'll be good to be out of the city for a little bit. My parents are driving me crazy, and parties just don't feel the same anymore."

Normal parties, not the ones where I screw your sister.

"How's the maple syrup business?" Ford asks as he glances at a duck walking along the deck.

"Hell if I know. I only occasionally glance at the financials when we have essential company meetings. I leave it to my family to run. That doesn't make them too happy, nor did my new ownership status of the Spinners thrill them. But trust me, maple syrup isn't in my calling. I mean, I keep a bottle in my kitchen out of loyalty but never open the disgusting thing."

"Brielle loves that stuff. It's a must every time she makes pancakes." He always smiles when he talks about his wife and kids.

I can imagine it must be a unique feeling, I've just never been drawn to the family lifestyle.

"How is the Spears crew?" I lean back in my chair to study my friend who seems completely at peace.

"Great. Connor is on summer break yet still hits the ice a few times a week, forward seems to be his position of choice. Sixteen is an age that requires a few extra bottles of beer, for me, not him. I swear that kid is going to give me my first gray hair." Ford and Brielle had Connor when they were very young, which makes it a little more fun that the age difference between father and son isn't so big. "Wyatt is still in the napping phase, and Brielle is always radiant when pregnant."

"A few more months, right? Is this your last one, or are you going for creating your own hockey team?" I'm generally interested, as their family is growing, and his gushing grin is *nearly* infectious on the matter.

"Nah, when this one arrives later this year, then we're done. Three boys and a dog are enough for us, plus my sister is around, so I'm sure she will add to the family gatherings soon enough."

My lips stall on the rim of my drink glass at the mention of Violet. Taking a shallow sip for appearances, I swallow a deep breath. "Didn't realize she was dating someone." I sound casual enough.

Inside of me, something feels tied to her, a connection, and not the wrists-knotted-to-my-headboard kind.

Truthfully, it was concerning how I woke to find her peacefully asleep next to me in my bed, naked. Either the bed was made for her, or she was made for the bed. I liked the way she looked wrapped in my sheets. I had to unravel us when I slowly slid out from the covers. I'm not used to that.

I have no right to be territorial about her dating life, but my interest is far too piqued.

"She's not seeing anyone. I just don't imagine her being single for long. Violet is smart, runs her own shop, and she's fun. I'm not blind, I know half the team had a thing for her, and Violet is relaxed, so she's easy to hang out with. I'm sure the mayor has a son or nephew somewhere for her, and I think the new sheriff in town has been eyeing her. I think he would pass my approval list."

Not going to lie, Violet made an impression on me and has lingered in my head. I can only agree with her brother's remarks. Well, except for the sheriff part. Other than his handcuffs, I doubt he would bring much to the table to keep Violet interested.

"Right," I manage to say.

Luckily, the waiter arrives to take our orders. Still, as Ford reads off the menu, my mind wanders to Violet. I've already failed this test of brunch with Ford a few moments in because she's all I can think about.

I don't owe Violet an apology. The setup of that night had clear rules. It wasn't intentional that I left her before she woke, but I had somewhere important to be. Not to mention, that would have been a slightly awkward morning after considering sex with her was… different. If I'm honest with myself, it was slower and more sensual at times than my usual play. Those parties are a temporary escape, but with Violet? It was like a whole other world.

Not apologizing to her doesn't exactly feel right either, and I want to rectify that.

Violet is a lethal combination if a man looks close enough. She knows what she wants, and that's sexy as hell. But she's also the kind of woman that any grandmother would invite over for tea. This combination of the two are not good for any man's head.

"Since you'll be in Lake Spark more often, maybe you'll set down some roots since hotel life can't be that fun."

"This week, I'm staying at the Dizzy Duck Inn here in town, and I'll probably get a weekend home here. I do want to be a bit hands-on with the team if they train here. At least, I want to be able to observe the players," I explain.

Ford hisses a sound. "You know that the team hates when the owner is around at practices."

"That's because most owners never played the game, but I'm different. Either way, I will make myself hidden if needed." This team will only be the best in my book, it's what I want, and I'll prove to everyone that having me as owner is well worth it.

"Good. I'll keep my eye out if any interesting real estate becomes available."

"Like I said, I'm not sure if small-town life is for me, but it's worth an investment," I repeat to calm his eagerness.

"Weren't you dating a real estate agent once?"

I scratch the back of my head. "Many years ago, for like two months, but she got clingy way too fast." Nor did she understand that I had no intention of sending her flowers and planning future holidays together.

"I can never keep up with your dating life."

"That's the point," I state with a tight smile. For the most part, people know that I have a good time, they're just not aware of the specifics.

Thank fuck for that. Ford would kill me.

I take a moment to look out across the lake where a line of pines frames the outline of the water. Lake Spark is beautiful, I'll give it that.

Lake Spark has been a business decision for the team, but maybe a little downtime would be good for me while I'm here. I've never given much time to nature, but they say it brings better focus.

Our food arrives a little while later.

"Thank you," I hear Ford tell the waiter.

I repeat the sentiment and stare down at my BLT sandwich.

"Looks good," I say while I debate how to attack the sandwich.

In truth, I'm not that hungry.

Probably because I was hoping he would bring up Violet a little more in conversation. It would be my practice to act indifferent around Ford, examine if I would ever feel guilt for betraying a friendship.

Instead, I'm left disappointed that I'm not awarded the opportunity.

"You should stop by our house later. Connor is having friends over, so I'm going to BBQ and have Spencer join."

I have to grin. "Oh yeah, your street where every homeowner is a professional sports legend, or you."

"Spencer retired, but come on, join us. We'll drink a few beers while we ensure my sixteen-year-old and his crew don't get out of line. Brielle would love it if you stopped by. You haven't seen her yet since she really started to show."

"I've never been one to turn down a social gathering." I take a bite of my sandwich. Something clicks in my brain, and I wipe my mouth and suggest, "I should bring something for Brielle. Fruit, flowers?"

Please say flowers.

"Just bring yourself."

That doesn't help.

I'm failing. Miserably.

Violet keeps seeping into my thoughts every time I look at Ford. Or it's the fact that I'm in Lake Spark and it has crossed my mind a million times that Violet lives here.

My brain flashes the image of her lying underneath me, and the way her breath hitched in surprise when I rolled us over in bed, or the fact that we barely left my sofa the first two rounds.

I scratch my cheek, realizing that I need to take matters into my own hands, especially if I'll be in Lake Spark more often.

"My mother would be disappointed if I show up to your BBQ empty-handed. I'm sure I'll find something in town."

"I mean, Violet's shop, The Flower Jar, has gifts as well as flowers. I'm sure she has something, plus it helps her business. I do my best to ensure she doesn't go bankrupt."

"Is that a concern?"

He scoffs a laugh. "No way. She's always busy, a lot of online orders. The Dizzy Duck Inn contacts her for flowers when people stay for a night and need that romantic touch. I'm just her big brother and want her to succeed, and all business helps."

Violet strikes me as an independent woman with strong shoulders. What her brother mentions sounds right on point.

"I'm going to assume, like all great places in Lake Spark, that I can find her store on Main Street?"

"Main Street, First Street, Pine Street, or Duck Lane, the only streets in Lake Spark, but they all run into Main or the lake."

"Quaint." I try to suppress a smile.

Ford grins. "Nah, just easy. Welcome to Lake Spark."

My lips quirk out at Ford's sentiment.

Easy.

Not exactly, but at least I won't get lost.

Because my next stop is finding Violet at her flower shop.

5

VIOLET

I stare at my sixteen-year-old nephew, Connor, who's tapping his fingers on the counter of my store, The Flower Jar, his chin resting against his propped elbow while he seems to be in deep contemplation.

It's summer, which means he should be having the time of his life. He's a popular kid, with good looks that keep his parents worried. It's no secret that every girl at his school harbors a crush on him. Add in the fact that he plays varsity hockey and I'm confident he thinks he's the messiah to some.

"You okay there? You seem kind of… lost." A bewildered smile stretches on my mouth as I count the individual sunflowers for my brother's order, thankful my apron catches the drops of water from the stems.

"Carnations look like roses, I don't get it."

Ah, yes, he's been debating which flowers to buy for the last five minutes.

I playfully hit his head with a sunflower. "They are not the same, and I've told you that many times. You need to go for roses if you want to impress a girl," I remind him.

The joys of your brother accidentally having a baby at young age means my nephew and I can hang out without it feeling like I'm just another parental figure. I was eleven when he was born. We have a special bond, closer to friendship, because I'm the cool aunt. He tells me things that he wouldn't tell his parents, although he's pretty damn close with them too.

"You're right. A single rose, red, classic, and it's more of a statement." He stands tall, confident with his choice.

My brow raises. "Who's the lucky lady?"

He shrugs a shoulder. "Just someone."

"Nothing to do with your pool party later?" I ask as I walk to the bucket on the floor filled with roses. I hold one up for his approval, and he nods.

"Maybe. Haven't decided if she's worthy or not, I'm keeping my options open."

I snort a laugh. We're going through a lot of roses this summer.

The chirp of a parrot reminds me that there is a bird in a cage in this place, not by choice.

"I'm a hostage," the bird parrots.

Connor laughs and glances at Nugget. "That animal is hysterical."

I shudder from the realization that I'm never alone here. "He isn't helping my phobia, but he belongs to the landlord, and the parrot isn't going anywhere. Just a shame I can't keep the blanket over his cage for longer periods."

"Oh, baby," Nugget chirps. I sigh from exasperation.

"When are you going to bring a guy to our house?" Connor asks.

Great question. There hasn't been anyone, well, not since that night in Chicago with Declan.

Declan.

The man with a foul mouth who leaves filthy memories in my head.

He worshiped my body like it meant something but left as if I was nothing.

Shaking my head, I focus on my nephew.

"If you bring a guy over, it will divert the attention away from me. I'm going to lose my mind if my dad tries to let me throw another party. I know his plan. Try and be relaxed, get my friends on his side so they only want to hang at our house. It's going to kill my dating life."

Pulling some ribbon off the spool, I smirk to myself. "I think that's the idea. Boohoo, your parents let you throw awesome parties that I hear girls talking about when I pick up a coffee at Jolly Joe's. Just trust me, you want that kind of dad. Growing up, I had rules on top of rules and couldn't tell my parents anything."

Our parents divorced, with my father being the major parental figure. For the most part, I shouldn't complain, except for the fact that I lived in the shadow of Ford's stellar career and his young fatherhood that was a constant point of contention between him and our dad.

"What did you do about the rules?"

"Waited until college, let loose like an animal, and made questionable choices," I state matter-of-factly before I point a finger at him. "Which you will *not* do."

Wrapping the silver ribbon around the rose, I'm kind of relieved that I'm closing up early today. There was a Saturday-morning rush, a wedding delivery, and an hour of chasing a supplier for a delivery time on my fresh orchids arriving next week.

Connor indicates with his watch that he wants to epay, but I wave him off. "Family discount," I say. He gives me his signature grin and begins to turn, but I clear my throat. "Forgetting something?"

He reaches for the sunflowers that I packed with green paper around the stems. "Keeping me out of trouble, Aunt Violet?"

"No. Your dad would kill us both if one of us forgets to bring your mom the dozen sunflowers that your dad wants hand-delivered." I tilt my hip out.

"Did you add an extra one from me?"

"Of course."

My nephew has moves, I'll give him that. Every time Ford orders Brielle flowers, Connor adds an extra flower, brings it to Brielle, and ensures she knows that the additional flower is from him. She turns to a puddle of goo every single time, while my brother just smirks with pride. It's ten times more extreme now that she's pregnant again; I heard there were tears last time.

"You're the best. See you at the party."

I offer a short little wave. "Yep."

Watching him leave, I sigh as I lean against my counter and scan my shop. A wave of satisfaction hits me, because The Flower Jar is mine. Well, for the most part. I had to lease the building, but I designed the interior space, manage the administration, and other than a few part-timers helping me out, I'm here pretty much six days a week. I can check off the box marked "small business owner," and I'm having a blast doing it.

But career is only one aspect of life.

Looking through my window, with gold stenciled letters on the glass, I see that Main Street is busier than normal, probably because it's tourist season. Illinois summer puts everyone in a good mood—until winter hits us. We sometimes improve in mood around February, with Valentine's day, before spring rolls in, which keeps us on our toes with unpredictable weather.

Fortunately, flowers are the key to brightening anyone's day, and they are available in my store all year round.

It's just… flowers are also the language of romance. I'm somehow part of everyone else's moments, yet I don't experience my own.

Maybe I'm a little envious when I watch Ford with his family. Who wouldn't be a little jealous?

Shaking away the thought that creeps into my mind more often than it should, I sigh and grab a broom to sweep the floor and prepare to close up.

A few minutes later, I step outside and grab a few buckets filled with flowers on display. The fresh air and sun are a welcome change. Sometimes I wonder if the sun and flowers are competing to turn someone's day around, it feels like today the sun wins.

Because the thing with flowers is that while you can buy yourself flowers, it doesn't have the same effect as if someone else would.

And right now, there is nobody in my life, not even close, only a memory of a night that lingers in my thoughts.

Heading back inside, I recount the list of things I need to do to close, and it's a welcome distraction.

It's twenty minutes later when I turn off the tablet for orders and payments then head back to the closet where I lock things away.

The sound of the bell over my front door rings to inform me that someone is here.

"Sorry, the options may be limited since I'm closing up," I call out, not looking up, as I'm too occupied with noticing how dirty my apron is today.

Untying the belt, I walk back onto the shop floor.

"It's okay, there is only one item I'm looking for."

That voice causes me to instantly freeze, except for my eyes that snap up to confirm that it's him, and I'm faced with a smirk as he leans against the counter, with sunglasses in his hand and wearing jeans and a light blue short-sleeved button-down shirt that accentuates his piercing eyes.

"Declan."

"Violet."

Hesitating, I take one step into the middle of my shop, doing my best to interpret his suave smirk and not combust at the same time.

He left a damn note on the pillow, with paper he'd folded into a bird, after a night of endless fun. I can't really be mad because that was what I signed up for, but still, it stung a little.

"Tie her up."

Declan instantly searches for the source of the words and finds Nugget perched in his cage. My face turns red from the choice of words this bird spits out at random moments.

"Someone is direct. I like it." Declan's cheeks heighten as he grins to himself.

I shake my head and smile tightly in embarrassment. "He is the culprit of my daily misery."

Declan's head tilts in different angles to study the bird. "I thought you have a bird phobia, so why am I staring at a parrot in a cage?"

"Nugget is part of the deal with my landlady. I get a decrease in rent if I keep the bird, since my landlady moved downstate to a condo that doesn't allow pets. His limited vocabulary that is barely appropriate is just a bonus." I'm sarcastic and huff out a breath.

"You're handsome." Nugget pecks his beak as he walks along his pole.

"Couldn't agree more," Declan responds.

Looking away, I hide my soft smile as I touch a lisianthus amongst a bunch of flowers. I do my best to occupy myself and erase the memory of Declan's mouth covering mine to block my moans while by back was on his couch. "I wasn't expecting you here. Is there something I can help you with?"

I can feel his gaze on me. "Thought I would stop by. I saw Ford, and he invited me to a BBQ. I would like to bring Brielle some flowers."

I swallow because now I know that I will have to be near him at my brother's house. I knew this day would come eventually.

"Well, uhm, okay, what do you have in mind?" I walk around the counter, avoiding glancing in his direction.

"What about sunflowers?"

I chortle a laugh. "Trust me, Brielle has enough of them. The men in her life enjoy buying her sunflowers." I peer up to find his eyes set on me and a subtle wry smile on his lips.

"Then maybe chocolates are a better idea," he mentions. I nod once and feel my mouth tug, wanting to smile gently. The air between us is peculiar, neither tense nor calming. He clears his throat."Truthfully, you're the item on my list that I came here for."

Heat swells in my body, and my brows raise in surprise. "Whatever do you mean?" I say, playing coy.

His jaw flexes side to side as he grins. "Since flowers for Brielle are a no-go, then maybe you can arrange something else for me? Can you have something delivered to the Dizzy Duck Inn?"

"As in what?" I'm curious. I watch as he picks up a small square card with my logo from the pile on the counter, and he flips it between his fingers.

"Any flowers will do, they're even optional, but the card is kind of crucial." He tips his head gently to the side and hands me the card.

An audible breath escapes me. "Sure. What am I writing?" I click a pen and pose my fingers, waiting for him to dictate.

"'About last night…'" He pauses when he notices that my fingers freeze mid-sentence, and I stop writing. Something inside of me boils. This man has some nerve, asking me to deliver flowers to some woman he spent the night with. "Shall I continue?" he asks.

I swallow, debating if I should throw him out of my store now, but something inside of me tells me to go on. It's the tone of his voice. "Next sentence." I remain defiant.

"'My answer is yes, Violet.'"

"What?"

"No, I mean, the card is from you, so you're signing your name."

I wave my pen between my fingers and look at him for answers. "I don't follow."

He stands confidently, and a pleasing smile graces his lips. "You're going to answer a question that I'll ask at the BBQ and send me the card one day real soon, flowers optional."

"Why the hell would I do that?"

"You'll see." It sounds like a delicious threat. He clears his throat as if he wants to switch topics. "I thought it would be good to clear the air."

I notice a wilted rose on my counter that I forgot to clean up earlier. Picking it up, I pluck one petal off. "Oh?" I pretend to be surprised. "Nothing to clear." I grip another petal, this time with a little more force.

Take the high road, Violet.

Declan's eyes squint to study me as I continue to tear. "*Yeah*, not sure that's true."

I grab the scissors. "Do you mean leaving before sunrise? Or the note folded as a bird that said *Coffee machine is ready, door will lock on your way out, thanks for a good night, Declan*." I cut the stem rather ceremoniously.

"Something like that." He reaches forward with a grin, cautiously wrapping his fingers around the scissors, causing our hands to touch and my body to jolt with electricity. "How about you put these down." He takes the scissors and sets them back on the side.

"Why apologize now? Are you worried you hurt my feelings? Never fear, I knew what I signed up for."

He runs his thumb along his chiseled jawline with a little bit of stubble, bringing my attention to his mouth that I want to kiss. "Still… I'm not sure I would have left had it not been for the fact that I needed to meet with my lawyer to finalize the paperwork to become owner of the Spinners." My spine straightens at his admission, because that *is* a crucial meeting. He seems to notice, as he angles his head to enable his eyes to catch mine. "I had a great night."

"Really? You only mentioned *good* in your little note on your pillow," I say rather dryly.

Declan chuckles from my humor. "I'm not one for notes. Anyway, I'm in town and thought I would stop by." He scans the room around him. "It smells like you. This place, I mean."

"Flowers do tend to have a fragrance."

His fingers glide along the countertop. "You did well here."

"Thanks." I stare over his shoulder and notice the old lady from the knitting club peeking into my store. "The town gossip is here. She spreads stories like wildfire but ensures they never leave the Lake Spark bubble." I wiggle my fingers at her with a bright smile which causes her to scurry off.

"If only she knew our little secret."

My eyes whip to Declan who has a sweltering gaze.

A brief pause floats between us. The air turns into a giddy awkwardness, but I'm not sure what I was expecting. I only know pieces of him; he's a mystery in some way still.

"I'm staying at the Dizzy Duck…"

A smile forms on my lips. "You mentioned when you had me writing a card that apparently I'm going to send to you."

My eyes narrow in on him, and I cross my arms over my chest. I wait for him to further explain, because I have no idea what he's up to. I mean, there are many reasons why he mentioned where he is staying, but none of them are good for me.

"I really should apologize."

I roll my eyes. "It's fine. I mean, you have your protocol, and you're the one who is a pro at these kinds of things."

"Violet, you're not just anyone." He sounds near adamant.

Frustration fills me to the brim. "Yeah, I know. I'm Ford Spears's little sister and have been branded as off-limits to any guy who plays any sport for a career."

The corner of Declan's mouth hitches up. "That, and you are… memorable."

It's impossible trying to interpret his words without feeling a twinge of hope. But I'm going to run in circles, and I'm positive Jolly Joe's has maple pecan ice cream today that is calling my name. Untangling from my untied apron, I hang it on the hook behind me.

"So why do you have me sending you flowers with a card?"

"I haven't decided yet, but it'll be good."

My eyes go bold at his suggestion. "Trouble?"

"Maybe." He's playing coy.

I huff a breathy laugh. "I'm not going to answer to that," I say firmly.

"Yet," he adds.

"If we're done here, then I think we made our peace and can move on."

I grab my purse and circle around my counter, only to find that Declan hasn't moved an inch. In fact, he gets even more comfortable in his lean against my property, with one foot crossed over his ankle.

"We're all good for your brother's BBQ? You're not going to look at me and think of my cock inside of you?" The words flow off his talented tongue so casually.

I feel my cheeks burn. "Really, you're off the hook. We had a night of fun, it is what it is. I'm sure you've enjoyed many parties since then." I motion with my arm to the door and hold my keys with my other hand.

He propels off my counter, following my cues. "I really appreciate your attitude with all of this, especially since I haven't been to any parties since." His tone is flippant.

My eyelids flutter as I look at him with disbelief.

He hooks his finger and glides it along my cheek in passing, touching me as if he is catching a distant memory. He smirks smugly, proud that he caught me off guard.

"You leave an impression and know the score—"

He's hinting at something, and I scoff a sound between my stretched lips, stopping his sentence. "You're kind of unbelievable. Gutsy, at that. Goodbye, Declan." I walk to the door and open it, with the bell making a noise, and wait for him to get a clue.

I'm not sure how I feel about the last few minutes, nor do I particularly want to question why my thighs feel tense in a good way or why on earth the mere touch of his finger against the curve of my face still feels like it may haunt me the rest of the day.

I don't dare look up at him as he leaves, and I think his swaggered walk out of my shop is from accomplishment.

He wants to occupy my thoughts, have a sense of hold over me, and simply feel like it's his doing that I toss and turn later.

But the joke is on him.

Because he didn't need to put in the effort.

I haven't been pining over him, yet I sure as hell haven't forgotten that I have the ability to make that man beg.

And that's what I intend to make him do.

6

VIOLET

Sitting at the table overlooking the lake, I glance at my brother who is busy flipping burgers while talking to his neighbor Spencer, a retired professional baseball player. Ignoring the group of teenagers in the pool, I focus my attention on Brielle and April, Spencer's wife.

"Are you sure you're okay manning the fort while Ford and I get away for a little bit?" Brielle double-checks while she pours me some wine, because it's conveniently my favorite and makes me more agreeable.

I willingly take the glass. "Of course, I'll keep an eye on Connor and play with my little nephew Wyatt. It's only a weekend, and it's still a few weeks away." As much as my dad acts like a grandfather, his relationship with Ford is different, more fraught at times, and our mom lives in Oregon since they divorced many years ago. I'm Ford's local family, and I don't want to let him down. Not to mention Brielle, who despite having a few years on me, is the closest thing to a best friend that I have in Lake Spark. We can talk for hours.

Brielle glances radiantly down at her growing belly. "I'm a planner. Well, except for Connor." She's glowing, and her brown hair seems to get more gorgeous as the pregnancy develops, I mean, her hair even flows in the wind perfectly.

"Two kids under the age of three, plus a teenager. I don't know how you do it." April flings her blonde ponytail behind her shoulder before she chomps on a tortilla chip.

"A busy house is the way we like it, but we're done after this one. Three boys will be plenty." She smiles as Ford comes to stand behind her with a plate of burgers, and she affectionately touches his shirt. I can't believe they were apart for ten years. They tried the whole co-parenting thing until they admitted that they're meant for more.

Spencer takes his place next to April, kissing her cheek.

I feel like an extra wheel, but I have my wine glass, so that's a plus.

"How was work? Didn't kill the bird yet?" my brother asks as he slides a burger onto my plate.

"You know Nugget is part of the deal. Didn't notice him much, as I was busy, but Connor stopped by."

"I know. I love the sunflowers," Brielle gushes.

Looking over at the pool, I point out the obvious. "Quite a boy-girl ratio happening over in the pool," I taunt my brother and indicate with my head to the teenagers where guys are outnumbered by far.

Spencer chortles a laugh. "Don't rile him, we just went over his master plan for being the cool dad and promising to keep the hockey team away from my daughter." Spencer's daughter Hadley is a few years younger than Connor and has an obvious crush.

"It will only make her want them more," April adds.

"How about we switch topics so I can sleep tonight?" Ford suggests as he sits down. Brielle asks him something related to the kids, but I only catch the end of their exchange when he mentions that Declan will be here soon. "Now that he owns the Spinners and is adamant that they train here in Lake Spark, maybe he'll be around more."

I nearly choke on my wine. Declan's name sparks warmth inside me, all because of one wild night and his surprise visit to my flower shop. But it's this new fact that I'm learning which has me thrown off my axis.

"You okay?" Brielle attempts to rub a circle on my back.

I pat my chest while my other hand holds onto the wine glass placed on the table. "Yeah, totally, just drank a little too fast," I assure her then focus my attention on Ford. "Around more?" I repeat, attempting to sound steady.

"Declan? He's here this week to help with the hockey camp, but he also wants the Spinners to train here next season. I'm trying to convince him to move here," Ford answers.

That man.

He's in my head.

Declan didn't mention more frequent visits to Lake Spark, only the Dizzy Duck Inn, which normally equates to temporary accommodation, as in a passing-through-town kind of thing.

I feel my face drop from the realization that this bothers me more than it should.

Meanwhile, the sound of an approaching car engine hits my ears, distracting me from my mind racing in a thousand directions. Luckily, my distraction is broken by one of Connor's friends who is walking into the yard with his thumb hiked over his shoulder as he calls out, "Con, your parties are always unreal. Not only are the adults here like former pro athletes, but now you have a guy show up in the newest Maserati who I am sure looks like Declan Dash." The teenager shakes his head with a grin.

Christ, of course Declan would drive a ridiculously expensive car. It fits perfectly with the image of playboy billionaire that everyone has stamped him with, and I'm still undecided on whether it's true or not.

I notice Brielle has a strange expression while she stares at me, but I ignore it.

I'm about to be tested.

Can I look at Declan with indifference when my brother is so close?

No. I. Can. Not.

There is no sense in even trying. I have stupid butterflies in my stomach because I did the horizontal, vertical, and upside down with the guy who I'm sure I will be passing the salad bowl to in about three minutes.

"Hey, Declan," my brother greets the guest of honor.

Declan swipes his sunglasses off as he walks into the yard, surveying the scene. There are teenagers splashing in the pool again, the sun is bright but beginning to dip low in the sky, and all the adults are around the table, ready to welcome this guy.

"Hey, everyone, looks like quite a setup," Declan mentions then hands Brielle a small bag with tissue paper. "This is for the lady of the house for keeping all the Spears crew together." He gives her a side hug before giving a high five to Spencer and a nod to April. His eyes pause on me for a second, then his focus is back on Brielle who is unraveling her box of chocolates. "Got something from Jolly Joe's. Your sister-in-law convinced me not to buy from her shop."

"You saw Declan today?" my brother asks, with creases forming on his forehead.

I nod. "Yeah, didn't think it was worth mentioning." My sight zips to Declan who has a subtle smirk on his mouth. "I knew Brielle was getting flowers already," I explain.

"But you always say that a person can never have enough flowers." Ford seems confused.

"True, but—" I begin.

Declan cuts in. "Don't give her a hard time. She was closing up and busy writing a card for an important order. Between the talking parrot and her need to focus on her delivery, then I'm sure I caught her at the wrong moment. Did you get that order out?" he asks me with a hint of smugness.

"How considerate of you to ask. You know, you should try a burger. Ford seasons it with his own special spice mix." I smile and do my best to keep this conversation moving and away from myself.

"Sounds delicious," Declan replies.

Ford hands him a plate, and Declan sits down just in time for everyone to offer him something.

My nephew walks to our table, seeming to be on a break from his afternoon of friends, flirting, and swimming. "Hey, Declan."

"There's our future hockey star." Declan and Connor bump fists together.

"When did you get the car? I wish Dad would go all-out." He looks at Declan with a bit of worship in his voice.

Declan pats Connor's arm. "First off, I can only fit one other person in that car, max. Your dad needs a good family car, and he still has a Jaguar for when he has a kid-free day."

"Dad won't let me drive it. I'm sure you'll be the cool guy and let me drive your car."

Ford scoffs, feigning hurt. "Oh my, Connor is the first kid whose parents won't let him drive fancy cars because he only just got his license."

"That car in our driveway isn't even on the market yet. This is going to skyrocket my popularity at school." Connor shakes his head then walks away, clearly annoyed that Ford isn't taking him seriously.

Declan points his finger in the air. "And that is why having kids is not on my radar."

"Never say never. By the way, are you still dating the model you met at some charity event?" Spencer pipes in.

"Nah, that ended like a year ago," Declan confirms.

Brielle shakes her head. "Admittedly, I can't keep up with your dating life, but I'm happy you're here. Speaking of dating..." Her voice raises an octave. "Sheriff Carter completely has a thing for Violet. He asked me when you normally take a lunch break when I was at the park the other day."

Here we go again. If the man has such interest, then he needs to make his move, as I've been hearing about this for months.

"Ooh, that is some high-quality Lake Spark stock, with deep connections," April points out.

Ford raises his hand. "He has my approval."

"She doesn't need your approval," Brielle says. "Now, if you will excuse me, I need to go get the ice cream out for the kids." She begins to stand, but I quickly beat her to it.

"Relax. I'll go, and I think if by kids you mean hormonal young adults, then yes, I know my instructions." I salute her then leave, heading straight inside.

I need air. Which makes no sense, as I've been outside by the lake for a good hour, but I need air free from Declan and the word *dating*.

I don't want confirmation that this guy has no plans to ever settle down, and I sure as hell don't need to hear about his dating history. Nor do I want to talk about my current lack of love life with him in attendance.

When I arrive in the kitchen, I blow out a breath and take a moment, pausing with my hand on the handle of the freezer. I remind myself that I knew what I signed up for on that night with Declan; it's like a freaking mantra in my head every time he enters my brain, which is a lot.

It was only one night.

Opening the freezer, I grab the boxes of ice cream sandwiches, and I have to smile to myself. This house is, literally, hangout central, and I don't even want to know what Connor is going to try when his parents are away for their babymoon.

I set the boxes on the counter, then go back to grab another that was stuck in the back of the freezer. Closing the freezer door, I jump when I find Declan leaning against the counter with arms crossed.

"Came to give you a hand," he states with a sly smirk.

Rolling my eyes, I stack the boxes. "No, you didn't. You probably excused yourself to use the little men's room with no intention to do that, and instead, you came to find me. Alone, for that matter."

"One, 'little' and me don't go in the same sentence, you know that. Two, you're right."

My hip dips out, and I lean against the adjacent counter while our eyes meet to linger for a few good seconds. We both have wry smiles on our faces as we stew in the fact that we did something so very intimate, because no-strings or not, history is something we now have.

"What do you want, Declan?" I sigh, with my half-stretched smile not fading, and I glance out the floor-to-ceiling windows to confirm that nobody is taking notice that we're inside.

"Did you keep the card?"

I shrug my shoulders. "It wasn't recycling day."

"Meet me every day this week at my hotel room."

My eyes shoot in his direction to find that he is dead serious.

"W-what?" I stutter.

He steps slowly once, twice, I lose count, but his hands land on either side of me to trap me between the counter and his body, causing a tingle to spread through my veins.

"We can repeat last time, enjoy the connection we have, have a little fun." His voice is low, and feeling his breath so close makes me weak in the knees.

"Ah, so this is your crazy suggestion that I should agree to?"

He threads his fingers into my hair by my ear. "A card with flowers is an extra touch, right?"

I laugh under my breath at how unbelievable he is, but at least he has me smiling. "I've never sent a guy flowers as a thank-you for sex. Not from me directly. I'm sure a few of my customers had me doing that. Normally, it's the guy sending flowers, though." I raise a brow at him.

"We don't do conventional." He smirks.

"No. You just proposition me inside my brother's house, which is a bold move. He may kill you one day if he ever finds out. Speaking of which, there are like baby monitors everywhere in this place," I whisper loudly in absolute amazement at his bravery.

Declan's fingers tap my hips as his eyes dip low to watch. "Living dangerously doesn't scare me."

"Clearly."

"What do you say, Vi? Tomorrow is Sunday, I know you're off. The sign on your door told me."

Geez, he's been thinking about this all afternoon.

My mouth opens, but I'm mute.

"I'm sure you have lunch breaks where you need a little more excitement than catching up on the gossip at the general store," he adds. "Or are you hoping for the sheriff to sweep you off your feet?"

I shake my head at the fact he was listening outside and seems to be slightly annoyed, or maybe that's my hidden wish.

This situation he's offering is enticing, but I'm not sure it's wise.

Laughter from outside breaks my gaze from the man in front of me, drawing my attention over his shoulder where I notice the adults outside, all happy in their solid marriages.

Pushing Declan away, I break free and walk to the cupboard that normally is home to the heavier stuff to drink.

"Damn it," I curse to myself when I see the shelves are empty. I forgot that Ford hides the good liquor when Connor has parties. Responsible parenting is screwing me over right now.

"You okay there?"

I hate that I can't suppress a grin, which is why I don't face him. "Yup." I recall another fact that I learned today. "Is it true?"

"That I want to fuck you in my hotel room? Yes." His tone is neutral.

My entertained smile doesn't fade. "I meant that Ford mentioned you might be in Lake Spark more often. You missed that detail earlier."

I feel his eyes studying me. "Is that a problem?"

Could be. Makes an escape harder, and the reminder of him will always be around me.

"Not at all," I lie.

My body trembles when I feel him step behind me, his talented fingers pressing lightly against my ass.

This man is shameless.

"What do you say?" His voice is a sweltering grovel that spreads across my skin, while he takes the opportunity to slide the strap of my dress back over my shoulder, as it fell slightly. I wish he would do that again.

Slowly turning on my toes, I face the devil that has me far too intrigued. "I think…" My tone is purposely a breathy, needy husk. "That the ice cream is going to melt." I smirk, satisfied, and walk to the ice cream.

I notice he puffs a breath. "You're the first woman to test me like this."

The bottle of maple syrup sitting on the counter near the olive oil catches my interest. The label has a picture of a cartoon bear wearing sunglasses, leaning against a tree. It's Declan's family's syrup. He really is unescapable.

Grabbing the boxes of ice cream, I slam them into Declan's direction for him to carry. "Make yourself useful, will you?"

"Will I be rewarded?" How does this man flirt so easily?

Walking in a slow stride past him, I poke my finger against his hard pecs. "Undecided."

He hisses a sound. "I'll be relentless."

"I'll be defiant."

Maybe a distraction and a good time is exactly what I need. I mean, my cheeks hurt from smiling so much today, despite my brain working overtime.

Declan's jaw flexes, and then a relaxed droll grin graces his lips. "I'll take the ice cream out."

I nod in approval, as I need him out of here so I can steal the bottle of syrup.

Because I know exactly how I'm going to use it… when I show up to his hotel room.

7

DECLAN

Hitting the rewind button on the screen, I watch the replay once more. It's from the final game of the season, when Toronto lost. I pay attention to their coach—our new coach—and his reaction to the loss in the final seconds. His frustration is a little too visible for my liking; he could work on adopting a poker face. If it wasn't for his contract, then I would have him gone. I just added another bullet point to my long list of notes; I need to discuss the coach's demeanor, probably with our general manager present. I know that I should leave training and strategy to the team, but I really feel my experience as a player can bring a lot to the table.

Closing my laptop, I sigh as I look around my hotel suite. I'm going to miss playing on the ice under pressure; now I'll be the guy that watches from behind the boards. Stretching my arms, I debate what to do, as I feel restless.

That I completely blame on Violet.

Honestly, my proposition was something not even planned, but after seeing her again, a split-second decision was made. She looked at peace in her flower shop, and that cute summer dress with straps that fall off her smooth skin was a complete bonus.

Last night at the BBQ, I did my best to stay out of Violet's way after the kitchen run-in, but my eyes kept circling back to her. The way she teases Ford is hysterical, and her laugh can make even a grumpy man delirious.

I wonder if I'll see her today.

My phone vibrates on my desk, and I pick it up to see my father's name flash across the screen. That's a solid tap of the red button. I'm not in the mood to talk to him and listen to how I should invest more of my time into the Dash empire.

Rubbing my face, I know I need to get out of this place and enjoy the sunny afternoon, with fresh air to fill my lungs. Before I get a chance to make a decision, I'm interrupted by a soft knock on my door.

Excitement hits me, because even a man who never falters under pressure enjoys the idea of a woman waiting for him. Walking to the door, I open it to find an empty hallway, and my eyes travel down to the floor where I notice a card lying on the carpet.

I recognize the logo of The Flower Jar right away and quickly bend down to pick it up and read the card.

My answer is yes, Violet

My grin stretches, and I stand to scan the hallway. I know she's here because I can feel her presence, and I swear I smell damn roses. "Where are you?"

Violet steps around the corner with a subtle smirk on her lips. Her hair is down, and she's wearing another summer dress. It's baby blue, and I make no mistake that there is a strap of a matching bra peeking out on her shoulder.

"I'm here. Really shouldn't be. But I'm here." Her voice is at ease, at least.

She walks toward me, but I reach out to grab her arm and yank her through the entry, closing the door with my foot.

"Where are the flowers?" I joke.

Violet assesses the suite before circling to face me. "You said they were optional, and I think I have something better."

I step closer to her, completely invested in the fact that she showed up. "Oh yeah?"

She nods seductively then crooks her finger and invites me to follow her as she walks backward to the bed. "You're playing a game." She grabs hold of my shirt, right before she pushes me onto the bed. "But..." She brings one leg to the side of my waist and swings the other one around to straddle me, and instantly my guy rises to the occasion. "Games normally require two players or more."

"More?" I croak out.

Violet chuckles and blushes. "In this case, only two." It comes out as a playful warning while her fingertips push against my chest, inviting me to lie on my back.

I prop myself up on my elbows, wanting to get a full view of her stunning body on top of me, determined about an idea in her head.

She reaches to the side where she had thrown her purse, causing her body to stretch across me and rub friction against my cock. I breathe to keep myself grounded. Pulling a glass bottle out of her purse, my head perks up in full attention.

"Why do you have a bottle of pure maple syrup?"

Violet flashes me a playful look. "Don't worry, I'm loyal to your family brand."

"That I can see, but why is that here?"

She begins to drag the fabric of my shirt up my stomach to my chest, encouraging me to take action, and I swiftly pull off my shirt without her moving an inch from sitting on top of my cock.

"I remember you mentioned your fear of maple syrup."

I chuckle, because I have no idea where she's going with this. "And?"

She lowers her dress halfway without a thought, revealing the matching bra that caught my attention already. "You see..." She ceremoniously twists the lid off the bottle. "As much as I'm cool with your note on a pillow in swan-shaped form, and your ludicrous requests that I send you flowers, I'm not that easy."

"Of course not," I assure her. No, I want to do more than ease her mind; I need to get rid of any doubts that I would even put her on the same level as a puck bunny. My hands rub warmth along her thighs, and not in a sensual way but a caring manner. Before I have a chance to tell her that she can set the rules, a drizzle of sticky syrup hits my stomach.

Glancing down, my jaw drops when I realize that she just poured Grizzly Dash syrup onto my body.

"I kind of like the idea of torturing you a little," she confesses while she tips the bottle to draw a line of syrup up to my chest.

"What in the world is in that mind of yours?" I'm already afraid of the sticky mess this is going to create. Tree sap is the glue of about ninety-nine problems, and Violet isn't one of them.

She leans down to press her hot mouth between my ribs and peers up, flicking her tongue along my skin. "Do I lick up or down?" It doesn't sound like a question, more of a taunt.

I groan from the agony she's causing me. All options have me anticipating her body underneath me.

The tip of her wet tongue darts out, and she slowly licks up one stroke before moving back down. "Hmm, I love maple." Her hum is like sex to the ears.

"Your plan is to torture me with syrup?" I close my eyes as I take in the feeling of her tongue tracing a line on my body, up and up, until I open my eyes to find our lips within kissing distance. I attempt to capture her mouth, but she only gives me her breath tracing my lips, fueling a sensitive wave of need inside of me.

"I should lick lower, shouldn't I?" Her whisper is sultry and teasing.

"You are something, Vi."

She pauses, and her mouth quirks up. "Nobody calls me Vi, except you."

"Sorry, I like it. Violet is perfect for you, kind of like you were destined to do something with flowers, but Vi, it's… like a vow that I'm not sure I should be taking." I half-laugh.

A beautiful smile appears on her lips. "You're distracting me from my mission."

"Oh, sorry, please do continue spreading the goo all over my body and doing wicked things," I encourage, only to moan when her tongue lands below my heart and slides lower.

Just watching her slither down my body has me about to break my invisible rope that I've tied myself in. I want to let her lead because this woman has some plans that I'm on board with.

"Still afraid of maple syrup?" she asks mid-stroke.

"Trust me, it will ruin the moment at some point. Your lips are going to be ridiculously sweet."

She flashes me a smirk. "Which lips?"

I chuckle because every moment with her is fun. I've already forgotten about my last hour of mulling over life choices.

"Lower," I plead.

She unhooks the button of my jeans and unzips my pants. "Like, this low?" Her mouth skims the rim of my boxers, and I tilt my hips up to brush my bulge against her hot mouth.

"If your plan was to make me painfully hard, then you've succeeded."

A low giggle in the back of her throat has me concerned. Her tongue swirls just below my navel before she pulls away and returns to straddling me. "That's a point for me then." She smirks slyly before swinging her legs off the bed to stand over me. "Oh dear," she pouts. "Declan is all sticky and hard. Such a shame that I only planned to taste the syrup."

Holy shit.

This is her game?

"Whoa, you're going to leave me hanging?"

She shakes her head. "I'm debating."

I'm about to hop up off the bed to take control of this situation, but I feel excess syrup running down the side of my body, and if I'm not careful then my sheets will become a mess.

"You're just going to leave?" My voice is filled with disbelief and cracks in fear.

"I guess I could leave a note on your pillow." She quirks her lips to the side.

I roll my eyes, completely taken in by her banter, but after her blatant rule-breaking, I'll gladly take my free shot when I notice a crystalized and shiny substance in her hair.

A winning grin spreads on my mouth, and I throw my arms behind my head to rest against. "You're not going anywhere."

"I'm not sure about that."

"Considering you have maple syrup in your hair, I'm fairly confident that you're staying right here."

Her fingers instantly go to her hair, and she pauses when she feels the goo. "Crap."

"See? Told you maple syrup is evil."

Grabbing my shirt from the side, I hold it to my body to avoid the floodgates of syrup spreading onto the mattress, then I stand and walk straight to her, drop the shirt, and frame her face with my hands.

She seems taken aback by my move, but positive, nonetheless.

Her lips are pink and swollen, sweet for sure. I want to kiss her, but I want to drive her crazy more.

I move to wrap my arm around her middle and pull her flush against me. Her breath catches when she feels the stickiness of my body bond to her skin.

"You're nice and messy now too," I proudly declare, and as tempting as it is to kiss her, I purposely don't.

A chortle escapes her lips. "I need a shower now."

"By all means, go on, but I think we both need to be cleaned up, and you seem like someone who cares about the Lake Spark water supply and lack of rain this summer."

Her forehead falls forward into the crook of my neck. "That's one point to you."

"So, we're keeping score?" I confirm.

"We'll call it a tie." Violet steps back. "Join me in the shower?" She offers me her hand.

"I mean, if you say please."

I'm already scooting her toward the bathroom.

————

THE WATER in the shower rains down, and steam is already filling the room.

We're both quick to discard our clothes, and I appreciate that we feel familiar enough around one another that it comes easily. Violet isn't shy, but then again, I don't think she ever is.

I hold the shower door open for her, as any gentleman should, and she steps in first, followed by me.

"Okay, I think I understand the fear of maple syrup. I just feel all… messy." She grabs a bottle of shampoo, and the idea of her smelling of my soap is kind of hot as hell.

"Maybe we should just go all out then and get you completely filthy," I murmur into her hair, letting my fingertips glide along the curves of her body. She swats me playfully, and I respect that she's keeping us grounded. "It all started with a trip to a tree farm, you know." I begin to lather soap against my stomach.

She grimaces over her shoulder up at me. "Do tell."

"I was seven, and my father was insistent that I attend a business meeting with him up in Canada. It just so happened to be at the tree farm where they collect sap, it's next to one of the hotels my father owns. There was a bucket of the stuff that was cooling after being boiled, and I'm not even sure how it happened, but I ended up with the glue all over my hands, and then I stupidly put my hands in my hair, and it just went downhill from there. Everything I touched stuck to me, and then we had to rip off things. It was traumatic."

Violet giggles. "That's it? No grizzly bear making an appearance? Just a lot of maple sap? Wow, thoroughly disappointing."

"Trust me, the memory haunts me. There was also a time when my cousin threw a can of maple syrup at me because I pushed him into a pool. Did you know the best way to store syrup is actually in a tin can, just like olive oil? Anyway, I once had a broken nose after a game with Toronto, and I kid you not, after the painkillers they gave me, I was hallucinating about that damn tree and a can."

She bursts out with another laugh. "Okay, okay, I believe you and shall never involve breakfast syrup in foreplay again." She feigns a serious tone.

I gently pull her hair in reaction before tickling her side and drawing her closer to me, with her back against my front and our slippery bodies now connected. My hand rests against her stomach, and I feel her exhale as she relaxes.

"You were a good player," she states.

"Oh yeah? You watch a lot of hockey?"

"How could I not? Even after Ford retired, his house is still hockey central."

A ping of guilt hits me that I'm lying to him. "You're very close with him."

"Yeah, I mean, Brielle is like a friend, and the kids are my nephews. I'm the peacemaker between Ford and our father, as they get along but not always. But most of all, Ford and I are there for one another. It wasn't easy when he and Brielle had Connor so young, and he was there for me when… you know, never mind. Let's not talk about him now. We're all allowed a dirty secret every now and then, so long as it doesn't hurt anyone." I get the sense that there is more as to how her brother has supported her, but something stopped her from explaining further.

"You're close with your parents?" she asks.

I chuckle. "Yes and no. My mother for sure, yes, and my father, well, he likes to put on the pressure that I got my hockey career but now it's time to take over the family business."

"He isn't a hockey fan?"

"At first, no. Then I went to a fancy prep school and played on the varsity team, and the school was really into hockey. Every game, the alumni would be there, and my father loved that. When I turned pro, he would attend a few games but always reminded me that it's only one chapter to my life."

"Huh, guess he isn't thrilled with your latest purchase."

I look up into the showerhead to wash my face. "Exactly."

It's a few moments of us in an embrace, with the sound of water filling the room, when I realize that I haven't really shared my family situation with many, but it comes easily when it's with her. I also recognize that I haven't asked her a simple question, and that maybe I should.

"What made you decide to say yes?"

"I need an escape, just like that night." Her arm raises behind her to loop around my neck, stretching her body in the process. "A repeat could be fun, and it's not like I'm occupied with someone else."

Planting my lips against her jawline, I slide my palm down her abs, wanting to feel her ready for me. "I'm not the kind of guy who can be much more than this," I warn her, because our boundaries are important.

She presses against the back of my hand to encourage me to move lower, guiding me to what she wants. "You've made that clear, yet I'm still here."

Maybe I should question her answer more, but it's good enough for me.

Feeling between her apex, I find her ready, and I swirl my finger around her clit which causes her hips to roll. My teeth nip at her shoulder while I feel her pussy. It's as if we're picking up right where we left off that night.

She reaches back to grip my length and give me a stroke. I groan from her touch and become eager to touch her everywhere.

She slowly turns around, twisting our bodies, yet my fingers don't leave her pussy. I marvel at her beauty, hair soaked and droplets of water outlining her face. Leaning down, I take what I've been waiting for.

A kiss.

Hard, yet absolutely tasting of maple syrup and lust.

My tongue swipes her lips before touching her tongue, and it only sets me off because I want more and then some. When she murmurs into my mouth, I steal all the air I can, while I walk her a step back to ensure she has the wall for stability. Our foreheads touch while our mouths part, with the drizzling droplets of water the only barrier between us, and I have no qualms about what I'm about to do to her in the shower.

Kneeling down, I lick between her thighs, and she moans at first touch. Throwing her leg over my shoulder, I enjoy lapping her up and tracing her bundle of nerves with my tongue. I loved having my head between her legs that night, and I think I suppressed the craving, but it's come out with a vengeance in this moment.

Her fingers entwine in my hair as she tilts her body against my mouth, and I like that she's greedy.

"I came here to make you beg, and I'm failing," she rasps.

My tongue stills against her clit, and I pull back to look up at her with a drowsy smile on her face. "I'm on my knees, and that's close enough."

I return to my task, hungry for more, and I dip my tongue inside of her, causing her hips to buck.

"Declan," she gasps.

My name on her lips; it's praise mixed with confirmation that she's getting lost in the moment too.

Images of last time flash in my mind, which only intensifies my drive to please her. I change the pattern of my tongue against her clit, which sends her into a convulsing state against my mouth.

Peering up, I watch as she comes undone until I feel it's safe to return to standing.

Placing my arm by her head against the wall, I can't stop staring at her mouth that's home to a sleepy satisfied smile.

"Hockey, fucking me with your tongue, any other talents?" She's breathless.

I kiss the corner of her mouth because I can, even though it's far too sweet for this moment. "You'll find out."

She laughs before she reaches for my cock, but I tsk her away. "Not today, sweetheart. Your evil maple syrup episode means that you're the bad girl, and now you have to wait for what you came for."

She loops her arms around my neck. "Oh, but I did come."

My response to her witty remark is turning the water off behind her. Otherwise, I may just say hell with it and literally fuck her.

———

A FEW MINUTES LATER, I'm perched on the edge of the desk in my room as I watch Violet tie her wet hair into a nest on top of her head.

"What do you say? Meet me here tomorrow on your lunch break?"

She's searching for her purse now. "Right, you had this whole meet-every-day-for-a-week proposition."

"You said yes," I remind her before I tear off a piece of paper from the stationary pad and begin to fumble with it.

"I did say yes. Guarantee me a sandwich and I may even show up on time." I enjoy her lighthearted tone.

"I'll even throw in a bag of chips."

"You're trouble."

She snags my gaze, and I toss the paper airplane that I just made —my other hidden talent being origami—in Violet's direction, which she catches. "The best-kept secrets normally are," I promise.

8

VIOLET

I hum as I scoop a spoonful of cooked rice into Nugget's bowl then place it in his cage, slightly taken aback that he doesn't seem to irritate me as much today.

The bell above the shop door informs me that someone is here.

"What in the world?" Brielle's perplexed voice causes me to look over my shoulder as I close the door to Nugget's cage.

"What?" I say before closing the container of rice that I brought from home.

Brielle sets her umbrella by the door before she walks over to lean against the counter, with her eyes never parting from my direction. "You're actually smiling while you feed the parrot."

"So?" I shrug as I walk behind the counter. I feel like my sister-in-law came to have a talk. "What brings you by on this dreary Monday morning?"

We both look out the window to see the rain pouring down. "It's supposed to be this way all week. Blah. I guess we needed the rain, and it doesn't really matter, Ford and Connor are at the ice rink all week for summer camp anyway, and something tells me that your free time is spent indoors with a certain former hockey player." She taps her nails on the counter.

My face tightens, and my eyes freeze on Brielle who isn't wasting time and going the direct route, proven by her smirk that she caught me off guard. "Oh? What would make you say that? Nothing is going on, and with whom? So many hockey players waltz in and out of Ford's life."

Brielle continues to tap a steady beat, with her face poised with confidence. "The one who is in Lake Spark for a week and graced our dinner table over the weekend." She raises a brow at me.

"And?"

"The old lady from the knitting club saw you two a little cozy in your store, then told someone at the general store when April just so happened to be there to overhear, who then informed me before the BBQ, which naturally meant that I was observing you with my lawyer eyes, and you failed, like completely. There is totally something between you and Declan Dash."

My jaw goes slack because that's one hell of a gossip train, and yeah, she's a lawyer, so squirming out of this may be tricky.

But the reality is that nothing is going on between Declan and me. We're only having fun, and nothing will come of it.

"Nothing is happening," I half-lie and pull out my purse to grab my lip balm, only to notice the paper airplane from yesterday, and I can't control the smile that tugs on my mouth.

Brielle, who is now rubbing circles on her belly, doesn't seem to believe me; I can tell by her stoic facial expression. "Look, say what you want, but if anything, whether serious, fun, or who knows what is brewing between you and Declan, then just know that Ford will lose his cool. He's seen every shitty choice his former teammates have made, and as much as Declan is a friend, it only means that Ford is even more critical of him when it comes to women. No, not even, when it comes to *you*."

"Like I said, nothing to worry about. Does Ford think something is going on?"

Brielle scoffs a laugh. "Please, it was the weekend, and we have a sixteen-year-old. His mind was occupied with that, so you're fine."

"You know, even if I was, you know, well, I'm allowed to have a little… fun," I justify.

"Of course you are, but not with your brother's friend. When it goes wrong, then it *really* goes wrong. Plus…" She reaches out to touch my hand on the counter. "You deserve a hell of a love story, not some guy who will make you laugh but never commit. Violet, you can keep telling me that life is great, but I know that's not true. Something is missing for you. Your mom never played a big role in your life, but you made peace with that long ago, probably because you have family here who adore you and need you. But I know you want to *experience* romance and family for yourself. You used to tell me about the husband and kids you want one day. After…"

I close my eyes because I don't want to hear her reminder of a disaster from not long ago. It's hard to accept that I have an absent mom and I bury myself into my brother's family. I'm watching everything that I want on a daily basis.

She licks her lips and takes a beat. "Since the…, you throw on a smile, but I think you believe you don't deserve more." Thankfully, she doesn't repeat the memory that I don't need today. Instead, she squeezes my hand for comfort. "One day you will realize, and I'm not sure Declan is the guy who would hold your hand and walk you into that happy ever after you've dreamed about."

Abruptly, I pull my hand away. "Geez, Brielle, you didn't even bring me a coffee from Jolly Joe's for this deep conversation." I roll my eyes.

"Want to send the pregnant lady out in the rain to go grab your coffee and a cinnamon roll so you'll listen?" She grins.

I cross my arms and pretend to be annoyed. "I mean, let's not get dramatic. You're probably on your way there anyhow."

"I am. Why don't you join me. Don't you have a lunch break soon?"

I smile awkwardly. "I do, but I have an appointment at one. Tilly is coming in to help this afternoon and will handle this place for an hour or so."

Brielle narrows her eyes in on me. "Appointment?"

"Yes. I need to deliver some flowers to the Dizzy Duck."

She scans the room. "Strange. I don't see any flowers ready for delivery."

"I still need to make the bouquet," I lie.

Brielle looks at her watch. "It's already 12:40."

For fuck's sake.

I throw on a fake smile and walk to the middle of my store and pull out a few flowers. "Making it now."

"Sure you are," she says, playing along.

With a sharp movement, I pull out a lily from one of the buckets on the floor. "I'd better get moving on this."

"You do that then, and just remember, fun is fun until either someone catches feelings or Ford discovers that your constant smile today is due to Declan."

"It's all fine because nothing is going on," I call out in an attempt to deter her thoughts once more, knowing it's pointless, but I felt a need to try.

———

I SLAM the bouquet of flowers that don't even match into Declan's hard chest the moment he opens the hotel room door.

"Don't get excited, I was trapped and had to make a bouquet to survive, and I'm not wasting flowers," I explain, and my eyes instantly land on the trays of food sitting on the table by the window in his suite.

Even though I beeline it to the food, I sure as hell notice that the man looks good in jeans and a t-shirt, and his jaw is more defined since he doesn't seem to have shaved today.

"Trust me, my entire body is riveted with excitement for these flowers," he says sarcastically as he closes the door. He sets the flowers on the desk and walks to the table. "You're late." He grins.

I'm already sitting down and examining what food we have. "Sorry, Brielle wanted to remind me that life can be puppies, babies, and sunshine." Looking up, I see that Declan has a confused expression on his face, as he should. "Ignore me. I'm late and starving."

He indicates for me to lift the cover of the tray, and I do so eagerly to find a burger and fries. "Figured you'll burn a ton of calories, so I'd better go all out."

A fry lands in my mouth and tastes heavenly. "I totally skipped breakfast this morning by accident. A bride was waiting at my door because she was eloping at the courthouse and forgot about flowers, then Brielle came by, and hell, I'm not even sure I'm caffeinated today." I shake the ketchup bottle because hunger is taking over my words and body.

"I'm a little scared what Monday-you looks like on coffee now." Declan sits down in front of me and removes the cover on his plate and reveals a BLT sandwich. "It's okay, I need to eat too. I'm training a group of ten-year-olds at 2:30, and something tells me that I need energy for that. I need a relaxing de-stressor too, but I think that's why you're here."

I throw a fry at him, but I can't help but beam at his humor. "I think you kind of enjoy helping at camp. Is it the first time that you're on the ice since the season ended?"

His face turns soft as he pauses for a moment. "I guess it is. It's slightly different, but maybe I didn't notice since playing hockey comes naturally." Declan flexes his jaw side to side and seems to be at peace with his realization.

"Kind of cool that you get to do something else with hockey now."

"I think everyone is waiting for me to fail." He laughs.

I take a break from chomping on my food and study him for a second. "Curse of a family name or…?"

"Nobody wants the rich guy to succeed. In truth, the whole owning-a-hockey-team thing leaves a lot of room for error. I'm not used to all these business meetings. It's kind of a relief this week being in Lake Spark and back on the ice."

I prop my head in my hand and appreciate his honesty on the topic. He notices that I'm staring, and his lips twist. "I feel like hockey players take on projects once they retire. When Ford retired, it was full-on Operation Win Back Brielle, and then family and the sports complex, it all keeps him busy. I guess owning a hockey team is your project?" I flash him an odd look. Partly because, for some reason deep within, it doesn't feel like he is convinced of his next chapter.

A sound escapes him, and our eyes lock for a thick moment. "You maybe have a point. It's going to be hard not to bring up Ford in conversation, isn't it?"

"Probably." I sigh.

"How did you end up as a florist?" Declan asks before grabbing a bottle of water.

I set my burger down, no qualms that I can eat like it's a night at home chillaxing. "After college, I wanted to start a business, and I've always loved flowers. I was never great at sports, but I did join a sorority, which might be the reasoning for some of my tendencies." I tilt my head to the side in contemplation.

"That's how you know Charlotte? From your sorority?" He looks at me, purely entertained.

"For sure. Anyway, despite the epic Friday-night parties, we had quite a lot of rules, including a promise to volunteer in the community. I volunteered to be a big sister to a girl in high school, Phoebe. She has Down Syndrome, and she loves flowers—tulips, in particular. Our weekly meetings were always at the botanical gardens, visiting florists, or planting flowers at her house. Her family moved to Vermont, but every year, I send her tulip bulbs to plant so in the spring she has them blooming. So anyway, after college and one business loan with Ford's help later, I put down roots here in Lake Spark."

Declan leans back in his chair, with his eyes surveying me, up and down, but in a way that feels almost captivated, and it sends a wave a warmth through me. I guess I forgot what it feels like to be the object of someone's sole attention; I'm always the one there for everyone else.

"I'm trying to figure out your flaw. Everything you say makes it difficult for me to believe that you have any, except we all have one."

I sigh. "Trust me, we all have cracks, even if you don't see them." I look away because I can't handle his eyes on me, maybe because now I feel that he is watching me closer.

"You're right. Just sometimes we manage to keep it to ourselves." His voice is gentle almost, and I swear I hear vulnerability, or maybe I wish for it because then I would feel even in this conversation.

"I'm pretty sure that I didn't come here for a burger and small talk." I smile nervously because it's best if I attempt to move us on to other matters.

"You're right. Stand up." I'm surprised how his tone switched to an order. Returning my gaze to him, I'm faced with his determination.

Wiping my hands quickly with the napkin, I stand up, very much aware that this man has no problem with dominance, but the playful smirk on the corner of his mouth is inviting and relaxed.

I slowly walk a few steps then plop myself onto the edge of the bed, sitting up straight like a polite woman would. "I believe you mentioned something about de-stressing." My eyes drift down to my finger where I'm tracing the lines of the duvet pattern. Nonetheless, I sense Declan vacate his chair, causing my chest to flutter.

The mattress dips when he sits down next to me, and when his hand lands on my thigh, I nearly shiver from his touch. An unbearable aching ignites between my legs, and I feel my nipples tighten. All of this because he placed his hand on my oh, so sensitive inner thigh.

My breath catches when I feel the pads of his fingers slide up my skin, taunting me of his impending touch between my legs.

Declan leans in to whisper near the shell of my ear. "Do you want to know a secret, Vi?"

"Yes." My breath feels heavy.

"All morning, you've been on my mind and how I want to touch you. I'm trying to be a good guy and let you have your lunch, but I don't want to be the good guy anymore." Declan's lips trail down my neck until he finds my collarbone that he traces with his tongue.

"Never be the good guy around me." My voice is filled with lust that I didn't realize could be so overpowering.

His head tilts up, and our lips meet for a slow kiss. An instant sizzle that sets off fireworks inside of me. Nothing is enough right now. I need more of his mouth, more of his hands. I need him to take me the way he's been thinking about since that night.

Our bodies tangle when he guides my leg to prop over his lap. His tongue is a delicious assault to my senses as he swipes gently the tip of my tongue.

We fall back onto the mattress, and our bodies curve against one another as we're trying to feel everything at once.

"Clothes off," I manage to say between kisses.

I'm searching for the straps of my dress that are midway down my arms now. I can't see because I refuse to let our mouths part.

Declan reaches between us to fumble with his zipper.

But just as we're about to remove all our barriers, a phone goes off.

"Ignore it," I plead and struggle to drag my lips away enough to speak.

"Not my phone," he mumbles into my mouth.

Shit.

I groan and reluctantly pull away. As much as I wish I could ignore it, I can't. It's still a workday, and I told Tilly to call if it was urgent.

Grabbing the phone from my bag, I quickly answer while I look down at Declan who has no plans on moving an inch. "Hey, Tilly." I sound almost out of breath. She answers on the other end and explains the issue that someone phoned in an order because they forgot their wife's fiftieth birthday party. "Yeah, no. I mean, I'll be there as soon as I can. Give me fifteen minutes. Just grab a bunch of dahlias for now. Okay? See you soon."

The moment I end my call, Declan is patting the mattress and inviting me back.

I throw on an over-the-top pout. "Sorry. I have to go. A last-minute order came in, and it's a big one. Need to go save some husband after he forgot his wife's surprise birthday party."

Declan blows out a big breath, and he returns to sitting. "Work of a superhero."

I begin to straighten my dress, severely disappointed in this change of events. "Raincheck?"

"Same time tomorrow?" he suggests.

I nod and rise from the bed. "I'll even come caffeinated and fed so we can skip to the good part."

Declan grins as he slides off the bed and approaches me, placing his hands on my shoulders, with his eyes so damn charming. "I think I like you wolfing down a burger and not afraid to ask questions."

"I have a hundred more."

"And I think I do too." He leans down to capture my mouth for a quick kiss, a sweet parting. "See you tomorrow."

I smile softly at him before I head to the door. "Maybe I'll send you a picture later. An apology for leaving."

"Wouldn't complain. But you don't owe me an apology. I left a note on the pillow, remember?"

I laugh to myself. "And I'm leaving you with a monster hard-on."

"Call us even."

I hold the door open as I look back at him. His head is low, and he wipes his hand across his jaw. His sexual frustration just makes him ten times hotter. "Hey, Dec."

He looks up with bright blue eyes. "Yeah?"

"You said earlier that everyone is waiting for you to fail." His head perks back slightly at my words. "I don't think you'll fail."

He seems taken aback by my words. "Why do you do that?"

"What?"

"Say things that are actually sincere."

I slant a shoulder up to my ear. "Why do you say things that remind me I can have the time of my life?"

"Because I'm selfish, and you haven't left my mind since that night." His blunt answer lingers in my mind for the rest of the day.

9

DECLAN

I hook my hands under the arms of an eight-year-old who just fell on the ice. As soon as he is up on two feet, he's gliding away from me as if nothing happened. That's pretty much what kids do, bounce back. Or at least, that's what I've noticed the last two days of helping at the kids' summer camp.

They skate around without a care in the world, and I'm kind of jealous. Being stuck in the crossroads of your life isn't exactly a clear-minded experience.

Skating to the boards, I watch as the group of mostly boys skates around to warm up. I don't have a clear plan about what I'll teach them today, but I feel like taking shots at the net is a basic good start.

"Don't forget that lunch is at one," Connor reminds me from off the ice. I glance at him and see that he's busy surveying his to-do list on his tablet. To my surprise, Ford didn't have to rope Connor into being a camp coordinator; he volunteered. Of course, he negotiated his hourly wage, so it's not exactly volunteering.

"Lunch?" I cock a brow.

He looks at me as if I'm crazy. "Yeah, with the kids. Some days you can do your own thing to have a break, but today is team build-ing, so enjoy your peanut-butter-and-jelly sandwich, or cheese sandwich if you have a peanut allergy. If you really feel like you want to live it up, then have a juice box too." His tone is mundane.

I rub the back of my neck and blow out a breath. I forgot, and I was kind of looking forward to lunch with Violet. Now I'll have to find a new time and wait even longer to see her.

"Not a problem," I lie. "Okay, make sure they're all lined up in five minutes. You should get your skates on, I want your help this morning," I tell him.

Connor looks up from the screen. "Really? You want my help?"

"Isn't that why you're here, Mr. Varsity Hockey Player?" I flash him a grin, as I can tell my request is boosting his ego a bit. In truth, he has talent, and he's going places. I feel confident enough to give him a little responsibility.

"Okay, I'll be right back."

I nod my head, and I quickly step off the ice to grab my phone from my bag. Quickly, I scroll down my contacts, then touch the screen to type.

ME

How caffeinated are you today? I won't be able to escape for lunch. What about room service at dinner time?

The moment I hit send, I realize that a dinner time slot is slightly risky. It leaves a gray area about what to do for the night—stay or go. It's the ambiguous no-man's land of fuck-buddy protocol. She sees the message instantly, and the dots move.

VIOLET

Oh, dinner...

Huh, she must be thinking it too.

I guess it could work.

7?

Sure.

Alright, see you then. Slightly disappointed I
never got a photo…

I throw in a crying emoji.

I had no free hands…

I chortle a laugh and quickly look around to check that nobody is
taking notice of me.

I can help you later.

How courteous. ;)

Have to go teach these kids, but I'll see you
later, if that bird doesn't get to you first…

Good luck! And if Nugget hasn't killed me
by now, then I think we're safe.

I smile to myself and place my phone back in the bag. Violet is
someone who I think, when all is said and done, after our little round
of weeklong fun ends, that she could be a friend. It's easy to talk to
her, never makes me feel a need to impress, and she's funny. The
drop-dead-gorgeous factor can't be denied either.

Only this week, I remind myself.

I don't do relationships. Hell, I can't even figure out what makes
me happy careerwise right now, but if I ever did a relationship, then I
suppose I would want the woman to be exactly like Violet. I guess
her future husband will be one lucky man. The idea of her with
someone else causes a sour feeling in my stomach, but I can't think
for too long.

Connor returns and sits on the bench to remove the skate guards.

"We're going to do two lines. I need your help keeping the kids
in order. After everyone has a turn, then we need to collect the pucks
and do another round. I don't want too many pucks lying around on
the ice, it's too much of a hazard with the kids," I explain.

"Sure."

Connor heads out onto the ice, but as I begin to move, I hear Ford call my name. I smile when I see him walking down the stairs.

"Go ahead and start, you got this," I call out to Connor.

"Putting my son to good use?" Ford grins before leaning against the boards.

"Absolutely. What has you in a good mood?" I wonder, as he seems happy today. Then again, Ford is normally very content these days.

Ford glances out onto the ice then back to me. "I was getting my coffee from Jolly Joe's. Remember the place where they put jellybeans in your coffee, and you never know which color you'll get?"

I wince from the idea of it, sounds disgusting.

"Anyway, the local real estate agent mentioned that this one house is going up on the market soon. If you're interested, then she can get you in before it hits the market."

"Why would I do that?" I play, entertained.

He slaps a hand against my shoulder. "Because if you are serious about the Spinners training here, then the Dizzy Duck Inn just won't do. Besides, doesn't the idea of fresh air and a lake house sound like a nice little escape?"

My brows bounce because he isn't wrong. "Send me the number of the agent, and I'll consider it."

"Great. You know Violet was a city girl until she moved here, and I think it's been great for her. A different scene completely changed her life. I mean, I'm sure having people she knows around helps. But you know people here."

There is something about his sentence that piques my interest. "Why did she need a change of scene?"

Ford scratches his cheek. "Everyone has a rough patch at some point. I guess I never told you about her car accident."

Immediately, I'm invested to learn more. "No, what accident?"

Ford waves me off. "It's a long story, but she's fine now." He indicates with his head to the group on the ice. "Connor may need some help. He's outnumbered, and those eight-year-olds are circling him. Time to go awe them."

I'm uneasy now. I want to discover what Violet never mentioned. In a feral sort of way, I feel responsible to know all her secrets, considering I am one of them.

But now isn't the moment for me to play detective. Thankfully, I'll see her tonight.

———

VIOLET SHAKES out her hair as she steps into my room. "It's pouring out there."

"Luckily, I have no plans of leaving these four walls," I tell her as I help her out of her rain poncho which has parrots on it. That's what I like about her, she brings humor to everything, including the things she hates. "I didn't order room service yet, wasn't sure what you would want to eat. No joke, I ate peanut butter and jelly for lunch."

"Grape or strawberry jelly?" she interrogates.

I scoff a sound. "Grape, of course. To be honest, I forgot how much I missed such a classic sandwich."

She giggles and walks to the table to grab the menu, taking notice of the paper crane I made while I waited for her. "They actually have a really good plate of nachos here. The steak is good too—oh, and the pumpkin tortellini is to die for."

"Just order a few things." I walk to the mini fridge to grab a beer, and I hold up the bottle of wine, but she shakes her head.

"I drove here, and it's raining. And staying the night is kind of out of the boundaries." She clicks the inside of her cheek.

I grin at her logic, because I was wondering if she picked up on the obstacle of a dinner meet-up, but once again, she is making this too easy for me.

She closes the menu. "Okay, you will be ordering us nachos and two steaks."

"I'm ordering?" I walk to her and grab the menu from her.

Violet pokes a finger into my chest. "Yes, because I already snuck my way up here to avoid Ted at reception. The last thing I need is someone recognizing my voice then starting the Lake Spark gossip train." She holds her finger up into the air. "Gotta love our little Lake Spark bubble."

"I guess. But lucky us, the inn went digital, and we can order via the TV." She gives me an unimpressed pout. "Which I'm excellent at using, so I will handle that order right now," I assure her, and her smile returns.

Two minutes later, we have food ordered and an ETA of forty-five minutes.

"Whatever shall we do while we wait?" Violet's tone is flippant as she begins to unbutton her blouse. The view sends a spiral of heat straight to my dick.

My voice lowers, and I step closer to her. "Getting you on your knees is an idea. Just throwing out options."

Violet's eyes dance as she tips her chin up. Instantly, I hook my finger under her jaw to bring her lips to mine.

Relief fills me, because apparently the craving to kiss her all day was of a higher magnitude than I realized.

It's the way she whimpers into my mouth because our lips refuse to part. Better yet, it's her murmur when our tongues untangle for a second, while she drapes her arms over my shoulders and my hands frame her hips, pulling her tight to me. I like it all.

We fall back onto the bed, and I yank down the blouse, stealing a glimpse of her purple bra in the process. Fucking lace.

I'm far too fortunate.

She begins to tug on the bottom of my t-shirt. "Was my mouth on your cock an option too?" she purrs.

Extremely fortunate.

"Absolutely, but I've been dying to fuck your pussy for far too long. Maybe a quick round?" I toss her over my lap to ensure she's straddling me. I want her to feel my hard dick thrusting between her legs.

But in a split second, the beautiful glint in her eyes entraps me, and suddenly, everything Ford said earlier runs through my brain.

The confident woman on top of me has a past, a puzzle piece that I want to find, when I have no right to.

Her face and movement still when she notices that I'm surveying her more intently, causing her eyes to narrow. "You okay?" she whispers.

An audible exhale escapes me because I don't recognize this version of myself. Sex always comes first, except in this moment.

I pull her down to me for an embrace and tuck her head under my chin. "I need to ask you something."

She retreats slightly and our eyes meet, hers fueled with concern. "What?"

"Ford mentioned something today about your accident."

Instantly, she crawls off me and stands, my body feeling the loss of her, and an inkling inside of me is desperate to get her back in my arms.

"My brother has a big mouth." She crosses her arms and appears very agitated; her nostrils even flare slightly.

I sit up, and the distance is just right that I can wrap my arms around her legs to force her to step forward. I peer up to her, resting my chin on her belly. "I don't know. Does he? I don't know what happened."

Violet doesn't seem to want to look at me, but I can see she's visibly annoyed, and I feel bad that it's my doing.

"I'm sorry, maybe it's not my place to ask." But I'm desperate for an answer, because I'm now too intrigued.

I run my hands along the sides of her body, tracing the curve of her ass, before wrapping around her again so she has no chance to escape.

But she does, because she squirms out of my hold and flops onto her back on the mattress like a starfish, which isn't half bad, because now I can just lie on my side and stare down at her.

"You want to know what happened?" She stares at the ceiling. "I destroy things. That's what I do."

My fingers find her loose hair, and I tuck it behind her ear. She doesn't flinch, but I can't seem to not touch her when she's around me. "I doubt you destroy things."

Her head turns sharply in my direction. "I was in an accident, with my ex. It was a few years ago. We were having an argument, and he ran a red light. Physically, everyone survived, except I had a broken rib and a few stitches from glass cutting me."

"Shit, sounds a bit more than a normal car accident."

I hear the longest sigh of my life escape her lips. "Well, the injuries were kind of the least of my problems. I discovered that I was the other woman."

My brows knit together as I try to understand. "What do you mean?"

"After the accident, I discovered he had a wife with a baby. The hospital phoned his emergency contact. I swear I didn't know. There wasn't even one sign. I met him when he just moved to the city for his new job. Apparently, it turned out his family was still back in Atlanta."

I cringe for her. "Ouch."

"I'm a horrible person. I played a role in destroying a child's family."

"You had no idea. It's the asshole's doing, not yours."

Violet laughs without humor. "That's what Ford said. My mom and I barely talk, my dad is fine with me but he sometimes lacks emotion. Ford is… Ford. My brother who is more than a brother, he fills in for what my parents lack. Which is why he was the one I called, and he met me at the hospital. If you ever wanted to see him ready to kill, then that was it. Which is why I'm thankful that he doesn't know what we're doing."

I bite my inner cheek and tense slightly, but it soon passes. "Don't let the asshole prevent you from moving on."

"It's not that I'm not open to dating, Dec. It's more that I currently enjoy knowing the clear lines of what to expect, less likely to lead to a surprise."

"Ah, you mean that party. You obviously enjoy sex but don't want to deal with the thought of getting hurt again."

She seems to ease. "Exactly. Just like this week, we have a deadline."

My finger grazes the skin around her navel. "Now I understand why you seem very comfortable with all the situations we find ourselves in."

Her lips quirk out, and it's freaking cute. "What about you? What could have possibly happened to make you so opposed to relationships?"

I lie back and bring my arms behind my head. "Easy. Nobody has given me a reason to believe that a relationship worthy of more is possible."

"That's called, you haven't found the one. You never got close to feeling like maybe that person is more than a friend with benefits?"

"Not entirely. I dated someone for a few months a couple of years back. It wasn't serious but more than benefits, I guess," I admit for the first time.

It grabs her interest, and now she's the one lying on her side to watch me. "What happened?"

"I discovered her hidden stockpile of birth control that she swore she was taking, and a lie like that is something you can't come back from. Trust is a big thing." Wow, I never realized I was keeping that in, and it feels damn good to have told someone else.

"That is bad. I couldn't agree more. Trust is everything." Violet grips the front of my shirt and yanks me, causing me to move until I'm hovering over her. "Look at us then. Two hopeless souls," she whispers.

"Nah, you still believe in love. Why else would you help people romance through flowers?"

The lines of her mouth stretch into a wry smile. "I never said I don't believe in love. I'm just on a temporary break from pursuing it."

I kiss her along her ribs once. "Thank fuck for that. You showed up to a party and ended up with me."

She hums while she licks her lips, and her eyes gawk at me. "Trust. Tell me the truth…" She's waiting for me, and I think I know what she's insinuating, but I'm not 100% sure. "How involved was fate that we ended up with one another's name?"

A deep chuckle rumbles in the back of my throat. Ah yes, I was wondering if she would ever ask. "Did I rig the magic of the bowls?"

Violet nods once, with the tip of her tongue darting out to the corner of her mouth, and she looks delicious.

"I didn't know you would be at the party, obviously. I can't confirm it, but as much as rules are rules, Brent is the one who pulled the names, and he knew that I might have had my eye on you…"

She laughs softly and tips her pelvis up against me. "A secret wink, folding the paper a certain way, the options are endless. Let's just leave it at that and focus on reliving what we did after our names ended up together."

I smirk at her suggestion and back off slightly to give myself room to sneak up her skirt and grip her panties. "Then we better get these off right now."

Because I won't let her leave until after I've buried deep inside of her.

10

VIOLET

Declan's expression is hungry and determined. The moment he tosses the flimsy fabric from his fingers, he's slowly crawling over me, causing the heat of his body to spread along my skin.

My entire body pulses from anticipation, only intensified when he kisses my lips for a long firm kiss before backing up. "Naked. Now."

Quickly, I discard all my remaining clothes while he works his shirt off.

"Tell me that you've been thinking about my cock inside of you all day." He coaxes my thighs open with his hand, and he slips his fingers along my pussy that is soaking for him. "I think you have, and I want to hear you say it." His sly smirk is nearly proud that he is responsible for my body's reaction.

"I have, and I'm disappointed that it's taken this long for you to fuck me again."

He growls, rubbing my arousal around my clit, and embarrassingly, I know I won't last long.

Scooting back, he looks down at me, his eyes pinned to my center, and he quickly decides what to do by using his hands to part my thighs wider, but I can't help but notice his tongue darts out to lick a line across his bottom lip.

I'm completely exposed, but it only turns me on more.

"Remember that night? Your heels stayed on, and I watched you. Do it right now, touch this soaking pussy in front of me." Declan's tone is purely demanding.

Without hesitation, I slide my fingers down my flat belly to touch myself. Nobody has watched me with as much intensity as he does. Gliding between my lips, my eyes hood closed as I sink into my own pleasure.

"Open your eyes, Vi. I need you to look at me while I watch."

I bite my lip because he won't let me take the easy way out. Forced to view the way he watches me while I touch myself adds a layer of pleasure, although it should make me self-conscious.

My toes dig into the bed, my lips roll in, and I open my eyes to be greeted by his gaze fixed on my pussy.

Slipping one finger inside of myself, he hisses in approval.

"Are you just going to watch?" My voice is sultry, a version of myself that I don't quite recognize, but I like challenging him.

I'm near a ledge, and Declan picks up on this, which causes him to take hold of my wrist, stopping me.

I'm left balancing on the edge while he brings my fingers to his mouth and sucks with a groan. His breath makes me eager to insist he moves between my legs.

"To hell with dinner. You taste good, and I intend on getting my fill. Are you this wet because you know that tonight your pussy is all mine?"

This man's mouth, gah! A dirty mouth suits him.

Words don't escape my lips, especially when his knuckles outline my pelvic bone.

"Hmm, so many options of how to make you come." My body curves into his touch, seeking more. "I should make you wait, it will make your orgasm better." His fingers move to my nipples, and he twists both while my hands work his buckle that he finally lets me handle. "Is there any part of your body that isn't gorgeous?"

I'm on fire, the sensitivity of my nipples sending a tight coil straight to my pussy.

"Please." The breathy plea escapes me.

Declan smirks, leans down, and captures one nipple into his mouth to suck and toy between his teeth.

"I like when you beg. You'll do that a lot tonight," he says against my skin.

I nod like a wanton woman overcome with desire.

He removes his pants and boxer briefs, and his cock stands at full attention. I enjoy watching him prepare himself to take me, with his hand gripping his cock for a few strokes while he grabs a condom from his wallet.

"But begging waits. This round we do quick; next round, not a fucking chance," he grits out while he slides the condom on.

Without any grace, he hooks under my knees to spread me out. "You're going to wrap these legs around me while I take you deep and hard. I know you can handle it." He slides his cock between my arousal and circles my clit, dragging his tip down to goad me, and I whimper in agony because I'm impatient and aching for him to be inside of me. I do my best to move under him to bring him within me. "Someone is needy for my cock. Want me to slide right into you?"

"Yes," I gasp, as I'm about to lose my patience.

He enters me, just the tip and retreats right back out. "Vi, you feel tight and so damn ready." He slides his cock back in and unapologetically thrusts deeper inside of me.

We grunt and moan together from the impact of his movement, and it only intensifies as he keeps his promise.

Fast. Hard. Mind-blowing.

NOT EVEN A MINUTE after collapsing from our orgasm, room service arrived. We had perfect timing, and I disappeared into the bathroom, as I was naked and wanted to clean up. Now, I wrap the terrycloth robe around my body and exit the bathroom to find we're alone, with dinner now set on the table.

I take an extra moment to admire how Declan looks like a man who threw his clothes on, with his hair slightly ruffled, but he wears the just-fucked look well.

He walks to me and runs his fingers into my hair. "Eat quick. We have round two to get to." His voice is gruff and laced with a sweltering request.

"Trust me, you will want to savor every bite of those nachos." I tow him along by gently holding the tips of his fingers.

We find ourselves, again, at a table with food. Dining out in public isn't really an option considering our dynamic, and to be honest, after what just went down, I'm not sure I would want everyone in public to see my glow. We both seem too obvious.

"Okay, you're right. The cheese is melted just right on this," he tells me mid-bite.

"How was the rink today?" I grab a chip.

He looks up at me and rolls his tongue along his inner cheek. "It was actually fun. Kids aren't afraid to be blunt, but it's kind of nice to see a bunch of little eyes staring at you like you can do no wrong."

"Maybe you picked the wrong career path and coaching kids is really your calling."

He chortles a laugh. "Nah, I don't have the energy for that. I need a little more… power struggle on the ice."

My face must turn cherry red because of his words; the only thing that my brain seems to connect is an obvious parallel. "You like power, huh." It's most definitely more of an observation than a question.

Declan narrows his gaze on me until it feels like a piercing sword, and that damn droll smirk returns. "It's a good thing to have. Something you care to share?"

"Well…" I steeple my hands on the table and sit straight, as if I'm behind a desk. "You felt the need to own a team, and if I recall that night, someone was leading, and it wasn't me. No complaints." I smile shyly and avoid looking at him, but I can't control it, and my smile stretches and stretches until I nearly laugh.

"Okay, someone has another idea in their dirty little mind." He's amused.

Clearing my throat, I know I will spit it out even though I shouldn't. "I wouldn't be surprised if you've had a dominant/submissive relationship with someone."

Now I have to watch him because it feels like the air evaporated from the room. The smile on his face disappears, and his eyes turn dark with a seriousness. For a few moments, he is lost in thought, and I can't figure out where his head is at.

He scoffs a sound before he abruptly stands up and circles around the table, and as if I'm weightless, he shifts my chair while I'm in it. His thumb lands on my bottom lip, and he drags my lip side to side.

I'm speechless because he has me completely entranced.

"You think you've figured me out. Is that what you want, Vi? To be always ready to go on your knees when I demand it?"

Holy fuck, his tone is pure authority mixed with confidence.

And for a reason I'm not quite sure, my body instantly agrees, with my head nodding once, while he dips his thumb into my mouth, encouraging me to suck.

"You would only ever come when I let you, and I would spank you when I want."

I'm mesmerized.

"Call you my good girl when we both know that you're anything but."

I gulp while my clit throbs, and at this moment, I will agree to anything if it means he touches me more right now. My entire body, down to my toes, craves this man.

His thumb pops out of my mouth, and he unzips his jeans, lowering them slowly as my eyes glue to his movement, and when his cock becomes free, his solid length is directly in front of my eyes, and my mouth salivates.

"Be a good girl right now and open that filthy mouth of yours," he husks, and with his free hand, he gently grabs the back of my head, pulling my hair to guide my mouth to his cock. He stops for one moment to search my eyes for consent, and I softly nod before he leads me to his cock.

I dart out my tongue and lick his tip.

"Suck," he demands.

I bring him deeper into my mouth, drawing with my tongue along his entire length, letting him lead when he pushes farther into my mouth until he reaches that sensitive part that warns us of my limit.

I peer up for approval, and the corner of his mouth tilts, while he brings his thumb to glide along my cheek, an almost caring gesture.

"You're beautiful with my cock in your mouth."

His words cause me to bob more, my mouth watering, and I have an overwhelming urge to bring my fingers between my legs for relief as I feel my upper thighs get messy.

I attempt to lower my free hand, but Declan ends that sentiment quickly by grabbing my wrist and holding me firm.

"I didn't say you could, and you didn't ask for permission."

Oh yeah, he's trying to prove a point.

I moan with a full mouth, but I'm mixed with emotion. It feels good to please someone, but I'm miserable that my clit is going untouched.

Without notice, Declan pulls me off his cock and holds my hair to force me to look up at him.

"To answer your question, you are perfect sub material…"

I blink because I think he's about to, well, I'm not sure, but my heart is beating extremely fast.

"But I'm not your dom." A disappointment pings at me, and that's a surprise, but so are his next words. "I'm nobody's dom." A sound escapes his lips, but his eyes don't leave me; he's staring at my swollen mouth. "As much I do like the idea of that lifestyle, have respect for anyone who can handle it, but it requires trust, patience, and most of all, time. There are rules, and you're in a sort of relationship. It's not for me." His head tilts slightly to the side. "…At this moment."

"Oh." My breathy answer is the only word that I manage to say, and it's not even a word of substance.

Declan leans down so our eyes are aligned. "It's extremely hot that you're open to a lot of things." He begins to untie my robe to reveal my naked body. "By all means, we can try a few things over the next few days, if that's what you want."

"I…" What am I trying to say? "It's not that I'm into it, I just… really thought if either of us had done that, then it's you."

A sinister chuckle escapes him. "Maybe one day. But right now, I need to fuck you again, because I'm still painfully hard, and I know you're wet and eager." He opens the flaps of my robe, and I'm splayed out naked, with the fabric hanging off my arms. "How about you ride me until I'm about to come, and then I come all over your beautiful ass that's red from the spanking I give you."

His hands travel down my body, spreading goosebumps across my skin.

"Yes, sir."

I giggle as he pulls me up out of the chair and takes us straight to the bed.

———

I KICK away Declan's foot as he tries to keep his leg over me to entrap me, but as tempting as this warm bed is, I know better and should head home soon. But one minute more won't cause any harm, I'm sure.

His arm adjusts around me as I lie with my head on the pillow.

"I think we can agree that we need to recover now," I say.

"Pff, speak for yourself. I'm a well-trained athlete with stamina for days."

I roll my eyes. "You're a *retired* athlete."

"Ouch."

"Yeah, because team owner sounds so drab."

Declan rolls to his side and props his head up against his arm. "I might be horrible at it. I can't even properly feed the woman I'm fucking like crazy."

I wave him off. "You'll be fine. I barely remember to feed the bird, and I'm still successful at my shop."

He reaches back with his free arm to grab his phone, and he begins to connect to the Bluetooth. "What are we listening to?" He pauses, and his nose scrunches up. "What's your musical taste?"

"Anything country or indie."

"Ah, you're a country girl. No wonder you like certain positions."

I laugh as he brings up a playlist and hits play.

"I'm curious, how in the world did you get into origami? Trust me when I say that it's the last thing I would ever expect your talented hands to do."

Declan gets comfortable between the covers again and peppers a few kisses along the curve of my shoulder. "My grandfather taught English in Japan. Picked up the art of origami and taught me."

"You're close with him?"

"Was. He passed a few years back. Now it's just my parents and me. My mom gets along with everyone, and for what it's worth, my dad isn't bad. He's just waiting for me to step up, and I have no plans to take over maple syrup and hotels. I've been avoiding his calls all week, to be honest."

This time, I'm the one to place a kiss along his arm, a sort of caress. "It's okay, everyone is allowed to have their Lake Spark escape before making key decisions. You know everyone on Ford's street kind of did that. Now you're here and can enjoy Illinois summer and coffee with jellybeans before finding your career path and talking with your dad."

"Illinois summer have just been rain for the past few days," he deadpans.

I wrap my arms around his bicep. "True, but there is an extremely hot florist on Main Street who might just be able to guide you with indoor activities."

"You're guiding me?" He pretends to be offended. "Other way

around, sweetheart. It's more like you have a perfect ass and bring good conversation."

"A winning combination," I retort.

He rolls us over so I'm underneath him. "That's kind of a problem."

I get the feeling there is something underneath his words, but I don't want to try and analyze. This is probably my cue to leave, anyway.

"On that note." I tap his nose with my finger. "I need to go and let you enjoy the warm chocolate chip cookies that they deliver at turndown service."

Leaving him in bed, I scramble to find my clothes.

"Are they good? I keep declining every time they offer the cookies."

I look at him, shocked, as I begin to dress. "They're delicious. I would stay here purely for the cookies. I mean, they are chocolate chip, and they even bring you a glass of cold milk. Come on, live a little."

He smiles to himself. "For you, I'll try. Maybe I can meet you for lunch, but I have a few team meetings about moving training here next season."

I work on the buttons of my blouse. "See? Every day here is getting you closer to your path and will help you let go of hockey-player you and welcome billionaire-team-owner you. Although technically, weren't you always a billionaire? You don't seem like one, except for the car, but you get my drift," I ramble.

"Your perspective is a nice change. People normally hate me or try to kiss my ass. You're just... blunt."

He sits up in the bed, and the sheet falls around his waist. *Yikes,* staring at his chest is not going to get us anywhere. I grab my bag from the chair and decide to steal the paper crane.

I hold it up. "I'll add it to my Declan Dash shrine."

He grins. "As long as it isn't a paper flower, then it's fine."

"Why?"

"Because the flowers in your store wilt and die. A paper flower lasts forever. My grandfather told me that the most romantic thing a guy can do is deliver a paper flower because it shows the relationship will endure time."

My eyes go wide as I think I've heard that before, but it's a beautiful thought, and I do my best to erase the image in my head of what it would be like if a paper flower were to appear in front of me.

After all, flings are temporary.

11

DECLAN

Gliding along the ice, I can't stop grinning as Ford tries to steal the puck as it travels between the passes of my stick. We're playing a little one-on-one before the kids hit the ice. God, I miss this. I really miss this.

"Go easy, we don't have padding on," Ford reminds me.

We're only in jeans and hoodies, but still, I'm putting up a fight with my offense and doing my best with my determination to score a goal.

Picking up speed, we make it across the blue line into the attacking zone, and I take my aim.

The moment the puck hits the net and I get my goal, I let go and slow my skating.

"Damn, you're too good," Ford curses from his loss.

Something about waking up early to hit the ice without any rules or structure is exactly what I needed to start my day today.

I slept great but woke to the smell of Violet in my room, and kind of wondered what it would be like to wake with her in my bed. Not like that night when I left before she woke up, but actually wake up and face one another.

Would she act shy? Or would she lead us into morning sex?

My vote is on the latter.

Stepping off the ice, Ford and I take a seat on the bench. "I think marketing wants to reschedule the photo op to around lunchtime. That's cool, right?" Ford asks as he grabs his water bottle. "'New Spinners' owner teaches kids how to play hockey,' that's probably their angle. Good for the facility and great for your team."

My brows raise. "Sounds about right. Sure, lunchtime is fine."

I already texted Violet that I wasn't sure of my schedule today.

"What did you get up to last night?" Ford asks, making small talk while he unlaces his skates.

Glancing up, I take a second more than I should to answer. I don't feel guilty for what I'm doing with his sister, we're consenting adults, but nonetheless, lying even when it makes perfect sense to do so doesn't feel great either.

"The usual. Room service, checked my stocks, and tried to watch a series."

"Sounds quiet. I'm slightly envious; even the dog was noisy last night at our house." Yet Ford still has a broad smile as he says that.

I chuckle once. "That's the way you like it."

He stands and points a finger at me. "True. One day you will see that hockey isn't everything."

"I'm counting the days," I say in a mundane tone.

He waves me off. "I'll be in my office and will see you in about thirty minutes to go over logistics for some of the proposals you made for pre-season training camp next year. We can video call your GM."

"Great," I call out as Ford heads off.

I arrived in Lake Spark with ideas, from schedules to a list of demands of what would be needed for the team to train well. For one, we need a full commitment for specific dates and office space for the coaching staff. I'm confident that we can make it all happen.

Glancing down at my watch to check my heartrate, I remember I have a little break before heading into the day full force. Grabbing my phone, I pull up Violet's name to type her a message.

ME
No go for lunch. Can we meet later tonight?

I see the dots bouncing in the chat. I know she's at her store, as she mentioned once needing to be there by eight in the morning.

VIOLET
Whatever will I do on my lunch break now?

I love her banter.

I'm sure you will figure something out. Just don't come, it will be better if you wait.

She sends me a few shocked emojis.

Pff. Fine.

7?

Should work. I'll pick something up on my way there. Ruin your room service standards with peasant food.

I scan the area to ensure that nobody notices the beaming smile that I'm wearing.

I'm a laid-back guy, you know that.

That you like to lie on your back? Why, yes, I do know that.

An audible laugh escapes me.

Says the woman who wears ridiculously expensive lingerie… Yeah, I noticed.

It's for a good cause.

I'm a cause now?

No. But my need for enjoyment is.

The image of her in my jersey twists me in a way that I don't like. I want to hate it... but damn, I entertain the idea in my head.

My fists form, and I want to bite my knuckles. I won't be able to get her out of my head. I mean, she's already there, but now it's the extremely X-rated version, complete with her moaning in my ear, that won't escape my thoughts.

A freaking kissing emoji.

Blowing out a breath, I do my best to bring relief to my body. I'm going to have blue balls all day, and I need to focus on something else.

Violet and I have playful chemistry, that's for sure, but the excitement that's inside me, as if I'm counting down the minutes until I see her, isn't because of attraction. Well, it is and it isn't. But I know being unable to filter what I say around her is a change from my other encounters with women, and the fact that her laugh is so freaking beautiful to hear is another plus.

Violet is the type of fling that if the circumstances were different, then I wouldn't be eager to give us a deadline. My stomach sinks from that thought; we're already halfway through the week.

Scratching my chin, I brush all thoughts aside, as I have a day to conquer.

———

OPENING the door of my room, I'm faced with Violet standing in the hall in her rain poncho again. It's been pouring all day; not that I went outside, it was meeting after meeting.

She holds up the takeout bag. "Turkey sandwiches from the deli at the general store, plus a bag of chips because I felt you earned it." She attempts to keep a straight face, but her wicked little smile is something she can't control.

As I grab the bag from her fingers, she steps forward, close to my body, and tips her chin up, with her eyes challenging me.

We're not going to move.

I reach behind her to grab the do-not-disturb sign and slide it on the outside handle.

"So strategic," she purrs in approval.

I push the door closed, our eyes never parting, and I carefully drop the bag onto the floor to the side, before I step forward, which causes her to walk back, right into the door.

"I'm not really hungry," she softly whispers.

"What a coincidence, neither am I."

I lean down to kiss her mouth and allow my hands to cradle her head to ensure I get the best possible angle, because kissing her is the best part of my day so far. Her lips are warm, yet there is a subtle taste of freaking blueberries.

"You taste like muffins," I note before kissing her again, because it's like a drug you could get addicted to, or at least I imagine this is what addiction feels like.

"That's because it's blueberry-muffin lip balm." Violet begins to remove the rain poncho and just throws it to the floor. I'm looking down at her poncho, when she gently clears her throat, and her eyes flash to inform me to take a closer look at her.

The moment I notice what she's wearing, I step away and rub

both of my hands over my face while I groan. "Are you kidding me?"

"It was on the floor of my closet needing a little more respect." She clucks the inside of her cheek.

A whistle escapes my lips as I take in the fact she is wearing shorts that shouldn't be legal and an old Spinners t-shirt which looks like it's been through hell and back, but it just makes it even hotter. It stops right above her belly button and slides off one shoulder, and she isn't wearing a bra. I know this because her pert little nipples are outlined through the shirt.

I was never into puck bunnies, and this outfit is skirting a few similarities. Many women would wear something similar and throw themselves at me at a bar or party after a game. But Violet? Violet is dressed like this with pure intentions; simply to make me smile and laugh.

So what if the consequences of her attempt will be dirty as fuck, but it's all about *why* she did this.

And that just makes me want her even more.

Stepping forward, our bodies are flush, and in one swift move, we work together, with my arms hoisting her up as her legs willingly wrap around my waist.

"Screw the bed, I'm taking you right here," I warn her.

WE EVENTUALLY MIGRATED to the bed and have been talking for what feels like hours. The shirt she tempted me with was lost then thrown back on after our last round, but the shorts haven't left the floor near the door.

"Happy Accident" by Tomberlin plays on my Bluetooth as we face one another on our sides and snack on chips and cookies, since turndown service stopped by.

"Are you still avoiding your dad's calls?" Violet asks, nibbling on a gooey cookie that draws my attention to her mouth,

I grab another potato chip from the little bag resting between us. "He tried to phone earlier, but I was saved by a photo session. I'll face him soon. I kind of need to switch gears, you know? In truth, the last few months have been… odd. I always knew I would need to retire, but I hate it, nonetheless. Then buying the team, sure, it's a thrill, but…"

"You're trying to fill a void," she says, finishing my sentence.

My eyes widen slightly because she gets it. "Something like that. Don't get me wrong, I'm excited, but it's not the same as being on the ice with a timer controlling your adrenaline as you try to score."

"Have you ever thought that now you get to experience hockey through a different lens? You'll probably still feel the adrenaline, but now you get to watch a game unfold and go home without a black eye too."

I flex my jaw side to side, as I'm slightly in awe that Violet analyzes things so clearly. "You read people well," I compliment.

Violet lies on her back and turns her head to face me as she rests against the pillow. I take the opportunity to grab a stray section of her hair and twirl it around my finger.

"I need to, in my line of work. I have to determine if flowers are needed for a happy or sad occasion. It's my sixth sense to figure out if a man is buying flowers for his mother, his lover who he is madly in love with, or if he is trying to get out of the doghouse. Then again, when a guy is trying to get out of the doghouse, then it's obvious."

I huff a laugh. "How so?"

A near evil smirk spreads on her lips that makes me want to kiss her again. "He tends to ask for the most expensive flowers."

I nuzzle into her neck while I laugh, as that makes sense.

She giggles and further explains, "If he shows up needing flowers for someone who he truly loves, then he normally has an idea which flowers are her favorite or at least gives me her favorite color to work with. But if the first thing he says to me is that he needs the most expensive flowers, then I know, I just know, and I hate it."

"What do you do?"

"Lie and actually give him the cheapest flowers but charge full price," she quips.

It sounds exactly like what she would do.

Her fingers begin to trace lazy patterns on my arm, and damn, I'm not sure when the last time was that I just lay in bed with someone and talked without any thought of the outside world. I'm used to gratification and get out. Instead, time slows, and I'm relaxed while we leave chip crumbs in the bed. We're in our own bubble.

Violet seems to get more comfortable, sinking into the mattress, and her face tells me that another round of questions will be shot my way, though I don't mind.

But she surprises me and sighs a relaxing breath. "Hear the rain?"

I try to focus, and despite the subtle music, the sound of pouring rain overtakes the background noise.

"Kind of calming," I admit.

"It's only June. I hope this isn't the indication for the season ahead. It's the high season in this little town, but I guess off-season for you; opposites connect."

I nip at her shoulder gently, because that's what our bodies are doing, following movements without thought. "When I played hockey, I could actually enjoy off-season, would go on vacation even, because I knew hockey training would be waiting for me at the end of the summer. I'm so out of my realm right now." I gently shake my head in irritation from that fact.

She taps her finger against my bare chest. "You're not. You're *adapting* to your new normal. Where is that confidence that you ooze? Throw it into your new chapter."

She steals my gaze because the conviction in her voice sounds far too natural.

"The confidence is there, I just seem to let down a wall or two around you." My voice grows soft and our eyes lock, hers filled with admiration and mine must show a fondness that I'm not used to feeling.

A long moment falls between us until Violet twists her body to look over her shoulder at the clock on the bedside table. "It's almost midnight." She begins to stir. "I need to get home."

I don't like the idea of her on the road at night in this rain. Hell, I know that's only partly true. I hate the idea of her leaving.

When her cute little ass is about to slide off the mattress, I quickly grab her arm to stop her. "You don't need to go."

Her brows knit together, and her eyes grow wary but are misted with a hint of delight, the perfect contradiction. "I should..." Her sentence hangs open.

"Nah, stay. I mean, it's raining, it's late, and I hear the foxes on the roads in this area are a complete killer this time of year." I list many reasons but none of them are the real reason.

Her mouth opens then shuts before a sound squeaks out. "I guess one night wouldn't hurt."

"We did it once before," I highlight.

Violet chuckles. "Kind of a different scenario, as we basically did the same thing, all night, over and over, thinking it would be a one-night kind of thing."

"I won't even leave a note on the pillow this time," I promise.

She tries to suppress her smile from my remark, but I see her cheeks heighten. "I am kind of tired."

"You're staying. It's a demand."

Violet nods once and returns to the mattress, crawling on all fours, with the sultry look on her face shooting me a warning. "I guess I'm staying, so we can definitely..." She straddles me and leans down to run her lips down the line of my stomach, tracing my muscles. Her breath spreads lower and lower, causing my cock to twitch. But just before she moves the sheet hanging low on my waist, her body slithers back up to align our eyes together. "Sleep. We're totally sleeping."

She flops to the side with exhaustion, grabbing my arm like a freaking teddy bear.

I lick my lips at her effort to always tease me. "Then the only question left is if you will be sleeping naked or want to borrow a shirt? Either way, you will be accessible so I can slip right into you when I wake up." I smirk, relieved that she's staying.

Because I'm selfish, and if I can stretch our boundaries for this week, then I damn well will.

12

VIOLET

Waking up on my side, I instantly feel a delightful heaviness between my legs. The feeling of skin-on-skin contact, so warm and firm. I murmur as I stretch my body out, which only gives a certain man's hand better access to my clit where Declan is currently working with his finger.

"Is this your way of waking me up?" I wonder and yawn.

Where Declan's lips are dragging along my back feels extra sensitive this morning or maybe it's the fact he hasn't shaved yet and is sporting some stubble. I'm in a daze, trapped between the heavenly sleep I had in this man's arms and his method of waking up which feels like a dream, because it's so damn good.

"I warned you that I needed you accessible." His gravelly morning voice is pure sin, and I feel my inner walls clench, even tighter when I feel his cock against my ass.

"You're a man of action." I look over my shoulder, and I wish the damn sun would come out to peek through the curtains and give me a better view of his face, but instead, it's raining out, and Declan looks serious, on a mission.

I chuckle to myself because that's not bad either. A blissful breath escapes me, that is until I notice the clock. "Shit, I need to get moving like now."

"We can do that." Declan teases my opening with the tip of his cock.

I groan with the struggle between giving in right now and responsibility.

"As in, I need to run home, shower and change, and grab my coffee before I open the store," I clarify, yet I don't make any effort to move.

"Shh, baby." He grinds his body into my hips.

Oh no, he said baby. The female population's weakness.

Five minutes later, after an orgasm to start my day, I'm getting dressed, and Declan emerges from the bathroom where he started the shower. He seems to be searching for some fresh clothes.

"Are you sure I can't order some breakfast for you?" he double-checks.

"No, I really need to head out, plus Jolly Joe's is calling. It's kind of an essential part of the day, otherwise people send out search parties if they notice you don't check in." I tie up my hair. "You haven't been yet since you've been in town? Yikes, you may want to fix that, otherwise people will talk."

"Maybe I'll stop by then. I would hate for people to think I'm some billionaire asshole," he jokes, but I hear the hidden truth, I think, because he does care, since he is the opposite of what many people think.

I shrug a shoulder. "You should." Looking around, I note that I have nothing left to throw on, and this is my moment to leave. "Well, I've gotta run."

We stare at one another, a giddy smile preventing us from saying any words, and the warm air wraps around us, pulling us closer in a magnetic force because we both take a step closer to each other.

Declan makes a sound, reaches out to snake his arm around my middle, and pulls me close. "Have a good day."

"You too."

He doesn't let me go, and I take the opportunity to run my fingers along his bare chest, staring at my actions before my eyes strike up to meet his.

"Morning-you is… different." Tender.

He rumbles a laugh. "Nah, I'm just admiring the view."

"I'll see you around." I feel butterflies, and it's preventing me from saying anything clever.

Our eyes linger, and we're making no effort to part.

"Get out of here before I throw you in the shower." At least Declan has the courage to move us along.

———

I'M lucky that on Thursdays, Tilly is at the store from open to close. It meant I had a little time to spare, which I'm thankful for, as I needed a long shower to recall all the ways my body was touched last night. Also, dry shampoo only gets you so far.

Stepping into Jolly Joe's, I'm in awe how half the town seems to cram in here in the mornings for breakfast, and again later in the day for ice cream. A retired judge created this place that resembles an old soda shop.

Walking straight to the counter, I order my flat white and an orange roll.

"What would you recommend?" Declan's voice surprises me as he arrives to stand by my side and pretends to look at the menu on the wall.

Instantly, my body eases, and my closed-mouth grin spreads. "What brings you here?"

"Someone mentioned this is a must, and I kind of worked up an appetite." He doesn't look at me and continues his ruse of studying the menu.

I straighten my posture and follow along, even though the edges of our arms just grazed and a breath that I didn't know I was holding releases. "I'm a fan of the orange rolls. Cinnamon roll base with an orange kick, it's a twist on a classic."

"I'll give it a go." He steps forward to order.

Looking around the place, it's noisy and a mix of people chatting and others in a rush. Nobody will notice us, or rather, it's easy to explain a coincidence that we are both at the best spot for coffee in town at the same time.

"Hey, Violet." A deep voice startles me, and I nearly jump in my spot. My attention transfers away from Declan, ahead of me ordering, and lands on Carter, the sheriff in town. "Usual order?" The man smiles at me.

He's Ford's age, and he does get points on the handsome front, if you go for the hundred-pushups-a-day kind of thing.

"Good morning, Sheriff." He's told me many times to call him by his first name, but I feel like I might get in trouble if I don't address him by his title in public. The rumors would spread like wildfire if someone heard me call him Carter.

"Flat white and an orange roll?"

My eyes narrow. "Yeah, you know my order?" I'm surprised.

"It's the little things that you should notice," he mentions.

A tap on my shoulder causes my eyes to dip to the side, and I notice a hand with a coffee in a to-go cup.

"Your order was ready," Declan mentions, with his eyes set on Carter.

"Thanks." I notice both men sizing one another up. "Uhm, this is Declan Dash. He played hockey with Ford, and he's here this week to help with the kids' summer camp."

"Sheriff Carter Mills." Carter offers his hand for a shake to Declan. "I've seen you in Lake Spark before. It's great that you're volunteering."

"Of course. I was stopping by for a coffee and ran into Violet. We go way back, thanks to her brother. I would trust this lady here with my life and coffee choices." A protective arm lands around my shoulders, I swear an act of possession.

Something Carter notices, as his eyes dance between us for a good beat. "Only in town for a few days?"

"Yeah, but I'll be here more in the future."

The testosterone of these guys is nearly overbearing.

I laugh nervously. "Well, it was great chatting with everyone, but I really need to head to The Flower Jar," I announce.

"Sure, I can walk you there if you like," Carter offers.

"Oh, that's not needed. A quick power walk and I'm there, considering it's only two blocks away." My eyes dart between the men in front of me.

Carter smiles politely at me. "You have a great day then."

"You too." I nod.

"See you around, Dec." I avoid looking at him and walk out.

But the quick stroll to The Flower Jar turns into a near sprint. As soon as I arrive, Tilly heads out on an errand, and I'm glad for the moment to breathe. I sigh, because I realize that I forgot my orange roll. I walk to Nugget's cage and see that Tilly handled replenishing his water and food this morning.

"Handsome," the bird chirps.

"Who is?" I ask, as if the bird understands me.

The bell rings, and the door to my store opens. "You forgot your breakfast," Declan announces.

I look warily at the parrot. Maybe he does understand more than I realize. He must have seen Declan through the window. It's a little too coincidental.

Ignoring the bird, I walk to Declan and take the bag. "Thanks."

"Your sheriff wanted to deliver it, but unfortunately for him, I was already holding the bag." He seems proud of himself. "Plus, I told him that I'm responsible for replenishing your nourishment since you had a *long* night last night."

I stop mid-bite, slightly concerned, because Declan probably would say that, but when he grins, I know he's messing with me, so I resume my path to calorie heaven.

"He's a good guy," I say with my mouth full, and I'm not sure why I said that.

Declan looks down at the cup of coffee in his hands. He doesn't want to respond to my statement, probably because we both know that I'm testing us to see if any jealousy arises. We're human, that's what we feel sometimes.

"This is good coffee."

I lick the corner of my mouth. "What color jellybean did you get?"

He shrugs. "I'm not at the bottom of my coffee yet. Is there a meaning if it's a particular color?"

"No, but rumor is that the purple ones are rare."

"Purple is violet, right?" He pulls up his phone from his pocket when it dings.

"It is. Shouldn't you be at the rink? I love having you here, but this is slightly jarring. I'm not used to guys delivering me carbs in my store, especially considering their tongue was inside me not even two hours ago."

Declan appears satisfied before he looks up from his screen. "Just enjoying an easy morning in this small town, perusing along Main Street with my coffee, and doing a good deed for a local citizen."

"Sure you are." I bring my hand to my hip, my smirk permanent.

"I don't need to be at the rink until ten. The real estate agent sent me an email that I can view a house later." He begins to type on his screen.

My breath catches. "Oh yeah, you might be moving here?" Fuckity ducks, that might be a little bit of a twister to our dynamic.

Declan's eyes lock on me when he realizes my brain is connecting dots. "More like a weekend house, when I need to be here for the team." His attempt to justify how this might not be awkward in the future is just that, an attempt, which means it doesn't always work.

I hum a sound. "Right." My T is sharp. "What house are you looking at?"

"It's on the other side of the lake, you can kind of see your brother's house from it. It's on…" He scrolls his email for the street name.

But I already know. "Owl Hill Lane," I say and take another sip of my coffee.

Declan's face screws up when he looks at me. "That's a very… storybook name. How did you know?"

"The landlady to this place used to live on that street. The house you're looking at is a great house, though it probably needs some changes."

"Will you come with me?" It shoots out of his mouth, taking us both aback.

"Tie her up," Nugget calls out.

We both look at the bird and back to one another. "He's super talkative in the mornings, ignore him."

"Who taught him that?" Declan is entertained.

I hold my palm up, urging him not to press with the questions. "I was too scared to ever ask. But, uhm, the house…"

Declan steps forward. "Come on, you know the area. I could use the advice."

"Is that a good idea?" My voice raises an octave.

He runs his thumb along the line of his jaw. "A horrible idea." He grins to himself. "But I don't care. Plus, if we weren't sleeping together, then you wouldn't hesitate. Besides, the agent is from Chicago selling on behalf of an estate, so they don't even know the quirky little details about this area. Please?" His eyes are pleading, with mischief thrown in.

A long sound escapes my lips as I puff out a breath. "Okay."
Not what I was going for.

"Great. I'll meet you there at 4."

"Yep." But my eyes turn cautious.

WE SLOWLY TRAIL behind the real estate agent dressed in a suit. Jimmy is in his forties and reminds me of the guy from that reality television show about California real estate that I watch. Everything he says feels like an upsell.

The house is empty of furniture and is incredibly big, but the view of the lake is to die for. Owning waterfront property is nowhere in my future. It's far too expensive, but I have a brother who lets me drop in at their pristine lake house at any time.

We all stop when the agent opens the sliding doors to reveal the backyard overlooking the lake. It's pouring rain yet again, so we admire the view from inside.

"The weather isn't cooperating, but on a good day, you'll get the sunrise and full sun until about mid-afternoon. The dock was renewed only a few years ago, and it's possible to add a pool if you really wanted, however the hot tub and sauna are perfect all year round. You've seen the house now. There is room to negotiate, I think, as they're looking for a quick sale," Jimmy explains.

"The only neighbor is the house up on the corner by the main road, right?" I ask to confirm. "The Joneses, and they're snowbirds, so they head down to Scottsdale in the winter," I add, as privacy is important for Declan.

"Something like that, I think. How about I leave you two alone for a few minutes to discuss?" Jimmy suggests.

I was introduced as a friend, but Jimmy has given me a few questionable glares about that definition, especially when Declan made a joke about the master suite shower being the right size for two, with room to bend over.

Declan nods. "That would be great."

I cross my arms and offer Jimmy an appreciative smile. The moment that he's out of sight, I roll my eyes at Declan.

"This is ridiculous," I inform him, yet I'm entertained. "One, that I'm here, and two, that you would need a house this size. This is a family house."

Declan smirks before he takes a step, right to the doorframe edge. "I need a house for entertaining." He seems to be reflecting.

I point out to the yard. "With a treehouse?"

He side-eyes me and shrugs. "I always wanted one. My parents were against it, always afraid I would fall out."

Huh, I wonder if he is attempting to grab hold of something he missed.

"Okay, but what are you going to need five bedrooms for?" I challenge.

Declan raises a brow at me. "I'm sure I'll have parties where people need to stay over."

My jaw drops, and I gasp. "Oh. My. God. You also host *those* kind of parties?"

His eyes grow bold, and he chuckles. "That's where your mind went? I was thinking of people staying over because they've had wine or beer and can't drive back to the city." Declan wraps his arm around my shoulders as he walks us back to the kitchen area. "And no, to answer your question, I leave the hosting to Brent."

Ease hits me, because for the past thirty seconds, an unknown jealousy boiled inside of me at the thought of him with someone else, both in his past or future.

I can't think about it, I have no right to. "What do you think of the kitchen?" I ask to keep us on the friends-looking-at-a-house situation.

We stop in the middle of the kitchen and lean against the island, and Declan purses his lips out as he studies the area. "I would probably need to update the appliances, and I'm not so sure about the countertops."

"You're right about the appliances," I agree. "But what's wrong with the counters?"

He rotates his body, with his hands instantly landing firmly on my waist, before he lifts me up onto the counter, stepping between my knees and leaning in with his hands on either side of me. Our body heat collides, as he is dangerously close, and our eyes hold in what feels like a fire starting.

"I'm not sure if it's sturdy enough for kitchen activities."

"You mean cutting vegetables?" I pretend not to understand.

Declan glances down at his finger skirting the edge of my dress. "I was thinking along the lines of straddling or bending over and holding onto the counter for support," he rasps.

"I don't want to know your future plans." It comes out playful, but really, it's the truth. Is he lost in this moment or thinking about his future romps in the kitchen with whoever isn't me?

"My only future plan involves grabbing dinner after this," he says it so casually, but his damn thumb is circling my inner thigh.

I scoff. "I'm kind of tired of room service and takeout. How about I'll cook at my place?" And twice in one day, we get the award for surprising us both, because I'm changing the scene on us and inviting him to my place, to cook. I'm not sure that's in the fuck-buddy manual, but whatever.

"Sounds good." He doesn't seem to mind, nor does he seem worried about the rulebook.

"Okay." I shake my head before thinking too deep. "But this counter, it's your deciding factor?"

"Would it be comfortable to lie on?" He sounds far too serious.

"I think you're going for uncomfortable, no?"

"Can you get a good grip?"

"I guess," I volley.

"Sturdy then?" He questions again before he slides my body to the edge.

This man is so inappropriate, and I love it.

The clearing of a throat breaks our little scene, and we both look to the side to find Jimmy.

"It's Naples quartz, that's the best of the best," he announces.

If only the earth would swallow me whole right now.

Declan smirks proudly then speaks directly to me in a low voice. "Let's get out here and head to your place."

13

DECLAN

Looking down at the wine bottle in one hand and a baguette in the other, I smile to myself. This day may go down in the record books for being notable. I sure as hell didn't plan on asking Violet to join me on my real estate appointment, but logic seems to go out the window when she's near. It was fun having her with me, even if she pointed out the obvious, that the house is fit for a family, not exactly something I'm planning on.

I was going to follow her in my car to her house, but I wanted to stop at the store to pick up some wine, and she asked if I could grab some fresh bread from the bakery section.

The door opens, and she has a lopsided smile and has changed into yoga pants and a t-shirt. "Welcome to my humble abode." She steps to the side to allow me to enter her house. It's small but has curb appeal.

I lean in to kiss her cheek, and I'm a guy that is throwing out moves that are not my usual, as proven by the fact that she makes a sound of surprise.

My eyes assess the living room, and it's not bad at all. It seems quite updated, and there is plenty of space considering she lives here alone. The design is simple, and I'm surprised that there aren't more flowers. In fact, all I see is a cactus when it comes to plants.

"I don't understand, where is your vase of flowers?" I say as I follow her to the kitchen, and my nose enjoys the smell of a home cooked meal.

"I've barely been home this week, that's why."

She gets to work on cutting the bread, and that's when I notice the parrot-shaped cookie jar. "For someone who told me that they hate birds, you've only been proving me wrong."

Violet quickly checks what I'm looking at and smiles softly. "Ford found it at an antique market with Brielle and thought it would be great for me. I hated it at first, but it's a damn good cookie jar, and I tend to bake cookies once a week."

"Oh yeah?"

"Uh-huh." Violet quickly looks over the pot with tomato sauce. "I don't really cook much, unless you count snacks as a meal, but you can't really go wrong with spaghetti."

"Sounds great."

She grabs a bowl for the bread. "So, are you going to put in an offer for the house?"

"Not sure yet. You may have had a point about the size."

Violet looks up at me with an arched brow. "You mean that the house is for a family, with a dog and maybe even chickens?"

Taking the bottle opener that was resting on the counter, I work the cork out. "Something like that. I have my place in the city, and that's admittedly a bachelor pad, but at some point, it would be nice to have a house with a yard."

"You mean a home?" She offers me two empty glasses.

"I guess."

"I know what you mean. I'm at Ford and Brielle's far too much, but I like sitting amongst their chaos and admiring their home life. One day I hope to have that, complete with kids and a dog."

Right, because she *is* the relationship type, once she's ready to head back to the market after she's over her break.

"My parents gave me a good life, and let's be honest, hockey isn't a cheap sport, but growing up, the house and all of that always felt… superficial."

"No treehouse either."

My cheeks tighten. "That too. Anyway, I'll think about the house. Tomorrow is my last day with the kids at camp."

Our eyes connect as we both suddenly remember our deadline. The sound of the pots simmering on the stove fills the void of our words.

"Better make tonight count then," she mentions softly.

"I'll stay another night tomorrow but then head back to the city on Saturday morning. One of the team sponsors wants to have dinner this weekend, and I can't really say no to that." I hand her a wine glass. "Hope you don't mind, but I intend to finish this bottle with you, which means I'm staying over. I would hate for the sheriff to go on a power trip and pull me over."

Her response is to laugh, and that makes me happy. Maybe the sheriff is potential for her, but this week, Violet is mine, and I don't tolerate any other man attempting to take what currently belongs to me. In hockey, your mission is to protect the puck, never let it out of your sight. That's Violet in this moment.

Violet walks into my arms and takes hold of one wine glass. "I would say we should toast, but this day is already one bizarre situation after another, so my money would be on that this would be an awkward toast." She sips from her glass.

I enjoy her straightforwardness. "Maybe." I take a sip of my own wine, bitter with a hint of berry.

"I think if the house will make you happy then go for it. Life is one big adventure, isn't it?"

God, I admire her positive outlook on life. She's just a good energy to be around. I need more people like that in my circle.

I set my wine glass down because I want both my arms around her; if our week is almost up, then I will glue myself to her tonight. She looks up at me and must sense that I have a lot on my mind.

"What are you thinking about?" she asks.

"Hockey," I lie. "This week, I got to physically do something, but now my association with hockey turns to corporate meetings."

"You'll get used to it. I guess your social calendar will open up too, so go check out some concerts or take a vacation. Decompress." She's listing ideas, but they're all enjoyed better if joined by someone who makes it more fun.

I don't like myself softening. It's happening. I feel it.

The water boils over on the spaghetti pot, and Violet is quick to take action, stepping out of my hold and giving us the space that we probably need. "Look at me, about to kill our meatless dinner. This is why Ford doesn't trust me with dinner duty."

Ford. The gentle reminder that Violet and I are supposed to be off-limits to one another. Then again, not many people share the details on who their current friend with benefits is. We also have to question if the thrill of him finding out plays a role in this attraction between Violet and me, because our chemistry is high and seamless, maybe even uncontrollable.

"Are you frowning? For a man about to eat the best sauce from a jar, you seem kind of down," she comments.

"I'm just lost in a lot of thoughts, and starving. I guess I didn't eat lunch today. There is this boy who wouldn't stop talking about his favorite player, and I got excited and listened, assuming it was me. Turns out his favorite player is Erikson, who is a forward. A shot to my ego, but I couldn't stop smiling. The kid has his whole future ahead of him and so much optimism. I'm kind of jealous."

Violet tips her hip out and gives me a knowing look. "Your problem is that you only look at the near future and not the far future, and your far future may just hold the dream that makes you optimistic again. Use that logic when you make your house decision… and ask for proof that the counters are quartz." She winks.

Of course she would be supportive, she's a team player. Except I think we tossed out the rulebook a few days ago, and I'm no longer sure what game we're playing.

———

SKATING BACKWARDS, I do my best to steal the puck from Connor, but the guy is fast and sharp. We decided to play a little one-on-one since it's my last day volunteering at the summer program, and the kids are eating their lunch before we do a round of working on coordination with a partner.

"Come on, old man, give me a challenge," Connor snickers.

In a flash, I overreach my arm to grab the puck with my stick, and although successful, I feel an old injury in my shoulder flare from the effort.

"Respect your elders," I chide through labored breath as I begin to circle my arm.

Connor gets the clue that we need to take a break, and we both pause near the crease.

"If it's any consolation, you're better than my dad on the ice."

I look up from leaning over with my hands on my thighs. "Thanks." *I think.*

"You look kind of tired, to be honest."

That's because I spent last night with your aunt.

After dinner, we attempted to watch a movie, then ditched that idea and headed straight to her room where we had a round before sleeping until early hours. Violet had to get to her store at seven because she had to prepare flowers for a wedding.

"I'm not tired," I lie. "I'm distracted." The moment it slips off my lips, I realize my error.

Connor shifts his stick to his other hand. "Why?"

"Nothing in particular."

"Well, figure it out, because your focus on the game sucks."

My eyes pop out at his boldness. "I'm not playing anymore; I don't need to have my head in the game."

"Yeah, you just own the team now, so I'm pretty positive you need to focus on that."

My head wobbles side to side, as the guy is right and I need solid concentration.

"You know that if you're distracted in Lake Spark then something is seriously screwed up. My dad says if you can't clear your head and enjoy your family in this town, then no magical place will save you." I hear his sarcasm.

"I will take that into consideration when I figure out if I'm fixable or not," I respond dryly.

"Won't you be back more often? You better figure it out fast."

Again, this sixteen-year-old is on point today, because the reality is that I will be back more regularly, and I'm not entirely sure where Violet fits in on the distraction front. I asked for a week, and our timer is up, but she won't be out of my life.

And that very much weighs on my mind for the rest of the day.

———

It's eight in the evening, and tomorrow, I check out from the Dizzy Duck Inn. Violet had to stay late at The Flower Jar, so we skipped dinner together. But the moment she walks through the door and sets the do-not-disturb sign on the handle, my hands frame her face to kiss her hard, as if I need to seal the imprint of her lips on mine.

She murmurs a sweet sound which is a contrast to my low, rumbled groan.

Pulling away, I cup her jaw with my hands, and she peers up at me, her eyes sparkly in this dimly lit room. "That's one way to welcome me," she rasps.

"No reason to hold back tonight."

She nods gently while our eyes lock, and this woman has me completely mesmerized.

"How do we end this week of fun?" Violet is searching for a clue of how tonight may go. Slow or fast? I don't have an answer.

Walking us back to the bed, I debate within myself how I like to take her the most… but I like every way.

But it's probably safer if we stick to our adventurous side.

"All fours, Vi. Show me that ass of yours."

A devious smirk appears on her lips before she complies, even going so far as making a show of lifting her skirt to indicate that she took off her panties at some point between her car and my room.

I go nearly feral and spank her with the palm of my hand, and her yelp turns into a whimper because I dive right in to lick her slit, nor do I begin with gentle strokes. Her body falls forward and her fingers claw the duvet. This is the way I like her.

At my mercy, knowing I will reward her.

Violet knows how to take, but she much prefers following my cues.

"I swear you taste like pure maple syrup." I rise up on my knees and run my finger along the corner of my mouth.

She glances over her shoulder with a mischievous look. "You hate maple syrup."

"Not if it's on you." I rub a circle on her ass, and I get another idea. "Can I take a photo of you like this? A little keepsake."

Violet flops like a pancake to her back and rests against her propped arms, her foot drawing a line up her leg, stopping mid-thigh. "Yes, but I thought for sure you would much prefer one with me touching myself."

I blow out a breath. "You *are* a wild little thing."

I'm hovering over her in a flash, and I decide the photo will have to wait; being buried deep inside of her takes priority.

All night becomes one long event of sex, rest, and sex again. Sometime around one in the morning, we finally zoned out for the night, but by six in the morning, I woke to find her peacefully sleeping. I couldn't help myself and decided to wake her up the one way we both enjoy. We go slow until I'm thrusting into her, because I won't let her leave this morning without a proper goodbye.

"I can't," she breathes out as I spoon around her from behind. That drowsy smile gracing her lips is beautiful when she turns to look back at me.

"You will come again, Vi. On my cock. Now be a good girl and squeeze." I push in deeper, with her arm looped back around my neck, while my other hand holds her hip in place.

"Dec, I'm going..." Her eyes hood closed while her pussy tightens around me.

The sound of her long moan is broken by my lips crashing down on hers as I feel her spasm.

My own release isn't far behind, and then we lie there in an entwined mess, making no effort to part, because this embrace with my dick relaxing inside of her feels too damn perfect. It should send me running when Violet lets go of my neck to link our hands together, but I only pull her closer to me.

———

WE DOZED OFF AGAIN, until I woke the moment that Violet slid out of bed.

Nature is playing a joke on us; bright sun and blue skies. That's not exactly how I feel, but then again, rain every day for the last week was as if nature were encouraging us to stay inside and do what we've done.

Violet emerges from the bathroom, pulling on her dress. I can tell she's avoiding me, or at least keeps her eyes angled away from my direction, even when she sits on the side of the bed.

"Were you going to sneak out?" The corner of my mouth stretches.

"Maybe. It's easier."

I touch her arm and invite her to look at me. "I guess this is…"

"Mm-hm." It's a long moment of holding one another through a gaze. "I'll be in Chicago next weekend to meet a friend," she nearly spits out.

"Will you?" Excitement underlines in my tone.

"We could meet for a coffee if you want? During the day. Public place. As friends do." She nibbles her bottom lip, but her face remains impartial, rather unsure.

Adjusting my body, I lean to kiss her shoulder and flash her my eyes that have won me fans. "I'll be seeing you for a coffee then."

A coffee meeting is one ambiguous setting because it could mean so many things. But at least I'll get to see her again, because going cold turkey on this woman seems too difficult to fathom, and at least this buys us a little more time.

14

——

VIOLET

——

The taste of cranberry hits my tongue as I take in the scene around me. Jupiter is the bar and restaurant that everyone wants to be at when you're in Chicago if you're young and successful. I've been a few times with Ford, as a lot of his former teammates would hang out here. The exposed brick walls with industrial lighting makes this place perfect for cocktails, and cosmopolitans are my favorite. It's late Saturday afternoon and there isn't an empty seat.

Looking up from my glass, I see Charlotte swallowed her martini in no time and is now sucking on her olive.

"I miss dressing up and drinking overpriced cocktails sometimes," I admit with a relaxing sigh.

"Small-town life not treating you well?" She gives me a skeptical glare before taking hold of her long hair to play with.

I grin to myself. "You won't be able to convince me to move back to the city. I'm very content where I am. It's just nice to be around all of this buzz and dress up." I give myself the once-over, and I'm rocking it in a tight black dress with a zipped V heading dangerously low between my cleavage. I matched the look with hoop earrings and black wedges with ties that wrap from my ankles up to my knee.

"We should totally check out this club that a friend recommended, he can get us on the list. It would be a lot of fun." Charlotte attempts to persuade me with her smile and flashing eyes.

"Maybe. I mean, I'm staying at your place, so why not." I shrug. "I'm meeting Declan tomorrow at ten for coffee, so I don't want to be out too late."

Charlotte instantly scoots to the edge of her seat and rests her chin on her propped arms resting on the small table, clearly invested in our conversation. "Tell me *everything*. I mean, I know how it all started. I still can't believe you convinced me to get you an invite to that party. I'm so proud of you," she nearly coos.

"I still can't believe it, but I'm happy I did. I wanted to be free for a night, and it was an adventure." Maybe to start with... "You know, I'm kind of relieved that I ended up with Declan's name that night. A stranger wouldn't have been the same."

Charlotte listens with a gaze of admiration. We can't talk specifics because of the NDA we signed, but we just know we both had an evening of satisfaction and happened to witness the names we pulled.

"But what happened the other week with Declan?" she presses.

My cheeks warm, and I can't help but blush. "We just had a little fun, that's it. Nothing more."

"But you're meeting for coffee tomorrow. Near his place?" She tips her head slightly to the side.

"I don't know, we still need to text details."

"You've been texting all week?"

I shake my head. "No, which is for the better, as maybe a Declan detox is good for me. We had a…" I can't even describe it.

Charlotte indicates to the waitress for another round of drinks by circling her finger between us and giving her best beaming smile, but Charlotte quickly diverts her attention back to me. "So, you just did the whole friends-with-benefits thing for a week and expect to move on?"

"Why not? You do it all the time," I challenge.

Charlotte chides with a sound. "That's because I don't ever see myself being in a long-term relationship. I don't believe we are made to be tied down to one person. You, on the other hand, moved to freaking nowhere just so you can take part in family dinners at your brother's house until you find Mr. Right and push out your own little monsters of joy."

I'm quick to justify. "I'm on a break from trying to find Prince Charming."

Charlotte grabs my own drink to sip. "No, you're not. Your thoughts still dream away, and since there are no prospects in town, then you allow yourself to have fun, but as soon as you realize that the future father of your kiddos is right in front of you, then I'm sure you will be hoping for the chance."

"Exactly. Declan isn't relationship material, plus Ford would freaking lose it."

Charlotte widens her arms, causing my drink to spill slightly over her hand. "Oh my God, the brother's-friend angle is hot. Totally forgot about that. Probably adds a layer to the sex appeal."

"I mean..." My face must make an odd look. "You're not wrong."

The waitress returns with our new round of drinks, and I'm eager to get a sip of my fresh cranberry cocktail.

"Do you really think that Declan is a no-go on the list of future prospects?"

I nearly cough up my drink. "Yes. He has stated it a few times that he can't be more than a fuck buddy and that was for a week. Besides, now he's busy with owning a team, which will entail travel, and he can't even decide on house purchases or what his next few months will look like. Imagine where a woman would come into that."

Charlotte nurses her fresh martini and leans back on the lounge chair. "Nothing happened to make you think maybe it could be more?"

His warm glances, the way our fingers entwined, the movement of our bodies as one flawless fit, natural conversation, laughter, and my chest fluttering. "Nope," I lie and drink from my glass to distract my thoughts.

"Okay, I just… I don't know. Everyone wants to see a gamechanger where the player turns lovestruck."

I roll my eyes. "Don't we all, but I will just guard my little heart, thank you very much."

Charlotte's phone dings, and she picks it up from the table to view. "A friend is nearby; I'm just going to mention that we're here in case they want to drop by. I think if we aim to be at the club by ten, then that should be good."

"Sure. I probably need to grab something to eat if I hope to have any chance of pacing myself."

"For sure, the food here is to die for. Let's order a bunch of appetizers."

Fifteen minutes later, we've ordered and are talking about planning a girls' getaway, when Charlotte throws on a leer that I recognize from our college days as flirty to someone over my shoulder. She is quick to stand and welcome her friend with open arms, and I instantly recognize that it's Brent. It's not too surprising, as they do hang out, amongst other things.

"There you are," he greets her and kisses her cheek, pulling her close, and I swear he squeezes her ass in the process. He looks at me with a suave grin. "Hey, Violet, it's been a while. I'm sure you remember Declan." He winks at me.

On cue, Declan appears at his side, and instantly my body feels transfixed. Like Brent, Declan is wearing a dress shirt, blazer, and dark jeans, with no tie, which means the top buttons are undone, and I could drool over the peek of his chest. Declan's piercing blue eyes strike my own, and his grin is perhaps the smoothest of the two men.

I stand because I was the only one sitting, but it gives ample opportunity for Declan to snake his arm around my middle and pull me close into a side hug. He presses a kiss on my cheek, near my ear, which sends a sensitive vibration all the way to my toes.

"Vi," he speaks my name with so much possession and heat.

It feels like everyone is staring at me, probably because I'm flushed. "I wasn't expecting you here. Thought I would only see you tomorrow." I smile.

"Truthfully, I didn't know you would be here until I was two blocks away and Brent got a text from Charlotte asking if he wanted to meet for drinks."

Charlotte reaches out to touch my arm. "I swear I thought Brent was flying solo tonight." I hear the sincerity in her tone.

"Don't want me here?" Declan teases me and ignores any response that I may have as he's guiding us to sit down. We both find ourselves seated tightly next to one another on the oversized chair, albeit a chair built only for one.

I nervously tuck some of my hair behind my ear. "It's actually a nice surprise. We just ordered a bunch of appetizers and are enjoying our drinks."

"I'll order us a round of whiskeys, be right back," Brent announces, and Charlotte follows him to the bar, probably to leave Declan and me alone.

Declan's eyes examine the room before settling on a view that seems to be me. "You're gorgeous tonight."

"Thanks. You look like you have plans this evening."

"Not particularly. Brent and I were heading for drinks and were going to see where the night takes us."

His fingertips land on my knee, and I shiver from his simple touch. "How was your week?" I ask.

"Meetings and more meetings, not to mention I asked the agent for an inspection of the house."

"Oh?" I grip my cosmo and take a quick sip. "Moving to Lake Spark seems likely then, even if only part-time."

A soft half-smile appears on his mouth. "Probably. Ford and I need to sign off on a few agreements, but the Spinners will have training next season in Lake Spark. How was your week? Nugget behaving? The sheriff checking in?" His jaw tenses for a second, and I can tell he's both teasing me and curious.

I clear my throat, kind of enjoying that I could make him squirm right now. "Nugget said duck it, which I think he meant fuck it, and I didn't see the sheriff, nor was I looking. My mission was coffee, bouquets, and letting my thighs rest after a week of strenuous exercise."

He nudges my shoulder with his. "Not forgetting about me?"

I look at him, a bit taken aback by his comment. "Is that what you want me to do?"

"No, not unless it's better for you." He isn't joking, and I don't like that.

"Well, it's not. Besides, I'll be running into you more often, so let's consider tonight practice, right?"

"Sure. This place is packed with people in the hockey industry. Have to keep my hands to myself unless we want rumors to fly."

"You're doing a poor job then," I tease him.

His response is to squeeze my knee. "Still up for coffee tomorrow? I was thinking of this little spot up near Lincoln Park that has an indoor conservatory with tropical flowers and birds."

It feels like he put in thought. "My favorite things, flowers and birds to give me nightmares, I love it."

He takes his scotch that Brent offers him as they reappear, but I still feel Declan's hand on my knee, and I don't think he has any plans of removing it.

Brent and Charlotte sit down across from us. "Charlotte and I have decided that after a few rounds here, we can all move on to the club," Brent explains with his arm hanging off the back of Charlotte's chair. I really need to ask her if more is going on between them.

"Which club?" Declan asks before his lips hit the rim of his glass.

"Eclipse," Charlotte states.

Declan's mouth pauses on his glass before he slowly lowers the drink, and his body seems to tense. "That's where you want to go?" he double-checks with Brent who smugly nods a yes.

"Violet already told me that she would go with me." Charlotte smiles tightly at Declan, nearly proud.

"It would be fun with these two," Brent adds.

Declan snaps his gaze to me. "You said you would go with Charlotte?"

"Yeah, why not?" I shrug.

His face turns serious. I swear I see a vein pulsing in his temple, and his eyes, good Lord, those eyes, so incredibly dark with possession.

Declan takes hold of my arm. "Excuse us for a second," he informs Brent and Charlotte.

He pulls me up before I can protest. Declan walks in a fast stride straight to the bathrooms, dragging me close behind. He scans the area to find that it's quiet and pushes me into a small bathroom with stone walls and acoustic music playing on the speakers.

"What the hell?" I say when I break free from his hold.

He locks the door, marches straight to me, and cradles my head in his hands. I'm beginning to believe that city-Declan is a man fueled by power, and when he's in Lake Spark, he is a man who lets down a wall or two. Both versions of him, I seem to adore.

"Why would you go to Eclipse with Charlotte?" His voice is clipped.

"Why not? I didn't know the name of the place. Charlotte just mentioned that she wanted to go to a club, and I said yes."

His face softens slightly. "Wait, what kind of club do you think she wanted to go to?"

"Music, dancing, I don't know." I'm trying to understand what is happening.

Declan pinches the bridge of his noise and smirks. "I can assure you that's not the kind of club she wants to go to."

"What do you me—" Then it hits me. "Oh." It drags out of me.

"Yeah, oh. Charlotte and Brent go there together. They like to have a lot of fun, the more the merrier. They also love to watch. My prediction is that Charlotte was going to spring this on you later in the night."

"I guess after the last party I went to with her, I might appear willing to tag along." Charlotte is spontaneous and likes to push my limits, but if we got there and I said no, then she wouldn't be mad. I glance down at my shoulder to avoid his gaze. "You're familiar with the club?"

He glances to the side. "In a past life, yes."

"What if I *do* want to go?"

"Not happening on my watch." He steps closer, heat radiating off his body. "It seems we both ended up with our friends either lying to ensure we met up tonight or they really are eager to watch us."

I chortle a laugh because, knowing Charlotte, it's probably option two. "Should we be flattered?"

Declan slides my hair to one side to expose the curve of my neck. "You should be. Me? I want to kill my friend out there."

"Why?"

"Because I don't want to share you or have anyone get a front-row seat to watch the way you come." His fingers glide along the skin of my shoulder, and I feel my panties getting wrecked.

My breath hitches when a ripple of arousal rolls through my body. "We were just a fling, right? I'm not sure you still get to stake a claim," I manage to rasp.

Declan dips his head down, and his teeth make contact with my skin to gently nip at my shoulder. "About that… what if we don't stop?"

Our eyes meet again. "What do you mean?"

"I'm not the guy for romantic sunsets, but I don't want this thing between us to end. Tell me you feel that way too." His hand grips my hair behind my neck to hold me in place, while his other hand skims up my thigh. "Tell me," he whispers with assertion.

"Were we really going to have coffee tomorrow?"

A sinister chuckle rumbles in his throat. "I was going to try. I do enjoy listening to you talk but how long we would have lasted there, I'm not sure. I had a busy week, but you stayed in my head. God, I hate the idea of anyone getting to see you looking like this."

"That's kind of how this goes when you're not with someone," I highlight the fact.

"I know, but I don't want our week to end. We're both single and enjoy one another, so why not keep it going?"

I smile, as I was hoping tomorrow at coffee that he would tell me he was miserable the last week without me, and it appears that is the case.

This time I'm the one stepping closer to him. "What are the rules this time?"

His thumb pushes against my bottom lip. "I don't know. We keep going, and when one of us can't handle it anymore, then we're open with the other and stop."

Risky. I know it is. But it's also exhilarating.

I nod gently in agreement.

"I guess no coffee tomorrow." He begins to grin and lolls his head gently to the side. "Or maybe that depends on when we actually get out of bed."

"I'm supposed to be staying with Charlotte," I counter with a grin.

In a flash, he spins my body to press my front against the sink, and our eyes lock in the mirror before his hand lands at the base of my throat to keep me in place. He urges my body to bend forward as he yanks at my panties under my dress.

"You're not staying with her. Nor are you going anywhere with her."

"What if I want to watch or be watched. Can we go if I promise nobody can touch me but you?" I'm challenging him or maybe deep down a desire swirls and inches to the surface.

The feeling of his hard cock nudges my lower back. "Are you trying to test me?" he grits out. "Not funny."

"Whatever will I do to occupy my Saturday night then?" I play coy.

The sound of his buckle weakens me in the knees. "Allow me to take you right here because fuck their idea of fun."

Staring at us in the mirror, I appreciate the fact that both of our faces demonstrate a lustful need for each other.

His hands dig into my hips to position me better in an angle, with the tip of his cock sliding along my slit. "Shit, condom."

"Pill," I answer. Concern flickers in his face, and I remember what he once shared with me. "I take it religiously, you can check my purse."

His face softens as he scoffs a sound. "Of everyone, I trust you the most." His tone is full of reverence.

"And we know that we're both safe, since…" We both look in the mirror and laugh. We had to prove our health check before the party, and we've only been with one another since.

"Watch in the mirror while I fuck you, Vi," he demands.

The moment he pushes into me, I'm thankful for the sink as my support.

"Watch us," he encourages. "We look good together."

Yeah. Yeah, we do.

Everything inside of me shoots a warning flare, but equally, instinct tells me to hang on because just maybe this could be more.

15

DECLAN

What have I done?

That's what comes to my mind when I stare down at Violet sleeping in my bed like she belongs here.

It slipped out of my mouth last night that we should keep seeing one another. I can't even blame it on a cloud of lust; it's what I want deep down. One night wasn't enough, one week wasn't enough, and whatever our timestamp will be from now on, I'm not sure that it will ever be enough.

Maybe I'm in the infatuation zone.

I gently trace my finger along her arm like a feather, careful not to wake her. I'm sure she could use the rest after what went down last night.

After the bathroom tryst, it was a quick change of plans. We had our fun in the bathroom, then quickly rushed out and said goodbye to our friends to move onto other plans. Our friends seemed to have been anticipating that, as they waited for us with smirks on their faces, although they seemed slightly disappointed that we wouldn't be joining them.

In another time, I would have been disappointed too. But I simply hate the idea of anyone watching Violet. It's a protective wave that just comes over me whenever she's involved. It unnerves me, as I'm not used to that.

A soft smile spreads on my lips as she snuggles closer with the pillow. Deciding that she isn't going to wake anytime soon, I throw on some shorts and a t-shirt then head to the kitchen to grab a coffee before I sit in my home office and flip open my laptop.

I might as well go through some work emails, because there are a lot. Between marketing, strategy, coaching staff, and a calendar that is getting filled with so many appointments, I'm getting drowned in the business.

My feet don't even get to touch the ice for any of it. At least I was able to help at Ford's summer camp, that gave me a few hours at the rink.

Pulling up the search bar, I type in my name to click on a few highlights of my old games. It's not so bad watching your past life.

That is until a voice points out the obvious. "Sending yourself into a bout of depression?" Violet walks into my office, wearing my shirt. I didn't leave one out, but I like that she dug through my drawer as if she owns the place.

I open my arm to invite her to sit on my lap. "You caught me. I should probably find a documentary on owning a team or something."

She slides right onto my lap, with her palm pressing against my chest. "Probably, but you do things your own way. Are you at least excited for your new adventure? I mean, sometimes I wonder."

"It's the next best thing to playing," I say honestly.

"Not coaching?"

I snicker a sound. "You know what I'm going to say, right?"

Violet shakes her head, oblivious.

"There is a hierarchy with a team, and owner trumps coach. I want to be on top."

She struggles to contain her laugh, but then it escapes her mouth, and the sound fills the room with a lightness that I need in my life.

"That is not a surprise," she reaffirms.

My head tilts to the side. "Thought you would think that way."

Her fingers play with the hairs at the back of my neck while we take a few seconds to stare at one another, because we didn't plan on this. A lopsided nervous smile appears on her mouth. "Uhm, about last night…"

"Yeah?" I'm curious how she is going to lead us into this conversation, which causes her to gawk her eyes at me because she knows that's exactly what I'm doing.

"It's okay if we got caught up in the moment…" She's struggling to beat around the bush.

"We can do casual." I swipe some of her hair behind her ear.

She bites the inside of her cheek. "Yeah, so casual… without Ford finding out."

"Probably wise." I'm not sure he would appreciate the sentiment of not being serious with his sister. "Which means I need to scrap the whole 'will you be my plus-one for a few social events I have coming up.'"

"What will you do then?" Her head perks up.

"Go solo."

"Okay. And the moment that I feel this isn't good for me, then I tell you."

I lean in to kiss her neck. "Likewise. Now, how about we go grab breakfast from that spot I told you about."

She lets out a laugh. "I think being with one another in public when we're not platonic is kind of against the point."

I grin at her. "Lucky for us, I have enough money to rent out their private room and ensure we have privacy. In an hour?"

Violet's arms loop around my neck to pull herself closer to me, her tits right below my face. "I have nothing to wear since you destroyed my clothes somewhere between the elevator and the kitchen."

"Two hours then, and I'll buy you a new outfit."

"Ooh, big spender, you should definitely make me earn it." This is her way of leading us into trouble. I know, because great minds think alike.

"Damn straight. Now sit on top of me and use my cock the way you want to."

Her sultry smirk informs me that she's on board and stands up only to swing one leg to the other side of my lap. In one swoop, she lifts my shirt off her body to be fully naked and on top of me.

I free my cock from my shorts and allow my mouth to trace the curve of her breasts.

"You know, last time I was here at your place, you left before I woke," she softly comments.

It catches me off guard, and I stop my trail on her breasts. Guilt hits me, but then I know it's a distant memory, because for some reason, I feel like something else defines us. I latch on to her nipple to kiss while her head falls back.

"I'll make it up to you, I promise," I say against her nipple. "Use me the way you need, Vi."

She aligns me with her opening and sinks down, her warm heat wrapping around me like a perfect glove.

No condoms with her is going to mess with my head, I know it, because I can never go back with her, and this feeling is pure indulgence, even more that it's a type of closeness that is intensified when you already care for someone.

"Declan, is this what you want?" Her sweet moan follows the rhythm of her slow thrusts.

I use my hands to bring her breasts together as she moves on top of me. "Yes, baby, exactly like this. Clench harder," I urge.

She clamps down, and my eyes nearly roll to the back of my head. This woman is sexual dynamite with a heart of gold. And I hate the fucking guy who will claim forever with her.

But right now, she is mine, which is why my lips crash against hers to ensure we are completely one, until she convulses around my length, taking my own orgasm with her.

———

I FASTEN my watch around my wrist, and Violet emerges from the bathroom in a summer dress that I had sent over from a boutique a few blocks down. I had them send over a few options, plus lingerie, in case we lose this dress too somehow in one of our morning escapades.

Violet looked concerned that my call to the boutique was so simple, then she eased when I assured her that I knew of the place because my cousin stayed here a few months ago and she studies fashion.

"Okay, I think I'm ready. I got a text from Charlotte that I can just get my car from her place whenever by asking the doorman for access to her garage. She's not at home, surprise, surprise." Violet's tone is the opposite of her words.

We look at one another with a knowing thought.

"They probably went to an after-party, and who knows where they are," I add.

Violet holds a hand up. "I don't want to know. Besides, I'm starving."

I walk behind her and gently pat her ass to scoot her out of my room. "As you should be."

My phone chimes a sound, and I pull it up from my pocket to see Ford is video calling me. "Shit." I show Violet the screen, and her eyes blaze.

Yet, instead of ignoring it, I answer, since Violet is out of view. "Hey, man." I smile. "What's going on?"

Ford looks like he's lying by his pool. "Just wanted to check if you're going to the team reunion leading up to pre-season games. I got the email from the team, and then another email from marketing about a press conference. I don't know, I just go with the flow, but thought I would touch base that you also got it so that we're on the same wavelength."

I scratch the back of my head while I balance the phone. Meanwhile, Violet smirks at me while she reaches for the buckle on my jeans to mess with me.

"Yeah, I saw something come in but didn't open it." I attempt to shoo her away to no avail, and I do my best not to crack a laugh in front of Ford, but he must pick up on something, as his face changes to entertainment.

"I think I'm interrupting?" He smirks.

Violet's face is pure mischief.

"No, it's okay. I was just heading out, need to get my day moving."

Her fingers curl into the waistband of my jeans, and I do my best to keep my face straight.

"I'll let you go then, and just give me a call next time you're in Lake Spark, we can grab a beer."

"For sure." My voice is strained.

The moment the call ends, Violet's head falls back as she laughs. Immediately, I tickle her which only causes her laughter to grow. "Are you kidding me? With your brother on the other end?"

"Oopsies." She flashes her eyes at me.

"What happened to a peaceful breakfast?" I ask.

She clings to the front of my shirt to yank me gently in her direction. "It went out the window the moment you joined me in the shower earlier."

"No, it went out the window the moment I saw you last night in that dress," I reply.

A lie. I've been thrown upside down since I pulled her name all those weeks ago.

16

DECLAN

Not going to deny it, there is a bit of pep to my step as I walk along Lake Spark's Main Street holding a tray of two coffees, intending to surprise Violet.

The sun is out, and my mood is great.

But since the other week after agreeing to keep seeing one another, then I've been in a damn good mood. We've been texting all week, but still, she doesn't know that I'm swinging through Lake Spark today.

With a satisfied grin on my mouth, I balance the tray of coffees, and with my other hand, I swipe my sunglasses off my face as I use my back to push the door to The Flower Jar open, with the bell announcing my arrival.

But then I instantly stop in my tracks when I hear Ford's voice deep in conversation about babies as he leans against the table where Violet is cutting a few stems.

Ford's head turns in my direction, while Violet looks up and smiles, but her eyes turn slightly fearful when they bounce between her brother and me.

"Hey, what are you doing here?" Ford, at least, seems happy to see me. "Didn't know you were in town."

"Hey." My greeting isn't as steady. "Yeah, I... was going to do another walkthrough with my realtor before placing an offer. A last-minute kind of thing."

"Sounds like you're ready to settle here, which is great." He looks around the shop then back at me. "What brings you to The Flower Jar?"

"I..." I'm not sure how to get myself out of this one. Violet is behind Ford's view and begins to gesture with her hands a steering wheel then points to Ford. "I... noticed your car." I think that's what she was going for, and she nods. "Yeah, noticed your car parked nearby and thought I would stop by to say hi."

"Cool." He hikes a thumb at his sister. "I was just telling Violet about the latest doctor's appointment for Brielle. This baby is going to be huge, the biggest yet."

"Fun," I simply state.

Ford's eyes turned puzzled when he notices the coffees in my hands. "What's with the second coffee?"

"Duck it," the parrot chirps.

We all look at the bird then awkwardly at one another, with Violet letting out a nervous laugh.

"Thought I would bring a coffee to my real estate agent," I lie.

"Jolly Joe's, excellent choice," Violet adds, but her eyes tell me she appreciates the effort that I'm bringing her favorite.

Ford walks to me and places his hand on my shoulder. "See? Lake Spark is rubbing off on you. I bet you're like the rest of us and on a mission to get a purple jellybean."

"Yeah... I heard they're rare," I reply. Just like Violet.

"If you want, you should stop by the rink later," he offers.

"Thanks, but I'm a bit short on time today, but I'll be back soon," I promise him.

Ford looks between Violet and me, and maybe he picks on the fact that I can't keep my hands off his sister when he isn't around. I'm not sure, but he seems to have a peculiar look flash across his face as we have a break in conversation.

That is until Violet disrupts the silence. "Just text me what time you and Brielle want to leave this weekend, and I'll be there."

Ford glances to Violet with appreciation. "Thanks." His sight lands on me again. "She's helping us out with babysitting. She's special, this one."

Okay, now I'm certain that he is trying to transmit a secret message to me.

I stand a bit taller as he says goodbye, looks at me skeptically, and walks out.

Violet and I look at one another, holding our breath, until she heaves a sigh when she feels the coast is clear.

Stepping forward, I bring the coffees to the table. "Wasn't anticipating him being here," I admit.

"Wasn't anticipating you being here." She smiles softly.

Offering her the coffee cup, I state the obvious. "That's called the element of surprise."

"Do you really have an appointment?" she wonders as she takes a sip of her drink.

My head bobs side to side. "Yes… only after I arranged it. I was hoping that I could steal you away for lunch."

"We might be destined to hide in the closet in the back since Tilly called in sick, so I'm here alone." She sits down on her stool to get comfortable.

"Doable." I allow myself to drown in the view of her for a few extra seconds. "Everything okay with Ford?"

"Yeah, he was just stopping by, going over the rules for the kids, and checking if I'm ready to hit the dating scene, as he would like to see me get out there more. That's when I told him that he shouldn't worry, as his hot friend is banging me against walls on a regular basis now." A smirk curls on her lips which informs me that she's messing with me, at least for the last sentence.

My phone vibrates in my pocket, and I hold up a finger to indicate for Violet to wait a second. Glancing at the screen, I groan when I see my father's name.

Violet scoffs a sound. "*Still* avoiding your parents?"

Tucking the phone back into my jeans pocket, I roll my eyes. "Kind of. My mother not so much, but my dad... It's just... I don't want to disappoint him or appear overly selfish, even though I know that is 100% what I am."

"Ah, so it's your issue, not his. You're afraid of what you might feel when you see him face to face and confront the fact that Declan Dash will not be taking over the family empire, despite being the only child and getting everything he normally wants." Her wry smile doesn't fade.

"Something like that." Swallowing the last sip of my cortado, a little pebble hits the lid. I take the lid off and have to grin. "A sign?" I show her the cup with the purple jellybean that must be covered in who knows what food coloring to have survived my coffee.

"Maybe." Violet swirls off her stool and walks around the counter to stand in front of me. "I guess things we believe are impossible don't seem so hard once it happens."

I narrow my eyes at this beautiful vixen in front of me. "Are you trying to connect the jellybean to my parents?"

Her lips quirk out. "Is it getting the wheels in your head turning?" She slips her arm around my waist.

"Maybe."

"Trust me, you will focus better once you face your parents."

I pinch her stomach and pull her closer. "I know you're right. I've been holding off on seeing them, but they want me to have dinner with them this weekend. What are the chances I can see you after to recover?"

"Zero, sadly. I'm babysitting my nephews and plan on enjoying the pool after they go to sleep."

I wince at the thought of her in a bikini alone and me nowhere in sight. "What an image in my head now."

"You know I appreciate that you stopped by and brought me coffee, it's cute."

"Babe, I'm not cute."

"You kind of are," she argues. "My point is that I wasn't sure when I would see you again, but here you are."

"Want to know a secret?" I whisper.

"Yes."

"I have no clue what I'm doing other than I had an urge to see you."

She checks nobody is outside. "Well, I *may* know the feeling. Now, follow me to the closet and let me blow your mind so you have something to think about when you see your parents."

———

MY MOTHER CAN'T STOP SMILING as she grabs a few vegetables from the tray on the table. She's a contrast to my father who hasn't said much, nor blinked as he continues to stare at me.

"Carrot?" She offers me the plate. I can tell she went to the salon today, as her blonde hair is partially curled, and her nails seem freshly painted.

I shake my head. "No, thanks."

"We are so happy you're finally joining us for dinner. I know you've been busy, but we always appreciate when you make a little time for us."

My lips stretch from her sentiment, and I glance at the wall of their dining room which has my signed jersey and a photo of me holding a trophy. "New?" I indicate with my head.

Dad chuckles. "You mean the shrine to our beloved, only, and firstborn son? Why, yes. That is exactly what your mother was going for." Even with his face stern, he manages to execute sarcasm with perfection.

It causes me to grin. "Should we just lay this all out on the table? I'm not planning on taking over the business. You know it's not about money, I have that from my own doing."

My mother touches my hand on the table. "We know, it's about what you enjoy. Right, Walter?" Her eyes aim a warning at my father.

He grabs hold of his scotch. "We let the boy enjoy his hockey career. He can't take a little time to give back to this family?"

"You have people who are by far more suited to handling maple syrup," I explain. "Besides, I'm still young and need to ensure I enjoy my life ahead."

Maybe Violet was right, and this isn't as bad as I had built up in my head. After the initial look from my father, walking into the dining room to a well-spread meal seemed like a piece of cake. Now words just flow out of me.

"You're the only one who can carry on the name," he nearly grumbles, "unless you get to work on settling down with someone to give us grandkids, but nothing you have done has ever indicated that's on your mind. Hell, you've never even introduced us to a woman."

"Now isn't the time to pressure him to settle down." My mother flashes him an unimpressed look before turning her attention to me. "Your father just had it in his heart that after your hockey career, you would spend more time with him to take on the company. But you kind of took us by surprise with your grand purchase."

"You mean the hockey team? Yeah, because if I can't play, then I still want to be involved. It's too much in my blood," I clarify.

"Of course, dear, but maybe you can find a way to balance your time a little." She's trying to offer an olive branch to the two men at this table.

"Heaven help us, Pearl, I probably would have to have a heart attack before Declan even considers."

I rub my forehead, now getting aggravated. "This is beginning to feel like a bad idea that I ca—"

"No!" my mother cuts me off. "We have to start somewhere. Your father's pride is just a little hurt that you don't want to take interest in his company. After so many years of watching you succeed on the ice, we thought you could bring that passion to the corporate table now that life will quiet down for you."

"I will succeed, on the business side of hockey. You both love maple syrup and dancing bears, while I love hockey; let's just agree to disagree. I'm sure we will eventually find something that we can all enjoy together," I say before I grab a stick of celery from the tray, because it's desperate times if you grab the freaking celery.

"What a wonderful way to look at it. So tell us, what will you do with the Spinners?" Give this woman an award for trying hard.

I crunch on the celery. "I'm moving trainings out to Lake Spark for better focus. I'm going to get a house there too."

She claps her hands together. "Get out of the city, that's a great idea."

My father makes a low grumbly sound. "A house there is always a good investment." Damn, he just gave me a compliment.

"We should go visit, Walter," my mom suggests.

"Suppose it's a good spot for a weekend away from the suburbs. Haven't been that way in years." Huh, he's more agreeable.

"Ford, remember him? He lives out there, along with a few other athletes," I add.

"Always liked Ford, he's a family man. You know, there used to be a maple syrup festival out there. Wonder whatever happened to it." He seems to be lost in thought, although calm.

My mom smiles widely at me, as it seems we are finding neutral ground, and seeing them does make the situation slightly easier to handle. Of course, I feel guilt that I'm not following my old man, but looking at these two, I know with certainty that they do love me. We just need to navigate our road a little better, and I sure as hell shouldn't shut them out.

A cheese plate is offered in front of me, and as I'm about to tuck in, my phone goes off on the table.

"No phones at the table," my mother chides.

I see an incoming video call from Violet, which is odd, because I know she's babysitting.

"Give me a minute, I kind of need to take this," I say before sliding off my chair and hitting the green button with my thumb. "Hey, Vi, what's going on?"

I vaguely hear my mom say, "*Ooh, a woman,*" in the background before I manage to leave the room and find a quiet spot in the main hallway at the bottom of the wraparound stairs.

"I'm totally fu—" She looks at Wyatt who she's bouncing in her arms. "Ducked. Totally ducked." Violet sets the toddler on the ground, and her face is a mask of pure panic, and she looks exhausted.

"What's going on?"

She attempts to breathe normally. "I told him he could have two friends over. Two guy friends and they could chill by the pool. Two." Violet grabs her hair in frustration before her eyes catch something off screen. "Oh no, Wyatt don't eat Puck's food." She sets the phone down on what seems to be the kitchen counter and is propped up against something so I get full view.

"Puck? What? Violet, you're scaring me."

The screen shows me that she rushed to Wyatt who is eating dog food from the bowl while a Labrador runs across the screen. She takes Wyatt into her arms and returns to the phone.

"I went upstairs to do bath time and get the cute kid ready for bed, only an hour later I came downstairs to find that the bad kid had multiplied two to God knows what number, and it's freaking Project X outside, with every teenager in a ten-mile radius."

"Shit. Connor is throwing a party?"

She nods her head repeatedly. "This is so bad. I swear I saw Spencer's daughter out there, which means he will go through the roof. I don't have it in me to call Ford. This is their last chance to be alone before they're a family of five, and hell, I know they volunteered for that, but Brielle doesn't deserve her weekend of relaxation to be ruined. I mean, I was sixteen once, I just need to think like them and be one step ahead. I can beat them at their little game."

I give her an awkward look. "What would sixteen-year-old you have been up to?"

Violet takes a moment to think as her lips curl into her mouth. "Bad. This is very bad." She glances off-screen again. "Puck, what do have in your mouth? What the duck is that can?" Violet looks back at the screen with her eyes blazed with more loss of what to do.

Her night is a disaster, far more than the mini storm happening in my parents' dining room.

A shaky breath escapes her mouth. "Maybe I just hose them all down?" Her voice squeaks.

In my mind, I walk through what I just talked about with my parents. I know they were subtly calling me out on my selfish move, but I'm ready to prove them wrong. Not just with hockey but also with the people that I care about.

I refuse to let Violet go through this alone.

"I'm at my parents' house, which means I can get to you in forty-five minutes. Hang on, I'm on my way."

17

DECLAN

Immediately, I rush to Violet who is walking down the stairs, while the music's pulsing base is low in the background.

"You didn't have to come," she says as she scratches the back of her head.

"I wasn't going to leave you alone in the trenches." I squeeze her arms for comfort.

"I got Wyatt to sleep, but I have no idea if the party outside will keep raging. It's so stupid, I know all I have to do is head out there and demand they all leave, but then…"

"You're no longer the cool aunt. Plus, in all honesty, I think the odds of a group of mostly 16-year-old-boys listening to the hot twenty-something woman are kind of slim. They might be distracted." I attempt to make her smile.

"I'm so angry. Connor has never put me in this position." I can easily sense that Violet is deeply disappointed.

I bring my arm around her shoulders, and we walk to the kitchen. "Let's come up with a game plan."

We head straight to the window by the kitchen sink to peek outside. The florescent-blue pool light gives us a view, along with the outside lighting around the deck where teenagers are gathered.

"At least they have good taste in music," Violet attempts to joke.

I listen closer, and my head naturally bobs. "Imagine Dragons are a solid choice. Heard they put on a good concert."

Violet focuses on me for a second. "I wanted to go, but tickets are hard to get."

I scoff. "I'll make it happen. Now let's focus."

We both examine the scene again.

"There are boys and girls, just great." She scowls. We both angle our heads as we observe the jungle outside. "I'm pretty positive that make-out central is happening over on the chaise lounge by the pool."

I grimace at the scene, but I search for Connor who is sitting on the top step of the pool, laughing as someone passes him a drink. Then his eyes dart across the pool, and I recognize Hadley, the next-door neighbor, who is Spencer's daughter.

"Could be worse, at least it's not our guy making out. What do we do about Hadley?"

"Sneak her back to her house, maybe I text April, but Hadley is harmless. She has a crush on Connor, so she stops by a lot. What are the chances they're all drinking alcohol?"

"Uh…" An awkward sound is the only thing I manage to respond with.

Violet groans. "I hope zero, but yeah, sixteen-year-old me knows better. I mean, I think Connor is responsible enough not to drink, but I can't say the same for his friends."

"The boat keys?"

Violet shakes her head. "Ford keeps the keys locked in his home office."

I blow out a long breath. "There is only way to do this…"

"Turn off the electricity?" she retorts.

"I'll be the bad guy."

"What?" She looks at me.

I nod. "Yeah, I'll be the bad guy and go out there and shut this shit down right away."

"We're a team in this." She wants to debate.

"There is also a sleeping toddler upstairs and a Labrador hyped up on who knows what."

She tilts her shoulder up. "Puck is always hyped up, he likes people."

I comb my fingers through my hair. "I'm going in."

Violet protests, but I'm already enraged on adrenaline. I kiss her forehead then walk away, noticing the fruit bowl, and I empty it before bringing it with me as I dart outside through the sliding doors.

The moment I'm outside, the music grows loud and is mixed with laughter. I charge straight for Connor, demanding on my journey that phones and keys go in the bowl to anyone who crosses my path, and I ignore the eyes all following my line of travel.

"Connor!" I yell out.

He glances up and then grins. "Hey, Declan, what are you doing—?"

I interject with a seething voice. "Ending this. Now."

Connor stands up and seems to be unfazed. "Come on, it's just a little gathering."

I yank the plastic cup from his hand. "Really?" I sniff the cup, and it smells like a mix of Kool-Aid and alcohol. "What the hell is this?"

"Just punch."

My eyes grow bold. "Screw that. We're not going to play stupid right now, so don't even try it. Hurry up, everyone, phones and keys in the bowl," I call out, then resume my conversation with Connor. "Where did you get this?"

His eyes dip low. "A friend brought it," he mumbles.

"Music off," I call out to the crew, and a few seconds later, the music fades. I have no misgivings that all eyes are on us or that someone is probably filming this as I heard a few people whisper, *"Oh my God, it's Declan Dash,"* but chose to ignore it.

"This isn't even your house, what are you going to do about it?" He stands tall, ready to challenge me.

I pinch my nose, purely entertained yet pissed, and I step closer to him. "Don't mess with me, Connor, I hold all the cards. Now is the time to send all your little friends packing, after you tell me who the hell is driving so we can ensure everyone gets home safe." I'm in a death-stare competition with a teenager, and this is not how I thought my night would go.

"You know how it is. Can't you just let us have a little fun?" he tries again.

My face doesn't flinch. "No. By all means, have fun, but not when your aunt is being kind enough to take care of you guys for the weekend because your mom and dad are away to enjoy a little quiet time before your new baby brother enters the world, which means, let's not upset your very pregnant mother. So wrap. This. Shit. Up. Now."

Connor grumbles but nods to a friend somewhere behind me. "Party's over." He sighs, and everyone begins to stir.

"This is how this is going to go. First, nobody gets their phone or keys until I'm 100% sure whoever the hell is driving is sober. Those phones? I don't want to see one single photo or video from this evening on it. Second, I'm not going to make you snitch who the hell brought the jungle juice, but I want to see every damn drop thrown out. Finally, I don't care how hungover you are tomorrow, because trust me, you will be, but you know it doesn't matter, because you're going to clean this place up, then you're going to volunteer at your aunt's flower shop for the next three weeks. I'm sure Nugget will appreciate you cleaning his cage. Now move." I cross my arms, proud that I'm standing firm, because this is every version of myself that I would have hated at his age.

He groans but gets moving.

———

HEAVING AN EXHAUSTING BREATH, I close the front door behind me after making sure the last of the teenagers are headed home safely. I'm pretty sure it's the eighteen-year-old with older brothers or a good fake ID who brought the punch, but I'm picking my battles tonight.

Violet's sitting at the bottom of the stairs with so much appreciation glazing over her eyes that it's not a surprise when she jumps up to throw her arms around me and plant a kiss on my lips, which I gladly take as my reward.

It's a long, hard kiss that nearly makes me forget the last hour.

"Thank you. Thank you. Thank you." She peppers kisses along my jawline.

"No problem."

She chortles. "Liar."

The sound of Connor entering through the back door breaks our attention, yet we seem to forget to detangle our arms. I made him walk Hadley to the property line next door because it's close. Spencer may kill us, and I wanted to throw Hadley one bone for the evening since she was the easiest of all the kids.

"You know there are baby monitor cameras like everywhere inside this place," he informs us, rather cool in tone.

Violet backs up like a hot potato. "Shit, forgot about that."

Connor slides onto a stool. "You guys are such amateurs. Lucky for you, I hacked the system and turned them off earlier this evening. Looks like I saved your little secret budding romance." He throws his feet up on the counter. "Oh, whatever will you do to repay me for that… or shall I just share the news with Dad tomorrow? He will *love* it."

"Oh my God, the jungle juice created a monster," Violet mumbles under her breath.

I walk straight to Connor and knock his feet off the counter with my hand. "Blackmailing me? Is that what you are trying to do?" I'm unfazed by his attempt.

"Let's call it even." Connor attempts to square off with me.

I wave my finger side to side at him. "Nope. Call it another stupid choice on your evening of bad decisions because…" I step into his space which seems to irritate him. "This game that you want to play, only I can score. First off, you didn't see anything, your aunt and I are friends who gave one another a hug. Alcohol confuses you, clearly. Also, you know that little hockey career that you want so badly? You're playing varsity this year, right?" I tap my finger on my chin. "I'm old friends with your coach. In fact, he often calls me for advice on players and rosters, and I would hate to forget your name in a momentary lapse of judgment."

Connor's face falls when he realizes that I hold the upper hand. "You wouldn't."

"I love a challenge. Oh yeah, and then there is, of course, the fact the Spinners will start training here in Lake Spark. That could be a total bonus for you… if you keep your head above water, that is."

He growls before he slides off the chair. "Fine. You two win… this round."

Connor storms off, and then I notice Violet with her jaw low and her eyes wide with amazement.

"Who are you tonight?" Her jaw snaps shut, and her lips curl into a smile. "Are you really friends with his coach?"

"Nah, I have no clue who he is, but Connor doesn't know that." I take a few steps and walk straight into her open arms. "He's going to be a little out of sorts tomorrow morning."

"I know. You'll stay? It's late, and I don't want you on the roads." There is so much care in her tone. "Nothing exciting will happen, since this is kind of my brother's house. There is a teething toddler upstairs, an overexcited dog, and a teenager who may just burn the world down, but ya know, we're just keeping it real." She pops her lips.

Something about that scenario sounds kind of appealing right now. I'm right where I should be.

"I'm not going anywhere," I promise.

———

WE STAYED up only for a little bit, recalling our own teenage years, which caused us to come to the same conclusion that we were both kind of wild. We fell asleep on the couch, which is for the best, as it appears more platonic, in case Connor was looking for more evidence. Now, we've been up for an hour thanks to Wyatt who decided seven is the ideal time to wake on the weekends.

He's bouncing on my lap as we sit at the dining table with his craft box. Wyatt is drawing with a thick crayon, while I fold paper and create a few origami animals for him. Occasionally, I glance up to watch Violet tidying up the kitchen, and to be honest, I kind of enjoy this whole setup.

I mean, even Wyatt's plate of cut-up toasted waffles and fruit were kind of tasty when he decided to feed me a few bites.

The feeling of wet slobber on my thigh brings my attention to Puck who just delivered his tennis ball to me... for the hundredth time.

"Hey, Vi, what's up with this dog? He won't stop chasing the ball."

"Well, he is a *retriever*. But you're right, and Ford is training him for some competition." Violet walks to the table with two fresh mugs of coffee. "Here you go, my superhero."

"Thanks."

This is a nice little routine. I don't remember my parents ever being this way. I mean, they love one another, but my dad's head would always be buried behind a newspaper while my mother looked on. It was never everyone at a table doing something together. Hell, even the dog wants in on the action.

Violet grabs a sheet of paper and attempts to fold, but then gives up. "I'll leave it to the pros. Anyway, I can't thank you enough."

"No problem. Are you going to tell Ford?" I wonder.

Her eyes flick to mine. "About us?"

I gently shake my head. "Connor," I clarify.

She sighs. "It's the responsible thing to do since he was drinking. I might leave out a few details. This will for sure take me down a notch on my nephew's cool list."

"And... about us?"

The tip of her tongue hits her upper lip. "I don't think Ford would think us being together is a good thing unless we are together-

together. No brother wants to hear about the friend with benefits, especially if it's with *their* friend."

"Right." I don't have an answer, nor do I like hers.

She smiles at me. "We never got a chance to chat about your parents. How was it?"

I pass another crayon to Wyatt. "Not bad at all. You were right, it was more in my head. I think we can find our way and maybe meet in the middle. I know I'm disappointing them, my dad for sure, but seeing one another face to face helped. They even got a little excited about Lake Spark."

Her face turns elated. "That's great. I'm so happy for you. I can only imagine that being the only child makes it more… sensitive for them. Can I ask if they wanted more children?"

"They did and tried, but it just never happened, unexplainable. I'm lucky Mom doesn't push the whole grandkids thing… yet. I can imagine that it's something she wants. I guess I don't win many points for being son of the year when it comes to them."

Violet props her foot up on her chair, bringing her knee up to her chest. "Don't assume. I'm sorry I took you away from them over something so silly. I feel like I should send flowers as an apology or something."

I chuckle. "My mom would lose her cool and get excited that a woman I know sent her flowers."

Violet laughs. "We can't have that, now, can we?"

Yet I wouldn't mind if they met Violet. She would make them smile and bring us all peace through her sunny perspective on life.

"Green," Wyatt says and points to another crayon.

Violet picks up a paper swan and examines it. "You have a lot of hidden skills."

"You know about my paper talent."

"No, I mean with kids too."

Before I can ponder, a grumbling Connor arrives down the stairs. "Aunt Violet, I don't feel too good."

I roll my eyes. "That's called regret."

Violet chuckles softly and gets up off the chair to walk to her nephew. She gives him a hug, even though the guy doesn't deserve it, then guides him to the kitchen island. "I made you a hangover cure." Violet grabs a glass with green liquid and a bottle of tabasco sauce.

"What the hell, why do I need that?" Connor sounds horrified.

"Trust me." She dabs a few drops of hot sauce into the glass then hands it to him.

Connor takes a quick sip then begins to gag. "I think I'm going to be sick." He runs to the bathroom down the hall.

Violet lets a relaxing breath escape while her shoulders lower. "Works every single time. He will feel so much better after it's all out, and then he will spend his morning cleaning up the backyard. What fun." She claps her hands together.

Looking around, I decide I'm comfortable right where I am. "I'll stick around… if you want."

She walks back to me, leans down, covers Wyatts eyes with her hand, and kisses me quickly on the lips. "Let me make you a real breakfast then, because I would love if you stayed."

Me too.

Because apparently this chaos is a side of life that I didn't realize could be appealing, especially if it has Violet shimmying her fine ass to the kitchen to cook us eggs.

18

VIOLET

I flop onto the couch, causing goldfish crackers to spill out of the bowl next to Wyatt who fell asleep beside Declan while they watched Cocomelon. This is a side of Declan that I wasn't expecting to see. Hell, I couldn't have predicted that this was how the weekend would go. I'm not sure why I called him in my moment of panic, but I felt like I could rely on him for advice or anything, and he delivered in full.

He could have rushed off by now, but instead, he's hanging out with us, and my heart warms at the gesture. I glance outside and see Connor is finished cleaning up, as he is walking with a full garbage bag to the back of the garage.

My eyes dart back to Declan while he squeezes a tennis ball, with Puck sitting at full attention and drool running down one side of his mouth.

"I really can't thank you enough. I know this is the last place you want to be." I feel like I'm repeating myself, but it's worth it.

Declan shrugs it off. "It's fine. Ford would want me to help you out during your dire time of need. Plus, this isn't so bad." He leans in closer to me and lowers his voice. "I mean, have you seen the snacks in the pantry here? It's a goldmine!"

I laugh softly, aware that Wyatt is napping, and we didn't have the heart to move him. "That's what happens when you have kids; your pantry becomes the key to utopia."

Declan leans back against the sofa with a wry smile. "You're really in your element now. I mean, the whole family thing. It suits you."

"Really? Because I feel like I sprouted a gray hair last night."

He finally tosses the ball for the dog who goes running. "Nah, you like the chaos. I kind of get it. I mean, you can't get lost in your own thoughts when you have all of this around you." He points between Wyatt and the dog, then looks for Connor.

His point of view isn't far off. "I think you're right," I agree.

"Some people have career aspirations on the forefront, and others have family aspirations. You and I are opposites."

"Hey, who says I don't want to start a flower empire?" I protest in jest.

He gives me wide eyes. "Do you?"

I think about it for not even a second. "No. I'm happy with one store and a talking parrot."

"Exactly, and I'm happy with anything hockey."

Right, this guy doesn't have his personal life as a priority anytime on the horizon. The reminder is good for me, otherwise the scene in front of me will begin to offer a slither of hope. How can I not be affected by Declan showing me his family-man persona, even if he has no idea that he seems to have it. He's been nothing but, well, swoony since he got here.

Connor enters the house, interrupting our conversation, luckily.

"I'm done," he declares.

He walks to the big chair opposite the sofa and flops onto it. "My head hurts."

Declan and I look at one another, knowing the familiar feeling.

"It will for a little bit, but I already ordered pizza because carbs are your friend." I know I should go harder on him, but I'm a softy when it comes to Connor.

"Drink more water. Just remember this feeling, because trust me, you never ever want to show up to practice or a game like this. You're way too young to go down this road," Declan conveys to him while he wraps his arm around Wyatt to pull him close in a snuggle. I'm not sure he even realizes what he's doing, it appears so second nature to him.

Again, I shake off the thought, because he's stated many times that he only does casual.

Connor crosses his arms and nestles deeper into the chair. "I know. I said I'm sorry, and it wasn't me who brought the alcohol."

"Hopefully you learned a lesson from this," I add.

"Yeah," Connor mumbles.

The sound of the front door opening and the dog running draws all our attention to Ford and Brielle entering the house. They're home early.

"Hey," Ford draws out while he sets their bags on the floor. He notices Wyatt sleeping, so keeps his voice low, and although he observes that Declan is here, he doesn't seem bothered.

Brielle saunters behind him with her natural smile, and her eyes dance between Declan and me. That's when I notice she's confident with her theory about us that she presented to me a while ago, as her lips roll in to hide her smile from Ford before she takes a few steps in front of him.

"Has Wyatt been sleeping long?" she asks as she studies the scene and does her best to keep the jumping Labrador at bay from her growing belly.

"Half-hour. You guys are home early," I say and stand up, nervously tucking my hands in the back pockets of my shorts.

"We left right after lunch and didn't have any traffic. Looks like Wyatt made a new friend." My brother's eyes land on Declan again.

"Yeah, do enlighten us with your explanation on Wyatt's new friend choice," Connor remarks to completely mess with us.

My eyes snap to Connor with a disapproving look. "How about you go grab another water, huh? You know how this is going to go." I indicate with my head that he should get out of here.

He groans but stalks out of the room, leaving his parents confused and looking curiously at me.

"We had a bit of a situation," I begin, and Brielle instantly looks panicked, so I hold my hand up to calm her. "It's fine, all fine. Connor got a little carried away with his friend quota for the evening, and it might have involved a little alcohol, but hey, he learned his lesson."

"What?!" Ford looks furious.

Damn it, I knew the easy story wouldn't work.

"I went to give Wyatt a bath, returned downstairs to find a party. Luckily Declan saved the night by ending it and making sure everyone got home safe."

Ford swipes his hair with his hands, while Brielle's head dips low.

"It was bound to happen. We were all his age once," Declan attempts to comfort them.

"I'm so sorry." Brielle seems mortified.

Ford glances off into the kitchen, and I can tell he is debating which talk to give. He lets out a breath and turns his attention to Declan. "Thanks, man, I owe you. I can imagine man-to-man worked better in that situation."

"It's no problem, you would have done the same." Declan gently moves Wyatt out of his way.

"You guys didn't call us?" Brielle wonders.

I offer her a sympathetic smile. "Now you know. *After* you enjoyed your little getaway." Her face is full of fondness and appreciation.

Declan stands and rubs a hand across his jaw. "I think I'm going to head out."

"Me too, since I think you guys have a fun evening ahead. Pizza should be here soon."

"Don't you two want to stay?" Ford asks.

Brielle places a hand on her husband's arm. "I think they want to run away after this."

"Exactly what she said," I tell my brother.

Declan and I begin to walk out of the room.

"Wait." Ford stops us in our tracks. We both look at him, slightly concerned. "Is something happening between you two?"

The question instantly makes my stomach swirl, as if we've been caught out, and I think it excites me, if I'm honest.

"Of course not." Declan is quick to laugh off his suggestion.

Even though I know it's for the best, I wish we didn't have to lie. "I knew Declan was in the area, and I needed a manly touch to deal with the varsity hockey team," I add.

Ford nods slowly and seems to buy it. Brielle, meanwhile, hides behind her hand over her mouth because she knows exactly what we're doing.

"Okay, I mean, if there was, I'm not sure I would be cool with it, to be honest." Ford still eyes us with caution.

I offer a fake smile. "Nothing to worry about then. Just friends."

He seems convinced, but I know we're leaving having told the biggest lie of the century.

———

UNLOCKING MY DOOR, I enter my home, with Declan hot on my heels. I'm lucky he had a weekend bag in his car when he went to visit his parents, because he didn't have to hesitate over logistics about staying at my place. After last night, I want to do something nice for him. He followed me home in his car, and I'm sure his Maserati will draw the attention of my nosy neighbors, but I don't really care.

"If you give me twenty minutes, I'll shower then cook dinner. I'm positive I have a stray Cheerio somewhere in my hair," I mention as I toss my keys into the bowl on the side table.

I feel arms wrapping around me from behind, because how dare I forget how insatiable this man is when the setting allows.

"Go enjoy a warm bath, and food will be here in a bit."

I glance over my shoulder with a raised brow. "What do you mean? I'm cooking."

"No, you're not. You deserve to rest and take it easy after what went down. In the car, I called the chef from the Dizzy Duck to send over some stuff." He says it so casually.

Twirling on the balls of my feet, I come face to face with Declan and rope my arms around his neck. "You should be the one taking it easy, and the chef from the Dizzy Duck just won a bunch of awards, and now you're saying he is sending over food?"

"And wine."

My mouth opens then closes. "Is this a connections thing or a threw-some-money-at-them kind of thing? People wait weeks for a reservation there." This is crazy. And expensive. But mostly sweet.

"Not us, babe. Now go relax." Declan slants his shoulder up while he encourages me to walk forward.

I don't unlink from around his neck, and instead, I stand on his toes as he walks, with me hanging off him. "Look at you. If I wasn't wise, then I would call you a romantic. You know, this really ruins my ability to thank you tonight. You've outshined me."

"That's hard to do," he promises.

But a few hours later, and it feels like I'm a tiny speck on the ability to impress. I'm for sure relaxed, and the food was delicious, right down to the drizzle of sauce on my chicken. I know thought went into the order because we got extra chocolate chip cookies that the inn leaves on pillows but are not on any menu. I feel like Declan asked for that just for me.

Drinking the last sips of wine from our glasses, we stand by the sink.

"Thank you for staying. I would have felt bad if you went back to the city and I didn't get to give you at least one orgasm this weekend."

He chuckles. "I'm swamped with meetings this week, but this is a perfect way to head into a new week. Besides, I kind of felt ending the weekend between us with brother bear giving me the stare down wasn't the way to leave things." Declan tips back his wine glass to finish the drink.

My eyes enjoy the reality that he's standing in my kitchen after a dinner where we laughed and talked. "Fun, right?"

"If he ever were to find out, because I'm not sure Connor is going to stay tight-lipped with his theory, then we need to come up with a story."

"What do you mean?" I hold my glass to my chest.

Declan folds his arms over his chest and leans against the edge of the sink with a suave grin. "Well, we can't exactly say how we started, now can we?"

"True. Nobody knows about that night except us, which means we are free to make up our own version of events."

"We ran into one another at the stadium, then…" he begins.

"Again, at a bar in the city…"

"Where I asked about things that scare you."

My cheeks warm because it seems neither one of us wants to change our sequence of events. "And we got to talking, then you showed up in Lake Spark at my flower shop, relieved that you would never have to impress me with a flower…"

"The bird said to tie you up, but you just wanted to tie me down, and your charming ways kind of wore at me."

The way he says it, with his eyes locked on me, sends a chill down my spine. It's a blur between what's real or pretend right now, especially when he steps closer. Only when I hear the glass clink against the bottom of the sink do I realize that Declan slid it away from my fingers. He cups my face between his palms, and he lowers his mouth onto mine to kiss me.

The kind of kiss that feels confirming.

I'm not sure for what, but I return his kiss with the same force.

My fingers curl into his shirt because I feel like I'm going dizzy or crazy, and I don't seem to mind.

Pulling gently away, his eyes have a glint that gives me no answers, other than the desire I see.

I interlink our hands, and without any words, walk us to my bedroom where I guide him to sit on the edge of my bed. He watches my every move as I lead, pleased when I drop down onto his lap to straddle him.

Declan's hands follow the curve of my hipbone down to my ass before he hoists me snug to his body, and instantly, I feel his cock through his jeans.

Our lips fuse together in a kiss that feels far more intimate than it should.

But it only fuels us because he rolls us until I'm on my back and underneath him. Then it feels as though the air snaps between us, a calm after a long day.

We enter a pattern of a kiss, then our eyes dancing, before planting another kiss at random spots on one another's body.

No need to rush or say anything, because our eyes say it all.

Sex isn't our priority, yet this feels like something to cherish.

We take our time caressing one another's bodies for what feels like forever, until Declan holds my gaze while he brings two fingers inside of me, and his thumb circles my clit. It's like a magnetic pull that neither one of us can control as my body follows his movements, writhing under his touch.

Slow, we never rush. We enjoy the taste of one another at the same time, and when he pushes inside of me with his cock, I get lost in him.

Because when I see our hands connected against the mattress as Declan moves inside of me—no dirty talk, just our breaths and moans merging into a synced sound—then I realize we're entering new territory that I'm not sure either one of us anticipated.

VIOLET

I trace my finger over the words on my phone.

DECLAN

I'm going to be in Lake Spark tomorrow.

That wasn't on the calendar. ;)

Fuck the calendar, we freeze time. I'll see you tomorrow. Spread yourself wide and be ready.

Some of us need to work, Mr. Impatient.

Fine. I'll pick us up dinner and you can meet me at my place. I got the keys. We have surfaces to test. ;)

What an offer…

And you love it.

I do, I really do. A smile dances on my lips as I place my phone flat on the table, as Ford will be here any moment. I'm waiting in

Catch 22 for dinner with my brother. He wanted to meet up after last week's babysitting weekend turned into an adventure not for the faint of heart. It's a little messed up, but despite my teenage nephew ending up with a hangover, I'm kind of happy that the weekend ended the way it did.

I got to experience another side of Declan, a softer side.

It's a big problem too, because it's hard to see the guy you're only supposed to be casual with as just that, when you were already feeling things, and then he swoops in like a knight in shining armor. Not to mention, when we came back to my house and we slept together that night, it felt as though our connection deepened.

We text every day, and when he was in Lake Spark a few days ago for a meeting, he came to my place after. I ate dinner while sitting on his lap because he wouldn't let my hand go.

"What has you in a good mood?" My brother greets me by placing his hand on my shoulder.

My body jolts as my brain tries to rewire my focus. "Oh, hey, you're here."

"Yeah, we said we were meeting at seven." He offers me a goofy look and slides onto the chair across from me.

"Sorry, I had a lot of orders today, and my brain is a little foggy," I fib.

He nods in understanding as he gets comfortable. "It's okay. Did Connor stop by on time to do his clean-up duties?"

"Yes. Nugget very much appreciates a new servant to his kingdom," I reflect with sarcasm.

My brother laughs. "I always appreciate your positive view of the world. Again, I'm sorry he got a little unruly. I assure you, I have him on Nugget, house, and training center duty for another week."

I wave him off. "Stop apologizing. We were all his age once, and I think he learned his lesson."

Ford smiles at the waitress who arrives at our table, and we both order our drinks, keeping it to soft drinks for now. When she walks away, my brother grins at me peculiarly.

"What's up with you?" I wonder as I grab a piece of bread from the basket.

"Nothing. It's been a while since you and I had a little one-on-one time. I haven't checked up on you enough lately—"

I hold up my hand, indicating for him to stop. "For that, I count my blessings," I tease.

Ford rolls his eyes. "I just mean, I felt I didn't need to, as you seem pretty happy. There isn't anyone new in your life?"

My heart jumps into my throat and gets stuck. I internally question why it's my heart and not my words, but I don't have time to analyze now; I need to deter Ford. I rip my bread into tiny pieces. "Nobody. It's just summer in Lake Spark, how can you not be happy?"

"It's been raining more days than I care to count." He looks at me blankly.

"And? Dancing in the rain can be good for the soul."

"Right." It drags out of him, as he doesn't seem to be buying it. "No idea what you're up to in your free time, but I hope it's nothing illegal. I would love for you to find someone to settle down with, you deserve it."

The waitress drops off our drinks, and we thank her but indicate we need more time to order.

"Where is this coming from?" I take a sip of my drink.

Ford rests his arms on the table. "I just… you kind of punished yourself for your last relationship, even though you are not to blame, and I've been waiting for the sign that you're ready to move on again. Lately, you seem to be in a good place, so I have to ask. Are you ready?"

My mouth opens but only air escapes. He has caught me off guard, but then honesty overwhelms me, along with a gushing smile. "I think… I am." Ready for a relationship, a real one. There is someone who has unintentionally given me a taste of how great it could be.

Ford wiggles his finger in the air. "I was hoping you would say that." He smiles to someone over my shoulder, and suddenly, I feel as though this is an odd situation. "Don't kill me. Brielle mentioned you might. But I kind of invited someone to dinner."

Oh my God, did he figure out that I'm seeing Declan? Is this his way of testing me?

"What do you mean?" I ask with caution.

Ford doesn't have the opportunity to answer, because he stands to greet the man arriving at our table. My eyes roam up, and I think I might kill my brother.

The sheriff.

"Hey, Violet, I was hoping to run into you." Carter smiles at me like I'm treasure. He's out of uniform, in dark jeans, and I notice a few eyes land on him, as natural good looks don't get ignored by humans.

Quickly, my eyes dart between both men before me and quickly connect the dots. "Hi. Let me guess, my brother mentioned I would be here..." I nervously smile.

Ford answers for him. "I ran into him at the general store and invited him to join us. Please, have a seat," he offers.

My entire body tightens from disappointment that the wrong man is in front of me, and the fact that Ford, although with good intentions, sprang this on me. To be fair, I may have mentioned months back that the sheriff could be a contender, but that was before Declan entered my life and raised the bar so disproportionally high that I'm not sure anyone can compare.

We all sit down, both guys in front of me very much ready for this evening that I've been tricked into.

"How was your day, Sheriff?" Ford asks.

Nervously I twirl hair around my finger. "Bet there were a lot of cats in trees to save," I attempt to joke, but my stomach feels numb.

What the hell do I do? I can't exactly say I'm taken, because then Ford would want to know by whom. Can't exactly say I'm sleeping with his friend, because no sister wants their brother to know about their sex life. Besides, Declan doesn't want more than this, whatever it is that we're doing.

Carter chuckles. "No cats today. Actually had to appear at the county courthouse to testify in a case on speeding tickets. I wasn't working the big bad streets of Lake Spark today." I hear the humor in his tone. "How is the flower business going?" Carter asks with interest.

"The usual. Men phoning in to ask for the right flowers to apologize. Brothers ordering flowers after their sisters threaten murder. Oops, shouldn't share that info with you, as I may soon be involved in a crime." A short laugh escapes me because this is just beyond bizarre.

"I'll go easy with the handcuffs," Carter jokes.

My brother chortles, while I stare blankly at these men.

Someone save me.

"You'll what?" A deep voice with an undertone of rage fills my ears.

No. Nope. This is not who I meant to save me.

My eyes turn to saucers and snap in the direction of the familiar voice that I love. "Declan." I sound unsteady.

Declan looms over our table, with his jaw tight and his eyes blazing with fury.

"Hey, man, I didn't know you would be here." My brother smiles while he stands to greet his friend with their ridiculous team handshake.

Declan looks at Ford, completely unimpressed. "I told you when I was at the rink earlier that I would be in town for the weekend, and you mentioned we should meet for a drink tonight."

My head gently falls into my hand as this is one colossal setup, and I shoot a death stare at my brother.

"You're right, perfect timing. We can leave these two alone and go grab a drink at the bar," Ford suggests.

Declan ignores him and grabs a free chair from the table next to us and slides it between Carter and me. "Or we could stay here. I'm sure your sister doesn't need two guys chaperoning her *date* from the bar. Might as well make it a group dinner, less awkward, you know."

Ford blinks then shrugs. "I mean, I guess."

I wave to the waitress passing. "Can I have a Chardonnay; I think my iced tea isn't going to cut it right now." I take a deep breath then briefly catch Declan's gaze directed at me which causes my body temperature to rise. "I thought I was having dinner with Ford, then by coincidence, our local sheriff showed up." I smile tightly to the table but feel a need to subtly explain to Declan.

"Well, this is fun," Carter lies, as the atmosphere of our table shifted the moment Declan showed up.

"Thrilling." Declan's gaze is a dagger at the sheriff.

"So, you're in Lake Spark tonight?" I ask Declan, confused because he told me that he would be here tomorrow.

"Yeah, sorry to crash this fun-filled evening, but your brother and I only want the best for you. Have to check the sheriff's intentions, don't we?" Declan offers a sweet vindictive smile.

Ford passes the breadbasket to Carter. "Forgive my friend. He looks at Violet like a sister, it's kind of hockey-team code. He's protective like me. But I'm sure the local *sheriff* is not the guy we need to worry about." Ford shoots Declan a warning glare.

"You know I'm off duty. I'm just Carter now." The poor guy seems to grasp the awkward situation that he unknowingly volunteered for.

"Lucky us," Declan mumbles. I kick his leg under the table because he isn't helping.

My wine arrives, and I puff out a breath before taking a long sip. "Uhm, so uh, Carter, what happened to the kindergarten teacher? I thought you were dating her for a while."

"She moved to Indiana about a year ago. You know, I can tell this evening kind of caught you off guard. I thought you weren't seeing anyone, and we run into one another all the time, then Ford mentioned we should all hang tonight..." Bless Carter for trying to smooth this over.

"Cute," Declan mutters under his breath.

"My sister isn't seeing anyone, otherwise I wouldn't dare try anything like this," Ford mentions.

I want to scream that I'm taken, but the man next to me is giving no indication that I can. Another sip of wine calls my name instead.

Ford's phone dings, and he pulls it out. "Sorry, I need to take this, it's Brielle. Be right back." Ford leaves me in the shark tank with the man I want who is emotionally unavailable and a man who wants to date me.

None of us take notice to Ford leaving, instead Carter bounces his gaze between Declan and me.

"What would a first date with you look like?" Declan asks. "Did Ford already check that off his list?" He's stiff beside me.

Carter smiles and doesn't seem tense about the atmosphere that could be cut by a knife. I guess the police academy taught him to stay cool under pressure. "I'd probably go traditional. Flowers, dinner, a rowboat out on the lake."

"She owns a flower shop. What kind of man buys flowers for the woman who sells flowers?" Declan counters.

I roll my eyes, wishing I could be swallowed whole by the ground underneath me.

Carter leans back on the chair. "The kind of man who seems to be more observant than Ford. You obviously feel you have a claim to Violet here. Clearly, something is going on between you two." Carter doesn't seem fazed and continues to smile softly.

Declan looks at me with serious eyes, and I know mine are pleading with him… and it's not to keep our secret, which surprises me.

My brother reappears in my sideview. "Sorry, I need to run. Wyatt isn't falling asleep, and Brielle is exhausted," Ford informs us all as he arrives back. He looks up from his phone and notices that the mood has shifted. "Drinks will have to wait. Declan, want to walk with me out?"

Carter cuts in, "You know, I need to run. I got a call from the station." He begins to stand.

"Oh, that's a shame. Maybe you two can meet for lunch or something soon," Ford suggests.

Carter looks at Declan for a few ticks then to me, yet we say nothing. He's giving us an opportunity to come clean, but we don't. "See you around, Violet."

"I'll call you." Ford waves goodbye to me. "I'll settle the bill on my way out. Make sure she's okay to drive home," he requests of Declan who nods once.

A few moments later, Declan and I are alone at the table, but I don't want to talk to him. A fury that I didn't know was brewing comes to the surface inside of me.

"I'm fine. I didn't even finish my wine." I grab my purse and stand. "I'm leaving."

"Why? You seem angry, when I'm the one who should be pissed."

Declan trails behind me as we leave the restaurant. Every step adds more power to my mood that's about to burst if he prods me too hard. All it takes is his hand landing on my elbow when we reach the parking lot, and I turn to face him with complete irritation.

"Why the hell should you be pissed? I had no clue that Ford was trying to set me up. I'm as surprised as anyone that the sheriff was here."

I notice Declan's tongue slide inside his mouth as his cheeks heighten. "You could have said you were seeing someone."

I laugh bitterly. "Is that what we're doing? Openly admitting this thing between us? Because last time I checked, you didn't want anything more than casual."

"We're not seeing other people," he points out.

"You could have told them back there that we're seeing one another, but you didn't. That just means that you want me to keep being your little secret. I was following your cues," I bite out and yank my arm from his hold.

I've never seen Declan angry except at a hockey game when he wanted to rip out the opposition. But right now, he looks furious, with a touch of disappointment and attachment that it's me he is dealing with.

"Don't put this all on me. You've also said that we are staying under the radar. Is that what you want? For me to tell Ford? Because you know he won't be thrilled. Even if I said that I would get down on my knee tomorrow with a ring and promise you ten kids, he won't be excited. And while I don't care so much about his opinion, I know you do."

I sigh. "But it doesn't mean that… I think tonight was the realization that you and I are at a crossroads."

Declan steps forward to rest my hands affectionately in the palm of his. "What does that mean?"

I lick my lips while I try to format my thoughts, as I have many swirling in my head, but then it hits me like lightning. "You're the guy who doesn't want a future with anyone, which is almost hysterical, because you're the guy who made me realize that I'm ready to have a future with someone."

The lights of the parking lot highlight the invisible punch to his gut as his face drops in sadness. "What are you saying?"

"It's hard to be casual with you because you give me a hint of what I want," I admit softly.

Silence overtakes us, and everything feels heavy, or at least my heart sinks to somewhere inside of me where it probably doesn't belong.

Declan releases an audible breath before he steps forward to kiss my cheek. "Okay, I hear you. I'll see you tomorrow." That's all he says which only infuriates me more.

I need more words from him, to understand where his head is at. Instead, he leaves me cold with no clarification.

My patience for this evening has run out, so I scoff a sound and walk away.

I BARELY SLEPT LAST NIGHT, yet here I am on a Saturday morning, having managed to smile while I had a few 9am pickups. Even Nugget has left me in silence, probably picking up on my dreadful mood.

Deep inside, I had hoped that Declan would follow me home and confess what he feels. But maybe I have it all wrong. I'm not even sure how we pick up today. We're at a turning point, which doesn't feel great because it's not going to end well for me, but damn, I've enjoyed our time together.

My phone rings, and I pick it up when I notice it's the reception from the Dizzy Duck Inn.

"Hey, Ted, what can I do for your today?" My voice lacks energy, but luckily, we have a good working relationship and are in contact throughout the week, so we've both had our bad days shown.

"Hi, Violet, I have a last-minute order from a guest. She would like a bouquet delivered here in town, something masculine, whatever the hell that means."

I grab a card from the pile. "Okay, what should the card say?"

"'Thank you for our special night, and I can't wait for this evening.'"

I frown. At least someone is having a better weekend. "Fine. Sounds romantic. I'll whip something up and have it delivered by two. Where am I sending it?"

"Apparently, that hockey guy moved into his lake house. Declan Dash."

My pen freezes on the card, and my world feels like it might break, which means I'm far too emotionally invested in the man who clearly had a great time last night after we argued.

I swallow a cry that wants to escape, say okay to Ted, then hang up and throw my pen across the room, before deciding that I will hand deliver these.

20

DECLAN

I sign the tablet for the delivery man who just dropped off my new mattress, along with linens. The rest of the furniture and my stuff will arrive next week. The man thanks me and heads back to his truck. Yawning, I take a look out at the lake, thankful it's sunny today. I stretch my arms over my head and reflect how no amount of coffee will cure me of how tired I am after last night.

What a disaster.

Murder came to mind the moment I realized that Violet was on a date. Even though it quickly became apparent that she was set up, I hate the idea of any man thinking Violet is available.

She's not. She's mine. And she's made it clear that she wants more.

I couldn't answer her, because I'm not good at digesting my feelings in a flash. Time to process, and a solid scotch is how I assess. So, I went to the Dizzy Duck, and over a scotch had the most unreal experience that's changed the road for Violet and me.

My head turns when I hear a new car arrive, and damn, my heart thumps with exhilaration because it's Violet.

I wasn't expecting her now, and I've been debating all day about how to approach her. Yet again, she is making this easy for me.

A smile begins to stretch on my lips, because she's in my view, getting out of her car with a bouquet of flowers that look like roses but are not. Her sneer is sexy as hell, and I can tell she is still pissed, which she has a right to be.

"Vi." Her name on my lips still feels far too good.

"You asshole!" She stomps my way before she throws the flowers at me, and my arms instantly come up to guard myself.

What the hell? She's plain vicious. I've never seen her this way. And it's one hell of a turn-on.

"Violet, what's going on?" I look at her with concern.

Her hands shove against my chest. "You have some nerve! We have one little argument and you—you…" She can't finish her sentence, instead she stomps on the flowers on the ground, destroying them further.

"Was it a little argument? I would hate to see your reaction after a big argument," I note in astonishment at what she's doing.

She shakes her head, and she looks near crushed.

"How dare you try to make a joke right now. I'm not the one who went to someone else when things got a little too real," she seethes out, with her hands on her hips.

"What in the world are you talking about?" My brows pinch together.

She scoffs a sound of disbelief. "Really? You're going to pretend nothing happened? The flowers are not from me, by the way. They are from someone who had a *special night* with you last night." Violet seems to be mocking the note that must be for the flowers.

I'm even more confused. "I'm so lost."

Violet with purpose opens the card and reads it aloud. "'Thank you for our special night, and I can't wait for this evening.'"

I try to puzzle piece last night together. What the hell did I do to have someone send me flowers and a card like that?

Oh.

She rips the card into a thousand pieces, while my confused state turns to watching her, because I'm entertained by her anger. It's cute and hot, slightly crazy, but I like that about her.

"Stop smirking. I can't believe this. This is how I find out that you…" She points a finger at me.

"That I what?" I step closer to her and wait for her answer.

A woman's voice interrupts the stare-off that Violet and I are having. "Declan, I don't know. I think we should go with a Portuguese-style backsplash in the laundry room." Her eyes peer down to the ground at my feet. "Oh, you got my flowers, I see. Well, kind of."

Violet glances at the woman then back to me, then returns to study the woman who smiles when she notices Violet. Her smile fades, then lines form on her forehead when her eyes fall again to the flowers on the ground, and she stares at them in bewilderment.

A laugh rumbles in my throat. "You sent me flowers, Mom?"

Watching all color drain from Violet's face is priceless.

My mother smiles shyly. "I did. Though, I was going for whole flowers instead of pieces."

Violet's hands cover her face, as she's horrified. "Your *mom* sent you these flowers?" Violet whispers.

"Why don't I give you two a minute," my mother suggests and pivots to head back into the house.

I tilt my head gently to the side as I watch guilt spread over Violet's face. "My mom came out to Lake Spark to see my house since my dad is away on business. She was getting in last night after dinner, that's why I didn't ask to see you. But I did see you, and then I was pissed and ready to kill the sheriff. To my surprise, my mother was a listening ear while I drowned myself in scotch."

Violet touches her forehead. "The special night?"

"She and I haven't had a good conversation like that in years." I shrug. "Maybe it was special."

"Oh no, I feel mortified." She glances at the flower graveyard at her feet. "I even went for the carnations instead of roses."

"You devil woman," I reply, while a smirk stays on my mouth. Her eyes meet mine, and I can tell that she feels guilty. "You really think that I would jump into bed with someone else?" Disappointment is apparent in my voice.

Violet lowers her head in near shame. "Truthfully, deep down, I don't. On the surface, I was angry, and then the flowers. It seemed easier to be furious."

I hook my fingers under her chin to guide her sight back to mine. "I just walked away."

A somberness glazes her eyes. "I didn't enjoy last night."

"Me neither."

"What's tonight? According to the card that I just shredded, your mom is looking forward to tonight."

A warm wave spreads across my chest, and even though I'm about to make a move that I've never done before, it feels right. I cup Violet's cheeks and her eyes turn soft. "I wasn't planning on my mom staying, but she's in town until tomorrow because I asked her to stay. Want to join us for dinner?"

Surprise flickers in her eyes, but a gentle smile appears. "You want me to meet your mom?"

"Yeah, you can't really say no now. I mean, you destroyed her sweet gesture," I tease.

Violet laughs, and her head falls forward to rest on my shoulder. "What a first impression. I'm so sorry."

"What do you say? I'll get us a private table at the Dizzy Duck."

Her beautiful eyes search my face for a clue because this is unfamiliar territory for us. "Are you sure?"

I don't hesitate. "Yeah. I was about to head into town to ask you, but you showed up here in a rage first."

"I killed the flowers. What kind of florist willingly murders flowers?" She's in a dazed state, either because she really does feel sorry for the flowers, but my money is on that I've thrown her off by my invite.

I stroke her cheek with my thumb to assure her that I'm sincere. "You know, I've never had a woman meet my mom." I try to sweeten the persuasion, realizing to myself that Violet is special.

It's not a clear answer to her question from last night, but it gives us a little direction. To where? I'm still not entirely sure, but I can't let her walk away just yet.

———

VIOLET SMOOTHS her light pink dress while she sits across from my mother. I can tell she put in effort. Violet has natural beauty, and she doesn't wear a lot of makeup, but her lips have a little gloss, and I think she curled her hair slightly. Violet apologized more times than I can count for destroying the flowers my mom ordered. They were quick to ease into conversation with one another.

"This is exciting, Violet. I've never had the privilege to meet someone in Declan's life. I've only seen pictures in the media of past… dates. Last night, my son couldn't stop talking about you," my mother explains, and already I might be regretting my decision about this evening.

"Really?" Violet is curious, and she rests her chin on her propped palm, intent on getting the full intel. "What did he say?"

"More wine, anyone?" I interrupt.

Both women tsk me away in unison.

"Well, I'm not sure a mother should break that trust, but you have his head in knots, for sure." My mom dips her fork into her salad.

My mom and I exchange of look of affection. In truth, I went to the Dizzy Duck, ordered a scotch, and found my mother in the bar having ordered a martini. Within two minutes, she asked if my bitter mood had to do with the woman I rescued the other week when I left their house, and I caved and admitted yes. Then the floodgates just opened, and it felt as though we could bond over something; the state of my dating life.

"Well, I can very much understand having your head in knots. It sometimes leads to a pool of flower petals at your feet." Violet plays with her food.

My mother laughs, as she's been enamored with Violet since moment one. "I should have realized that there is only one florist in Lake Spark. The dots just didn't connect in my head."

"It's okay, next time flowers are on me. You'll be back often?" Violet asks.

"Maybe. My son said I can decorate his new place as a project to keep me occupied and out of his love life," my mom teases.

Violet smiles and looks at me, confirming that this is all going well.

"My mom has a talent for interior design," I mention.

"Declan, stop. It's not a talent. More that I know where to hang all of your hockey photos and throw some fancy tile around it," she says, brushing me off.

I shake my head. "Nah, she's good at it."

"Figuring out where to place Declan's thousands of photos is a difficult task. Have to go in chronological order," Violet comments with a bit of tongue and cheek. "Don't even get me started on the trophies. Shelving is key, but it's already carrying his big ego."

My mother eats it all up, and I have to grin that these two women are having a good time at my expense.

Violet gently touches my shoulder. "I'll be right back, just going to head to the ladies' room."

I stand up and pull out her chair before placing a kiss on her cheek, watching her every step, with my mouth in a permanent stretched line.

"She's a delight," my mom says to break my attention.

I sit down again and look at my mom. "She is."

"I can understand why you were out of sorts last night after you two had a disagreement. You look like a man captivated, and most of all, happy. Why would you let that go?"

I grab my glass of wine that I've been pacing myself to drink. "I don't want to, but eventually, we'll hit a wall where she wants more. There are a few things. I mean, her brother, I'll be traveling for games, and most of all, she wants the whole family-and-marriage thing."

My mother sits straighter in her chair as she makes an agreeing sound. "The thing is, Declan, you don't need to rush into things, but since you're taking little steps, then maybe you're curious. You've never been remotely serious about a woman, but here I am meeting Violet. That's a step that you don't seem to mind. Sometimes the things we think we don't want, we just haven't looked at close enough..."

"And the only way to get close is to take steps in that direction," I reflect.

"Ah, so you were listening last night. I wasn't sure if the scotch drowned out my voice or if you actually cherished my wise words."

Setting my wine glass down, I admit that last night made me ponder. "I can't believe I'm talking to you about her." This is something I would never have anticipated.

My mom brings her hand over her heart. "Me neither. But sometimes someone enters our lives that strengthens other relationships. You are totally besotted by her, it's so refreshing to see. Your eyes never leave her, and I'm not blind, I know you two are playing footsy under the table."

"Stop it. Like, please, let's talk about something else," I plead but can't stop grinning.

"Fine, but somewhere inside of you, you're too curious, that's why you're not running away."

I lick my lips, aware that's what my mind is doing.

Violet returns to the table, and I pull out her chair. "You saved me," I whisper.

"From what?" Violet murmurs.

"His mother. Now tell me, are you a fan of maple syrup?" Mom asks Violet.

Violet laughs. "Of course. I think I can ease him back onto the stuff." Violet points her thumb to me.

"No, you can't," I interject.

She makes a sound of doubt. "I think I can. We've been trying a few meal ideas with syrup to see if we can bring back his taste for maple."

"Such as what?" My mother appreciates Violet's playful demeanor.

"Afternoon snacks." She winks at me.

Great, now I can replay the maple-syrup fiasco in my hotel room from our weeks way back... freaking love it.

"You know, I've talked about you a lot this weekend, but now I realize that I don't actually know when the spark between you two happened. What was the moment that started it all?" my mother innocently asks.

Violet and I look at one another and try to suppress our grins. We sure as hell can't tell my mom about the type of party we were at.

"It was a party, actually," Violet seriously states. What? For so many reasons, nobody can know how we started, it's going with us to the grave. Violet notices my panic, but then a playful smile curls on her lips. "A murder mystery party, and he had the clue on a piece of paper."

Smooth move.

"What was the clue?" My mother drinks from her water glass.

"'The one you are after is closer than you think,'" I softly answer, while Violet's eyes catch mine.

———

"I'LL SEE YOU TOMORROW, MOM." I hug her goodbye as we stand from the table, since we just wrapped up dessert.

"You're going back to your house? All you have is a mattress." She's puzzled.

I grin. "That's all we need."

Violet's face turns cherry red, and she covers her face with her hand.

"Well, you two have fun then." My mother gives me a humorous discerning look.

The two women of my life also hug goodbye, and I tell Violet that I'll pull up my car so it's a quick escape.

The moment Violet slides onto the front seat, she's near bashful. I don't think I've seen her this shy.

But at last, I can kiss her senseless, and I don't hesitate and crash my mouth onto hers which she responds with a purring sound and her tongue asking for entrance. As much as I want to make out with her in the parking lot, we need to get home.

"Hi," I greet her into our calmness.

"Hi," she whispers.

I reach over for the seat belt and pull it across her body to ensure she's secure in my car, because I may need to speed us back.

The click of the buckle warns me that I have to leave the warmth of her body that I touched in the process with my own, and it sends an array of emotions around me. I shiver and realize I'm in deep with her.

Straightening in my seat, I lean my head against the headrest but look to her. "We probably have a lot to talk about after this weekend."

Her fingers interlace with mine on the middle console. "We do, but let's get out of here."

"Agreed."

I hit the accelerator with vigor, and we're off on the road around the lake. I'm aware that any wild animal may run across the road, but still, I take the initiative to drive one-handed and rest my other hand on Violet's thigh to drag up the hem of her skirt.

"Declan, careful, or I may just drive you crazy." Her voice tells me that she loves it.

"Be my guest."

Her hand slides to the side and cups my cock through my pants, and now I'm aching to spring free.

With my eyes on the road, one hand on the steering wheel, I allow my fingers to slide into her panties where I feel her warm and aroused, which sends an eager wave of want through me.

"Have you been this way all night?" A sheepish grin forms on my mouth, but my eyes remain on the road.

"Yes," she breathes and squeezes my firm length.

"Watch it, I'm the one driving. A hard-on has the same effect as driving under the influence."

She laughs before she slides off her panties then parts her thighs open, inviting my hand back. "No, it doesn't."

My head bobs to the side. "There must be truth to it."

"Fine, then I'll tell my mouth to behave." That seductive voice of hers can burn the whole world down.

"Great. Doesn't mean I need to. Ride my fingers, Vi," I demand, seeking more when my long finger gets coated in her need for me.

A moan escapes her lips, while she wiggles around my fingers. Her one hand never leaves my cock and the other wraps around my wrist for support.

"Don't you want me to wait until we're at your house?" she breathes but continues to guide my fingers.

"No, you will come many times tonight."

"But I want my first orgasm tonight to be *with* you."

I quickly glance her way to find her face flushed and her dress ruffled by her waist. Christ, I'm going to lose focus. She's perfection, and it's making my dick go near senseless. A fog of lust is taking over me.

"Well, aren't you such a good girl," I rasp.

The flashing of police lights appears in my rearview mirror, and then the sound of the siren goes once, indicating that we need to stop. *Shit.*

"What did we do?" Violet sounds panicked.

My fingers sadly retreat out of her. "You've been a bad girl, and public indecency is calling your name," I tease while I pull us over, reminding myself to stay calm. To my surprise, Violet just laughs. "They're probably just checking that I'm under the limit," I assure Violet who tries to adjust her dress.

Lowering my window, I wait for the police officer to arrive.

When he arrives, I have to roll my lips in tightly because I'm trying not to sneer at this dude.

Of course, it's Sheriff Wants-My-Violet Carter.

21

DECLAN

"Well, well, well, isn't this surprising." There is pure cynicism in Carter's voice as he leans against my car with his arm against the side of my window frame. "Of course, it would be you two that I pull over."

"Hi." Violet awkwardly wiggles her fingers for a curt wave.

I want to tell him to back the fuck off my priceless car, but I'm in no position to do so. Instead, I throw on a fake smile. "What can we do for you, Officer?"

"You two been drinking?" The headlights from his car allow us to see that this guy is enjoying his power trip.

"I'm the designated driver," I say. "I had one glass of wine while we had dinner with my mother."

Carter's eyes grow wide. "Already meeting the folks, Violet?" He whistles his surprise.

"Something like that." My girl politely smiles and folds her hands on her lap.

"You two move fast, considering yesterday was denial central."

"Do we? We could just be two friends who go for dinner with one another's parents," Violet says, playing it cool.

Carter knocks on the hood of my car and glances away, seeming to be a bit disappointed that we're the people he pulled over.

"Were we speeding?" I ask to try and figure out what is going on.

"No, just at the limit."

Violet gently touches my arm as she leans in to get a better view of Carter. "We're being mindful of the deer that cross at night." She smiles.

"I bet you are." He studies us, and his eyes catch the sight of something in my car, but I'm not sure what. He stalls for a second before he bites his cheek then purses his lips out. "Let me guess, Ford has no clue you two are in this expensive car together on a Saturday night post dinner time?"

"It's a Maserati, not even on the market yet," I correct him. "And Ford doesn't need to know every detail of our days, now does he?" I give Carter a soft warning glare, realizing he kind of has the upper hand right now.

"It would make one hell of a story, the Spinners owner gets pulled over with the sister of his former teammate," he highlights.

Fuck my patience, I'm getting annoyed, but Violet senses it and squeezes my arm to keep me at bay. Instead, my nostrils only flare slightly as my knuckles tighten around the wheel.

"Your point?" I calmly grit out.

He sighs and rolls his eyes. "No point. Just you two are really shit at keeping under the radar." His fist knocks on the hood of my car. "Well, your not-yet-on-the-market car has one of the taillights out, you should have that looked at."

Carter begins to step away, clearly done drawing this all out.

"That's it, Officer?" Violet asks, clearly puzzled.

"Yeah, that's it."

"Oh," she pouts. "I was kind of looking forward to the locked-in-handcuffs part." Violet smirks to herself, while my mouth parts open at the brazen fearlessness this woman has; it makes me proud. This is the kind of person that makes every day an adventure, and that gives you something to be excited for what tomorrow may bring.

Carter steps back on his heels to study us. "I strongly urge you both to get on home, otherwise I will write you both up for indecency."

"Why the hell would you do that?" I spit out.

He shakes his head, clearly exasperated with us. "Clean up the floor of your car," he informs us before he walks away, mumbling something inaudible in the process.

My head turns to Violet who is repeating his words, as if she is trying to solve a riddle, then her eyes dart to the floor of my car and she gasps. "Oh my." She leans over and picks something up, then holds it in the air with a wide smirk.

A satisfied grin takes over me, because I have no problem with the sheriff witnessing the proof that Violet is all mine.

"He saw your panties."

Violet bursts out laughing, and it grows hysteric.

I turn the engine back on, soaking in the last few minutes, with an uncontrollable smile on my face. "Let's get out of here. I can't believe you made a handcuff joke, you're trying to get us arrested."

Her laugh vibrates through the car, and damn, it flows through my body, awakening the obvious.

I don't enjoy my days without her.

———

It should be me leading Violet, yet I'm following her as a man completely captivated by her beauty and spirit.

The moonlight outlines her gentle smirk that feels defenseless to me as she tugs me along. We walk into my bare bedroom that only has a mattress on the wood floor, plus some linens because I thought ahead. Hell, we couldn't even turn on a light if we wanted because I'm waiting for the electrician to install the new lighting. But there is something special about a mattress on the floor in an oversized master bedroom, with high ceilings and the night sky the backdrop of the woman guiding us as if she's the queen of the house.

Violet is the image of someone who belongs here.

I stop to watch Violet walk to the French doors to observe the moon reflecting off the lake and outlining the trees surrounding the water. I rub my fingers over my jaw as I admire the view, and I don't mean of the lake.

The past month or so, I've been letting go of physically playing hockey on a professional level, and my time has been replaced with Violet floating into my life. She occupies my thoughts and makes me feel free in the moment.

I'm lucky.

I take a few steps and wrap my arms around her from behind, feeling her melt against me as I rest my chin on her shoulder. "I believe you said we have surfaces to test," she rasps and sways in my arms.

We both look out into the sky, soaking in this moment of our embrace. "That can wait. I'd much rather take you right here."

She slowly turns to face me before snaking her arms around my middle. "Also a good idea."

I comb my fingers through her hair and settle to hold her head before leaning down to kiss her on the lips. Slow, tender, and giving her a side of me that I can't seem to shake, nor do I want to try.

If a kiss were a breath, then this is the only thing I would need to live, and that isn't half bad.

Violet croons as she reangles her lips before kissing me back with a firmness that feels like it carries far more than a physical need.

We part only to gather air, but my lips stay near, tracing the corner of her mouth while I inhale her floral scent.

"Everything lately…" she whispers.

My breath halts somewhere in my chest before a smile ghosts my lips. "I know."

"Declan—"

"Shh," I soothe her before backing her up against the glass to kiss her with more insistence.

My lips are cemented to hers while I unbutton my shirt, starting with one button and moving slow, but halfway I give up and speed up my movement. It allows me the chance to yank and pull at her dress and bra until it's mostly off her body, and she voluntarily makes a move which enables her to step out of the pool of fabric at her feet. She's so incredibly stunning, and she's naked and showered in moonlight. I lift her up to ensure her back lands against the window, with her arms linking around my neck for stability or just to pull me close to her.

"You're too beautiful," I remark between hurried kisses.

"You've mentioned a few times." Her legs tighten around my waist which adds friction to my already-eager cock that presses against her belly.

All day I've been imagining plunging inside of her, and I'm not quite sure why it hasn't happened yet, except I want to enjoy every second with her and drag this out.

I bury my head into her neck before trailing my lips down to her breast.

Violet throws her head back in a moan and offers it all to me.

"Please," she begs. "I just need all of you tonight."

"You wouldn't get anything less," I promise before spinning us around and heading straight to the mattress where we fall.

I slide down the mattress and take hold of her ankles to part her legs. "This isn't bad at all, Vi. The image of you in the middle of my new bed, naked, with my head between your legs."

Violet gets comfortable, wiggling her body to settle into the mattress, with her hair splayed out against the pillow. She brings her arms above her head as she peers down at me. "Is that what's happening," she taunts me.

I growl before I drop onto my stomach, and I slam my mouth against her center, instantly causing her body to buck from contact and her mouth to call out my name. My tongue and fingers work her into a state that has her completely surrendering to me, and it only ups my own keenness for more.

Her toes curl into the sheets and her nails dig into the pillows when I finally send her trembling underneath my touch, but I don't let her come down from her release.

As she quakes, I move to hover over her, offering her a soft kiss against her lips while my hand aligns my cock with her opening.

"I need to bury myself in you and never leave," I whisper against her cheek while I push into her.

She whimpers as her pussy wraps around me, the best possible fit. "Don't say never." Violet isn't teasing, she's honestly beseeching, before she leans up to capture my lips for a kiss.

We move together as one, careful to soak in every moment of our turning point. Words are on the tip of my tongue, but I'm not sure what and they don't come out.

Which is fine, as we drown in one another anyways.

————

THIS IS SOMETHING SPECIAL, lying on the mattress with a naked Violet against my chest and her head tucked under my chin, tangled in a sheet, while the sun begins to rise outside the curtainless windows.

This house is mine, but my first night in it will always be ours.

Ours.

The tickle of her fingertips painting lines against my skin reminds me that we've been shadowing one another. One of us wakes, then so does the other. One of us falls asleep, and the other follows.

But something about daylight is more confronting.

"Dec," she says my name softly, and her gaze rises to study my face.

"Sleep."

"I can't, and you can't either."

The faintness of a smile forms on my mouth. "True." I kiss the top of her head, and I stroke her long hair with my fingers.

"This weekend has been… a lot. I mean, there was the sheriff on two incidents, our disagreement, murdered carnations, dinner with your mother… last night. For most people, it would be whiplash, but for us, it feels… like us. It makes sense somehow; I just haven't figured it out."

I snort a laugh. "Trust me, in no universe does this weekend make sense."

"Oh." She was expecting me to say something else.

I roll us so she's underneath me, and I lie on my side to look down at her. "Tell me what's really on your mind."

"Our lines… they're blurry."

"I agree… but this feels right."

Finally, a line forms on her mouth that pleases me. "What are we doing?" Her question is like a song, as her tone is floaty. She's trying to hide how scared she is to ask.

This time, I think I'm the one who may blush as my head falls forward and the tip of my nose nuzzles her shoulder. "Everything we never meant to." I'm being honest.

God, I love when she wraps her arms around my neck.

"I meant what I said. I do want a future. I can't see someone casually forever, I'll want more. You're giving me pieces, mixed messages, acting like we're more than we are. But stop it if there is no thought behind it."

I collapse to my back in defeat. "I don't think when I'm around you, that's new."

Violet straddles me while she holds a knotted sheet by her breasts. Her on top of me like this doesn't help us. My dick is going haywire, and my mind is hypnotized by her.

"Declan, we're over the blue line because we are no longer casual, and you know that too."

I plant my hands on her waist while I lick my lips and contemplate what to say exactly, especially after she just threw in a hockey reference. "You're telling me that we're heading for the big game now?" Why the hell don't I feel petrified?

She nods, with a cute wry smile, then to add more damage, she swirls her finger against my chest, reminding me how I can't get enough of her touch, her pure radiance that she gives us which feels like it's all for me. "You know, hockey is a really fast sport. Always go go go, but we don't need to move as fast as hockey. All I'm saying is that things have changed."

When she lifts her finger, I capture it between my teeth for a little bite and growl before kissing it softly. "What if I say I agree?"

"Then we should probably talk about what that means." She rotates her pussy on top of my cock.

This isn't fair, she's using her bewitching powers. I love it.

"You're no one else's."

She chuckles. "I haven't been since our names were written on two pieces of paper."

"You can tell the sheriff to take a hike."

"I think he got the clue that I'm sleeping with a possessive billionaire."

"Possessive billionaire *boyfriend*," I correct her.

"Ooh, boyfriend," she counters and fails to hide her laugh; therefore, I tickle her side.

Why is this conversation flowing so easily? We're playful yet serious, and my body is relaxed.

"I don't want to hide you," I say.

Her long finger taps my mouth. "You told your mother about me."

I blow her finger away. "Don't make a big deal about it." I roll my eyes and grin because it's completely the opposite.

"Yes, sir."

I come up to sitting so we're eye to eye, our bodies tight together with the sheet still wrapped around her. "I don't want to hide you," I repeat.

Her smile fades, but she seems content as her head gently tips to the side. "You know what that means."

"Yeah, I do," I confirm.

"When do we tell him?"

"Next time I'm in town. I have to head back to the city later, and I think Ford requires a bit more of a thought-out process."

"Okay."

We hold one another, with our eyes set and our smiles mirroring one another.

"Good, now let me take you the way a boyfriend should." I slap her ass and tilt my body up.

"You act like it's your first time doing that." She flashes her eyes at me.

I groan from how she has the ability to tease me.

Yet again, I flip us so she is caged underneath me. "You're right. But you're the first one that matters," I tell her sincerely. Because I care for her, I see more than just now with her, but it's too cloudy to define what our future holds. Her eyes pierce mine with recognition and affection. "I want you, and I will give you more. I can't make promises, but I can't let you go just yet. You get that, right?"

Her hand comes up to touch my cheek in that way that always instantly gives me warmth and lights something in my chest. "I know."

It's a few long seconds of staring, with the glimmer of fondness apparent in our eyes.

"Now let's figure out a way to untangle you from this sheet, it's in the way."

She squeals in delight as my hands begin to roam, while we both ignore the fact that maybe we should think this through more.

22

DECLAN

Pacing my living room, I look out onto the lake on this sunny summer day. My cell phone is to one ear while I listen to my assistant list what is on the agenda for the week ahead, mostly media opportunities as we begin to gear up for the new season.

"I need you to make sure the team dinner is moved here to Lake Spark. I want both veterans and current players to meet here in the area. We need to set the team up for a new mindset and focus. The coaching staff should be there too, all team staff really. Oh, and make sure I meet with the head coach and general manager in the next week; it's time to set out what I expect and warn him of what happens if he doesn't deliver."

Glancing over my shoulder, I see Violet sitting on the sofa, leaning over to buckle the clasp of her shoe around her ankle. Violet notices that I'm watching and flashes me a sexy smirk.

How I managed to get furniture into this house during the last week, I'm not entirely sure, but I'm positive money played a role, and I don't exactly mind, because it meant I could focus on other things, including the dark-haired beauty in front of me.

My mind whips back to my assistant who promises to send me a short list of locations for the dinner by end of day. "Thanks," I say. "I'll be back in the city tomorrow, and we can meet at ten to set up the agenda for the months ahead, especially aligning with away games." After a quick goodbye, I hang up and walk eagerly to the couch where I lean down to steal a warm kiss from Violet.

She gives me a pointed look with a grin hinted on her lips. "It's Sunday, and you're all business. Your poor assistant."

I sit down and drag her legs over my thighs to help with her other shoe. "Rex can handle it; besides, I ignored him all week because I was occupied with you."

After leaving Violet last week to head back to the city, I had a constant need to see her again. I missed her, if I'm being honest. When I drove up to Lake Spark yesterday, then that was it, we didn't leave my house since the second she arrived. We ate, laughed, and moved together slowly, except for that moment in the shower which was out-of-this-world intense.

Violet taps my shoulder and fails to control a smile. "A rather good choice." Her head lolls slightly as she studies me. "I'm also happy to see that you're stepping into your role. Business-Declan may just surprise you with how much you enjoy it. I'm sure your father would be impressed too."

"Or upset that I'm flaunting my skills for other uses."

"Nah, you have a certain element when you're on the phone discussing your team that's only admirable. To the point, yet sentiment undertones your demands. It's kind of hot as hell too."

I interlace our fingers and approve of the sight of us connected. "I have a big dinner coming up. Will you come as my plus-one?"

Her lips role in but her smile stays put. "It's kind of public."

"You no longer mind. You've been seen at your brother's games before. I sure as hell love this." I'm used to the cameras and also the numerous times the press decided whoever on my arm was a worthy news story. This time I'm casual about it, because with Violet, it feels like the logical next step, and I want to flaunt how lucky I am.

Her brows raise at me. "Which leads us to the elephant in the room that we said we would conquer this weekend."

I grimace at the thought. "Ford."

She nods gently. "It's Sunday morning, so he's with Connor at the rink doing a little one-on-one time. I told him I would stop by like I sometimes do."

I swipe my hands through my hair and blow out a breath. "I'll grab my keys and we can head there."

Her delicate fingers from her other hand plays with my hairline along my forehead. "I'm not nervous," she states calmly.

"I don't get anxious."

She squinches her face in doubt. "Never?"

Getting lost in her eyes, I realize she's right. Violet makes me nervous. She makes me want things that I never gave much thought, and I'm not even sure what those things are. When I'm with her, even the happiness outweighs the scary feelings that occasionally breach my bubble where I'm completely enamored by her.

I swallow and pretend she isn't seeing through me. "Never," I lie.

Gently, I slide to my side so her back lands on the sofa cushions and I can enjoy Violet underneath me for a minute more. Her eyes twinkle with wonder, and I'm just reminded of how beautiful she is, and as cliché as it is, that goes for both inside and out.

"How am I doing on the boyfriend front?" I run my hand along her curves while I stare down at her.

"You had breakfast delivered after you wore me out last night and had chocolate chip cookies from the Dizzy Duck delivered before bedtime. Meh, can't complain." She's teasing me.

I kiss her again real quick. "I can't buy you flowers, and the hot air balloon was already booked last night," I deadpan, and she chuckles softly.

Violet does that thing again, where she glides her fingers down my cheek and soothes me whether she is trying or not. "I prefer lying in bed, wearing your shirt, and reading a book while you go over hockey articles... The cookies were a nice touch, though." Her honesty creating the perfect answer slays me every time. She seals her sentimentality by tipping her mouth up to kiss me. "Declan," she purrs against my lips.

"Hmm?" I return the move.

"I…" she begins then pauses for a second. Whatever thought she had leaves, and she kisses me again, this time with a little more fire.

We make a good team that way. We both give and take, letting the moment lead, but always ending with both of us satisfied.

It's a balance.

For the first time in a long time, I feel grounded, and that's a damn fine feeling.

———

"WE'RE REALLY JUST GOING to wing it?" Violet asks as we walk through the sports complex. There are people here, but it's by no means busy.

My shoulders slack. "I guess. Is there a good way to say, 'Hey buddy, I'm seeing your sister, and that's been happening for a while now. By the way, she gives amazing head'?" While I'm serious, it's only on the surface. She *is* amazing but for so many reasons not even related to her talents in bed.

She playfully nudges my arm. "I feel like we should have prepared ourselves for this a little more. Oh well, I see him up ahead by the entrance to the ice." Violet now seems a little anxious, but I think it's more because she's been waiting all week for us to do this, not so much because she's worried for Ford's reaction.

We both assess the scene and notice that Ford has his arms crossed as he watches his son on the ice.

Connor brakes with his skates. "Is that better?"

Ford narrows his eyes at his son. "Connor, I don't care how you play today, not every moment is about preparing for a hockey career. I'm more concerned that you're tired, and I'm wondering if you were really home in your room at midnight last night."

"You're always on my case," Connor rebuffs and begins to toss the puck side to side with his stick.

"Because you threw a party," Ford exclaims, with his hands coming out.

"That was weeks ago!" Connor counters before he skates away.

Violet and I approach Ford with caution. "All good?" Violent touches Ford's shoulder. "I thought we were past the timeline for party punishment."

He sighs. "Oh, we were. That was until I discovered he borrowed my Jaguar when I was sleeping the other weekend." Ford gives us a forced smile. "What brings you two here? Did you run into one another on the way in?" he wonders.

Ford and I look out on the ice and see Connor make a sharp swing with his stick, and the puck lands in the net. Damn, that guy is fast and sharp.

Connor skates back to us. "Look what we have here." He waves sheepishly as his eyes bounce between Violet and me.

Violet isn't having it, and she rolls her eyes. "Heard you've been giving your dad a hard time." She gives her nephew a knowing glare in a fun sort of way. He knows she loves him like crazy.

"Dad's being unreasonable."

I reach out to nudge his arm in comfort. "It's his job," I reiterate the obvious. "Good move out there. You should try coming a little more from the left."

Connor fumes, and his face turns hard. "I don't need your critique."

Violet interjects. "Cool down, he was giving you a compliment and a pointer."

Ford shakes his head at Connor. "I don't know what's up with you, but I think we'll wrap up this session," he suggests, circling his finger in the air and huffing a breath.

Connor throws his stick on purpose.

"Why don't you skate it off and let your dad have a moment," I suggest.

Biggest fucking mistake ever.

Connor drives his sight to Ford. "Dad." He grabs his attention. "Declan and Aunt Violet are hooking up."

Violet's face drops, and I shake my head that this is how this is going to unravel.

"What?" Ford stammers.

"Yeah, and Declan threatened my career," Connor proudly announces before skating off.

Violet puffs out a long breath before she drops her head to hands. "That's not… not what Declan did."

My jaw clenches side to side as I take in the fact that a hormonal teenager just outed us.

Ford's fists form balls as they hang by his sides, and he turns his gaze sharply to me. "What the hell is my son talking about?"

I scratch the back of my head then sigh, as the best way forward right now is to own up to the situation. "Violet and I…" I take her hand to make a statement. "We're together."

Ford's eyes laser focus on our hands. "What?"

"Ford, don't be ridiculous," Violet says. "We're adults, and we're allowed to see one another."

"How?" he grits out. "How did this happen?"

"We ran into one another that one time at the stadium a few months back, and then we…" My face screws up. "A murder mystery party." I throw that out there, and Violet tries hard to hide her chortle.

"The colonel in the kitchen with the wrench kind of thing," she adds.

Ford's eyes change to pure venom. "Fuck you, Declan." Before I can process, Ford lunges forward and takes hold of my shirt.

"Ford!" Violet gasps.

"What the hell, man." My words fall on deaf ears.

We stumble onto the ice in a scuffle, sliding around, as neither one of us has skates on. "There is no way I'm okay with this."

I do my best to shake Ford off me. "Then talk to me like a normal friend," I raise my voice.

Ford steps back but keeps his grip on my shirt, his gaze completely furious. "*Friend?* Are you kidding me? You know she's off limits."

"You're no longer playing hockey, and neither am I," I justify and push him away.

"Doesn't matter." He's unamused. "The rule is for life. Besides, we kind of work together now in some way. You crossed a line!"

I huff out a breath to calm myself. I wasn't expecting confetti, but this is the worst-case scenario by far. "We can't control the way we feel," I highlight.

Ford pinches the bridge of his nose. "You have a reputation that I sure as hell witnessed on a few accounts. You really want to tell me you're in a relationship with Violet? Screw that, you don't do relationships, since you only ever think about yourself."

"That's not true. Did I not play as a team, am I not supporting a team?"

"Don't compare hockey to Violet," he shouts.

"Stop it, you two!" Violet watches, horrified, from the sidelines.

Ford looks at her and points to me. "No! You're my little sister, and you deserve the best." He throws his arms in the air. "I knew it. I had a feeling you two were up to something, but I wanted to be so wrong. This guy here only looks for his momentary good time."

"People change," I mention.

It causes him to laugh. "Oh yeah? You really want to tell me that you intend to settle down with a wife, kids, and a kickass Labrador who retrieves like crazy?"

"What's your point?" I'm getting angry.

He looks between us, as if we've gone insane. "Have you really grasped what Violet deserves? I mean, can you honestly look her in the eyes and say that your relationship will go exactly where she wants it to go?"

My heart flinches from his words. A sharp knife wound.

"Relax, Ford, we're not even there," Violet explains, but I hear uneasiness in her tone. "We're enjoying one another and seeing where this can go."

"Fantastic. Get emotionally invested, only to walk directly into heartache. Because, Violet, you wouldn't be here telling me about you and Declan if you were just having fun. I know you too well. Deep down you want more, you want it all and believe maybe he can

give you that. You're lying to yourself if you try to tell me otherwise," Ford lectures.

I adjust my shoulders as reality seems to shower down on me,
especially when Violet goes mute, and she doesn't blink. Her brother
just threw a bucket of reality onto her.

Hell, maybe I've been lying to myself too, because I know what
kind of future Violet wants, and we're not on the same page, but I
can't seem to push her away because of our magnetic pull.

The momentary silence is broken by Ford continuing on his
tangent. "And threatening my son? What the hell?"

Now I'm aggravated. "Come on, it's not like that. Really, Connor
was drinking and tried to blackmail us…" As soon as that rolls of my
tongue, I realize this sounds incredibly bad.

Ford throws his hands in the air in disbelief. "I don't know what
to think right now. The fact my son has the balls or the fact that my
friend is using my sister—"

I interject. "I'm not using her."

Connor skates over. "Yeah, my vote is that you should focus on
bad-boy Declan since we all know that I'm freaking awesome
anyhow," he announces as he slowly skates on by, clearly satisfied
with the chaos he started. His smug grin is a reminder of me on a few
occasions.

"Don't get excited. There is a long conversation happening later,"
Ford calls out as Connor skates to the other side. Ford returns his
death stare to me. "That's why you two are here together? To inform
me of this forsaken blessed union?"

"Stop this. You're being overdramatic." I swipe my jaw with my
thumb and wonder why we're still standing on the ice.

"She's my sister."

"I'm aware."

"Are you two done now?" Violet reminds us that she's here. We
both glance to her and see that her hands are stationed on her hips.
"I'm an adult, and you either accept this or not."

Ford growls in frustration. "Violet, I know you're an adult. But
you're my little sister who I owe so much to, and I simply can't

ignore this protective need I have to watch out for you. Brother bear is here to stay, so get used to it. My point isn't that I'm pissed that you two are together; I'm *livid* because you're with a guy who will only break your heart."

"Stop saying that," I insist.

"Fine. Tell me you both want the same long game," he challenges.

My mouth opens, but only a sound croaks out.

Ford watches me and scoffs a sound. "Thought so." He steps into me to ensure only I can hear and whispers, "If you care even an ounce about her at all, then you'll be honest with her."

Then he leaves me there to ponder in my own fumes.

———

WE HAVEN'T SAID one thing since we walked from the rink back to the car. Violet and I move side by side with our arms occasionally grazing. As we approach my car, I turn to her and notice her eyes dip low as she avoids facing me.

"That was not how I expected it to go," she mumbles with a weak laugh. Her hair blocks half her face, but now I'm far too familiar with her and recognize that she's somber and affected by the last fifteen minutes.

If this were after a hockey game, I would be running on adrenaline and energized to say anything. Yet Ford is right, this isn't hockey, and Violet is a whole other scale.

Maybe that's why I feel empty inside, my chest hollow, which is crazy because my heart is beating far too fast.

I touch her shoulder. "He has a point."

This hurts. It feels like misery. An impending doom.

When Violet flicks her gaze up to me, I see a glaze of sadness over her blue eyes. "I don't want him to have a point."

"Neither do I, but…"

Tears well in her eyes, and she steps forward to claw my shirt.

"Be honest with me, Vi," I rasp with urgency. "I know what's going on in my head in this very moment, but I need to know what you're thinking."

"It's not in my head, Declan." Her words startle me, because it means they come from a deeper place. "I'm giving you pieces of my heart, all for a chance."

My thumb brushes a teardrop away from her cheek. "A chance that I want the longest game there is?" I finish her thought.

She nods softly. "I don't want to be that woman who thinks you will change for them. I know you don't really want kids or a wife, and still I signed up for more with you because it feels better than nothing. But… you have the pieces of my heart in your hand. It's up to you…"

"To figure out if I'll break them or not." I cup her head in my hands to plant a long kiss on her forehead. "He's right. I feel a lot for you, which means I shouldn't lead you on. I need to be 100% sure of our direction, that we're on the same path. It's only fair to you that my head is clear."

We stand there, completely heavy in our reality, and it feels like the ground below us is quicksand.

"I need a timeout," I whisper my request. "A little break."

Violet sniffles another cry as she nods before turning to walk away.

This isn't goodbye, but at this moment, I can't give her the answer she needs.

23

VIOLET

I use my spoon to play with the jellybean that sank to the bottom of my coffee. I'm sure it weighs heavy like my heart.

"How do you not need caffeine right now? You've barely drank anything," Brielle mentions as she stirs the tea bag in her mug.

We're sitting in Jolly Joe's, and I'm sure I must look a state. I'm in yoga pants, a cute-enough hoodie, and a messy bun.

"I'm not that thirsty or hungry lately," I tell her honestly.

She sighs in understanding. "Haven't heard from him at all?"

I glance up from my drink while my thumb plays with the mug handle. "It's only been a few days, but why should I?" I laugh to myself. "Then again, Declan is very good at mixed messages, so maybe I should be surprised that he hasn't reached out."

"Violet, I don't know what to say. I was rooting for you two, but maybe Ford made a valid point. Why ride the train if the destination is wrong?"

For the experience, for the adventure. Sometimes we are attached to someone and refuse to let go.

"Maybe I don't want kids or a husband one day."

Brielle gives me a pointed look because she's calling my bluff. "It hurts, I'm sure. You never know, maybe he'll realize his priorities in life have changed. At least then it would be from his own initiative and not an ultimatum."

I reach up and tighten my bun. "All valid points, but it doesn't change the fact that I feel hollow inside and wish I wasn't so willing to fall for him, but he made me feel… special and that something more was possible."

She reaches across the table to squeeze my hand. "Remember the good parts."

I nod, but my bottom lip trembles as I feel a cry about to break which has become routine lately.

Brielle smiles at someone over my shoulder. "Hey."

I turn my head to see April and her daughter Hadley. "Hey, you two, how are things?" April beams a smile. Her eyes whip to Brielle who I catch mouthing not to ask about Declan. "The flower shop all good?" April's tone is hesitant as she tries to figure out the dynamics.

I growl a sound. "It's okay, Brielle, no need to worry about upsetting my little heart. That's already been done by a man who, under that bachelor-hockey-player persona, is surprisingly romantic. But never fear, my beloved brother was right, and Declan Dash is bad news." I string my words together, as that anger resurfaces inside of me. At least I made it to 3pm today.

"Yikes," April simply answers.

"Eat ice cream, that's what I do every time hockey players break my heart," Hadley says, as if she has experience, and she's only fourteen. "Ooh, they have maple pecan today." She notices the board and heads to the counter.

"Maple pecan," I echo, with my lips quivering.

"Oh crap, a trigger," Brielle winces.

I blow out a breath, but tears pool in my eyes.

"How the hell is maple a trigger?" April questions Brielle.

"Because Declan's family—" Brielle explains.

"Owns a maple syrup company, and he hates maple syrup, except when we…" I wail a sob and drop my head onto my arms on the table, which would be hysterical to most.

April looks at me blankly. "I think this is a sister-in-law pep-talk moment. I'm going to, uh, go grab some non-tree-related ice cream." She mouths good luck to Brielle and leaves us.

"Why don't you come stay at our house for a few days?" Brielle suggests as she rubs my arms where they're crossed on the middle of the table.

My head pops up. "No, I don't want to hear Ford give me any more of his life wisdom, and your son, I love my nephew, but Connor is really turning into a little shit." My head flops down.

"He is, isn't he," Brielle reflects with a fond smile on her face. "He's going to be one of those hockey players with a bad reputation off the ice, I feel it in my bones. I'm already waiting for him to come home with a tattoo because he used a fake ID to get one." She takes a sip of her tea, calm with her predicament.

The corner of my mouth stretches. "Sounds like something he would do."

"I promise you that one day it will feel like the storm has moved on."

I straighten my spine to sit up. "I was so happy. I'm not sure I'll get that again."

"You will. Besides, you're talking as though you'll never see or hear from Declan again. He'll be in Lake Spark more than he won't. Eventually you two will need to face one another to clear the air. But I still believe there is hope."

"Why are you so optimistic?"

Brielle twists her lips and stifles her smile. "Just a feeling I have that will make sense one day, but right now, you should function with confidence and dress to kill. It drives guys crazy, and their brains begin to rewire to think properly. It's like a button is pushed."

I shrug a shoulder. "This is my first time out of the house other than the flower shop," I admit.

"Then do something to change that routine."

"You're probably right, I can't live in this cloud forever. Especially since I don't know what timeline I'm working with, and I'm not sure biology would let me wait forever."

Brielle smiles softly at me. "Would you wait forever?"

My lips purse together. "That's a long time. But I know that it will be hard to match the last few months, and unless it's Declan, then it won't be the same."

That I'm sure of.

———

YANKING UP MY STRAPLESS DRESS, I'm severely doubting my choice of attire. My strapless bra is giving me zero support, and the red on my lips feels a shade too dark. This is what I get for letting Charlotte dress me up.

Now I'm swaying my hips to Bonobo's "Nightline" in a busy club in Chicago, all because I took Brielle's advice to heart. At least I look and feel hot, I've noticed a few eyes land on me, but nobody is of interest because they're not Declan.

"I'm sorry I haven't made it out to Lake Spark lately," Charlotte apologizes over the music as she dances. She's in hot pink and hard to miss.

I wave her off. "It's fine. I wanted to get out of Lake Spark, and last time I checked, the club scene is minimal there."

"Someone needs to tap into that market, there must be a demand."

My shoulders slant up to my ears. "Doubt it."

"Come on, I'm dying of thirst." She grabs my hand and guides me off the dancefloor to the bar.

"Two gin and tonics," she calls out to the man behind the bar before turning her attention to me. "Doesn't a small town mean you're going to run into the man who shall not be named sooner rather than later?"

I bite my bottom lip. "Maybe. Then again, all he has to do is avoid Main Street and we're safe for a while."

Charlotte laughs. "Brent thinks Declan is hung up on you."

My heart patters from the thought, and my head perks up. "Really?"

"Yep." She smiles at the barman for delivering our drinks.

"Declan even skipped the last party, if you know what I mean." She lifts her brows.

"Oh?"

"Totally."

I take a sip of my drink. "I almost told him I love him during morning sex." The confession falls off my tongue.

Charlotte looks at me with affection. "I'm happy you get to experience that—love, I mean. But I'm sorry it's turning out like this."

"Maybe it's for the better that I froze and kept my words in. Makes this all easier, right?"

She shrugs at my thought.

I take another long drink and assess the room, only to return to the door, and my gaze freezes. "You didn't tell anyone we would be here, right?" I check with Charlotte because this is too much of coincidence.

Declan walks into the club with a beautiful brunette by his side. He smiles at one of the barmen as if they're familiar with one another.

"No, why?" Charlotte looks over her shoulder, only to scoff a disapproving sound. "Forget small town, seems Chicago isn't big enough not to run into each other. Who's the chick?"

I want to run to him and shove him into the wall from the level of anger boiling inside of me.

"Don't know, don't care," I lie and quickly take a sip of my drink. "We're not together, he's free to do what he wants." Bullshit too. Is this what his "timeout" looks like? Did he just move on? No wonder he hasn't reached out.

Aggressively, I stir the straw in my glass and an ice cube falls out.

"Forget him, Violet. We can get out of here right now and go somewhere to forget him."

"I'm not going to a sex club," I protest.

"Okay, okay. Just throwing out options."

I do my best to avoid glancing at Declan, but it's hard as he's a cross between business-Declan and Lake Spark-Declan, in jeans and a blazer.

"Damn it," I curse to myself and down another long sip of my drink.

"His loss," Charlotte reaffirms. "The audacity to go around town with *her*."

I search for the bartender, ignoring Charlotte clearing her throat.

"Violet." A warm deep masculine voice says my name, and it wraps around every fiber in my body. *My Declan*. His hand on my lower back molds to me instantly, a button pressed into the world we created.

My eyes flick up to Declan, and the room seems to stop.

"I see Brent, I'll be back," Charlotte mumbles then leaves. Neither Declan nor I take much notice.

"Declan," I say softly.

His eyes drop then draw a line back up, and an approving smirk ghosts his lips. "You look *really* stunning."

For a second, I nearly blush, giddy from his praise, but I know better. I search for the brunette but can't find her.

"She's my cousin. *Blood-related* cousin." Declan seemed to notice my curiosity and answers my thoughts.

But I won't melt to a puddle. "It's okay, you don't owe me an explanation. We're on a break."

His hand jolts me forward a step, closer to him. "Really, my cousin who studies fashion, the reason I knew which boutique to call when you stayed at my condo, that's her. She's in the city for a few days to meet up with friends. There is nobody else, understand?"

I barely nod because somewhere in that sentence a beacon of hope shot out at me.

"Why didn't you let me know that you'd be in the city?" He looks pained.

I scoff a sound of annoyance. "Why haven't you contacted me?"

His face tenses, and his lips purse out while he takes a long breath. "It's complicated. I want to be sure."

"Of what?"

His head lolls gently to the side, and his eyes send heat across my skin before he leans in to whisper in my ear, "You look really good."

My body trembles from feeling him so close, wanting more.

"Changing the topic, great." I look up to the ceiling then back to him. "You still need time, that's fine, but don't look at me as if you're about to devour me."

He smirks and slides the outside of his thumb across his slightly stubbled chin. "Want to get out of here and head back to my place?"

My eyes grow wide. "No, Declan, meaningless sex isn't going to help us right now."

He grabs my elbow with a little force that catches me off guard but feels safe all the same. "It can never be meaningless with you."

Declan's twisting into my thoughts and feelings again, hope hitting me from all directions. I deserve to have it all, I remind myself.

But this is too good, seeing him again, his hand on me, his eyes possessive.

"How was your day?" I ask, as if we're chatting over coffee, in an attempt to re-center us to neutral.

"Fine. I had an interview for a magazine profile on my new ownership gig."

"Good. You can confirm you're single and readership will skyrocket." I don't know why that just spit out of my mouth. The alcohol must be hitting me.

His look turns unimpressed. "I'm not single. We're on a break." Declan's words nearly sound seething. "Tell me the sheriff or some asshole with flowers hasn't already attempted to make a move."

"No. Why are we even going over this? Our situation hasn't changed. I want to give you time, but you are touching me and saying these things that send me right back on the mixed-message train." I down my drink to the last drop.

His hand drops from my arm, and I hate that it's my doing that I feel the loss of his touch.

"Violet, let's get out of here," he says again, adamant.

I cross my arms over my chest, doing my best to stay firm. "No way." I can't help the smile that wants to grace my lips because his persistence sends a swirl of fun tumbling inside my belly. "We're not helping ourselves if we fall into bed together right now."

His eyes dip down to me while he smirks. "Say that again and I might just throw you over my shoulder."

Run far away from this man's charm. Do it now. Save yourself.

"Find me when you have a clear message and know what to do with my heart," I declare before I walk away from him, and I may look proud on the outside, but inside I'm desperate for him to proclaim everything I want to hear.

24

DECLAN

I knock on Brent's door at ten in the morning, hoping he has time to head out for brunch. I sure as hell could use a distraction.

I barely slept. I mean, how could I? Running into Violet last night was both a blessing and a curse. I've been avoiding sending her a message or giving her a call for two weeks, because I knew it would just confirm what I fear… Letting her go is the last thing I want.

But I need to be sure of so many things because stringing her along for an end game with different rules would crush her, and believe it or not, hurting her just isn't an option in my playbook.

Damn, what I would have given for her to come home with me and to wake with her in my arms before I order in breakfast from this little French bistro nearby. We would have talked about our weeks, and she'd listen to my hockey talk because she gets it and has interest. She would sit on my lap while she explains how much her nephew drives her crazy, but her pure affection would be apparent. One of us would say something wicked, and domesticated-us would be thrown out the window. That's my ideal Sunday.

Instead, Brent opens the door while he's pulling a t-shirt on. "Hey, you look like shit."

"Thanks. Exactly what every man wants to hear." I follow him inside and immediately hear giggling.

Charlotte pops her head up over the back of the sofa wearing only a bra. "Morning." She smiles, completely unfazed by her state of undress.

Immediately another woman appears next to her. "Morning." The brunette smiles as she attempts to zip up her dress.

My eyes bug out as I turn my focus to my friend who grins proudly. "It was a good night," Brent reflects as he leans against the wall.

"And a good morning," Charlotte adds.

"Clearly eventful," I deadpan. My eyes turn to Charlotte who rests her chin on her folded arms on the back of the sofa. Something dawns on me. "Where's Violet?" She was staying with Charlotte, I assume.

"She stayed at my place. You know she doesn't like to play." She pouts.

I pinch the bridge of my nose in frustration. "You let her go back to your apartment when she'd been drinking?" The disapproval runs strong in my voice.

Brent slaps a hand on my shoulder. "Relax, we dropped her off in the taxi on the way here."

"Where is she now?"

"Probably on her way back to Lake Spark. She wanted to leave early, something about needing to escape you and preparing begonias or something like that," Charlotte explains.

"Who's Violet?" the random third wheel dares to ask.

Brent chuckles, and Charlotte stares at me blankly, almost waiting. When I don't say anything, she says, "The woman that this guy is in love with."

I sigh, because I can't deny it.

"He just needs time to 'think.'" Charlotte uses air quotes.

The random woman angles her head to study me. "Aren't you that hockey guy who owns a team now?"

"NDA," Brent clucks his tongue and chides her a warning light-heartedly.

I point at her and look at Brent. "Who is this?"

"Jenna," he answers.

"Gemma," she corrects him.

"Gemma," he repeats with a tight smile. "Sorry, Gemma, Declan here is a little out of sorts and has morphed into someone with an emotional backbone."

Charlotte turns to Gemma who is sitting on her knees, invested in our conversation. "Declan used to be as adventurous as us, but then he hooked up with Violet, and since then has been a monogamous lovesick puppy—until he turned into an asshole to think over his feelings."

Brent squeezes my shoulder. "Don't be too hard on him. He's never been this obsessed with a woman before. I mean, hell, one time on a video call, he wouldn't shut up about babysitting with Violet and some dog. He smiled the entire time. This isn't the guy I've known all these years. If I ask about his sex life, he shuts me up, as if his time with Violet is so sacred."

I give him the death stare. "Why did I bother coming by to see if you wanted to grab brunch?" I wonder.

"I did work up an appetite, but I can't handle listening to your Violet woes for another meal. Not when it's so obvious. You literally called me the other day because you were standing outside the window of Tiffany's trying to imagine if buying a ring is something you could see in your future."

"You what?!" Charlotte sits up in full intention.

My hands come up to defend myself. "It was a moment."

"Yeah, and what about having the contractor fix a treehouse, even though you don't have kids? Manifesting or what?" Brent adds.

"Aww, a treehouse for little Violets and Declans," Charlotte coos to tease me.

"The treehouse was already on the property, so why take it

down?" I shrug, but really, there was maybe something screaming inside of me that one day, just maybe…

"You're putting yourself through these moments because somewhere inside you do want to imagine it." Brent walks to his bar on the side and holds up a half-empty bottle of champagne. "Mimosas?" Everyone ignores him.

"What else has he done?" Charlotte asks Brent. These two as a team are a headache.

"He's avoided Ford, sent his assistant to a meeting in Lake Spark so he didn't have to go, made a shitload of paper animals. This man is losing his focus. Bad news for his hockey empire." Brent is trying to put pressure on me, I can tell.

"She loves you, you know." Charlotte's words strike me.

"Why do you say that?" I pry.

"She nearly told you, but then you went on your break a few hours later."

My mind runs through that day. In bed… she almost told me something. God, I wish I heard her say it. I would hold onto that forever.

"I'm not sure you should have told me that," I say softly.

Charlotte stands up and grabs a shirt of Brent's hanging off a cushion. "Nah, something tells me this will make a good maid-of-honor speech one day."

"This is so romantic. How did you meet Violet?" Gemma asks as she grabs her purse.

"She's my buddy's little sister."

"Their sparks started when he grabbed her name from a bowl at my party." Brent grins then sighs. "Someone had to do the good Lord's work."

I shake my head. "That's my cue to get out of here."

"Fine, I'll send up a bagel if I order some. Just remember that your ideal world isn't having a bagel with me, it's with someone else. Oh, and imagine that, you could actually have it all." Brent plants both his hands on my shoulders to square my vision to him. "It's okay to admit what you enjoy is actually everything we were always against… Besides, I'll just go wild for the both of us."

For the first time this morning, I nearly laugh, because it feels as though ease is forming inside of me.

———

HEADING BACK UPSTAIRS, I take a long shower before I walk into my closet to search for a suit that I'm after. I'm supposed to drive out this afternoon to meet with my parents for some event at their country club.

I slide hangers to one side until I spot my suit in a dry-cleaning bag. I forgot this was delivered a while back. I bring the hanger off the rail and carry the suit to my bed where I work the bag off. I notice an envelope attached to the neck of the hanger. The dry cleaner always puts things that are found in pockets in an envelope.

Opening the envelope, my body comes alive at the sight of the catalyst for my current state.

Taking the two small sheets of paper out, I unfold them to find Violet's name and my own.

Because I'm the guy who decided to keep our names that were in a bowl. Deep down, I know why, too.

She was always going to be more than one night.

Now it's time to do something about it.

25

DECLAN

Brielle smiles warmly at me as she balances Wyatt on her hip and grabs a treat from the jar for Puck who is jumping up on his back paws.

"He's been waiting for you, you know," she mentions.

"Ford or the dog?"

She laughs. "Both. Ford will be down in a minute. Want something to drink?"

"Nah, it's okay." I take a seat at the kitchen island, scanning the area. Every time I'm here, I'm reminded what a home looks and feels like. Toys scattered on the floor, an overzealous dog wagging his tail, and the music from upstairs which means Connor is home.

"Thanks for the maple syrup." She indicates with her head at the new bottle on the counter.

It's a glass bottle with gold foil around the cork. "It's a special edition, all the way from Quebec," I explain.

She tickles her son. "This guy loves it on his waffles and pancakes. It's so strange too, because we had like a full bottle, then suddenly it disappeared. "

A light feeling hits me because I know exactly what happened to it.

"How much longer?" I indicate to her belly.

"Too long, still another month… but you didn't come here to make small talk or discuss hockey with Ford, did you?" She gives me a pointed look.

Wyatt points to me. "Paper bird."

"What?" Brielle asks her son, grabbing his little hand.

"We made paper animals together that one time, didn't we, buddy." I smile at him.

He proudly nods his head.

"Oh yeah, I remember that now. The weekend we all want to forget." Brielle exhales a long breath.

Except me, I kind of enjoyed that weekend a lot.

The sound of footsteps coming down the stairs is slightly daunting. I'm not sure what mood Ford is in, but I need to talk to him if I have any chance of saving a friendship and possibly more.

"Hey." His tone is neutral as he walks to Brielle and takes Wyatt from her arms. "Connor is asking about laundry. Really, he can do it himself, you know that, right?" he tells Brielle.

She grins and pats his shoulder. "But then we end up with destroyed clothes. Trust me, it's better this way. He's probably asking about his jersey. I'll go." She begins to walk away but pauses and clears her throat. "Be nice." She smiles tightly at her husband.

We both watch her leave, but then I notice that Ford has an affectionate smile tracing his lips. "It never gets old, this chaos," he states fondly.

"I can only imagine."

He looks at me cautiously. "What brings you by?"

His calm demeanor catches me off guard, considering last time I saw him he wanted to rip me to shreds. Then again, that's a talent many hockey players have; we eventually cool off after outbursts that are mostly warranted. I sit up on the chair. "A few things. An apology, a request, and a use of the friend card."

Ford chortles as he grabs a box of animal crackers sitting on the counter. "Ballsy, but that's just you."

"Ford, I owe you an apology for going behind your back."

"You're not sorry," he informs me matter-of-factly, with the corner of his mouth twisting.

I tilt my head to the side in contemplation. "You're right. Sneaking behind your back was never an issue for me, nor would I have sought out your approval."

His face turns serious. "I'm not going to go in circles about that. What matters right now is that my sister has a broken heart and that's all your doing."

My shoulders drop, and I sigh. "That's why I'm here."

Ford slams the box of animal crackers on the counter rather abruptly. "Gentle, Daddy," Wyatt reprimands him.

Ford smiles sweetly at his little boy. "I'm sorry, sometimes Daddy is so strong that he doesn't recognize his force, something other big boys should be aware of."

I roll my eyes at his humor. "Remember I've taken you down a time or two."

"Let's stay focused. Are our future dinners going to be awkward as…" He glances at his son. "Duck? Or is this the part where you try to tell me that you've seen the light." Ford snaps up a cracker with his mouth when Wyatt offers one.

"A bit of both."

He raises one brow at me. "Let's discuss this in the living room so this one can play."

I nod, and we walk to the living area where Wyatt runs straight to his blocks, Puck walks to me to deliver a tennis ball, and Ford gets comfy in his big chair as he continues to snack on animal crackers.

"You made a point, one that we needed to hear," I begin.

"Violet is more than a sister to me. She's part of our support network, she's crucial in Connor's life, and I see her almost daily. I will never let her settle for less, she deserves it all. You have to get that. She wants the husband, the kids, any pet but a parrot, and I just don't see how you can provide those things."

I lean forward and rest my elbows on my knees. "I don't know either… but I want to."

"Want and will are two different things."

"Which is why I've thought about the future every waking second since that day. I won't apologize, but I can't walk away from Violet. Life is too good with her in it. I'm happy for once, and it isn't because of hockey. It's her."

Ford takes a long pause as he studies me, with his gaze fixed. "I don't doubt that you two have fun or that you care, but life is more than the present."

"Which is why I wanted to be sure, and it can't be a thought but a feeling… It doesn't matter anyway, it all leads back to Vi."

"Are you telling me that you've changed? Because I've witnessed some unsavory things when it comes to your partying ways, especially if Brent is involved, and I have to be honest, it's going to take a hell of a lot to caution before I'm convinced that you've changed."

My lips purse out. "Fair enough, but it's not you I have to convince."

A hint of a smile appears on Ford's lips. Maybe I'm saying all the right words. "You're telling me that one day you want to marry Violet and have kids?"

Looking around and seeing the dog knock Wyatt down into his blocks, only for him to squeal in delight, I can't help but smile at what surrounds me, a glimpse of what I could have. "Maybe not tomorrow, but yeah, that's what I can see in the future."

His eyes widen with reality sinking in. "I'll be da—ducked."

"It's cliché, but it's because of someone that my entire view of life altered, and that someone is Violet."

"You promise not to freak out again?" he asks.

"I promise."

"You came to me first; why not go straight to Violet?"

I grin to myself and toss the ball again for Puck. "I'm crazy about your sister, but not so crazy about another showdown with you. I'm here because I value our friendship, and a wise man knows you'd better be on good terms with your girlfriend's brother. I need you to know that I only want to make her happy, and there isn't anything I wouldn't do for her."

Ford continues to stare at me, eating another cracker. He offers me the box. I wave him off. "Have a cracker, trust me."

He's adamant, and now isn't the time to test him. I grab a cracker that's really a cookie, but whatever. Taking a bite, it isn't bad.

"Delicious, right?" Ford insists.

"Surprisingly."

"So how are you going to win back my sister?" He's interrogating me now.

Connor enters the room and gives me a scowl before he flops onto the opposite end of the sofa and points at me with his thumb. "We're back on friendly terms with him? *Really*, Dad?" I can't tell if he really isn't amused or if he's just riling me up.

Ford's gaze slides to Connor. "Yes, Declan was just about to enlighten us how he is going to impress your aunt, because surprisingly, I may be shipping them as a couple *if* he gets his act together."

"He better go big, because he sure as hell put her in a shitty mood all week," Connor says before he steals the box of crackers from Ford. Clearly, I discovered the Spears family snack of choice.

Ford gives him a disapproving look. "Language in front of the young one. We should give Declan the benefit of the doubt, I'm sure he has grand plans."

I look between them. "Actually, I do, and I kind of need Connor's help."

"Really? Now you want my dating expertise?" Connor's voice is pure attitude.

"Expertise? Hardly. Your ability to scheme? Yes," I answer.

Connor and Ford look at one another before breaking out in grins.

There is only one way in my mind for how I'm going to ensure that Violet knows she's the one.

26

VIOLET

Arranging the row of newly potted plants that I received in this morning's shipment, I admire how a green cactus is a safe bet. It's green, dry, and sends the message that this is not a romantic plant. This is the plant for people who only want to give occasional attention to it.

Apparently, plants scream, but we can't hear it. Kind of like me lately. I'm yelling inside, waiting for clarity, hoping for a fantasy. Everyone looks on with sympathy, maybe even pity for the woman who fell for the playboy hockey star. I wish I could say that I'll prove them all wrong.

"It sucks, Nugget," I voice.

The bird looks at me with I swear surprise that I've given him extra attention in the last week, but anything to keep me occupied, even if that means giving spare thought to the parrot who I'm sure wants to kill me.

The bell over the door rings, and I'm ready to throw that bell onto the street. Every. Single. Time. Hope ignites inside of me that maybe it's Declan.

I frown when I see Connor walking in. "Oh, it's you."

"Geez, someone is in a mood." He frowns.

"Sorry, it's been a day."

"More like a few weeks, but it's okay, you'll be okay."

Lines form on my forehead. "What makes you say that?"

Connor looks around the room and drops his gym duffel bag on the floor. "Didn't you get the message?"

"What message?" I say as I walk to my station.

"I'm here because I assume you ignored the message."

I blow out an exasperated breath. "I'm lost."

He begins to search my table, and he notices a pile of cards, and it grabs my attention. Tilly was working earlier, I must have missed the orders. Crap, I now potentially have clients waiting. Frantically, I lift the papers. Tomorrow. Tomorrow. Today.

My eyes scan the order.

No flowers, only a card, it says for the instructions. To write on the card:

Declan, thank you for last night. My answer is still yes, Violet.

He was here. Declan was here.

My stomach sinks, and then a faint line forms on my mouth because it's the same note from when he first came into my store, but I'm lost about what this means.

"That message," Connor points out.

I narrow my eyes at him. "How do you know?"

"Don't ask. It's time to go." He pulls out rope from his gym bag and a strip of fabric that I can assume is a blindfold.

"What the hell is going on?" I'm half curious and slightly scared.

"Trust me, I've been asking myself the same thing since Declan showed up for a *talk* with my dad."

A smile tugs at my mouth. "He went to Ford?" That must be promising, right?

"Close up shop and let's go."

———

I CAN'T SEE, my wrists are tied, and my nephew's driving is not for the faint of heart. I don't remember this many turns around the lake.

"Will you just tell me where we're going?"

"It's a surprise."

"Is this really necessary, the rope?" I wiggle my wrists in the air.

Connor laughs. "I think so."

He speeds up as the car turns to the right. "Easy, tiger, I'm going to be sick."

"Not in Dad's car."

My mouth gapes open. "We're in the Jaguar? Does your dad know?" I sure as hell didn't, considering I've been blindfolded since I locked the door to my store, and although it felt like a sports car, Ford never ever lets Connor drive it.

"This is for a good cause." That's a no, Ford has no clue his son stole the car.

I breathe to myself. "Please, can we drive a little smoother?"

"Relax, we're here," he informs me as he begins to slow the car.

I have no idea where we are, I was too distracted by Connor's driving.

The moment the car comes to a halt, I breathe out a sigh of relief. I was getting a little queasy, and I have zero patience for this mystery.

I hear Connor get out of the car, and a few seconds later, he opens my door to help me out.

"Goods delivered," he calls out.

Connor guides me by my arm, and we take a few steps in the afternoon sun. It feels like we're on a driveway.

"What the hell?" Declan yells in the distance, and he sounds horrified, but I can only hide a smile. I hear his voice, which means he's here. He delivered a message, he saw Ford, he has Connor involved, these are all positive indications. "Why is your aunt tied up and blindfolded?"

Oh, this wasn't part of the plan.

I hear the stomp of feet, and I think Declan is marching toward us.

"You said I could do it my way," Connor protests.

My hands are yanked, and instantly I feel Declan's familiar fingers fiddling with the knot. "I said you could come up with whatever story you needed to get your aunt here because you're her soft spot."

"I added a little interpretation," he gripes. "Trust me, this is by far more memorable. Far less boring too," Connor justifies.

The rope falls from my wrists, but all I feel is the warmth of Declan near, and my heart is on a rollercoaster. Fingers sneak under the blindfold and lift the dark fabric. My eyes take a moment to adjust to the light, and I'm greeted with eyes that possess me in the most delicious way possible.

"He went rogue on us. You okay?" Declan asks with concern as he assesses my body.

I blink a few times. "I'm fine." I smile nervously. "Not sure what's going on, though." I look around to see that I'm at Declan's house.

Declan glares to my nephew. "I'll take over from here."

"Sure. Want to keep the rope?" Connor asks casually.

Declan gives him a stunned look. "No, I don't want to keep the rope," he mocks. "One of these days you're going to give one of us a heart attack."

"Just keeping it real." He flashes us a peace sign and heads back to the car.

Declan ruefully shakes his head, and I roll my lips in because an overpowering smile wants to beam on my face. Declan is here in front of me.

He waits a few moments until Connor starts the engine before he focuses on me again. "Hi." He sounds tender and near shy. Ooh, timid is a side of him I haven't yet seen, and I'm here for it.

"Hi," I softly answer.

"Give me two minutes. I was supposed to be waiting out back, but then I saw you were kidnapped and had to intervene."

"Chivalrous," I state, one-toned. "I'll wait," I reassure him.

He offers me an appreciative smile and jogs back to the backyard.

For the next two minutes, I nervously wait outside, kicking a few pebbles and breathing to myself until I look at my watch and there is no more stalling.

My walk isn't slow as I circle around his house, and then my heart falls… so hard.

A path of flowers lead to the treehouse. Not just flowers, but paper flowers.

Different colors, mostly purple. One flower after another. I chuckle because he's lucky it isn't windy today.

I follow the line of flowers until I reach the steps of the treehouse. My face turns puzzled, as the structure looks different, refreshed, upgraded, and a far cry from what it was when we first saw this house.

Climbing the few steps, I enter the treehouse to find more paper flowers all leading to a bowl on a new rug in the middle of the room. Declan is leaning against the wall with one ankle crossed over the other and his hands in his pockets, a man confident with his move, maybe even calm.

Our eyes meet, and my chest is visibly moving.

One step, and another.

He tips his head to indicate that I should investigate something on the floor. My eyes peer down to find our names on two pieces of paper in the bowl. They're not new, they're the originals… from that night.

"I kept them," he states softly.

"Why?" I can't tear my eyes away from what started this all.

Declan walks to me and places his hand on my shoulder, and the fingers on his other hand hook under my chin to guide my eyes to his. "Life's always been a game to me. Turns out, the championship game that I've been after is the one that I have with you. I always win, which means I've been waiting to score, with you and the life we can have."

Am I floating? Is this real?

He continues to speak, with every word wrapping around me. "I knew you would be something, and I didn't want to forget our night together. I held onto paper, for crying out loud."

I shrug and smile. "You do a lot of things with paper," I tease him.

He smiles as he steps closer, threading his fingers into my hair to ensure I can't escape, even though I wouldn't want to. "But only you get paper flowers."

I glance around before returning to meet his eyes and smile, with emotion taking over. "Aren't paper flowers for forever?"

Declan's eyes stayed locked with mine. "That's the point."

"What are you saying?" I try not to sound like I'm going to jump into his arms.

"It's only you, Violet. I'm not going to let you go, and I refuse to break your heart, so I had to be sure. It turns out, the things you want are what I want, as long it's with you and only you, because I love you."

I step closer then stall. "I should be angry at you, not give in so easily when you do something as perfect as this. But is it wrong that I just want to walk into your arms, because then the last few weeks become history and my misery is over?"

He nods once. "I can't answer because I'll be biased."

Slowly, I step into his embrace and loop my arms around his neck. "Are you sure about us?"

He snorts a laugh. "I fixed up a treehouse, and other than right now, I don't intend to be in here again, so I'm going to assume this is for our next generation."

"I don't want to have kids soon, I just… eventually."

"We have time. We have to train our dog first." He smirks.

I'm still hesitant, but I'm about to burst. "You won't get bored with me?"

"Not a chance." He yanks me forward by my middle. "Though maybe let's avoid any parties, clubs, or suggestions that Charlotte and Brent might give us too."

This time I chuckle. "Couldn't agree more."

"I can't say sorry about the last few weeks. I wish I didn't have to give us the distance, but I owed it to us to ensure we are the long game."

"I get it. I was patiently waiting on the offside." I know he loves when I make hockey references.

"I love you, Violet. I thought hockey was my life, and I got thrown into a void when I retired, but it turns out, real fulfillment is you."

His words take me by surprise. I always kind of assumed that I would be the first to say it. The feeling has been bubbling inside of me, but it feels safe to admit the truth. "I love you too."

"Good, we've established that. Now let me kiss you," he nearly growls.

Our mouths slam together for a deep and passionate kiss. He steals my breath and saves me when I lose my balance, because this man's swoon has swept me off my feet.

He hoists me up, and I wrap my legs around his waist, instantly feeling his hard length.

"I brought pillows," he mumbles.

I glance down. "Oh, you want to do this here?" I kiss him again.

"I thought it would be special."

"For sure. We can get a splinter in my ass, and the squirrels can watch us too." I love being playful with this man.

He squeezes my behind. "Your ass might be in the air."

My head falls back in a laugh, and his mouth lands on my throat to spread the warmth of his breath across my skin. "I don't care how we do this, I just need you."

"It's been too long," he whispers against my skin.

"I'm sure we will make up for that," I husk right before he walks me to the wall of the treehouse to keep me trapped between his body and the wood.

Turns out, christening the treehouse is *nearly* as amazing as hearing him tell me that our future is together.

27

DECLAN

Violet's eyes are cloudy with lust as she leans her head against the headrest while she stares at me, with our fingers interlaced on the seat between us. We're in the back of the car while a driver is up front.

"You never get nervous, so I won't even ask." She smirks.

Feathering my hair with my fingers, I think I'm set in my suit. Violet looks stunning in a deep blue satin dress that plunges in the front, just a shade above scandalous.

"It'll be a good night. You left some clothes at my place, right?" I ask with a mischievous grin.

Since a few weeks ago when we decided to go all in, I'm not afraid to take steps. One of them is that Violet needs to keep stuff at my place, as it makes logistics easier. Besides, give it a month or two and she'll be moving into my lake house.

"Yes, sir. Toothbrush and all." I want to kiss her coy smile off her face. I lean in to capture her mouth before retreating.

"Just stay close tonight, okay?" I request.

She scoffs. "I'm sure you will be way too busy to notice me. Everyone will want to talk to you, it's the team dinner."

Inhaling a deep breath, I can't help but smile. "Crazy, huh?

People coming to me, not because I'm the star player but because I'm the one in charge."

Violet brushes the sleeve of my blazer with her fingers. "Just the way you like it."

"My parents are slowly accepting my new career. You softened the deal a little. They seem less concerned that I'm destined for a life of debauchery. You know, my dad phoned the mayor of Lake Spark."

"Oh yeah? Why?" Violet looks entertained.

"He wanted to insist that Jolly Joe's starts to use Grizzly Dash maple syrup for their recipes. It's a local syrup now, since his son is a Lake Spark resident. Then, to sweeten the deal, he promised to sponsor next summer's festival, with Dash branding and all."

Violet laughs. "Sounds like him." My parents adore her, and that's based only on the few times we've seen them lately.

"If only he knew how we make use of the family brand," she taunts.

"You wicked woman."

She glances at the partition between us and the driver, before she unbuckles her seatbelt and swings her leg over my lap to straddle me, a pool of satin now resting up by her waist, giving me a fantastic glimpse of her thighs.

"I am wicked," she promises. "Whatever will you do about that?" she rasps.

My fingers claw her bottom, and she gasps from surprise. "Want me to show up completely hard?" I warn her.

"Now, now, I can't wrinkle this dress, so you need to be on your best behavior." She jabs her finger into my chest then bops my nose, right before she slithers down my body and begins to work my belt.

"Violet." It comes out as a pleasurable curse.

"Doesn't mean *I* need to be on good behavior. Guess I will have to swallow and not miss a single drop."

"Fuck me." My body is at her mercy, letting her lead the way, instantly reacting when her mouth finds my tip and her tongue swirls. Blood rushes down to below my naval and a dizzy spell hits me, knowing the best relaxation is about to descend upon me.

Violet moans as she strokes and bobs on my cock.

Sometimes the way that Violet gives a blowjob makes even me lose my mind, way beyond any fantasy, and that takes a lot. But she's sexy, beautiful, talented, and likes to give as much as she receives.

And she's mine. All mine.

A sharp breath hits me, and I know this won't take long. There's something about this setting and the fact we are short on time that tells my brain to hurry up, but it doesn't matter, as my body already feels the release that is purely due to Violet.

My hands gently cup her head, because she took a while to do her hair for tonight; I'm considerate that way. Framing her jaw with the palms of my hands, I hold her in place while I come inside her mouth as she wraps her lips tighter around my length.

She stays on me until she fulfills her promise of every last drop.

I release her, and she leans back to lick her lips and give me a satisfied smirk.

Tucking myself back in and zipping up, a relaxing breath escapes me. "You are special, you know that?"

"You've mentioned that about a hundred times lately, but by all means, tell me again."

"Thank God Ford isn't sitting at our table. You know I can't speak to him after you do these things to me." Because this scene has happened a few times as of late. How I survived Sunday dinner last week, I'm still not sure. I guess I focused on Puck's tennis ball more than I should have, stress relief for both of us.

Ford is on board about us, or at least he's slowly adapting to the fact that Violet and I are a couple who are cemented by a promise to move at our own speed but with a destination that we both want.

The car slows down just as Violet finishes applying a fresh coat of lipstick. "You've got this. Tonight's your night."

"It's better because you're here."

"Just give me a sign if you need to be saved, otherwise I will be your arm candy all night, at your command." She smiles proudly.

"There will be photographers, so we're going pretty official." I grin.

"Can't wait to read the headlines," she teases.

"Come on," I say. Stepping out of the car, I button my blazer and offer my hand to Violet to help her out. The moment she's standing, I admire the curve of her bare shoulder which will drive me crazy. My hand finds a protective spot on her lower back as we begin to walk toward the team photographers stationed outside the restaurant, ready for a photo op.

Violet offers me her signature smile and brings her arm around me for a side hug.

Before I have a chance to remind her how breathtaking she looks tonight, there are already flashes going off.

In general, this is a private affair, except for the team marketing department that never misses a beat.

We give them what they want, the affectionate embrace, with our eyes telling their own story as we look at one another. I would say that we're putting on a show, but this is actually us.

Luckily, we usher that along quickly and head inside to the private banquet room that we rented.

Violet holds me firmly. "You're going to rock your speech. I'm proud of you."

I kiss her cheek. "I haven't done anything yet."

"I already know you're going to rally the troops."

"What makes you so sure?" We both take a glass of champagne that's offered to us by a passing waiter.

She turns toward me and offers her glass for a toast. "Because you're now playing for your favorite team. The you-and-me team, and as a proud member, I can say that you have an excellent positive mindset. It's infectious."

I tilt my head side to side, glancing around for a second to see everyone who contributes to the Spinners. "I like our team, the you-and-me one." I clink our glasses.

We both take a sip, and our eyes dance in a funny waltz, with wry smiles on our faces.

"We're ridiculously too cute. We have to stop this." She pretends to be annoyed. "Even I can't handle it. Go, go out there and be inspirational yet firm, and a little fear for the rookies might be good for them." Her lips purse out in doubt.

I chuckle under my breath. "You're keeping me sharp."

She winks at me before she indicates that she's going to say hi to her brother. I watch her walk away, and I'm still in awe at how perfect she is for me.

Then it hits me.

Playing hockey was my life, but never has a goal been so clear with nothing in the way. Both career wise and in my personal life. It's because of Violet that I've saved the best play for last, because she's my breakaway to the greatest win of my life.

EPILOGUE: VIOLET

FOUR YEARS LATER

Handing over the bouquet of red roses to the young man, I smile. "Here you are."

He grins at me while the bell announces someone entering the store.

"I think Hadley will love them. Thanks again." He holds the flowers up before turning to leave, crossing paths with Connor who just arrived. I notice both men square their shoulders and puff out their chests. Connor is 100% Ford, which means the glare he possesses right now is some sort of territorial claim.

Connor continues his stride to my table, while the other young man leaves. "Why was O'Keefe here? He mentioned Hadley's name."

I suppress my grin that wants to appear. "Because he bought her flowers, as she has a dance audition, or show, maybe a date. Is that… a problem?"

"He's an ass, but whatever. If he wants to get flowers for Princess Snark, then he can be my guest." He adjusts his neck, clearly agitated.

I tap my nails on the roll of ribbon, figuring out the best way to approach this. Ah, hell. "For someone who often declares that your next-door neighbor is an annoying creature, it's odd that you seem a little… bothered."

"Totally not. Hadley is a complete headache, and now I nearly feel sorry for O'Keefe that he wants to sign himself up for time with her. Then again, he was booted from the varsity hockey team when he was in our junior year, so maybe he is resorting to desperate measures to find someone willing to date him."

I shake my head, exasperated from prying for details because it will be one big circle. "Not everyone is like you, Mr. Just Voted Newest Player to Watch in the Hockey League." He's been drafted from college hockey to the pros, to the Spinners, which despite what people may think, neither his father nor uncle played a role in that.

He can't control his proud smirk. "Talent is talent."

Walking to the bucket of sunflowers, I begin to count the flowers. "Thirteen, right?"

"Make it fourteen. Mom loses it when I say Wyatt also got her a flower."

"You have the seven-year-old in on your ploys now too?" I'm impressed.

"Of course." Connor walks to Nugget's cage and peers in. "This guy causing you any trouble?" he asks me.

I laugh. "No, he doesn't age. I was kind of hoping he would nap more and then I could pretend that he isn't here plotting ways to murder me. Instead, he speaks words, lots of words."

Declan bought out the building as a wedding gift to me, and he even negotiated a new home for Nugget. Yet, when it came down to it, I couldn't let my faithful parrot go, so Nugget got to stay.

"You love it," Connor reminds me.

"That's what Declan tells me." I circle back around to my workstation and roll out some wrapping paper for the bouquet of sunflowers.

Connor taps Nugget's cage while the bird angles his head in various ways. "Where is your husband these days?" Declan and I have been married for two years, after a beautiful wedding which was by no means small here in Lake Spark.

"He'll be arriving back from out of town. He was out in Arizona for a few league meetings. Don't worry, he'll be at family dinner tonight." We all meet up at least a couple times a month, but sometimes we're missing Connor or Declan due to hockey life.

But it's June, which means everyone is on downtime. Well, at least, once Declan is back this afternoon, then I get him all to myself for a few weeks.

Luckily, tomorrow is Sunday which means we will not be leaving our bed. He's always extra insistent that we stay in our little bubble after he returns from business travel. I can't complain. We just need to survive a chaotic dinner first.

———

"I SAY we bail five minutes after dessert is served," Declan murmurs into my ear while my eyes roam the outside table to ensure nobody notices how my husband hasn't removed his hand from my thigh for the last five minutes and his voice is thick with need for me.

I smile tightly, avoiding glancing at him. "Ten," I counter.

He growls low into my ear, giving up in defeat before he leans back on his chair.

The lake is quiet on this early evening, but the backyard of Ford's house is anything but. Puck circles the table with his wagging tail, desperate for any handouts, while my near-four-year-old nephew Alex sings a song that makes no sense. Meanwhile, my other nephew Wyatt protests to my brother that he should be allowed to play more hockey.

"Dude, relax. One more year, then you can start to really play games that mean something. Don't rush it. You'll be living in my shadow anyway, so good luck with that," Connor informs him.

Brielle instantly reproaches him. "Connor."

Ford touches his wife's arm affectionately. "Relax, our son has a good point. Spears boys are exceptional hockey players, all eyes are on them."

I sputter my sip of wine that I'm drinking. "You sound ridiculous. It's not like it's genetic."

Ford makes a sound of doubt.

"Come on, it's not like some men have some magical hockey swimmers. If that's the case, then good luck, because one day, we—" I gesture between Declan and me "—may just produce our own little hockey team that could outshine your crew purely because my husband also has hockey swimmers."

Declan winces before guiding my waving hand back to the table. "Can we not talk about my… in front of your brother?"

"Yeah, please don't. I'm going to need therapy for this." Ford shakes his head while he folds his arms on the table.

"We really should pivot into a new topic," Brielle suggests. "By the way, I saw your parents, Declan. They mentioned looking at real estate out here. They were having lunch at Jolly Joe's."

My eyes snap to Declan. "What?"

He nervously offers me a tight smile. "They mentioned, but I forgot to tell you." I mean, I love Pearl and Walter, but his parents living so close? I don't know. Naked backyard sex will just feel too risky, in case they stop by to borrow eggs.

"Ooh, someone is going to get an earful on the drive home." Connor winks and clucks his tongue at Declan.

Declan gawks at my nephew. "Or not, as there is nothing more to say. By the way, how is the signing bonus my team paid you? Reminding you to mind your own business?"

I snicker a laugh, as these two always tease one another but are close.

Ford sets a hand on Connor's shoulder, as they are sitting next to one another. "Connor knows he is on the straight and narrow now. A little less partying and staying humble."

Connor just rolls his eyes. "Let me just grab my fictitious guitar and we can all sing Kumbaya together."

Declan and I glance at one another, and we both roll our eyes, entertained.

"Why do I fear the years ahead?" Ford says to the sky.

"Because my husband may have hockey swimmers like you, and we're your competition on producing the future hockey leaders of our world," I deadpan.

My brother looks at me, pretending to be unimpressed, yet he can't control the trace of a smile on his face.

All while my husband glides his fingers along my thigh, informing me that he has plans for me tonight.

———

It's an hour later when we're back at the house, and the moment we make it through the door from the garage to the hall, Declan's hands are on me, and our bodies are flush together as he walks us forward, with him behind me. His hot breath spreads just below my ear in that sensitive spot before he kisses the nape of my neck.

"I've missed you," he whispers.

"It's been three days but three days too many." I hum a sound when his fingers drag the hem of my dress up as we continue to head toward the stairs. We may just burst from the overpowering urge to forge our reunion together, literally.

"My favorite part of returning home to you is when I get you naked and take you, with our hands and our wedding rings linked together. It's the reminder that you're always waiting because you're mine."

I reach behind my back to yank on his belt. "Wedding rings do tend to symbolize that. So do some collars, but you're not a fan of that," I taunt him.

His chuckle rumbles against the back of my neck, and he fists some of my hair. "Naked. Now," he barks.

"You're so impatient." I begin to shimmy my cotton dress to the ground, and my eyes catch the outside patio lighting, which flashes an image of backyard sex, and then my head spins into a different direction. "Your parents," I state.

Declan stops his own clothing removal in a heartbeat, because admittedly, I just ruined the mood. "It's not a big deal," he insists.

"I just didn't realize." Really, it is that, because I guess it's a minor thing in the grand scheme of things.

Declan guides my body to face him, and I'm standing before him in my bra and panties. "They might have said something the other week, but I didn't think they were serious."

"Okay." I blink several times. "Why do they want to move?"

His fingertips cascade down my arms to link our fingers together, and he gives me one gentle yank to bring our bodies close again. "Because they made a grandchild remark."

"And? They often do." In a gentle not pushy kind of way, more of "do we need to plan our year around any potential development" kind of way.

A peculiar look flashes across his face, with the sexiest most endearing smile appearing on his lips. "I didn't remind them to be quiet." Declan kisses the outside of my hand and steps closer, letting go of my hands to cradle my face. "Instead, I smiled to myself." His thumb runs along my bottom lip, my heart thumping like crazy, because a balloon of hope fills my chest.

"What are you trying to say?" My eyes narrow as I try to read his mood.

"I've been thinking about it a lot lately, and don't you dare think your little 'my husband has the good hockey genes' speech back there is any influence," he warns.

"Influence over what, exactly?" Feelings swell because we've always respected that we didn't want kids right away, we have time, but I've been feeling the desire lately. I never wanted to push, but now it seems…

Declan drops one hand to my belly. "I want to put a baby inside of you."

A warm smile instantly hits me, as my entire body enters a new state of happiness. Maybe we'll be lucky to one day get pregnant, maybe not, but right now, we're on the same page and timeline, and that feels like a positive start to a new chapter for us.

"I couldn't focus during my meetings because I've been thinking about it for a while, but I'm ready, and you better believe that this place is turning into baby-making central."

I leap into his arms and kiss him with so much excitement. "We don't need to make it a big thing, let's just do what we always do, minus birth control."

He's walking us to the stairs. "To hell with that. The number of times that I'm going to have you on your back with legs in the air will be way above our daily average."

I kiss him again, inhaling his love, feeling so incredibly lucky that this man is my husband.

$$\overline{}$$

EPILOGUE: DECLAN

$$\overline{}$$

ANOTHER THREE YEARS LATER

"Shh," Violet shushes as I pump into her with a little force while I spoon her from behind.

It's afternoon, and we have a window of opportunity while our daughter Willow takes her nap. She's two years old now, and she's going to be the spitting image of Violet when she's older. Everyone adores her. My parents insist on watching her at least twice a week, and her cousins are excited to have a girl in the family.

I cover Violet's mouth with mine to keep our sounds under control. We are two souls with a little less sleep, a hell of a lot more patience, and this is our moment to close out the world and just be us, together.

We just entered the off-season, so I'll have a little more time with my girls.

Violet moans wildly into my neck as her body begins to shiver around my cock.

"Declan," she breathes out.

"Let go, baby, come on."

Her pussy contracts around me, and it causes a wave of pleasure to flow through me. I won't be far behind her release. Violet reaches behind to link her arm around my neck as she draws out our kiss.

There is nothing like being naked in bed with the woman you love at two in the afternoon while the house is quiet except for the sound of our skin slapping together and my dick sliding in and out of her. I've waited my whole life for this.

Finally, when we lie here, tangled together, tempted to fall asleep after great sex, we smile fondly at one another. "I fucking love you," I remind her and swipe away hair from her forehead.

"I love you too. Do you think we can get thirty minutes of sleep? Will our daughter give us that today?"

This is my favorite part of the day, touching base with my wife while I'm still inside of her.

"I think so. She played a lot this morning, had her pancakes with maple syrup, which means she had a sugar high and crashed right on time after lunch."

"She loves the family brand." Violet grins at me before kissing my lips. My parents lose it every single time we send them a photo of Willow eating maple syrup; it's the highlight of their day.

"But I think we should attempt to get another round in since you promised we can try for the next kid." I want this. Watching Violet pregnant, then the moment Willow entered our lives was a gamechanger. I don't want to stop growing our family. I dive in to kiss her mouth then speak against her lips. "Close your eyes."

"Sleep," she insists.

We both sigh a satisfied breath and get comfortable, ready for a power nap.

An hour later, the Dash family is rested and ready to conquer the rest of our day. Violet and I decide to pack up Willow and head into town to grab some things for dinner, plus Violet wants to check on The Flower Jar. It's a quiet day, so not many people are on Main Street.

We stop at The Flower Jar first. I hold our daughter and approach Nugget's cage at a safe distance. Our daughter instantly squeals in delight, meanwhile Violet chats with the new assistant who works in the store.

My phone vibrates in my pocket, and I balance Willow in one arm to pull up my phone without even looking at the call display. "Dash," I answer.

I listen while the team publicist and general manager talk on the other end of the phone, explaining the latest news that will bring attention to the Spinners. They're doing this as a courtesy due to my connection to the team. When she mentions Connor's name, my jaw juts out. That kid is making all of us age too soon. My nephew follows the whole "play hard and party harder" philosophy. A lot like me when I was his age. The number of times the team publicist has had to do damage control lately has made me want to throttle Connor, but he's just too damn good of an athlete and is related to my wife.

After the team publicist finishes her explanation, and we hang up, I shake my head in pure aggravation, yet I chuckle to myself for the potential fallout coming Connor's way. Before I can process the information, I hear the bell over the door announcing a customer, and my daughter's grabby hands reaching behind me breaks my thought.

"Connor!" Violet greets him with a hug.

Of course, he shows up to see his favorite aunt when he returns to town from his latest adventure.

I walk toward them because I feel a conversation coming. "Hey, Connor." I don't blink.

He looks at me cautiously, probably not expecting me here. "Hey." Yep, it's an awkward hey.

"How was your trip?" Violet asks as she signs off on an order form and hands it to her assistant.

"Yes. Do tell." There is no enthusiasm in my voice.

Connor scratches the back of his head. "It was… Vegas."

Violet looks at me, slightly thrown off that Connor seems to be acting weird.

"And? You had a big group going, right?" Violet does her best to keep the conversation moving.

Connor swipes his hand across his jaw. "Something kind of happened."

Now I smirk to myself, while my wife notices in…

Three.

Two.

One…

She grabs Connor's wrist to examine his new accessory. "What the hell is this?"

"I kind of wanted to see you first before my parents find out," he begins. "I'm going to need a lot of sunflowers."

Violet shakes his hand. "Why do you have a wedding ring?"

He takes a deep breath. "I kind of… got married."

My wife's jaw drops open as she releases his wrist. "You don't have a girlfriend. You have flings. Now you're telling me that you went to Vegas and got married?"

His lack of words coming out of his mouth confirms Violet's question.

Violet enters freakout mode and quickly glances at our daughter, reminding herself of our child's impressionable ears. "What the duck, Connor!"

"Duck it," the parrot volleys.

Connor stays mute, but his face says it all. None of this was planned.

"And who might the lucky bride be?" I ask, knowing full well that my fury for his private life making the news is minor compared to his parents who are about to have a heart attack.

Connor inhales deeply. "Hadley."

No wonder the media is going to go crazy. I can see the headlines now: "Hockey Royalty Elopes in Vegas with the Daughter of a Baseball Legend."

WAITING TO WIN

Age. It's just a number. And in case you are wondering, the math adds up, just barely. It isn't Lake Spark age-defying water. Waiting to Win can be read as a standalone as I always focus on one couple. But if you've been following the town of Lake Spark then you first met Hadley and Connor in their parents' stories. Hadley is Spencer's daughter (Worth the Chance) and Connor is Brielle and Ford's son (Worth the Wait) whom they had when they were teenagers. Basically, the parents in this book are still rocking their prime, and the kids are no longer kids.

If you are already familiar with Connor and Hadley, then you are in for a treat, as their romance was always there in the making!

1

CONNOR

Arriving late because I got sidetracked, I slide into my chair and swipe my sunglasses off my eyes. I can't help but smirk at the men sitting across the outdoor table from me, overlooking Lake Spark at Catch 22, a local establishment with a decent menu. The dark emerald-blue lake is calm today, and the pines lining the backdrop are green from recent rain.

And these men? They may be embracing a casual day with jeans and t-shirts, but their seething stare has become a constant occurrence.

But I'm the golden ticket, and they know it.

"What lovely weather we're having for May in Illinois. Probably means it'll snow next week, but it's the small wins, right?" I calmly say as I cross my arms and feel a victorious grin form.

"Cut the bullshit, Connor." My Uncle Declan is the first to speak, and that doesn't really surprise me. His stake in my hockey career is a little high, considering he owns the Spinners. He's never afraid to voice his disapproval, yet he has a soft spot for me. How can he not? He married my aunt Violet, and she's the best. More like a friend since we're closer in age, plus her flower shop provides the flowers that I need to charm the female population around here.

Sitting next to my uncle is my father. Ford Spears and Declan Dash are hockey legends; they played together years ago and never left hockey behind. My father owns the sports complex nearby where the Spinners train, and these two are also true partners in crime.

Which is unlucky for me most of the time.

My dad sighs. "Why are we having this conversation yet again?" While he isn't my agent, he voluntarily took on an unofficial role as my manager and trainer without the title, lucky me. He can throw in the dad card too, yet I've never minded. My father and mother had me when they were young, which means the age difference makes it a hell of a lot easier to connect sometimes. My parents did a lot for me, that I'll never forget. So, if he wants to help guide my career, then so be it.

But right now? These two men are ganging up on me.

Uncle Declan slides his drink to the side and leans against the table, scanning the area to ensure nobody is taking notice of us. Even if they did, Lake Spark is a small town that respects keeping gossip within our bubble. "I'm begging you, for all our sakes, to cool it down with the partying," he states.

"You're landing in too many media reports and not for the reasons that make your mother happy," my father adds. He's pulling out the big guns, mentioning my mother who I buy flowers for on a regular basis because she's amazing.

Still, I roll my eyes. "We made it to the playoffs, even after our shitty season, so of course, the team was going to celebrate," I justify. What a shame we were out in the second round.

"There is a photo of you taking shots next to the goalie while lying on a bar top," my uncle deadpans.

I shrug a shoulder. "So? I'm in my twenties. What else would I be doing to celebrate?"

My father shakes his head from my answer while he slides his hand along his brow.

Good ole' Uncle Declan points a finger at me. "I swear I could strangle you." He doesn't mean it. He has to play bad cop when he's in business mode. At family events, he'll just turn off his work switch and be uncle extraordinaire, complete with a side hug and jokes.

"It's off-season now. I'm strongly suggesting that you lie low. Try to straighten up your image a bit. You want to be in the media because of your skill, not because of your off-ice antics," my dad points out.

He may present a valid point. It took years to prove I earned a spot on the team due to talent, not connections. Hockey may be family tradition, but my abilities have made me MVP for two seasons straight. I'm a damn good defenseman. And so what, sometimes media throws in the hottest bachelor title. If you have good looks, then celebrate it.

"Relax, I have one more thing, then I'll focus on sleeping in, hanging with my little brothers, and hitting the gym." My parents got back together when I was ten, and my little brothers came a few years later. When I return to Lake Spark, even though I have my own place, I'm at my parents' a lot, and the house is chaos, with kids running around and a Labrador who is enjoying his final years.

The two in front of me glance at one another with a puzzled look.

Lifting his nose, my father asks with a hardened stare, "What's one more thing?"

My grin stretches. "Vegas. The boys and I are heading there tomorrow for Briggs's birthday. Don't worry, I'll be back for family dinner by the weekend."

Both men wince at my statement before shaking their heads in disapproval. But then my father forms a soft smile for someone who seems to be standing behind me.

"Hey, Hadley," he greets her.

My body tightens, and her name wipes my cocky grin right off my face. Keeping my eyes set on the table, I choose to ignore the fact that Hadley Crews, with her long silky hair with caramel highlights and sparkly blue eyes, is stopping at our table to say hello to my father because she's a good girl like that.

"Hi, Mr. S and Mr. D." Her polite tone makes me grip my denim-clad thighs.

Hadley is a few years younger than me, my next-door neighbor growing up, and the daughter of a former baseball star. She's also anything but polite… when it comes to me.

"Christ, how many times do we have to tell you, it's Ford and Declan. We're too young for that mister crap," my father corrects her, because our parents are best friends, down to our moms sipping a dry white on weekends together.

She chuckles softly. "I know, but still."

"Brielle, my sister, and your mom are hysterical. They go on and on about that class you teach," my father mentions.

"Ballet barre? They come every week, work up a sweat, then hit Jolly Joe's right after class for cake. Balance, I guess." Hadley can't help but gush because she loves her mom, and well, probably loves my mom also, then add my aunt to that list too. In return, they have her on a pedestal of greatness.

"Brielle keeps asking me to check out her toned body," my father reflects.

I cringe at the thought. "Get it together," I mutter. "None of us want to know what you and Mom get up to."

"Passion doesn't die, Son." He chuckles at me then turns his attention back to the thorn in my side. "Grabbing lunch, Hadley?"

"Yeah, I'm just meeting Isla for a quick bite then heading back to the dance studio. I'm teaching a group of eighty-year-olds this afternoon."

Uncle Declan interjects and speaks to me. "See? Work ethic and helping the senior population. You could learn a lesson or two from her."

I scoff a laugh. "Trust me, I'm sure underneath her heart of gold, her mouth spits out wicked things." It flies off my mouth too easily.

The men at the table stare at me blankly, and Hadley's eyes snap to me with distaste apparent on her face; I know because I glance up to catch her soft lips form a tight line. She may be an elegant ballerina that teaches dance in our little town, but her eyes have a tint of wildness, the type that can make a man come undone if he isn't careful. She's always been the ballerina who dances with her hair down to Guns 'n' Roses. And her dark polished nails? They dig into skin as if she doesn't want to let go. But that's our little secret, one she wishes we didn't share.

One of the men sitting across from me clears their throat, attempting to break the stiff tension now gracing our table.

Hadley throws on a smile for their benefit. "I hope you both enjoy your lunch despite sitting with this menace. See you around."

"Yeah, he is special, this one." My father flashes me an over-the-top grin before turning back to my nemesis. "Oh, and thanks for babysitting the boys last weekend," my father remarks.

"Maybe we can add babysitting my nephew here. I'll pay extra," my uncle adds.

"There isn't enough money in the world for that," she states dryly before walking away. She's right too. Because she hates me, and hell knows, I've given her a bucketful of reasons, which is why she'll never change her mind.

My relatives have the audacity to chuckle at her comment, which causes me to give them an unimpressed look.

My father smiles. "You two are always the same. Ever since you were kids. Not sure why. I mean, she had the world's biggest crush on you."

"And?" I can't care.

"Grow some maturity is what your dad is saying. You may actually realize that she is quite a joy to be around, and you've just been flirting with her," my uncle has the audacity to casually mention before he looks at his phone.

My face stays blank. "I'm not flirting."

"Thank God. Spencer would kill you." My dad is only half-joking. Spencer, Hadley's dad, probably would. I'm like 90% certain that he might hate me due to my wild teenage years or the fact he doesn't like the idea of any guy around his princess... and I don't mind one bit.

Ignoring what they say, my eyes scan the room and land on Hadley with her friend Isla sitting at a table. Internally, fear forms that Isla is inviting Hadley to Vegas. These are the hazards of Isla hanging with the team, since her older brother is our winger and my best friend.

Why the fuck does Hadley have to be a vision? Even when she's wearing an oversized shirt that falls off the curve of her shoulder, then she's in those tight little dance pants, and I bet she's sporting a leotard underneath too. Nobody knows how she gets under my skin or how in another life she deserves to be my queen.

"Vegas, Connor. Best behavior," my uncle grits out as a reminder.

Memo received.

"What happens there, stays there." I turn my attention to him with an overdone smile.

"Connor," my father warns.

"Relax." I humor them, or maybe I consider their concerns… for a second.

I haven't decided because my eyes flick briefly back to Hadley, the delicate flower with a feisty tongue who is tucking a lock of loose hair behind her ear while the waiter flirts with her. I bet he would never be able to make her scowl the way I do.

My eyes pin on my uncle and father. "I hear your advice loud and clear, and I'll follow it *after* Vegas," I promise.

2

HADLEY

"**I** know it sounds crazy, but it felt like someone was watching me," I say as I play with the wrapper of the straw.

Isla tightens her ponytail. "What do you mean? At the dance studio?"

"Yeah. I was doing my usual self-practice. Just dancing a modern piece to music on the speakers, in my own little world, but then I swear someone was outside watching. I had the backdoor to the studio open, but when I looked, nobody was there. Maybe I'm paranoid. Then again, I also didn't feel unsafe, you know?"

She shrugs. "I mean, Lake Spark is one of the safest places to be."

"True."

I've lived here my whole life. I also grew up in that dance studio, and after my teacher Ms. Romy moved to Colorado, my father bought the place and gifted me the studio when I finished up my dance degree over at the university in Hollows nearby. I turned down a spot at a professional dance company, as it wasn't for me. I don't like rigid routine, and I love my family too much to be far. Teaching is my calling, as proven by the fact that it's been a few years and I'm still happy.

The waiter returns to take our orders. I go for a chicken salad sandwich, it's my favorite at Catch 22, and Isla orders a Caesar salad.

The moment the waiter leaves us, Isla is in action mode while I down my glass of water. "Pause your gallon-a-day hydration for a sec, we have business to discuss."

"Hydration is key for my dewy skin," I playfully defend.

Isla crosses her arms on the table and looks at me with enthusiasm. "*So,* Vegas." She flashes her eyes at me.

"What about it?"

Isla is a few years older than me, but it doesn't deter our friendship. Her brother plays for the Spinners, and she's close with the team, as she works for Ford at the training arena in project management for the summer camp that he runs.

"Come on, it's my brother's birthday. I can't not go to Vegas. But I *do* need a trusted sidekick with me."

A half-smile forms on my mouth. "As much as I love a good party, I'm not… sure."

"Because of a certain player who is sitting somewhere in this restaurant?" Isla's face screws up, and she pretends to search.

I huff out a breath, and my eyes do a quick travel to land on Connor Spears, the carbon monoxide of my air. His piercing brown eyes don't affect me, nor do his cunning grin or well-defined biceps. And so be it if his hair is the kind of shade of light blondish-brown that I like, not quite as dark as his ruthless heart.

I hate the off-season. It means I have to see his face around town more than usual, and it exceeds my tolerance quota for the guy.

My eyes journey back to Isla. "Trust me, I could care less if I have to witness his partying antics or flavor-of-the-week puck bunny."

Isla offers me a pained look. "Did you two ever talk about—"

My palm flies up to stop her. "Please don't mention it." I groan from the pure memory of a time I should have known better.

She nods in agreement to my request. "Then it's settled. You will pack your sexiest dress and come with. The private plane that my brother arranged leaves tomorrow at lunch, and we should be back the day after."

Picking up my phone, I see my screensaver. It's my dad, mom, and little brother Ashton. It's an old photo, which you could tell because Pickles, the beagle that lived to a hundred, is in the photo. I loved that dog. He was almost the best part of my dad marrying April, except April became my mom and nothing tops that. My biological mom was never in the picture, a fling of my dad's. She even signed away her rights the moment I was born. But I don't care, because it means my dad and I ended up with the person who I consider to be my real mom, and they had my little brother one day after my ninth birthday.

I bet if I told my mom that I was going to Vegas, she'd help me pack. My parents are the kind of people that you can throw back a drink with while listening to good music. They encourage living life to the fullest.

"I guess I should get out of the house," I say. "Plus, I do want to get another small tattoo, which I could get in Vegas in the morning before we go." I already have a small pair of ballet slippers, and a baseball because my dad was a pitcher. I would like to add a few tiny shooting stars somewhere. I keep my tattoos hidden in intimate spots near my hip bone. There are great tattoo artists in Vegas, so it would be a bonus for this trip.

"That would be fun, and you should get out of the house. You live with your parents."

I give my friend a pointed look. "By choice," I correct her. Why give up a great room in a beautiful house with an indoor pool, family, and a mom who cooks to professional standards?

Isla reaches across the table to take my hand between her palms. "Please, Hadley, I don't get along with the other girls in the group. I need someone who can dance all night and tell a good joke. I think Cann has a thing for you too."

"Shawn Cann, the center?"

She nods.

"Not interested. Besides, my dad would go through the roof if I ever introduced a hockey player as a boyfriend. He witnessed too many of Connor's varsity team parties next door, and it's only gotten worse since then, and his opinion has only grown since then thanks to the asshole over there."

Isla can't help but smirk. "A party. Is that how you and—"

"You are bad. Don't bring him up. Con is his nickname, and trust me when I say it's purely fitting for his personality too." Connor is the opposite of what he seems, but few people know that, and I don't call myself lucky that I'm one of those people. "Your pitch to get me to Vegas really sucks," I tease her.

Isla sits up and clears her throat. "You're right. Okay, how about my brother is getting you and me a luxurious suite with a hot tub, full breakfast, and unlimited champagne."

My eyes slightly bug out, as I'm impressed. "You should have led with that."

"Come on, please? You know I'm not a big party girl, but this sounds like something fun and out of my norm, plus it's my brother's birthday." She brings her hands together in a pleading gesture.

I debate for a few seconds, but it doesn't take long. "Fine." A grin slowly forms.

She nearly squeals. "It will be unforgettable."

"I'm sure." I look at my phone and see the time is near one. "I'll get someone to sub my classes tomorrow. Be sure to have a glass of champagne ready the moment I walk onto that plane." My eyes side-line to Connor who is standing up from the table with his family. "I'll need it," I murmur softly.

ISLA HANDS me a glass of champagne as I settle in my seat post takeoff on this private plane, and I adjust my black dress; it's casual, but I know it turns heads. Already, the party seems to be going, so I'm not sure many would notice anyhow. Shots of tequila are being poured, and a few women are sitting on hockey players' laps.

Why I signed myself up for this, I'm not entirely sure. Maybe it's growing up with professional athletes always around me, but I appreciate that these guys have an unusual life. I guess that I have more understanding than most, which is why I'm often invited to their social gatherings. Most of the guys here are good men who treat Isla and me with respect and as a friend. They're fun to hang around with too.

Well, all except one.

Connor is sitting by the window with a nice pair of jeans and a baby-blue button-down. It nearly makes me miss his glared look of steel or appreciate how baby blue brings out his eyes. But the scotch in his hand has me thrown. The image itself makes me chortle.

Scotch is a man's drink. And I've seen Connor as a boy, the next-door neighbor who made fun of my ballet costumes when I was a little girl, to the teenager whose parties I would crash and he would shoo me away. The guy who lived and breathed hockey his whole life and gave roses to girls, with a charming grin plastered on his face. God, I had such a crush on him. Made worse when I was fourteen and his uncle forced Connor to walk me home after Connor's party got busted, then he surprised me and kissed me on the cheek.

His parents are the sweetest and are good to me. They raised him well, which is why it doesn't make sense that, when it comes to me, Connor is…

Our eyes connect, and for a mere second, I could swear something underlying is there, and I hate my treacherous heart for jumping.

Isla breaks my focus by nudging my arm with hers. "Drink up. Tequila is next, and it's calling our name."

I laugh. "We should pace ourselves."

"Don't you want to be a little numb and hungover when you get your tattoo tomorrow?"

"You're getting a tattoo?" Shawn asks, having overheard as he flops onto a seat nearby. He has a sweet smile, so it's a shame I seem to be drawn to hardened looks.

I offer him a polite smile. "Yeah, I think so. I've been wanting it for a while, but I didn't have the right moment. I actually got my last tattoo with my dad, and he got one too—a baseball glove with names of everyone in the family."

"Your dad is cool like that. He comes to our games sometimes, but in truth, I used to watch him play baseball. He was a really talented pitcher. Where are you getting the tattoo?" He swipes his hand across his jaw in a suave manner. "Let me guess, your inner thigh?"

The sound of a cough breaks our conversation, and my eyes sideline to the culprit. Connor gives his teammate a death glare. "I'm confident princess tippy-toes keeps her tattoo destinations above the waist."

My eyes roll before I down a long sip of champagne. Of course, this would happen. My favorite villain always surprises me when he decides to go possessive on me, as if he has a fucking right. He doesn't. Yet he still takes it upon himself.

"Or I enjoy very intimate locations. Hidden, private, slightly questionable for the tattoo artist," I challenge with my eyes set on Connor whose jaw clenches slightly.

"If you need someone to hold your hand, I'm there," Shawn volunteers with a grin.

Isla makes a sound of approval.

Connor, on the other hand, is quick to stand up. "Cann, now," he orders and indicates to follow him.

Shawn gives me a rueful shake of his head before he agrees and follows Connor to the other part of the plane behind a curtain.

Leaning back in my chair, I sigh and finish my champagne down to the last drop.

Isla leans in to whisper, "Remind me again, what the hell is Connor's problem?"

"Hell if I know." I puff out a breath and offer my glass for replenishment, while I attempt to fog out the memory of that one time, when his hands and lips landed on me.

But I was just a little mistake, and we've hated one another since.

Which is why I stare at my champagne flute, confused as to why Connor Spears is berating his teammate for merely glancing at me.

For a jerk who hates me, his possessive streak is *sometimes* endearing.

Definitely infuriating, and I sure as hell will let him know. Which is why I unbuckle my seatbelt and stand.

● **3**

CONNOR

Roughly, I pull across the curtain dividing the plane and step into Shawn's space.

"What the hell was that back there?" I grit out at my teammate.

His mouth curves. "I was just talking with Hadley, because I bet that dancer knows how to bend and—"

"Shut the fuck up." I grab his shirt near the collar from pure instinct. "Stay away from her," I nearly snarl, and I hate that I care.

Shawn squints his eyes before he smirks. "Oh yeah, someone mentioned you get a little crazy when it involves her. You should seal that deal, Con. She's sports dynasty, hot as hell, and flexible, the kind of woman that I'm sure my dick would thoroughly enjoy."

I push him against the side of a seat, enraged somewhere inside of me. "Say that again and I will gladly break something, since we don't need your arm during the off-season." Shawn just chuckles. "Listen, it was your first season with us, but everyone knows to leave her alone. It's a team rule," I attempt to rationalize, and I roll my shoulder back.

He raises a brow. "You mean your rule, and everyone just follows because they're too scared of who your daddy and uncle are."

I tighten my grip on his shirt. "Think whatever the hell you want, I'll gladly prove you wrong."

"Whatever, Connor. She's an adult, and from what I hear, she hates your guts, so let me just walk back in there and offer her a drink." Christ, this dude is pushing me. I always thought he was half-decent, but now he's just irritating me to the max.

Before I can shoot off another warning, the curtain slides open in one abrupt swoosh, and our eyes land on Hadley who is leaning against the divider with her hand over her head and hip tipped out, and her tits are perked up because of her dress. Well, this is just agony; she looks like a pinup girl full of sass. My dick stirs against the zipper of my jeans, knowing her pissed-off look is for me, and that's just exciting.

She throws an overdone smile at Shawn. "Do you mind giving your teammate and me a moment?"

Shawn looks between us and chuckles. "Sure. Body shots later?"

My muscles clench from every word this guy directs toward her.

Hadley smiles tightly. "Maybe."

With my teammate walking past her, and I'm sure as hell confident he purposely brushes against her shoulder in passing, Hadley steps into my space, and in one movement, closes the curtain again before her hand returns to her hip with her dark blue nails tapping the curve of her waist.

But I've been here before with her, and it's on.

"You're breaking the rules, Hadley," I chide as my eyes transfix on her face that doesn't move an inch.

"Ah yes, your imaginary rules that you believe I follow," she muses.

I wave my long finger side to side. "Staying away from one another is about the only thing we agree on, so why are you here?"

She steps forward and stands tall to appear unaffected by me. "To enjoy your pleasant holier-than-thou company, of course." Sarcasm suits her, damn it. "Unlike you, your teammates and my best friend find me a little more than tolerable, so here I am, because I don't give a rat's ass if you care or not." There is a little bite to her tone.

"Feisty Hadley, lucky me," I mock.

Her mouth changes shape to a sultry look. "Someone will be lucky. I didn't even offer yet, but I may let Shawn trace the spot of my new tattoo with his tongue," she rasps.

Willpower.

It's taking a ton of willpower not to snap right now. She's riling me up because she seems to think I'm affected, and she can't know her theory is true.

But I'll play her little game. I pretend to look at my watch. "You should send him my way if he needs directions, considering we both know that my tongue and hands are far too familiar with your body."

"And don't I regret it," she snipes.

In a flash, I step forward and trap her between the side of a vacant seat and my body, our breaths mingle, and her chin rises from surprise. My head lolls to the side gently, and if I were to move an inch, then her mouth would be mine. "Trust me, I'm honored that you gave me your V-card." I pretend to be touched because she can never know the real truth.

Two palms land against my chest because I delivered a low blow, even I know that. Trust me, I'm already disgusted with myself.

"Don't dredge up our past mistakes," Hadley seethes, and I notice the rhythm of her chest moving while her scornful gaze feels like fire on me. "You're the biggest asshole on this plane."

"Big and me do go hand in hand," I taunt.

She growls. "Your ego is a piece of work, and your arrogant tendencies aren't the least bit refreshing. Anything but original, actually. This is how this is going to go, Connor. You'll let me drink, dance, play blackjack, and do whatever the hell I want in peace. Watch all you want, because we both know you're like a child upset that his toy got taken away."

A deep chuckle roars in the back of my throat. "You're a toy now?"

Hadley shakes her head, clearly exasperated. She looks away then back to me, with her eyes softening. "Insufferable, that's what you are." For a second, I hear sadness in her tone, and I nearly falter because I do actually hate that she was hurt and it's my doing.

But I stay strong.

When she pivots to leave, I grab her arm, and she looks down then draws her sight up. "Just… not Shawn. He's bad news." My voice grows delicate, because as much as we're one another's despair, a protectiveness that I have no right to feel hits me when she's around.

She scoffs a sound. "No, Connor… you're bad news, and I swear, if I had it in me, then I would find a way to destroy you." It takes me a moment to digest her honesty, but then she snickers and walks a step before glancing over her shoulder. "I'll be sure to ask you to pass the salt when I decide to do body shots with your teammate."

She turns her back and leaves, so maybe she doesn't hear my growl. She's impossible, agonizing, and beautiful when she snarls.

Having her on this trip, not my choice, is the work of the devil. That's the only thing I can come up with when I decide another scotch is calling my name.

———

THAT WAS A NEAR EXCRUCIATING FLIGHT, but luckily, other than a few drinks, everyone kept it steady, as we all know we have a long night ahead.

Now we are in Vegas, and I'm sitting on the sofa in the luxurious penthouse that we rented, complete with a rooftop pool. After checking into the hotel and freshening up, we got straight into the celebratory mood. I'm sitting on a sofa, overlooking the Vegas skyline as the sun hangs low to the west.

My friend and teammate, Briggs Chase, hands me a fresh drink with a grin. "God, I'm having a good time. No Vaughn Madden in sight." That's his archnemesis on the ice, the guy who got Briggs a ten-minute misconduct penalty during our game with Tampa.

"You're still going on about that? He is actually quite a good guy off the ice." Briggs gives me a death stare, and I give up.

He tips his nose in Hadley's direction. "You going to survive?"

I stare into the presumably gin and tonic that he placed in my hands. "Always do. I'm feeling lucky tonight. Let's head straight to the blackjack table when we head down."

He feigns a sound of doubt. "I don't know, man, can't be late for the strippers."

I scoff. "I'll take a hard pass."

Briggs raises his brows at me. "Why? Because you want to stick around to deter Shawn from getting his own private show from a certain dancer?"

"Fuck that. She isn't my problem." I hate that there is frustration in my voice.

Choosing to ignore the giggles of the girls in our group, lining up shots near the snack buffet, I know the daggers I feel on my back can only be coming from one person on this trip.

I don't dare search for her with my eyes. Not when my mind is replaying how this all started a few years ago.

Glaring at my mother, I'm not impressed with this set-up as she sits by my side in the theater while we wait for the show to start. "Why the hell am I here again?" I ask her.

She adjusts her sunglasses resting on the top of her hair framing her face. "Because we are neighbors and friends. Everyone on our street supports one another. We go to Hudson's football games, everyone comes to your hockey games, and now we are here for Spencer and April and for their daughter."

"I come home for the weekend, and you have me watching little kids in tutus." I'm very unimpressed.

My mother leans in. "If you stay in our house for the weekend, then you follow our rules," she chides.

"I'll go stay at the Dizzy Duck Inn," I counter.

Her frown informs me that she isn't having it. "You can suck it up for an hour or two. Besides, you missed Hadley's eighteenth birthday party." She stresses the word eighteenth.

"And?" It comes out flat. She's the neighbor who has crushed on me for years. Sure, I've noticed that she's no longer a little girl.

Instead, she's easy on the eyes, and I've done my damnedest to block her out of my head when she shows up to any family gathering or party I used to throw at my parents' house.

The lights flicker, indicating that the show is about to start. I lean in to whisper to my mother, "This is my chance to escape."

She grips my arm, preventing me from standing. "No, you won't."

I begin to grumble, but the curtain rises and music starts, an alternative rendition of a song by The Police. My eyes land on the ballerina dancing solo on her pattering toes in her pointy slippers, and my lips twitch when I notice there isn't an ounce of baby pink on her like you would expect. Her shoes are blue satin, and everything else on her tight body is black. Her hair partly up and her eyeliner strong, she's beautiful and mesmerizing as her leg stretches into the air in a long line. My eyes adjust to register that it's Hadley. My breath cuts when I realize my fear has come true.

She's worth looking at, roping me in, and now is entirely legal.

Suddenly, I'm invested in this dance show.

I don't need to glance to my side, and I couldn't tear my eyes away even if I tried. My mother gently clears her throat. "Thought so," she mumbles. I hate how she can read my mind; she walked me into this trap willingly.

Hadley spins in a turn, and when she lands perfectly on her feet, I swear that for a mere second our eyes connect, with the bright stage light sparking in the corner of my eyes.

The light of a match. That's what this is.

Blinking, I bring myself into the present when someone clinks a glass. "All right, everyone, we have a birthday to celebrate and Vegas to conquer. Tequila, anyone?" The whole group erupts in cheers before someone turns up the music full blast.

It doesn't take long for things to spiral from there.

It's when I turn my head that I see, across the room, Hadley is clearly in good spirits, sucking on a slice of lime, and I realize it's near enraging that she can be the life of a party. She's laidback, doesn't try to be anything she isn't, a free spirit, complete with a kind heart—as long as it doesn't involve me. Her presence here isn't because of who's here or that she wants to be associated with a name; she's here because she wants to enjoy life.

Watching her is glorious torture.

Curiosity gets the best of me, and I stand up to walk casually in her direction, partly to annoy her and the other part giving me one hit of enjoyment.

In the process, a random woman touches my arm. "Con, you should totally go in the pool with us," she coos.

I don't even bother giving her a look. "Nah, I didn't come to Vegas to go swimming," I say.

Briggs arrives by my side and throws an arm around my shoulder as he holds a bottle of tequila in his other hand.

The woman tries not to show her disappointment. "Who knows where the night will go, right?" Her blonde hair flicks in front of me as she spins to turn her attention to a friend.

My quest leads me closer to my target. Hadley peers up to meet my eyes with disapproval. "Go away," she groans in warning.

Briggs fills her empty shot glass. "You two better get it together. We haven't even hit the club yet or sung happy birthday. Call it my birthday wish that you two call a truce."

"As the responsible one, he's right, Hadley," I say, sounding condescending.

"Spare me. Oh look, there's a stripper pole in the room. Let me go experiment with my life choices." She begins to walk, but I step in her way.

"Sure, we both know you love to make daddy proud," I say, and I don't know why.

Hadley shakes her head as she bites her bottom lip because she's pissed and probably knows she's drawing my sight straight to her delectable mouth. Briggs awkwardly stands there with his lips quirked out while he freezes and holds the bottle up.

"What planet did you wake up on? Your family's Labrador has more manners than you," she snipes.

"You two are at it again?" Isla intercepts as she arrives and rests her hand on Hadley's shoulder. "I swear, I'm about to lock you two in a closet together."

"Maybe we should give them an ultimatum," Briggs ponders.

Isla throws her arms up. "Or just give them another shot. It will loosen them up eventually."

"I don't know, Hadley is already mentioning a career on the pole," I comment dryly, but the image inside my head is driving me nuts.

Frustrated, Hadley abruptly hands her glass to Briggs. "One more. Obviously, Prince Charming isn't going to arrive, throw me over his shoulder, and save me."

"You shouldn't have come, princess tippy-toes." I hand my glass to Briggs, with my eyes drilling in on Hadley.

In the corner of my eye, Briggs looks at Isla to double-check this is a smooth plan. Isla responds with her eyes gawking, which causes Briggs to hold up the bottle. "You guys only get another shot if you give it to one another. Call it a truce," he informs us with a smirk.

Well played, but fine.

Hadley grumbles.

I take the two filled glasses from Isla. "I'm sure Hadley can follow my lead, she has before."

"That comment just made me not care how the hell I get my shot, as long as you become a blur," she boils.

I grin, satisfied, as I step closer and hold up the glass. Our eyes lock before her lips press against the rim of the glass that I hold, and her fingers wrap around my wrist to keep me steady as I slowly tip back the liquid. The electric shock hits us both. I feel it in my bones, especially as our eyes linger for an extra second. When she swallows, I don't release the glass. I enjoy this connection that doesn't feel alcohol-infused, even though it must be. She doesn't seem to be escaping either, and that's of her own accord. Hot energy shoots down to below my navel because this woman is a curse.

When I finally bring the glass away, she instantly reestablishes contact by bringing my other hand with my shot glass up, and the corner of her mouth tugs, but she won't commit to a smile, not for me.

Our eyes stay pierced as the shot comes to my lips. She stands on her toes as she guides the alcohol to me. The shot comes to my lips, and she slowly eases the liquid into my mouth, and my free arm wraps around her middle to keep her in a firm stance, causing our bodies to press together. We stand in this embrace longer than we should, the music in the background fading away as my attention is on Hadley.

I refuse to believe that anything less substantial is causing me to feel dizzy. My current state is her doing, purely from a spark in her hazel eyes. But whatever the reason, she gets her wish, because the night becomes a blur...

Until the next morning, that is, when I feel my favorite little vixen in bed next to me.

HADLEY

A brick. Why does my head feel like a brick?

My stomach doesn't feel too great either.

My eyes flick open to find my face is half smashed against an admittedly comfortable pillow. This bed is warm, unusually warm for being under the covers, almost as if there is a heater next to me. From behind me, in fact. I begin to stretch out my body, but my foot hits the skin of a leg.

Not my leg.

Rolling over, my eyes widen when I see Connor groggily waking up on the other side of the bed, his eyes already in a blinking frenzy, as he is a few seconds ahead of me.

Oh no.

Instantly, I jab his shoulder, and his response is a low grumble, but he begins to stir awake.

I'm an idiot. Why am I alerting his attention? I should just sneak on out of here and ignore the fact that we…

Wait, what did we do?

"Connor," I shriek in a loud whisper.

"What?" His voice is scratchy against his throat, but something must connect in his head because he jackknifes up to sitting. "Why are you in my bed?" Connor's tone is gruff, with an edge that would be sexy if it wasn't for the detail that it's him speaking.

We look at one another, horrified, then his eyes dip down, which causes my own attention to follow his line of sight.

I'm gripping the duvet around my body, but one glance and it appears I'm naked, proven when I lift the blanket slightly and confirm that I'm only wearing a thong… and he's wearing nothing, which is why I slam the blanket back down into position, because I don't need a reminder of his size even in downtime.

"What the hell did we do?" I begin to panic.

He scratches the back of his head. "I… did we?"

I shrug my shoulders and shriek, "We're both pretty much naked!"

He has the audacity to half-smirk. "Got a glimpse, huh?"

I growl in frustration. "I vaguely remember last night, but I'm missing moments." My eyes scan the room, and I see empty water bottles which causes me to knit my brows together. "Oh, gee, we were responsible and stayed hydrated," I deflate with sarcasm.

"Relax." His hand indicates to stay calm. "You would feel it if you decided to ride my pony again."

Shaking my head, I choose to ignore his ridiculous comment and search for my phone that I hear vibrating. Luckily, it's under my pillow.

I see Isla's name on the screen and pick up, careful to bring the phone to my ear so the devil doesn't hear.

"Hey, Isla," I calmly greet her. "What the hell happened?" My voice does a 180, pitching higher at the end.

My friend laughs. "What do you mean? You're the one not in our room. I was scared I needed to send out a search party. But then I remembered that you left the party with Mr. Nobody's Eyes Shall Ever Land on You But His, so I knew you were safe."

I glance over my shoulder and notice Connor doesn't seem stressed by the fact we're sharing a bed, with no recollection of events.

"I left the party with Connor?" That can't be right.

"You two were doing shots. It seemed to loosen you two up, you were both even laughing about childhood memories at one point, certainly didn't want to kill one another. When Shawn asked if you wanted to do a body shot, Connor threw you over his shoulder, you giggled, and you dared Connor that he wouldn't carry you out to save you. It was kind of cute."

I vaguely remember Connor carrying me out of the party and a dare… but that was when we were in an elevator. Oh no. Nope.

"You let me leave with him? I swear, I may be revoking your friend card," I huff.

"Hey! I called you twenty minutes later, and you said that Connor was taking you to get your tattoo." Strange. I have no new tattoos. "Then you sent me a text later saying not to wait up as you were having an unforgettable night."

I try to remember. "I don't recall any of that."

"Well, I'm assuming that you and him…"

"Don't even say it," I grit out and feel Connor's eyes on me.

"Okay, well, thought I'd check if you want to have breakfast?" Isla asks, and the thought of food just makes me want to heave or it's the presence of the man behind me, I'm not sure.

I roll my eyes, and a long exhale escapes me. I reach for the bottle of water near the bed, and that's when I notice something. It's new, *very* new.

"Uh, you go ahead. I'll come to our room soon." I manage to string a sentence together, end the call, and toss the phone to the side while my sight locks on my finger that's sporting a diamond ring. A gorgeous, albeit new ring.

"Breakfast sounds good, I'm starving," Connor casually mentions as he yawns and stretches his arms over his head like this is a daily occurrence.

My head turns sharply to stare at him full-on, and I hold up my hand. "What the hell is this?"

It catches him off guard, and his jaw goes slack, but only a croaky sound escapes him before he looks down and notices a band on his finger. "Oh, shit."

My stomach drops, and a meltdown is fast approaching. "Tell me we didn't," I plead.

He gives me a sympathetic look. "I can't."

I shove him with my hands and the blanket drops slightly down my breasts before I save myself. "Do you remember last night?"

Connor gives me a funny look as he scratches the back of his head. "Parts."

"Which parts?" I'm furious.

"Not the part where you apparently got your childhood wish." He examines his finger and leans back against the headboard. "The one where I'm your husband."

I groan and quickly slide off the bed, taking the blanket with me, only allowing myself one glance at his impressive package, before giving him a glare. "We did not get married!"

He examines the scene before his eyes discover something, then he leans to the side to grab it from his bedside table. Connor chortles a sound and holds up the paper. "According to this, we are husband and wife." Why is there a hint of a smug shade across his lips?

"No!" I look up to the ceiling.

Connor scrubs a hand across his face. "I'm sure this is not what my uncle had in mind for staying on the straight and narrow."

I could scream, but instead, I head directly for the bathroom and abruptly close the door behind me, ensuring I lock it. Walking straight to the mirror, I rub my face and attempt to calm myself down. I look like a trainwreck, yet I have a glow on my cheeks, and this ring is a blinding accessory that is somewhat flipping perfect on my finger, but no, nuh-uh, I am not Connor's wife!

"What have I done?" I whisper as my thoughts head into a memory from when I was eighteen and why Connor Spears can never be my husband.

Connor grips the steering wheel, internally preparing himself as he pauses before he starts the engine, probably because I'm sitting in the front seat. The air between us feels heightened. For the longest time, I thought the guy was neutral about me, has never given me any indica-

tion we could be anything more or less, except lately. First, when he showed up at my dance show, and then the other week when our families went out to dinner to celebrate being drafted. It was near unbearable because I kept catching that his eyes were on me, and our gaze held while his lips tugged, as though my sight on him is something he enjoys.

And here we are because we were both watching our little brothers play T-ball, and our parents wanted to take the team out for pizza and ice cream after. We love our brothers, but not a group of kids their age. Connor and I just looked at one another, agreeing on our version of hell, and made up excuses for why we couldn't go. A promised attendance at a party for him, and tired for me because I rehearsed for six hours yesterday.

So here's Connor, driving me home.

He is also my answer, and he might have appeared in my fantasies a few times too. Well, a lot. But right now, it isn't just that. Something is causing me to want to orbit around him more than usual.

Connor backs the car up and drives us away. "Come on, let's get you out of here, Sprinkles." He gave me that nickname when I was thirteen, and I hate it as much as I love it.

"Why do you call me that?"

"Because you used to bring me cupcakes when you had a ridiculous crush, and you smelled of icing and cake. Sprinkles seemed fitting."

A smile begins to stretch on my mouth.

"Can I go to the party with you?" I try my luck.

He scoffs and doesn't even bat an eye as he focuses on the road. "Not a chance."

"Why not?" I ask, defensive.

"Because that's the deal we've always had. I've tolerated you because our parents are friends, and I know your dad would want me to keep an eye on you. That means no parties because I can't watch you every second, and you're a distraction to most."

The corner of my mouth tugs that he called me a distraction.

"Am I distraction to you?" I glance to him and notice the twist on the corner of his mouth.

"Yes." He's blunter than I anticipated, but I love his answer.

Silence overwhelms the car since he just admitted that I'm something.

I sigh and rest my head against the headrest. "I need a moment, and I'm not ready to go home. I'll only think about my future there."

He glances sidelong at me for a quick second before returning his focus to the road. It feels as though the mention of my future fueled compassion inside of him. "Come on, I know a place for that."

"Okay." A giddy feeling hits me.

It's a few minutes later when he pulls off onto a side road then up a hill where he parks. It's empty and dark, but I only feel safe around him. We get out, and the engine is off but his car still plays music, and when I follow him to sit on the back of his car where he opened the hatch, a bit of light from the car highlights his face, and the sky is speckled with stars.

"I come here to think of my future all the time." He sighs.

I turn to him, and he mirrors my move. "Do you ever find it exhausting?" I begin. "The whole hockey career thing? Don't you just want to wake up and play without any pressure?"

He seems to study me for a second. "Not often. I've wanted to go pro since I first touched the ice. Why do you ask?"

"There was someone who watched my dance showcase a few weeks ago, and they offered me a spot in their company in New York, even without an audition," I admit.

Connor touches my shoulder gently, and it surprises me, but it's welcomed. "That's great... or isn't it?"

I shake my head. "I don't want to go, it's not for me. Too much pressure, but I don't want to let down my parents. I mean, I know they would support me no matter what, but it's just a thought in my head, you know?"

"I do. My uncle and dad are a constant reminder of what I need to achieve, and they don't even mean to be." He sighs.

"I guess we have something in common then. Being good at something but struggling to fully breathe." I can't stop staring at him.

He twirls the end of my hair around his finger and attempts to focus his eyes on my hair, but they only flick up again.

This is my moment.

"Do you find me attractive?" I ask, and I'm not shy about it.

He scoffs a sound before biting his inner cheek, desperately trying to hide his entertained smirk. "Where is this coming from?"

"Answer me." My tone is short.

He avoids looking at me and instead wraps my strand of hair tighter. "Hadley, you're a beautiful girl. You don't need me to tell you that."

I smile to myself with satisfaction and confidence before I interlace our hands on the floor of the trunk, catching him off guard, but he doesn't pull away. "I thought so. Do you want to kiss me?"

"I'm not answering that." There is a hint of a grin on his mouth. "What is this about?"

"I'm no longer a kid," I remind him.

"I've noticed."

"Help me," I rasp, barely a whisper.

His eyes linger on our joined hands. "With what?" he asks softly. Maybe I make him nervous or maybe his brain is already connecting the dots.

"Kiss me because I'm too scared to." My bold declaration surprises even me.

Connor's sight rockets back up to mine, and he tilts his head slightly to the side, the light highlighting his concerned face. "You don't seem scared now."

"Kiss me," I repeat my request.

His eyes sideline, only to return to me with heat in his gaze. "Hadley, I've done a hell of a job avoiding you lately because the ideas in my head don't make me a gentleman, and here you are throwing it all at me. I won't be the guy to walk away noble, I'm too selfish."

"And?" I'm not concerned.

He debates for a few seconds, clearly having an internal struggle. "I've tried to warn you. Fuck it," he seems to curse to himself right before his lips slam onto mine.

His kiss is an explosion of my heart. A command that he leads. So damn firm and better than all of my dreams combined.

I've kissed guys before, but nothing like this. My whole body is alive, and his tongue swipes into my mouth with clear direction, causing me to melt. Then it only gets better when it turns fervent. We don't pull away nor stop.

It escalates until we're lying down in the back of his car. His hand finds my leg, and I feel it in my bones that we won't stop. I pause for a second, and his head jolts back to attempt to read my face.

"Just go slow." My eyes gently gawk at him to ensure he understands that I want more.

But his head gently tilts when a realization hits him. "You're..."

"Don't be surprised."

"Fuck," he groans before swiping a hand through his hair. "I'm the last person you should be with now. My moral standing to take you right home is non-existent." He begins to create space between us, but I grab his wrist.

"You're not other guys... you're..." It trails off, and I lean in closer to him to run my hand along his arm. "Or would you rather I find some other guy?" I challenge, and instantly I see a sort of possessiveness roar in his eyes.

"Hadley," he warns. "Don't do that either. It should be with someone who cares."

I bring his hand that I'm holding by the wrist and plant it on my bare thigh just below the hem of my skirt. "Like you. You care." His eyes turn tense, and his jaw tightens, but he doesn't remove his hand. "Connor, I want it to be you," I whisper my insistence.

"Don't throw this offer at me, Sprinkles." His voice has an edge to it.

I lean in to close our distance, and it can't be my imagination that I feel his pulse quickening. "Why? Because it's enticing?" I husk then brush my lips along his jawline.

"You're not just some hookup," he whispers as he brings the fingers on his other hand to splay against my throat to hold me in place. His gesture is demanding yet soft.

"How so?"

Connor lifts the corner of his mouth as the fingers on my thigh begin to swivel a lazy design on my leg, as if he is contemplating a few ideas, and my whole body tingles while his lips remain nearly touching my own. "Don't make me say it." His voice sounds desperate.

The last few minutes have proven that my attraction is not one-sided. We've grown up with one another, at a distance yet so close too. And it seems we both want the same thing.

"Fuck me, I shouldn't be doing this here with you. You deserve more." He seems to be talking to himself.

He grabs the blanket from the side, and I have a wary look.

It causes him to laugh. "Relax, it's in here because I went with some friends to the beach." Ah, so not for another conquest, except he just highlighted that I'm not just anyone. Nerves hit me, but I feel comfortable and ready.

He lies on his side while I'm on my back. "Have you really thought about me like this?" I hear vulnerability in my voice.

A smirk forms on his mouth, but it's an earnest and natural look. "I have. Too many times to count."

I try to control my smile, and we take a few seconds of staring at one another, soaking in our realization that after years of knowing one another, here we are together in a different manner. My fingers begin to work at my clothes, but he stops me.

"You're going to have to tell me if I'm not gentle enough or I need to slow down. Don't lie to me. You understand?" He's insistent.

I nod once, and he does something that surprises me; he kisses my cheek so tenderly, like the time he walked me home once. Then he peels off his hoodie and shirt, placing his balled-up clothes near my head before digging into his wallet for a condom. He helps slide my panties off while I peel off my sweater, and I lie back across the seats.

His lips are already trailing my body, heading lower to my most intimate spot. I shiver from the thought of what he is about to do.

"I know this is only a favor." My breath shakes as I try to reassure him as he hovers over me, but I'm desperately wishing for more.

Connor glances up before he returns to a higher destination, where he hooks his finger under my chin to guide my eyes to meet his. "It's a little more than that. A lot more than that." He dips his head down to capture my lips again. "You're giving me something, and I will never let you forget it. You're not just anyone. You were always going to be more than something to me."

His words make my heart soar. I've been hoping for the moment we would confess our feelings, and now it's a reality.

Shaking my head and throwing water on my face, I do my best to forget the way he kept his promise to go gentle and slow. Urged me to look at him and claw his back when pain hit, and his answer was to distract me by kissing me deeper, to the point that I felt he had control of my breath and body. After, he ditched his party and opted to lie with me for what felt like ages. He covered me with his hoodie, stroking my hair with his fingers as he laid on his side, reminding me that I was okay, before we reminisced about many things growing up as next-door neighbors and our future careers. We unleashed a promising start with one another.

Connor told me that we should see one another again. His parents had a relationship when we were that age, and it made him believe we could have been possible. He showered me with kisses every chance he got. It felt like I was on top of the world.

But then the next morning, he appeared in my room completely different, eager to find his hoodie, and he made his thoughts clear.

"We were a mistake.

Forget last night ever happened, we will never be anything."

It's been vile hatred since then.

Patting my cheek, I blow out a breath and throw on a hotel robe. Bracing myself, I know I need to face the man in the other room.

Opening the door, I'm surprised to find Connor sitting up against the headboard with only boxer briefs on and perusing a room service menu.

Great, he wants to have the marriage talk shirtless, just freaking awesome.

"Hey there, Wifey." He smirks as he pats the spot next to him on the bed, inviting me to join him.

I cross my arms, determined not to move an inch. "I am not your wife."

He hums a sound. "Our marriage certificate and rings say otherwise, so…" It drags, and his chipper tone has me concerned.

"We'll get it annulled."

"Can we, though, considering we might have consumed our blessed union?" He's taunting me.

Why is he sitting there cool as a cucumber?

"We didn't." I would have felt it. He isn't easily forgettable, even when alcohol is involved. "Besides, we can file for a divorce," I counter.

He slides off the mattress, making a skeptical noise. I gulp when I watch him slowly take a few strides in my direction, and my sanity checks out for a second as I drink in the view of his muscles and chest. "We shall do no such thing, Sprinkles," he states.

Reality hits me again when he calls me a name I haven't heard in years, and it throws me off. "W-what?" I stammer.

Connor brings his fingers to my hair and gently tucks a few strands behind my ear, as if he is a sensitive creature, but before I can enjoy any cozy feelings from his touch, I blow away his finger.

"The thing is, I need to keep it positive in the media for a while, and I know you don't want to break dear old mom and dad's hearts by informing them that you became a Vegas cliché. Not to mention, the parents of those little gremlins you teach have a lot of opinions. Since we know what this is, then I think it's best that we…" I'm already shaking my head, and my hands form fists from aggravation. I can't muster any words. "Stay married for a while," he confirms my suspicion.

"Why would I want that misery?" I snicker, with our eyes in a standoff.

"We won't even manage to end this marriage fast enough before our parents find out. Let's not break their hearts until we mentally prepare them that our marriage was doomed from the start," he explains.

I growl because he may have a point. Plus, I'm in no clear mind right now to find a divorce lawyer. Or see the look on my father's face, probably filled with disappointment that I went away and came back in need of a divorce.

"It's the off-season, I'm sure you can fake it for the summer."

I laugh to myself that this is my life, but then I remember what this guy did to me. "You're right." I fake a sweet smile. "Being your wife sounds like a real delight. I can make your life dismal all in the name of marriage." I pat his hard chest with satisfaction at the new plan forming in my head, all because the idea of destroying him feels like a relief, and the opportunity is here.

He sneers. "I can't wait to see you try. How about you save it for after our news hits Lake Spark that you're the new Mrs. Connor Spears, okay?"

"Whatever you say, dear husband." A contrite smile hits my lips because he will not get the upper hand.

He'll see.

5

CONNOR

Sliding into the backseat of the limo that's taking us to the private airport, I notice instantly that Isla and Hadley are deep in discussion that abruptly stops when I arrive. My inkling is that I was the main topic, but married or not, I'm confident Hadley talks about me and how to use a pitchfork on a regular basis. Since they are facing me, I get a prime view of my wife. It's the first time I'm seeing my dear wife since she left my room to go change and grab her bag.

"There you are, it's been unbearable the last hour without you. Forgot how much you love backseats." A cheeky look is planted on my face, and I offer it to Hadley while Briggs slides in next to me.

"Save it," she mutters to me with a shade of disdain for my reference.

Isla looks back and forth between us. "She wasn't joking, was she?" Isla asks me, deeply concerned.

Briggs slides a glance at me. "About what?"

Isla chortles. "Haven't you heard the news? These two got hitched." She points between us.

"Funny." He doesn't believe her.

The car begins to move, and I lean forward to gently touch

Hadley's knee because I can. "Go on, we're amongst friends, they can share our joy."

The glint in Hadley's eyes is pure venom, and I love it.

Did I mean to become someone's husband? No.

Do I hate that it's Hadley? Well, no.

My rule has always been to keep her at a distance for reasons that I don't care to think about today. So be it, fate threw us a wild card by making us husband and wife. I'm going to soak in these accidental nuptials that mean I get to have her close. I might as well. Call it selfish. My reasons to keep her away are still valid, but maybe I should have always kept her close with a difficult escape, à la marriage.

Hadley takes a deep breath. "Connor and I are husband and wife. Our night was unforgettable… *clearly*." Hmm, I could do with a little more enthusiasm in her tone, but we'll work on it.

"No shit." Briggs looks at me in awe. "That's what you two got up to?"

"What can I say? Sprinkles here always had her heart set on me, and I caved." I sit back with ease and satisfaction.

"But you two wanted to kill one another yesterday, so is this like… what is this exactly?" He's confused, as he should be.

Hadley crosses her arms and keeps her sight fixed on me. "Please, Con, do tell us the romantic tale of how I became your wife. It better be good, since you seemed to woo me in the span of only a few hours."

"Alcohol," Isla deadpans an answer.

I cluck the inside of my cheek with my tongue and point to Isla before I spew out a story. "Cute. But I'm positive it was Sprinkles here reliving the time I was forced to walk her home after my uncle ended my impromptu party. I was sixteen. I kissed her cheek when I said good night, to make her dreams come true, and told her she smelled of cupcakes with sprinkles, the kind she would bring me when she baked."

"You never said that," Hadley interjects with surprise in her tone.

"I was thinking it," I explain. "Anyway, since then she vowed that I would be her husband, and last night, somewhere between her attempt to give me a lap dance and her request to search for cupcakes with sprinkles, I gave in. I mean, what's better than having a wife who can bend and smells of cupcakes, am I right?"

Briggs scoffs a laugh. "You better come up with a better story when your parents find out."

"I would kill to have a front-row seat at that family dinner." Isla nudges Hadley's arm.

"But seriously, you two are going to end this thing, right?" Briggs hands me a bottle of water.

"Nope," I state proudly.

Hadley throws him a sweet overdone smile. "I'm moving into Connor's house that he bought a while back. It's the off-season, so I'm sure I can keep him occupied and make him feel so incredibly lucky to be my husband that it may feel like irritation, so much so that he will be begging to leave our happy house."

I grin at her humor. Two can play our game, and I'm ready.

"*Right*, I guess we need to… celebrate?" Briggs isn't sure.

"Yeah, we should get a few photos for the happy day. I guess you don't have any wedding photos?" Isla's voice raises an octave.

I reach for my cell phone in my pocket. "Funny you should mention that. I was scrolling through my phone, piecing together what happened last night—I have the receipt for the ring, by the way. Tiffany's in the hotel, not bad taste if I may say. Anyhow, I came across this gem of a photo." I unlock my screen, swipe, and show Hadley and Isla my phone.

Hadley's eyes bug out as she examines the evidence from our night. We are in a Vegas chapel, and if it weren't for the fact that our eyes are clearly in a haze of alcohol, then it would be kind of believable. Because I'm looking down at her with affection while she peers up with admiration and an arm wrapped around my neck, with cheap plastic flowers in her hand.

"Oh boy," Isla mumbles.

My wife's breath catches as I take the phone back, and the fact that I'm calling her my wife hits me for a second. *What the hell am I doing?* This woman annoys me, and she can never know the things in my head, but I guess I'm making her villain fantasy come true, because I'm tying her into marriage with me… and that just fuels my pleasure from this situation.

Arriving at the airfield, we park on the tarmac near the plane.

"I'll ask the staff for champagne," Isla offers and still seems uneasy about this situation as she gives me a death glare mixed with a smile. As she should, she's Hadley's best friend.

"We'll go first then let you two love birds make a grand entrance," Briggs suggests as the car door opens.

"Sure, make sure Shawn gets a front-row seat," I call out as Hadley and I continue to give one another an icy stare.

"Real mature," she mumbles.

"You bring out the best in me." I slide out and offer her my hand. "Come on, Wife, don't smile too hard. I would hate for your cheeks to strain; they're important for certain activities."

Yanking her up out of the car, she squeezes my hand. "Gag. Your dick is not going near my mouth. In fact, we didn't even establish rules for that aspect of our blessed union."

"There are none. Let's just put on a good show, and consider it practice for our family."

Hadley rumbles another sound because she knows I'm right and begins to step in front of me up the stairs. My head tilts slightly to check out her ass because it's worth a look, and I'm going to reap all my husbandly perks.

Up the stairs I go, and I come to stand by my wife who looks at everyone. Our moment of opportunity is here. I slide my arm around her middle, gently squeezing her ass in the process which causes her to yelp softly. I bring her close to me with a bright smile glued on my face.

"Is the champagne out, boys?" I ask the plane.

"What are we celebrating?" Shawn asks as he holds up an empty flute, waiting for an attendant to fill his glass.

I lean down to kiss the top of my wife's head because we have a part to play, and it may be years later, but fuck it,

Hadley still smells like cupcakes. "You tell them," I encourage her.

She giggles awkwardly to herself before loosening her tight smile a smidgen. "We got married last night… I'm Mrs. Connor Spears." Hadley shows her ring finger, and everyone goes silent for a few seconds, until cheers erupt, and the sound of a cork follows after.

My hockey crowd may be easy, but Hadley and I can agree on one thing; our families will be, by no means, a breeze.

———

It was a quick flight back to Lake Spark. Sure, people had questions, but Hadley and I stayed firm that we were married, with no plans to write this down as a drunk mistake. We had feelings bubbling over after years watching one another grow up. It may be a fairytale we spew, but there is some half-truth to it. I also know that we are running out of time before our news goes public, which is why I drove us straight to my Aunt Violet's floral shop, The Flower Jar.

I'm close with my aunt Violet; she was only eleven when I was born, and the age difference makes her more like a friend.

Hadley is grabbing some items from the general store or Jolly Joe's, the bakery nearby, that she mentioned were essential for dinner, and we agreed to meet back here. Walking into The Flower Jar, the bell instantly announces my arrival.

"Connor!" My aunt Violet is quick to greet me with a hug. Her dark hair is down today, and she never looks like a woman who only got two hours of sleep due to having a kid; she's a natural beauty.

I notice my uncle near the parrot's cage, holding my three-year-old cousin Willow, my goddaughter. He steps closer to us, and I feel like his face is stoic because he already knows. "Hey, Connor." He doesn't blink, which raises caution in me. I was hoping to speak with Aunt Violet alone, since she's my sounding board.

"Hey," is all I can offer him, and it's awkward, can't deny that.

"How was your trip?" my aunt asks as she signs off on an order form and hands it to the assistant.

"Yes. Do tell." Crap. My Uncle Declan for sure knows. I can tell he is waiting for me to spill the beans.

I scratch the back of my neck. "It was… Vegas."

My aunt looks at her husband, as she seems thrown off by my answer. Her eyes swim back to me. "And? You had a big group going, right?" She tries to keep the conversation moving.

I swipe my hand across my jaw. "Something kind of happened."

My aunt grabs my wrist when she notices something, then examines my finger. "What the hell is this?"

"I kind of wanted to see you first before my parents find out," I begin. "I'm going to

need a lot of sunflowers." That's my flower of choice that I give my mom when I want to butter her up, and it works. Every. Single. Time.

She shakes my hand. "Why do you have a wedding ring on?"

I take a deep breath. "I kind of… got married."

Her jaw drops open as she releases my wrist like a hot potato. "You don't have a girlfriend. You have flings. Now you're telling me that you went to Vegas and got married?"

I can't answer. Instead, I notice that she quickly glances to my cousin, reminding us all that we need to keep our words appropriate. My cousin's three-year-old brain is like a little sponge, it's crazy.

"What the duck, Connor!"

"Duck it," the parrot volleys.

Nope. Still not sure what to say.

"And who might the lucky bride be?" my uncle asks, even though I can tell he is already brushed up on the info.

I take a deep inhale. "Hadley."

"What the duck!" my aunt repeats her earlier sentiment.

Uncle Declan, or Declan in this situation because I know he is in business mode, puts my cousin down then walks to me and places his hands on my shoulders. Shit, he is in super-serious mode.

"The team publicist called me just now. You have exactly three hours before this hits the media." He waves his long finger at me. "You tell your parents. *Now*."

"I am. Hence the need for a bouquet of flowers." I raise a brow at him.

"You're going to need the entire bucket of sunflowers. A bouquet isn't going to cut it." My aunt sounds panicked.

I flash her a grin. "You're right. I need a bouquet for my new mother-in-law too, so whatever April likes."

Declan blows out a breath. "What happened?"

I shrug out of his hold. "Don't worry. We're staying married, at least for the off-season. I'm sure this will be positive press."

Declan pauses for a second and seems to be thinking. "You're right. We can work this angle to our advantage. Maybe you two can have a photoshoot, make this somewhat believable. But you're right. Baseball royalty marries hockey royalty, throw in the Spinners a few times in the interview, and it could be good. You're settling down." He's trying to convince himself it's a grand idea, but really, that's the angle I was going for.

"See? The bachelor settles down." I grimace and turn all my attention to my aunt, because Declan can stew in his plans without me. "So, about those flowers. Let's just go all out, shall we?"

She points the stem of a sunflower at me. "Your dad and mom are going to lose it."

My lips quirk out as I think about it. "No, they won't. Or at least they'll get over it fast. They love Hadley, they've been shipping us for years. It's their dream come true."

She shakes her head at me. "No, not like this. They will be heart-broken that they missed your wedding, didn't get to do all of that traditional stuff." She growls to herself. "Duck it, Violet, do not speak like this is a real marriage." Scolding herself seems to bring her into a more focused mode. "Connor, don't be stupid. I don't know what you and Hadley are playing at, but don't break her heart."

"Trust me. It's cold as can be for me," I promise.

"Then how are you going to explain this to your parents? They won't be on board with a fake marriage," she adds softly.

I sigh. "You're right. That's why Hadley and I are kind of going all in on this. We have a story, can fake it for a few hours in their presence, so I'm going to need those flowers."

She turns sharply to her husband. "Do something," she instructs.

Declan raises his hands in surrender. "No can do. The last thing I want is a quickie wedding and divorce in the press for my star player. Besides..." He snorts a laugh. "These two kids will come to realize they have a good thing underneath those angsty jabs."

"I mean…" My aunt's face softens. "You have a point." Her eyes whip back in my direction. "Fine. I'll go along with this, but I mean it… don't break her heart," she warns again.

A little late for that. I already did long ago.

I swallow. "Sure."

My aunt begins to grab flowers. "Okay, so most expensive flowers, no family discount—"

"Whoa, why no family discount?" I protest.

She raises her brows at me. "You're in the doghouse. Now let's just get these flowers to impress gathered."

The bell to the shop rings, and I turn to see my wife walk in with a bag from the general store.

"I got supplies," Hadley announces.

"I'm getting the flowers," I explain.

Hadley gives me a glare. "At least one of us is smart. Flowers won't be enough." She turns to my aunt. "No offense, we need bigger guns." Her attention returns to me. "I got wine for the moms. Open it as soon as we arrive."

"Genius." I snap my fingers.

My aunt walks around her table and straight to Hadley to give her a hug. "Mazel tov. Welcome to the family." I shake my head since my family doesn't have a single Jewish relative.

Hadley nervously laughs once as she accepts the hug. "Thanks."

My aunt steps back and looks affectionately at Hadley. "I should have known if my nephew ever decided to elope that it would be with you, only you." Now she's just being dramatic.

"Uh," Hadley's voice cracks. "Okay."

Checking my watch, I know we have to get moving. The clock is rolling. "Flowers, Aunt Vi, please. Our parents were having dinner together anyway, so they will be blindsided when we show up together, and we have to knock this off the list."

"Wine, flowers, and a damn good story is what you two need," my uncle says with a cheeky grin. "Good luck walking into the lions' den."

———

We stand outside Hadley's home, since it's her parents hosting tonight's dinner. She's fanning a hand in her face to calm herself down while a bottle of wine hangs from her other hand. I'm holding an armful of flowers.

"Ugh, this is not the conversation to be having while hungover. Or am I still slightly drunk? I don't know, but here we are." Hadley groans again.

I scrub a hand across my face. "This day is almost done."

"Just, we ease them into this. When you pour the second glass of wine, then we break the news. Just keep topping up their glasses," she explains.

I have to laugh. "Our moms are easy. Remember your sweet sixteenth?"

She looks at me, and after a second, a smile cracks. "God, they were tipsy on cosmos, then did karaoke. It was so embarrassing."

"But they really belted out Taylor Swift to perfection," I add.

We take a moment to look at one another. Maybe it's the first time today that we really sink into the fact that we are husband and wife. For a second, I could swear her smile is for me or the fact that we share memories.

Hadley clears her throat. "Okay, in we go. I'll pack a bag to take to your house between dinner and dessert or something."

I whistle a breath. "I love the confidence that we'll make it to dessert."

She nods in acknowledgment before opening the door. Right

away we hear our moms in the kitchen area. We slowly make our way to the kitchen where our moms are busy with a glass of wine in hand and nibbling on the cheese board.

Immediately, their eyes light up when they see us.

"Oh, you arrived… together." My mother's eyebrows knit close, but her smile remains bright as she comes to hug me, and I hand her the sunflowers. "And with flowers too."

"Of course," I state simply before walking to April to hand her pink dahlias.

April looks at me, skeptical. "Oh, thanks." Her eyes dart to my mother. "Why is your son handing me flowers? Connor and flowers are never a good sign."

My mother shrugs. "I don't know. Mysterious."

"For hosting dinner. Oh, wow, look at that melted brie," Hadley says in an attempt to divert their attention.

"We brought wine," I announce, and Hadley is quick to showcase the bottle in her hand right before she reaches for their glasses to fill, because we came prepared with a twist-top bottle and don't care about mixing wine at this point.

My mom plants a hand on her hip then walks to April to stand next to her. They both focus on Hadley and me.

"They're up to something," April states and studies the scene.

Hadley laughs nervously as she hands back their glasses. "Don't be silly. Just a normal night."

"What's going on?" My mother gladly takes the wine, and her smile doesn't fade.

Hadley arrives at my side and nudges my shoulder. "Abort plan, just spit it out," she mumbles.

I bring my hand to rest on her lower back to ease her concern. "Okay."

"You both were in Vegas, right? How was it?" April asks as she takes a sip from her glass.

"About that…" I wrap an arm around Hadley's shoulder for a side hug. "We have some news…"

6

HADLEY

y heart is pounding so loud. This feels more profound than waking up hitched to the guy next to me.

Why did Connor have to start by saying we have some news?

His mother's hands fly to her mouth before she takes a moment to gather her thoughts. "It's okay, we're here for you both. Your father and I, we were in your very shoes, and we were even younger."

I glance to Connor, confused, and then a lightbulb goes off in his head. "We're not pregnant," he clarifies.

His mom takes hold of the counter and sighs in relief. "Phew. It's not that."

"Why does your mind even go there? They're not together!" my mom squeaks at her friend.

Connor's mom, Brielle, chortles then smiles warmly. "Come on, they've had a thing for one another. It's not out of reach." I hate that everyone thinks we have a *thing*. "I mean, just the other day, I caught my son staring at her dancing in her studio."

My eyes snap to Connor because I realize that he is my mystery watcher. He avoids my gaze, but it doesn't matter. Something inside of me spurs warmth. I'm not surprised it's him. I should have known, and I'm not sure why.

"Okay, so maybe it wouldn't be so bad these two together. Kind of cute. The whole neighbor thing. I mean, I'm positive they kissed or something when they were younger. Caught him sneaking out of her room." My mom crosses her arms and seems to be relaxing.

"Mom!" I shriek. I had no idea that she knew about that, it was when he told me we were a mistake. Oh my God, she's a freaking detective when it comes to me. Dear Lord, I hope she hasn't pieced together that I lost my V-card to Connor. "You knew?"

"Whoa, knew what?" Brielle asks.

"Oh boy, we're going into the vault of memories," Connor reflects almost fondly while he scratches the back of his neck.

My mom waves us off. "Nothing. I know nothing. Or at least, I've never and will never mention it to Spencer. *So,* what is the news, you two?"

Connor and I look at one another, and I give him a nod to just rip this band-aid off.

"Perhaps we gather the dads?" he suggests, and even I hear the nerves in his voice.

"For what?" My father's voice startles me, and I turn to see him arrive at the kitchen island with a beer bottle in hand. His eyes land on Connor, and I can see he isn't thrilled that he's touching me.

"What's going on?" Ford arrives by his side with a smile.

I feel the warmth of a hand entwine with mine, and I peer down to see Connor's and my hands together. I attempt to ignore that it's an image that looks right, and instead take a deep breath to give me courage.

But before I get a chance to announce our news, my husband does something incredibly stupid.

"Aren't you going to welcome me to the family, *Dad?*" He directs his question to my father as he holds up my hand with a shiny diamond ring on it.

The gasps in the room come from the moms, while Ford freezes, and my dad? Shit. Spencer Crews is a man who was a star pitcher and handled pressure well. Curveballs were his expertise. This curveball? Not so much.

I've never seen him so angry in my life. His jaw ticks, his fist clenches. That beer bottle he was enjoying? Slammed down onto the counter.

"Why is my daughter wearing a wedding ring?" he grits out.

I speak before Connor can. "Because we eloped. Last night. In Vegas."

The room goes deathly silent, and my heart may just break from the look on my father's face. I can't read him. I hate that uncertainty. Disappointment is the last thing that I would ever want from him. It's why I agreed to stay married, as I thought a quick annulment would be worse, and I may have also stayed married for a little revenge, but mostly not to break my father's heart.

"We decided that we didn't want to be apart. We cemented our feelings," Connor explains and pulls me into a tight side hug.

"Are you kidding me right now?" Ford gives his son a hardened look. "What in the world would make you think that every parent in this room wouldn't want to be given a clue that you two were getting hitched?"

"Because then I would have stopped it." My dad glares at my husband.

"Maybe we should take a breather, have some wine," Brielle says. "I mean, Ford, we eloped… plus, everyone… we are all family now," she points out, attempting to bring some light to this conversation. She flashes me a reassuring smile. I guess she's on our team. Then again, she doesn't get mad about anything.

My mom steps forward. "I just don't get it. I mean, your whole life you've talked about how you want a big wedding, fancy dress, cupcakes, and flowers. Vegas, it isn't you."

I step out of Connor's hold, because somewhere inside of me I'm cracking. That *is* my dream wedding. Nothing about this situation is something I fantasized about. I don't even remember my wedding. I glance over my shoulder to Connor who has a shade of guilt in his eyes.

Licking my lips, I do my best to carry this situation forward. "We didn't want to wait. But we can still have a big wedding later."

"I didn't even get to throw you a bridal shower! You know, with cookies, tea, and lingerie," my mom cries.

The dads in the room groan. "Do not put lingerie, bridal showers, and Connor into the same scenario when it involves our daughter," my father implores my mom.

She shrugs, then the corner of her mouth hitches up. "At least she married her prince. She's dreamt of him since she was six."

Shaking my head, I don't need the reminder that I was a naïve girl with a silly crush.

"We're relatives." Brielle nudges my mom's shoulder before my mom wraps an arm around her for a hug.

"No warm feelings right now." My dad seems stressed. "I warned you that your hockey-playing son should stay away from my little girl," he seethes to his friend.

Ford rolls his eyes. "Yeah, when they were teenagers! They are legal adults now who drink and know how to sign their name on a marriage certificate. We need to focus on the now. They're married."

"Yeah, and your son didn't have the respect to speak to me before he made my daughter his bride!" My father is furious.

"I would have. It's just… passion and love caught us in a moment," Connor explains.

My dad rubs his temples. "Do. Not. Speak of passion and my daughter to me. If it weren't for the fact that you are Ford's son, then I swear I would kill you right now."

"That's a little harsh. I'm great son-in-law material." Connor doesn't seem fazed by my dad, and inside of me I want to laugh, because that's just Connor, always wanting a good time. And in this moment, as dreadful as it is, he's a beacon of humor that we all need.

"Let's calm down." Ford gestures his hands out to my dad and Connor, who look like they are ready to square off.

In that moment, my brother Ashton, along with Connor's brothers Wyatt and Alex, walk into the house from out back, where they must have been playing basketball.

"Mom, I'm hungry. Is dinner ready?" My brother walks to me to give me a hug—we're a hugging family.

"Uh, in a little bit, kiddo," my mom says uneasily.

"Why is everyone looking at Connor? What did he do now?" Wyatt asks as he grabs crackers from the counter.

Alex is only seven and shy when adults are around, so he only gives Connor a hug then runs to his mom.

"I think all the kids under the age of eighteen need to go to the other room. Go play on the game console or something," Ford suggests.

Wyatt snorts a laugh. "You never let us game around dinner time. What's with the ring?" he asks, indicating with his head to Connor's hand.

My brother Ashton looks at me, and his eyes pop down to my hand that I attempt to cover. "You have one too."

Wyatt begins to laugh. "No way, you two. Classic."

My brother tucks his fist and brings it to his chest. "Yes! The downfall of the princess. Finally, Hadley does something to upset the parents."

I look at him, a little surprised that's how he views me, but then roll a shoulder as well. Daddy's princess isn't just a phrase.

"Boys. Out. Now," Ford repeats himself.

Our brothers stumble out of the room, which doesn't do much for breaking the tension in the air.

Connor wraps his arm around me from the side again, and my body seems to be growing accustomed to this. I might even find it comforting. *Oh no.*

"If you want to end this marriage then say the word, blink, give me a secret code, I don't know, anything, and I'll have my lawyers on it so fast," my father offers.

My mom walks to him and places her hand lovingly on his shoulder. "Stop it. Relax and accept this is what it is, and we are here to support them."

"She's too young to be married." His eyes seem sad as he connects his gaze with my mom.

My mom touches his cheek. "But old enough to make decisions for herself."

Ugh, there is a breach in my heart. I should just scream that I'm making a stupid mistake, but when I catch Connor in my side view, with remorse and tenderness on his face, then I pause because the words can't escape me, and I can't even question why.

"Don't worry, I'll take care of her. It's all I will do." Connor doesn't sound like he's acting; why doesn't he sound less convincing?

My father's eyes catch with Connor's, and the room goes eerily quiet.

"You. Me. You best believe that we're talking one on one this week." My father's voice is full of an edginess I've never heard before. It's only when his gaze transfers to me that his face grows delicate. "If he doesn't make you happy then I'll kill him," he announces before he storms out of the room.

I open my mouth to call out something, but my mom indicates for me to stay quiet. "Give him a little space. A day. Maybe three. I don't know, eternity seems a stretch. Just give him a little breathing room to digest this news."

"News that I'm still undecided about." Ford stretches with his hands behind his head. "I mean, love to have you in the family, Hadley. I knew you two little rascals' constant jabbing was a sign of something. It's just... wow." He breathes out and swipes a hand through his hair. "This came out of nowhere. Marriage is big. My son and I will be having a talk about responsibilities very soon."

"A lot of talks. Thrilling," Connor mumbles.

Brielle brings her hands together. "I think we can declare dinner... postponed." She grabs the entire bottle of wine. "We'll reschedule for a day when hunting my son doesn't seem to be on the agenda."

"I second that. Oh my, I guess this means you're going to live with your husband." My mom looks at me blankly then seems to shake it off. "Now I need to figure out a wedding gift." My mom deflates and sits on a chair at the kitchen island. She then enthusiastically waves to Brielle. "We should book them the honeymoon suite at the Dizzy Duck in town."

"I love that idea!" Brielle grins.

I lean gently into Connor's space. "If they mention consummating the marriage, run," I mumble under my breath.

"No shit," he responds, with his face concerned as he stares at our moms' excitement.

"I think you both should head out and enjoy your wedding week… Gosh, I did not just say that." Ford blows out a breath.

I turn to face Connor, and he must see my exhaustion and somber mood. I've just experienced whiplash several times over. He does something that surprises me; he leans in to kiss my forehead. Softly, sweetly, and I don't feel a shade of falseness.

"Come on, Sprinkles," he whispers and takes my hand.

I do my best to suppress the light feeling I feel when our palms touch.

———

LUCKILY, I followed Connor in my car, so we were saved from awkward conversation. Connor has a house in a subdivision in the hills, overlooking the lake, heavily wooded but with barely any neighbors. Mostly, it's sports guys who train here or vacation homes that are only filled in peak summer season. By no means are these houses cookie cutter; they all sell for a solid seven figures.

I've been here once when he had a party, and Isla dragged me along. It's a modern place, which I know his mom had a hand in decorating.

It doesn't matter. I can barely see straight from exhaustion.

Arriving at the front door, Connor looks at me, and his lips twitch right before he steps forward and is quick to throw me over the shoulder before I can protest. "Carrying the bride over the threshold, right?"

I can't help but let a giggle escape. My traitorous body seems to enjoy his effort, even if it is to tease me. "Put me down," I tell him. I don't think I mean it, but I can't let him know my enjoyment from this.

He twirls me around before setting me at the bottom of the stairs. "Welcome home."

"Home," I scoff before I walk straight up the stairs with Connor in tow.

"The guest room doesn't have any sheets on the bed," he states.

I turn at the top of the stairs to face him, stopping him from taking the final step as my body acts as a gate to the upstairs hall. "Where are the sheets?" I sound only slightly agitated.

"Hell if I know. The housekeeper that comes once a week takes care of that stuff." Of course, he wouldn't be capable of living independently. His whole life he's been doted on by his mother and most women within a fifty-mile radius.

I huff out a breath, and I'm past the point of caring. I march down the hall directly to his room, and yeah, I know it's his room because my radar just sends me on roads that lead to Connor Spears.

Ignoring him, I slide up my dress and swing it to the side where it lands on the floor. I walk straight to the dresser, taking my bra off in the process before I open the drawer, not afraid about what I might find, grab one of his t-shirts, and throw it on.

He doesn't say anything, just watches me from where he stands in the doorway, enthralled, even though I ensured that he could only see my back in the process.

I flop onto the soft bed, landing on my stomach, already feeling like heaven hit my head. "I just don't care anymore. I've slept two hours in a forty-eight-hour period, got married by mistake, broke my father's heart, and have you as my husband. I'm tired and want to sleep. It's a dire situation that I'm sleeping in your bed, even though make no mistake, I'm not a puck bunny that you bring home, so burn this damn mattress tomorrow."

He snickers, and I get a glimpse of him peeling his shirt up and over his head as he walks toward the bed. "It's a new mattress, Sprinkles. Get a new one every year due to wear n' tear."

I may be drowsy on tiredness but even I hear the humor in his tone.

"Good. A new mattress is one less thing we need to worry about." I begin to close my eyes on the indulgent pillow that my cheek rests against.

His chuckle is low and in the back of his throat as I feel his body cause the mattress to dip. "Sharing a bed was in your plan. That's good. I wouldn't have it any other way."

He places his phone to the side, and I vaguely hear him mention he got an email about a photoshoot tomorrow, but my eyes give out and sleep takes over, as I lie in Connor Spears's bed, my doting husband.

7

HADLEY

I sit in the booth at Jolly Joe's, the old soda shop in town that decided jellybeans in coffee for luck and surprise would be what people remember about the hotspot. Well, that, and the amazing ice cream, cinnamon buns, and every carb imaginable.

Overlooking Main Street, I lean my head against the window while I hold my mug of coffee. Admittedly, I sneaked out before Connor woke. I may have crooked my head a few times to study the way he sleeps on his stomach, yet his muscles still stayed flexed with pure shoulder perfection. He smirks in his sleep too; must have been imaging ways to kill me, except I now know his secret.

"Earth to Hadley." A voice breaks my thought. Looking up, I see Isla waving a hand in front of me. "Shouldn't you be cooking a warm breakfast for your *husband* who you are currently dreaming about?" she says, enjoying teasing me.

I roll my eyes and take a sip of coffee. "He'll survive. I am sure he has his mom on speed dial if his housekeeper can't solve his cooking and cleaning needs. Besides, I had a class of toddlers to teach first thing this morning. Also, I wanted to catch up with you before I get roped into this photoshoot. Leave it to Connor's uncle and dad to turn this around real fast. I woke this morning to about a gazillion emails about an interview with my husband about our blessed union."

"Oh yeah? How is that going to go?"

"Fake it till we make it, right?" I shrug.

Isla squints her eyes at me. "You know, alcohol… it tends to bring out our inner inhibitions…"

My palm flies up to stop her. "Do not lecture me. Besides, after the shock when we told our parents wore off, our moms are in a glow of happiness. I'm not going to ruin that in less than a day by saying I'm getting a divorce."

"Your dad?"

A long exhale escapes me. "He… isn't pleased."

"So then why didn't you tell him it was a mistake?"

"I was going to, but then I figured an accidental marriage is even worse."

Isla looks at me, not believing my words. "What's the game plan? You married my boss's son and brother's teammate. Classic move, Hadley." Her sly grin plays on her lips.

I cross my arms. "Turns out Connor is my mystery watcher at my dance studio. His mom let it slip. Either he still harbors a little crush, finds me attractive, or has some twisted perverted thought in his head. My vote is on the latter. All of those options are excellent for using to my advantage to bring him to his downfall. Then, before hockey season starts again, kaboom, our marriage ends with his little feelings in pieces." My hands accompany with gestures.

Isla laughs, almost hysterically. "Kaboom could also be that you two want to stay married because you both enjoy it."

I'm about to protest, but my phone vibrates on the table. Flipping the phone to check the screen, I see Connor texted.

CONNOR

SOS. Where are you?

My eyes bug out from instinct, and I quickly type back.

ME

Oh dear, did you miss me when you woke up? I had to teach a class. I'm surprised you weren't lurking outside, since we know that's your favorite pastime.

Says the woman who threw on my shirt with no bra on in front of me. Easy as a breeze. I think someone enjoys being watched.

Shove it.

Mouth or pussy?

I choose to ignore his crass comment.

I'll see you at the photoshoot thing.

I'm already at my parents' house. Need you here now. We have a situation.

What kind of situation?

The moms...

I growl in frustration and choose to ignore my phone for a second. He's being overdramatic.

"Apparently there is an emergency for the photoshoot, and someone can't put his big boy pants on and handle it himself," I tell Isla.

My phone pings and a photo pops up. Studying the image, I shake my head. Clearly someone didn't get the memo that the photo session was going for casual, as the patio table at Connor's parents' house, my neighbors, is covered in flowers, cupcakes, and I'm positive the balloons are filled with confetti.

Growling, I know I need to head there sooner than later.

On my way.

Cooperative.

"Looks like I need to head there now. I'll let you know how it goes," I say as I gather my purse.

"Enjoy the honeymoon phase. Have an O or two for me." Isla smirks as she sips on her coffee.

I give her a warning glare. "Don't… I learned my lesson once… but maybe I need to sacrifice an orgasm to make him pay. I'll do it if makes him weak." It causes Isla to laugh again as I leave.

Inside me, something tingles from the thought of Connor having his wicked way with me, and I hate that the image flashes in my head. I should be stronger when he's involved.

———

LOOKING IN THE MIRROR, I try to suppress the smile that wants to spread. My palms rest against my belly as I study myself from different angles.

Arriving at Connor's parents', my mother quickly ushered me to the guest room to get dressed, as the hair and makeup lady was waiting for me. I didn't realize we were going all out. I don't even want to know how this dress was chosen or by who. It fits me to a T, and although not a wedding dress, it could be if you were going for dressy casual in white. It dips down my back, cuts off just below my knee, and I feel beautiful.

"I can't wait to see the photos. You're so stunning." My mom arrives by my side, holding up a necklace. "Here," she says as she brings the jewelry around my neck. "Your dad gave this to me on our first anniversary. I was saving it for your wedding… which I missed." Her happy tone dips to disapproval before her smile returns. "So, I will give it to you now and be sure to steal some photos."

I touch the pendant with a small diamond and smile tenderly at her. "Thank you, I love it." And I feel kind of guilty too. She wanted to save it for a special occasion, but I guess to her, this is. "How early were you up this morning?"

"Oh, it's nothing." She waves me off.

I throw her a funny look. "There is a cupcake tower downstairs."

And she made it because she's an excellent cook and baker, even works in nutrition.

"I'm up early anyhow. Besides, you used to go on and on about cupcake towers for weddings."

"This is a photoshoot… one that you and Brielle invited yourselves to." I laugh.

She brings her fingers together to show size. "We are a little excited for you and Connor."

"Clearly," I deadpan.

My mother touches my curled hair that is mostly down. "You know, love hides under the surface. We don't always embrace it in the right way first, but once you uncover it, then it can be amazing and long-lasting."

"Is this our marriage talk?"

She nods once with a closed-mouth smile. "It is. Also, remember your father and I couldn't stand one another until we realized it was because we were completely right for each other. Soulmates."

"So you've mentioned at every opportunity that arises."

My mom gives me a loving knowing look. "I'm not sure what you two are up to, but I see it. The potential, I mean, and I'm here for it."

She is dead serious, and I'm taken aback slightly by her conviction. There's experience behind her words, which means her advice isn't to be ignored. That unnerves me slightly, as it means there may be truth to what she says.

Clearing my throat, I decide that we should probably get on with this day. "I guess there is a fancy journalist and photographer downstairs that I should get to."

She nods, and we leave the room to walk down the stairs and head outside into the beautiful day. The Spears home is much like my own childhood home. On the lake, with a dock, but they have an outside swimming pool, whereas we have an inside one. Connor and I both grew up in a life of love from our parents who did their best to give us more than most but keep us humble.

Our parents, two photographers, a journalist, and Declan is here, probably under the ruse of uncle duty. They are all huddled around the table full of refreshments.

But in the corner of my eye, I spot Connor and my dad deep in conversation near the willow tree and away from everyone. It strikes me that they seem serious yet they're speaking in hushed tones, and I wonder what they are discussing.

My father peers up, and he seems to pause instantly in his sentence, with fondness flooding his face.

Connor is wearing a linen dress shirt and khaki pants. His back is to me, but when he notices my father hypnotized, Connor glances over his shoulder. He does a double take before he slowly turns to face me. His eyes draw a line up and down my body, and his lips tug from a smile he can't commit to. But when he steps forward, abandoning my father, his eyes lighten before he gets to me, stops, and touches my elbows with his fingertips, sending a current through my blood.

"You look beautiful." His voice dips low, ensuring nobody can hear. "Then again, I wouldn't marry anything less."

I give him an unimpressed look. Maybe because for a moment, I thought he was being sincere, or he was then ruined it. Both options enrage me somewhere deep within.

Glancing around, I realize we have an audience. I chuckle softly. "Wow, what a spread."

My eyes nearly bug out at the abundance of fresh flowers, and Connor notices. "They roped my aunt Violet into this event; she dropped them off this morning. Peach-colored roses for Sprinkles, apparently that was in your wedding dream diary."

"Oh God, I guess my mom really did dig that up. I made that when I was like seven, by the way."

"Don't worry, my mom went off the rails too. See the dog?" He tips his head to Puck, their family's yellow Labrador, who is sporting a little bandana around his neck. "Dressed up for the occasion."

I snort a laugh before I fix my gaze on my father who walks to us. "Hi, Daddy."

"You look so pretty," he notes.

I blush because the two men in my life are staring at me as if I'm something special. "It's just a dress. Not a wedding dress or anything," I say, trying to downplay it.

"Still." He shrugs.

Lifting my shoulders, I look between them. "Everything okay? You two seemed to be in quite a discussion."

My father plants a hand on Connor's shoulder, causing Con to tense slightly. "Peachy. Just reminding my son-in-law what I expect. You are precious goods and deserve the best. I'm confident he won't do anything I wouldn't do. Warned him I'm too young to be a grandpa. The usual talk."

I don't believe a single word he says. Spencer Crews doesn't say peachy unless sarcasm is the root. I smile anyway because he clearly doesn't want to clue me in.

"Don't worry, she's in excellent hands." Connor's death glare lands on my father.

Lines crease my forehead. "Okay, you two are acting weird."

Connor smiles at me and then playfully pinches my cheek. "All is fine. Your dad and I were debating if the batting cages or ice rink should be our next bonding session."

My father touches my shoulder. "Had to be a hockey player that you married, huh," he states warmly.

"Okay, kids, they want to get started with this. Ready?" Ford calls out.

My father gives me a nod before leaving to give Connor and me a moment.

It takes a few seconds for Connor to refocus, as his eyes are locked on me, and he seems to be pondering something.

"Pretend. You're good at that," I remind him of our day ahead.

A sincere grin spreads on his face, and it unnerves me. "We just go with it?"

"Well, we have no other choice. We sure as hell didn't rehearse this for weeks on end, considering two days ago neither one of us had marriage on the mind."

He leans in to kiss my forehead, and it catches me off guard until he mumbles against my skin, making it clear that it's all part of the act. "Showtime."

Ford, Connor's uncle, and a journalist arrive before us.

"Hi, Hadley, I'm Julia, the reporter and old friend of Declan's. He called, giving me the first chance to jump on this wonderful news. Sam, over there, is my photographer, and Rupert is his assistant. Congratulations on the marriage." Julia seems sweet, but growing up with a famous dad, I'm wary of reporters. Julia looks to be a few years older than me. I'm sure if my husband wasn't tied down to me, she would be his type.

I smile politely. "Hi, nice to meet you."

"Why don't we sit down, chat for the article, and then we'll have a photo session after. Pretend the camera isn't there." Her overdone smile doesn't do it for me, but I play along.

"Of course," I reply.

We begin to follow her to the seating area on the other side of the deck, but Ford and Declan gently touch Connor's arm to stop us.

"Marriage equals better focus for you, which equates to a better team, and the Spinners are going to be a winning team next season," his uncle Declan mutters, a reminder to Connor. It seems they have an agenda. But then Declan relaxes and gently slaps Connor's shoulder. "Hot damn, you two kids look great together."

"We'll be by the refreshment table reining in your mothers. Just holler if you need anything. A balloon, a cute Labrador, a rose, maybe champagne. It will be a great hour that makes up for the lack of wedding festivities that you denied your mother who labored for hours to bring you into the world, only to have her son elope." Ford smiles tightly.

"This right here is exhibit A of why we did." Connor throws a smirk to his father.

I have to laugh. Apparently, our marriage has made our parents a little crazy, but a good warm-hug kind of crazy.

Connor and I take a seat in front of Julia, and Connor instantly interlinks our hands. He's going all in.

"Thank you both for meeting with me. I love that we are doing this at your childhood home, Connor. Considering you both grew up together as neighbors and your parents are close friends. Did you two ever feel like your relationship was a sort of arrangement or pushed from them?" Julia begins in the deep end.

Connor laughs. "*Oh yeah*, every BBQ was a discussion about our future." He is completely joking.

I unlink our hands and place my palm on his thigh. "Isn't he a funny one? No, I don't think they did. Of course, it might be a dream come true for them slightly, but we are the product of our own feelings and attraction."

"Considering Connor was living quite a big bachelor life last season and now he has a wife, many might say this is sudden."

Connor reconnects our hands, almost to counter my every move. "Everyone loves a second chance, right?"

"Oh, so you two are a second-chance story? You dated before?" Julia asks.

I laugh nervously. "You can say something like that. How could I live next to this hockey god growing up and not have had a thing for him? And since he has a thing for dancers, preferably the kind who keep their clothes on, then I think we can let the cat out of the bag and admit that we acted on it before. It's not like we went to Vegas and acted careless." My smile is far too easy for these half-lies.

Connor seems to enjoy my explanation. "She keeps me focused, this one. We were celebrating my good season and talking about how next season will be even better, then I realized that I can't do this whole 'will she or won't she finally commit to my charm' thing. I told her how I felt, and she said that I was right like always, and she wanted all in. We've known one another since she was in elementary school, we don't need to go slow."

"That really sounds like a whirlwind, but we also can't deny the obvious. Connor, you come from a family of hockey professionals, a star player yourself, and Hadley is the daughter of a baseball legend. Surely, a grand wedding would have been in order. This is sports royalty at its best," Julia comments, and I'm sure Connor's uncle fed her that line.

I retreat my hand from Connor's and return to his thigh that I clench, and he nearly yelps but keeps his smile. "Sometimes romance is better when it's between two people," I tell the reporter. "Besides, we're here today at the spot where we grew up. Where Connor here would throw his teenage parties and walk me home. Always the perfect gentleman."

"I would always be in the pool, and she would stop by with cupcakes decorated with sprinkles, throwing in indecent proposals that I just couldn't deny," he adds with that grin that could make a woman faint. Instantly, I squeeze his thigh with a bit of aggression.

"This is so cute. You're both young; what plans do you have for newlywed life?" Julia asks as she adjusts her sunglasses on top of her head.

Connor nuzzles his nose into my cheek for show. "Practice for family expansion, of course."

I nearly choke, and I'm positive my father over by the iced-tea pitcher just stretched his neck in agitation.

I nuzzle Connor back with my nose. "Con, I'm sure that's a given. But I think what she meant was honeymoon or not." I turn to Julia. "Probably down to the Florida Keys for some beach time. Nothing like a string bikini and a hockey player on your arm, right?"

"I think most women will be jealous of you, Hadley. Considering the Spinners are stars on and off the ice with those fun videos on social media. Connor is somewhat of a sex symbol, especially amongst romance readers who peg him for hockey boyfriend material in a book."

Connor smirks proudly and relaxes his shoulders. "Am I? Nice." I gently elbow him. "I mean, they better get in line. My wife is my one and only. Connor Spears is committed and tied down."

"He loves being tied down," I deadpan.

Julia's eyes have curiosity in them, as if she is investigating the dynamic between Connor and me. Good for her, she might actually be good at her job.

Or we may just have calmed her skepticism when the photo session goes into full swing, and I find myself sitting at the end of the dock with Connor next to me and a request that we kiss for the camera…

8

CONNOR

With our feet hanging over the edge of the dock while we sit, my arm is firmly wrapped around my wife while we look out at Lake Spark. Hadley's head leans against my shoulder, and I can't help but kiss the top of her hair. It's not my fault that she's in prime position for a chaste kiss.

"Could we have a photo of you both kissing?" The photographer raises his request from where he stands at the start of the dock.

"I'm sure my wife can handle a little public affection," I call out since they're not close enough to hear.

Hadley grumbles a sound only I can hear. "Of course, our first kiss as husband and wife would be with our parents spectating."

"Except they don't know that, *and* it's not really our first kiss in general," I give her in recap, "but enough going down memory lane."

"Don't remind me of my naïve self and your douchebag tendencies. Careful, the lake is deep here, I would hate for you to fall in. Then again, I didn't sign a prenup, so that's your bad if something should happen."

My finger curls, and I capture her chin to tip up and guide her gaze to me. "I would take you with me. You enjoy getting wet around me." I give her a contrite grin.

"Wishful thinking, Con."

"Let's deliver the fairytale, shall we? Committed, loving, insanely handsy." My fingers land on her thigh, dragging the fabric of her dress up slightly to touch her silky skin right above her knee, feeling her body flinch, then seeing her mouth thin into a line as she tries to hold a breath because she enjoys this but will never admit it.

"Just kiss me," she grits out, but it feels like an act.

Gladly.

Dipping my head down, I press my lips softly against her bottom lip, taking a moment to feel the connection that I remember from years ago. I take more, kissing her top lip, feeling her kiss back, letting go of her tightly wound rope and giving me something that makes me feral inside, needy for more. I make no mistake that she kisses me back, and when I dip my tongue inside her mouth to meet hers, I feel no protest. A little moan vibrates in the back of her throat, and damn, that's a sound I like. I tilt my mouth to cover hers in a different angle, only to feel a new jolt of electricity that makes me go slightly blank.

This isn't a hard kiss, but the damage is the same. Kissing her gently, I brush her lips with mine as I pull away very slowly, wishing I could prolong this.

I like her quiet this way, with my mouth on hers. She's more receptive, slightly bewitching, but also mine to kiss.

My eyes skim down to see her plump lips, and I smirk to myself from accomplishment, especially when her breath grows shallow. Taking my thumb, I rub a circle on her bottom lip to touch where I kissed her.

"Not bad," I rasp.

I don't let her chin go and keep her face in my hold while her tongue darts out to lick the corner of her mouth.

"Somewhat decent," she lies and avoids looking at me, but her flushed cheeks inform me that she may have felt the buzz flowing between us. Dislike sometimes makes passion more attuned.

"You know, we haven't discussed certain needs we might have

during our marriage." I throw that out there because I love riling this woman.

Hadley places her hands on both of my shoulders and digs her nails into the fabric of my shirt. Any bystander watching would assume we are being a cute couple who can't keep our hands off one another, but that's not the reality I'm facing.

"Oh, trust me, you're going to need to work a little harder than *oh by the way, honey, I need to release one out*," she mocks me.

"Don't worry, I assumed you wouldn't be so easy. But just so you know, if you need to unwind, I'm able and willing since we *are* sharing a bed. I'm loving my shirt-and-thong look you have going at night," I compliment.

"Can we end this conversation considering who is in earshot?" she suggests.

I glance over at our parents. We should have known that our parents, oh so wise, saw this coming; Hadley and me together in any form. They've patiently been waiting, well, except Spencer, but you can't win them all.

I release her chin and move to stand, offering Hadley my hand. She accepts, willingly, and I yank her up. I can't help it and give her the once-over for the hundredth time, but she's absolutely gorgeous; it's natural too.

She seems to notice I'm a man who observes. "You okay there?"

"Yeah, you just really… look beautiful." I can't even turn it into a jab because it's the honest truth.

Hadley blinks a few times, and when I don't add on a retort, she seems to understand that I'm being sincere. "Thanks. You're not bad yourself." I nod once, not sure what to say. "This is kind of crazy, right? All of this." It sounds like she's letting down her defenses for a moment.

"A little crazy," I admit.

She scans the area and then lands her sight back on me. "Part of me hates that this is pretend. The other part wonders how deep into the fantasy I should go. You're trouble, Connor Spears, and you know it." She has some serious conviction in that statement, but I like the way her eyes have a sparkly glint and the line on her mouth stays stretched when she says that.

"And you're insufferable most of the time, lucky me," I answer softly.

Hadley is right, though. She should have run when she had the chance, but now everyone can get off my back, except her, and I don't mind that. Our game of rivals is just that, and I'd play it forever if it means that I at least get to have her words and sight directed at me. She just doesn't realize, and that's my doing.

In the corner of my eye, I see the photographer approaching us again for closeups. I encircle my arm around Hadley's waist and pull her close and tight to my body, enjoying the way she molds to me. She'll always have to look up because of our height difference, I just hope the marvel in her eyes will always remain.

———

BY THE TIME we wrapped up the photoshoot, ate cupcakes, and avoided champagne toasts with our parents who are planning joint family holidays, we were tired. Hadley took a few more items from her house to bring to mine, which just means she'll get more established at my place, harder for her to escape too.

I helped take a few bags from her car inside, refusing to give up the location of spare sheets for the guest room because I might have an inkling where they actually are. I led her to my room and cleared out some space in my closet instead.

She may hate me, but last night when she slept and unknowingly rolled into my arms, I couldn't help picture what it would be like to have her naked and under me… again.

I have every intention of driving her wild. She can get under my skin, then I will get under hers. That's marriage, right? Two-sided bliss.

After a shower and a check of my schedule for the week, I enter my kitchen to find Hadley in shorts, a t-shirt, and sitting at the kitchen island with a sewing needle and thread.

"Already getting domesticated on me?" I inquire as I open the fridge for a beer.

She snorts a laugh. "Never for you." Closing the door to the fridge and grabbing the bottle opener, I study her while she seems focused on cutting thread. Hadley must notice, as she pulls her eyes up. "Yes?" There's a little attitude in her tone.

"What are you doing?" I throw the bottle cap to the side.

"I need to sew the ribbons on my new pointe shoes."

Sipping my beer, I picture her in my head on her toes, spinning around for me until she lands on my lap. She's a great ballerina. Even though she dances a lot of styles, ballet is where she's kind of extra hot, and she dances flawlessly but adds her own alternative flare to her song choices and choreography.

She raises a brow at me. "Why did you watch me the other day?"

Ah, I knew this was coming. My mother gave away my secret, that she caught me surveying Hadley when I ran into my mom on the street, the reason I was delayed meeting my dad and uncle.

"I might not enjoy your presence, but you have talent."

She seems to be debating if my answer is worthy of her approval. "It's strange."

I slant my shoulder up in doubt. "You shouldn't dance with the door open; anybody can watch." I set my beer bottle down.

"It gets warm in the studio. I wanted some air."

I begin to walk slowly to her, determined to try something. "I'll buy you an air conditioner, consider it a present for *my wife*. But what I meant was, any guy could watch."

A sly smirk forms on her mouth that I want to devour. "Ah, can't have that now, can we? Connor throws a fit at the idea of another man watching." Her tone is taunting me, and I don't like that one bit.

I circle around the island, getting closer to my target. "Hadley, while we're married, no man will look at you." I slide the pink satin ribbons off the counter. My eyes stay connected with hers while I tie the ribbons together.

Her eyes slide down, but then quickly back up. "What are you doing? I need those."

A sinister scoff leaves my mouth. "I'll buy you a new pair, twenty if you want. We need these for something else right now."

My hands land on either side of her legs, then I slide the chair so she is squared off with me.

She isn't protesting, and that's a positive sign.

"Do you know what I think?" she husks.

"Humor me." I pull the knot on the ribbons ceremoniously.

Her head lolls slightly to the side. "You enjoy watching me because it makes you hard, doesn't it, even though you're supposed to despise me." Her sultry voice should be a crime.

Ignoring her valid observation, I get to work. "Hands, Hadley," I demand.

To my utter amazement, she lifts her hands together, wrists tight, offering herself as the prize.

I whistle in approval. "Well, well, well, someone is a good girl and listens to her husband." I begin to wrap the ribbon around her wrists.

"Or you just followed instructions and are working a little harder than saying you need to tug one out." Her reminder of what she said earlier causes me to smirk. "Plus, I have a weakness for curiosity," she states blandly.

Scoffing a sound, I decide to call her out. "Or you're just as twisted as me. I know you found the sheets for the guest room, so you could make yourself cozy in one of those rooms, yet the sheets haven't been touched." I flash her knowing eyes, but she doesn't break. I tighten the ribbon around her wrists. "You want to know why I really observed you dancing the other day?"

Her tongue swirls across her bottom lip as she nods.

I cup her jaw in my palm, with my thumb sliding along the curve of her face. "Because we may irritate one another, but I was your first, and your disdain for me, mixed with your legs wide open, is an image any man would think about. Now, spread," I nearly growl.

Hadley's jaw hangs low, but our eyes stay locked. Her tied wrists rest against her chest. I can't read her right now. Maybe I've pushed too soon.

"You didn't say please," she scolds.

No hesitation from me. "Please."

Her knees part open, and I glance down, figuring out how to strip her. One button and a zip. Should be easy. This stool at the island? Not so much. In a swift move, I lift her into my arms and plant her on the counter where her back rests against the marble while I spread her wide again.

With no elegance, I begin to work the button and zipper. "Arms above your head," I order.

She willingly complies, and I slide down her shorts. My fingers skirt the fabric of her panties, feeling her warmth and arousal radiating through the cotton while a soft moan escapes her lips, which causes me to focus my attention on her mouth.

Gosh, I want to kiss her again, but this isn't that kind of release. This is about power and testing how easily she succumbs to me.

She's crumbling, and I love that I have that effect on her.

I hiss a sound as I watch her eyes hood closed. "For someone who doesn't like me, you sure seem eager." My finger slips under the fabric to slide along her pussy, and the touch instantly shoots desire straight to my groin. She's soaking, and I'm already satisfied that I'm the reason. "My oh my, my wife wants this." I circle her clit, and her hips buck from the contact. "I wonder if you still taste like cupcakes. Is that what you want? My tongue on you?"

"Connor," she gasps. "I swear the only reason I'm here is because orgasms are essential for living and tequila made you my husband."

I chuckle because I love when she's feisty. "But babe, I'm a giver. Don't worry, I'm going to be a good husband tonight," I promise.

She can't protest because I lean down and swipe my tongue up her heat, tasting my confirmation. Her hips bolt up from the contact, and her lips gasp a breath. She's sweet and at my surrender, everything I was hoping for. I dip my tongue inside then swirl back up, her little moans encouraging me. I feast on her, nip on her clit, then circle again until I find a rhythm that leaves her jolting underneath my tongue.

I hook my arms under her legs and bring her forward to the edge of the counter. "You taste good," I murmur against her inner thigh.

Her body writhes and attempts to arch up to encourage me to use my tongue some more. I want to make her come, and I will, but not yet.

"Then don't stop," she breathes.

It causes me to widen my eyes due to her insistence. Hovering over her body, I fist some of her hair around my hand and carefully guide her up to sitting. "I won't. But you need to work for it a little."

She raises her brows. "You tied me up. Whatever would you like me to do?" Sass. That's my girl.

I plant my hands on her hips and hoist her off the counter. "Knees," I demand. She sighs but yet again complies, while I lower my basketball shorts and boxer briefs. "Mouth."

Her eyes blaze with a hint of surprise, but she only licks her lips before she parts them to welcome my cock into her mouth. I bring my tip to her lips and the edge of her tongue greets my head.

"Damn. You're a sight. My little dancer, wrapped up and willing." But I step back and instead weave my fingers into her hair. "Would you like that? Having my cock inside your mouth? Your lips wrapped around me? Because you would look good with your mouth full and getting destroyed." My words cause her to moan sharply, and I raise a brow. "Bet you wish you could touch your pussy now. Tell me that you need my tongue on you." Words don't escape her lips, as she seems lost in a daze. "It's okay, I'll check for you."

She smirks with pleasure. "How giving." I still sense some sarcasm, but she's an equal partner in this scene. A far cry from her first time with me, definitely not innocent.

I lift her back onto the edge of the counter, taking my cock in my hand to give it a stroke, while she spreads her legs, and my tongue finds a home on her clit.

"Connor, right there, please."

Her moaning my name, pleading, is music to my dick. A perfect melody that I plan on putting on repeat.

I work toward my own release while I take care of her until she's shaking against my tongue, cursing out my name, with her head fallen back as she convulses on the kitchen counter. I keep my tongue on her, and my balls tighten before I still and unload onto her inner thigh.

Rising and then leaning over her, I'm panting as my forehead falls against hers, using one another for support, as she has no use of her hands. We both have labored breathing and say nothing, instead melting into a pile of orgasmic bliss. It takes about thirty seconds for me to adjust that this actually happened, then I reach for a kitchen towel to wipe her thigh, with the flicker of a memory of the last time I did this with her. She was shy and innocent, and I made her mine. For that night at least. Before untying her ribbon, noting that I really do owe her new ones.

We don't say anything, even when she hops off the counter and swoops up her shorts, and I pull up my own.

She walks away, and I rub my face as I try to find my feet, as I'm trapped between endorphins and unsure of what to say to her. It doesn't matter, as she is already halfway upstairs.

I decide to give her a little space while she takes a shower, then when she emerges from the bathroom in another one of my shirts, I relax a little more and lie back against the headboard, watching her approach the bed.

"You okay?" I check.

She laughs once. "More than." She hops onto the bed then does something that surprises me; she straddles my hips, and my dick is instantly intrigued. Her finger pokes out and jabs my chest. "Downstairs was appreciated because now I know that you *do* want me." She swivels her covered pussy on top of my cock, and my breathing grows labored. "I fully intend to drive you insane, so thank you for the intel, Con." Hadley dry humps the fuck out of me in one sensual move, a wave of her hips churning as she tosses her hair behind her back, causing her chest to perk out. "Mmm, someone is hard. A shame he's not getting anything." She gently pats my cheek. "Night-night, Husband."

Then she's off me, rolls to her side of the bed, and turns away from me. Leaving me with a massive hard-on that I'm going to have to rub out in the shower.

Great, my determination paid off only partly tonight. But what the hell happens tomorrow? She's up to something, and I will bring her to her knees again, that I'm sure of.

9

HADLEY

Banging my pointe shoe against the counter in one hand, I press the button on the blender for my breakfast smoothie using my other hand. I have no qualms that this will ruin any sleep-in plans that my dear husband may have envisioned.

A proud smirk takes over me when I notice him walk down the stairs, though shirtless, and scratching the back of his scruffy morning hair. He seems rather grumbly, and I don't mind. The man is the king of mixed signals, because what in the world was last night? I'll never look at ribbon the same way.

The drilling of the blender sounds like my agonizing heart. I'm slightly disappointed that I caved so easily yesterday. Then again, Connor is the one who faltered first, right? Yet, I gave him the power…

"Uh, what in the world is going on? It's not even nine," he groggily calls out over the noise and walks to the cupboard to take out his protein powder.

I stop my noise for a second. "Some of us work all year round. I need to teach old ladies tap dance this morning."

"Fine, but must you do it making all this commotion?"

I offer him a pointed look. "I always have a smoothie for breakfast when I can. Vitamins are important, just like staying hydrated. And my shoes? I need to break them in."

He smiles to himself as if he is reflecting, and his gaze falls low to my waist. "Ah yes, your shoes." He clucks his tongue. Not even two minutes in and he is reminding me of last night.

I hold up the blender cylinder. "Shake? It's banana, avocado, oat milk, spinach, mint extract, some Brazilian herb, and a hell of a lot of contempt for you."

Connor walks my way with a swagger in his step, then purposely brushes his arm across my body, sending a tingle to my nipples as he reaches for a glass behind me, our eyes in a deadlock. "Aww, you're the sweetest. Both figuratively and literally." Oh crap, he has a saccharine tone, and his grin is too charming for this early in the day. My defenses are too weak before lunchtime.

But I will stand firm. "Let me state the obvious. So what? We had an orgasm. It might happen while we are husband and wife. It is what it is. But make no mistake, it's not me weakening my resolve, because I didn't magically forget what an asshole you were the first time around." His grin disappears and his jaw moves side to side. He hates when I remind him of that, I've learned that pretty quickly.

Stepping away from the joint bubble of space that we created, I walk to the other side of the kitchen to grab a massive water bottle and my to-go cup to pour my shake into. Twisting the cap, I ignore Connor who is like a lost puppy right now, unsure of what to do.

But then I freeze mid-twist when he pipes up.

"Let me put in the effort."

I slowly turn, with fear running down my spine. "What do you mean effort?" My eyes land on Connor leaning against the counter, ankles and arms crossed, and that cunning look is back.

"Let's call a truce. If we are going to be married for a bit, then let me show you that I can be a *good husband,*" he casually mentions, and my mind flashes to his use of the label last night and hate that my body responds positively.

Shaking my head, I huff out a breath. "I don't have time for this.

Whatever game you want to play today, have fun. I need to get to my studio," I declare and grab my shoes and drink in a hurry.

I vaguely hear him mention that he will see me at noon.

———

THE OLD LADIES WERE HYSTERICAL. They always are. Tap dancing isn't my go-to choice of style, and I'm counting on one of the teenagers from my dance company to start teaching in the summer. But something about teaching a classic dance number à la "Singing in the Rain" always puts a smile on everyone's face. After their morning class, I worked on invoices. It's a weekday, so other than adults and toddlers in the morning, my days are fairly free, as it's summer, so I have a lighter schedule.

I threw Radiohead on my Bluetooth, put on my new shoes, and ignored the fact that the new ribbons are a little stretched. It doesn't matter, I get lost in my movement with nobody around. Swaying to the music and seeing where my body flows. I do this for a solid twenty minutes.

I'm landing from my pirouette when I get startled. "What the hell?"

Connor is leaning against the doorframe to the back door with his hands in his pockets, a man confident and eager to show power. Connor's eyes are filled with… sizzling heat, darker than normal. "You look good twirling around with my wedding ring on your finger." I tip my head to the side slightly, waiting for him to explain why he's here. "I guess being your husband gave me the privilege to watch you."

"Without lurking, oh gee, lucky me," I retort and turn the music off. I walk to a chair in the corner to unwrap my shoes. "Why are you here?"

"I'm taking you to lunch, of course."

I glance up as I slip one slipper off then massage the pads on my toes, a soft whimper escaping me as I notice a blister forming. "You're not taking me to lunch." I continue to my other foot.

"Truce and effort, remember?" He steps in my direction, examining my foot. "You okay?"

I look at him like he's crazy. "It's a blister. I'll survive," I answer rather dryly. In truth, I'm far too curious what "good husband" Connor is like.

"Come on, Jolly Joe's? Catch 22? Dizzy Duck? What do you want to eat? You need to eat, you've worked up an appetite."

My eyes bug out at his insistence, but my heart also flutters at his concern. "You sound like my mother. Next thing I know you're chasing me to go see a doctor about my allergies."

"You have allergies?"

I shrug as I grab my sandals. "I don't know, still need to test. It's probably just hay fever or something. Again, not going to die, to your dismay."

He offers me his arm, and his demeanor in the last five minutes is unnerving me. I don't like when he's unapologetically sweet or even appears to be. Still, my traitor of a subconscious disagrees with my thought, and I offer Connor my hand to pull me up. His strength causes me to shoot up like a rocket, and I stumble forward. His arms instantly balance me while my face buries into his chest. Inhaling, I make a note to figure out his laundry detergent; it's a delicious fresh smell, not too masculine.

We cling to one another a second more than we should. Oh, how I hate the way every fiber inside of me clings to him like a magnet.

"Lock up and let's go," he requests softly.

Stepping back, I feign a frown. "If I must."

A minute later, we are walking down Main Street, with the spring air fresh and the sun shining down, arm in arm because Connor believes I hate it, but I know he, and even I, might enjoy it. I notice a few spectators surveying us as we stroll down the sidewalk.

"Do you feel like everyone is watching us?" I whisper to Connor.

"I'm me. Of course they are."

I snort a laugh because he's serious, yet he means it light-heartedly. Connor enjoys being popular, but he also tries to use it to his advantage, both on the ice and when he helps out with charities.

Ford and Brielle raised a man of character, just not when it comes to me.

"Relax," he assures me. "We just hit the news, so give it a few days."

I pull out my phone from my side pocket to look at the few headlines that I noticed after tap class.

"It's positive, I guess." I begin to read the headlines.

Hockey MVP Marries Baseball Princess in Shocking Vegas Wedding!

Curveball! Connor Spears Elopes with Former Baseball Star's Daughter.

Hockey's Favorite Bachelor Marries in Secret.

Connor Spears is Officially a Husband.

Two Famous Sports Families are Now United by Marriage.

"Oh, here is the article from Julia."

Like a sheet of black ice, the public never saw the nuptials between Connor Spears and Hadley Crews coming. The reality is that these two are a match made in heaven. Connor, the son of former hockey player Ford Spears and his wife Brielle, plus nephew of The Spinners owner Declan Dash, has always proven he is worthy to be on the road to becoming the future captain of The Spinners. His off-ice antics gave him a notorious track record for enjoying life, but he's now even more determined and committed both on and off the ice thanks to the love of his life. Hadley, daughter of former baseball star Spencer Crews and his wife April, is not only accustomed to pro-athlete life, but grew up with Connor as neighbors. Some may call it Vegas magic, but those close to them have always known about the soft spot these two share and are not surprised by this romantic elopement. The couple plan on making their home in Lake Spark where The Spinners train and to be close to their families. The female population may be sad that Connor's off the market, but we look forward to watching sports' newest hot couple appear at future events together.

"Who writes this fluff?" I comment.

"Julia," he answers dryly.

"Yeah, no shit. But this sounds so…" I stare down at the accompanying photo, and I don't even remember anyone taking this. It's Connor kissing my forehead and a smile that even I know isn't fake is hinted on my lips. Our hands are connected and hanging between us as I lean my head against his shoulder. If it wasn't for the fact that this article has me boiling, then I might just admit that, gosh, we look good together… I mean, we are a photogenic couple, which tends to happen when two people are good-looking. And it looks like a stolen moment between husband and wife, so kudos to the photographer for doing his damn job.

"It's a little sappy, but it does the trick. It's a good article. I'm sure our moms are framing it as we speak." Connor isn't fazed by this.

I grumble a sound and stomp a few steps as we continue to walk. "I guess it's… what we needed."

"It will blow over in a few days when Shawn Cann does something stupid to land in the media." He leads us and motions up ahead to Jolly Joe's. "Grilled cheese?"

"Sounds good, actually."

A few minutes later, we are sitting in a booth by the jukebox that's barely used in Jolly Joe's.

"Is this going to become a frequent occurrence? Lunch?" I ask one-toned and drop my straw into my iced tea.

"I do think humans eat lunch, so yes." He's being coy.

"I mean you, me, lunch."

Connor crosses his arms on the table. "Get used to it, Sprinkles. I'm going all in on this. I know you hate it, which is why I love it."

"Wonderful." I'm not at all serious.

He bows his head and an almost shy half-smile forms. "Can I ask you something?"

"Might as well or it may be a long lunch."

"Are you 100% certain that we didn't… in Vegas…" His face strains before his eyes draw a line up to mine. "I mean, we probably didn't use birth control."

I'm amused by this. "You mean, am I sure that we didn't have sex in our drunken haze? Or am I sure that I'm not miraculously pregnant?"

He isn't entertained by my statement, and he rolls his eyes to the side.

I snort a laugh. "Connor, your dick isn't that magical. No immaculate conception happened, so yeah, I'm sure. Why do you even ask?"

His head bobs side to side. "I think we can both agree that we share a similar history in that department."

I think about it for a second then realize. "Ah, you mean that you're the product of an accidental pregnancy and so am I?"

"Exactly that. Don't get me wrong, I love my parents and they love me. But I know I wasn't planned and ruined their life only slightly." He's only partly joking. "And you, well…"

"Also a surprise. Although my dad was in his mid-twenties, not eighteen like your mom."

"Do you ever wonder about, well, I know April is your mom, but…" He treads delicately with his words.

I stir my drink. "April is my mom, I don't need biology for that. My birth mom is purely someone who birthed me. She never wanted me, so I will never give her a second thought, and I'm completely at peace with it. She had options when she got pregnant but chose my dad, who gave me the best life, so in a way I appreciate it."

Connor swipes a hand across his jaw, and I notice that he's growing out a little stubble, and it's kind of sexy. I felt his five-o clock shadow against my thighs last night, and I cross my legs from the thought.

"That's a good way to evaluate it. You are such a daddy's girl too."

I laugh, appreciating how easy our conversation is going, how open we can be. "I am," I admit proudly.

"I have to go the rink at the training center this afternoon. I promised Wyatt some ice time, plus I want to talk to my dad about summer camp this year."

A sincere smile beams on my face. Connor's good with his brothers. Like me, we pack an age difference with our young siblings, but that makes it more fun. "You're volunteering this year at summer camp?"

"Always. My dad has been running it for years, and I have to give back. We have a few extra weeks this year because we have more inner-city kids coming out, it'll be good." There hasn't been an ounce of fakeness in him in the last ten minutes. I dare say that he's being endearing right now.

I recall something in my head and bite my lip. "Weren't you a camp counselor once for the summer camp?"

Connor leans back and brings his hands behind his head with a glimmering smile. "Yeah, when I was sixteen. The summer my aunt and uncle were sneaking around, and my dad had no clue. It was awesome," he reflects fondly.

I have to laugh, because of course he loves mischief, and that summer he caused a lot.

And that's just how our conversation goes for the next hour. A memory, a laugh, one topic blending into another, everything easy.

By the time he's paid the bill and we are walking back to my studio, I almost forgot that I find the guy insufferable on the edges. Instead, I'm conflicted inside.

Our arms brush as we move in a leisurely stroll down the sidewalk, appearing like a perfect couple. When the man up ahead locks his car, he gives me a nod, and I return the gesture.

"Care to explain why Harry, the sheriff's brother, greeted you with a nod?" my broody husband requests.

I smirk to myself before I pull his arm to stop walking, because I want to see his face. "We used to date."

There we go, the territorial glare begins to brew on Connor's face. "As in…"

I cross my arms over my chest and stand tall. "As in did I sleep with him? Believe it or not but you may have been my first but not my last. It was like one month of dating, and he's now with someone he met in college."

"He doesn't seem like your type. He looks like an ass. Then

again, you had a phase. I remember when you dated O'Keefe who didn't even bother getting you roses."

My eyes turn surprised. "That was when I was like seventeen, and he brought me flowers for my dance recital. How the hell do you remember that?"

Connor rubs his shoulder. "I don't know."

Rolling my eyes, I get us moving again because maybe I'm reading too much into it. "I don't really care about your opinions on my dating history, since I know I've kissed a lot of frogs, including you." I flash him a pointed look that he appreciates because he enjoys when I offer him snipes on a continuous basis.

It's a silent block that we walk, but I don't mind. It's kind of peaceful. I hate to say that we are more comfortable with one another as the hours since our time in Vegas pass. Then again, comfort isn't our issue, because even when arguing we're comfortable.

After I enter the security code, he holds the door to the studio open for me. "I can stop by the grocery store on my way home from the rink. What do you want for dinner?"

I'm melting into a pile of goo. Who is this guy? Oh yeah, the man who thinks being a good husband is the way to break me. Except, he looks far too convincing right now, and I've actually lost what's happening. I need to take a breather, create some space.

"Oh, don't worry, I'll grab a salad from the store. Weekdays are pretty busy for me. Four to nine pm are primal dance class times, so don't expect me back until later," I explain, even though it's kind of a lie, as I'm on my summer schedule.

A wave of disappointment glazes in his eyes. "That makes sense. I'll leave you something in the fridge."

I nod once. He leans in, and I pray to myself he doesn't do what I think he's going to do.

Don't. Please don't. No. Yes. I mean, really don't.

He places a small kiss on my cheek as a parting.

It's the type of affection that is concerning to a woman like me. Because it's effective and sends a whisper inside me, awakening a small beacon of hope that maybe we could be everything.

10

CONNOR

Gently pulling the back of my brother's shirt as he leaves the ice, a proud smile takes over my face. "You're getting good, kid."

Wyatt glances over his shoulder with excitement in his eyes. "Oh yeah?" He's only ten, so I'm not going to tell him he could work on his swiping of the stick from the left during a pass.

"Might even be half as good as me one day," I tease him as we flop onto the bench and begin to untie the laces of our skates.

"Ha. Wishful thinking. You don't want me to steal your light." Wyatt pulls a skate off.

This guy is 100% me when I was his age. Now that it's the off-season, it will be good to hit the ice with him a little more. It's not like I can take him to a bar with me.

"You are completely in the doghouse, by the way. Mom and Dad can't stop talking about you and Hadley."

"Oh yeah?" A sheepish smirk hits me before I take a sip from my water bottle. I figured as much. I would question it if they didn't get thrown off their axis a bit.

He nods. "I even escaped my chores because they didn't notice.

In fact, Mom even fed Puck and crossed it off my chore chart, not even realizing she did it for me. Same with putting my laundry away."

"You should be thanking me then."

Wyatt scoffs a sound at me. "Dude, you married my babysitter."

I muss his hair. "Hadley *was* your babysitter when you were younger. Now she watches Alex occasionally with you reading a book in your room since you feel you're too mature for a babysitter."

"Whatever, if she wants to marry you, then good luck to her. Anyhow, Mom and Dad can't stop talking about you. Even when they think I'm not listening."

A curious grin takes over me. "Good or bad?"

Wyatt scoffs. "Well, Dad had to calm Mom down when she wanted to buy a toaster for your new bride. Something about it being a traditional wedding gift. Dad stopped her, and then she said he was right, she needs to go bigger, so she started looking at honeymoon destinations. She's completely hyped up on your news."

I scratch my stubbled jaw and can totally picture my mom doing that.

"*Dad* needs to talk with your brother," our father's voice breaks the conversation. We both look up to see our dad towering over us. He gives a pointed look to my little brother. "Go to my office, have a snack, and we'll leave in a little bit so we're back in time for dinner with your mom and little brother."

Wyatt hops up and throws on a beaming smile. "Someone is getting a talk," he taunts me and nearly skips away happy.

It only makes me entertained, and I look at my father. "I was going to find you, figured you would be in your office."

He hums a sound and comes to sit next to me, scanning the area to ensure nobody else is in earshot. "Let's have a chat, *Son*."

I roll my eyes to the side but my grin stays. "Oh boy, here we go."

"Now that the shock has worn off and I realize that you and Hadley weren't joking with us, then I think we should talk."

I hold up my hand to show him my ring. "You mean about this? My marriage." It still astonishes me how easy it is to say that.

He gives me an unimpressed look. "Connor, I don't care how you two kids ended up married." Drunk, that's how, but I'm not going to highlight that. "What I care about is that you put in the effort to *stay* in a lasting marriage."

My grin fades as his words hit me a little more than I was expecting. "Go on," I say softly because I owe him this. Even more, I owe it to myself. I've been living in the moment the past few days, but maybe someone needs to pour a dash of reality on me.

"You play hockey, and that's a team sport. But the greatest team that you will ever be on is the one with your wife." He's serious, but I can't help it because it's so cheesy that I burst out laughing. "Connor Spears, I'm serious. Communication, practice, and determination to make it forever are the qualities you want in a marriage."

I hold my hand for him to stop. "Come on, Dad, even you can admit this is a stretch on the ridiculous side? Didn't you rehearse this? Come up with a different angle?"

His lips purse out then he pauses before he too has a line stretching on the corner of his mouth. "You get my point, though, right?"

"I hear you."

He affectionately touches my shoulder. "Do you? Because you have a bonus in this situation. You've known your new bride since she was a little girl, and you were the boy who would pull her pigtails. Spencer and April are not only neighbors and friends, but they also care for you as if you were family, and we feel the same for Hadley. You've watched Hadley flourish into a woman, and she watched you turn into a man. Not many spouses can say that."

As touching as his speech is, he's killing me here. "You lost me at Hadley flourished into a woman. Seriously, you have a few years before Wyatt starts to date. Work on this." I gently nudge his shoulder. But when all is said and done, he is right.

My father laughs. "Fine. Let me keep it basic. You be there for

Hadley, you treat her like a queen and with the outmost respect. I don't care if in your head you did this because of the talk we had the other week. You will stay married, not because I don't want my son divorced before he's twenty-five. No, you will stay married because you've both been blind. She cares for you, more than she wants to admit, but I bet my life that if she thought today would be your last then she would be honest, and you would do the same."

I begin to protest, but my words are trapped at the bottom of my throat.

He continues our heart-to-heart. "She's wrapped you so tightly around her finger that you don't even realize."

My bitter laugh interrupts him. "What if I have always realized?" I'm sincere in my answer. My father's words only scrape the surface of the obvious that my consciousness decided to hide away.

He smiles gently. "I've seen the way you get, and it's only with her. You get one soulmate in your life; don't be stupid and ruin your chance to keep her."

He might be disappointed in a few months when Hadley and I call it quits, except nowhere in the last forty-eight hours, other than saying we would be temporary, have I actually *believed* we would be temporary.

"Uh-oh, my first born is pondering. I can tell by the troubled scowl appearing on his face." He stands and grins in accomplishment. "There. Talk done." He points at me. "Don't forget, charity hockey game next weekend to raise money for puppies." He walks away, knowing damn well my brain is now working in overtime.

The truth is it doesn't take much to think about. I know his points are valid. The only problem is that Hadley and I are so far gone on our game of cat and mouse that I don't know where to begin to unravel what we're doing.

It feels like a long car ride before I stop at my aunt Violet's flower shop. She normally has an answer when I need one.

Entering The Flower Jar, she smirks as she arranges a bouquet of mostly purple blooms in a vase, her eyes staying focused on adjusting the height of the flowers. "What brings my newly married nephew to me today?" she asks.

"Duck it," the parrot in the cage chirps. He doesn't know many words, but the ones he does are very questionable. My aunt had to keep the bird when she took over the building from the landlady, and despite telling everyone she hated the parrot, when Uncle Declan bought the building from the landlady and promised to get rid of the bird, Aunt Violet said Nugget could stay.

I walk to Nugget's cage and cluck my tongue on the roof of my mouth to grab his attention before I answer my aunt Violet. "Flowers."

"Again? Did your old schmooze-your-mom trick fail?"

I throw her a glance over my shoulder. "Nah, that worked well. I need flowers for my wife." I walk over to my aunt's workstation; this is probably her last order since she should be closed now.

She stills mid flower tuck and raises a brow at me. "Flowers because you enjoy teasing her or flowers because you actually want to make her smile?"

My jaw goes slack because my aunt is going to break me down too. "The latter," I admit. Instantly, our eyes hold, and I know she's studying me.

Her hip tips out, and she gives me a closed-mouth smile. "Ah, that's right. Hadley is your wife now, which means she's madly in love with you and won't throw them at you?" She taps a purple flower.

"Have your theories, but I don't know, I feel like... I need to change the playbook a bit. Shake it up." I'm supposed to be a good husband to annoy her, but now I know it's because I want to convince her, I'm not entirely sure of what because we shouldn't be the end game, even if we're meant to be.

"Sometimes we realize it's true love a little later." She indicates her head to a bouquet behind me. "Pick one. She likes roses, especially single roses because it's simple and more fitting for a dancer, she says. Hadley orders one for each of her dancers at the year-end recital."

That sounds like something she would do, she's thoughtful like that.

"Then the red one it is, but make it six."

"Classic." My aunt walks to the bucket on the ground. "Remember when you helped me out here one summer?"

I snort a laugh. "You mean when I was grounded for throwing a party when you were watching us and had to volunteer my services? Yeah, I remember."

"I made you study the meanings of flowers, especially the significance of numbers and roses. Funny that you pick six."

Damn, she's good.

I awkwardly rub the back of my neck. "Is it so wrong that a husband asks for six roses?"

She ceremoniously snips her scissors for the wrapping paper. "Not at all. I'm just happy that your inner emotions chose the number six, which I know you know means 'I want to be yours.' Someone is hopelessly romantic for their new wife, I'd say."

So what? I'm using other methods to state the obvious. It's far easier than saying it.

"Maybe," I play coy.

My aunt laughs wickedly. "If your new playbook is to woo your wife into staying your wife, then you are off to the right start. Do you know what I think?" She adjusts her stance. "You're going to hear it anyhow. You woke up married by accident and now you're trying to decide the path to convince her to stay."

I heave a long sigh. "Have you ever been in a situation where something feels too right but you know it won't work?" Not after what happened.

She laughs as she tapes the paper. "You mean, did my now husband feel he wasn't relationship material, even though we were explosive together? Yeah, I've been in

that situation, but eventually you can't ignore that plans and feelings change, and you might just be inseparable."

I tap the counter and stare down at the roses. I feel like I'm crawling in my skin. I'm beginning to think that I've done something so wrong, that it's too late and the damage has been done, that I can't make Hadley fall for me. But I think I should try, really try. It's what I would have done all those years ago. It would have been easier, as she was already mine then.

"I hope you're right," I nearly whisper.

Maybe it's time to fix a mistake.

———

I'M BURIED amongst a pile of deliveries and presents when Hadley returns home.

"What in the world?" She drops her keys on the counter and surveys the breakfast-nook area.

"Wedding gifts. News spreads fast, and now we have sponsors and anyone who is anyone in hockey sending us stuff," I explain as I open another package and pull out his-and-hers t-shirts and drop them like a hot potato.

Hadley studies the contents on the chairs and tables. "We have to donate some of this stuff. What would we do with a basket of a hundred candy bars? And do we really need *another* blender?"

I play with the card for the next gift. "You could always hoard this stuff and save it for when we decide to part ways." I'm testing the waters.

She clears her throat and chooses to ignore my comment and instead opens a neatly wrapped box. "This is from Piper and Hudson." Our parents' neighbors and April's uncle and aunt. "I can tell it's from Piper's boutique."

"Oh yeah?" I'm invested because Piper owns a...

"Of course, she sends this." Hadley holds up a black mesh nightie that leaves little to the imagination, since Piper owns a lingerie boutique.

I nod once. "Not bad, someone understood the assignment."

Hadley looks at me, horrified. "They are our neighbors! They're family to me."

I lean forward to swipe the card. "'To Hadley and Connor, enjoy the honeymoon phase. We are so delighted with the news. You two were always adorable. Hugs, Piper (and Hudson).'"

"Didn't someone send us matching flannel pajamas that cover every inch or something?" She searches the pile of presents.

"Actually, yes, over there by the chair." I point.

She gets sidetracked by looking at the matching champagne flutes with our names engraved on them, and then examines the fruit basket. "Seriously, what do we do with this stuff?"

I shrug a shoulder. "Let me call someone tomorrow. Some of this stuff is from sponsors. I'm sure they want us to post a selfie in our pajamas on a Sunday morning with some ridiculous scented candle lit and mug in hand."

Hadley laughs, then her eyes land on the roses and her face scrunches in confusion. "Your aunt sent more flowers?"

I lean back in my chair and watch her gently pick up the stems to smell the flowers.

"Nah, I was at her shop and thought I should get something for my wife since I'm a good husband."

Her eyes flick in my direction, and she smirks to herself as she taps the petals against her cheek. "Going all in on that, huh?"

"You love it." I don't blink.

Hadley tips her nose up, and she seems to be in contemplation. "Excuse me." She drops the roses then slides something off the table before leaving me alone amongst the mountain of congratulations.

But I'm not done with this conversation, which is why I follow her. She's already in the bathroom when I make it to our bedroom, and even I know not to interrupt a woman when she's in the bathroom with the door locked.

Instead, I hop onto the bed and kick up my feet to get comfortable. I'll just wait, and luckily, it isn't long, because precisely a minute later, the lock clicks, then the door opens to reveal Hadley in black make-me-instantly-hard lingerie as she leans against the doorframe.

This design should be a crime. It's a little dress that ends just barely below her ass, and those straps appear easy to slide down. I don't get a chance to debate that, as my eyes are drawn to the plunging line between her breasts that are pert from the fabric pushing her tits together.

"You want to be a good husband, then I'll play that game and be your good wife, even dress the part, when I go to bed *to sleep*." Her sexy-as-fuck smirk causes me to propel off the bed.

Don't falter... yet.

"You know what I think, Sprinkles?"

"Your ploy to take me to lunch and charm me with roses has backfired? And yeah, I know what six roses means. I worked one summer for your aunt, and she made me study that chart like it was the exam of my life."

I chuckle under my breath as I stride my way to her. "I don't think my plan has backfired. Because I'm kind of confident that the walls you and I built around one another, you actually want to burn them down."

I stand right in front of her and plant my hands firmly on her hips then pull her forward, which causes her breath to catch, but it does the job because her mouth is now in a kissable distance, and I feel her breath spread along the line of my neck.

Her eyes sparkle with intrigue, and when her mouth parts open, I can't help but trace her jawline with the pad of my thumb. It feels as though she's entranced by me, and by all means, I get a kick out of being the one to possess her, but ultimately, it's the fact she trusts to let me lead.

"Hmm? Isn't that what you want? For me to break down that wall you have when it concerns me? Even for a night?" My voice is heavily laced with lust as I set my sight on her mouth.

"Sometimes my head spins around you. Unlike dance where I can control it and land perfectly, with you I don't know how," she admits in a whisper.

I step closer to bring our bodies flush. "I can show you how," I husk.

She shakes her head, but a smirk appears before she meets me halfway because she stands on the balls of her feet as she offers me her mouth, the mouth that I cover with my own.

Because I have every intention of grounding her through a kiss, followed by laying her on the bed.

11

HADLEY

Why am I doing this again?

I am voluntarily surrendering to him because this man knows how to curse me with a stare, and it's not even a vile curse. Instead, he is shaking me and waking up every dormant feeling that I have for him.

I changed into expensive lingerie because I like teasing him. I wanted him to suffer, look but not touch. We all have a weakness, and mine is the way his eyes fill with a warm possession when I'm the object he stares at.

Which is why I am standing right here locked in a lip tango with my husband.

Connor's lips firmly kiss mine, with his tongue requesting entry, and I eagerly give. We always want what we probably shouldn't have. Except, I never say no to ice cream, so the same rule can apply to the only man who kisses me with electricity.

Because Connor's kisses seep through my veins and sink me down, and my body comes alive when his lips are on mine, something I hate to admit.

My body curves into his as his arm tightens around my waist and his kiss deepens. We sizzle together, and maybe through the years, we've both feared that.

We kissed for the camera, we made one another come, but an intimate kiss like this? It's our first in this chapter of our lives, and it's from our own initiative.

I murmur a sound of enjoyment as my eyes remain closed so I can drown in this kiss and in his arms, ignoring any warning flare looming in the back of my head. If I'm giving into this moment, then I'm going all in.

Even when he begins to walk us back toward the bed, I'm lost in a spellbinding moment. That is until his mouth leaves my lips and skims down my throat, and his free hand spreads along the back of my neck like I'm his to claim.

"You drive me crazy," he hums as he nuzzles into my neck, creating a sensitive wave that cascades down to my nipples.

"My life's mission," I whisper in retort, but really, I should scream ditto.

He growls and hoists me up, my legs naturally wrapping around his waist, and a sound escapes me because I feel he's more than ready.

A flimsy strap falls off my shoulder, and it only encourages Connor to trail his mouth along my collarbone, causing my head to fall back and my thighs to bind tighter around him.

It's a worthless move on my part, because a few seconds later, he plops me onto the bed and hovers over me with his eyes hungry and my heart growing heavy—the good kind.

I watch as Connor peels his t-shirt up, and I bite my lip from the show. There is a reason why women peg him as the hockey player with looks. I can't decide if I should focus on his arms or chest; it's a hard choice, so I choose the dangerous one and lock my gaze with his smoldering eyes.

The corner of his mouth tugs when he combs a few strands of hair behind my ear. I hate when he's sweet like that—no, I don't, but I should. I'm a woman who has self-respect, I remember what he did, but I can't seem to shake that there is a reason, and we're no longer as young and foolish. Maybe he was meant for a second…

I shake my head. "This is just sex," I lie.

He smirks. "Sure, whatever you need to tell yourself."

"Can you just, I don't know, step up your cocky ego factor? You seem to have left it at the door, and it's confusing, distracting, kind of infuriating," I begin to mumble and pout.

He pauses as he holds his weight over me. His head falls forward when he laughs, then he glances up to study my face. "You want me to be an asshole during sex?"

"No," I stutter. "Just… you're sending mixed messages. I don't know if this…"

Something sparks inside of him, and in a swift move, he grabs my wrists and pins them above my head. "This is me about to take you with a ring on your finger that confirms you are my wife, so I intend to fuck you the way a wife deserves to be fucked. Is that clear enough for you?"

I'm speechless because he has determination in his tone to prove me wrong from whatever doubt is floating in my head.

Gathering my bearings, I remain firm. "It's just sex."

He lets go of my wrists and sighs. "Fine. The choice is yours; you lead, or you let me prove you wrong."

My pussy squeezes from the thought of what that could entail, but emotionally, I'm not sure I'm ready. "On your back," I demand. The safer option, that's what I choose.

He tips his head slightly to the side. "This could be fun." He complies by standing, removing his jeans, then lying on the bed.

I quickly swing my legs to straddle him, and from instinct, my hips roll to ride his boxers. The matching panties to this baby doll are barely a layer, and I feel everything against my heat. My senses are heightened, and I should beg for him to touch my bundle of nerves to get some form of release.

I assess my fingers as I walk them up his stomach then stop at his chest. Leaning down, I place a kiss next to my hand. His skin is warm, and my hair falls along his body, tickling his skin, but it's his hand that is stroking my behind and drawing up to my lower back in mollifying circles that drives me wild.

He's boosting me through touch.

Lifting my shoulders back up, I hold his gaze as I slide the straps off my arms and inch down the lingerie. He sits up to kiss my breast, and I hiss a breath when his lips latch onto a nipple, and he sneaks his fingers between us to stroke my pussy.

He groans but keeps his mouth on me. "You're so wet for me," he murmurs between switching breasts.

I breathe out to pace myself. I'm aching for a release to come quickly.

"Mmhmm." It's a cop-out answer, but I'm too lost on his fingertips that circle my clit. Then he dips one finger inside of me and my head falls onto his shoulder from the intense feeling.

"I think you're desperate for my cock. Always have been."

I want to hate his sweltering words, but I'm already half gone.

I reach between us and sneak into the waistband of his boxer briefs, setting his cock free and wrapping my fingers around him. His throaty moan appeases me, and I'm desperate to do more to him.

One stroke then two.

We're touching each other and working ourselves into a frenzy.

"We have too much on," I whisper.

"I agree."

Quickly, we both discard any remaining scraps of cloth, then I'm back on him, sitting together face to face and his cock sliding between my center, getting soaked in my arousal. The tip of his cock is dangerously close to my entrance and our foreheads touch while we take a moment to digest that we're about to do this.

"We're good?" he asks gently. "I've never…"

My heart is palpitating, and my breath runs wild. Fuck, why does he have to make me feel like this is special. I'm his first for something, wife and no condom.

"Considering you think I can get pregnant from immaculate conception, then I think you're a little late to ask, but yeah, we're fine."

Mischief twinkles in his eyes. "Then ride me."

A short laugh escapes me. Half of him just said that because he is goofy that way, while the other part is because he means it.

Positioning myself over him, I slowly press down, and everything inside of me coils from the instant gratification of having him inside me. I move and move until he's filled me up, with my inner walls clenched around him.

"You feel so fucking good," he grits out, and his hands grip my hips to hold me in place.

I'm nearly stuck on top of him as I adjust to his size, but then I move an inch, then a little more, until I lift myself back up to his tip and root myself back down on him.

I do this a few times until I find a rhythm that feels right.

He gently slaps my ass and then palms a soothing circle.

"Use me. Take what you want. It's all yours," he whispers.

That sensitive demeanor is back, but I don't argue.

I meet him on thrusts, when I'm halfway down and he tips up, with the angle hitting the right buttons inside me, and I moan while he groans. I'm not sure I can feel my legs anymore, everything is barreling to my pussy, and I'm on fire in the best possible way.

Maybe he notices, or maybe he's just being dominant, but he grips my hips with vigor then pulls me close and flips us so he's on top, all without ever leaving me.

"I lied. I'm taking over."

A drowsy sound escapes me. "Surprise, surprise, you lied," I tease with an underlying truth.

"Hadley," he warns.

My response is to reach up and frame his face affectionately while he picks up our speed. My toes dip into the muscle of his ass, widening my legs, and my clit enjoys the friction of his body rubbing against me.

"Eyes on me," he demands.

Our eyes meet and lock, and my heart reminds me that it's still beating and all of my energy hasn't, in fact, flowed to my pussy. This feels like entrapment; I'm under him with no escape and his eyes are a shackle. But there is nowhere else that I would rather be.

We stay in this trance until our rhythm is uncontrollable, and I know I'm near the end. I use my fingers to play with myself to help me reach the destination at the same time.

"I'm coming inside of you. Need to mark you, and I fully intend to use those ribbons again if it means you won't be showering tonight. All night, you will have to feel me." Ah, there is his cocky comment that I needed to hear, except it's hopelessly hot.

"Figured you would go barbarian on me." I smirk and moan.

He leans down and kisses my mouth, gently biting the corner. "Call it perks of being your husband."

"Then do it. Leave. Me. Dripping," I gravel out, wildly eager for his words to come to fruition.

"Good wife." He places a kiss on my cheek before focusing on taking us to the finish line.

I close my eyes and see stars, with my body exploding.

When all is said and done, he stays seated between my legs, as our connection doesn't break even when I feel his warmth trickling down my thigh. I lie there taking in the post-orgasm bliss. I can't help the faint smile that wants to form as I rake my fingers through Connor's hair where he rests his head against my chest, his ear near my heart.

Living the fantasy is completely okay if it's only for a little bit, right?

⬤ 12

—

HADLEY

—

I let out a deep breath as I brace myself to walk down the stairs and into the kitchen where Connor is busy making a smoothie, I can hear the blender. Taking the plunge, I walk down a step and recall last night. After he rolled off me, we didn't say anything, and sleep took over. Sure, I may have noticed how his arm clung around me during the night while he slept and I pretended to sleep. Nor did I slip out of his hold.

As I walk into the kitchen, Connor pauses the button on the blender. He offers me a warm half-smile that makes me feel all light inside.

"Morning, I'm making you a shake," he mentions.

Instantly, I freeze then study the counter where I see my favorite ingredients, banana and peanut butter mostly. "Why?" I ask cautiously.

He flashes me a cunning grin as he grabs a clean glass from the counter and goes a little over the top when he pours the contents into the glass. "Being thoughtful, of course."

I smile tightly and take the drink he offers. "Let's not make a big deal about last night, okay?"

Connor chuckles as he grabs a glass for himself. "*Yeah... you* kind of mentioned last night." He crosses one ankle over the other as he leans against the counter. "Doesn't mean that I agree. So, here's the deal, Sprinkles." The rim of his shake hits his lips, and he takes a sip, even smacks his lips together for good measure. "I'm going all in on proving to you that we might as well admit this thing between us and knock down a wall or two. If you're going to be a little slower to step up and be a team player, then so be it."

Holy shit, he was serious.

"A ring, an orgasm, and flannel pajamas with our names on it doesn't change the fact that I should probably be a little wary of the sudden change of mood, considering our past." I drink from my smoothie and hum out a sound. Damn, that's good.

Connor sets his drink down and strolls my way. He lifts my glass from my hold and sets it down on the counter next to me. "Sprinkles, you're not a teenager anymore. I was an ass. Want me to get on my knees and admit it a hundred times?"

I tip my nose up. "Why were you?"

"Let it go. At some point you have to decide if holding a grudge or moving on for something better is more worth it." He raises his brows at me, waiting for an answer, one I don't give. "What's it going to be?"

I scoff. "It doesn't work like that. Not at the snap of your fingers. We're married, so I'll consider it, that's it." I give him a hardened look, but inside I'm melting, my defenses are breaking, and the dam holding everything in is on the verge of collapse, including my pussy that is eager this morning for Connor's touch.

The back of his palm glides along my cheek, and he smirks from accomplishment. "That's a start."

I shake my head gently, kind of exhausted that this is how my day is starting. Not energy-wise tired, more like my mind is muddled and I haven't even had coffee today yet.

"I'll take care of all of this." He indicates his head to the pile of gifts, some we haven't even opened yet.

I shrug a shoulder. "Maybe first we should see what everything is?" There could be some cute stuff, and I always need sweatshirts, plus it's not every day you get wedding presents to gawk at. "We won't keep all of this, and I don't have time to write thank-you notes."

"I'll have someone handle that. By the way, I have a charity game this weekend. You'll be there, right?"

"Oh." I'm taken aback. "I guess your wife should be there, uhm, sure. What's the charity?"

He grins. "A dog rescue shelter. Which is awesome since I know you can't be mad at me if I'm holding a puppy."

It causes me to grin and bob my head side to side. "You're kind of right. I wish my parents got a new dog after Pickles passed, but it just isn't the same."

Connor touches my shoulder. "He was the laziest dog ever."

I laugh. "Oh boy, he was. Then again, Puck is like a retriever on speed."

He laughs too. "My dad trained him for dog competitions. Biggest mistake, he's like addicted to chasing balls."

"Maybe we should have a joint calendar or something? Then we can plan events where we need to make an appearance as the perfect couple. My studio has a summer dance show at the summer festival, so you should probably be there. Oh, and family events."

He slides his arm around my shoulders. "Look at us, going all official with a shared calendar."

I chortle. "Uhm, I'm positive we can't get more official than a marriage certificate and rings."

"True. We're in the honeymoon phase, so may I make a suggestion?"

Skepticism takes over, yet I'm still enticed. "What?"

He begins to spin me slowly around. "We should be at it like rabbits. It's tradition."

Heat spreads through my body as he places my hands on the counter with my back to his front.

Yikes, I should be a little more resistant, but his breath caressing the back of my neck feels far too good, especially when his teeth scrape my earlobe.

"What the hell, why not," I sigh in defeat, and my body is already two steps ahead of my brain, and I press against his cock while he reaches for my front.

When I glance over my shoulder, Connor acts fast and captures my lips for a kiss, as if he knew he had a small window of opportunity.

Morning kisses, this is very new for us. He's a bit more sensual than I anticipated.

That is until my yoga pants are yanked lower, and he aligns himself with me.

"Hold on to the counter," he instructs.

I do as I'm told and look forward as I feel him plunge inside of me before he pumps. My entire body jolts on every move, my hands spread along the counter for more support, and as his robust movements intensify, I accidentally knock over my smoothie and neither of us seem to care.

"Connor." I'm not even sure if it's a beg or plea. We're moving fast, and I want it all. "Turn me around," I decide.

We quickly smack our lips together for a kiss before he retreats out and guides me over to the cabinet and traps me there. I lift my leg, and he enters me, stretching my leg farther.

He peeks down then at me with impressed eyes, and they grow bold when I lift my leg even higher.

"Benefits of having me as your wife. I'm flexible." My breath is heavy.

"Benefits of having me as your husband. I have stamina and can act fast when needed."

We both laugh for a second before we go at it with pure abandon until I'm shaking around his length, and he chases me not long after by unloading inside of me.

We stand there, draped around each other, completely spent and satisfied.

———

"You have the newlywed glow," Isla remarks as she leans against the ballet barre at my studio in workout gear, waiting for my ballet barre class for adults.

I attempt to avoid her gaze because I need to hide a ridiculous smile. "I don't," I deny. But I know the opposite is true. There was yesterday in the kitchen, then last night we might have gone another round after lights out in bed. This morning, I might have let him join me in the shower too.

It's bad. I'm addicted. But for an unexplained reason, I don't feel like I should run.

"I'm cautious," I reaffirm out loud.

"Sure, but you look like someone who can barely walk due to living her best life."

I have to laugh at her observation while I connect my phone to Bluetooth. "Maybe tone down the orgasm accusations, I have to deal with our moms in like two minutes."

"Oh please, knowing you and Connor can't keep your hands off one another would fuel April and Brielle's souls. They already texted me asking when we can throw a late bridal shower."

"What?"

She gives me a knowing nod. "I'm responsible for inviting all the girlfriends and wives of the hockey team." I'm not surprised, they text Isla like she's a daughter on a normal week, which I love, since other than her brother, Isla doesn't have a lot of family.

"Well… I guess it could be fun." I can't decide.

Isla has a sheepish grin. "You're kind of enjoying this wild ride you walked right into, huh?"

I croak out a sound. "It's not like there's been a boring minute lately."

"Admit it, of all the guys on that hockey team that you could have woken up married to, you're happy it's Connor."

"Relieved may be more like it," I admit.

She chuckles as she stretches her arm over her head. "Mark my words, Hadley Crews Spears. That guy isn't your accidental husband, he's your forever husband."

Before I can think of an answer, Isla tips her head to the door. "Speak of the devils." Isla offers a funny smile as my mom and Brielle enter my studio, along with two other ladies who join the class.

My mom walks to me and gives me a hug, along with Brielle. "You shouldn't be here, you should be on your honeymoon," my mom mentions.

"That will come later, I guess."

She waves a finger in front of me. "I know. But since you made the choice to elope *without* your parents present..." There is that disproving tone, and here comes her bright cheery smile. "Brielle and I have taken the liberty to explore options that something is done to celebrate your marriage."

Brielle hands me an envelope. "For you and Connor."

I examine it with curiosity and see it's a fancy envelope that's closed by a traditional stamp that requires melting a stick of wax that I used to do as a kid at the craft station at Pioneer Park nearby. My eyes nearly bug out when I notice the letters H & C engraved on the stamp.

Taking the card out, I begin to read then stop. "Did you two seriously just hand me an invite for my own wedding?"

Brielle bounces her shoulders. "We're just presenting options. We can't do *nothing*. It's not a wedding, per se, it's a celebration, wedding-ish."

I read out the card. "'Mr. and Mrs. Spencer Crews and Mr. and Mrs. Ford Spears warmly invite you to celebrate the *unexpected* marriage of their children Hadley Crews and Connors Spears at the Dizzy Duck Inn in Lake Spark.'" My jaw goes slack. "You even put hockey sticks on the invitation?"

"I thought it was a nice touch, actually. It was Brielle's idea to add that little phrase at the end." My mother is in her element.

"'He was always waiting to win her heart.'" I read it aloud in utter disbelief that they mocked up an invite and made it so sweet that I might get a toothache... but I'm grinning.

My mom turns to Isla. "I think the bridal shower is off. We're going bigger with a party if they agree. We'll meet for the second round of invites."

Isla bursts out laughing.

I have to fan myself because, as ridiculous as this is, my mom and Brielle look deliriously happy.

I hold the invite up. "We'll talk about this after class, now get to the barre."

Heading to my little table where I store my phone, I quickly send a text.

Me: Options for a real wedding-ish. Our moms created an example invite.

I take a photo of the invitation and send it to Connor.

Instantly, he types back.

Connor: What are the chances they actually booked the venue already?

Me: Probable. They've gone a little loco, but they seem so ecstatic.

Connor: I bet you my dad would order a tux for the dog.

Me: I guess this might be better than them planning our honeymoon.

Connor: Rumor has it that's a work-in-progress.

Me: Uh oh… Well, I gotta go teach.

Connor: Sure, hey… the invite is for well in the future, you know…

I still for a second. I did notice it's in a few months but didn't think much about it. Connor and I spoke of a timeline, but I'm not sure something ever connected that we have one.

I type a lie.

Me: I didn't notice…

Connor: Liar. Guess I'll just have to spank you later.

A goofy grin hits my face, and I set my phone on silent and hit play on the dance class playlist.

———

THE NEXT DAY, I find myself with a sandwich wrap sitting near the gazebo at the end of Main Street with my dad next to me. His request for a quick bite and walk wasn't unusual considering we always do stuff together, but the last few days he's been a bit distant. This chat over turkey and honey mustard feels a little more stiff than normal.

"Ashton is bummed he is missing your husband's charity game with puppies, but I have tickets for a baseball game in the city and need to make an appearance since it's my old team." The way my dad says husband causes my cheeks to raise.

"Puppies make people happy," I state blandly.

My father tosses the paper wrapper from his sandwich in the nearby trash can then turns his attention to me. "You okay with your mom going a little overboard with pushing a wedding-ish, if that's what we're calling it?"

I laugh. "Sure, she can plan away, but that doesn't mean it will happen. Are you okay with her acting crazy?"

"Sure. In this fictional wedding, would I get to have a dance as father of the bride?"

I interlink our arms. "Of course. Is that what has you down? Missing your father-of-the-bride responsibilities? Because if you say that's what has you in a mood, then I might not believe you."

"You didn't have the wedding I would have expected, but you're right. I'm just worried that you married for the wrong reasons."

I quirk my lips out. "Stop scowling, it's bad for your age lines. Besides, I thought you and Connor had a little chat the other day. Are you worried about something?"

My father's eyes glaze with a mood that I can't quite distinguish. "He never asked me for your hand in marriage, never went through my vigorous tests, and I needed to be sure that he will do anything for you."

"And?"

He pauses for a second. "It's nothing. Can you blame me for being protective? How are your first days as husband and wife? Wait..." He recoils when he realizes what he asked. "Don't answer that."

I chuckle and hold his arm tighter. "You know I think I've been lucky. You gave me the best life, kind of a breeze. The only thing that was a surprise was when you met Mom. I guess what I'm saying is I finally threw the unexpected at us. Surprise!" I splay my hands out.

He attempts to smile, but it slips, and he dips his gaze down. "Nearly gave me a heart attack too, and I'm not even fifty, so thanks for that."

"I'm your favorite daughter, you'll forgive me," I tease.

"You're my only daughter," he reminds me.

In the corner of my eye, I see Connor approaching us. I had mentioned via text that I was going to grab a bite with my dad today.

I offer him a curt wave to let him know that I see him. His eyes land on my father, and like every man who sees my father when they ever tried to enter my life, his eyes fill with a humorous fear.

My father stands to greet my husband. "Connor," he states.

"Spencer."

Lines furrow on my face because these two together are far too much testosterone, even for them. Connor kisses my cheek, and I swear my father is still adjusting to the scene, and truthfully, so am I, considering this time last week I would have swatted Connor away with a growly comment.

"You two should maybe go do a gym session or something together," I suggest to them. "You used to do that. One trip to Vegas and it feels like I need to lock you two in a room or something. I know, what about golf?"

"Golf isn't a sport," they both say in unison.

My hands fly up to calm them. "Okay, well, at least you both agree on something."

Both men stand taller, and my dad puffs his shoulders out. "We agree on a lot of things, Hadley. Like we both agree that you are something special and deserve only the best." He slaps a hand on Connor's shoulder. "Don't we, *son*."

Connor is amused by my father's expression. "Absolutely."

"I think I'll leave you two love birds alone. I need to pick up your brother from a friend's house." My dad steps to me and offers me his arm for a hug. "Let him take care of you," he mumbles. Our embrace breaks, and I see the sincerity in his eyes that throws me off. I realize that he and Connor are more alike than I ever thought; they are kings of mixed messages.

He gives a nod to Connor who returns the gesture. A secret code that only they seem to know.

I watch the man who was always my number one walk away as I stand next to the man who takes that spot in a different way. The profoundness of this moment stings my heart. I guess this is what growing up feels like. Because we never stop, even when we're in our twenties. We constantly evolve and change…

Even the ones who broke your heart the first time around.

They may not be the same, which is why another layer falls to the ground as far as Connor is concerned. Because what if he really was right the other day? If I let down a wall or two, he could be everything.

No better time than now to discover if he's right, especially since he's already my husband…

13

CONNOR

I'm not used to eating this late, but Hadley mentioned earlier that she would be finished at eight tonight, and after meeting her at the park earlier, she seemed a bit more distant than normal. Not frosty around me per usual but lost in thought.

I was in town, running an errand, when I texted to ask if she wanted to grab a bite, and she mentioned she was already at the park. I took it as an invite, but arriving, I saw that I was interrupting a moment between her and Spencer, and I have no clue what. She didn't say much after, and I accepted the silence when I walked her back to her studio.

Glancing down at the stove, I can see the vegetables and chicken are tender for the curry that I've made. I grab the small bowl of cashew nuts and toss them in when I hear the door to the garage open, and a minute later, Hadley enters.

"Wow." Hadley's voice sounds different. She walks slowly to the other side of the kitchen island and sets her giant water bottle down; the lines on the bottle indicate she is right on track for her hydration scheme. "You cook?" Her brows raise.

I smirk to myself because I aim to impress. "I do. Need to ensure

I'm eating good macros during game season. I figured you might have skipped dinner."

Her brows stay fixed in an arch as she seems taken aback. "You waited for me?"

"Yeah." I turn the stove off. "It's a mild yellow curry and rice."

Her eyes relax, and a warm smile forms as she sits down on the bar stool. "It looks delicious." A sound rumbles in her throat. "Is this your good-husband thing? Cooking?"

"Maybe." I wink at her before I dish out the food. I figure we can keep it simple and eat at the counter.

She bites her inner cheek as she watches me place the plate in front of her and remains somewhat in awe that I cook. I find my spot next to her and hand her a fork.

"Okay, here I go, I'm digging in," she announces before she brings a forkful of food to her mouth to blow on then carefully takes a bite. Hadley stalls as she chews, watching me, because she knows I'm waiting for my appraisal. She swallows, and her face stays neutral. "It's… good." Her facial expression relaxes.

"I know."

"I don't even want to know what you do when you actually try to impress a girl," she mentions before her fork dishes up another bite.

I study her for a second while I eat my own bite. "Not this. This is casual-weekday Connor."

"As opposed to puck-bunny Fridays?"

Ah, so she's fishing into my dating history.

"Cute. And no, cooking is reserved for wives."

"You've only ever had one wife."

I point my fork at her. "Smart."

Hadley sets her fork down and her look of hesitation returns before she surveys the room. "More gifts?"

"Ridiculous, huh?"

"Depends. Are there any big water bottles? I could use a new one."

I laugh because I appreciate that she doesn't care for fancy things, she's all practical.

"You know, other than your ridiculous request for birthday cakes, party dresses, and a dance studio in your house, contrary to what people would assume, you're not a spoiled princess."

She rests her chin onto her propped arm. "First off, cake is important for the soul, so it better be good. Second, dresses are key for many situations; weddings, birthdays, proms, impromptu elopements. And finally, the small dance studio in my parents' house was all my dad's idea when I was six."

I scratch my end-of-day stubble on my chin at the mention of her father. He gave me the father-of-the-bride speech the other day, nothing I wasn't prepared for or couldn't handle, but our relationship is one of understanding—ensure Hadley has the best life.

"You okay? Seemed like you were kind of out of it after seeing your dad," I pry.

"I'm fine." She's lying, but I let it go.

We stew for a few beats in silence, just playing with our food. I'm not sure we're that hungry.

But then she does something that catches me off guard. She lunges forward on the chair, cups my face with both hands, and plants her lips on mine.

It takes a moment to digest what is happening, but then I close my eyes and give back as much she gives, which is a lot. I snake my arm around her middle to keep her close. Her lips nearly suck the life out of me, it's a bruising kiss, and we both moan a sound of satisfaction. She's fervent and determined, I'm not sure of what, but I'm sure as hell along for the ride. I'm lost in this kiss that she owns.

The sound of our lips parting is what causes me to open my lids and see her swollen lips.

"I'm deciding," she states. My eyes widen slightly because she has my full attention, and her eyes meet mine. Hers filled with adventure and mine filled with hope. "About you. This husband-and-wife thing, as if we could actually work."

I swivel my stool to allow me to have her in full view and for my fingertips to rest on her lower arm. "Why not go all in and see if we can prove ourselves wrong?"

An audible breath escapes her lips. "People change, but I don't want to be on the receiving end if you haven't. I wanted to make you suffer, and I'm sure you had some other plan too. But the difference between you and me is that I can't survive you hurting me a second time around."

I squeeze her arm, because nothing I say will rewind the clock, all I can do is be honest. "I want to prove you wrong. Maybe waking up married was our odd way of getting a fresh start."

She slides off the chair, leaving my fingers vacant. Hadley walks a few steps before throwing her arms up in the air. "I'm cautious and still deciding," she gripes and leaves me with the hope that maybe she's softening to me.

————

CIRCLING AROUND THE RANGE ROVER, I open the door for my wife. She's busy typing away on her phone, and it kind of annoys me. "I might throw that phone somewhere. You've been on it non-stop since we got in the car," I tell her.

Hadley tosses the phone in her bag, a Spinners tote. "I know, I know. It's my little brother. He has some biology project for his summer science club he's taking part in that I need to help him with." I relax because we both have a soft spot for little brothers.

Offering her my hand, she gently shakes her head and smirks at my effort to be a gentleman, before she slides her palm onto mine and we begin to walk. Although we parked in a quiet spot behind the training center, in about one minute, we'll be surrounded by my dad's marketing team, hockey guys, and puppies.

I'm wearing my jersey, and I'm thankful that she got her jersey less than twenty-four hours after our marriage was announced, because the marketing department acted quick and sent over something for Hadley, and now she's wearing my number 19 with the word husband on the back. Paired with her jeans and hair only partly up thanks to her sunglasses, I can only conclude that I'm lucky to have a sexy-fox wife.

"I guess it's a few photo ops, then I'll go change for the friendly hockey match. We're only going to do a one-period game." It's for charity, the local shelter where my parents adopted Puck from. A few guys from my team are here, along with a few veterans, including my dad and uncle.

Hadley snorts a laugh. "Isla and the marketing department are geniuses. I'm positive this setup got every female from the 18-35 demographic here within a fifty-mile radius."

I shrug a shoulder before I open the side door. "Happy to oblige using my good looks if it means it helps a little furball find a home."

She stops and tips her nose up, giving me a knowing look. "As much as I could call you out, I know that you are actually being noble here. We both know you're going to milk the attention for the sake of a good cause."

I bring my hand to my heart. "Most definitely isn't for the female popularity. I'm a taken and tied-down man now."

She chuckles under her breath, and I follow her in. Instantly, we see the main entrance covered in balloons and a table to one side with various cookies, both for humans and canines. There is a pen of dogs playing with toys on the other side of the hall.

Already Briggs is holding a yellow Lab puppy, and Shawn is holding a mixed breed that doesn't appear to be a puppy at all. They smile for the photographer, yet the smile on their faces is purely natural, because how can you not be happy right now?

We are quickly ushered by one of the coordinators to one of the dog pens, and before we know it, I'm holding a mixed Labrador breed that is older, but a hundred pounds is easy for me, so I cradle him like a baby. Hadley is cooing and rubbing his belly, but the dog just looks at her with a blank stare.

"This dog is way too chill," I note.

"He seems to be one of the few on this earth that enjoys your company. Isn't he lovable?" She scratches his chin.

Glancing down at the dog in my arms that's wearing a bandana and this guy is sucking me in. "I need you to pull the wife card."

"Wife card?" Hadley wonders.

"Rule the house, tell me no, remind me that we don't need a dog," I explain.

She giggles, and the way her hand touches my shoulder feels good. But the last few days she's been softening around me, and we just... flow.

We ignore the camera going off around us.

"Oh, I have no problem saying no to you," she jokes. "But I also see cookies over there, so I dunno... priorities." She slants her shoulders up.

"You two are adorable!" Brianne, one of the wives of a veteran from my dad's years, says as she greets us, with her meticulous blonde hair. She was young when she married then; I can imagine she still isn't pushing forty yet.

"Hey, it's been a long time," I greet her and bounce the dog gently as I cradle him.

She turns her attention to Hadley. "I'm Brianne O'Shae, my husband is playing today. He used to play for the Spinners. Congratulations, you two! Did the team reach out about the wives' club? You are in for a wild ride at games. A few rules, but mostly everyone is decent."

Hadley glances sidelong to me, slightly panicked. "Someone will be in touch, I'm sure," I say.

She awkwardly smiles to Brianne. "I'm sure we will be fine. I watched my mom handle my dad for a few years before he retired from baseball."

The bubbly woman in front of us touches Hadley's shoulder. "Oh, that's right. You'll be a pro then. Okay, well, you two are the cutest. Loving the social media boost that it's giving the team." She shimmies away, and her burst of sunshine makes us need a second to come down.

Briggs arrives next to me, now dog-free. "How's married life, you two?"

"Joyous," Hadley answers, with smile fixed and one-tone voice.

Briggs chuckles, and we both watch Hadley meander on over to the cookie table where Isla is busy checking her tablet.

I make faces at the dog in my arms, and he opens his mouth as if he wants to talk but then nuzzles into my chest. This guy knows how to give marketing what they need; social media will go crazy for this.

"Not going to lie, it's a little strange seeing you two together and being kind of sweet. I mean, you both always flirted, it was some serious foreplay we all witnessed, but this is… damn. You're completely into this." He speaks low so only I can hear.

"I am," I admit honestly without hesitation.

My friend grins at me. "Maybe this will help keep your head in the game next season." He nudges my arm because being an ass sometimes is our play.

"I'll be better. You just need to get laid, and then you can play at my level," I joke.

"Yeah, this is why you shouldn't have eloped. I was counting on a hot bridesmaid who needed her night rocked."

One of the volunteers comes to take the dog out of my arms, and I kind of miss him already as they walk away.

Briggs and I begin to walk toward the locker rooms. "I'm still debating how we can turn this all around and still have a bachelor party post-'oops I got married,'" he comments.

My lips quirk out. "Are we talking like beers with the boys or full-out 'Hadley would rip my balls off' kind of party?"

"You lost your right to strippers when you signed your name in Vegas. Doesn't mean we all have to suffer," he teases, but then he turns serious. "Nah, we'll check out a brewery or something. Your dad and I have already been texting to maybe arrange something."

"I'm happy my life is turning around everyone's social calendars," I quip.

"I bet. Now let's go play some hockey."

An hour later, after getting on my equipment, some warming up, some photos with dogs on the ice, and waving to some fans who came out, I find myself near the center line to the right. This is low-key friendly, so no fancy lights, more of a practice than anything. I'm playing against my dad and Shawn, plus a few others, so nothing like making this an easy game.

I skate toward my position on the ice, and my sight sidelines to Shawn who is skating next to me.

Shawn begins to speak to me. "I've been trying to figure out what wedding gift to get you. I'm thinking a vibrator is probably what your wife needs since she's with you."

My blood begins to boil, but I know I need to take the high road. "Classy. Aiming low at a charity game."

We both line up. Me as right defense on the blue line and Shawn on the opposite side as left defense.

The referee blows the whistle, and my sight focuses on guarding his ass, following him is not my ideal, but I have dogs to save and a wife to impress.

Telling hockey players to play for fun is kind of pointless. The retired veterans have a point to prove that they're still young, the new players want to show enthusiasm, and wingers just want to be an ass.

We're five minutes in and every block and chase is making me work.

My only relief is when I notice Hadley sitting in the stands watching me. It feels like extra support, makes me focus better, and she could be part of my formula to always win. I ignore any flag in my head about timelines or next season, especially when she wiggles her fingers at me because she caught me looking.

But now we're going into another play, and Shawn is pissing me off again with his radiating aggression.

"You know, I'm confident if I'd gotten her drunk enough that she would have married me too."

"Fuck off. That's not what it is," I grit out.

"Right. She'd probably spread her legs too."

I drop my stick and shove him without thought, my protective instinct in full swing. "Do not speak of my wife that way." My gloves come off.

"Touchy, Spears. I would be too if I had girl with a tight body like that."

I push him again before all hell breaks loose, and we take turns in headlocks. We scuffle, and the referee blows the whistle before players are ripping us apart.

"Box," the ref informs me as he brakes on his skates next to me. "Instigating, two-minute penalty."

Great. I got sent to the penalty box during a charity game.

14

CONNOR

Briggs sits on a sofa in one of the spare offices, with a yellow Lab puppy on his lap as he attempts to be the peacemaker after the game.

"Seriously, it may be the off-season, but if our captain or coach were here, then you two would be dead. What kind of shitty sportsmanship was that out there?" Briggs continues to lecture us as he continues to stroke the puppy.

"Dude, are you seriously going to keep that puppy on your lap as you attempt to get us to listen?" I point out the obvious as I adjust the ice pack on my shoulder and lean into the lounger.

He doesn't stop. "Yep. This fluffball is like therapy. We should totally get a team dog."

"Well, why don't we have Connor ask his uncle since we know he has the connections," Shawn throws out the shade as he touches his roughed-up arm.

"Fuck you, man, I earned my spot."

"He kind of did. We need his skills," my friend says, supporting me.

Shawn looks between us, completely unamused.

"Don't say anything about my wife, and then we won't have any future problems," I suggest.

"Fine. But you realize I could say she's standing over there in a turtleneck and you would lose it. You are so fucking whipped it's unbelievable. You better get it together before next season or I will have no problem highlighting to the press about your Vegas accident, considering they are all shipping your romance as if it was years in the making."

"Go ahead. We'll be the proof that you're lying, you'll see," I promise.

Right on cue, there is a knock on the door and Hadley peeks in. "Sorry to interrupt, I came to check on my husband."

Hearing her say husband, meaning me, is good. I'm already used to it.

Shawn shakes his head and stands. "You know, it doesn't matter if you have a ring on her finger, you would have ended up in the penalty box for her even before." He walks out, giving Hadley a fake smile.

"He might have a point," Briggs adds before he too leaves.

Hadley patiently waits for them to exit before closing the door behind her. She approaches me with caution, reaching out and debating if she should touch my shoulder when I stand.

"You ended up in the penalty box during a charity game for puppies," she states the obvious, with underlying amusement in her tone. "Was it because…"

I peer down at her as I adjust the ice pack, but she takes over with her hands and holds it just right. "Doesn't matter."

"Kind of does. Besides, Briggs already texted Isla about why you went berserk out there, so I know."

I shake my head gently. Of course he did. "Siblings."

"Want to know a secret that I really hate to admit?" She moves so she is squared off with me, our middles flush and her voice raspy.

I'm fully invested to discover her secrets. "Go on."

"I don't condone violence in any shape or form… but knowing you were maybe defending my honor slightly, then well..." She kisses my cheek. Who does that? The woman who knows any touch can send a man spiraling, that's who. "It's kind of hot," her voice husks.

"Oh yeah?" My voice is mixed with desire, because her saying that motivates both my heart and cock.

I should kiss her, but her eyes twinkle in a way they did the other night, with adventure and chance glazing her eyes. I should let her lead this moment.

"I'm being cautious," she states softly, with vulnerability seeping into her voice.

"As in?"

A slow delicious smirk begins to stretch on her mouth. "The husband-and-wife thing. We can try and see where it goes. The whole letting down our walls as if we actually enjoy one another part. I'm just not jumping fully in without hesitation, but okay, might as well make it bearable between us."

I give up on the ice pack as it falls to the floor. "What are your conditions?" I grin because she wouldn't make it this easy, and she shouldn't, considering our history. I bring my hand to the back of her neck so I'm in position to slam my lips down on hers after she answers.

She steps forward and rises on her toes, drawing me in, bringing our mouths closer. I feel her breath, and it encourages me to brush my lips along her cheek.

"We might have consummated the marriage, and we might be sharing a bed." Her sultry tone is a killer. "I might go to bed every night in next to nothing." The image sounds like heaven. She's reeling me in, and my thumb blots her bottom lip.

I swallow. "Uh-huh."

"But Connor, no entanglements until you work for it. Woo the hell out of me. Show me why the women peg you as their romance hockey guy. Until further notice, you get nada except a kiss."

My stomach sinks. She's brutal. Vicious. And fine, I'll do it because I want to see where we'll go.

I groan a sound. "Fine."

"Fine?" She doubts me.

"Yeah, fine. Are spankings off the table?" I tease her.

She hums. "I guess one or two would be fine." She flashes her eyes at me. "Now kiss me."

I slam my mouth onto hers and ensure that it's firm, deep, and long. Inescapable is what I'm aiming for.

I love when she kisses me back. It only reconfirms that I'm not delusional, and maybe I'm right. I might have pushed her away over the years, but she always wanted to be mine, even if she couldn't admit it.

Reluctantly pulling away, I enjoy how her arms hang around my neck. "You're going to go all out at bedtime, aren't you?"

"You mean wear your jersey and nothing else? Absolutely." Her saccharine tone is already misery. Her chin tips down, and I know she's looking at my hard cock. "Oops. Poor guy." She fakes concern with that gorgeous grin of hers.

"We so need to adopt a therapy dog now. My dick is going to be so turned on by you constantly that I fear I may go blind since he has to wait."

Her head falls back in laughter, and it is music to my ears. Hadley unhooks from around me, and all I can do is admire her, as I feel it in my bones that this has to be our time.

She glances over her shoulder on her way out the door. "I'll give you a second and meet you out by the dogs."

"How giving of you." I roll my eyes.

A few minutes later and I find her by the same Labrador mix that I held earlier. Before I get a chance to tease her that she's attached, the woman in her thirties who volunteers notices me.

"I was just telling your wife about Ace. He's one of our older dogs. Only four, but too old for most. He's up to date on his shots and he is chipped. He was abandoned in an apartment a few towns over."

Hadley's face turns sad and my own heart tugs. "That's horrible. We also had a dog growing up that my mom adopted when he was older." Hadley pets Ace's head, with his eyes sullen.

I swipe a hand through my hair then pull at the back, struggling to walk us away. "I-I mean, surely, he could…"

Hadley shoots me a hard stare. "Don't. You travel during game season."

I shrug. "You wouldn't be alone if we got a dog."

Her eyes bug out. "Dogs are as big a commitment as marriage." She ensures only I can see that her eyes flash, indicating that we're already in new territory; why bring another into life to it?

"You're right," I calmly voice.

Her eyes bounce between the dog and me. "Maybe my mom and dad would be interested. They are surely ready to get another dog, my brother wants one."

Ace wags his tail and angles his head to the side.

"I know, buddy, you had a connection to Connor." Hadley's melting. It's made worse when his eyes travel to me.

"Boy, he likes you two," the volunteer states the obvious.

My voice cracks because I'm caving at high speed.

"No." Hadley pinches the bridge of her nose. "I'm supposed to use the wife card." She winces as she says that.

The volunteer pipes in. "If it helps, you wouldn't be able to take him home today. We have a required waiting period to ensure that new owners think through their decision. During the waiting period, he is on reserve. But he also has to finish his basic training that all our dogs take part in before adoption, and that doesn't end for a few weeks."

Hadley's eyes shoot to me with hope, but she doesn't want to admit it.

A dog wasn't really on my radar, but this guy is calling to us with his wagging tail and pleading eyes. Maybe Hadley's right, her parents are better suited.

"Come on, we should go." It pains me to say it.

She nods, and we begin to say goodbye to the dog, but he stands on his back legs and rests his front paws on the pen.

Hadley and I look at one another, and in unison we blurt out, "Maybe."

———

"I MEAN, even if we don't work out, we can share custody. During the hockey season, I'll take care of him." Hadley speaks while she's in the bathroom, with the door ajar to the bedroom as she does her nightly routine, which I noticed a few days ago requires a lot of creams.

I scoff as I scroll through my phone in bed, shirtless. "If we don't work out. Thanks for the vote of confidence," I call out.

She emerges through the door, turning the light off to the bathroom. I drop my face into my hand because this isn't fair. Hadley is wearing an old cut-off Lake Spark Summer Festival shirt and panties, and the best part is that she doesn't even make a big deal about it.

"Well, we can't get Ace for a while, so maybe we will come to our senses," she mentions as she crawls into bed.

"I feel like I'm betraying Puck." I'm completely serious. He's the family dog, although he has a special kinship with my dad.

She smiles at me as she fluffs her pillow. "By the way, I was kind of curious what that hockey wife said, so I checked my email and realized like three different coordinators from your team e-mailed me. Welcome emails, protocols, schedules, and they need a copy of my passport."

"Yeah, probably for booking travel. Remember, I travel to that great country to the north for games," I explain.

"You mean during game season, which is *after* the off-season." The way she says that has me worried, and I turn my body to her.

"I thought we no longer have a timeline." I narrow my eyes at her.

She slithers lower into the bed to get comfortable. "I said I'm being cautious and let's see what happens if we make somewhat of an effort," she corrects me.

"Well, I'm not worried."

Hadley rolls to lie on her side. "I noticed. We are heading into dog-parent territory."

I follow her indication and get into the same position in bed, facing her. "You're in the lead here. Nothing beyond kissing, *except* you didn't specify where." I squint one eye.

She playfully shoves my arm, and I grimace from slight discomfort. "Shit. Forgot about your shoulder and defending my honor."

"You said it was hot."

"It was." She hooks her leg over my hip and begins to stroke her fingers gently over my biceps. "You for sure earned cuddle time."

I snort a laugh. "If that's the only thing on offer then get closer, Sprinkles."

Hadley shimmies nearer until our bodies meet, and she guides my arm over her. "Shh, don't make a big deal that I've traded in ripping your throat out for cuddling."

"It'll be our secret. I have good arms for this, though."

"I remember." Her words hit me because I know she means all those years ago when we had a special night—up until the point I initiated our war.

My lips twitch. "It's a different time now," I promise softly and kiss the top of her head.

I'll woo her like she requested and win, but I would just throw her over my shoulder kicking anyhow, because I have no plans of letting her go again. Our marriage may have been an accident, but divorce won't be in our cards.

15

HADLEY

I count the number of bee-print leotards in the box that was just delivered. This has been my day today. Sitting on my knees, checking on all the costumes that came in for the upcoming summer show, after my doctor's appointment for my annual checkup this morning. Slamming my pen down after I cross off my list, I glance to Isla who writes down a number on her list, as I roped her in somehow since she was working from home this afternoon.

"I think everything is here," I confirm.

"Cool." Isla swings her feet to enable her to sit cross-legged on the floor, and she takes a sip from her water bottle. "Did I tell you that Ford said he is sending me to a conference later in the year down in Florida? It's especially for organizing sporting events, it should be good."

"Sounds awesome. If it's near a beach, then I might just tag along."

"Tampa or nearby, I forget the exact location. Perfect for my bikini that I intend to pack. I actually checked the schedule, and I think the Spinners have an away game there the same week. Assuming you're still in your wife glory, then you should totally come."

A line stretches on my closed mouth at the way she said that. "Assuming?"

Isla flicks her hair behind her shoulder and smiles. "What's going on with hubby? Don't blame the canines, you two were completely easy and in your own bliss the other week. Thank you too for giving the marketing department enough material to break the internet."

I begin to pull my hair up into a bun as I recall how Connor and I are falling into a routine. He makes me my breakfast smoothie, we check in during the day, we laugh over late dinners, and go to bed not to sleep. "It's nothing. The hockey game was fun, minus Connor ending up in timeout like a toddler. You did a great job organizing it. We might even adopt one of the dogs or convince my parents to."

Isla begins to fan herself. "Oh my, if you adopt a dog together, this would absolutely blow up our socials. That's me being 'trying to advance my career' Isla. Your best friend has to point out the obvious…" She trails off, and I look at her, entertained and waiting. "You are totally committing to making this work between you and Connor. What in the world changed?"

I slide a box to the side. "It's more… I don't know. I owe it to myself to try and make it work since we're married. But something my dad said made wheels in my head turn toward where we all deserve a second chance, and maybe my brain got fried when we kind of, you know, the other day."

Her entire face blazes with so much interest. "What now then?"

"He has to prove to me that I won't get hurt. I'm not jumping full swing in, I'm dipping my toes in a little bit first," I attempt to justify. My feelings are there, but I've built a barrier.

Standing up, I pretend to wipe dirt off my legs, as I'm satisfied that I got through the boxes and can start handing them off to the dancers in the coming days.

"As long as you believe you are making the right move. I mean, despite watching you two over the years nearly murder each other, I don't think Connor would ever let anything happen to you, not then or now."

My jaw goes slack, and I touch my cheek as I listen to her state the obvious, what everyone, including myself, has always known. "Anyhow, we're married and kind of living together, so I might as well see him give his best shot."

"What is his version of best shot when it isn't hockey?" she wonders.

My face screws. "No clue, but he texted me earlier that I need to be ready soon, which is fine, as I'm letting one of the teenagers take on more responsibilities with teaching."

"What's the dress code?"

My shoulders bounce. "He didn't say. I'm sure in his mind less is better, zips are preferred, and my purse should be able to fit handcuffs."

"I dunno, is there also room for the blindfold?" Connor's voice takes over the atmosphere from where he's standing behind me. Is it possible to already see his smug smirk? I'm positive he has one.

Isla attempts to hide her smile. "That's my cue to leave."

We both stand and she walks by me while I remain frozen, not because I'm mortified—I'm not. It's because a flutter travels through me, and my heart thrums from excitement that Connor has plans for me.

I give Isla a nod in acknowledgment before I spin on my feet to face Connor who is leaning against the doorframe as if he owns the place, and his mouth confirms the image that I had in my head.

"I'm sure you'll keep her in line." Isla snorts a laugh when she walks past Connor, leaving us alone.

"You're early," I say, attempting to steady my voice.

He does that move I like, where his eyes dip low, then he bashfully glances up with a suave grin. "I don't know the rules around kidnapping since we're married. Is that kidnapping then? Anyway, there has been a change of plans."

"Oh?"

His hand that was resting behind his back comes up, and I chuckle instantly because a blindfold is dangling from his finger.

"What can I say? You know me so well," he explains.

Now I'm anticipating what he is up to.

———

I'M KIND OF DISAPPOINTED that Connor hasn't used the blindfold yet. Not exactly thrilled that I didn't get a chance for a shower either, but he insisted I was fine in jeans and a t-shirt.

We're driving along the winding road around the lake, and we are not heading in the direction of the house. He has "Follow You" by Beyond the Horizon on his speakers, and I could see him training to this.

I attempt to meander my gaze to the backseat, but immediately, he tsks me. "Eyes forward," he demands as he focuses on the road. "Or you get the blindfold early."

My fingers tap on my thighs. "I have no clues to work with."

"That's the point of a surprise."

I scoff as I lean against the window of the car. "Haven't we had enough surprises lately?"

A grin tugs on his lips. "This one is planned."

"Give me something to work with."

"I can tell you what we're *not* doing." He glances sideways toward me then back to the road.

I give him an unimpressed look. "Helpful." Nothing is further from the truth, but I'm curious. "Go on."

That confident look plays on the corner of his mouth again. "Well, no Dizzy Duck Inn, because that's your parents' and my aunt and uncle's spot, for reasons I don't particularly want to know." I smile because he is so right. "The lagoon is like sacred territory for my own parents, so I can never take anyone there," he adds.

My smile vanishes, and he notices. "Uh, I mean, not that there are a lot of anyones, just… yeah, can't save myself there." He gives a pained expression before he tilts his head. "I thought about taking you to the city, looked for tickets to the Joffrey Ballet, but they're not in season in the summer, except for a public show in Millennial Park, plus we don't get much privacy in the city."

My eyes nearly bug out because he put thought into it, and I'm surprised he even knows where to look for ballet tickets; surely, he must have an assistant who helps him. "So, where does that leave us?" I ask.

"Back to our own place."

We drive a few minutes more, and he parks off the road next to the woods. I'm fairly confident that we shouldn't be here, but Connor isn't one for rules.

He indicates for me to wait a second when he turns the engine off, and I patiently stay seated until he circles the car to open the door.

Connor holds up the blindfold with a cheeky smile. "It's time."

I can't even attempt to give him a scowl because the stirring emotions are running wild inside of me, as there is significance here. It's been a hot minute—okay, months—since I was on a date with anyone, and what woman wouldn't be in good spirits when her husband tries to surprise her? I'm not immune, even I know that.

My hand molds into his palm and I stand, turning on my heel to allow him to wrap the black fabric around my eyes. Connor knows how to tighten a knot, and my brain instantly registers that fact with heat swirling inside of me.

"I didn't blindfold you on the road because that's pure hell on the turns, but you won't be this way for long, although we can keep this blindfold for other activities later tonight if you want," he casually mentions, and I feel him step away and hear the hatch of his car open.

"Wishful thinking," I call out.

He returns, and next thing I know he is guiding me. The ground feels uneven and rough, and occasionally I feel long grass against my ankles or I step on a large pebble.

"I have an inkling where we are, but really, where the hell are we? Don't we need to worry about, I don't know, foxes or raccoons? The old lady from the grocery store mentioned the coyotes in the area are getting bold," I list.

Connor just chuckles as he helps me step up a rock. "Isn't that what you want? You can feed me to the foxes."

"That was before we got drunk and reckless. You might be growing on me a smidgen since then."

"I think I'm growing on you a full nine inches," he retorts.

I giggle, and without notice, he hoists me up and throws me over one shoulder. I can feel he is carrying something in his other arm. Damn, I love his arm strength.

It's a few steps, then he twirls me around for effect before plopping me down on a spot. I can feel him step away for a few seconds, and I wait, noticing the somersault in my belly and the way my pulse has changed in the last few minutes; it's eagerness.

His fingers feel like feathers, yet they leave a gentle imprint on my shoulders as he half turns me in one direction before his digits sneak under the cloth to untie my blindfold. "Open your eyes, Sprinkles," he whispers as the fabric falls.

It only takes the flick of my eyes opening and two blinks for me to be awestruck. I'm overwhelmed about where to look because there is the backdrop of the lake and woodlands below since we seem to be up on a hill, and right here in front of me where Connor must have been earlier because there's a blanket and a few lanterns. I notice the box that keeps food warm and realize that must have been in the back of his car the whole time.

"Oh." It softly escapes my lips before I turn my head to find that Connor has been watching me this whole time, with his foot on a log and face stoic.

"Uh." He shyly strokes his jawline with his thumb. "Doesn't this place seem familiar? Although, last time we might have stayed in my car."

Looking around, I *knew* this place was familiar. I know why too. A profoundness hits me, and I do my best to keep it in by biting the inside of my lip. "You mean, do I remember being here at night with you once?" In truth, this brings up mixed emotions, and I'm not entirely sure if this is the place for us to be.

A fondness hits him, and his head tilts low while his eyes perk up. "Yeah." His voice is soft. It seems he chose this place for a reason.

A silence floats between us because we don't need many words in relation to the significance of this place. It was a beautiful night, but it started our years of hate too. I glance around again at the view. I think I'll choose to remember the good, which is why I turn back to him with a small half-smile.

"I haven't even pulled out the big guns yet," he says.

I cross my arms. "Oh yeah? What might that be?"

He indicates with his head to go sit on the blanket, and I easily follow instruction.

He is busy grabbing items from the food box. "We're not really supposed to light anything that burns here, but I'm sure the forest ranger will let me off when I get him season tickets."

I can't even tell if he's joking. My eyes trail down to see he is holding a small tinfoil-wrapped casserole dish, and it looks familiar, the writing on the top anyways. "What is that?"

"My gamechanger for tonight."

"Leave it to you to think food can sway me."

Connor takes a seat next to me, with our elbows grazing, and he hands me the box. "You're mom's famous mac 'n' cheese."

"Really?" I'm completely thrown off because it's such an original and sweet gesture.

He nods, with his subtle smirk permanent, because he's satisfied with my facial expressions. "I know how much you love that stuff, and since you're not living at home anymore, I figured you might miss it. I asked for her help for dinner, and yeah, the squeal and aws nearly burst my eardrums."

My cheeks hurt from how much I'm smiling. I can picture it all in my head. "I bet. She probably went overboard too."

"Oh, she did," he confirms. "We also have zucchini pancakes. There is no logic to the menu other than she said they were your favorites."

It's thoughtful that he reached out to her.

A silence takes over as our eyes catch and silly looks grace our faces. I decide to pipe up and admit the truth. "You might get points for how this night is starting."

"Does that hurt? Giving me a compliment?" He nudges my shoulder with his.

I touch my arm, then my stomach, followed by my legs. "Everything seems to be okay."

"That sucks, I was kind of hoping you needed me to tend to your wounds."

Reaching out, I hook a finger under his chin to bring his mouth in my direction. Our foreheads touch and our eyes connect. I could kiss him, but I enjoy keeping him captivated like this. He's partly in suspense if I'll bring my lips to his or if this location is a good idea at all.

Dance has been the passion of my life. The best dance, however, is the one where Connor and my lips trace and brush one another's, with our breathing entwined, while our noses nuzzle the lines of our cheeks. The most unchoreographed dance is my favorite, and that's him.

"You're making it hard, Connor Spears," I rasp. "I'm supposed to make you work *really* hard."

"Well, Hadley *Spears*, sometimes a clear shot appears, and you take it." He returns my tone.

I'll let him off on the hockey reference because the sport is part of the blueprint of who he is, and I don't mind. I kiss the corner of his mouth, nothing too sensual; it would be respectable enough for my grandparents, but it drives this man crazy.

Giving us some space, I retreat and decide to get our conversation moving and enjoy this picnic that is in a prime location for the upcoming sunset to the west. "You'll always play for the Spinners?"

He shrugs before he reaches to the side for a bottle of wine. "My contract is actually for one more year. I'm an unrestricted free agent which means next year it's about the right contract and whichever team offers it. I would like to stay with the Spinners, but I'm not sure my prospects are great. Nobody here wants me to be captain considering my family connection to the team. Careerwise, it will be better if I find a new team."

Oh, away from Lake Spark.

I touch his shoulder to comfort him while he works on the bottle, because he has talent, and it would be a loss if people thought only of potential bias. "I can see that… uhm… I guess your wife would follow you where your team would be?" I never thought about that, and I'm not questioning why I seem invested in the topic, but then again, a timeline kind of vanished somewhere in my head.

His fingers still on the bottle mid-pour. "I would hope so. Then again, I travel for more than half the games. Hockey is a lot more grueling on the schedule than other sports."

"Yet you want a dog," I state the obvious.

"Between our families, I'm confident he would have plenty of places to stay and be happy, even if I'm away. It's better than living at the shelter."

"You really want him, huh?" I have to gush because Connor is like a kid waiting for Santa, and it's all for the sake of saving a cute dog. Some people would call that being a man of character or having a heart of gold, and in this case, it's all true.

He gives me a pointed look. "Even if you want me crucified, I know you would take care of him."

"Kind of correct. I'm used to hectic families, with pets included."

Connor hands me a glass of red wine. "It's kind of cool."

I nod. "Considering I don't have many cousins, then yes, I'm lucky that our little family provided the full effect. Twins run in my father's side, but he lost his twin brother young. My mom was an only child, though."

He pauses for a second and looks at me with interest. "Twins? So, we're having like ten kids." He looks into his glass of wine, nearly somber.

"Whoa, relax, twins means two, not ten, and I'm still years away from wanting to swell my ankles to push out a baby or three. But anyway, I guess you and I are family people. Didn't Violet make you godfather to her daughter?"

His brows bounce. "I'm sure she and Declan argued over that one, but yeah, I'm Willow's godfather. Happy to be the stellar influence she needs." He isn't afraid to put himself in a different light if it means humor.

Connor's soft smile returns. "We have something else in common." He holds out his glass for a toast. "We now have the same last name, and I think it's the next best thing to a leash for keeping you tied to me and in line."

I chortle yet clink our glasses. Possession is completely a turn-on for me, and I have no problem admitting that, which is why it's worthy of a toast. The sweltering in his sentence creates an ache between my thighs too.

Leaning my head against his shoulder, I interlace our arms and let a relaxing breath escape while we look forward at the horizon.

I'm beginning to wonder if our whole situation may actually be luck on our side. Because right now, he feels like the Connor that I kept locked in my dreams, but this time, I open my eyes and he's still there.

16

CONNOR

She's easing into me, tearing off a few layers, and right now I feel like I'm being the man I should have always been to her.

I'm following her lead, but I would kill to lay her down right now, but that's not what tonight is about. Tonight is a sort of truce to move on, with the possibilities endless.

The thing is, I've always been the guy who can be charming when dating someone, but tonight is confronting that maybe I've always done it for show, because with Hadley, it's very different. My entire body comes alive, and I truly mean every romantic gesture that I'm making.

We eat dinner, and it must be true that food brings comfort. It dawned on me earlier that even though Hadley is a grown woman, our situation kind of called for an impromptu move in a flash. She doesn't seem to mind, but still, I wanted to do something for her to remind her of her old home.

With the sun setting, the orange hue fades, revealing a starry sky. The lanterns were a nice touch if I do say so myself.

Lying down on the blanket, we look at the sky with hopes of finding a shooting star. She gently jabs her finger into my hand, and I can tell she is testing the waters for me to weave our hands together. I follow her cues and slip her fingers through mine.

"Maybe we're idiots and should get out of Lake Spark. See the world. Or maybe that's why we do stupid things, we were out of our habitat," she muses with humor mixed in her tone.

I chuckle and sling her leg over mine. "Speak for yourself. I'm on the road half the year, although mostly I don't see much. Besides, nobody bothers us here except our parents." I'm happy she asked about my career earlier. My schedule isn't for the faint of heart, though she doesn't seem deterred. Then again, I'm not sure what timeline for us exists in her head.

She sighs but it seems peaceful. "Do you think having memories together from our younger selves is a curse? Like, it's hard to differentiate between adult us and younger us?"

"I fucking hope not. I promise, I look at you and only think about those tiny tattoos on your skin that I can explore before my tongue runs up to your pussy." Fuck, I'm supposed to keep us above board, not get us sidetracked.

"Is that where your mind is at?" she teases.

I huff out a breath and flip us to ensure she is under me. "Yes and no. You are a feisty woman who I kind of admire, who can dish out what she takes and isn't afraid to knock me down a peg or two."

"I'm only feisty when it's you."

"I noticed. I'm only pulling out ridiculous moves in the romance department when it's with you, so congrats, we bring out the best in one another," I promise.

Her body writhes under me, and my cock instantly reminds me that he's alive and waiting. "Even though we get two timelines," she says, "I have one little fantasy years in the making that you kind of need to make come true."

"What might that be?" I play along.

She reaches out to claw her fingers into my shirt. "Kiss me under the stars again, just like last time we were here."

I pretend to debate her request, but then I'm lowering my mouth, happy to oblige. Kissing her is an addiction. It doesn't matter if she's in a foul or pleasant mood, I want her mouth both on mine and wrapped around me. I want my name to escape her lips as she pleads, and her mouth should always look like I've ruined her in the best possible way.

I groan as she runs the tip of her tongue along mine, and she pulls her body up, pressing her breasts against my chest. It can never be just a simple kiss with her, Hadley must know that.

"Let me make you come." I scrape my teeth gently below her ear because it always makes her shiver from the tickle of my short scruff.

A chuckle rumbles in the back of her throat, but it only makes her neck elongate, and she's offering me more opportunity to trail my mouth on her body.

"You seem very eager," she hums.

No shit. I'm scolding myself that I'm not better behaved.

I slip my hand between our bodies to enable my fingers to search for the zipper of her jeans. "Hadley, whether we were arguing or perfectly content with each other, making you come is the best way to leave you speechless."

She isn't stopping me, and my fingers dip into her damp and warm panties, and I rumble a sound when my fingers get drenched in her arousal. I'm already going dizzy from the thought of my tongue enjoying every drop of her.

"We're in the middle of nowhere, and I swear I just heard an owl or some wild creature," she observes.

I continue to stroke her, feeling her tremble under my touch. "I'm the fucking wild creature, so let me have my way." My voice is filled with reverence.

"Are you about to have a hissy fit?" Hadley has the audacity to taunt me right now.

My response is to spear a digit inside of her that instantly causes her breath to halt and her internal walls to wind tightly around my finger. "Depends, do I get to have you coming all over my hand?"

She struggles to form words as I slip my thumb between us to ensure her clit continues to receive the attention it deserves. Her breath hitches again, and her mouth parts open as her body responds to my touch.

"I guess it's the least I can let you do since you did arrange a romantic picnic under the stars. You're such a softie when it comes to dating."

"Whoa, you have the audacity to tease me right now? I'm by no means soft." I'll show her.

In a flash, I yank down her jeans and panties until they're stuck around one of her ankles, then knock her knees to part to give me a canvas because I'm on my stomach in no time, with my arms hooked under her thighs. My mouth covers her pussy, my tongue flicking her clit before drawing circles. I could get high just from the taste of her. I'm trying to ignore how hard I am, but it just makes me determined.

"Connor," she bellows out, her fingers clawing my hair.

Briefly, I glance up. "You will come all over my tongue and you will not look away while I do it."

Her eyes drop to watch me. "Fine, yes, don't stop," she nearly slurs before another moan escapes her.

My fingers dig into her thighs while I keep her splayed open, and I continue to lick her senseless. I could spend hours feasting on her and I wouldn't get bored.

"Remind me who this pussy belongs to," I murmur as I grasp for air.

"Someone who managed to get a ring on my finger." Her voice strains as she pieces a sentence together.

I still my tongue on her pussy before retreating my head back.

Hadley giggles, and with her face flushed and highlighted from the lanterns, I'm only wanting to devour her even more.

"Say my name," I grit out in demand because I hate leaving her pussy unsatisfied.

She touches herself with her finger and my eyes have a full view of Hadley playing and ensuring I watch. Her finger swirls where my tongue just was. "Hmm… I think my pussy *might* belong to this guy I kind of woke up with."

"Hadley," I snarl with an uncontrollable grin.

"Connor," she says matter-of-factly. "In this moment, my pussy is all *yours*."

"It always was."

Her hips buckle from the work of her finger. "Debatable."

I shake my head and growl before I push her hand away and continue on my quest. I don't ease her into her oncoming orgasm; I lick that spot and repeat over and over until she's convulsing on my mouth. I don't stop even when she's shaking. I continue to lick her relentlessly as her body pulses and she curses my name. Only when I feel her weaken do I finally move back to enjoy the view of her body completely spent, with a drowsy smile curling on her lips. I help slide her pants back up before I dip my mouth down to kiss her, knowing she's tasting herself on my lips.

Ignoring my dick that wants to break free against the fabric of my jeans, I take the high road. "Should we swing by Jolly Joe's for a sundae on the way home?" I pretend the last few minutes didn't happen, just to rile her.

"Was I not your dessert?" She throws on a pout for effect.

"Not even close. I need you swallowing me, before you insist I come inside of you so you can watch my come drip down your thighs, then you take your finger and swipe it up into your mouth while I watch you suck it all off. That's dessert."

Her jaw drops open, and her eyes grow into saucers. She has no clue the dirty thoughts I harbor for her.

Reaching to my side, I pick up my wine and take a sip before getting cozy on the blanket and welcoming her back in my arms, because I'm a fucking gentleman.

———

WALKING BACK INTO THE HOUSE, I don't understand why Hadley is so quiet. We laughed some more while we looked at the stars and talked about wanting to visit Iceland or Norway. By the time it was midnight, we realized that ice cream wouldn't be in our cards and instead drove home on the dark roads with good music playing in the car.

Maybe I should have been concerned that she didn't say much in the car, but a permanent half-smile was glued to her face when she occasionally glanced my way.

But as we walk into our bedroom, she seems stressed.

She pivots to face me and points a finger to confront me. "I detest you!"

What the fuck is this turnaround?

"No, you don't, but enlighten me. What have I done now?" I scratch my cheek and remain calm, ignoring the whiplash that I should be experiencing.

"You were romantic and giving and everything I shouldn't enjoy." She seems angrier with herself than anything.

My lips quirk out as I step closer to stand off with her; we're good at this. "That's a bad thing?"

"Yes! I shouldn't let you have it so easy," she nearly squeals.

I take hold of her wrists by wrapping my hands around them. "Are you making it easy? Because we have two very different interpretations."

The spark in her eyes is beautiful and promising.

"You should have to work harder, but…" Her lips roll in, and she appears frustrated, yet her demeanor is folding.

I raise a brow because victory is mine. "Uh-oh, was someone affected by my date planning?"

She rolls her eyes to the side. "You do not get to win."

Releasing a wrist, I snake my arm around her waist to pull her flush to me. "Right, someone wanted me to make them swoon and go slow."

"I never said slow," she corrects me. "Be an asshole right now. Don't be the guy that I kind of really want to pounce on, nor do I want to wait," she bites out.

Leaning in to whisper with purpose, I notice goosebumps form on her skin. "Babe, you know we can always fuck angry. But my money is on that you want me to fuck you like we matter, because we do."

She attempts to push me, but my hands are quick to cup her head while her eyes lock with mine, the twinkle not fading but now mixed with recognition. Her frown disperses into history and the corner of her mouth tugs.

"Do we matter?" She's breathless from my simple yet true statement.

"Yeah," I answer softly.

We stand there, nobody making a move because we're waiting for her internal debate to end. It doesn't take long before she jumps onto me with our mouths sewing together. It's a bolt of lightning that causes me to stumble back a step or two.

"It's not fair." She speaks against my lips, as neither one of us wants to part. "I crumble around you in no time."

I carry her a few more steps before I toss her onto the bed, and I peel off my t-shirt. "Welcome to the club."

I'm over her with my hands running wild all over her body, letting her work her clothes off because she'll do it faster.

When she's down to her bra, she leans up while I dip my mouth down to capture her in another kiss. Hadley is busy yanking her panties off, and I reach behind to unclasp her bra. I love her naked, but it's distracting, and right now, I just want to plunge right into her.

Luckily, we are two minds alike, and she wraps her legs around my waist to help gravity pull me to her faster. I brace myself over her and bring the tip of my cock to glide around the proof that I make her crazy. She moans when the head of my cock rubs friction against her sensitive spot, and I groan from the fact she's soaking.

Our mouths fuse at the same time as I align myself and enter, sinking into her and feeling instant relief because she's tight, warm, mine, and if I have it my way, nobody else will ever touch her again.

I pump in and out, slamming back in until I'm balls deep, and a sharp moan escapes her lips.

"Shit, did I hurt you?" I study her face with concern in my voice.

A playful dazed look appears on her mouth. "The contrary. It's okay, you can go hard. I just need you inside of me."

I place a gentle kiss on the corner of her mouth and skim my lips down her neck before I continue my thrusts that have me feeling like I'm incapable of breathing unless I get to come inside of her.

Her skin feels searing under my touch, and I'm tumbling toward a release too damn fast. Her hands come to gently hold each of my cheeks while our eyes lock, and I'm deep, with nowhere else to go. She tightens her legs around me to hold me in and clenches her walls. Everything magnifies in intensity when the corner of my eye catches the sight of her wedding ring on her finger, and it makes me go feral.

I'm so far gone that it feels like an explosion when we finally get there together.

It takes a solid minute or two before I'm even capable of rolling off her, only to drag her with me because we are sweaty, our breathing rapid, and I want her head resting on my chest with my fingers combing through the strands of her hair.

Instantly, her fingertips begin to draw lazy patterns along my pec, even though our hearts are racing.

Hadley purrs a sound against my chest that vibrates against my heart, especially when it turns into a drawl of low laughter.

I squeeze her closer. "Yes?"

I notice her looking at her wedding ring. "Nothing. I'm just… content, I guess. Didn't think that was possible with you."

I contemplate what might be going on in her head, and I narrow it down to our first bad experience. I once laid with her and promised that we could see one another again, I would find a way to make it work I said, only to backtrack hours later for reasons she can't know. I shake that memory out of my head, ignoring the consequences of that night, and choose to focus on the present.

Kissing the top of her hair, I inhale the scent of fresh lake air mixed with sex. "I'm actually quite enjoyable when you break a wall down or two." She makes a sound and stays molded to me in a perfect fit. "But seriously, you don't, what was it… detest me?" I tickle my fingers along her arms.

"Ha-ha," she mocks mundanely. "I'm getting used to this. Us being like this. It feels very natural, yet kind of… exhilarating."

"That's a positive," I point out.

"I realize that." She peers up to greet me with a unique wonder, and I respond by giving her a quick kiss.

"You're beautiful, you know that?" I whisper right before I steal one more kiss.

She makes a funny face because she goes nearly shy. "Don't throw classic lines at me."

"I wouldn't dare. I'm just giving you the truth."

Hadley buries her face against my chest before planting a quick kiss against my skin. "Tell me something that's true and I don't know."

I think for a few seconds. "Even with no Vegas, we eventually would have found our way to one another."

A sound of doubt escapes her lips. "Why are you certain?"

"Because that's just the kind of chemistry we have. We're right for one another in love or hate, and I'm not sure the barrier between us was never going to be long enough to keep me away forever." I speak to myself more than her, maybe she notices.

"I think we need sleep. You make it sound like I wanted to keep you away, but it wasn't always like that, and in this very moment, I want you as close as possible." She snuggles against me, letting out a relaxing sigh, and even though I can't see, I know her eyes are gently closing.

I stroke her hair and stare at the ceiling, with my thoughts running rampant.

I always knew one of us would have caved at some point, even though I had my own private vow when it concerned her, she just doesn't know. Now, a knot twists in the pit of my stomach that we'll be okay because she is taking a step with me, and I broke my internal vow.

17

CONNOR

The way Hadley's lips twist when she's watching videos of my old hockey games is spellbinding. Games where I lost my cool seem to be her favorite. Nah, who am I kidding, it's me in my pre-game suit that she loves the most. A sort of smirk tilts on her lips, as if it's typical of me, yet she finds it irresistible. The best part is that she has no idea that I've caught her yet again watching in what she thinks is secret.

She sits on the couch in the living room with her knees tucked under and ear pods in while she holds her phone screen.

Here comes my favorite part.

Walking on my toes, I sneak up behind her and reach over the back of the sofa to shake her shoulders. Instantly, she shrieks and brings her hand to touch my arm that's wrapping around her as I playfully bite her cheek.

"Connor," she squeals my name.

I hop over the back of the couch because I'm smooth like that and land next to her on the cushions, only to encourage her to swing her legs over to rest on my lap.

"This is classic. My very own superfan, and it's none other than you," I note.

She pinches my arm. "Simmer down that ego, I'm just… curious."

"It's not a little bit that you're wondering why everyone is obsessed with our team? Or maybe you love that interview I did with a nine-year-old which melted the hearts of many." I bring a hand to my chest.

She rolls her eyes. "I never realized that *perhaps* you play kind of a cool sport, plus once you watch one video, then the app's algorithm sends you down a rabbit hole of more videos." It's cute the way she tries to play this down.

The last few days we have talked about aspects of our careers that we probably didn't realize. We went off track when I caught her glancing at photos of me in a suit when traveling between games; her bottom lip always gets attacked when she stares at those photos.

I stroke her thigh with my hand as we just relax together on the sofa. "The guys will be here any second, then I'll start the grill." The goal is to hang out, but I'm sure we'll end up re-watching a few games from last season.

"Cool. I'll stay for a drink then leave you guys be." She gently combs the hair behind my ear, a soothing touch that I love.

"We have cake at least. Our moms dropped off a box when I was in the shower and you were at the store." I flash my eyes at her because I'm entertained.

She giggles. "They did a wedding cake testing without us, didn't they?"

I grin. "Just in case, plus they're getting ballsy."

"But they are happy, and they would shut it down in a heartbeat if we asked them to. I'm convinced they enjoy messing with us. *Yet*, I really want to see how far they'll go." I couldn't agree more, which is why I smile. Hadley gets more comfortable on her spot. "Which cake are we having?"

"No clue." I shrug.

Just like that, we fall into a moment. One where our eyes linger and the lines on our mouths are in a permanent tilt. This is when I enjoy gliding my thumb along her cheek that causes her eyes to flutter at me with a glittery ember glazing in her eyes. Lowering my head, I gently nip at the tip of her nose, eager to get us lost in a deep kiss.

But the sound of the doorbell causes us both to groan because we can't stay in our moment of bliss.

Struggling to get off the couch together feels good because she's here, in my house that we now share, and we just move around one another in a perfect pattern.

Apparently, we are good hostesses together too.

Hadley set the television to the right channel, while I offered beers. I worked the grill, and she tossed a salad.

"You're okay if I steal him away in a few weeks? Bachelor day and all," Briggs asks Hadley as he refills his plate with food as we put one of our late-season games on pause.

Hadley stabs another cheese cube with a toothpick to snack on. "Yeah, sure. Just don't tell me what happens on it, okay?"

"I would say relax since your dad and Ford will be there, plus your one neighbor is invited too," he explains.

"Hudson Arrows? Yeah, he's friends with my dad, and our street is small," I explain.

"Those guys are legends and know how to party if needed, so you may want to be afraid." He winks at her.

"Oh, I know, I've witnessed far too many holiday parties. By the way, what is with the hate in this room for Vaughn? I don't even need to look at the screen and I know when he's on, as you all say, '*fucking Vaughn.*'" She attempts to deepen and lower her voice.

I grab another beer from the fridge. "I get along with him, but he and Briggs don't see eye to eye. Rumor is that next season is his last down in Tampa, then he will either retire or maybe come back to us. Our current coach likes him."

"But Vaughn is past his prime. A complete douche too." Briggs crosses his arms, agitated. "That asshole got me out of the game in our playoffs. I couldn't play the last four minutes."

I slap a hand on his shoulder. "Relax, we'll worry about him next season."

One of the guys sitting in the living room calls out, letting us know they are going to press play again. Briggs grumbles his way back, and I take the opportunity to quickly check in with Hadley.

"You good?" I ask as my eyes narrow in on her, and I step close enough that I can bring an arm around her.

She checks the screen behind me then focuses on me again. "Totally. I've been sipping on Chardonnay while you guys swear at the screen every two seconds."

I laugh. "Are you tipsy?"

She tilts her head to the side in doubt. "Maybe." She leans in to pretend to whisper, "I get kind of handsy when I'm tipsy."

"Oh yeah?" I'm very interested in this side of her.

She nods and a droll sound escapes her. "Like full-on 'I'm making plans in my head for how to mount you later' handsy."

I snort a sound, as she's definitely feeling light right now. "I will gladly take part in this."

Hadley stands up on her toes and brings one leg high up above my waist. Those dancing skills are a gift from the heavens.

"I'll leave you guys to enjoy the game. Me and my wine will be in the bathtub soaking and preparing for later." She kisses me sensually on the lips and my entire body feels aflutter with anticipation.

"Get a room," someone calls out, and I only grin more.

Hadley gives me a sultry look before she touches my chest with her fingertips in parting and walks away with an overdone sway that looks perfect on her.

I can't wait for later when I can plunge into her warm heat and see stars when I come while she screams my name.

I blow out a breath to recenter myself and turn my attention to the TV screen. Picking up my beer bottle, I walk back into the open living room to join the guys.

It's a slew of expletives and commentary right off the bat. I'm able to get into the game until my phone vibrates in my pocket. Pulling it out, I see that it's a reminder for next week.

Hadley has a summer dance show, then we're having dinner with her parents after.

I don't remember discussing this, but the joint calendar doesn't lie. It's a sacred tool for any marriage. I may be young, but I realized that quick.

The difference is that most people don't fear dinner with the in-laws the way I do. Because Spencer Crews may just be the reason that I lose it all.

18

HADLEY

Pride hits me as I watch little girls in tutus and bumblebee wings wobble back to their parents after having performed to a crowd of *awws* and *ohs*. We performed in the outside theatre here in Lake Spark for the summer festival. I somehow knew the little kids would be the ones to steal the show. The teenagers on their ballet pointe shoes performing elegantly to a *Midsummer Night's Dream* theme didn't really hold a candle to the cuteness over-load of bumblebees twirling.

Still, I made sure we performed five numbers of various dance genres to please the crowd on this weekend mid-afternoon. One of my girls was sick, so I had to fill in on the dance front too. I was kind of hoping to have stayed choreographer today, because I didn't want my dance company to feel like I was stealing their thunder. I did my best to stay in the back.

A pair of hands that I've become accustomed to and that blaze excitement at every touch sneaks up around me and winds around my waist. Like always, I sink into Connor's touch. What a wild contrast to before Vegas.

"These are for you," he murmurs against my cheek before

placing a respectable peck on my lips. His other hand holds out a single peach-colored rose. "Well done."

I gladly take the flower and feel my cheeks blush at the same time. Sweet Connor is, well, cute, but strangely eerie in a wonderful way. I'm not used to him this way, but it's nothing to complain about, especially when my eyes trail up to watch him lift his sunglasses off his eyes. Gosh, he is extra sexy when he's been sitting in the sun all day.

"Thank you." My eyes travel back to the rose that I twirl between my fingers. "I'm all done here. Dancers have been returned to their respective owners," I joke.

He raises a brow and a gleam that melts my panties graces his face. "Including you? I'm on board with being your respective owner."

I chuckle at his ability to send us on a train of dirty thoughts. "Easy there. My parents are somewhere around here."

"I know. I was sitting with them. We were thinking instead of going out for dinner that maybe we just pick up some takeout from Catch 22 and head to our house for dinner. Sound good?"

"Perfect. I wasn't really in the mood to sit in a restaurant all night."

He brings his arm around my shoulders, and we begin to walk side by side. "Cool. I'll call them with our order, and we can pick that up on the way back. Your parents will grab the wine."

"You bet we will," my mother announces. My parents and little brother walk toward us with bright smiles on their faces.

I'm quickly met with hugs. "You were magnificent as always out there," my dad mentions.

"So beautiful," my mother adds.

The compliments stop when I look at my brother who is busy on his phone. It only makes me smile, though. I bet this was his idea of the worst Saturday ever. Ashton is at that funny age where you're no longer a kid but hate being a teenager.

"Thanks for your kind words," I tease him.

He glances up from his screen with a scowl. "I didn't say anything."

"I know," I deadpan.

"Hey, can you help me with my biology project later? Won't take long," he requests.

I shake my head that we fly past into new subjects. "Sure," I promise.

"How about we meet in an hour or so?" Connor suggests while he studies his watch.

"Sounds good," my father agrees.

"I'll send you the alarm code in case you get there before us," Connor adds.

My eyes whip to him with an awkward look plastered on my face. "Do we really want them to have the code?" I mumble, knowing my parents can hear, and they're entertained.

My mom gives me a fake unimpressed look. "You mean so we can unexpectedly show up at random times and ruin your newlywed phase?"

"*Yeah*, I think you guys can wait a few minutes. It's lovely weather," Connor comments.

After one more round of hugs, we divide up. Connor and I are on our way to the parking lot, but he takes hold of my hand and yanks me in another direction.

"What's up?" I wonder.

"We have a few minutes to spare." He begins to tow me in the direction of the Ferris wheel, and a twinkling star inside of me travels from my heart to my stomach. "Come on. One time around."

It would be impossible to scrape the giddy look off my face, from the time he suggests his romantic scene to the moment that I'm sitting next to him in one of the cars on our way up to overlook Lake Spark.

Interlinking our arms, I cozy up close to him and rest my head against his shoulder and a deep long relaxing breath escapes me.

"Connor Spears, what am I going to do with you?" I say softly, with my words sounding floaty. Probably, because I need to pinch myself that this isn't a dream.

"I could give you a list of about a hundred options if that helps you," he offers.

I rest our connected hands on my lap and admire our wedding rings. A happy accident in the end. I was supposed to be watchful and cautious around him, but I only seem to be falling in the best possible way.

"It's not so bad… being married… to you," I state flatly, but I mean so much more.

His deep, smooth chuckle rumbles in the back of his throat. "Why thank you, I think."

We glance briefly at one another with sheepish smirks. Then our balloon that kept us at a distance bursts when he leans down to kiss me like it always matters. Soft to start, then his lips take me on a journey to being commanded. I love every second of it.

"Mmm," I hum because I feel as though I'm drowning in a pool of glitter. Inside, everything sparkles. We're being sappy, but our nights in bed are anything but.

Getting comfortable in my seat, we approach the top of the wheel and both look out ahead when the car stops. Something tells me he may have bought us a little extra time up here.

"It's hard to imagine living anywhere else," I note. Connor makes a sound but doesn't answer, and I feel his muscles tighten slightly. I realize why. "If you transfer teams in a year, then… we will figure it out." That's the best that I can say.

He kisses the top of my head affectionately. "Someone is thinking long run," he teases, but I hear the vulnerability.

"Maybe I am." It comes out faint.

"You know, the off-season is when I should be relaxing and resetting my mind and body for next season. I was *deeply* concerned when we woke up in Vegas that plan went out the window." I hear the humor drenched in his sentence. "But I think it's worked out quite all right." Now that part was just honesty, and it causes me to ensure our eyes meet and lock.

"I think so too," I agree.

We both lean in, with our foreheads touching, and I've never felt so alive.

"What kind of guy would I be if I don't kiss you at the top of a Ferris wheel overlooking the lake?" The desperation in his voice causes my cheeks to heat up.

"I don't know, you've been the guy to not kiss me before," I taunt him.

His response is to growl and bring his hand to cup my cheek, demanding my full attention. "That was another time. Tell me we're past that."

I slowly nod without hesitation that we are. It must make him happy because before I can register, his lips are on mine, and I'm certain it's his way of sealing my confirmation.

No going back.

But it doesn't cross my mind anyway.

———

SITTING OUTSIDE at the table on the deck of the house, we all are in a filled-belly slumber. Dinner was delicious, partly because I didn't have to cook, and the bottle of wine that my mom picked out was a perfect pairing.

Now we're taking a rest before ice cream for dessert.

My eyes break away from the candle keeping mosquitos away and draw a line to my mother.

"Okay, so I've planned for a wedding dress fitting in Chicago just in case, and of course, your grandmothers and Isla could join us," my mom casually mentions.

I squint an eye, debating if she is just riling me up or if she is dead serious.

"Already married," I say one-toned.

"But don't you want a princess wedding dress?"

I look to my father for help and to simmer her down. He gets the clue and touches my mother's arm. "Relax. Tonight is just dinner, no party talk." I mouth thank you. "So, what's the plan, kiddos? For the rest of the summer before hockey season? With the summer show out of the way, you have fewer dance classes to teach."

"I just want to take it easy," I say before taking a sip of my wine.

Connor squeezes my other hand that he hasn't let go of. "We should go somewhere for vacation. I'm thinking island, tropical, cocktails, bikini—"

"That's my daughter," my father adds on the list in a stern voice.

I can't control my grin because these two together are kind of hilarious. A perfect team if they allow it.

"We'll see. Also, depends on if we adopt a dog or not," I add.

My mom holds up her hand. "I'm all for babysitting the pooch, but we're just not keen on getting a dog right now."

"I know. Besides, I could use some company when Connor is off on the road for games. Maybe a dog is exactly what we need. If he's calm enough, then he can come to the studio with me." I flash my eyes at Connor, as I'm sure that news will make him happy.

I can see the hint of a victorious wry smile on his lips before they wrap around the rim of his beer bottle.

Looking around, I feel lucky in this moment. Or at least content. We're all enjoying the little things in life, with some form of elation on our faces. It's a perfect night too, as we can see the stars.

"Hadley, come on," my little brother groans from the patio door.

I stand, holding onto my wine glass because no way am I forfeiting this delicious vino for a biology project. "I'll be back. I promised to look at his project for summer science club," I announce.

I quickly lean down to kiss Connor's cheek and leave them to talk amongst themselves. I hear the mention of visiting a casino for the bachelor party, and it only makes me grin more.

Walking into the house, I head straight to the sofa where Ashton is scrolling on his tablet. I flop onto the cushion next to him and prepare myself for a doozy.

"All right, show me your wizardly knowledge," I tell him.

He begins typing away with his finger. "I need your blood type," he orders.

"Oh, uh… I don't know… wait, actually, I do know. I had bloodwork done recently for my allergy tests." I grab my phone that's resting on the charging station on the side table. "Can I see what you're working on?" I ask, curious.

"Nothing special. We're going over blood groups and pairings. I'm filling out a family chart. I've just been waiting on you, but you've been too busy being married."

I roll my eyes because he loves Connor. Who wouldn't want a superstar hockey player as their new brother-in-law?

"Mom told me hers, and dad's I found in his wallet," he further explains.

"You were snooping again?" I call him out on his admission.

He is quick to defend. "So? It's educational."

I shake my head as I pull up blood test results that produced nada on the allergy front, which is a good thing.

"I'll be back, nature calls." He hands me the tablet and disappears down the hall.

My curiosity gets the best of me, and I begin to look at the chart. There is a list of possible and impossible combinations. Huh, interesting. I remember studying this all back in middle school, but it is purely a blip in my memory.

Reading between the tablet and my phone, I search for my blood type then return my sight to the scientific table on the screen. I double-check then triple for good measure.

But my face falls, right before my heart quickens and an uneasy feeling stirs in my stomach. I freeze, and it feels like a crack is forming somewhere.

It must be a minute or two until I'm shaken out of my daze. I peer up and find Connor looking down at me.

"I'm just grabbing dessert. You okay?" His relaxed facial expression disappears when he looks into my eyes.

I toss the tablet to the side and stand up, ignoring Connor. I walk into the kitchen and begin to pace.

"What's wrong?" Concern is apparent in his voice.

"The mosquitos are getting vicious," my mother points out as she and my father enter through the sliding door.

The mood vanishes when they notice me standing in the kitchen, mostly in a bewildered state.

"What's up?" my father asks.

I stare at him for a long second. "Ashton's biology project. Have you seen it?"

He shrugs. "No, he mentioned it, but I haven't seen it yet."

I'm unable to blink or move, I just stare at him. "It's about blood types. How if your father is one type, your mother another, then their kids will have X type." I study him to see if his eyes change, but it feels like we're in a standoff. "I got my blood type the other week when I went to the doctor, routine tests, nothing really. Surprised it never came up before, actually." There it is, a heaviness glazing his eyes, fear combined with revelation. A bitter laugh escapes me. "According to my little brother's project, you have type O blood, but the thing is…"

I vaguely hear my brother walk into the room, but my mother ushers him away to somewhere else, grasping the gravity of this situation.

"Hadley." My father says my name as if he's carrying the weight of years on his back.

Connor steps closer to me, but I step back, as I need space to process.

"If both parents are type O, they can never have kids who are type A. Since my birth mom did do something right and left us with her medical history, then we know her type, which means it can't be possible that I'm type A… but I am."

I never knew it was possible to hear glass breaking if no glass is even present. But that's what is happening in this very moment as my father's face falls and tears pool in his eyes.

"It's not what you think," he says, his voice breaking.

Connor steps closer to me to touch my arm. "Hadley, why don't you sit down."

"Sit down!" I squeak out with so much strain inside my body. "Oh my God, it's true, isn't it? You're not really my father." I begin to lose my footing as panic takes over.

"I am. It's complicated," he admits.

I shake my head in disbelief. This isn't happening. "No, no, this is some joke."

"Hear him out," Connor pleads softly.

My eyes snap to him in surprise, why would Connor say that? He should be as astonished as I am. I yank my arm away from his touch. Something clicks in my head. "You knew!"

The immediate pain in Connor's face is my answer.

"Since when?" I ask, with a tear falling down my cheek.

Connor swallows and his fists hang by his sides. He glances to my dad then back to me. "For a while." He's avoiding the answer.

I push him out of frustration. "Tell me the truth."

Connor grabs my wrists, softly, tenderly, as if he can see I'm fragile and he won't be the one to break me. "A few years." His jaw tightens. "The morning after we…" he whispers.

But his attempt fails because I break.

19

CONNOR

I am a con.

It's not just a nickname.

I kept her away when all I wanted was to have her closer.

Now she's in front of me combusting from life-altering news, and my heart is breaking for her.

Hadley's eyes blaze with fury as they slowly travel between me and her father. She's not sure what to do with this information.

Her hands find her hair and she claws the strands as she shakes her head. "W-wait, I don't… where the fuck do I begin right now?"

"Hadley, it's really not what it seems," her dad attempts to soften the blow.

"Not what it seems?" she yells. "Are you kidding me? You're not… and my husband knew this whole time!" Hadley is enraged, and she has every right to be.

I step to her, but she moves farther away, giving me a warning glare to stand back. "Let him explain," I attempt to suggest.

She shakes her head, hysterical from this news. "I don't understand," she cries.

"You're my daughter. In every way that matters, you're my daughter. But if you really want to look at biology, then we are related, just not as father and daughter. My brother was a twin, just not identical. Technically, you're my niece…" Spencer drops the bomb.

Hadley stares at him blankly, connecting dots in her head. "You mean my uncle, your brother, the one who died?"

He nods. "He wanted me to raise you as my own, and I did just that since you were barely able to walk, and I never looked back. My brother never wanted me to tell you. Still, I thought about telling you, but I was scared because you're *my* daughter." The agony on his face is apparent, and I feel for him in this moment.

Tears stream down Hadley's face, and I try once again to reach out to her, only to be rebuffed quickly by her taking another step back. I just want to hold her in my arms right now. She doesn't need to stand by herself. I'll take care of her.

"Unbelievable… I had a biological mother who didn't want me, a dad I never got to know, and only now I learn of this," she wails.

"I'm so sorry. You must know it's from love." Spencer swipes a hand across his jaw before wiping a tear away.

Hadley looks at him with pure hurt. "Who else knows?"

"Your grandparents, Mom, a friend, lawyers… and apparently Connor." He sighs.

Her sharp gaze returns to me. "Why does he say it like that?"

My shoulders sink, and I know nothing I say will ease her pain. "A few years ago, when I came to you that morning, I snuck in to surprise you, but I accidentally overheard your parents talking. They didn't realize I was there, obviously, and they were debating telling you since you had just turned eighteen. Spencer didn't know I knew until I told him the day after we got married."

A gasp escapes her lips and fresh tears form. "That's what you two were talking about so intensely?"

"Yes," I whisper.

She lunges forward and takes hold of my shirt in pure rage. "Were you ever going to fucking tell me? Or were you just going to stay married to me and keep this secret?"

I take hold of her wrists and ensure our eyes engage. "Hadley, you have to understand—"

"No," she interjects firmly.

"What can I do right now to make this better for you?" Spencer requests with sadness in his voice yet standing strong because he won't ever let her go.

Her sobs fill the room. "Go away," she whispers with deep pain flooding her face.

"Hadley." He tips his head to the side, hopeful the conversation won't stop.

"I can't be here right now." Hadley's voice cracks right before she just flees the kitchen, leaving us there.

I want to go after her, but I feel she needs a minute. Instead, my hands slam down on the counter from pure anger that she's hurting and I'm not even sure who's at fault.

"You'll keep an eye on her?" Spencer requests faintly with his voice unsteady.

I only half glance over my shoulder. "Of course." He doesn't even need to ask.

"Take care of her. I'll be back," he promises.

I do my best to give him a comforting look. "I know, Spencer. I think right now she needs space to take it all in."

He sniffles and stands there for a long heavy minute before leaving me to ponder how I'm going to support Hadley in this very moment. I'm not exactly in her good graces, but she deserves to know the entire truth.

I reach for the liquor cabinet and pour myself a shot of bourbon, down it, then pour another, but this one is for Hadley, to help calm her nerves.

I head straight to our room to find the door closed and locked. I knock gently with hope she'll let me in. "Hadley, your dad is gone. It's just you and me. Let me in."

She doesn't answer, but I hear her crying into a pillow, the sound muffled.

I take a deep breath, step back, then use my weight to press against the door to break it open. It's actually easier than I antici-pated. Only a little of the alcohol spills over onto my hand in the process.

My move takes her by surprise, and she sits up in the bed, her face red and puffy. She may be a mess, but she is still a beautiful disaster.

"Get out," she demands.

I hold up the glass of alcohol. "No." I walk to the bed and set it on the bedside table. "Here. This will help you calm down."

She goes quiet again, and I make no effort to sit on the bed with her, as I'm waiting for her clues for how to approach her.

Her eyes are sunken with pure sadness. "You knew," she states, still in disbelief.

"Yeah."

"Is that why you came to my room and said I was a mistake?"

I lick my lips, because the truth fucking hurts, and I hate saying it all out loud. It's like a knife wound when you hear the words. "Yes."

"You're an asshole."

I agree, but I felt my arms were always twisted. "Hadley, it wasn't my truth to tell. You know that too."

"So you just pushed me away?"

I laugh bitterly to myself. "Don't you see?" I sit on the bed and take hold of her face between my hands because she has to under-stand my reasoning, I won't have it any other way. "I've been trying my damnedest to break your heart all these years to actually ensure it stays mended." My voice breaks because I'm aching too.

"That's why you hated me?"

"I never fucking hated you. The opposite. But I couldn't have you close because I didn't know if I could keep the secret. It's not my place to tell you, and your relationship with your dad is every-thing to you."

She laughs then takes hold of my hands to remove them from her cheeks. "What was your big plan, Connor? Never tell me, even though I'm your wife?" she snarls.

I stand up again and pinch the bridge of my nose. "Truthfully? You want the honest truth?"

"Yes," she bites out.

"I wasn't going to tell you. I just knew that if you ever found out that it would be harder for you to leave me if we are married." I raise my voice because the truth is confronting.

Her jaw goes slack from my admission, and it feels like the air in the room evaporated.

"Wow." She huffs a breath before she looks to the side then brings her sight back to me. "Get out."

"No." I stand there, defiant.

"I can't be near you right now," she volleys.

I grab the throw blanket from the end of the bed and lie down on the floor. "Tough luck. I'll sleep on the floor, but I'm not leaving you alone."

Hadley goes speechless at my move.

I pretend to get comfortable on the floor, then after a minute peer up by the edge of the bed. "Will you throw me a pillow? You know you want to." I'm trying to see if a glimmer of relief is deep within her somewhere.

She just sits there frozen, aware that I'm serious. I won't be moving an inch from here. I'm staying firm.

Slowly and unsure, she tosses me a pillow.

We both lie down on our spots in silence for a solid ten minutes, because that is what she needs right now.

Until I break our silence. "Deep down, you know it's true. It wasn't my secret to share."

A new round of sniffling tears fills the room. "Maybe you're right, but it doesn't change the fact that I'm broken right now."

I sit up to observe her. "I won't let you break," I softly confirm.

Hadley props herself up on her elbows to look down at me. "I don't know what to think right now. But Connor…"

"Yeah?"

"Just hold me," she sobs.

I'm lying next to her in a flash, curling her tightly to my body as

I swipe away the tears with my thumb and stroke her messy tear-drenched hair. There is no place I would rather be.

"Did we ever have a chance to be something real?" she asks as she buries her face into my chest.

I continue to touch her in hopes of soothing her. "It's not a chance. We *are* something real," I assure her.

"I'm so confused," she mumbles into my shirt, and I can hear that her energy is nearly gone.

"I promise you, we'll get through this. I'm not leaving you."

Then I hold her all night, not sure what tomorrow may bring.

HADLEY

Numb.

That's what I feel.

Not long ago, I woke up in a Vegas hotel room with no recollection of the events of the night before. This time, my body is in a similar state physically, but make no mistake, I remember every second from last night.

A ton a bricks didn't hit me; they came crumbling down around me. It's no wonder I struggle to gather energy to move from this bed. I attempt to stretch, but my hand pokes a firm body.

Connor.

I have two things to process; my dad who lied and my husband who lied. I'm not sure where to begin.

My eyes widen to take in the view of Connor perched on the edge of the bed with a mug in his hand. He must have been waiting for me to wake up, as he looks showered and dressed in a fresh t-shirt and jeans. His hair has this ruffled wave that screams he has an edgy side.

"Hi." His greeting sounds so delicate.

I drag my body up to sitting and sigh. He offers me the mug of tea, but I indicate with my hand no. Instead, I opt to bring my knees to my chest to hold onto.

"Tell me it was a nightmare," I whisper.

"I can't say it didn't happen, but I don't believe it's a nightmare." He sets the mug on the bedside table and brings his hand to my knee, but I flinch. I'm uncertain what to feel, and he must pick up on the signs. "I'm so sorry."

I glance away, choosing not to say anything, but I do listen, and I hear a man whose voice is filled with remorse.

He continues, "Hadley, you have to know that I did what I thought was right. Spencer loves you more than anyone, only ever puts you first, and it wasn't my secret to share."

I scoff as fresh tears pool in my eyes, and my stomach twists because his point may be valid. "I have so many reasons to be upset. My da—" Why can't I say it? I move up the list. "You knew and pushed me away by making me feel like I was nothing."

"It fucking hurt, trust me."

"Oh, poor you," I mock before sliding angrily off the bed, feeling wrath building inside of me, and it's ready to bubble over. "You know, maybe we would have had something amazing if we didn't lose those years when you decided the best policy was to treat me like the enemy."

Connor stands, my words clearly hitting him hard. "I realize that. I can't turn back the clock, and we will still have something amazing. I *want* to have something amazing with you."

A sob escapes me because I'm so damn torn between the deceit and the emotion that I feel right now when he looks at me. He believes in his pleading words.

My fingers tangle into my hair as if I'm grasping at straws. It's frustration. "Connor, I don't have the strength to deal with you and also my da—" Another sob escapes me.

Connor is in front of me with his hands on my shoulders in no time. "Your dad is still your dad. You know better than anyone that biology doesn't mean a thing. Look at April, she's your mom, and you think nothing less. Spencer is even more of a parent because he's all you've ever known, and you are related in some way. Your real dad wanted it like this because they all love you so much."

I sniffle. I understand his logic, as it floated into my head a few times when I woke during the night. "I just don't know why he never told me or why he never planned to tell me if it hadn't been for a stupid science project."

The pad of Connor's thumb swipes a tear off my cheek. "Because he only sees you as *his* daughter, and he didn't want to lose that connection. He was scared."

I snuggle my cheek into the palm of his hand. "I just need to process it all."

He nods gently and guides me to muffle my snotty tears into his chest without a care in the world that I'm destroying his shirt in the process. "I'm not going anywhere. You can push me away, but I'll only return," he promises.

A new overwhelming flood hits me, with thoughts racing into my head from all directions. I step out of his hold and throw my arms up. "This is such a mess."

"It doesn't have to be."

I sneer at the humor in that. "Connor, it is. You and I are married because of a drunk night in Vegas. A night that I don't even really remember. Do you know how messed up that is? I didn't even have a wedding dress or a big cake or so many things—"

"But you had the groom who would do anything for you," he cuts me off, and the glimmer in his eyes is there. It's more than caring, it's… dare I say love? I see it for the first time, a gleam of hope and insistence. Maybe it's always been there, but I only really see it now when I'm trying to cling to anything to keep me from falling.

The bedroom feels smaller as our eyes stay connected, and the thumping of my heart returns. A beacon that maybe one day every-thing will be okay surfaces purely because of his damn eyes.

It just won't be okay today.

"How do I pick up the pieces?" I ask softly.

Connor takes one step before he drops to his knees and wraps his arms around my thighs, with his ear resting against my belly. "You let me do it."

His selfless words strike me, and I run my fingers through his hair. I'm clearly affected but still unsure if what he did is noble or plain fucked up.

Lucky for him, right now, I won't push him away. It doesn't mean I'm fully committing either.

We stand there for a solid minute as I try to connect dots. The truth was clearly always there. Little clues that now make sense. It just wasn't obvious at the time. The lack of baby photos, the photo of my uncle on the mantle, the timeline and story of when he passed away due to an accident, or when my parents had Ashton and it felt like pregnancy was something new for both of my parents. There were signs in retrospect.

The best thing I can do right now is take a hot shower alone. I begin to shuffle out of Connor's hold. "I'm going to shower. Alone."

He slowly stands, observing me and doing his best to assess me. Good luck with that, because I don't even know what I'm feeling or thinking anymore.

———

IT's an hour later when I emerge from the bathroom in a towel and find that Connor is sitting on the bed with his arms resting over his knees and feet firmly planted on the floor.

"You don't need to be waiting on me or watching my every move," I comment.

The corner of his mouth tilts up. "Since when do I listen to you?"

A slither of amusement attempts to break through my darkness inside. "I thought you had a meeting for the summer camp for kids that you're volunteering at?"

Connor leans back on his arms, his body now half splayed on the bed. "You're trying to get rid of me, but that ain't happening. I told them that I wouldn't be in today, that something came up."

"Oh." I stand on my spot, now studying him.

This will be my life until I find some form of closure surrounding the men in my life. Connor won't relent until I'm at peace, even if he's part of the reason that I'm in this state.

But in my shower, it kept circling in my head what he has repeated several times. The truth wasn't his secret to tell. I've attempted to imagine myself in his shoes, and to be honest, I'm not sure what I would've done.

So, I've decided for now that I'll have a temporary truce in my head when it comes to Connor and focus on my dad. Doesn't mean it's back to roses and sunshine with Connor, but I'm not going to run away.

And right now, Connor is before me trying to help.

I need him too.

To hollow the numbness.

I take a few confident strides to him, stopping short of his knees. He brings his body up, as I have his full attention.

Dropping onto his lap, I swing my leg over to staddle him. I settle in his lap and feel his length twitch and grow hard against the apex of my thighs. Connor doesn't move, including his eyes that are pinned to mine. He's going to let me lead because he knows this is what I want.

Bringing my hands to cradle his face, I splay my fingers along his jaw and cheek while I press my body to his and take command. "I don't want to think right now, just... feel alive," I rasp in desperation.

"Then use me," he whispers adamantly.

I bring my lips to his and kiss him with intention. It's warm and sensual, grounding me, and it stops the spinning in my world right now. I press harder against his lips with a force that causes the towel around me to loosen and fall gently. Ignoring it, I begin to ride on top of Connor, my hips moving in waves to feel friction against my pussy.

Connor gets his shirt off before our lips are glued to one another again, and his hands run down the sides of my body to find a home on my hips.

My arms rest on his strong shoulders, and our position only encourages him to lower his mouth to my breast. With the towel now fallen to my waist, he has prime access to my breasts, which is why he is eager to swirl his tongue around one nipple. I moan, with my entire body feeling extra sensitive, except for the pounding ache of my clit and the dampness between my thighs.

I'm turning greedy too, and I guide his mouth to my other breast. I want his mouth and fingers everywhere; it won't be enough.

When he's done teasing my hard nipple that only intensifies my senses, he leaves a trail of hurried kisses up my neck to find my mouth again. I close my eyes and let myself get lost in this momentary ecstasy.

Keeping my legs wrapped around him, he rolls us until I'm underneath him, and the towel gets lost in the process, leaving me naked. He drags my arms over my head, pressed against the mattress as our lips skim one another and stay in a dance.

"I'll do anything you want." His voice is full of lust as he traps my bottom lip with a featherlike brush of his lips.

My hips tilt up to feel his hard shaft, and I can't get a release fast enough.

"I just need you inside of me," I whisper as we thrust our bodies together.

"Then I'll take you."

I break my wrists away from his hand that had them pinned and find the zipper of his jeans, urging him to undo them, and the desperation inside of me to touch his bare cock is overwhelming. He slides them off in record time and then I receive my wish, with my hand wrapping around his long length, enjoying his gasp that vibrates against our open mouths that touch.

Taking charge, I urge him to his back and crawl on top of him.

I plunge down onto his cock with pure abandon, closing my eyes and focusing only on the feeling of being full. I move up and down, finding the right angle that hits the spot I like.

My hair falls over my shoulders as I tip my head back and close my eyes. I don't dare dip my gaze down to see Connor. It would make it far too intense.

Too real.

And I need an escape.

But I ignore my internal warning because fire builds below my navel, and I feel like I'm at the edge of a cliff. Glancing down, I'm met with a pair of protective eyes that sends a flame up to my heart.

Connor watches with pure admiration as I fuck him. As if I'm a queen.

He has patience because I know it's a struggle for him to let me lead when we're intimate like this. I don't mind, I like it like that, it's kind of a turn-on. But right now, I need the control.

I slide up and down, dragging from his base to the tip, knowing it gives him pleasure as much as it does for me. At first, I thought that I needed slow, but I have frustration swirling in me, which is why I need to work out some stress, and I pick up the pace.

Connor uses his upper body strength to sit up, which allows me to wrap my arms around his neck, drawing his mouth back to mine while I swivel my hips and tighten around his length, every thrust more charged than the one before.

My breath turns to a near pant, and his answer is to cover my mouth with his, as if he will give me air, but it only causes the passion between us to intensify.

We move together, with my breasts pressed against his chest and his arms tightly wound around my middle, bringing his length deeper inside of me. His own breathing turns heavy as he follows my cues and meets me on every thrust.

A shade of contentment hits me, because in this moment, my mind goes blank, and my body feels alive. I quickly spiral into temporary relief when I convulse around him, not even noticing that he chases his own release to the end. My body goes weak, but he has me. He stays inside while his hand rubs soothing circles on my back, and he kisses the curve of my shoulder.

Connor doesn't say anything, he just holds me because my body is spent and filled.

I lose track of time, but he eventually kisses along my jaw before gently flipping me so I'm on my back and he can pull out. Connor grabs the duvet and brings it over my body while he leans on his side to observe me again. However, I only feel his eyes on me, since I stare at the ceiling.

His finger, like a feather, traces the lines of my shoulder to the base of my neck. "I'm not leaving you."

"You've mentioned."

"I'll make sure nobody bothers you today if that's what you want."

I turn my head to the side to look at him. "You mean my father?"

His lips purse out. "He wants to see you."

A scornful yet humorous smirk curls on my lips. "I forgot that you two are close now."

Connor's head falls, and he rubs the back of his neck. "I did what I thought was right."

A long silence overtakes us.

"You and me? I'm cautious still. I'm here and not running away, but that doesn't mean I can forget. That's where you and I are," I clarify.

He drags his thumb across my bottom lip before his fingers dive through my hair to the back of my head to bring me to his lips for a confirming kiss. "I'll take it."

———

A SHORT WHILE LATER, I'm dressed in a hoodie and yoga pants when I stall at the entrance to the kitchen to find my father sitting at the kitchen counter.

He attempts to offer me a gentle comforting half-smile, and he holds his hands up in surrender. "I come in peace. Connor let me in. He ran to the store."

My husband clearly isn't following my instructions for the day. I walk to the coffee machine, but I give up because I doubt that I will be able to taste much due to the irrational amount of crying that has transpired today.

"I needed to see that you're okay," he laments.

I lean against the counter and feel defeated. "I'm alive."

A long breath leaves his lips. "This doesn't change anything. You'll always be my daughter. I was the one who watched you grow, raised you, and love you more than you can even measure."

The sting in my eyes returns, which informs me that tears are coming. "You and I have always been close. Why didn't you just... tell me?" I feel so hopeless.

"I promised my brother Camden. It was his dying wish that I raise you as my own, and that meant never telling you. He thought losing another parent since your biological mother was never in the picture was the right move. We're not identical twins, which might explain why we don't have the same blood type." His head gently lolls to the side. "I owed him his wish, and it was the best gift I ever got... just don't tell your brother that," he says, attempting to make me smile. "I don't want anything to change between us. I'm still your dad." I notice it now, how his eyes look as though he hasn't slept in days.

"How do we move on?" I barely whisper.

"Whatever way you want. Either way, you're just as much my daughter now as you were before you found out," he promises.

It makes me break into a sob, mostly because I hear how much it's true. This man loves fearlessly, and I've always been lucky to be his little girl. I just can't figure out if my identity is now different.

I wipe away a tear with the back of my hand and sniffle. "I believe you, but I just need to process."

"I get that. I'll follow your lead, but I'm not going anywhere."

I can't help it, the corner of my mouth tugs with a need to smile through my tears and aching cheeks. "Damn, you and Connor are too alike. I keep hearing that sentence."

My dad smirks to himself. "He's a good guy."

My eyes nearly bug out. "Did you just say that?"

He scoffs and a droll smile forms. "After you both got married, and he told me he knew, I was scared. Took me off guard, but then he promised that you wouldn't get hurt, and it turns out we're on the same team. Then when you arrived for the photos for that article, we both looked at you, so beautiful, and it was apparent that he will take care of you the way I would expect."

I would say that it doesn't make sense, considering Connor hated me then, but it turns out he never hated me at all. He's been harboring his feelings for me, and everyone could see except me.

My dad continues, "I attempted to give him a lecture when he informed me that he knew, but no shit, your husband literally told me, 'Don't bother with the lecture, Spencer. I have every intention of ensuring she's well taken care of and has a happy life. I'll do whatever it takes. Hadley's heart is mine, so get used to it.'"

I chortle because that sounds like him. "Always assumed you weren't his biggest fan."

"I don't like hockey players. There's a difference."

"News flash, that's his career." I appreciate that our conversation moves in a comforting way, as though we may be all right, even if we're not there yet.

My dad scratches his cheek. "He's one of the good ones. Connor kept the secret for far too long to protect you, so he is as good as gold to me. Because he sees exactly what I do. You adore your family, and we adore you. We thought it was the right thing to do."

I notice that my tears have subsided and I'm at last blinking normally. "Time will tell if it is."

The sound of Connor coming in through the garage door brings our attention to him. He walks in carrying a tray of coffees and a bag of what is probably pastries. Connor's eyes bounce between my dad and me, unsure of the scene.

Connor clears his throat. "Hey." It's an awkward greeting, probably because he knows he conspired.

I give him a pointed look. "Ambushing me?" I indicate to my father.

Connor sets the tray down and his face stays neutral. "He wanted to talk to you, and I thought it would maybe help."

My father stands up. "I think we've talked enough today, as I know it's a lot to take in. I'll leave you two alone." He walks to me and brings his arm out, hoping for a hug, but I don't move and his arm falls, his face disappointed. "I'll check in again tomorrow. I love you, Hadley."

I nod that I heard him and watch him leave, touching Connor's shoulder in passing. My heart cracking but not broken.

Connor steps in my direction with that look that is pure confidence. "You're not angry with me. Even if you don't want to admit it, you needed to hear from Spencer."

It wasn't horrible, better than last night, just… it's raw.

I grumble a sound before I begin to stomp out of the kitchen. "Space and time, Con. That's the only way we'll all come out of this," I declare.

21

CONNOR

Skating across the ice, I hate that I left Hadley at home. Well, she might be celebrating. She's been itching to have some space for a few days now. I could tell that she is growing tired of my constant check-ins and chivalrous gestures, like bringing her favorite coffee from Jolly Joe's or cooking for her even if she isn't that hungry. The only thing she doesn't seem to mind is when I'm inside of her.

I just didn't want to leave her alone, considering how the past week has gone.

But she insisted that I stay committed to my duties of volunteering at my dad's summer hockey camp for developing skills, plus I need to ensure that I stay in shape by keeping up with my workouts, as the new season is fast approaching, and I don't want my mind out of the game.

Briggs skates around me like a shark until he brakes. We both helped earlier with the kids, but now it's our time to run a few drills. Nothing too strenuous.

"Do you think Vaughn will retire or trade next season?" my friend asks as he bounces the puck on his stick.

I swivel my skates back and forth as we talk in place. "Does it matter? He isn't that bad of a guy, and we might need him if we want a chance at the cup. We won't know until end of next season. He's still signed with Tampa."

"Easy for you to say. You get along with the guy, and it isn't your position that they would trade."

"I can be off the team. It might be for the best," I admit.

He glances up, taken aback that I said that. "What's up with you?"

I hold my stick out to circle my wrists. "I'm just saying maybe getting away from Lake Spark would be good for me, for Hadley too." A bit of fresh perspective, change of scene, no parents around us.

Briggs laughs. "Nah, you two are complete family people, plus your uncle would be pissed if his team loses their star defender."

I give him an unimpressed look. "It's not always up to him." I'm kind of offended he said that. He's always had my back while I proved my abilities.

"Sorry, man, just being honest with you. Ready for the bachelor party?" He grins.

He wasn't joking, it's happening. In two weeks. I have no clue what the hell is up, and I'm kind of scared. Never underestimate Briggs, or my dad. My entire life my dad has attempted to be relatable and cool due to having me young. I can only imagine that he'll put in the extra effort to hang with the boys.

My head falls and my nose squinches as I debate if I can figure out any hints. "I'm fucking terrified."

"Also cool if the father of the bride comes? Spencer sent me a text that he wasn't sure he should be there."

That doesn't really surprise me considering what's gone down. "It's totally fine." I mean it too. Hadley loves him, and although they haven't spoken much lately, I believe they will be okay. His intentions have always been pure. "All is good," I confirm again.

He touches my shoulder as we skate to the rink exit. "I fucking love ya, man, which is why I can tease you that your mom is here with your juice box."

I laugh to myself and smile at my mom who is, in fact, standing by the rink holding up a bottle of water, indicating that she has brought me a drink so we can talk.

"Playdate's over, buddy," I reply in good jest.

"Good. I'm going to hit the spa at the Dizzy Duck Inn for a massage. That new masseuse they have is magical with her hands and her mouth."

"I didn't just hear that, Briggs Chase." My mom smiles sweetly, and I have to chuckle.

Briggs gives her his signature grin. "Sorry, Brielle, you know I'm just trying to find a woman of your caliber, but the pickings are slim here." He's just purposely annoying me now, because yeah, I've heard the guys mention how they think my mom is hot, which causes me to cringe.

"Such a charmer as always, Briggsy," she replies with her arms crossed.

He brings a hand to his heart. "I save it all for you in another life where Ford doesn't exist."

"Fuck off," I tell him.

He and my mom both laugh because annoying me is a pastime they enjoy.

Shaking my head, I get busy on my skates, taking them off, then head toward my mother to sit with her.

"I was visiting your dad in his office and saw my firstborn, so had to stop to say hello." Her voice is breezy.

I lean in and pretend to scan the room. "It's okay, you can say I'm your favorite son."

She feigns an unimpressed scowl. "Funny. Seriously, I feel like we haven't touched base much lately, and I know when you get married that your wife becomes number one, just don't forget about me."

"Couldn't if I tried," I assure her. "And sorry, I've just been tied up in a few things."

My mom touches my shoulder with affection. "Everything okay?

I thought everything is going fine. I mean, I've never seen you so happy. Marriage suits you."

"Really?"

"You have a glow."

I roll my eyes. "You and Dad need to work on these sappy speeches."

"Fair enough. But all good? Hadley had a substitute for her ballet class this week, and April seems out of sorts too, but I get the feeling that I shouldn't press." Concern is apparent in her voice.

I blow out a breath and briefly look down at my hands where my wedding ring sticks out. Marriage *does* suit me. "All good. She's just under the weather," I lie. It's not my place to inform anyone about Hadley and Spencer, and I don't think Hadley wants anyone to know. She mentioned not even telling Isla.

"Flu or…" It trails out of her mouth.

An exhausted breath now escapes me. "Relax, we meant it when we said that we're not with child, nor plan on being in the near future."

She gives me a sympathetic look. "Sorry, my mind tends to go there." I get it, I do. Being pregnant at eighteen must impact you in many ways. "If there is anything I can do, then just tell me," she offers.

"Thanks, but I've got it covered." My mom chortles, and it causes me to look at her peculiarly. "What?" I wonder.

She wraps an arm around my shoulders and keeps me locked in a side hug as we look out over the empty ice. "Of course you do. Love is when you put someone else first, and that's all you ever do when it concerns Hadley Crews, now Spears."

A proud partial smile attempts to break out on my lips. Reflecting on all my choices, although not always ideal, my mom is right, because I'd make the same choice again. Ultimately, putting Hadley first is my only goal.

"If only she saw it that way," I softly say to myself.

Not quiet enough, as my mom looks at me with alarm before she eases into advice that I know she is about to dish out. "Marriage isn't easy. What does help is ensuring you remind the other how much you love and care, say it over and over, louder if you can. Don't ever assume it's clear. We need to be showered in proclamations of love."

I bring a hand to my forehead and shake my head slightly side to side. These heart-to-hearts with my parents are killing me. Way too saccharine for my liking yet ridiculously informative.

Because if I look back at it, I've done many actions to show how much I feel for Hadley, yet I haven't stated the obvious. Maybe I took it for granted and never told her how I really feel, assuming she got the hint.

I can't afford to get it wrong now. Not when she's uncertain of how to move forward.

"Duly noted, Mom," I comment. "Great talk as always." I give her a little fist bump.

"Go. You have a wife waiting for you."

"Yeah… yeah, I do." My words linger in the air.

———

WHEN I ARRIVE HOME, I'm relieved to see that Hadley ate something, as there is a half-eaten sandwich on a plate in the kitchen. That's what I call progress. Especially since she told me that she was going to check in at her studio and go for a walk. She's attempting to find some normalcy again.

Heading to our room, I know she's there since her car is here, and her phone was downstairs by the charger. The moment that I'm standing at our bedroom door, I see her resting on her side with an e-reader on the mattress.

"Hey," I say as I walk into the room and remove my watch at the same time. My intention is to get comfy with her and have a relaxing evening.

"Hi." She sounds deflated. I guess maybe we haven't made progress.

I slide onto the bed to spoon her from behind. She's wearing a light summer tank top dress which means I have ample opportunity to brush my lips along the curve of her shoulder. "I was thinking… maybe we should get out of Lake Spark for a few days."

Hadley glances over her shoulder at me, and I take the moment to capture her chin with my crooked finger. "What do you mean?" she asks, curious.

"One of my teammates is back in Sweden for the summer and invited me to his family lake house there. Maybe it would be a good escape. The summer is ticking, and I'll have to start preparing for the season soon."

"Sweden?"

"Why not?" I shrug then tip my mouth down to trace her lips with mine.

"I'm not sure. Kind of feels like I'm running away."

"Sulking around here isn't the answer either," I point out.

Her eyes turn into saucers. "Really?" She's unimpressed. "I think I have valid reasons."

I do something that I know will calm her down. My hand journeys along her oblique around to her belly, stopping just below her navel, causing her dress to creep up slightly. Meanwhile, I drag my teeth on her skin as I travel down her neck with the occasional playful nip. I feel the goosebumps spread against her warm skin.

"Think of me holding a puppy, think happy thoughts," I tease her. I circle my fingers around the sweet spot below her belly button that drives up her anticipation for me to go lower and makes her hum in response. I turn serious again. "Did you talk to your father today?"

She growls but stays put against my body. "Why do you care so much?"

"Because you and I have a good thing going. It will be even better if you are at peace with him."

She throws a scowl in my direction. "Don't be noble," she demands.

I smirk in response. "I'm not. I'm being a selfish motherfucker who wants to see you completely content." I kiss her shoulder, determined to drive her wild.

"You need me happy so I don't ruin this marriage and your image and hockey season and our parents' hearts…" she lists.

I huff from frustration that she doesn't seem to get it, and my head falls forward for a second to gather my strength. "I don't care about any of that, and if you didn't get that memo, then I'm failing somewhere. Sometimes you just want to stop the world for someone because you put them first."

"Why would you do that?" she volleys back.

"Because you love them." It slips out of my mouth.

Her head instantly perks up, and her eyes blaze with realization.

It hits me that I'm confessing it all. I own up to it because the words come too easily. "Yeah, Hadley… I love you." Might as well state the obvious.

Her frown disperses, and the corners of her mouth curve up, with her eyes lighting up and softening. "You love me?"

My eyes bounce side to side because she is full of questions tonight. "Yes." I bring my palm to her cheek and encourage her face to move in my direction so I can entrap her with a kiss. I lean down and kiss her slowly, ensuring my tongue dips into her mouth to make this memorable.

I enjoy the way she sinks into my touch, allowing me to kiss her the way she deserves. We have history and a future. It was always going to be her.

Pulling away, I notice her eyes mesmerized and a wry smile on her lips. "You love me," she echoes.

It causes me to chuckle softly because she seems to be in a daze, but I'm not complaining about that. It feels exceptional that for the first time in days she seems happy, and it's my doing.

I'm not expecting her to say it back, and I don't give her the opportunity anyhow.

Dipping my head down, I capture her lips again while my fingers urge her cotton dress up. I don't drag this out; I pull her panties to the side and slip my fingers between her thighs and stroke her bundle of nerves that has her whimpering into my mouth. My proclamation did something to her, because she's slick with want, and it's easy for me to plunge my finger inside of her.

"Shall I prove it to you too?" I rasp and trail my mouth along her collarbone to the middle of her cleavage, recognizing the way her body shivers. "Show you that your pussy is mine?"

"Connor." Her body writhes.

My answer is to add another finger inside of her while the pad of my thumb softly rubs circles on her clit. In response she begins to ride my hand.

But when she breathes my name, it always makes me a little untamed.

"I love you," I whisper against her skin and begin to take my cock out. I'm eager to be inside of her heat, filling her up, letting go because I'm free from hiding anything from her. "I love you," I repeat as I bring my body over hers and align myself.

"Connor." Both of her hands come to frame my face in a tender manner.

Hadley lifts her knees high, offering herself to me, and I settle right where I belong. I start slow, keeping our eyes locked as I begin to make love to her, which is new for me. This is different. Very different.

Something inside of her jolts like lightning, and she lifts up to kiss me hard while I thrust in and out of her. I move deeper and harder in response, with her dress now tangled and loose around her body and revealing her bare breasts as she lies back. My mouth kisses any spot that I can find.

"You like this? Me inside of you because it means something?"

She burrows into my forearm planted next to her head on the mattress, gently biting, me with a beautiful droll smile on her lips.

"Answer me," I grit out.

"Yes," she gasps.

"You can be angry at me whenever you want," I begin as I pick up the pace. "Just remember that I've always been waiting for you, you're my end game." Her toes dig into the cheeks of my ass as she tightens around me, trying to bring me deeper. "Don't you see, beautiful girl…"

Her moans and the way her body vibrates beneath me tells me that she's close, which is good because for this round we have to come together. I grab her one arm and pin it above her head then bring the other between us, and she knows exactly what to do as she begins to touch herself.

"Don't I see what?" Her voice strains as she tries to balance breathing and the moan that rips through her.

My body tightens and fire spreads through me. A satisfied smirk appears on my lips. "It may have felt like a game all this time, but I've been purposely waiting," I manage to grunt out, as my own release is impending.

We kiss once more, a messy kiss.

"You're the only game that I've been waiting to win," I whisper into her ear.

And it sends us down the spiral of ecstasy as I come so hard until I collapse on top of her with my heart about to burst.

I do my best to roll us to our sides and stay inside of her so we don't lose our connection.

We lie there, in silence, staring at one another, letting our fingers roam.

Then it's there. Her lips twitch and her eyes flick up to meet mine while her arm snakes around my neck.

She fails miserably at trying to hide her smile, especially when I kiss the tip of her nose.

Her mouth cracks open with a sound, but the words don't follow until a beat later. "You're something special, Connor Spears."

I grin with smugness. "I know I am." Being cocky makes her smile, and right now she doesn't want to return my declaration, which I don't mind. You need a clear mind when you say it.

"I think we'll be more than okay," she whispers a promise.

I brush a few strands of hair away from her eyes. "Only when you make peace with *everyone*," I remind her.

Because otherwise, she may break, and if I can't fix that, then it feels like I didn't protect her at all.

22

HADLEY

Staring aimlessly into my coffee mug, I dive my spoon into the drink in search of my jellybean. That's why people come here, after all—for the jellybean in their coffee. I hope it's purple, they normally bring luck.

"Hey, girl," Isla's voice causes me to look up and see she is standing over me with a to-go cup in hand. I wasn't expecting her, and I haven't been the greatest friend lately.

"Hey." I softly smile back. "Want to join me?"

"For a little bit. I need to get back to the sports complex, as we are getting ready for our pre-season marketing strategy." She slides into the booth across from me. "I'm happy to see that you're still alive. I was getting worried."

I tilt my head slightly to the side and my smile feels strained. "Sorry about that. Had some family stuff."

"Everything okay?" Isla inquires before her lips purse on the rim of her cup.

I thought about reaching out to her many times. The support of a friend is key to a friendship. But the secret that put me in my current state is one that I don't exactly want to share. The fewer people who know the truth the better, because if I'm honest to myself, I understand my dad's logic. I wouldn't want any reason for anyone to think he is anything less than the dream dad he is. Not to mention, I have someone to share this all with… Connor.

A soft smile toys on the corners of my lips at the thought of him. I was taken aback when he told me he loved me. It was a beautiful moment and stirred a lot inside of me. While I didn't say it back, he was at peace with that, and it didn't alter our mood. It's not that I don't feel strongly for him, I do. More than anyone. Just in that very moment, I felt being lost in his embrace was the only answer.

My smile stretches, though, because wow, he said it first. Not only that, but it also lightens the gray that's been looming over me lately.

"Earth to Hadley." Isla waves a hand in front of my face, and my gaze zooms to her as she laughs. "Wow, your giddy look is hopefully contagious, and I hope I find myself a hockey player who sends me in a daze like you… preferably after a *long* night."

I bring my hand to my cheek and attempt to hide my blush. "What can I say? I scored myself a good husband. Besides, you're surrounded by hockey players, you have options."

She wiggles her long finger back and forth. "No. The ones that hang around Lake Spark are too close to where I work. They are a no-go." I bounce my shoulder up in agreement. She changes the topic. "Are you getting nervous for game season? It's a long and exhausting one, with pre-season games and potential playoffs later in the season."

I bite my bottom lip. "Truthfully, it hasn't crossed my mind. At least, it probably should a little more. I've just been distracted."

"I can tell."

"I kind of originally didn't plan to be around for game season, but now… that plan has changed. I also just assumed it would be kind of like my dad when he played baseball."

Isla's face goes crooked. "Hockey is a totally different realm. Longer season, more games, more injuries, a hell of a lot more fights. Connor will need the emotional and mental support for sure, and you'll need to get used to him not always around." She speaks from experience with her brother.

I take in her suggestion and recognize that I can add it to the list of trying to figure out how to move forward with my current life.

"Damn, I should have gotten a cinnamon roll while I'm here." Isla peruses the menu on the wall behind the counter.

"They are delicious," I note.

She studies me for a second and seems to debate her words. "You've lost a little weight. Are you sure everything is okay?" Isla reaches across the table to touch the back of my hand. "Or is it just that you're working out a little extra with your partner?"

I snort a laugh. "Something like that."

I feel someone arrive near my side, and they tower over us. "Oh hey, Mr. C," Isla greets him.

My dad offers her a warm smile. "Hey, Isla."

Isla scoots off the seat. "You can steal her back. I actually just popped in for a coffee on my way back to the office."

"Thanks," he replies.

Isla waves goodbye to me, and I promise to text her soon, but my stomach flips when my father replaces Isla in the seat across from me. There is no way around it. In plain terms, I've been avoiding him.

His eyes carry a seriousness and love combined. "Saw you sitting here when I was walking down Main Street."

I hold up my mug. "Caffeine. The code word to open the door to my soul."

The corner of his mouth tilts. "Not long ago, you would sit here and demand a sundae after your ballet classes."

"Hmm, I still demand sundaes." I do my best to keep our conversation bright because I believe we will eventually be okay.

"Hadley." He breathes a long breath. "I can't keep repeating myself, but I will if that's what you need."

My fingers curl up and my palm faces him low on the table to stop him. "I would rather we didn't rehash what we both now know." The truth and his reasonings.

He nods in relief.

I lean over the table. "I think I'm beginning to realize that sometimes life gives us a boost in the direction of unlocking a truth."

"It does," he agrees.

"I'm living two parallels right now. With Connor, it was a Vegas wedding that led to more. With you, it was a science project that led to a change in our dynamic."

"I don't want there to be a change," he protests in a low gritty voice.

I scan Jolly Joe's and see we are basically alone, as it's a weekday, except for some tourists over by the jukebox taking photos of the interior.

I blink several times to ensure tears won't fall. "You are my dad, but I don't feel anything for the person who is biologically my dad, you know? And I think what I struggle with is… I feel guilty about that."

"Hadley, you don't need to. It's what my brother would have wanted," he assures me.

"Isn't that twisted? He gave me away so easily."

My father shakes his head. "It wasn't like that at all. He knew he wasn't going to make it, so he made the choice to give you the best life, a selfless choice."

I lick my lips as my mouth feels suddenly dry. "I'm trying to wrap my head around that."

My dad sulks, as he is balancing patience and wanting to scream, I can tell.

"You know, Connor seems to think that we should get out of Lake Spark for a few days for a change of scene," I inform him.

"I think he might have a good suggestion."

"He wants to go to Sweden." I half laugh because a simple bed-and-breakfast somewhere warm would have sufficed.

It causes my father to grin. "I would say I should be concerned that he wants to take you far away, but I know he has to be back here before he starts training for pre-season."

I puff a breath from the reminder of my husband's career and what it will entail for me. "I remember watching your baseball games—well, the snacks might have been my highlight, but I remember. I was so proud, and you would always come say hi before a game. Something tells me hockey is a little different. I'll be clenching my seat every time they get out of line."

"I'll be there holding your hand then," he offers in a tone of pure affection.

A closed-mouth smile hits me as natural as a breeze. "I would like that. I might be cursing half the time, but we abolished the swear jar many years ago."

There it is, a natural laugh and ease between us. "It's okay, I'll join you. At some point, we get past things that are no longer what they always were. No more Pioneer Park that you loved to go to, no more tooth fairy bills, and no more treating you like a kid. But I promise, the moment you come to me and say you need anything, then you'll still be my little girl, and I'll take care of you."

Emotion floods through my veins. Spencer Crews is a good man. I glance away to try and hide a tear. "April is my mom, and I never even think of my biological one. It's just, I know my biological dad didn't think the same way and wanted the best for me, which is why I feel so guilty that I wish I didn't know because I'm perfectly content that you are my dad in all aspects. But I *do* know, and it just lingers in my thoughts." I feel like I'm repeating myself, but at least I'm being open.

"Trust me, I wish I could make you feel better," he swears.

I quickly wipe a token tear away. "I know."

A long silence hits us. What more can we say? We'll be going in circles.

"Want me to order a sundae? The one in the kitchen sink? It always used to make you feel better." My dad tries to capture my gaze with a sympathetic half-smile on his mouth.

God, I appreciate that this can't be easy for him and that he's trying.

"Go on. Just make sure they add peanut butter to the banana part."

"Oh, I'll steal the jar if they don't," he promises.

Sometimes an old-fashioned heart-to-heart over ice cream is what we need.

———

RETURNING HOME, I overhear Connor in discussion with someone in the living room, and I slowly approach, only to stall before the corner so they don't see me.

"I hate being in this position as both team owner and your uncle. I don't enjoy having the sense that you want to sign to another team after next season, especially after your marriage news is really spinning your image in a positive light." It's Declan, I recognize his voice right away.

"Look, my heart is with the team. But I'll never get to be captain of the Spinners, you know that. Everyone will assume bias," Connor explains.

"Just play like you are worthy, then it isn't a problem," Declan reminds him.

Connor scoffs. "We both know that isn't true. Besides, if our coach doesn't shape up this season, then it's another year of my career where I miss the opportunity to skate during playoffs and for a cup. I have career goals."

Declan growls, and when I peek around the corner, I see he is rubbing his face in aggravation. "Look, I shouldn't be telling you this, but we're off the record as family right now. I doubt we'll have the same head coach or general manager after next season. Not if I have anything to say about it. Just hang on a little longer. You even have a wife now, and I'm sure Hadley doesn't want to leave Lake Spark."

I clear my throat, announcing my arrival. "Hadley can speak for herself."

Both men whip their attention my way. Declan appears guilty, as if he was caught, and Connor smirks because he enjoys when I have a backbone.

"Sorry. You know where I'm coming from," Declan apologizes. "I'll leave you two be." He tips his head to Connor while he stares at me. "Talk a little sense into him, will ya?"

I grimace. "I think we both know that Connor will do what Connor wants to do."

Declan sighs. "Story of my life."

With Declan leaving us, I stride in Connor's direction, carefully, as I can tell he is sailing on rough waters right now.

"All good?" I ask, even though it feels like a pointless question.

"It's fine," he lies and walks to the kitchen. "This happens a lot. The lines get blurred between me and him." Connor grabs a beer from the fridge, and I hop up to perch on the edge of the counter.

My sympathetic look hasn't faded yet. "I think you and I have had a day."

His eyes narrow in on me with intrigue. "What happened to you?"

"My dad and I talked. It was needed, but I still feel a little over-whelmed. Need to find my bearings, I guess," I explain and stare at my dangling feet.

"It will get better," he assures me.

I sit tall and throw on an overdone smile. "I'm sure it will. Especially since I think I will take you up on the offer to get out of town. It seems that you could use a getaway too."

Connor sets his beer bottle down and approaches me with a smoldering gaze. "Oh yeah?"

I nod and quirk my lips. "Yeah. I figure you have two more weeks before you really hit the gym and ice hardcore to get ready for the season. A last-minute trip. No Sweden, though. I sent my passport off for renewal and it isn't back yet. Can we settle on, I don't know, Florida Keys or something?"

Connor brings his hands to the counter on either side of my body and leans in to bring our mouths within touching distance, but not quite. An agonizing move, but also enticing for me to attempt to brush my lips against his.

"You in a bikini, it's a deal."

Our lips meld together for a delicious kiss, which leads to him pulling me to the edge and using his hands to guide my legs around his waist.

This is what we need. A new setting to bring some clarity.

23

HADLEY

The feeling of lips grazing along my naked spine and moving up tickles, yet I respond by humming a sound of approval. I'm lying on my stomach, tangled in a sheet that isn't even covering half of my body.

Morning light floods into the room since the balcony doors are open to our own private little beach down in the Florida Keys. I've slept in pure bliss, but someone felt the need to wake me up in a delicious manner, with his hand now journeying up the back of my thigh.

I attempt to push him away playfully. "Sleep. It's more important."

Connor's answer is to take his fingers and sneak up under the sheet to claw my ass instead of spanking me. "Wake up. I have things I need you for." His voice is pure sin.

I decide to flutter my eyes fully open, and I flop over in bed. I'm greeted with Connor ready for the day ahead, with a subtle glean of sweat on his skin. He must have gone for a run or did his thousands of push-ups this morning.

"You don't need me awake for that. I might actually enjoy it when I'm in my slumber and you take me from behind," I tell him in a drowsy state.

He leans down to give me a kiss. "Oh, I'm familiar, but I meant breakfast arrived, and you wanted to walk around Key West today."

I slowly crawl up to my elbows. "Ah yes, vacation things."

He slides off the bed and begins to take his tank off. "I'll grab a quick shower then we can get going."

"Okay, I'll throw on some clothes if I must and attack those pancakes that I see over on the breakfast tray." I begin to scooch out of bed and abandon the sheet in the process. I stand up and stretch my arms overhead, releasing a long comforting sigh.

My husband stares at me with hungry eyes and arms crossed. "As much as I love watching you display your tits to me, I love seeing you relaxed and happy even more."

I grab the silk robe hanging off the back of a chair. "I guess… I am." The tropical way of life seems to suit me or at least destress me.

We've been here only a few days, but the change of scene has helped a lot. Only at the airport leaving Illinois did someone recognize Connor, and since it was a ten-year-old, Connor agreed to sign something for him. After that, we've been in our own bubble in an exclusive tiny resort in the middle keys and taking day trips to Key West or snorkeling. I've noticed since we have some distance from Lake Spark, our families, and hockey that it isn't just me who needed a few days of shutting off. Connor has hockey on his brain far more than I realized. Not in a bad way, but in an ambitious manner. He's determined to conquer his goals.

Connor peeks out around the bathroom door with the shower now running. "Want to join me?"

I'm in a faceoff with the pancake on the tray, wondering if it's a good idea. "Nah, you go ahead, otherwise we'll never get out of here."

Pushing the cart of food outside and parking it next to the table, I sit down and enjoy the quiet morning and the gentle breeze. My eyes lock down on my wrist, and something connects in my brain for what might be a great idea. For months, I've wanted another tattoo, but I want to make it more significant. It's a good while of contemplation and nibbling on food before Connor emerges with sunglasses in hand and ready to go.

"See? You could have joined me in the shower since we're still not going to get out of here on time," he teases me, but he leans over from behind to kiss me upside down while he slides his palm down the middle of my breasts.

I tip my head up to give him a better angle for a kiss. "You're right," I murmur against his lips.

His response is one more peck on my lips, and then he circles around the table to sit down. "It's all good. We can go hang by the pool if you really want."

I smile. "What do you want to do?"

"Nothing in particular, just to see where the day goes." He pours a little pepper onto his eggs.

"Connor, you seem less anxious about hockey too while we're here," I say, being honest.

He runs his tongue along his inner cheek. "Maybe so. It's not that I'm apprehensive, I just want to feel that my career is going up, not stalled. It's hard when your family is so involved."

I grab my glass of freshly squeezed orange juice and lean back in the chair. "I admit that the last few years, I didn't always follow your career other than wanting to throw something at the screen if I saw you on TV. But since I now admittedly pay closer attention, I can without a doubt say that you have talent. You're not just the next-door neighbor who played hockey; you are the man destined to rule hockey."

His lips twist at my observation. "I like hearing that."

I snort a laugh. "You like hearing anything that boosts your ego."

Connor's smoldering grin comes out in full force as he rests his elbows on the table, but his eyes pin to me with a heavy gravity sinking him down. "Hadley, we'll be okay if I sign to another team after next season, right? I mean, it's rare that a player is with the same team his entire career, it's pure numbers that don't lie. I know how close you are with your family, and you have your dance studio…"

Without hesitation, I slide off my seat and circle the table to land right in his lap where I loop my arm around his neck. "All of our beach walks and visiting eclectic boutiques has had me thinking about a lot of things." A soft reassuring smile hits my lips. "The dance studio is a non-issue. I can manage it from afar with other teachers in my place and teach during the off-season. I can also dance anywhere. Our family will also always be there waiting for us. I never imagined that this would be a conversation that you and I would have."

He's listening to me but worry fills his eyes. "What do you mean?"

"I can't say we're happening fast because we've known one another our whole lives. We're doing a lot of things out of order too. No matter how hard I try to shake it, the idea of you and me just stays glued to everything in my body."

Relief hits him. "Still not 100% sure what you're trying to say."

I kiss his forehead. "I'm open to whatever gets thrown at us."

He offers me his mouth for a kiss and our lips meet. A life with Connor is one of the clearest things in this moment of my life.

"Don't make a big deal about it." I might sound blasé. "But I love you too." I haven't told him until now.

But I feel as though this is my moment to do so, I want to. He follows my lead and pretends that we didn't just seal our fate.

"Thought you did," he answers, casual as can be, trying to hide his smile as he grabs a stick of bacon.

We're not going to make a big deal about this, because that's just us. We accidentally went full speed ahead, only to retrace the steps to that end point, and that's okay.

———

WALKING hand in hand down the busy street of pedestrians, bikes, and occasional roosters pecking around, I ignore the fact that I'm only slightly buzzed from the afternoon margarita that I just enjoyed with my burrito. We are having such a good time. There are literally no hours on the clock down here in the Keys. We don't plan and just follow the trail of what takes our interest.

"Should we send a postcard to your dad?" Connor jokes when we pass a tower of cards, but I know that it's his way of starting the conversation of the topic that he hasn't pressed me on since we've been down here.

I stall, and it causes him to turn his body to me. That shallow feeling in my stomach returns, but it feels more faded than recent weeks. "I really don't want anything to change between my dad and me."

Connor reaches up to tuck a few strands of my hair behind my ear before running his fingers along my arm. "Then it won't. It's up to you."

"It's just with the truth there and having told him how I feel, I'm not sure we can bury this all. Am I overthinking this?" I try to string my thoughts together.

"Hadley, you can bury something, but it will always be there in the spot that you left it. Instead, we do things to prove that we've moved forward, and then what you buried suddenly feels less heavy and behind a hidden wall. You're staying married to me, that shows we've moved forward, hasn't it?"

My lips press together because I admire his thoughts. I would never in my wildest dreams have anticipated him having this train of thought, but he's a lot more than a hockey dude and the former villain of my life.

I step to him and rest my hand on his shoulder while his arm snakes around my middle. "I'm kind of lucky to have you, but I think you realize that."

Connor tips his nose up in a cool kind of nod of recognition.

"The past few days and the ability to clear my head a bit has me realizing that I do want to move forward. Spencer is my dad in all ways," I declare with ease.

Connor's face softens. "That's wonderful to hear."

"I just need to find the key to help us confirm that."

Connor brings his arm around my shoulders, and we continue to walk. "You'll think of something."

It's a few blocks farther when we are confronted with a tattoo parlor, one that I've read about with rave reviews. I pull on Connor's arm, indicating for him to stop.

"I want a tattoo."

His eyes nearly bug out. "As in… now… or…"

I chuckle and lick my lips. "I've been thinking about it for a while. Remember? Vegas? I was going to get one there but got really sidetracked."

Connor indicates for me to stop. "Watch it, Wifey, you gained a husband, which I consider the best sidetrack shenanigans there are."

A bright smile spreads on my mouth. "Couldn't agree more." I interlink our arms and guide us straight to the door. "But I still want my tattoo, and this place is supposed to be phenomenal. Just a small one, a special one."

It makes sense for me. This isn't a spontaneous thought, but the meaning has changed.

I get yanked back when I realize that Connor isn't following me. Glancing to my side, I see that he appears nervous or agitated, with his feet rooted down. "Are you okay?"

"Why don't I just wait out here?" he offers.

"If they can see me now without an appointment, then it might be a good hour."

"I'll go grab a drink or pick out some souvenirs, I don't know. Anything other than looking at needles."

My face blazes with realization. "How did I not know that you're afraid of needles?"

He shrugs. "No big deal. I mean, you should do this. It's in an appropriate spot? I won't need to punch the artist after because he's seen your pussy or something, right?"

I giggle and point the side of my wrist. "Won't even see me half-naked," I promise.

Connor leans in and kisses my cheek. "I'll be waiting for you then."

I grab the back of his neck and yank him forward so I can crash my lips onto his in a bruising kiss. He deserves more than a delicate kiss goodbye. I slip my tongue in and swirl while I press my body against his, holding us tight. "Go pick out something for tonight when I can't touch the bandage of my tattoo but can lie in bed at your mercy," I purr.

That puts him in a good mood.

———

SITTING in the hammock next to our hotel room, Connor stares down, hypnotized by the clear bandage as we sit side by side with our feet on the ground and the sunset fast approaching.

"I can take the bandage off later tonight. Since it's only black ink and small, then it doesn't need so much time," I explain.

He hasn't stopped glancing at the design since he picked me up. The tattoo is visible through the Saniderm bandage. It's a few stars along the line from my wrist bone and up my forearm. They're small, and you would only notice if you were searching or happened to catch a glance.

But it isn't the stars that has him sentimental. I added tiny letters and numbers inside the stars. One is the initials of my dad, SC. Another star has the number 19; my husband's jersey number when he became my husband. That was a bit of a surprise for him, and me too, as I wasn't planning on it, but it felt right.

"I'm speechless," he reiterates again.

"I've noticed," I tease him.

Connor cups my cheek with his hand, drawing a circle on my skin with the pad of his thumb, holding my gaze as he kneels down before me, his eyes full of intention. My heart is on a rollercoaster, as he has me transfixed.

"Hadley Spears. I know you are kind of already my wife, but

marry me for real. Let's have a real wedding, the kind you wrote about in your diary when you crushed on me when you were seven."

I bring a hand to my mouth and gasp fake shock. "You mean a wedding with a unicorn theme and a magical cupcake tower?"

His laugh is deep and magical. "Okay, we may need to re-examine a few things… but a *real* wedding? One that you deserve to remember."

My hands frame his face, and I dive my head down to kiss him. "I absolutely love that idea." It's always kind of bugged me that I don't remember when I said I do or missed out on a few wedding traditions.

I throw my arms around his neck, and he falls back onto the sand, taking me with him. It doesn't take long for Connor to lead us inside where we tumble and miss the bed, opting to fall on the floor without a care in the world. He finds his way between my legs, first with his mouth and then with his cock. Screw the fancy bed, we just need the floor when we're this delirious with happiness.

Afterwards, we don't move from the floor and remain in a tangled mess. "The moms are going to lose it," he mentions, nearly out of breath.

"Oh, but we love it."

———

It's our last day of tropical life, but we can't wait another night to speak to our parents. There is no sugarcoating it, Connor and I are family people through and through.

Connor and I get cozy around the breakfast table to ensure we both fit in the phone screen. It takes two rings before my mom answers, and not so surprising, Brielle is with her, as they normally have coffee on Saturday morning together.

"Hey! You two look like lounge lizards," my mom notes.

"You both look good," Brielle adds as she attempts to equal the screen share with my mom.

I smile. "Thanks. Look, we're going to be quick. Don't make a big deal about it, but I kind of know you both probably have been plotting this anyway," I begin.

"We want to do a real wedding," Connor finishes my sentence in a melancholy tone to mess with them before swiping a few fingers across his jaw.

The sound of shrieking instantly causes me to lower the phone and stare at Connor who is shaking his head ruefully. Bringing my phone back up, I throw on a polite smile.

"Say no more. We can get invites out, confirm our reservation at the Dizzy Duck, and ask Piper to design a dress that she may have already started," my mom lists, and it causes me to burst out laughing because of course she had our neighbor designing a dress.

Connor gives them a thumbs up. "Cool. Just remember the father of the bride pays," he jokes.

"Connor," Brielle scolds him.

I see my dad peeking over their heads, attempting to see the screen.

"Can I talk to dad?" I request, and my mom hands him the phone. Connor takes my hand in his under the table to give me a comforting squeeze.

"Hey, princess. We're going on the real wedding train, huh?"

"Yep. I can see Mom is going to be busy the rest of the day." I indicate over his shoulder, as I can see in the background my mom already discussing plans with Brielle. In a strange modern-technology way, we have a bit of privacy. "Uhm, so I kind of did something while we're down here." I swallow.

My dad gives Connor a hardened look. "What the hell did you two kids do now?" He's messing with us.

"This one is all her idea," Connor promises.

I hold my wrist up to the camera so my dad can see. "It turns out my husband is a horrible replacement for tattoo partners. You are a lot better at going with me to get tattoos together, but I needed to do this one on my own and in my own time."

My father squints his eyes. "Is that—?"

"Connor's hockey number and... your initials." His mouth falls as the magnitude of the meaning overwhelms him. "Because you're my dad, the one and only, always a part of me," I confirm.

Tears swell in his eyes, and I notice that my mom quiets down as she observes. All eyes are on my dad and me. "No need to wait. We'll be okay," I tell him in what must feel like code words to the outside world.

But right now, everything fits perfectly. A fleeting few months brought a lifetime ahead of us.

(24)

CONNOR

The room erupts in low cheers as I arrive at the Vegas hotel penthouse. A mix of friends, teammates, and in an odd twist to the traditional bachelor party, my dad and his friends, including my father-in-law, are in attendance.

This should be completely awkward, especially since Briggs played a role in organizing this evening. But I know there will be no strippers or anything questionable since, well, I'm already married.

Instead, the room is set up with poker tables, a private bar, and a buffet of food to finish off our night. Because all day we've been on the go. A helicopter ride over the canyon, car racing at the speedway, and a scavenger hunt that led us back to the chapel where I got hitched yet don't remember.

Briggs grins as he walks over to me with a bottle in one hand, offering me his hand to pull me into a bear hug. "Keeping it real and giving us a little déjà vu. Oh, and I controlled the guest list, so, sorry, I did not invite Vaugh."

"That's kind of a dick move. He'll be at the wedding, you know. Unlike you, I consider him a friend. He volunteered once at the summer camp for kids." It's a lost cause, and Briggs takes a swig of his beer bottle. "We're going to play poker?" I ask.

"Yeah, and I'm going to give a not-safe-for-the-dads speech." He winks and cheekily grins, leaving before I can protest, but my half-glare and grin are apparent.

Briggs passes my dad who is approaching me with a whiskey in hand. It's kind of unusual to see him letting loose a little. He's always been easy to hang out with, but he's more of a BBQ type of guy.

He pats my shoulder. "Enjoying your day?"

"For sure."

"Your brothers are not thrilled about missing out, but they are way too young for this. Your uncle wishes he was here," he comments.

My lips quirk out. "I get it. Kind of inappropriate for the owner of the Spinners to be at my bachelor party if word got out."

My dad rubs my shoulder. "He did ensure we have the best whiskey available and sent some cigars our way."

I chortle. "I think you're living in your element right now. You didn't have a bachelor party when you eloped. Plus, you're off the hook from dad duty for the weekend."

"Whoa there, Son. I'm never off the hook from dad duty. I'm here to ensure you keep it respectable, as I know you will." His tone is humorous.

"Lies," I joke. "I'm a good cover. Now go, go enjoy owning the night."

His response is to chuckle.

As soon as he's off, Spencer is before me. Except, unlike my father, Spencer's smile is subtle. "This is a bit opposite to the lady's high tea bridal shower," he notes while he looks into his scotch glass.

I laugh. "I don't think Hadley minds. Besides, she had a wedding dress fitting today." We are throwing together a wedding in record time because pre-season games start soon, and we didn't want to wait until next summer, because that's what the calendar will do to us, make us wait. Luckily, our moms were ready to go, and this ship is sailing.

Spencer now breaks out in a grin. "Want my advice?"

I smirk shyly. "I'll hear it anyhow."

"Next off-season, take it easy."

I clap my hands together, eager for a drink. "Oh my God, I couldn't agree more."

One of my teammates brings me the scotch bottle to freshen up my drink. I've been pacing myself all day, and luckily, we had a big lunch too.

Someone turns the music down, and Briggs hits his glass with a cocktail straw to draw silence into the room. "Gentlemen, the sun has set, and we're heading into the night. Bring your A-game to the poker tournament that we have planned and enjoy the drinks. We're all here because of this man right here." Briggs points his glass in my direction. "Back in May, a bunch of us came out here for my birthday. What we didn't expect was that our boy Con would decide to ditch the party, carrying his future bride out over his shoulder."

A bunch of guys begin to cheer while I stand in the middle of the room, patiently accepting the roast that my friend is about to give me.

"For those of us lucky enough to witness the many quarrels between the love birds, then you will know that the bride and groom have *very dirty* mouths." Some guys begin to whistle, but my eyes bug out and signal to Briggs to mind the dads. "We can only imagine what that wedding night was like." More woots, but my jaw tightens, and Briggs notices before he glances to my dad and Spencer, but his smug grin doesn't fade since they're just eating up this speech. "Apologies, Ford and Spencer. Kids these days, am I right? Getting to the good stuff before committing to their vows."

My head falls as I give up, but I appreciate that everything is in good jest.

"But seriously, Connor, man." Briggs's tone turns serious. "I wasn't going to let you be shackled down without a good sendoff, so here we are. I've reluctantly called off the strippers, except for two, but they're heading straight to my room, since we're going to keep this classy. Let's open some champagne and have a good night. Cheers."

Everyone clinks their glasses before the music gets turned up again. Over the next few hours, we play poker, smoke cigars, and feel light thanks to the whiskey.

I appreciate everyone turning out and the effort put in to tonight, but somewhere between two and three in the morning, I decide that the DJ can play on without me, and I head back to my room.

I don't take much notice when I open the door, as I am busy unbuttoning my shirt, but I'm startled when a light flicks on, and I see Hadley sitting in the chair in the corner.

"You may want to lock the door." Her tone is pure sultry, and my eyes fill with desire as I give her the once-over.

It can't be the alcohol that has me imagining that she's in shorts that barely pass as clothes, a bra top, and her ballet pointe shoes that she dyed black. The ribbons lead a path up her calf.

I'm fully invested in this moment. "What are you doing here?" She should be back in Illinois.

Hadley propels from the chair and strides my way with a sway to her hips, drawing me in and building the need I have for her inside of me.

She reaches out to claw my shirt. "Decided I wanted to surprise you, so I flew out. Now sit down." Her stern demand swelters desire between us, and this dominant side is new to me, but I'm all for witnessing it.

A smirk toys on my lips, and I exaggerate the way that I sit down, informing her that I'm listening.

She walks back to me and leans down to chase my lips with hers, ensuring they never touch, but I feel her breath cascading down my chin and neck. "If we're going to have a real wedding, then you should have a real bachelor party… lap dance included."

My eyes widen, as I'm impressed that this is the angle she's going for. "I agreed to no strippers, so my wife decided she would fill the role?" I cock my head to the side.

"Something like that… but I've also never danced for you."

I grab her wrists, and I'm eager to take charge, even though this is her show. "You have, you just didn't realize."

The corner of her mouth pulls. "Well, this time it's with intention."

She drops low into a squat, balancing on her toes, before slowly slithering her way up my body, ensuring her breasts rub against my body, creating friction to my cock in passing. Next thing I know she's straddling me, with her upper body falling back in a curve because she's flexible and wants to offer me her body.

My eyes survey her like a canvas, eager to press my lips on the cleavage of her breast, but just as I lean in to scrape her skin with my lips, she sits up and brings her hands to her long hair. I get completely lost in her flawless transitions, especially when she rests her hands on my shoulders and reaches one leg behind her to the sky while she leans into me on one foot. She stays in this position while her mouth travels lower down my chest, pausing when her warm mouth covers my hard cock through my jeans.

I would love to be inside of her right now, that's the only clear thought that I have in this moment.

She peers up at me with mischief and flops around with her back now to me as she grinds against my body, grabbing my hand to part her thighs open. If we weren't alone, then the entire room would see her covered pussy on offer.

Taking the liberty, I unhook the bra top, and she leans forward to cover her breasts when the fabric falls. But she doesn't just gently push her body forward, she brings her ass to the air as her palms land on the floor.

I shudder from the image and the growing ache my dick is experiencing. Hadley is erotic in this moment and magnificent, but most of all, she's my wife.

I spank her because her behind is screaming to be touched, and she responds by swinging her hair over as her body draws back up. Hadley does a little turn on her toes to face me, and my eyes wander straight to her breasts with pebbled rocks peeking out at me. I fucking love her eyes that are filled with a sexiness that's new.

My hand finds her hip, and she drags my palm up to one of her beautiful globes while her hips move in a wave. I'm going to enjoy my prize, which is why I squeeze her breast, and her head falls back with a seductive smile.

I'm entranced by every inch of her in this very second, and when she tips her body forward and drops down to another squat with her knees out, I'm tempted to pull her onto my lap.

Her tongue darting out to lick her lips has me intrigued, especially when she begins to unzip my jeans and force the fabric down.

I bring my hands behind my head as I watch her fingers wrap around my length to give me a stroke and then her breath is on the tip of my cock. My eyes hood closed as I take in the feeling of her lips wrapping around my tip.

"Such a good girl," I praise.

She hums a sound as she takes me farther into her mouth, her nails digging into my waist to keep her steady as she brings me deep, only to drag her tongue back up in her wet mouth.

"Damn," I breathe heavily.

It only encourages her to repeat that move a few times more until she gags once, then she finds a rhythm by bopping her head to pick up the pace.

"I'm positive this isn't how a lap dance should go," I state.

The sound of Hadley's lips popping off my cock has me glancing down, and I fist some of her hair as I admire her swollen lips with a little drool on the side of her mouth.

"Positive you want to fuck me too," she says, being sassy.

I cock a brow. "Be a good girl then and ride my cock."

She smirks slyly and slowly stands when I reluctantly let her hair go. Once she stands, she pivots which means that I am unable to see her face. She hooks her fingers under the band of her flimsy shorts, and she leans forward, with her ass in the air as she drags the fabric down her thighs to her ankles, and she steps out of them. The entire move, allowing me to see her glistening pussy and the crack of her ass.

My body buzzes with heat and a swirling desire to plunge inside of her.

Hadley steps back and sits on my lap, with her back tight to me and her pointed toes against the floor. Her hands find my fingers, and she drags them through her arousal. "Am I ready enough for you?" she rasps.

I growl into her cheek then playfully nip her skin before I drag my teeth to scrape the lobe of her ear. "Perfectly wet. Now slide down on top of me, you fucking bad girl."

The feeling of her heat taking me in sends my eyes to the back of my head because she's snug and mine. My little vixen rides me slow until I square her hips and guide her to bounce. Then it turns wild, with our relentless effort to go harder and faster. She squeezes tighter, and my answer is to flick her clit with my fingers to drive her crazy. Her moans entice me to take control of her body and throw her on the bed, but I let her stay on top because she is the initiator tonight.

But then she glances over her shoulder and buries her head into my neck, with her heavy breath mixed with her moan. Her body is about to crumble in my arms as she vibrates around my cock from an orgasm. I hold her tight as my release ripples through me shortly after.

We're a couple tangled on a chair, and I didn't even get to kiss her lips yet.

I hook my finger under her chin to guide her to me and kiss her with passion and appreciation. When I pull away, I smirk when I whisper, "You are some surprise."

"I'm only here to please," she says, sarcastic.

It's a few minutes later when we crawl into bed naked, and Hadley finds her way into my arms, with her head against my chest. I begin to stroke her hair, because as much as I'm exhausted, I don't want this night to end.

"I'm happy we remember moments now with each other." I laugh under my breath.

"It's better." Her nail traces my pec. "Kind of sucks that I don't remember if we were handsy with one another when we got married."

"We'll make up for it. Besides, if it didn't happen this way, then

I'm sure you would have cut my hand off that night and never ended up as my wife."

Hadley half-laughs. "Ooh, that would have been bad. The world needs your hand. I need your hand."

"Ha-ha." I squeeze her tighter.

She looks up at me, and it's sentimental. "I love you."

"I love you too." I kiss her real quick. "Not that's it's a competition or anything, but I did say it first, and we should note that," I tease her.

Hadley's answer is to pinch me. "Not everything is a game, you know."

"If it was, then I would just win," I answer blankly.

"Lucky me." She stares at me intently for an extra second. "No really, lucky me." Then she cements our lips together.

Because she is everything that I knew was worth waiting for.

25

HADLEY

Okay, I'm doing this again.

I stare at myself in the mirror. I'm in a white dress, this time for a real-ish wedding.

My wedding.

The white dress is fitted and just long enough. The lace and silk are subtle, simple yet elegant. My hair is down except for one side pulled up slightly, with a peach rose in my hair, and I skipped the veil. I'm confident that the extravagant wedding and reception downstairs at the Dizzy Duck Inn will make up for my lack of a princess gown.

Any minute now, I will walk down the aisle to marry my husband again, with memories to replay in my head for the future ahead.

I needed a moment to myself before my dad comes to collect me and bring me down the aisle. My mom agreed a few moments of reflection would be a nice idea. Who am I kidding? She needed to go shed a tear and yell at the caterer to ensure the cupcake tower is taller.

A smile already hits me from everyone being so happy.

The gentle knock on my door puzzles me, as I thought for sure I had a few more minutes before showtime.

"Hadley, let me in." Connor speaks low, as if he doesn't want to be discovered.

"Connor?" I sound surprised.

I open the door, and he slides right through the crack, only to close the door and gape his mouth open at the sight of me. I steal his breath as he admires me, and I mirror his sentiment, as he always looks suave in a suit, like the man he was always going to be.

"Beautiful," he rasps before he strides a few steps in my direction.

I already feel the butterflies, every cliché for a wedding spinning through my body. "Here we are, Mr. Spears."

"Again… Don't worry, everything is going smoothly. Isla is your maid of honor extraordinaire, with 90% of the single hockey players here eyeing her like crazy. My mom quickly checked on Ace." Because we adopted him when the shelter phoned to say that he still didn't have a family. The little dude loves his life with us, plus he's good company when Connor will be away more and I need to cuddle in bed. "Our brothers have managed to be respectable ushers. Everything is in check."

"Then what brings you here?" I sound very curious.

He begins to chuckle as his lips stay closed, then he waves his phone up in his hand. "I kind of have a pre-ceremony present." Connor indicates with his head that I should follow him to sit on the end of the bed.

"Really? You want us to go at it right now? It took a solid two hours to look like this," I feign disbelief.

He gives me an odd glance. "That's not it. This is something…" Connor swipes his screen and shows me an email. "Significant."

I read the email from Briggs.

Con,

Only you could get me to give you two wedding presents for two different weddings in the span of a few months. However, this is perhaps going down as legendary. We're all idiots. You know those Elvis chapels? They save videos for six months…

…Yeah, I watched. Isla too.

Briggs

My eyes snap to Connor who has a grin. "Our… first wedding?" I'm unsure how I feel about this.

He nods. "Yep. Do you really want to watch it? It isn't long."

"Uhm… is it a good idea? Did you watch it?"

"No."

I roll my lips in and debate for a millisecond. "Who the hell are we kidding? Press that play button."

Connor laughs and does what I say. I squeeze his arm and keep him close as we sit tight to get a full view.

Then my brows furrow when he presses play.

The screen shows me that Connor is handing over a paper and his credit card to the chapel clerk, while I am on his back piggyback style.

"Ah yes, I think we had to get a license at the county office which is conveniently open late, and there are about ten chapels within a three-block radius."

"So, we just walked across the street?" I wonder.

We both angle our heads as we try to figure out how we found ourselves in such a predicament. "Sounds about right."

On the screen, he sets me down when the lady behind the desk indicates for us to walk down the aisle. My head now falls to my hands when the video shows me jumping onto Connor's front, straddling his waist, with my arms linked around his neck. Then he walks us down the aisle in that very position.

"Wow, you were eager." He smirks at me. "Oh look, we're getting to the good part. Elvis is making an appearance."

We both watch the video as we arrive at the end of the of the aisle, with a man in a costume ready to seal the deal. Connor lowers me, and we look at one another.

Suddenly sound begins on the video.

"Should we be questioning this more?" I ask Connor, clearly under the influence of tequila and holding fake flowers.

"Were you when we were making out with my hand up your dress

in the elevator at the hotel after we fought then gave in?" he chal-lenges, and it doesn't sound like he's sober, not by a long shot.

I shrug my shoulder. "Meh, you're right." I face Elvis. "We can do this. He has already told me he doesn't hate me... I think. Wait, did I admit that I want him too?"

Connor scoffs a laugh. "Damn straight you did, you pushed me against a wall to kiss me again."

I smile and point a finger at Connor. "I totally did. After you told me you didn't hate me at all, and I should be yours."

"You should be, Sprinkles." Connor nearly sounds offended.

I coo a sound. "You called me Sprinkles."

We share another affectionate look before we grab one another's faces with our hands to kiss hard and fast, not taking notice of the man trying to marry us.

Elvis observes us blankly then gets into character again, complete with a chuckle and voice that clearly isn't his own. "You kids ready to shake it? We'll make it quick so you can take this to the marriage bed."

Connor and I pull away from one another in a state of buzz and realization.

"Be mine forever," Connor states.

"Do we get to have a dog? I can wear your jersey too, right" I ask far too seriously.

Connor wraps an arm around my middle to keep us close. "Anything you want. I'll get a diamond ring after in the hotel store. We should totally get another bottle of tequila to celebrate that we're doing what we were always meant to."

"Yesss, tequila. Naked too. Naked tequila for our wedding night," I agree with excitement.

"You two seem like cool cats. But I gotta keep this cruising, we have another couple waiting in some medieval costumes, and we try to keep this short." Elvis is doing his best to move us along.

"Fast version," Connor snaps at Elvis then returns his gaze to me.

Elvis chuckles again. "Take her to be your bride?"

"Yes." Connor's answer is quick and sharp.

Elvis directs his attention to me. "Take him to be your husband?"

"Yes," I reply with vigor.

"I pronounce you husband and wife. Love her tender and love lives forever." He leans to the side to grab rose petals before he throws them at us. "Crystal at the front desk will take your picture. Have a blast."

Then we kiss and nearly skip down the aisle.

I lean my head against Connor's as he turns his phone off and the room is silent.

"That was…" he begins.

My eyes widen and my lips curl in as I'm struggling to come up with words. "Kind of a trainwreck."

He kisses the top of my head as he nudges my arm. "We're not watching that ever again, are we?" Connor seems to be on my wavelength.

"I don't think so, unless we're playing naked tequila."

We both let a laugh escape.

"You were totally into it, though," he points out.

I gasp at his accusation. "You were the one leading us. It was completely you pushing that wedding," I lie and try to control my grin.

"Who the fuck cares how it got us there. We're married and where we're meant to be."

Our eyes lock in a sentimental gaze. "So we are."

"We get a redo today."

I gently shake my head. "Thank the heavens for that. I have a feeling this wedding is the one that I'll always want to remember."

"No Elvis in sight," he promises.

I huff a sound. "But we're getting Briggs instead," I deadpan, because we don't actually need someone official since that deed is done, but it's just as scary as a fake Elvis but equally perfect too.

Standing up off the bed, I smooth my dress, and Connor joins me as he adjusts his tie.

"My wife," he whispers.

"My husband," I reply.

We both lean in for one last soft kiss on the lips before Connor walks to the door, and just as he opens it, my father is standing there with his fist up, about to knock.

My dad swims his eyes between us. "Really, you two? Couldn't just give your parents one traditional element for this wedding?" He is half serious but maybe kind of annoyed.

Connor and I both shrug as my father brushes past Connor then turns to lead my husband out. "The groom isn't supposed to see the bride before the wedding. Bye now."

I try to suppress my laugh and so does Connor.

We only follow our own path and rules.

Always have.

EPILOGUE: HADLEY

Squeezing my dad's hand for dear life, I wince when I see my husband scuffling with the winger from the opposite team against the boards. I do my best to return to my neutral face, hence why my dad's hand is getting ripped off.

I should have stayed up in the wives' room where nobody would be able to witness my observation of Connor during a game. But I need to feel closer, and it's kind of, well, exhilarating next to the ice.

That is, until my husband gets the whistle from the ref for cross-checking the other team's winger, Vaughn Madden. Just great, now I'm going to hear Briggs complaining about this for days, while Connor just takes the high road.

I breathe softly to stay calm. You never have any idea when a camera or fan might catch you.

Thankfully it's a home game, so my dad, keeping to his promise, stays close. Ford and Brielle are sitting up in a private room with Declan to watch the game.

"Number 19, two minutes," the ref calls out Connor's trip to the penalty box.

I bite my tongue, as I can tell Connor is now more pissed, and he will be sulking in the penalty box in the minutes to come.

"It's fine. He already scored twice, and we still have a period to go," my father leans in to assure me.

I huff. "He'll be grumbly later." Never with me, though. Connor may be an aggressive cocky ass on the ice, but he is the polar opposite when at home.

Grabbing my purse that I had set on the floor, I search for my lip balm, only to smile softly to myself when Connor's wedding ring hanging around my neck swings in the air. He's not allowed to wear rings during games. He brings it with him on the road, but when it's a home game, it's safe around my neck until after the game when I'm waiting by the locker room.

My dad rubs my shoulders as the next two minutes fly by, and then Connor is whizzing across the ice, outskating the other team that is eager to block him.

"What did I miss? I heard booing," Isla asks as she slides back onto the seat next to me.

"You picked the worst moment to go to the bathroom, which by the way, are you okay? You do that a lot," I'm a little curt, but the ref's earlier call has me livid.

"Feisty. Sorry if nature calls," she defends.

"I'll give you two a minute, and I'll go grab some snacks." My dad seemed to have a hint that Isla and I need a little space.

My eyes travel from the ice to Isla who looks a little pale. "What's up with you?" I wonder.

"Nothing." She's lying.

Drawing a line from her to the ice then back, it registers to me that we're playing Tampa tonight.

"Nothing to do with who's on the ice?" My brows raise.

She shakes her head, but it feels as though it's a struggle.

I touch her arm. "Spill it."

It feels as though the floodgates are opening and her face relaxes. "You know how I had that conference in Tampa a while ago?"

"Yeah, the one where you got stuck there because of a hurricane."

She nods. "I wasn't exactly alone when I safely rode out the storm in a hotel."

Excitement spreads through me. "You were riding someone else during the storm, weren't you?"

Isla bites her bottom lip. "It's not ideal."

"Why not? It's great. You are allowed to have fun. Who was it?" I inquire with deep curiosity.

She laughs nervously. "The guy who just put your husband in the penalty box."

My jaw goes slack. "Vaughn Madden?"

Guilt floods her face, and she brings her hand to her forehead. "Nobody can know. Especially since my brother isn't a fan. It was a one-time thing."

"Really? I mean, he's not hard on the eyes. Long-distance isn't ideal, but it's no different than if he played here in Lake Spark and had to travel for the season." I feel like I'm getting carried away.

Proven by the fact that Isla places her hand over mine on her arm. "Take a chill pill. It really was a one-time spur-of-the-moment kind of thing. He wasn't even there when I woke up."

"What an ass." Now my sour mood has returned.

"Can we forget about it?" she pleads.

I roll my eyes and feel frustrated for her. "Fine. But give him a piece of your mind after the game. You're entitled to that."

"No, Hadley. We're all entitled to a no-strings night. Now, will you focus on your man who is back on the ice and already intercepted a pass?" She smiles softly.

My attention moves forward to watch the ice where my husband has rejoined the game. "Damn. He has talent," I comment in awe, because it never gets old, the way he always goes straight back into it.

The game is a win for us, and I find myself waiting outside the press room, staring at a television screen mounted on the wall, watching as reporters ask my husband questions for post-game analysis.

There's something about Connor slightly flushed from the exercise, mixed with wet hair and a grin, that has my panties melting.

"Look, off the ice, I consider Vaughn Madden a friend. We played together before, and he was at my wedding. On the ice, we're not always friends, but that also means we can push one another's boundaries more easily, as the trust is there. It just happened that tonight the Spinners played better, with a tight defense, partly because I wasn't afraid to go in strong," Connor speaks into a mic.

Another reporter asks a question that I can only hear a mumble of.

It causes Connor to grin. "Yeah, we have a few days off for Christmas, but I'll use that to do a mini reset. I don't want my head out of the game since we are back next week playing, but it is my first Christmas as a married man, so I intend to enjoy that with my wife."

I love that answer. Even more, I love that it wraps up the round of questions, and Connor is walking straight to the hall to me, with the cameras still following him.

He kisses me real quick while I take my necklace off to return his ring. "Good game," I congratulate.

"Would have been better if I didn't get that penalty," he rumbles a sound.

I massage his shoulder. "Relax, forget about it as soon as we're out of here. Besides, you have a turkey to roast tomorrow."

He half-laughs. "Thanks for volunteering us to host."

"It's tradition that the newlyweds host," I counter.

"Since when?" he challenges.

"Mmm, since I made up that rule." I interlace our arms as we walk toward the players' parking lot underneath the arena. "Besides, we have a dog at home that would hate to miss out."

Connor chuckles again. "Sure, we'll host dinner for twenty because our dog might have hurt feelings."

I rest my head on Connor's shoulder as we walk, enjoying our post-game routine. Especially since I know hard and fast sex is coming later.

———

STARING down at the kitchen counter, I give Connor knowing eyes. "See? Christmas dinner is easy as pie."

He removes more foil with a grin. "That's because your version of cooking is having your mom do everything and bring it over in tin dishes."

I splay my hands out. "Delegating is cooking."

Connor walks a step toward me to pull me close, and his fingers entwine in my hair as he jerks me forward for a kiss. "You're a genius. Briggs is bringing beer, my mom pie, and our little brothers will be annoying shits as always. Not to mention my aunt and uncle will bring my cute little goddaughter and her persistence to ask one hundred times if a turkey is an animal." He loves it, he does.

"Sounds wonderful. Isla already brought the wine and is changing out of her yoga pants. I'll go change too since your hoodie doesn't feel like festive attire."

He draws me in for another kiss just as we feel Ace jump at our feet. We both look down, and Connor sighs. "I'll give him a quick walk and keep him out of the kitchen."

"Great."

We both part to head our separate ways, but he tows me back since he doesn't let go of my hand. "I love you," he reminds me.

"I love you too." I blush every time.

A minute later, I'm upstairs on my way to find a sweater dress, but I hear a sniffle. Knowing Isla was using the guest bedroom, I decide to check on her.

"Isla?"

The door is slightly ajar, so I take the liberty to push it farther open, and I find my friend sitting on the edge of the bed, wiping a tear away.

Instantly, I'm concerned. "What's wrong?"

"Hadley, I need to tell you something," she sniffles. "I can't keep it in anymore."

"You're scaring me," I inform her and sit next to her, touching her arm in comfort. "It's okay. If you don't like my attempt at a charcuterie board, you can tell me. Is that what it is?"

She smiles through her tears. "It's delicious, just my stomach didn't agree."

I frown. "Oh gosh, I can't afford to poison people at dinner tonight, not when a hockey team is relying on two of the guys present."

"They'll be fine. It's me. All me. I'm pregnant."

My eyes wash over her body to study if she is joking with me, but she isn't. I'm frozen from shock. "W-what?"

"A few months, actually."

"Huh?" I'm speechless. "How."

"A hurricane," she hiccups.

My eyes drive side to side as I register the timeline. "As in…"

She blows out a long breath. "Nobody knows. Not even…" She can't seem to muster the name.

But I can, and this is a twist. "Vaughn Madden," I croak out.

And she nods.

<hr>

BONUS SCENE

<hr>

CONNOR – 5 YEARS LATER

Opening the door to my hotel room, I sense my wife's presence instantly. I wasn't planning on Hadley being here, but when I left the stadium thirty minutes ago to find a text from her that I had a surprise in my room, then I knew it would be her—she's my sixth sense.

While she doesn't travel with me for away games since it isn't allowed, she does attend the random game in destinations that are fun and warm and stays in my room, which is allowed. Which is why I'm slightly puzzled that she showed up here in Denver at the end of January. It's the opposite of warm.

I've stayed with the Spinners my entire career so far, which means Hadley traveled from Illinois. But here she is leaning against the desk in the hotel room with a peculiar look on her face.

"Couldn't wait another week to see me?" I tease her and walk straight into her arms.

My fingers weave into her hair and bring her in for a deep and warm kiss. It's been days since I've touched her, and the feeling never fades. That reunion moment after time away, it keeps us alive.

When I pull back, I can see that she has a shy smile and she peers down.

"You okay?" I smile to myself, as she is kind of adorable.

"Yeah, just since you have to go on to Detroit, it would be next week when I see you for bye week," she explains.

I'm looking forward to mid-season bye week for a few days off. A bunch of guys are heading down to Mexico, but I just want to relax at home with Hadley. I'll catch Wyatt's varsity hockey game too and check in with Alex who decided hockey wasn't for him at all.

My wife nibbles on her bottom lip, debating something.

I take her hands in mine, determined to get to the bottom of this. "What's going on?"

"I couldn't wait to tell you something…"

Squinting my eyes, I'm not a clue further on the mystery.

She gathers where my brain is at and continues. "Remember Christmas?"

My brows raise, as I'm shocked she would even question that. I had three days off, and we didn't leave bed except for family dinner on Christmas Day. We even pulled over on the side of the road at one point. That's our rhythm during hockey season; days away from one another, contrasted by days that I live inside her.

"Up there on my list of best days of my life." I walk her to the bed to sit down.

"Yeah, so, uh, we also decided that we would… you know… try the baby-making thing…" She's waiting for me to catch up, and the glimmer in her eye informs why she might be here.

"Prime window when we need to try is now?" I wonder.

She shakes her head. "We're kind of already a few steps ahead."

Shit.

Didn't see that coming. But damn, my smile beams. "You're pregnant?"

She nods before happy tears pool in her eyes. "Found out yesterday, and I'm going crazy not telling anyone."

Pulling her into my arms, I kiss the hell out of her. This is wonderful news. Great news is exactly what I needed, it was a rough game and loss tonight .

"Well, this is amazing." I'm nearly speechless.

"I didn't have time to find a cute little jersey with your number that says baby, and the dog kind of buried the pregnancy test somewhere in the yard, I'm not even joking. But I did take three more tests at the airport for fun." Hadley shrugs her shoulders, and she's adorable.

I hold her close and fall back, keeping her tight against my chest. "We're going to be parents," I breathe out as I take in the news.

"Yeah. I guess I'm about six weeks. I called the doctor and demanded that we have an appointment next week since you'll be home."

I squeeze her tighter and kiss the top of her head. "You know, a week might be enough time to get little jerseys. I think we have some people who would appreciate them."

Hadley looks up to meet my gaze and splays her palm against my chest. "Our parents are going to flip."

STANDING outside the door to my parents' house, Hadley fidgets with the presents in the bag.

"Will you relax?" I place my hand on her upper back. Normally, we just walk right in, but we stalled when Hadley had a nervous freakout when my hand hit the door handle.

"Sorry. It's not every day we tell our parents that they're going to be grandparents." She's a little sassy, but I'll take it. She had her head over a toilet most of the morning.

I also know that she's been dying to tell our moms, and I want her to, even though it's early. She needs a support network until I'm back at the end of season.

"Who do you think is going to combust first?" I ask.

Hadley throws me an entertained look. "My money is on your mom."

I wiggle my long finger side to side. "Nah, I'm betting on your mom."

"We shall see."

The door flies open to my mother on the other side. "Oh, hello. What are you two doing out here? You never come to the front door." She looks at us peculiarly.

"Oh." I scratch the back of my head. "Felt like shaking it up since there is a pile of snow over there," I lie. As proven by the fact my mom peeks her head out the door to examine the driveway that was clearly shoveled earlier today.

"Right." Her tone informs me she doesn't believe us. "Come in, you two. Both of your brothers are starving, and your mom, Hadley, went overboard with dinner and wine."

I guide my wife inside and whisper, "Showtime."

After a round of hellos, we all find ourselves at the dining table where we left presents on our parents' plates. Since it's a school week, our brothers just grabbed some food and went to go work on their homework.

Hadley leans in to speak softly into my ear. "One of the moms are on to us."

"How do you know?" I whisper back.

"Wine. Blue cheese in the salad. Things I can't consume." She's overreacting, but it's cute.

I rub a soothing circle on her back. "Ugh, common ingredients at a dinner."

Hadley throws me a death stare. "Presents. Now."

I laugh and lazily hit my wine glass with a knife to grab everyone's attention. All eyes are on me, and I stand up with wine glass in hand.

"Good to be back for a few days," I begin. "As you can see, we left you each a present, so perhaps open them?" I'm not one for speeches.

"At the same time," Hadley adds and touches my arm.

Our parents glance at one another, curious yet with gentle smiles on their faces. I notice April squeezing Spencer's hand for dear life on the table.

Slowly the tissue paper finds its way to the floor, and everyone is lifting little hockey jerseys up.

My mother is the first to gasp before she beams a smile.

April coos and grins. "This is wonderful. I mean, I'm going to be a young grandma, but this is awesome. I'm so happy for you both. I was picking up the vibes." She nudges Spencer's shoulder. "Didn't I tell you she had a glow the other day at lunch?"

"Not a glow. Just post-vomiting color," Hadley states bluntly.

"How are you feeling? How far along?" my mother begins to list.

Hadley squeezes my arm and returns to sitting to be close with her as we take in our parents' faces. "A lot of morning sickness. I'm about eight weeks, and we had an ultrasound yesterday since Connor is home for a few days."

My eyes drive to my dad who claps his hands together. "This is great news. Like *really* great news. My son is going to be a dad." He blows out a breath. "Crazy but amazing."

All our attention turns to Spencer who seems to be transfixed by the tiny shirt in front of him. He's awfully quiet, and his face is neutral.

April rubs his arm. "Alive there, *Grandpa*?"

Then it happens.

Spencer Crews cracks. A tear, then he swipes it away.

Everyone is surprised by his clearly emotional reaction to our news. It would be entertaining to most, but it feels somewhat fitting considering his relationship with Hadley.

My wife stands up and circles around the table to kneel down and hug him. "Yeah, Dad, you're going to be a grandfather. If it's anything like your dad skills, then you're going to be an amazing grandfather."

They share a moment together and hug.

"You're going to be a great mom. My daughter is going to be a mom," he reflects, with a smile spreading.

"There is kind of one more little detail," Hadley informs him, with fingers coming up to indicate a smidge in length.

"Oh?" he says, curious.

Hadley stands again and walks back to me, taking a seat next to me. We interlace our fingers on the table and prepare for the gasps about to hit our ears.

"Twins skip a generation," I inform the table and wait for someone to get the hint. I see that little detail beginning to register in our parents' heads. I decide to add fuel to the fire. "Due date is right before season starts, but we're going to need all the help we can get."

"Twins?" Spencer's jaw drops.

It's a total myth that twins skip generations, but I'm not about to highlight to my father-in-law that either his daughter's eggs or my super sperm decided two babies would be in our cards.

"Surprise," Hadley announces.

The table erupts in a lot of comments and sounds of celebration. It's good to see everyone happy. But the best part is watching my wife completely elated by the scene in front of us and the fact that she's carrying our children.

Really, though, I didn't factor twins anywhere into our game that turned into more. No, like, this is coming from the blindside, but really, it's the perfect play.

Leaning in, Hadley's and my foreheads touch, and I have to grin because I'm going to rock this dad thing with her, because I only play to win.

WAITING TO SLEIGH

A Holiday Novella

1

BRIGGS

I'm sitting on the bench in the locker room, tying my shoes after hockey practice. I shoot a glare over my shoulder to my best friend and teammate, Connor.

"It's the right move," I reiterate.

"Can't you take a hint, Briggs? She isn't interested," he says in an attempt to deter me as he musses his showered hair.

Now I'm just annoyed. "You said that about Hadley, and now she's your wife," I point out.

A proud grin hits his face as he stands and grabs his coat. "Okay, you're right. So, what, you just keep booking appointments with Ivy in the hopes that she'll cave?"

"Exactly. I was hoping the photo of me in my jersey holding a puppy would have softened her a bit, but she's been radio silent." I shake my head in disappointment. I thought that was for sure a smooth move.

This all started over the summer when I had a one-night stand with a beauty I met at the summer festival here in Lake Spark, Illinois during the off-season. It was our intention to be only that, a one-night stand. Hell, we didn't even exchange full names, and nothing she said gave any indication that she knew anything about hockey. It was a spontaneous explosion between two people. An extraordinary night, with chemistry off the charts. I was disappointed that we kept to our promise of one night only. But then I decided to head to the Dizzy Duck Inn here in our small town, and I walked into my massage appointment for hands that could deep-tissue the fuck out of my aching shoulders, and I was confronted with the new masseuse, Ivy Tinsel, aka my one-night stand. Then I was hooked.

Naturally, her name raised a brow because it's very… festive. She hates it. Her blonde hair is silky, she smells of nutmeg, and her brown eyes pull me in. Lucky for me, we are always in a setting that screams to get intimate, down to the dim lighting, rainforest music, and incense. Except, she's adamant that I was a one-time thing.

Which means sadly, for me, she wants to keep it professional. Fine. I switched up my game plan and booked massages, only to arrive and use my time to talk with her instead.

"Will you ever give up?" Connor asks as we begin to walk out of the locker room.

"Nah, I'm relentless. Plus, I see the twinkle in her eye. She's dying for another night with the Briggsy."

Connor chuckles. "No wonder she won't agree to a date. Listen to yourself."

"Come on, man, you know I don't waste my A-game when in your presence. When you're not around, then I'm all fire to conquer my conquest. I've got a few days off coming up next week for Christmas, then I have ample opportunity to win her over with some hot cocoa or take her ice skating by the gazebo."

Connor stalls before we reach the door leaving the players' changing room. "Damn, you really want her or at least she isn't just a one-night thing."

I swipe my hand through my brown hair. "God no, I see potential, and it's driving me crazy."

He slaps a hand on my shoulder. "Maybe a little holiday magic is all you need then."

I can only hope.

———

AFTER THE RECEPTIONIST of the Dizzy Duck Inn spa brought me a glass of mint-flavored water, she led me to my treatment room to wait for Ivy and instructed me to undress and lie down, then wrap a sheet over my lower body.

Hopping up on the massage table, I lie on my side, ignoring the attendant's request; I stay fully dressed not to scare Ivy away at first. I'm eager to chat with my favorite Lake Spark citizen. A grin is fixed on my face as I glance at my watch and know any second that door will open to her rolling her eyes, yet she can never hide her grin.

A feeling in my chest jumps when the door handle turns, and when the door opens, Ivy enters the room with hesitation but the promising look that she's entertained. I have to laugh because she's wearing a Santa hat, along with her matching cotton slacks and top.

Her palm flies up. "I know, I know. This hat plus my name just makes it more ridiculous. But tis the holiday season, and someone at the Dizzy Duck staff meeting was insistent that we get into the holiday cheer."

"I love it. But Santa, I've been on the naughty list." I throw on a fake pout.

Ivy crosses her arms as she stands in the middle of the room. It isn't fair how she doesn't even need to try, but she's turning me on simply by lifting her full chest up by resting her arms beneath them. I peer down then draw a line with my eyes back up to her lips that have fresh gloss. I bet she did that for me.

We stare at one another for a few beats, taking in the fact that we're alone again. It's been a few weeks since I've seen her due to away games. Doesn't mean I haven't sent the occasional text, because luck was on my side when I discovered she takes dance classes from Hadley, Connor's wife. Stealing Ivy's number was the highlight of my day.

Ivy gives me a knowing look as she takes a few steps to the side table where she keeps her oils and pretends to be interested in a bottle. "Let me guess, no massage? Or are we going to attempt to at least get ten minutes of massage time in?"

"I do love having your hands on me, and I am feeling a little achy from practice earlier," I say, mesmerized by her presence.

Her eyes snap to me with concern. "Are you okay?"

A warm reassuring smile spreads on my lips. "I will be if you agree to go for coffee with me."

Ivy's concern fades to a wry smile. "Briggs, if you didn't come here for a massage then you might as well go."

"I know the deal. No massage, then I'm not allowed to pay either."

She scoffs. "I am not a whore."

I chuckle from the inside joke between us. I get it. It feels weird for me to show up and want to talk then pay a bill after.

Doing the right thing for all of humanity, I begin to unbutton my shirt, and I notice the way her eyes lift and her lips part open. "Massage it is," I announce. Then I overdo my sigh. "I'm deeply disappointed that me in my hockey jersey holding a puppy didn't persuade you." I slide off the table to hang my shirt on a hanger in the corner before I get to work on my pants. I glance over my shoulder to catch her stealing a glimpse. I didn't follow instruction and undress before she came in, but I like giving her a show.

"Oh, uh, puppies… right. It was cute. But I'm not into hockey, you know that," she says, attempting to deter me.

I stride a few steps back to the massage table in only my boxer briefs with a satisfied smirk on my lips. "It wounds me every time you say that. Guess you will just need to go in harder with your hands."

My innuendo causes a hint of a smile on her lips. "Tea tree mixed with coconut oil?" She's trying to distract us.

"Sure."

"Why are you here again?" she wonders out loud. "Don't you have a team physical therapist for this stuff?"

"They're not you. You're good for my muscles and my plan for winning your heart," I casually mention as I get comfortable on my stomach. My lines are cheesy as fuck, but I'm trying here.

"Briggs, I'm flattered, really. But..."

I prop myself up on my forearms. "But what? We're already past the awkward first-date questions. I know you hate that your parents named you Ivy, considering your last name. You do love the holidays, though. Your favorite drink is peppermint hot cocoa, and you enjoy dance in your free time. I also know you actually love puppies, and you like me too, hence why I am positive you saved the photo I sent. Just like you know that I have a sister that I adore, I love coffee with nut-flavored undertones, and that I might have the car, the career, and almost everything... I just don't have the girl who makes me smile."

Over the course of months of appointments, I've discovered little pieces about her, and I love it.

Ivy's palms land on my upper back, encouraging me to lie down, but it's the feeling of her hands against my skin that calms me. She pauses for a second, as if she feels the electrical current between us too.

"Why don't you just relax, Briggs. Think of, I don't know, snowflakes or ice. You play hockey, you must enjoy ice." She begins to dig her thumbs into my skin in search of my deeper muscles.

"I love ice, especially if I get to take a cube and draw a path on your skin of where my mouth plans to go," I inform her because flirting tends to happen between us.

Except this time, her hands abruptly halt.

2

IVY

My, oh, my, Briggs is painting an image in my head.

Heat flushes through my body from his words. A sensitive ripple coils around my nipples and cascades down my body to cause an ache between my legs. I remember the buzz between us when we shared that one night that was kind of fueled by tequila.

I do enjoy his attention, his words, his attempts.

But I can't imagine that dating a hockey star is for me. I mean, he's barely around as it is, due to away games. Except when he is around… he's here.

It's just, dating a hockey player seems to entail a lot of phone sex, lonely nights, and a calendar dictated by hockey. I already know the sex would be phenomenal, and Briggs does seem as though he is a hopeless romantic. It's just kind of out of my realm. What does he see in me?

However, it would be a lie to deny that over the past few months, I've gotten to know Briggs Chase. With his brown hair that is a little long in the back, but short enough that he couldn't tie it up, and his grin accompanies his lustful brown eyes, and that short stubbled beard is something that I've thought about tickling my skin on a few accounts.

Butterflies fluttered inside me when I saw his name on the schedule. My colleagues all find it cute.

I consider Briggs and I friends who met by chance, then our friendship blossomed at my place of work. Yet right now, I'm doing a horrible job of hiding my attraction.

My half-assed attempt to rub circles over his back to spread the oil is the first sign that I'm melting like a pile of snow. The second sign is sentences that are on the tip of my tongue but don't flow out; instead, I croak a sound.

Briggs takes it as his cue to roll to his back, which doesn't help this situation, as I get a clear view of his bare chest, along with a tattoo of his hockey number, 23.

"Briggs." I sound raspy.

My eyes become fixed on my wrists that he encircles with his fingers to hold. "One coffee," he pleads.

"I don't think that's a good idea." I feel as though I'm on repeat.

He lowers his head in disappointment. "I'm dying here. If you don't say yes at some point, then I swear my game-winning juju will be fucked, and then the Spinners can blame it on you."

I lick my lips because his humor makes me smile. "Oh no, I'm cursing the Spinners," I play along.

That droll grin, the one I adore, returns to his mouth. I admit that like every woman with a pulse in this country, I follow the team's social media, and damn, Briggs looks suave in a suit pre-game. He's also improving his speed as the season progresses, because apparently now I'm into hockey.

I must be crazy to have this man throwing himself at me and making all attempts to woo me, yet I keep denying him.

It's just safer. My little heart wants the whole tree, plus the star on top. I don't want to be his toy that he loses interest in. I've seen the media and his history with models and puck bunnies.

"Shall we get back to this massage?" I try to return us to neutral ground.

He heaves a long exhausting breath. "Okay." He sounds so deflated.

It takes a good minute, but we find our way into patient and masseuse roles. Except guilt hits me when I study the lines of his body more than I would anyone else or the way concern hits me when I notice the bruises from that hard crash against the boards the other day in their game against Seattle.

I touch him softly, more a caress, and he doesn't seem to mind. Blinking my eyes a few times, I do my best to shake away the image of my lips trailing over his skin.

Fantasy and reality get mixed when he's around. A voice in my head screams, *here is your Christmas present.*

Instead, we connect through my touch for the next forty-five minutes, aware that the air in the room is thick with desire. I should be insistent that he asks for someone else next time, but then I would be disappointed.

I give my fingers one last swirl along his spine. "All done," I whisper.

Briggs murmurs a sound; he might be half asleep. It tends to happen to a lot of people during massages, as they're so relaxed.

I rush to pour him a glass of water so he can hydrate and offer it to him after he slowly sits up.

"Your hands are magical," he compliments as he takes the drink, causing our fingers to brush against one another, and that tingle returns to my body.

"Thanks. I had to go easy since you're quite bruised from that hit with O'Shae the other day."

Briggs raises a brow. "You were watching the game?" He sounds surprised and hopeful.

My faces blushes from my slip. "I, uh, caught part of the game… it was on TV at the bar," I lie. In truth, I was at home in my pajamas with a fresh plate of cookies with the red and green sprinkles on them, right on time for the start of the game, but he doesn't need the specifics.

He doesn't buy my lie, and a victorious smirk takes over his mouth. "Okay, my last attempt for the day. What about stopping by the team holiday party? I can put you on the guest list."

"That's sweet of you, but actually, I was already invited by Hadley since she's going with Connor. Just haven't decided if I'll go or not," I admit and slant a shoulder up.

Hope fills Briggs's eyes. "See? We all want you there."

"Maybe," is all I manage to say.

———

STARING in the mirror in the dance studio, I debate if my hair should be up or down if I go to the holiday party. Maybe I shouldn't be entertaining this idea, but I'm curious as to how far I'll go with Briggs. After seeing him yesterday, I feel as though my bubble is about to pop. There isn't an ounce of resolve left in me, and maybe a holiday fling is better than nothing, as long as boundaries are clear. Or maybe it's the winter magic that surrounds me and gives me a nudge to take a risk.

With the other dancers from the adult ballet barre class clearing out of the studio, Hadley walks toward me with a smile on her face as she adjusts the bun on her head. "I would say it's my class that has you glowing, but I kind of heard a rumor that Briggs made another attempt to sway you."

She leans on the barre next to me and looks at me curiously. I would assume Briggs told her husband that I declined his attempts yet again.

A smile plays on my lips. "Are you sure it's okay if I go to the party?"

"For sure. Besides, Declan's wife Violet is in this class too, and since Declan owns the Spinners, then you are even more connected. Isla will be there too, I'm not sure where she was today. It's the third time she's missed class lately."

Isla is Briggs's sister, and she is also sweet and happens to be shipping for me to give her brother a chance.

"I'm not being crazy, am I? I mean, keeping Briggs at a distance is the right move considering his history," I ask in an attempt to seek reinforcement of my theory.

Hadley's face screws up as she debates what to say. "Does the guy party? Sure. Not always solo? Also, sure. *But* he has also calmed down this season, and he is completely crushing on you. I've never seen him like this. Sometimes people change, so maybe he deserves a chance."

I grab my sweater hanging on a barre. "How do you handle all the travel and women throwing themselves at the team?"

"Easy. Trust. Besides, the travel thing isn't as bad as I thought. It makes the homecoming amazing, if you know what I mean." She flashes her eyes at me.

I beam a smile because Hadley looks infectiously happy. "What should I wear?"

"Hmm, something that screams 'Briggs Chase, I'm waiting for you...' otherwise known as a black dress and some silver or blue tinsel thrown around your neck."

I nibble my bottom lip. "I think I can do that, the outfit-idea part. But I'm only going so I can experience this holiday party that everyone raves about. After all, I do love gingerbread cookies."

She touches my arm in comfort. "Sure, you do." Clearly, she doesn't believe me.

Nor should she.

———

CAUTIOUSLY, I examine the table of gingerbread cookies as music plays softly in the background. Apparently, some of the team had to decorate the cookies, and now all the guests need to guess who created which.

The party is at Catch 22, a restaurant here in Lake Spark on the water; the team rented out the entire venue. There is an overabundance of garland with lights and a model train doing loops around the base of a tree in the corner, decorated with blue and silver.

I jot down a few jersey numbers on the ballots to assign them to the boxes next to the cookies on the table. I have no clue who would be responsible for which one, only that a lot of the gingerbread people are missing… actual faces. It causes me to giggle to myself.

"You look great."

Glancing to my side, I see Hadley who is also in black, with a silver pendant around her neck, and Isla trails behind her in a dark blue sweater dress and boots.

"I love this color on you," Isla adds as she studies my dress. It's long-sleeved but cut low to show a bit of cleavage, except I threw on a blue scarf with a little silver tinsel.

"Thank you. You both look gorgeous. Quite a turnout," I mention as I scan the room. Everyone is laughing and enjoying drinks.

"Come on, lets grab some drinks," Hadley suggests, and we follow her to the bar where she promptly orders three eggnogs.

Isla nudges my arm. "The guys are doing a few team photos, in case you're wondering where my brother might be."

"Oh, uhm, I'm not. I came for the experience and heard the buffet is delicious."

Both ladies give me an amused look while Hadley passes us the glasses of eggnog that the barman sets in front of her.

We clink our glasses and then take a sip, but I struggle to swallow. "Wow, that's strong," I say.

"Cognac, I think, or is it brandy?" Hadley tastes her lips.

I notice Isla instantly spitting her drink back into the glass then pretending to drink.

"I'll be right back, I see my father-in-law waving to me," Hadley excuses herself before leaving us.

I tilt my head to the side as I study Isla. "Want to get a little air?" I suggest.

She takes a deep breath. "Sure." She sets her drink down, whereas I carry mine with. We head straight to the outside deck that has heaters and hanging lights.

"You okay?" I check in with her as we stop at the railing to look out at the half-frozen lake.

"Mm-hm." Isla seems distracted, and although I've only known her a few months since I moved to Lake Spark last spring, I would consider us friends.

"You know, if you ever need an ear…" I begin, and she glances sidelong at me, but I decide not to push, as I have a sister who has been pregnant twice, and the signs are there. Instead, I opt for a change of subject. "This is a wonderful party. You helped organize it, right?" She works in marketing for the training complex where the team trains.

"I did." She seems to shake whatever thought was in her head and smiles brightly at me. "Happy to see you here. I'm sure Briggs will be thrilled when he realizes you showed up. He's a great guy, you know."

My breath cuts out, as I don't know how to answer. "He seems like it." With the truth, apparently.

"Funny too, and I'm sure he would go all out on a date. But you don't need to hear his sister try to convince you."

"Truthfully, I don't need to be convinced."

Her head perks up, and her eyes widen. "Are you saying that you would actually want to date him?"

My cheeks rise as I feel an avalanche of denial falling to reveal reality. "I'm saying…" An indescribable sound croaks out of me. "Yes, okay? Yes, Briggs Chase has worn me down, and yes, I want to go out with him." It spews out of my mouth.

"So you'll go to coffee with me?" Briggs's voice roars from behind me.

Isla smiles like a Cheshire cat before patting my shoulder and walking off. She must have known he was standing there.

I go still from being caught out, but my cheeks warm as I prepare to spin on my heel to face him. I don't need to, as he is already circling around to land right in front of me, with a smoldering gaze and smirk.

"Hi." I wiggle my fingers in a little awkward wave. "Didn't see you there." I attempt to avoid his eyes on me but fail.

His smirk grows. "Good thing you didn't. You also didn't see that you're standing under mistletoe either."

My eyes shoot up to see that we are, in fact, standing under mistletoe.

3

BRIGGS

V ictory is mine.

Ivy's cheeks tighten as she slowly angles her eyes lower, avoiding looking at me. It may be partially dark out here, but the hanging holiday lights allow me to see that she's blushing. Freaking adorable.

My smirk fuses into a grin of satisfaction. "So, you *do* want to go on a date with me?"

Her eyes flick up to meet mine at last. "I guess there's no way out of this one, is there?" A playful smile forms on her lips.

I shake my head. "Not a chance."

She snickers then quickly drinks a long sip from her eggnog that she then places on the railing. She winces before she licks her lips. "It's not that you wore me down or anything. It's more that it's winter, and I love winter, and tis the season, so why not enjoy another little night together, right?" She seems to be rambling, but I caught a key part of her sentence.

Stepping closer to her, I swear the air between us is sizzling. "Whoa there, snowflake, I believe I've been begging you for a coffee, and now you're upgrading us to nighttime activities," I tease her, but in truth, I fucking love that idea.

Now she laughs nervously, but her smile doesn't disappear. "I'm not sure what I'm saying. It just seemed like the idea popped into my head, you know, a little holiday fling." She focuses on twisting that silver tree tinsel around her neck.

Gently, I touch her shoulder. "Snowflake, stop using the word little. It doesn't exist around me." That earns me a laugh. "And I'm not interested in a fling, most certainly not with someone in Lake Spark, that's just plain risky. Our one night is already an anomaly for me. To do it again…" I cluck my tongue. "Whatever will I do when it's off-season and we run into one another every day at Jolly Joe's for iced coffee? Nuh-uh, a fling isn't in our cards," I explain.

Her eyes light up with surprise. "I'm not sure I'm the kind of girl hockey players date."

I scoff. "What does that even mean? Should we maybe step back a few paces and focus on the important stuff, like how we are standing under a plant that is insistent we kiss?"

Ivy and I both briefly look up at the mistletoe again, then our eyes draw a line down, meeting one another in a gaze. "As much as I'm all for tradition…" She quickly scans the area before her eyes land back on me. "I'm not one for an audience."

Ah, that makes sense. Anybody could see us, and making out with her probably isn't a wise move at a team event.

I do the next best thing. I step closer and softly nudge her closer to my direction, then I lean down, careful to ensure my breath traces her jawline, right before I plant a soft kiss on her cheek. It's taking a lot of control right now, but if her soft cheek is any indication of what a real kiss between two people who want to take a real chance may be, then I'm the luckiest man alive.

Slowly pulling away, I notice the way she's beaming. I guess I have a few moves to impress her. Leaning up on my toes, I pull the mistletoe carefully off the hook. "We'll need this for our coffee date."

"Yeah, about that."

Back on my feet, I study her curiously. "No going back now, you admitted the truth."

She laughs and reaches out to touch my sweater, and I like that. Her fingers belong on me. "Any chance we could maybe skip to the good part? I kind of had this fantasy in my head that you would give me the night of my life again. If I'm going to go out of my comfort zone, then I'm going all out. We can have a wild night and do coffee after."

"Dating in reverse," I state blankly.

Ivy snaps her fingers. "Yeah, exactly."

"What the hell did I do to get on Santa's good list?" I wonder. This woman just surprised me in one hell of an exciting way, taking me completely from the offside.

Her fingers curl into my sweater. "You were persistent, and sometimes we just can't control the spark we feel for someone. Want to know a little secret?"

"Absolutely."

She leans into me, needing to stand on her toes because she's shorter. Her mouth finds my ear to whisper, "I desperately wanted to keep ignoring you, but I broke because it's just too much."

My lips tilt up at her honesty. For a moment, I appreciate her genuine words. She isn't trying to schmooze me like many women do, purely because I play professional hockey. I want her even more right now.

"I don't want to sound too forward, but how about I drive us out of here in an hour. I need to make some rounds at this thing, but then we can disappear," I suggest.

"A perfect idea," she agrees.

I trail my thumb along her face before I hold out the plastic berries. "Don't forget the mistletoe, snowflake."

IT'S AN HOUR LATER, and Ivy is waiting for me by my car on this snowy night. She has a shy smile on her face, yet still looks confident with her choice.

She chose to give our chemistry a chance.

I'm not entirely sure what she has in mind for our wild night, but I'm here for it. Nowhere in my head is this going to be another one-night thing. I haven't even kissed her again, and I'm putting my money on that we're a sure thing.

Approaching her, I offer her my grin that breaks hearts. My hands find her arms to rub a little warmth. "It's cold, I should warm you up."

She raises her brow. "Wow, you really got to the point," she jokes.

I chuckle. "No, I mean, let's get you in the car."

Her hand leaves her pocket to show me that she kept the mistletoe. "I think we need to do something else first." She quickly searches the scene to find that we're alone since we left after the toasts, then she holds it up, and I make a feral sound I don't quite recognize.

I dip my head down to capture her lips, and the moment our mouths touch, I'm done. This is it, what I've been waiting for, and it doesn't disappoint. My pursuit was all for good reason. I remember our electrical current, but it's better now. It's something leading us to a new direction. Her lips mold to mine and follow every angle I lead us on. Her mouth eagerly gives me entry to dip my tongue inside, and her tongue duels with mine. I bring her body closer to mine by snaking my arm around her middle to pull her close, and her moan into my mouth drives me crazy.

I've never actually kissed under the mistletoe. Hell, I'm surprised I even recognized the goddamn plant, but fuck, I've been missing out if this is the kind of kisses it delivers.

Ivy gently pulls away to gasp a breath. "Worth the wait," she whispers.

"By far," I whisper back. "Car. Now," I order. I need to get us out of here.

She nods, and I let her into the front seat of my SUV, then I'm quick to get to the driver's side to warm up the car. While we wait for the engine to heat, I turn to her and love how her lips look thoroughly kissed and plump.

"Do you mind if we go to my place? Even though we're starting practice an hour later than normal tomorrow, it's still ten," I explain.

"Sure."

My finger caresses the back of her palm that rests on the middle console. "No pressure or anything, we could watch a movie." My voice nearly strains from that half-ass attempt to be a gentleman, but I would do it for her.

She laughs, as she knows me by now and seems to be aware of my effort. "No movie needed, unless you want to make one."

My eyes bug out, because I can't tell if she's serious or not. Our one night was wild, but in a lustful mystery kind of way. "You're showing me a new side. I pegged you as being shy."

"Resistant to your charms doesn't mean I'm shy in the bedroom."

I swipe a hand through my hair and blow out a breath. "Ivy, hell, what have I walked into," I say before I turn to the wheel.

Luckily, the rest of the drive is overtaken by classic holiday tunes on the radio and talking about her brother and sister who live not far from here but will be away during the holidays due to their spouses' families, and her parents are on a trip to Hawaii.

When we get to my house, I recognize something inside of me that I don't feel very often—nerves.

Ivy wanders a few steps ahead of me and examines the surroundings. We walk into the kitchen.

"Drink?" I offer.

"No." She slides off her coat and tosses it on a stool by the kitchen island. I make the same move.

"I could put on the fireplace."

She cocks her head gently to the side. "Enticing." She slips off her shoes, and I repeat her actions.

But then I lose it. I charge forward and slide my hand through her hair to take hold of the back of her neck and bring her to me, enabling me to slam my lips onto hers.

Then it's on.

Our kisses steal our breaths. Clothes are getting tugged then ripped off. We walk toward the sofa, as my house is open-plan, but we don't part because our mouths stay in a constant tango with one another.

It's only when we fall onto the couch and create a little space between us so I can peel my shirt off that I take a look at the view of her stunning body… and the fact she is wearing matching red-and-green lace panties and bra.

"I don't even know where to start with my tongue. I want to lick every inch of you," I rasp.

Her bottom lip drops as a response from my words. "Wow, that's an image."

Throwing my shirt to the floor, I'm back on my journey. "Does that make you wet?"

"Maybe," she says, acting coy.

I pin her arms above her head on the cushions. "Don't lie to me. I have full plans to touch you, and I'll discover the truth. If you're a bad girl, then I might just have to spank you."

She writhes and curves against me. "Oh my, I do need a good spanking every now and then."

I curse under my breath, as she's going to be my undoing. Releasing her wrists, my mouth finds her neck that I kiss then gently nip at before working my way down, planting kiss after kiss to her breasts. I take hold of her nipple through the lace, and she moans instantly. My opposite hand forms around her breast to feel that they're heavy, with her nipples forming hard pebbles, eager for attention.

My mouth moves while I twist one nipple between my fingers. Her moans encourage me, which is why I slither down her body, leaving a trail of kisses, and pay extra attention just below her navel.

Taking hold of her legs, I spread her wide and find a position between her thighs. I've thought of taking her like this so many times while jerking off. Ivy is the solitude in my head when I need to destress and have relief.

I dive right in, inhaling her scent, a mix of cinnamon and something indescribable. I lick over the lace to her clit, and her hips buck up.

"Fuck, Briggs."

"You want more, baby?" I murmur.

"I need your tongue on me."

A sinful chuckle escapes me. "That's the plan, but my tongue won't just be on you, it will be *in* you."

She laces her fingers through my hair as I move the fabric to the side, and then I really get a taste of her. First with one lick up the entire line of her slit, and then I circle her clit. "You are so fucking tasty."

"I won't last long." She's breathless.

"Oh, don't you worry, we'll be at this all night."

My tongue explores inside of her, before I replace it with a finger, and my tongue finds home on her clit, finding a pattern that has her body trembling while my finger pumps in and out of her. Her pussy is soft, soaking, and soon it will be all mine.

I add another finger and do my best to find that internal button that will have her seeing stars.

"So fucking close," she coos.

I work harder on her clit, sucking and flicking my tongue. It doesn't take long for her to shudder against my mouth as an orgasm rips through her, my name escaping her lips a few times.

I stay on her clit until she calms, then back away with pride. "You are incredibly sexy when you come."

A drowsy smile is fixed on her mouth. "Don't you remember what I'm like when your cock is inside of me?"

"Even better." My fingers work the zipper of my jeans, and a little relief hits me when my cock breaks free. It was strained against the fabric, as I am so fucking hard and ready. I give myself a few strokes, and she watches me with intrigue.

"Don't just stare, snowflake. Get on your knees for me." She eagerly complies and slides off the couch, taking a spot between my legs as I sit on the edge of the cushions. "Bra off. I want to see your fantastic tits."

Her eyes have a hint of mischief as she reaches behind to unhook her bra, and then it's on the floor. With her breasts pert and facing me, she takes hold of her hair and brings it to one side. "Will you hold my hair?"

"More than, I'll guide you when I'm deep inside your mouth."

She licks her lips and then finds my tip, instantly drinking up a few drops for a taste before she slides me between her lips, taking more of my shaft on every long stroke. Her hand takes hold of my base, and my head tips back from the feeling of her moist mouth wrapped around me. Heat travels to my groin, and I know that as painful as my hard-on is, it's even more painful that I'll probably come sooner than I would hope. That's what a long wait does.

Ivy bobs her head, making noises like she enjoys my cock deep in her mouth, hitting the back of her throat. She goes at it for a bit while I guide her head, and when I know if I'm not careful that a release will hit me, that's I pull her off, her lips swollen.

"I need to fuck you," I say, honest, and then search for my jeans for a condom, but she stops me.

"I'm on the pill and I'm clean. You?"

"All good. Now lie on your back and spread those legs, baby." As she crawls back onto the sofa, I softly swat her ass in the process. "Such a good girl," I compliment.

"Just fuck me like I'm bad."

I look up the ceiling, thanking whatever may be up in the skies.

Then I'm sliding into her heat, first letting my cock play with her clit before working myself into her inch by inch. Her pussy fits me like a glove. It takes a moment to settle inside of her, as she's snug and tight. We both feel the connection tying us together, and it draws our eyes to meet before we steal a kiss. As much as this is sex, I can't help but notice that it feels a little more than that.

Her legs span slightly wider as I thrust deep. The movement is a jolt between us that causes moans to escape our mouths in unison. My senses experience a euphoria of sensitivity that is making me dizzy and relentless to pump in and out of her.

"Tell me you enjoy this feeling. Tell me this is what you've been fantasizing about." I'm confident it sounds more like begging than a demand.

The pads of Ivy's fingers touch my cheek. "I promise you… this is far better than what I imagined. And yes, I *really* enjoy your cock inside of me."

I rumble a low chuckle before picking up the pace as she wraps her legs tighter around me. "This round is hard and deep. Next round, I want you on all fours in my bed."

"Is that before or after I crawl to your bedroom?" She's toying with me, but hot damn, I love her humor. I was expecting sweet, but she's spicy as a clove hitting your tongue.

My head falls forward as I grin. "I swear I'm about to come so hard that you might be feeling me for days," I nearly pant.

It only makes her smile, and then we both get lost in our entanglement.

4

IVY

olling over, I find a vacant yet warm spot in the bed. My eyes shoot open to find Briggs emerging from his en-suite bathroom with a towel wrapped around his waist. This isn't a bad view at all. Our original one-night stand didn't even last a full night, since he left early in the morning. Not this time. No, this time we stayed curled against one another in a tight embrace.

My mind recalls last night. First on the sofa, a make-out session on the stairs, two times in his bed, both on all fours and on my stomach. I should be aching, but I'm only craving more. He's an addiction to something I'm not used to—a sexy hockey player making me come.

His eyes have a glint in them while he studies me. "I know I'm the reason you have that soft smile on your lips, but I would still love to hear what you're envisioning."

I adjust the sheet draped carelessly across my body. "Just remembering…" It's a singsong tone.

"Which part? There were a lot," he mentions as he sits on the mattress to throw on a pair of socks.

"Everything."

He glances over his shoulder then quickly leans down to give me a chaste kiss. "That's good. I would hate for you to wake up feeling regret."

My mouth tugs slightly at his comment, because it's the opposite. "Hardly," I promise.

My answer pleases him, and his grin comes out to greet me. "Listen, I hate that I need to run, but we have practice. What are the chances I can meet you this afternoon for that coffee?"

I sit up, as he has my attention. "Oh, right, we're doing everything opposite. Sex first then coffee. Uhm, I think I might have a window around lunchtime."

"That's good, as we have a break at one, and then we meet again at three to go over plays. Jolly Joe's at one? Tonight I head out with the team for an away game."

That disappoints me slightly, but at least I get him for coffee to explore what exactly this is between us. "Deal."

He steals another kiss from me, and I enjoy his soft warm lips on mine, plus the smell of his shower gel, slightly potent to wake me up. "I need to run, but just take your time to wake up, shower, grab some breakfast downstairs, snoop around, whatever you want." He has mischief on his face, and it makes me fall a little more.

"Sounds good."

When he winks at me before he leaves, I fall back onto the fluffy mattress and pillows with a heavenly sigh, feeling like the luckiest woman alive.

———

WAITING PATIENTLY in a booth at Jolly Joe's off Main Street, I can't hide this gushing smile that hasn't left my face. This soda-shop-styled café that is an ice-cream-lover's dream in the summer has been transformed into what feels to be the North Pole hopped on doo-wop. But it's Briggs Chase that put this smile on my face.

He arrives and saunters straight to our table where he slides onto the bench beside me, which takes me by surprise. I guess he wants to be close, as proven by the fact he wraps his arm around my shoulders. This feels like a public display that I'm not quite ready for, yet I don't flinch.

"I'm surprised you managed to walk in here," he jokes.

I laugh. "Well, sometimes we ache for all the right reasons. I did work up an appetite, though. How was practice?"

"Good. I think we have a good chance tomorrow against Phoenix. Then next week we have a home game, then three days off at Christmas before we're back at it."

"Sounds strenuous. I ordered us lattes with peppermint candy canes, if that's okay. I ordered you decaf because I know that most athletes only drink caffeine in the mornings, and I'm too scared to mess with your rhythm," I explain and maybe I'm a little shy.

Briggs gives me side-eye. "You've been reading about athletes? Since when?"

"A few months ago, when this hot hockey player showed up to an appointment." I don't deny it.

He enjoys my answer and leans in to kiss my lips softly. "That's kind of sweet. By the way, are you still thinking of starting that physical therapy course?"

He remembers. Then again, we've had so many discussions during our massage appointments that he does know a lot about me. I'm familiar with him. He wants a puppy desperately, especially since Connor got a new dog.

"Yeah, I can actually start in the January semester, so I'll take a few classes," I reply.

"If you need someone to practice on, then I'm all game. By the way, I kind of need to wrap my head around the fact that you massage other dudes." A protective and possessive look glazes over his face.

It's sexy as hell, but I need to highlight the obvious. "Well, it is my job. Has it always bothered you?"

"Kinda, but now I can make a claim to you."

Swoon.

I swallow. "I assure you, you are the only one where I get slightly inappropriate with. Everyone else is aboveboard professional."

The waitress drops off our coffees, and we both order a soup for lunch, and Briggs adds on a chicken salad sandwich, plus boiled eggs, not even on the menu, because he needs protein.

"I was wondering if you would come to my home game next week," he casually invites me.

My eyes widen slightly. It sounds so official, but it kind of proves to me that he's thinking a longer timeframe than just this week. Maybe there is hope for something more longstanding. "Isn't that kind of a big deal?"

He shrugs before his hand disappears under the table to caress my thigh, and heat spreads along my spine. His lips come to tease my earlobe with a gently nibble. "It's hot as hell."

"Do a lot of girls come to see your games?"

"Nope. I don't invite anyone. You're the first."

Wow, that's… special.

My face burns from the realization that we're jumping into the deep end. Then again, we've been slowly building up to this point over months. "I'll think about it," I promise.

A shade of disappointment subtly appears on his face. All I can do is connect our hands under the table to squeeze his hand gently in assurance.

For a few seconds, silence hits us, but then another smile dances on my lips when I look at the whipped cream on my latte. I take hold of the candy cane and bring it to my mouth with a dollop of cream.

"Mmm, this is what winter tastes of. This and you on my lips," I declare.

"Watching you right now is the gateway to hell since I can't take you right here on the table." His voice is sweltering.

"Think of me in a turtleneck with elves on it."

He chuckles. "Not helping, as it just fuels my naughty-student fantasy."

I laugh because the banter between us brings me so much joy. "I'm enjoying this… coffee together."

"Me too." He squeezes me closer. "I'm counting on it being the first of many."

"I'm slightly scared, but let's see where this goes. I have hesitations," I admit.

Briggs's eyes narrow in on me. "Such as?"

"You're away a lot, and I'm not sure how to handle that."

"But in the off-season, I'm nearly 100% yours, at your beck and call," he counters.

That's true. "Little steps?" I make him promise.

Reluctantly he nods before kissing my cheek, as if he is a perfect gentleman.

———

THE NEXT DAY, I return from work to find a gift outside my front door—a bouquet of red poinsettias and roses from The Flower Jar here in Lake Spark. I quickly grab the card to read it.

Still thinking about you. It's driving me crazy, so I guess I'll take it out on the ice. You might be good for the Spinners' juju after all.

Dirty kisses, Briggs

I snort a laugh at his card. It's effective, though, as I head inside, throw on some pajamas, and turn the television on to watch the game.

He's right. Briggs is a beast on the ice tonight. He scores a point in the second period and scuffles with another player in the third period, with Briggs coming out on top and without a penalty. The Spinners win which brings a permanent smile on my face, as I'm happy for him.

Grabbing my phone, I debate what I can do for him. Then it's a no-brainer. I slide my cardigan and the strap of my camisole top off my shoulders until my cleavage is in full view, then I raise my phone high to take a photo of me with puckered lips then send it to Briggs with a message.

> Me after watching a hot hockey player on
> television win a game.

I can imagine he has team meetings and a press conference after the game, so it's a good fifteen minutes before a text back comes in.

BRIGGS

You're wicked. Not even giving me a full view. Quickly changing now then have team stuff but should be able to call you when I'm back at the hotel in a little bit.

Okay. But was I talking about you or the guy in the other jersey?

Ha-ha. You'll be over my lap when I get back, with my palm firmly planted on that ass.

If that's what you want your prize to be.

He keeps his word, and shortly later, he calls on video, and my heart swells, I swear.

I'm lying in bed expecting this to be kinky, but then he surprises me.

Briggs is on his bed and looks exhausted, yet his smile is unique, a different shade of contentment and affection, plus it's all for me. "How are you today, snowflake?" It isn't an "I want you naked" kind of question; it's a genuine, earnest question.

"I'm good. I'm happy you had a good game and walked away without too many bruises."

"It was a great game, and next week with a few days off will be even better. Can't wait to see you."

"Me too." I'm excited. Then I say something I didn't plan on saying. "Wanna know a little secret?"

The corners of his mouth stretch. "Always."

"I miss you a little."

His face turns elated. "Me too."

"That's a good sign, right?"

"Very."

Is this becoming a whirlwind romance or is it just lust? That's what I can't figure out.

———

BRIGGS DOESN'T KNOW that I'm here. Once he was back in Lake Spark, we managed to get a few coffee dates and late dinners in. I always stay at his house due to his schedule, but I don't mind.

Hadley was right. The distance makes everything more intense in the best possible way. Because the moment Briggs and I laid eyes on one another when he returned, it was a searing gaze that lit a fire between us, and we combusted against the door of his kitchen.

I can do this, I think I can. Is that what it is? When something is right with someone, that we learn to adapt to the situation? Because that's what this feels like.

Which is also the reason that I'm sitting in the stands to watch the Spinners play during a home game, their last before Christmas, and it's against Tampa. I heard Briggs mention a few times how much he hates Vaughn Madden from the other team, but the fact that only two minutes in and they're already in a violent pursuit for the puck which just proves that it's a fact. It only goes downhill from there when the enforcer and wingers join in.

I wonder if Briggs senses that I'm here, but with this type of crowd, he hasn't spotted me yet.

But when a play ends and the clock is frozen, he takes his helmet off and scans the crowd, and his eyes land on me. A boyish grin appears on his face when he notices, and he shakes his head ruefully because I surprised him by wearing his jersey.

It's as if I'm committing to him on a whole other scale. Some people do things such as move in, get a ring, or meet the parents. In our case, I'm putting on his sacred jersey which means I'm his, and I'm open to seeing if we can go all in.

● 5

BRIGGS

She's wearing my jersey. Fuck yeah, Ivy's wearing my jersey.

That's hopeful, and she's officially my lucky charm.

Connor nudges my arm in passing. "Eyes on the game, buddy."

"It's good. I've moved on from your mom, I got myself a girl," I tease him because his mom had him young, and well, Brielle Spears is pretty much hot, and even though she's happily married to his dad, the whole team messes with Connor about their crush on her.

"Fuck off and focus on your girl," he hisses in good humor. But then he brakes next to me to look up in the stands, and he touches my pads. "Damn, you did it. You finally persuaded her to give you a chance, *and* you've lasted more than a week. Is she long-term material? The future Mrs. Chase? Whatever it is, get your focus back on the game and bring her to Christmas dinner where we can drill her with questions." He skates away, but I enjoy the idea of bringing her as my plus-one on Christmas Day.

She is something long-standing, and also my good-luck charm, as proven by the fact that we won the game. Barely, but we won.

IVY QUIRKS her lips out as we wait at the door for someone to let us in. It was an easy invite for Christmas dinner since Ivy didn't have any plans. Her family is away, and besides, the whole crew will be here. Connor has two little brothers who are still in school, as well as his parents who I consider almost my own. Hadley has a little brother too, plus her parents. Then we have my sister who is best friends with Hadley, not to mention at least two dogs will be running around. And to top it off, Connor's aunt and uncle will stop by with their toddler. All the men here are connected to professional sports, mostly hockey. Connor's uncle even owns our team.

The door opens, and Hadley answers with a big smile and a yellow Labrador jumping at her side. "Welcome to the chaos."

"Good to be here," I say, and Ivy hands over two bottles of wine.

"Thanks for having me," she tells Hadley.

I make a mental note that Ivy takes dance classes from Hadley, and I should insist on Ivy giving me a private show one of these days.

"Happy you could make it. Take no offense if we forget about you two; we are trying to wrangle all the kids and dogs. I'm fairly confident the turkey won't ever make it to the table, but at least we have wine," she muses with her face going crooked in amusement.

Ivy smiles at me, and we walk into the house, disposing of our coats in the front hall. I search for my sister in the sea of people spread out through the living room that we walk into, but don't spot her.

"You okay?" Ivy asks.

"Yeah, I just can't seem to find Isla." She was acting weird at breakfast. Ivy wanted to give me some space so I could have breakfast with Isla and exchange gifts. My gift for Ivy is later. But breakfast was kind of a bust, as Isla wasn't very hungry and seemed lost in her thoughts.

Hadley overhears my comment. "Oh, uh, Isla is… upstairs… changing." Ivy and Hadley exchange an odd look, and I remind myself to ask about that, as something feels up.

Ignoring it for now, I walk toward Connor in the kitchen who holds out a beer for me. "Getting serious, buddy. It's nice to see you didn't arrive solo."

I take a sip of my beer as I lean against the counter and admire how Ivy seamlessly fits in with everyone. "Got my holiday wish. I think she's feeling it too, I mean that this is going somewhere."

"You've been circling one another for months, might as well go all in. Not going slow, that's for sure, if you're bringing her to my Christmas dinner, which by the way, I didn't cook."

I slap a hand on his shoulder. "Good. We won't get food poisoning. Anyhow, I'm happy she came with me. I thought I might have to convince her a little more, but she's here willingly. It's awesome because we don't have a lot of time before the team is on the road again."

"It sucks that we have an away game on New Year's Eve," Connor highlights.

"Fuck, I know. I'm going to ask her to meet me in Denver."

Connor nods. "You should. Hadley is going to meet me there. We get like twelve hours between one game and hopping on a plane for the next one."

I shake my head and blow out a long breath. "If Ivy can handle that, then she's for sure a keeper."

Across the room, she throws me a gentle smile, and I tip my bottle at her in acknowledgment.

Dinner is a success, with a lot of laughs and great food. It turned into hours, but I was itching to get away with Ivy so I could give her a gift.

With my hand rooted on her thigh under the table, occasionally needing to shoo away an eager Labrador searching for morsels, I squeeze Ivy's thigh, indicating it's time to go. I can't help but notice my sister seems quieter than normal.

"You good?" I ask, as she's sitting across from me.

Isla looks up from her plate. "Perfect," she lies.

"Meet me in the kitchen?" I request.

My little sister rolls her eyes but obliges, and Ivy gives me a comforting look.

When I find myself alone in the kitchen area with Isla, I'm quick to ask as her head hangs low, "What's going on with you? Is it Ivy? You're not a fan?"

Isla's head instantly perks up. "Oh, gosh no, I think she's wonderful. You two look good together, and I'm happy your efforts finally paid off." She sounds convincing.

"Then what is it?" I wonder.

She sighs. "It's… nothing. Let's just enjoy the holidays, and we can meet up after New Year's for a coffee or something."

I'm not liking the sound of this, but she doesn't seem to want me to push. "Sure."

Isla gives me a weak smile and walks away.

Ivy walks over to me and touches Isla's shoulder in passing. "All good?"

I throw my hands up. "I guess. Nothing I can deal with now."

She places her fingers against my upper arm. "Shall we escape then? I'm having a great time, but I also know we have limited time before you leave again."

I kiss her forehead. "A great idea."

IVY ROLLS INTO ME, tucking her head right below my chin, with her hair splayed across my chest the way I like it, her fingers exploring my skin in the process. Best of all, we're naked in my bed. This is how I always want to spend my time off.

"I was thinking," I begin and brush my fingers along the curve of her shoulder. "I really want to do New Year's with you. Can I fly you out to Denver?"

She glances up at me. "Wow, that's an offer."

"Please." I fake a pout.

She shuffles in the bed until she's straddling me. "If I say yes, does that enter us into serious territory?" She slides her lips to the side, arching a brow.

"So what if it does?" I watch my fingers find her hips. "I'm in a sport that moves fast, and that's the way I like it in my life. Except, it's been a long while since I've had anyone to move fast with."

Ivy blushes again, and that only makes my desire for her peak even more.

"I'm scared. Everything that made me say no to you for months now feels like history. It vanished. But it feels right." She leans down to kiss my lips really quick, but as she backs away, I hold her arms firmly so she can't escape.

"Good. Now open your present." I indicate with my head to the pillow next to us.

She looks at me peculiarly and then lifts the pillow. "This was here the whole time?" She lifts the long, slim blue box with a ribbon.

"You were distracted."

She laughs before carefully pulling on the bow. When she pops the lid off, she gasps. "I can't accept this."

I begin to take the necklace out of the box. It's silver with two charms, a snowflake and a hockey stick. "Just a little something," I say. "We're by no means rushing into engagement rings or eloping like my good friend Connor, but flowers wouldn't suffice."

She allows me to sit up and place the necklace around her neck.

"My gift feels so small in comparison."

"You still being here is a gift, considering you had ideas of wild nights and flings."

She flashes me unimpressed eyes. "I had a momentary error in judgment."

The necklace looks perfect on her, which she notices as she glances down and traps the charms between her fingers.

I swipe a few strands of her hair behind her shoulder. "What are you feeling now about us?"

Her shy smile returns. "I enjoy what's happening between us. I just... I'm scared too, you know?"

"That's fair."

"Anyway, I owe you a gift. It's nothing in comparison, but it's something..." She flashes her eyes at me and leans over to the bedside table to pull something out of the drawer. I love how she doesn't mind making herself at home here.

She hands me a card. I'm curious as I open it. Then I read the card and grin. "You got me a dog… kind of."

Ivy shrugs a shoulder. "It's a virtual dog. Well, actually, you could meet him or her if you are ever in the area, but you're sponsoring a dog who's in training to be a service dog. You'll get photos and updates. I figured you travel too much for a real one."

"This is really cool."

"There's more." She encourages me to flip the card over, and when I do, I growl a sound. "This is a great gift too."

It's a promise of a sexy outfit and massage.

I set the card to the side and wrap my arms around her middle to pull her on top of me. "You're something special. Caring, sweet, and the right kind of wild."

"Nah, wild would be letting you do that thing we talked about last night. You know, where you flip me to my stomach and take—"

I shut her up with a kiss.

6

IVY

Nervously, I pace the hotel room. I'm standing in heels and lingerie, a satin nightie in maroon red. Sadly, Briggs's team lost, so I'm sure he isn't in the best of moods, but it's also New Year's Eve.

The click of the door draws my attention to Briggs entering the room. Admittedly, he looks more somber than normal, with his head hanging low, but then his eyes strike up to land on me and a slow droll smile forms on his face.

"This is some welcome," he says as he drops his small bag to the side.

He looks exhausted yet still eager for the night ahead.

I walk in a seductive sway to meet him in the middle of the suite. "I'm sorry for your loss—wait, is that the right thing to say?"

"Say whatever you want, but right now…" He wraps his arms around me to lift me off the ground, and he twirls me around. "I just want to get lost in you."

I purr a sound. "If that's what you need."

He sets me down and begins to unbutton his suit jacket, tossing it to the nearby chair. I patiently wait and watch, especially when he begins to unclip his cufflinks. Nibbling my bottom lip, I debate if now is the moment to tell him what I've been thinking. Rip off the band-aid.

His eyes stay fixed on me, I'm his bullseye, and I don't mind one bit. "You're thinking something."

I nod gently and do my best to avoid his gaze, but I'm sucked back into his sight. It's impossible to fight the pull between us. Once I let my wall down the other week, it was as if my chance to go back was erased.

I heave a sigh. "Should we get this talk out of the way?"

Briggs tips his head gently to the side, his look serious. "This doesn't sound promising."

Taking a deep breath, I go for it. "The whole way here, I was doing a lot of thinking." I drilled Hadley on the plane with a lot of questions about what it's like to be in a relationship with a hockey player. "In the summer, when you and I hooked up, it was just a little fun. When I discovered who you are, it was a red flag. I just didn't see how I would fit into your life or even gave you a chance to prove to me that you're not the image in my head. Anyway, I need to be sure that I can handle this life that you lead."

He steps closer, with his gaze piercing me. "What exactly are you saying?" He doesn't sound thrilled.

I reach out to grab the tips of his fingers. "I really want to try. I want to go all in. I'm going all in," I breathe confidently.

There is no point in trying to read his face, as his mouth is on me in a flash. A ravenous kiss that takes over my soul. It's hard, messy, and he has a point to prove. As if I'm a fool to even doubt him or us.

He sucks the air out of me before struggling to part from my lips. "You had me scared there for a moment."

I give him a peculiar look then chortle. "Why would I be waiting for you dressed like this if that was what I was going to do?"

His head bobs side to side. "Solid point." Then his mouth is skimming down my throat and teasing my collarbone before he takes hold of one thin strap between his teeth and pulls it down my shoulder until it rests loosely on my arm. He drops to his knees, nudging with his nose to lift the hem of my nightie, creating a sensitive ripple to travel through my core.

"What are you doing?" My breath grows heavy.

"I need a taste. I'm starving," he murmurs before his tongue darts out to travel up my thigh.

My entire body becomes searing hot with a need for him, especially when I glance down to find him coaxing my thighs wider, and his mouth finds my clit. The vision of him on his knees feasting on me causes me to lose my balance, and my hands land on his shoulders, as I'm already shaking.

"Shouldn't I be on my knees? You've had a long day." I mean it, but my voice is far too sultry.

"I'd rather you follow my lead and let me do as I please." He gently bites my inner thigh before returning to my pussy.

A moan from my mouth fills the room, especially as I feel myself racing toward an orgasm.

Briggs peers up with a sinister glare. "Lie on the bed for me and let me watch you."

I'm going to obey because he deserves it after that game where his coach made some bad calls, as did the refs. I find my way to the bed and back up to the headboard while Briggs goes to sit on the chair to stare at me. I know exactly what he wants which is why I spread my legs so he has a view of my pussy, and I lower my nightie slightly so he can see my breasts, with my nipples hard and eager for touch.

"I love to see how wet you are for me. Touch yourself."

My fingers land on my nipples to twist, but I'm aching too much between my legs, which is why one hand travels straight to my clit so I can play. "I'd much rather have you touch me." Yet, it's completely arousing having him watch me, especially when he unzips his pants and takes his hard cock out to stroke. My entire mouth waters, and a need overpowers me to do more.

"That will come, baby. I just love seeing how you play with yourself when I'm not around. It's not the same as the videos that you most definitely will be sending me when I'm on the road."

My body lights up with new fire. "Briggs, please," I beg as I continue to work myself into a frenzy.

He stands but doesn't move an inch closer to the bed. "Bring yourself nearly there."

I do as he says. "See? I obey," I muse.

A smirk appears on his lips. "I know you do. But I need you primed and ready before I take you deep. I need to destress from today, and most of all, I need to show you how happy I am that you're mine."

I bite my lip, loving every word he says. "I don't want to wait anymore, please," I plead again. "I need you inside of me, making me feel full."

Briggs walks to the bed, grabs hold of my ankles, then yanks me to the end, with my ass aligning with the edge of the mattress, and then he's hovering over me, his tip finding home, and he slides into me.

We moan together, as it's been a few days, which feels like eternity.

He pumps in and out relentlessly while I shower kisses along his shoulder. Then he moves to his side, taking me with, and we gravitate toward the middle of the bed. At this point, my lingerie is tangled around my body and waist, but I don't care, because Briggs and I are facing one another as he moves inside of me.

A gentler side of him sweeps over his body, and suddenly, this experience feels new. He slows down, our eyes connect, and our hands interlace as we find a rhythm together.

"I want this after every game," he whispers.

I hum a sound. It's a wonderful idea but unrealistic, yet we can dream. "I'll take you inside of me at any moment. I just love it."

"Tell me to fill you up." His breath grows labored.

"Come inside of me."

It makes us go wild again, and our thrusts grow vigorous until we crumple and shiver, wrapped in one another.

———

BRIGGS'S HEAD rests against my belly as we lie in bed. I'm stroking his hair as we wait for the clock to turn midnight. We both actually want to sleep, but we felt it's only right to ring in the new year together.

My eyes zip to the champagne on ice, then back to the man whom I have deep feeling for.

A box of chocolates and a protein bar rests on top of the duvet. "What is your New Year's resolution?" I ask.

He draws circles against the satin on my stomach. "Many things. Mostly to score more and enjoy the year with you."

I giggle. "I'm your good-luck charm, remember? You'll score more."

He grins at me before he moves to trap me under him, his forearms landing on either side of my head before he plants a few kisses over my face then neck.

"What's yours?"

I smile. "Can I steal yours? Enjoy the year with you?"

"Sure."

We stay in this position for a few minutes, with random soft kisses and whispered sweet nothings. It's only when Briggs drags himself away to sit up in bed that I realize the clock is almost midnight. He takes hold of the bottle to unwind the cork wire. Neither one of us plan to drink much, but a sip or two for good luck seems to be in order.

I sit up too and rest my chin on his shoulder from behind to observe his work on the champagne bottle.

He glances down at his watch and fiddles with it to bring up the seconds on the screen, and then we both count down from ten.

"Happy New Year," we say in unison when the clock strikes twelve.

The cork of the bottle goes pop and spills out, which makes me squeal slightly, only to be shushed by Briggs kissing me. "Happy New Year, baby," he says against my lips.

"May you have a meaningful year," I whisper back before I loop my arm around his neck when I move to sit in his lap.

He pours us two glasses and hands me one. "A toast."

"To you. For being persistent until I broke." I smile.

He smiles in accomplishment. "I am talented." We clink our glasses, but he keeps them in place. "To us. I'm sure this year will be even better since I caught my prize, my snowflake."

"Cheers."

The champagne is good, but now that we fulfilled a New Year's tradition, we set our glasses off to the side and return to bed. Turning the lights off, it's only then that we realize there are fireworks in the night sky outside. Briggs quickly hops out of bed to pull one layer of curtains open to ensure we can see the fireworks a little bit.

But then he's back in bed and under the covers with me. I snuggle into him, and he drapes his arm around me.

"I feel a lot for you." It escapes my lips, and I'm not entirely sure he even heard me.

But then he kisses the top of my hair. "I feel it between us too."

I lean up to seal us with a kiss. "Get some sleep, you have a busy day tomorrow."

"Which is why I plan on starting it by slipping into you and waking you up with my cock taking you."

"My dream come true," I retort, but really, it's the way I love it.

Throwing a few items into my suitcase, I'm relieved it's bye week. It means that I have the chance to unwind for a few days, which is why me and a few guys from the team, plus our significant others, are heading to Mexico for a few days to soak in some sun.

Except, I can't seem to get my mind in vacation mode.

My girlfriend walks into my bedroom. "My suitcase is downstairs, and I'm ready. Although the snow falling outside is a little worrisome. Hope the flights are okay. They say a snowstorm is coming."

Ivy's presence is reason number one that I'm uneasy right now, or is it reason number two?

Either way, she instantly picks up on my mood. She touches my arm in an affectionate manner. "What's up?"

I sigh and bring my thumb up to rub my chin. "I'm struggling to get into the vacation mindset, considering…"

She sits on the end of my bed next to my open suitcase. "Your sister?"

I growl from the reminder, and in fact, fists form at my sides. "Should I be feeling guilty that we're escaping while she's stuck here and pregnant?" Because that's what was up over the holidays; my single sister is unexpectedly pregnant.

Ivy gives me a pained look. "She's a big girl. Besides, Isla would want you to go. She isn't due for a few more months and seems at peace with her decision."

"When I get my hands on whoever knocked her up, then I swear…" My sister is keeping quiet on who the father is.

Ivy reaches for my hand. "We all know, the entire town knows, that you're ready to murder someone. But you've got to respect Isla's choices." Which is not to tell me who the father is.

I grumble a sound because I know she's right. Taking a breath to calm myself, I attempt to let go of problem number one.

My girlfriend's eyes narrow; she's on to me. "What else is bothering you?"

I was going to wait until she's lying next to me in a bikini with cocktail in hand to spring the other thought that's been floating in my head, but I don't think I'm going to last the plane journey, especially if I have plans to take part in the mile-high club with her. Our agenda is looking quite full.

I sit next to her on the bed, and she naturally scoots over. Taking her hand in mine, I admire the way our hands look when they're interlaced together. One day there will be a big ring on her finger, but first, we need to take some other steps.

"I wanted to talk to you about something on this trip, but I guess there's no better time than now."

"Oh? What is it?"

Bless her wild, wicked heart that she's either playing it cool or really is clueless.

"You're here most of the time. Let's make it official, move in with me."

Her eyes blaze with what I can only describe as happiness. "You want me to move in?" That gorgeous smile of hers slowly stretches.

"Yeah, waiting for me when I'm here and spending every minute possible with me during the off-season."

She throws her arms around my neck and kisses me. "Yes." Another kiss. "Absolutely, yes."

My entire body relaxes because that was the answer I was hoping for. I wasn't sure if I was moving too fast, but it seems we're on the same page.

Our phones both get a ping, and that's unusual, so we both quickly dig our phones from our pockets to find a message.

I groan at the screen, as does Ivy.

"It seems our trip isn't happening," I say. Our flight is canceled due to weather, which is always a risk when traveling in Illinois winter. Since we only have bye week, then any delays or cancellations basically means the trip isn't going to happen, as we can't afford to lose time or move dates around.

"Another time," she tells me. I appreciate her effort to stay positive by keeping that soft smile on her lips, but I know we're both disappointed.

Then it hits me.

I push my suitcase off the bed and pull Ivy to me so we fall back on the mattress. "Looks like we'll just need to ride out the storm in bed—*our* bed. Body heat to keep us warm for days on end."

She crawls on top of me, straddling me with a leg on each side of me. "This could be fun. We have to try that pair of handcuffs that I know you packed and were going to surprise me with. Similar to the fact that I planned on reliving that night from a few weeks ago, with the blindfold."

Instantly, my dick is at full attention.

"I don't even know where we should begin on this sex fest that's about to happen." I throw out a pretend sigh of exhaustion, but it's all in good fun.

Ivy peers down to her fingers dancing around my heart. "How about we start slow and sensual… because I love you."

She melts me and slays me, better than the Lake Spark city council protecting us from Midwest snow with snowplows.

I reach up to wrap my hand around the back of her neck. "I love you too. Now let me show you, snowflake."

This is what I've been waiting for. All it took was some mistletoe to be the key for us to unravel, so we could become what I hoped together. It's even better than my imagination.

Which is why we don't leave bed, except for the bathroom and to get food. We hold one another, make plans, and see who will initiate the next round. This is how we get through the next two days of being locked in our house during a snowstorm.

I've always loved winter. Now it's even better.

Ivy's going to be my wife one day, I'm sure of it.

It's also why I lie comfortably in bed, completely spent, with her in my arms softly sleeping and my thoughts floating in and out. I'm one lucky son of a bitch, but I can't help but still wonder who I'm going to kill in my sister's honor…

WAITING TO PLAY

1

VAUGHN

O h no.

My sober state is doing absolutely zero to deter my wandering eyes.

I was stuck wondering about this curiosity last night at the wedding of my buddy Connor. And it seems that I'm doing it again at this brunch for out-of-town guests.

It might be a cliché, but damn, the maid of honor is hot... and single. Couldn't tear my sight away if I tried.

I kind of ignore the tiny detail that she's also the sister of my nemesis on the ice, but maybe I get my kicks out of the idea that Briggs Chase would flip.

Isla is beautiful and has natural blonde hair that has a bounce when she swivels her hips on the dance floor, because, yeah, I noticed. I'm sure she's been to plenty of her brother's hockey games, but I never really got a chance to notice because we only play the Spinners up here in Illinois so many times a season. And even though they're technically a Chicago team, the owner just moved them to Lake Spark. I'm based down in Florida where the weather is warm and winter's a dream.

Connor and Hadley had a Vegas wedding a few months ago that

they didn't quite remember, so they had a redo in Lake Spark, and now we are all thrown together for this over-the-top wedding weekend. The last few days have been kind of unreal considering Connor's dad is a hockey legend, it's his Uncle Declan who owns the Spinners, and Connor himself is making waves as a hockey star. This meant that the guest list was nothing less than the best of our league.

Then there is his teammate who wants to kill me on a normal day. I guess it's fair, as I've thrown Briggs down in a few scuffles, including a penalty that cost him an important game. Which is why his glare is strong when I'm around.

His sister, Isla, doesn't give me a glare, though. Instead, I was picking up flirty vibes from across the room. Unfortunately, she was on maid-of-honor duty most of the time, so I didn't really get a chance to talk to her. My effort to take her back to my hotel room last night was thwarted when I heard her mention that she was going to stay at Hadley's parents' house to be up early to help prepare brunch. What kind of maid of honor does that? Shouldn't she be partying into the early hours, drinking a tequila too many, and walking barefoot as she carries her heels, preferable back to my room?

I have three hours before I need to head to the airport because I have training tomorrow. This morning is my only chance to talk to the woman whose name is Isla, like an island. An island I would love to be deserted on… with her.

A hand lands on my shoulder, drawing me out of staring at Isla helping the bride's mother adjust a few trays of coffee cake.

"How is Lake Spark treating you, Vaughn?" Declan asks as he hands me a mimosa. I'm sure he would want me on their team if I'm looking for a career change.

A knowing smirk hitches on the corner of my mouth. "You mean, would I be tempted to make this small little town a permanent spot?"

He grins. For the most part, he's a good guy. Another hockey legend who retired young then bought a team because he was already worth probably billions from his family. "While I could tell you that you have a spot on my team whether you retire this season or not, we both know it wouldn't be appropriate. Although, before you dive into that ridiculous table-sized charcuterie board, I should mention that in the event that you retire, if you're interested, our general manager isn't very popular according to the media."

The thought does create a mental note that I stick in the back of my head. I know my hockey career is dying down. I'm in my mid-thirties, and maybe I have one or two seasons left, but it depends on how I play this coming season. Still, I don't want to think about it now. I examine the over-the-top charcuterie table, complete with fruit, cheese, meats, breads, and nuts, and that's not even including the dessert table. My gaze darts back to Declan. "Oh, look at that, they have a quiche section." I do my best to deter him. "You made your point."

He smiles tightly. "I came to say hi and because I wanted to check in with you. I merely meant to ask if everyone has been hospitable." Only partly a lie, I think.

"Sure, you did." Okay, I sound skeptical, while my eyes scan the room to find the woman with a bright smile that could get me in trouble, but she disappeared.

"Isla went to check on Ace." The man read my mind. My eyes sideline to him, and he shrugs. "It's okay, your secret is safe with me."

"Ace?"

"The dog. Connor and Hadley's dog. My family has a thing for ensuring our Labradors dress for the occasion." He shakes his head, as he seems to find it ridiculous.

"Right." I spot my exit at the sliding door.

"Isla's brother is helping Ford with something, so go quickly. It's your window of opportunity, which is good because I need Briggs in tip-top shape for pre-season games, so I'd rather he doesn't catch you within a ten-foot radius of his sister," Declan gives me a warning, yet a smile is hinted on his lips.

"I'm going to get some fresh air," I say and walk away.

"I'm sure," Declan mumbles.

I make my way outside to find Isla grumbling at the Lab-mix dog that just wants to play.

"Come on, Ace. Can't you do this for like one hour?" She's talking to the dog as she tries to tie on his bandana that has the date of the wedding and Connor and Hadley's names. Isla is oblivious that I'm approaching.

I wait for her to notice, and I soak in the view of Lake Spark, with pristine dark blue water and pine trees outlining the lake. The dock looks like it gets good use. I can't imagine that the small power boat at the end of the dock stays out all year, as they actually have four seasons in Illinois.

Isla grumbles once more as she kneels down because the dog lies on his back with his paws in the air. "This shouldn't be part of maid-of-honor duty."

Clearing my throat, her head perks up, and an awkward smile graces her mouth. "Oh, hey, you don't happen to have some magic skill to get this dog to cooperate, do you?"

"Sorry, Isla. I left my dog-whisperer talents at home."

It earns me a laugh, and she stands up, abandoning her efforts. Isla doesn't seem shy around me, and her face lightens when I'm here. A cute kind of bashful.

"It's okay." She steps closer to me, scans the area, then pretends to whisper. "I'm kind of hoping when the dog catches sight of that ridiculous cold-meat section inside that he will make a rookie move and land himself in the doghouse."

I rumble a laugh. "That sounds like a plan we need to initiate."

Isla brings her hand to her hip and tips her nose up. "We?"

I gently roll my shoulder back, relaxing, because I'm liking the ease of our conversation so far. "I didn't get much chance to talk to you last night. All I know is that your Briggs's sister, best friend of the bride, and you work in marketing at the Spinners training facility. For all I know, you actually hate hockey."

She tilts her head slightly with a hum that drills straight to my groin. "Well, you know I can't hate hockey considering that's my brother's career. You know, the brother who I'm positive would like to rip you into shreds, and that's when he's having a great day. The brother who will lose it if he glances outside to see we're talking."

I forgot I had a mimosa in my hand and use this opportunity to take a sip. "You're just being polite to an out-of-town guest." I'm unfazed.

"Fair enough." A gleam flares in her eyes before she takes the mimosa from my hand, with her fingers briefly sweeping across my knuckles, and her touch has far more impact on my body than I should want. Then her lips purse against the rim and she drinks from my glass. I love how the shyness I thought she had seems to have been obliterated into a sexiness that I don't even think she means to be transmitting. "Ready for your new season?"

"I am. After a trip to the Turks and Caicos back in June, I've been developing my skills all summer."

"On or off the ice?" Now, now, that was 100% a playful inuendo that I fully support.

My grin stretches. "Are you this forward with all out-of-town guests or do I get special treatment?"

"I don't know what you're thinking, but I meant did you try cooking or sewing over the summer?" She's coy, and her smirk doesn't fade.

"Is that what you did this summer?"

She scoffs. "My summer was enjoying the lake, coffees at Jolly Joe's with jellybeans with an obscure food coloring that means you get a surprise at the end of every coffee, and calming down my friend because she accidentally married a guy. Typical Lake Spark shenanigans."

"Sounds tranquil." I take back my glass of spiked orange juice.

We both watch the dog run to the other Labrador that I think belongs to Connor's parents. "Not my problem anymore." She seems relieved the dog is gone and drops the bandana to the ground. "Connor and Hadley stayed at the Dizzy Duck Inn last night to have a wedding night, even though they've already had one or three. It meant their furbaby stayed here."

"That makes sense. You didn't get much chance to party last night," I comment.

A beaming smile spreads on her face. "I enjoyed last night, just didn't hit the dance floor too often. I really wanted to help the happy couple's parents with everything, not to mention Hadley's dress required assistance once or twice. But I don't mind, they are all family to me, the closest thing except for Briggs. I mean, I got to talk to a lot of people."

I admire her selflessness wrapped in every word. "You talked to everyone except me."

She holds her finger up. "Wrong. I talked to everyone except any hockey player who doesn't play on the Spinners and happens to be single, and my deep study of the guest list and table arrangements meant there were four men who fell into that category. Those are the ones I didn't get to talk to, including you, Vaughn Madden."

"Ouch. Unlucky for them, good news for me." We both glance out across the lake and seem to find a peaceful moment. "I've only been here a few times. I volunteered once at the summer camp and partook in a developmental skills camp. But that was a few years ago. A shame my trip is short this time around."

"Probably for the best. Winter is fast approaching."

My face turns puzzled. "It's only early September."

A deep rumble of a laugh escapes her lips. "It's Illinois, it could be flurries of snow or beach weather come October. We are not graced with Florida weather."

"Are you ever in Florida?" I'm a winger, which means being forward is natural.

She laughs, and it vibrates down my spine again and my attraction spikes. "Funny you should ask. I'm actually going down to Tampa in November for a conference." That's my city, and this must be a sign.

"November is a good time. You can escape the temperatures beginning to change here, in exchange for warm weather down there. The chance for hurricanes is not very likely either."

Isla doesn't say anything, instead keeping her wry smile as she studies me. "A shame we weren't sitting at the same table last night so you could give me some tips on places to go to, as I'm staying a few extra days, but there was a clear instruction for the seating chart that you and my brother were not to be at the same table."

"You seem to have a different view of me than your brother," I point out.

"It takes a lot for me to dislike someone. You haven't given me any reason, because I know what happens on the ice is all part of a game," she explains.

"Give me your phone." I hold out my hand, curling my fingers, indicating that she should hand it over.

Isla winces. "Sorry, I left it inside."

I dig into my pocket to grab my cell to type in her number, but we are interrupted by the sound of cheers, as it seems Connor and Hadley have arrived.

"That's our cue to head back in and discover if the smoked cheese is better than the Swiss in the cheese section. Besides… I might have forgotten my number." Isla smirks before she begins to step away, and instantly I reach out to touch her elbow and stop her.

For a moment, her gaze flicks up and I can't form words. But then it spits out. "When you're down in Florida, we should try and meet up."

Isla chortles and her jaw moves side to side. "Not a good idea."

"Why? Don't trust yourself around me?" I wonder.

"Something like that."

She leaves my grasp, but I'm still drawn to her like a magnet, even when she strides away. Isla's right, she shouldn't trust herself around me. I'm the guy who isn't searching for much except gratification that hopefully involves her dress on the floor and good conversation.

By the time I follow her back inside, Isla's vanished into the room of people. It's a solid half-hour later when Connor is talking to me that I spot Isla again.

"It really means a lot that you came out for the wedding." Connor hands me a new champagne flute.

"No problem. A bit smug, though, don't you think? I sent a wedding present after your Vegas nuptials, and now I need to do it all over again because you decided to remember it this time?" I smirk at him.

He smiles. "Give a donation to charity instead and you'll get over it. You shouldn't be sending me any gifts at all, considering in a few weeks when the season starts, I'm going to conquer you on the ice when we eventually have a game together on the roster."

My brows pinch together. "Wishful thinking, buddy."

His response is to chuckle then pat my shoulder before heading to the next guest. I inspect my watch and realize I should be heading out of here to make my flight. However, my feet don't move when I catch sight of Isla holding a small plate of food, and she approaches me with caution, probably searching for her brother.

"The Swiss cheese is the winner, and did you remember your number yet?" I tell her, and her gorgeous lips are getting harassed by her tongue swiping to the corner of her mouth.

"Really having memory problems today. Who are you again?" She's teasing me, and I laugh at her humor. "And duly noted about the cheese. Have a safe flight, Vaughn." Is that a sultry look she's giving me? It's a fine way to end the morning.

A shame I don't get more. It's okay, though, there is always next time. I'm an athlete for a reason; I'm determined to win.

EARLY NOVEMBER

Well, this is just not what I planned.

Not by what's about to go down, but by the fact our home game has been postponed and rescheduled for later in the season due to a late-season hurricane that's approaching.

However, this situation also means I got lucky. Really lucky.

My thumb traces the text message on the screen.

CONNOR

Saw the game highlights. You holding up
with the hurricane approaching? Hadley is
losing her cool because her best friend is
down there for a conference and didn't get
a flight back. Tell me something that can
calm my wife down?

ME

The hurricane? Yeah, well, it's only a
category one. People were buying
hurricane cakes at the grocery store earlier.
Hadley's friend will be okay. Most hotels are
prepared for this, or maybe she's
somewhere out of the flood zone. Do you
know which hotel?

CONNOR

I think Isla is staying at the Pelican Blue. I'll
tell Hadley to relax. Good luck!

I smirk to myself, because my buddy casually mentioning the intel on Isla was exactly what I needed to perk up my current state that landed me in this hotel a few hours later. He may have been thinking about the maid of honor's safety, but in reality, he unknowingly handed me the information I needed to get me here, sitting with a bottle of beer in hand, waiting for the prize that I wanted to claim already weeks ago.

Normally, I don't really drink much during the season, but a beer is perfectly fine right now. I focus on my drink, yet I feel her sit down at the bar, unaware of my presence.

The gripe that escapes her lips is my undoing, I swear.

"Dry white, please. Of course, this is my life. The one time I decide to mix work with a few vacation days in the sun, a hurricane decides to trap me in a hotel," she grumbles to the barman.

I bite my lip, as I'm entertained while I listen to her complain. I wasn't lying to Connor, this hotel is hurricane-proof, has a great generator, and a hurricane doesn't seem to faze the staff either. We're safe.

Is Isla safe from me? Not so much.

Rotating on my barstool, I face her, and she's sporting hot-as-hell yoga pants and a cute sweatshirt.

"It could be worse. You could be trapped in a hotel with me, because we just didn't get enough time during our last stint."

Her eyes whip to me and shock hits her that I'm sitting in front of her, before her lips curl into a smirk that spells trouble for the both of us.

ISLA

Why is Vaughn Madden sitting next to me in a hotel bar during a hurricane? And why do my instincts feel as though being trapped suddenly doesn't seem so bad?

I stare at him, intrigued or impressed by this twist of fate. However, his devilish grin and the glint in his blue eyes inform me that there is no fate involved. In fact, he hinted with persistence back at the wedding that it wouldn't be the last time we saw one another. Damn, his dirty blond hair is a length that is short, but I could still comb my fingers through that wave on top.

"Isn't this a coincidence," I state as my head lolls to the side gently, with zero conviction in my voice.

"Hardly," he says bluntly. "Your concerned friends let it slip that you were staying here, they don't know that I'm seeing you, though. And lucky for you, the league has postponed our upcoming home game. Mother Nature just conspired with me, clearly angry that you never gave me your number, Isla," he chides before he takes a sip of his drink.

"Hurricane-sized angry?" Doubt casts over my face before I quickly nod a thanks to the barman for my wine that he sets in front of me.

Vaughn leans against the bar, very confident with whatever he has up his sleeve. "You know, a late-season hurricane in November is extremely rare. Only a handful have hit Florida. But it might pass us and hit south or could stall, which would prolong our presence with one another."

I scoff a sound. "Tell that to the airport that closed, and now I'm stuck here because of Hurricane Nora."

"With me," he points out.

I play with the stem of my wine glass. "How convenient." I try to suppress the smile itching to escape my lips, but I can't.

The tips of his fingers touch near my elbow, catching me by surprise, and my eyes dart to see the proof that our skin is touching, yet I already feel a flutter in my belly.

It's not that I was playing hard to get or not very interested back during the wedding weekend. My gut was just telling me that it wouldn't really go anywhere, not to mention I was so busy with everything. But in truth, I'm attracted to him, far too much.

"It is *very* convenient. Wasn't planning on this occurrence at all." Vaughn's voice sounds playful, yet there seems to be an underlying truth.

"Neither was I. However, now would be the time to highlight what plan you conspired and is floating in your head."

"Dirty things." He's direct.

I have to chortle because he won't even try to hide it. "I figured." A silence overtakes us, and we both glance to the television mounted on the wall, with a weather report on display. "I've never been in a hurricane before," I mention.

"You know, they used to only give hurricanes female names, but then they stopped. However, it's a historical fact that female hurricanes are by far more dangerous."

I snicker. "Maybe I should be scared then."

His fingers gently brush just below my elbow. "Don't be scared. It's really a minor one, won't even hit during high tide. Tomorrow it will probably be sunny with no wind," he explains, and I appreciate that it seems he is trying to ease my concerns. He ends our touch so he can lean back on his barstool and get comfortable, as neither one of us can go anywhere.

"I'm not scared at all, so I won't need your strong arms to hold me. I'm from the Midwest, I've been through plenty of tornadoes."

Vaughn lifts his finger. "Now, a tornado and a hurricane are not the same thing, and once you realize that, then I'll be here with my strong arms, willing to hold you."

Warm heat hits my face, and I glance up to attempt to read his eyes, but my cheeks feel so tight from the wry smile I'm trying to keep tame. "You've been through a tornado? Where are you actually from? You've only played for Tampa for a short while, right?" I take a sip of my wine, hoping to ease my curiosity of where this will all lead.

"I'm from Colorado, and I've been down here for nearly seven years. Hence, my expertise on weather."

"Maybe I'll appreciate it when the lights go out."

He leans in. "Hurricane or not, the lights will be going out." It's a low gravelly husk that makes my body tingle.

Again, I have to laugh. "What is this, really? It's not like you've been thinking about me for two months, so if you found out I'm here and thought what the hell, let's have some fun, then you are…" My lips quirk out, debating what to say, but I love honesty. "Not exactly mistaken." I have no qualms about enjoying sex.

Now he chuckles. "Thought so."

We look at one another with ridiculous smiles, a connection that feels far too natural. To some, he may appear way too cocky, but I can tell it's all in good jest.

"Why aren't you at your home? You do live here," I point out.

"Well, as much as this is probably going to be an easy hurricane, the only anticipation that I have is in regards to you, when I discovered that you were here." He grabs a handful of nuts from the bowl on the bar. "And by chance, you're staying in the hotel that a buddy of mine invested in."

Lines form on my forehead. "Did he help you land a room here then?"

Vaughn shakes his head. "Nah, me sitting before you about to blow your mind is all thanks to your friends freaking out about you being safe and my determined ability to nab a room using my celebrity status."

A fond smile takes over me. "Hadley and Connor are great people. All of them are. Their parents, uncles and aunts, even the dogs. They're family to me."

A shade of interest and care hits his face while his gorgeous eyes narrow. "You don't come from a big family?"

I tuck a few strands of hair behind my ear and look down at the floor then back up. "No, not at all. It's me and Briggs. Our dad took off before I was born, and our mom, well, decided she didn't want to be a mom and left when I was five, so we lived with our grandmother who passed a few years back. Never heard from either of our parents again, and truthfully, never want to." Wow, I just laid it all out there, and it feels like a relieving whoosh.

Vaughn reaches out to touch my shoulder gently in a comforting manner. "Sorry to hear. I understand you completely. Our dad wasn't around at all, except for the random times he would float in and out of our lives, always in trouble. Our mom really did it all as a single mom, but now she lives in New Mexico with a new husband, so we don't see her much, as she is more occupied with her new marriage, and to be honest, has kind of forgotten us, as though we don't exist."

"We?"

"My older brother, Stone. He used to play hockey too, actually. We have a sports gene or something. Now, he lives in Chicago. We're pretty close."

"Older brothers can be great. Briggs and I are close, as you've figured out."

He chuckles again, this time deeper and at the back of his throat. "Oh, I know. But I don't particularly care about his opinions."

I grab some peanuts. "That was always clear."

"What is it you do exactly at the sports complex?" Vaughn wonders, and I like that we are, in a way, getting to know one another.

"I work in marketing. At first, it was for the summer camps that Ford runs, mostly for kids and charity events. Then it was the development summer training for young pro athletes. However, since the Spinners moved to Lake Spark to train, I liaison often with the team marketing department. I'm super lucky that Ford is my boss, as he is a good one, laid back and lets me come up with my own ideas. Trusts me until I have the end product," I explain.

Vaughn's lips purse out as he thinks about something. "Sounds kind of fun. I wanted to study sports management in college, but I was drafted at twenty so couldn't finish. A shame, because I have only a few years, if at all, playing before I need to shift gears."

"Well, you're not the first guy to be in that situation."

It's darker than it should be in here because the hurricane shutters are closed as a precaution, but I think it's late afternoon. I'm losing track of time because we're picking up right where we left off two months ago.

"I wouldn't have figured that you would manage to get yourself here, with determination flooding your eyes," I note.

"You know, many people stress before a storm, but I always felt rest is key."

I raise a brow at him. "You need rest, yet here you are."

A suave grin appears to curl on the corner of his lips that look soft, and his dimples are my downfall, causing my inner walls to tighten. "Ah, so you're saying I won't be getting rest?"

Swirling on the stool to face me head-on, he plants his hands down on the edges of my seat to ensure I have no escape.

"Truthfully, I'm still kind of thrown by the fact you appeared here during a storm," I admit.

"Shall I lay it out for you?"

I nod once purely to play along.

"I think you're more than gorgeous, and your flirting game is strong. I'm not looking for serious, not now. Not even casual. But a night is something I can do, and I enjoy that it's a little more than that. Talking to you is easy."

I study Vaughn for a solid few seconds. "I don't want you to think that I do this all the time. I may enjoy a lot of things, but I'm not easy. Since my last relationship, I accepted that there is no sense in planning or defining lines. I'm more concerned these days about work, ensuring I'm first in line for the fresh cinnamon rolls at Jolly Joe's, and trying to survive Hadley's barre Pilates classes. I'm not a model or anything like that." I feel like I'm in good shape, and I'm confident with my looks, yet still I don't spend hours on my appearance.

This time it's Vaughn who swipes a few strands of hair behind my ear.

"A girl who isn't afraid of breakfast pastry, you say?" Did he even hear me? "I dated models, and it's not for me," he adds.

I chortle and use my hands to indicate my outfit. "Great, your standard is models, and here I am before you in yoga pants and a sweatshirt."

His dimples appear again from his wide smile. I really do love dimples. "Oh, but your sweatshirt literally says 'A Simple Woman' with an icon of a donut, wine, and a hockey puck with sticks. That indicates that you're exactly the woman I need."

My face falls into my hand where my arm is propped on the bar, slightly embarrassed by my outfit choice, but I'm having a blast. "Least it's not my 'I like life in the penalty box' sweatshirt."

His eyes grow bold. "We can make that happen."

I search the room and see only a few people here, mostly watching the television or checking their phones. "Shouldn't we seek safety or something?"

"We're fine. Almost everyone is staying on the second floor, so not too high because of wind, and we're okay from flooding even if it rains a lot."

"You thought through all aspects, huh?"

"Even included snacks, flashlights, and bottled water," Vaughn deadpans.

I lean in to whisper, "What a thoughtful person. So..." My voice turns awkward, as I'm not sure what is next—well, I'm aware what is next, but I'm trying not to appear too eager.

He answers for me. "Take my hand and let's head upstairs." His tone is straightforward. He's past trying to persuade me; he knows that he has me. "But you might want to bring your suitcase so we can be kind citizens and let others have your room."

Good judgment is way beyond me. I think I was committed the moment I turned to find him next to me.

Which is why I easily take his offered hand.

———

QUICKLY, I grabbed my things and checked myself in the mirror before I went to Vaughn's room which was only a few doors down. I told the front desk they can have my room back very aware that I appeared in a rush and eager. Arriving, Vaughn lets me in with a sly smile. Behind him, I see he is watching the radar on the screen. It's raining outside, and I notice the trees blowing, but it's tame so far compared to the storm fronts that pass through Illinois.

Vaughn turns the TV off and throws the remote onto the bed before he strides my way with an overpowering heat in his eyes. My chest is on fire from my heart rate that's higher than normal because I love the pure purpose that seems to have possessed him.

We bypass small talk, and he grabs the hair at the back of my head to yank me forward, a power move that tells me he has a dominant side. When his lips slam down on mine, I'm already sinking into this moment.

He kisses hard yet tantalizing, his tongue swiping into my mouth, and it's the right amount of tickle against the tip of my tongue. A hum draws out from the back of my throat because I'm eager for his mouth to explore more. The feeling of his hands framing my face to ensure I can't escape is a sexy move that I enjoy.

We gently part to lock our eyes and check in with one another, only for him to growl and meld our lips together. The man devours me through a kiss, and inside, my body screams more, more, more.

But I refuse to just stand here, which is why my hands begin to roam his body, searching for the bottom of his t-shirt so I can encourage us to keep moving. I tug then yank as we walk in a circle with our mouths never parting. That is, until we must, to pull his shirt up and off. I can't help myself and lean slightly back so I can give him the once-over, and my pussy clenches from the view of his chiseled chest and stomach, and the tattoos on his shoulder and chest; a small black Celtic pattern. My fingers trail the lines of definition on his skin, biting my lip in the process because he is magnificent.

"Isla, you clearly see something you like, and I refuse to be the only one undressing here. Let's get this off of you." Vaughn begins to guide the fabric of my sweatshirt and tank top up, and when that's off, his eyes laser in on my pink lace bra. I've always been lucky with my cleavage, a perfect C cup.

Taking the liberty, I crawl onto the bed on all fours and glance over my shoulder as Vaughn watches, then I crook a finger to invite him to join me.

"Damn, which one of us is luckier tonight?" he says right before he grabs hold of my hips to flip my body onto my back, causing me to squeal in delight. He hooks his fingers around the waistband of my yoga pants and tugs them down and off. Vaughn's gaze rakes over my body, and he nibbles his bottom lip as he gently shakes his head in approval, clearly satisfied with the view. When my fingers begin to draw circles on my cleavage and I drag one hand down below my navel, his eyes grow big and his patience breaks. He is over me in no time, with his hands pinning my wrists to the mattress.

"I bet you're ready to go." He's sure of himself.

My head dips back into a pillow as I offer my neck to Vaughn, which he gladly trails his mouth with the occasional nip before heading lower to my breasts. His lips skim my skin and send vibrations down my body, causing a tight knot to form between my legs.

"This round you might not need to work so hard." My breath is heavy. "But something tells me somewhere between round three and four, you're going to have to use that tongue of yours and go incredibly slow."

A deep chuckle leaves his lips. "Babe, that's already going to happen this round. So spread those thighs of yours."

Obeying, I soak in the feeling of his tongue circling a nipple through the lace, while his hand delves between us, and he slides his fingers into my panties, instantly hitting the aching spot that I desperately want relief from. His hard cock rests against my inner thigh, and I just want to wrap my legs around him.

"Fucking hell, you're drenched," he notes with a rasp.

"I guess that happens when you're around, and I know any moment you will demand I get on my knees to suck you off."

Something about this man breaks open the doors inside me, making me let go of all inhibitions. The attraction between us feels like luck, because this simmering need to go wild is unbearable to most.

Vaughn curses under his breath. "You're a mind reader, which is why you know a spanking is going to come to you next round when you're lying over my lap with my hand tangled in your hair." Then he's slithering down my body, ready to prove a point.

He roughly pulls the lace to the side right before his tongue flicks against my clit, and his finger finds my entrance. My entire body writhes under him as I moan in response.

Vaughn isn't going to treat me like a delicate flower, and I'm completely here for that. Heat sends a wave through my body, desperate for him to continue.

"You taste so fucking good. Now, let me make you come," he urges before his tongue returns to my bundle of nerves that will unravel me. I don't even question why we're moving so fast; I guess our attraction is the type that combusts.

He adds another finger inside of me, and I swear I'm getting dizzy with overpowering lust.

I hum in approval, enjoying every second until I vibrate against his mouth, and he grips my hips down to keep me stable. He even interlaces our fingers against the mattress to steady me, or rather, be possessive. Either way, I'm not complaining. Give the man a reward for allowing me a few seconds to recover.

But we are a blazing flame, and he flips me over to my stomach and tilts my hips up. The moment the tip of his cock explores my pussy to coat his length before he circles around my entrance, I'm desperate for a new orgasm. When he fills me up with his cock I must appear as a woman wantoned by neediness.

His first thrust feels far too good, pleasure that I'm not quite sure I could have ever fathomed. We're on a wild train due to our eagerness.

We're fast, primal, and raw with one another.

It's only when he curses to himself that I'm broken from my cloud of ecstasy.

His breath is already heavy. "Condom, Isla. We completely forgot. I'm safe but…"

I have a strong instinct of trust with him, and I'm not logical right now. "I'm on the pill. Safe. Now don't stop." I string words together in a sentence.

His crusade to thrust into me with abandon continues. "Isla, I'm going to fuck you so deep that you'll discover new spots that make you want to scream and come all over my cock."

Him inside of me with no condom. Bare and hard. It only ups the ante between us, and my moan is as loud as the wind outside.

———

Lying in bed, I catch the protein bar that Vaughn just threw at me. "Really?" I'm entertained.

He smirks to himself. "Gotta keep us strong for the night ahead… but really, I forgot I had one in my bag."

It causes me to smile as the lights flicker because the storm is going to hit us in the next hour. The outer bands are already overhead.

Vaughn throws his phone onto the chair. "We will miss the eye but looks like we might get the right side of the storm." He joins me back on the bed.

"I'm not worried."

"See? That's what the safety of my cock does. Calms you down."

I breathe out a sound as the corners of my mouth hitch up. We're both lying on our sides, resting from round three. I feel this is the moment to highlight the obvious.

"What happens tonight is what it is, okay?"

"Absolutely," he agrees. "We're making up for our missed opportunity during the wedding reception."

"We can pretend nothing ever happened," I add confidently. Deep down, I think that's what I want too. Our lives barely overlap. "Even if you have a game against my brother." Okay, I ignore that our paths will cross then.

Vaughn bobs his head side to side. "I don't know. It would really throw your brother's game off." I give him a death stare, and his response is to touch my shoulder. "Relax. You're right. I'll even make it easier and be gone by the time you wake."

Oh.

"That's maybe for the best." There's disappointment somewhere within me, even though I initiated this conversation, but I choose to ignore it.

Vaughn grabs the protein bar from my fingers and throws it to the side before he pulls my body flush on top of him, causing me to lean onto him. It's warm, and ooh, I'm going to enjoy myself tonight.

"What are the chances I can get you to ride me reverse cowgirl right now?" he mumbles into the top of my head, nuzzling my hair.

The thought of what his fingers could do to me while I ride him is too overwhelming. "Very high," I tell him, and instantly the tip of his finger comes to play with my clit, creating that internal agony of needing a release again. He encourages me to get in position.

The rain pours outside, the wind picks up, and there is an unusual feeling in the air. I'm not sure if it's the change of air pressure or the fact that tonight is one that I will remember, because I am truly happy by this very planned coincidence.

Which is why I'm grateful he keeps his word. Because when I wake, Vaugh Madden is gone, just like the hurricane that passed.

3

ISLA

My nails strum against the wood of my dining room table as I stare at my laptop screen. This is all pointless. I know I'm not going to learn any new facts. I squeeze my knee closer to my chest and sigh as I rub the back of my neck before I glance to my side.

Sometimes in life, you just have an uncontrollable feeling that you're right.

The pregnancy test taunts me from where it's lying on the table. Unceremoniously, I flip the test over to see the answer.

Positive.

It's not even a big deal because in my head I already believed it. The test is confirmation that I was right.

I felt it in my bones that something was off. The dizzy spell after the staff meeting. The slight case of nausea when I was at the general store picking up groceries. By the time my period never came, my head had already done the calculation. It never once occurred to me that maybe it could be a flu or virus; it was straight-up intuition that I was pregnant. A different feeling.

I thought the pill was enough. Obviously not.

Here I am blankly searching up on the internet what to expect over the coming weeks, with a realization that I need to get an appointment on my calendar to see the doctor and check on everything. Sure, I'm aware that I have options, but for me, this is the decision I'm making.

My groan this time is longer, and I bite my bottom lip to stop it.

I should be focusing on buying gifts for the holidays. Yet my eyes dart between a positive pregnancy test and the screen that tells me I'm carrying a blueberry-sized human, the creation of Vaughn and me.

Moving to stand up, I walk to my kitchen to grab a devil's-food chocolate-mint cookie from the box. Taking a bite, the sugar relief does fuck all to relax me.

I pull out my phone to call my doctor and make an appointment in two weeks.

Once that is done, I text Hadley.

> Sorry. Can't make it to barre class tomorrow, a bit of a cold is coming on with chills.

It's a lie, but alas, the internet told me to stay away from certain exercises during the first trimester.

HADLEY
> Oh. Need anything? The moms will miss you at coffeetime after class.

I laugh to myself, because it looks like I can join the moms club. But then an affectionate smile overcomes me. Hadley's mom April, plus her mother-in-law Brielle, and her husband's aunt Violet would only be supportive, probably constantly asking if I'm okay too.

I'm not ready for that.

> Another time. Sleep is calling my name.

So is figuring out how to tell my baby daddy.

Sweet dreams.

I have Vaughn's number, but neither one of us have texted since that night in Florida. And tonight, I'm not ready to try and reach out. How does one break the news?

I better come up with a way and fast.

———

SITTING in the waiting room at the doctor's office, I fully recognize that scrolling on my phone to check out how Vaughn played during last night's game against Boston is not the way I should be heading into this appointment. Nor is getting side-tracked that he is so ridiculously handsome in his pre-game suit that it's all over social media.

The door to the doctor's office opens, and I freeze when I see Violet. Not only is she now related to Hadley through marriage, but she's also the wife of the owner of the Spinners, and a friend in a way, as she joins the Pilates classes. She's only a few years older than me.

Her face grows crooked as she takes off her wool hat to reveal her dark hair. "Hey, Isla… uhm… didn't expect to see you here."

Because she's about five months pregnant with her second child, so of course she's at the OB/GYN's office.

I give her an awkward look because I already see she's puzzle-pieced things together in her head, and saying I'm here for a yearly gyno check-up doesn't seem like it's going to cut it.

Throwing my arms up in a loss, I ask for a favor. "What are the chances we can keep this visit between us? Like, completely sealed so not even your husband is aware. I'm not ready for the world to know."

Violet comes to sit next to me in the waiting room, and she nudges my shoulder with her own. "Absolutely. I never saw you here… Is this why you missed barre?" She rejoined when she hit her second trimester and skips a few more strenuous exercises. Then again, she doesn't need to exercise at all—she's stunning.

I pull out my devil's-food cookie box and grab one before offering her the box. She takes one on offer. "Something like that. This *obviously* wasn't planned." I hold my hand up. "Please don't ask about the father."

She quirks her lips out. "Does he know?"

I shake my head. "I'm kind of wrapping my head around the fact that I need to stock up on diapers before telling him. Another point for me, we're *obviously* not in a relationship."

"I gathered." She touches my arm to comfort me. "He has a right to know at some point, don't you think?"

I nod in agreement. "I'm trying to focus on one thing at a time."

Violet smiles warmly. "Okay, are you excited? Babies are a lot of work but oh so fun. And pregnancy can be the best time of your life too."

The corners of my mouth curve up. "Actually…" A radiant smile hits me. "I am excited. Other than Briggs, I don't really have any biological family, and well, this baby will be helping my family grow. Plus, I might have already looked at some baby clothes online, and well… they're so cuuuute."

She laughs. "I know. We have a bunch of girl stuff if you end up having a girl. It's a boy this time around, so I get to shop all over again."

My eyes drift down to my still-flat stomach, curious if it's a boy or girl inside of me. "Time will tell."

The door opens to the corridor for the exam rooms and a nurse appears. "Isla Chase?"

"That's me." I stand up and look to Violet who gives me an assuring smile.

"My appointment isn't for a while if you don't want to go in alone."

It's really sweet of her to offer. "It's okay, I think I need to do this solo."

"You've got this," she offers in encouragement.

I take a deep breath and leave her to follow the nurse who takes me to an exam room, where a minute later, I'm sitting anxiously on an exam table with a paper gown, and the doctor arrives.

"Hi, Isla, I'm Dr. Forest." The woman in her forties smiles. "Yes, like the forest with trees and deer."

"It's a fun name," I say. "Not easy to forget. I'm sure you get a lot of jokes about Bambi."

She smirks at my humor and glances down at her tablet. "Okay, so what brings you in today?"

"Shouldn't you know, since you're looking at my file?" I sound kind of surprised.

Dr. Forest laughs. "I do know, but I would like you to confirm it."

"That's kind of your job. To corroborate that a pregnancy test at home claims that I'm pregnant."

She sets her tablet to the side to grab some gloves, still smiling. "Sounds like I don't need to tell you that your blood work came back also positive, and HCG levels put you at about seven weeks, but we're going to have a look because your file said that you had an ovary looked at a few years ago for a cyst, but everything checked out."

An audible breath escapes me. "Pregnancy, yay," I flatly say and give myself a weak fist pump.

Dr. Forest pauses to look at me. "You're not sure about this pregnancy? We can, of course, discuss options."

I shake my head no. "I'm ready for this, the baby, I mean. It is what I want. It's just... this was really unplanned. Like, 'surprise November hurricane, a hotel room with a hot hockey player who just so happens to be your brother's enemy' kind of unplanned. So... yeah... not exactly sure how to celebrate this one."

She rolls a machine toward the exam table. "Wow, that's quite a..." She debates what to say. "I can understand why your thoughts may be everywhere."

"You're telling me," I snort.

"How about we focus on you. How are you feeling?"

My head bobbles side to side. "Tired, nauseous, but so far, doable."

"Good. If you lie down, I'm going to do an internal ultrasound to check on baby."

I begin to lie down, with my pulse quickening. Lying on my back, I attempt a few relaxing breaths.

"I'm going to start now," I hear her say.

But it feels like the thrum of my heart is taking over my ears because I'm a good kind of nervous. I can only imagine what's about to happen. And when the swooshing sound of a fast heartbeat overtakes my nerves, tears instantly sting my eyes.

I look up on the screen where the doctor is pointing to a blob. "Healthy baby right here."

A warm tear falls down my cheek. I'm instantly in love. Life-changing emotions hit me in a giant wave.

She zooms in and tilts her head in various ways. "Is there a point to me confirming how far along you are, as you mentioned the one-night hurricane kind of thing?" I appreciate that she has humor.

"Least we can easily calculate, right?" I shrug, with my eyes laser focused on the screen.

"Yes, but don't forget, pregnancy starts from the date of your last period."

I raise my long finger. "Yep, got that. I'm quite aware how pregnancy works, which is kind of funny, as you would think I'd have had sense to double up on the birth control, but hey, we're not always wise."

"Normally you should be okay on the pill, but sometimes, travel or not taking the pill on time can decrease efficiency."

"You're telling me that eastern standard time, that one hour ahead of us, really screwed me over?" I'm sarcastic. I'm 100% sure that I forgot a pill.

Dr. Forest takes a few screenshots. "I don't think analyzing what went wrong will help. You have a healthy baby inside of you, and you seem at peace with that."

"You're right." I finally tear my eyes away from the screen. "Do I get to take home the photos."

She smiles widely at me as she slowly brings the wand out. "I'll do even better and upload the video and photos to the medical app. You can share it with…"

I hold my hand up. "The father? Yeah, that's taking a little time to process in my head, how to tell him."

"That's up to you."

"Yep." I pop the P, well aware that I can't rely on the excuse that I was waiting to confirm with the doctor anymore.

———

I PACE MY LIVING ROOM, while I struggle to hit send with my thumb. Instead, I type a text then delete and do this on repeat.

Hey, long time. Is it okay if I call you?

Obvious, Isla, obvious.

Hey, Vaugh, it's been a while. Nice goal last night.

Perhaps a good opening.

We need to talk.

Again, horrible.

Hope you're doing well. I know we said we would leave the hurricane night as a one-night thing. But we kind of have a situation…

That will just make him freak out.

Photo of ultrasound. *SURPRISE.*

That will just give him a heart attack.

"Just call him," I scold myself. In person is better, but there is no way that can logistically happen in the next few days.

My phone rings, and I see it's my brother calling. Briggs is in St. Louis for a game tomorrow. Guilt hits me because I feel like I might disappoint him. He's my older brother, but at times we're inseparable, and he supports me in so many ways. I don't want to let him down, and I know a surprise pregnancy isn't on his list of wants for his sister. And he will for sure kill Vaughn. Still, I answer.

"Hey, Sis, how is your cold going?" It sounds like he's walking.

"Fine. Ready for your game?"

I'm not telling anyone until I inform Vaughn. It's the right thing to do.

"For sure. The Spinners are playing somewhat better than last year." He's not afraid to be cocky.

"I know. It's a marketing gold mine. Thanks for that." Maybe he can hear my smile.

"Someone mentioned that you weren't at work today. Everything good?"

"Spying on me? Damn it, why does my brother have to practice at my place of work."

He growls in frustration. "How about you just answer me."

"How about you tell me how your 'operation win over your masseuse' is going?" I counter.

He's ridiculously hung up on his masseuse who doesn't want to give him the time of day. But now he is going full swing trying to win her over. I had to take extra photos of him in his hockey uniform holding a puppy with a Santa hat.

"I'm going to get that date. Just you watch. Now, work?"

I'm aware that I can't squirm my way out of this.

"Relax. I went to the doctor to check on this sinus infection. Just a virus that will pass," I lie.

In about seven or eight months.

"Okay, take it easy. I'm going to grab some dinner with the guys. Send me your Xmas wish list, by the way. Two weeks to go, I need to figure all that stuff out."

I already bought him his gift. I saw it in October. A remote-control car that delivers beer bottles from the kitchen. It's simple yet him. Briggs will go all out; he always buys me expensive stuff I don't need.

"Sure. I'll think of something. Good luck tomorrow."

"Love ya, Sis."

"Love you, too."

You're going to be a great uncle, I think to myself. I pull up the ultrasound photos on my phone, with a smile tugging on my mouth again.

"It's time to do this," I say to myself. Vaughn has a right to know. This baby deserves to have a chance to get to know their father. I also want to be ready if Vaughn wants no part in this. I can do it without him. I'm going to give him an out. I just hope he doesn't take it. I *pray* he doesn't take it. I want to believe that there are good fathers in this world. Nothing like my own.

I purse my lips and blow out a breath, ready to rip the band-aid off.

My thumb hits his name and the call button. My entire body is about to burst with nerves. He didn't have a game tonight, so hopefully he answers.

It takes three rings before his phone picks up. I could scream that this is going to happen.

"Hello?" A woman's voice answers, she sounds my age.

Every feeling inside of me collapses to my stomach.

"Hello?" she repeats. "Hey, babe, don't forget we're meeting Sam for drinks in an hour," she seems to call out to someone in the background.

Babe?

No, no, no. Tell me he isn't seeing someone. Maybe, I guess, he could have met someone, it's been a while since our night.

"Oh, uh, I'm looking for Vaughn," I nearly croak out.

"He's a bit busy, if you know what I mean." Her voice is like a purr of a taunt. I don't like it. No clue her name, but I already want to wipe that smug leer off her face that probably has lip gloss and over-done foundation.

"Do you… do you know when he might be available?" I nearly stutter, but I'm desperate now because he is within reach, so close to his phone, he's there… just not alone.

"Listen, Irene, Isabel, whatever name that came up on Vaughn's phone. A request from Vaughn, unless you're his publicist or from the team, then he isn't available. In fact, he will be quite occupied later, so don't bother calling back… ever." She hangs up on me.

I stand there speechless with my phone to my ear, unable to move. This is the worst-case scenario. Vaughn has moved on and really wants us to forget about that night.

My hand gently touches my navel. It will be hard to do that; we have a reminder.

A tightness forms in my throat and a cry is working its way toward an escape.

"It's just you and me, kid. It'll be okay."

For now, I need to focus on my pregnancy. Telling Vaughn is no longer a priority, at least not any time soon. Feels like I need to recover and come up with a new plan.

● 4

VAUGHN

Sliding the door of the balcony closed behind me, I wish I wasn't leaving the Gulf water views of this penthouse downtown. Especially since my eyes land on the woman who causes pure aggravation, tapping her finger against the screen of my phone.

"What the hell?" I snipe as I approach her with speed. I had my phone on the charger while I went outside to say hi to a few guys since this is my neighbor's place, and a soft drink before sunset sounded somewhat relaxing.

The bleach-blonde woman instantly pouts her plump lips that are in no way natural. Amber has been the headache that never goes away. Borderline crazy if I'm being honest, maybe even stalkerish. She is also friends with my neighbor's girlfriend, which makes her sometimes inescapable. I wouldn't have come had I known she would be here.

"Baby, I was just checking that your battery was full so I could bring you your cell, of course." She purses her lips then perks out her tits that I have zero interest in.

I snap my phone out of her hand with fake white-tipped nails. "What did you do?"

"Nothing." She plays innocent, but I can sense a lie.

One mistake from six months ago, a drunken mistake, not even a full-on performance. More like in a haze of tequila, apparently, I kissed her, and here I am with her claws never letting go.

I examine my phone. "How did you unlock my phone? Do you know my password? Did someone call me?" I ask, because the call log is open, although I don't see anything new. She seems like someone who would erase the evidence.

"Of course not, silly." She touches my arm and flutters her lashes with an overdone giggle that I'm not buying. I'm pretty sure she is a replica of the doll that my teammate's daughter plays with.

"Then why is my screen open?" I grit out.

She squeezes my arm right before I rip away from her touch. "Oh, that. Wrong number, a cold call of someone trying to sell you hurricane shutters for next season." She's avoiding the total breach of privacy.

Shaking my head, I'm not going with this. "Really?" I cast my doubt. "My number is unlisted." My eyes narrow in on her for an answer. "Besides, my phone doesn't show any new calls. Did you delete it?"

"Did I?" She begins to twirl hair around her finger, playing innocent.

I pinch the bridge of my nose, beyond frustrated. "I don't know what clue to give you that I'm not interested, nor ever will I ever be interested."

She steps closer to reach for my hands, but I step back. "Come on, baby, we can go for drinks, relax. I'll give you a massage, maybe a little bit more." She bounces her shoulders in pride, as if she just gave me the best offer.

In another world it would be enticing... if it was from another woman. Isla, to be exact.

"I swear to God, I'm losing a brain cell right now." I was speaking to myself, but her puffed-out cheeks indicates she heard me and is no longer happy.

Luckily, a hand lands on my shoulder; it's my buddy Scott.

"Didn't realize my girlfriend invited crazy, sorry about that," he mutters to me. Then he throws on an overdone smile. "Hey, Amber, how about you go find my girlfriend in the kitchen and stay there. This guy is probably on a plane tomorrow for his next game and just needs… well, not you."

Amber seems pissed off and sharply pivots to storm off to the kitchen, flicking her hair in the process. I turn to Scott and sigh an exhausted breath.

He winces at me. "Sorry, I didn't realize she was stopping by. I wish Nicole would warn me about these things, or even better, ditch Amber altogether. But you know Nicole, has to be kind to everyone, and Amber was in her sorority."

I laugh without humor. "She's batshit crazy."

Scott grins to himself. "That and I think you still have your mind on someone… anonymous hurricane girl."

My mouth stretches slightly at the memory of Isla. I haven't told anyone about who she is exactly, just briefly mentioned my fling during a hurricane.

"You know I'm focusing on the season." Partly a lie, since I think of Isla every single time I need a release with my hand.

"Doesn't mean she can't occupy your thoughts. Have you texted her?"

I slide my phone, now fully charged, albeit touched by Satan, into my jeans pocket.

"Nah, we had a blast but agreed to keep it at that," I reiterate what I've mentioned before.

Scott drinks from his beer before he tips it at me. "Should I head into the kitchen to get you a drink so you can stand clear of psycho?"

I wave a hand. "Not feeling it, and besides, I think Amber killed the mood for any casual hangouts. I'm going to head back home. Could use the extra sleep," I explain.

He gives me a comforting nod. "Okay, have a good game up in Memphis."

"Thanks." I scratch my cheek. "Kind of full-on during December, on the road most of the time."

"Good. It just means you can focus, right?"

"Yeah, I'll see ya."

After heading out and back to my place, I ensure my security system is on to prevent any unwelcome guests. I would move states just to live in peace.

Heading straight to my sofa, I flop onto the cushions and turn on the television which instantly has hockey highlights on the sports channel.

Scott is right, I should be able to focus.

But I can't, I really can't.

I need to play harder to prove that I still have skill. Everyone is predicting this will be my last season—hell, even in my head I'm predicting it too. I just don't say it out loud, as that makes it too real.

I've thought about what's ahead. Back at Connor's wedding, his uncle mentioned a possibility for a spot somewhere within the Spinners organization. I'm sure a lot of teams will be vying for my attention to be involved next season in a non-athletic sense. However, Declan runs a tight ship, a team that has a large group of fans and that gives back to the community. Their social media presence draws a lot of eyes to the Spinners…

Social media is marketing, marketing is… Isla.

My eyes dart up to the screen that shows the hockey league's schedule for the coming two weeks.

I scoff a half-smile to myself when I read what I am already well aware of. We have a game against the Spinners coming up on the schedule, the last game before Christmas. It's at their home arena.

Which means that the probability of seeing Isla is disproportionately high.

Grabbing my phone from my pocket, I debate unlocking it to type a message. It isn't a good idea to check in with Isla, it will probably make my focus on the game diminish. She could be a distraction. I'm confident that we agreed on the right plan of action; nothing.

But I'm bound to see her, even a glimpse of her. Surely, she'll either be working or sitting behind the boards to watch her brother.

I'll try to give her a nod or something when I'm skating by—wait, no, if her brother saw that, he would go mental. I promised Isla I wouldn't rile him for the sake of goals.

Maybe I should send a text. I mean, we will be in the same zip code again. It's just stating the obvious. Connor and I text, and even though we have to play against one another, off the ice we're friends. Which is why he sent me a "looking forward to seeing you in Lake Spark" text.

Isla and I can be friends. That we can do.

Growling, I toss my phone to the side. My life is one of confusion right now, no point in dragging another factor into that.

———

SKATING onto the ice at the Spinners arena after a last-minute team huddle, I find myself facing off with Briggs.

"Vaughn," he says my name rather curtly.

"Briggs. Hope you woke up on the right side of the bed to keep your head in the game." I bend down to get in position.

He mirrors the move. "Oh, I did, with a beautiful woman right beside me. So, I'm fully ready to swipe that Florida vitamin D right off your pretty-boy face."

It's on the tip of my tongue to retort with something about Isla. But I can't, I have too much respect for her. It would be so easy, though.

"Only makes us stronger," I dryly reply.

The referee drops the puck, and it's on.

For the next few minutes, it's a constant back and forth on the ice with Briggs.

Then it happens.

I push Briggs into the boards, and a few seconds later, Connor is behind me. I have to keep friendship aside for the moment, and I aim low to pin Connor against the boards, gripping his shirt in the process. Helmets fall off as one arm elbows into Briggs, and Connor begins to scuffle with me. It's always a moment of high adrenaline when these incidents happen. Your body just reacts the way it needs to, even if it's a bit more aggressive than you would ever be. Which is why I give it my all.

Briggs ends up on the ice and his stick out of reach. Connor, now pissed, aims a little too high with his stick, landing on me. The ref blows the whistle, and Connor is sent to the penalty box for two minutes, which gives us a power play.

"Asshole," Briggs seethes as he skates off from me.

"Yet here I am, still on the ice to ensure you're in misery," I call out.

Finally getting a chance to breathe and shake off that outburst, I notice movement in the corner of my eye, then fully examine the scene before me.

Isla's walking down the stairs to go sit with Hadley who is right behind the boards. The rink cam showed Hadley a few times on the screen. It's marketing gold. Isla has no idea I'm staring at her. But she's here, which means she's watching the game, wearing her brother's jersey number… can't fault her for that.

As much as I want to attract her attention, I have a game to win.

Maybe after the game, I'll be able to subtly say hi.

5

ISLA

"What did I miss? I heard booing," I ask as I slide back onto the seat next to Hadley.

"You picked the worst moment to go to the bathroom, which by the way, are you okay? You do that a lot lately." She sounds frustrated with the game.

"Feisty. Sorry if nature calls," I defend.

It's been a few weeks since I found out about my pregnancy, and I still haven't told my friend. Part of me isn't ready, because it leads to questions, and I know that the baby will become a central topic for every coffee date. It makes it all even more real.

Hadley's dad, who was sitting next to her, excuses himself with the cover of finding snacks. I get the feeling he is giving us a moment alone so we can talk, even though he has no clue that my news will require a full-on play-by-play.

My nerves are rocketing because Vaughn is here. I'm thankful for the helmet which blocks me from staring at his smoldering eyes. It will also hurt less, because seeing him is like a knife to my body. It's clear he is in a relationship with someone and wants to keep to our word and forget our night.

The thought of this situation causes me to feel a little tight.

"What's up with you?" Hadley wonders. She must be picking up on my somber mood.

"Nothing," I lie but also sigh.

Hadley seems to be studying me as I stare aimlessly at a patch of ice.

"Nothing to do with who is on the ice?" Her eyes go bold.

It's a struggle, however I manage to shake my head.

She touches my arm. "Spill it."

An overwhelming feeling takes over me, and it just rolls off my tongue. "You know how I had that conference in Tampa a while ago?"

"Yeah, the one where you got stuck there because of a hurricane."

I nod. "I wasn't exactly alone when I safely rode out the storm in a hotel."

She seems invested in this gossip. "You were riding someone during the storm, weren't you?"

I bite my bottom lip. "It's not ideal," I admit.

"Why not? It's great. You are allowed to have fun. Who was it?" She's far too curious.

I nervously scoff a laugh, very well aware that I shouldn't give her clues to who this baby's father is, the baby that nobody knows I'm having. "The guy who just put your husband in the penalty box."

Hadley's jaw drops. "Vaughn Madden?"

I scrub a hand across my cheek. "Nobody can know. Especially since my brother isn't a fan. It was a one-time kind of thing."

"Really? I mean, he's not bad on the eyes. Long-distance isn't ideal, but it's no different than if he played here in Lake Spark and has to travel for the season." This is probably why I didn't tell her; she's excited for a probability that will never happen.

I place my hand on her arm, needing to calm her. "Take a chill pill. It really was a one-time spur-of-the-moment kind of thing. He wasn't even there when I woke up."

"What an jerk." Hadley isn't impressed.

"Can we forget about it?" I attempt to plead. We both notice Connor leave the box to hop back onto the ice.

She rolls her eyes. "Fine. But give him a piece of your mind after the game. You're entitled to that."

"No, Hadley. We're all entitled to a no-strings night, and we agreed on the morning protocol. Now, will you focus on your man who just intercepted the pass?" I try to refocus her attention.

I'm very well aware that I might run into Vaughn after this game.

I SHOULDN'T DO THIS. Not after that call. But I need to make one more attempt.

It's the least I can do for him or her who is currently in my belly and causing my stomach to swirl. It's as though the baby can pick up that I'm anxious and decided to make my stomach flop with nerves a few extra times.

I'm standing in the hall near the locker rooms for the opposition, thankful that I'm able to be back here. Still, I do my best to blend in and stay out of the way. The Spinners won, which means Vaughn probably isn't in the best of moods. However, quite frankly, his dickish move of having someone else deliver the message that I'm never to contact him again causes me to not particularly care about his precious post-game feelings.

I nervously fidget with my fingers as I wait, reminding myself that I need to do this. My head perks up when I hear the door to the locker room open and a few players leave, but not Vaughn.

Oh great, let's draw this process out.

I'm not sure how many times I glance at the door when it opens with a brief excitement that I can cut the tether on this situation off. Finally, the door opens, and my chest tightens at the sight of a freshly showered Vaughn in a navy-blue suit. I want to scold myself for melting a little at the image before me.

His head hangs low until it doesn't. His eyes zap up because he caught sight of me in the corner of his eye. It surprises me that his mouth tugs, as if he's happy to see me. He quickly scans the area to see if anyone would notice, but everyone seems busy with their own tasks. Vaughn takes a few steps in my direction.

"Hey, Isla." His voice sounds soft. "Thought I might see you here."

"Hi." I give a ridiculous little wave like I'm a schoolgirl with a crush, but I clear my throat when sense hits me. "Uhm, listen, I know you don't really want to see me—"

"What?" Lines form on his forehead.

I glance away because his blue eyes on me feel too much, almost as if I should let him off easy. "Come on, Vaughn, I'm a big girl and got the memo that we are very much forgetting… late-season hurricanes." I can't muster the words to describe our explosive night.

He reaches out his fingers to gently touch my shoulder, and again, he studies the hall to make sure we're under the radar. "Again, what?"

"Your… a woman delivered the message that you are very much occupied and—"

Vaughn looks at me as if I'm an alien. "I'm sorry, I'm *very* lost. I know I didn't text, which is kind of a shitty move considering we were bound to run into one another tonight. But I don't understand about a woman delivering a message."

I roll my eyes. "It's okay, you don't owe me an explanation."

He seems to be thinking and then something dawns on him before he pinches the bridge of his nose. "Oh no. Ugh," he grumbles. "Did this woman sound like Barbie?"

I lift a shoulder to my ear. "I guess."

"Isla, she's no one."

I hold my hand up. "You don't need to justify it."

"Really." He's adamant, and his eyes bug out. "My neighbor has a crazy woman who visits their house, and she won't get the hint that I'm not interested. She had my phone. You must be the call that she erased from my call log."

I could cry. Hope fills me to the brim; this is a promising turn of events.

"She called you babe and said you two had to go somewhere for drinks." I need to double-check that this beacon of light isn't a lie.

He scoffs a sound. "Trust me, that never happened."

"You only talk to women who are your publicist or from the team she told me," I list.

Vaughn shakes his head. "Wishful thinking on her part."

"I was never to call you again."

"Jesus, that sounds like her… wait, you called me? Why?" The corner of his mouth snags up, and he seems pleased with that news.

Tucking a few strands of hair behind my ear, I bite my lip. I can do this. "I can imagine you have to get on a plane with your team soon." I'm stalling.

He tips his head down, then back up to capture my gaze. "Actually no, we're about to go on a three-day break for the holidays, and I'm going to see my brother in the city tomorrow morning."

"Oh?" My voice rises on octave.

Vaughn licks his lips and his dimples shine, creating the illusion of a sweltering look of trouble. "We were kind of adamant about leaving things the way they were, so I'm not going to tell you my room at the Dizzy Duck is number 107." The mischief in his voice while his gaze pierces straight through me is almost too much, I'm forgetting my mission.

I need to stay on track, not lose my panties.

Tightly, I smile, soaking in the fact that we had a classic miscommunication mix-up, and he just gave the sign that he would bend our promise a little. Honored as I am, sex is really the last thing that should be occupying my brain… yet it's crossing my mind.

Flicking my eyes up, attempting to ground my feet and stay strong, I shoot out an alternative. "Maybe a coffee or something… I don't mean that kind of something, not that I have complaints, it's just we could chat." Holy hell, I'm rambling.

I must look like a confused squirrel who really could nibble on him right about now.

Yet, Vaughn's eyes burn me with a type of affection that could be my misfortune. "Sure. Send me a text of where to meet you."

Our eyes are trapped in a holdout for a few seconds, but then I offer him a half-smile and walk away.

———

WAITING IN JOLLY JOE'S, the soda-shop-styled diner, with my tea mug in one hand, I scroll through my phone to admire the ultrasound photos. It never gets old, that feeling of astonishment.

That's what I will do, tell Vaughn, then show him my phone as proof.

It's not a cute announcement, but we're not a couple. We're two people who accidentally made a child.

The door opens, and Vaughn gives me a nod. He's now in jeans and a winter coat that he takes off to hang on the coatrack while he stomps his boots on the mat.

I laugh to myself as he approaches me with a stride that everyone calls swagger, complete with a suave smirk that oozes coolness, and my biggest fear comes alive when I notice that determination burns in his eyes. For what? I can only imagine, as I'm smart.

Vaughn slides into the booth seat across from me. "Welcome to Midwest winter. I would say I hope you can handle it, but your job is literally on ice," I joke.

He rubs his hands together for warmth. "True. Were you waiting long?"

"Not at all." My eyes dip down to my tea that I've barely touched, as I'm doing my best to cut caffeine for the pregnancy. Drawing a line back up to Vaughn who is now studying the menu, I take a deep breath. "Sorry about your loss, the game. I didn't get a chance to tell you since we got occupied trying to figure out the mystery of why I wanted to kill you."

He raises his brows entertained. "You wanted to kill me?"

"I thought you were not being a gentleman."

"I'm always a gentleman. Your body should know that."

Crap, did Jolly Joe's crank up the radiator? Because I'm refusing to believe that my body warms due to Vaughn's ability to make me weak and the fact that our banter just flows.

Snap out of it, Isla.

"Uhm, maybe we can keep this coffee… I don't know, as friends?"

A shade of disappointment is hinted on his face, and he eases his attempt to flirt. "Sure. What do you recommend?"

"Anything. Are you hungry?"

"We ate a few things after the game to restore calories. That's kind of boring stuff, wild rice and salmon."

I push down the menu he holds to the table. "Then try the grilled cheese with curly fries." I can steal a few fries.

"I shall follow your expertise."

That awkward air floats around us again in silence. It's crisp and could easily break if we just give into our attraction. A few images flicker in my mind of that night, and my mouth nearly waters.

Vaughn waves a hand in front of my face. "You okay? You seem to be deep in thought."

"Yeah, just, uh, forgot that the gossip train runs strong in Lake Spark, and my brother could discover I'm enjoying an evening snack with you."

"Enjoying? That puts me at ease."

I quirk my lips out then wave him off. "It doesn't matter. He's busy with his new girlfriend, and he doesn't get angry at Connor for talking to you, so why should I be any different, since you and I are just two people who are chatting over grilled cheese."

Vaughn folds his arms over his chest. "That we are. So why did you call the other week?"

Shit, I *nearly* forgot why I'm here.

"I saw your game with Memphis and thought I would check in. Tampa isn't having the best of seasons this year."

He rakes a hand through his hair. "We've had better. Why do I sense that isn't really the reason why you called?"

The waitress arrives, interrupting my opening to answer. Vaughn orders, and I ask for warm cherry cobbler with vanilla ice cream, although I can't stomach so much.

A screeching sound of a child hits our ears, which draws our attention to a young family leaving their table and a baby that looks near one getting pulled out of their highchair.

"Yikes. I'm so happy that I get to enjoy dinners in peace," Vaughn notes.

His comment instantly causes my eyes to whip back in his direction. "You don't like kids?" Doom hits me, then I remind myself that I always said I could do this all alone if I had to.

"Only if I can return them to their owners. Don't get me wrong, I think it's great when kids are at a game or I help out at a camp, but babies are a whole different ballgame. I see my teammates with kids, and I'm not ready to give up the life I have for that."

I cough once to rid the fear that is taking over my body like an exorcism. "So, one day you do want kids?"

Vaughn shrugs. "I can't think that far ahead. I'm not really sure that I would be a great dad anyhow, I don't think I even have it in me. Right now, my focus needs to be on my last season and gulping down this grilled cheese that my table companion has raved about."

I attempt to offer him a closed-mouth smile, but it wilts far too quickly. Vaughn has just in plain terms stated that he doesn't enjoy or want kids. He needs to focus on his career. I'm circling back to earlier in the day of imagining the worst-case scenario.

"Oh… we forgot to ask them to include onions. It makes it so much better." Give me the award for avoidance.

However, this is perhaps the biggest news that I could share in someone's life. What I'm about to say will alter his life completely, whether he is involved or not.

"I'll ask them to add some." He moves to slide out of the booth, but I reach out to grip his wrist to keep him from leaving. Vaughn looks at my adamant hand on his wrist then to me.

"You know, I think I have a better idea. We can ask for it to-go."

"To-go?" A smirk begins to stretch on his mouth, and he looks impressed. "Sounds like a plan."

Great, throw me in the horrible-human category.

———

WE WALK to the parking lot because I'm not sure what I'm doing except filibustering. I need more time to figure out where his head is at.

"Are you excited to see your brother for Christmas?" I ask as we walk side by side, with the snow crunching at our feet and twinkly white holiday lights hanging all over Main Street. He's holding the takeout bag as we walk.

"Absolutely, we're going to kick back with a few beers, and Stone is cooking a turkey. Way too much food for us, but we have college football to watch. It's sort of a tradition. Growing up, we had simple Christmases, all of our mom's savings went into hockey. Then when my brother went pro, followed by me, we still chose to keep it simple. Between hockey, endorsements, PR commitments, and fancy events, it just feels so good to sit back and relax."

God, I can relate. "I hear ya. It was kind of the same for Briggs and me, or at least until our grandmother got a job typing up hospital records. It paid well, and life kind of changed a little. I had a scholarship at college, and I'm relieved about that. It meant I wasn't relying on her."

Our shoulders occasionally touch on our leisurely stroll, and we slow down as we approach my car, not wanting this conversation to end.

"You have a strong head on your shoulders, Isla." His praise causes my cheeks to lift, because I think I needed to hear that; it's the only way I can be now.

"I can imagine you must be able to relate. It must get lonely focusing on hockey. You don't ever want to have people waiting for you when you come home?" I'm testing him again.

He stalls in his step, and it causes me to side-eye him to investigate the look on his face, highlighted by the streetlight.

"Why do you ask? You're not holding out that maybe I want

more, are you?" I hear the concern in his voice, and it only confirms my theory. Yet he isn't harsh either. Maybe he feels it too, that beyond our attraction we're able to connect on a different level that feels like a relief since he can relate to so many things.

My head goes side to side. "Not at all. Just asking." I don't dare ask him if he would have been happy or confused if he had answered the phone. "I needed to call," I mumble to myself, only realizing the thought in my head escaped my lips.

"Right, how come you called?" A deep low sound escapes his mouth in contemplation. "I guess I would have been a little confused if I had answered, as we kind of had a plan to leave it at one night, but I was also debating sending you a message."

I think of a fib. "Because we knew we would run into one another."

"Yeah. There isn't much more that I can offer." He sounds serious, but his smile remains gentle.

"Except screwing me. You've implied it once or twice tonight," I tease him.

He laughs. "Well, that is on offer. We're laidback around each other and are well aware that we're not going to be anything more than a hookup… maybe two."

Except we made a baby.

The words to make the announcement seem to be vanishing. I'm too scared, as his views are clear. A baby is the last thing he wants. I knew this was a possibility, but I hate the thought that another father figure has failed me.

"So, this is me." I indicate my car.

Vaughn nods as he steps forward, guiding me until my back rests against the door of my small SUV. There is heat blazing between us, despite our breath visible in the cold air. "It is. Going to offer me a ride?" He came by taxi.

"I think that would get us in trouble." I grin to myself.

His fingers adjust the wool hat on my head. "I'm starving."

My head lolls gently to the side to swipe my cheek along his hand. "A good thing you have the food then."

Vaughn sets the bag on the top of my car. "Except that's not what I'm hungry for."

I snort a laugh. "That's a ridiculous line, and you know it."

He nods in agreement, his eyes pleading like a man entranced. In this moment, I hold the cards more than he will ever know.

My brain is crossing wires, and I do the stupidest thing I can think of.

I take hold of his coat and yank him forward so that we can share a kiss. However, I know better. Instead, our lips are within breathing distance, tracing one another, both eager for more. A brush of our lips gives us a hint of what could be our night. A feathered-feeling reminder that our attraction is dangerous… but I won't give in.

Which is why I nuzzle his nose and inhale his scent, as if it will give me strength for the months ahead.

"I think," I whisper, "we're in a risky situation. I had every intention to drive you to the Dizzy Duck and get out of my car with you. But it's better if we say goodbye here, trust me."

"I disagree," he chides softly.

His lips nip at the corner of my mouth, and I retreat slightly.

Taking a breath, I do what's best because I'm far too petrified right now due to our conversation tonight. "Bye, Vaughn," I simply say.

Because I can't tell him about the baby.

I'm the first to arrive at Hadley and Connor's house for Christmas dinner. Funnily enough, I was on wine duty. Not that I can have any, but I think I picked up a few excellent bottles. Quickly excusing myself after trying some cheese from the charcuterie board, I went upstairs to change, as I was still in my yoga pants and sweatshirt to conquer this winter day. Now, I just want to change into something cute.

Instead, I'm sitting on the edge of the bed in the guest room and a waterfall of tears hits me.

I didn't tell Vaughn. I'm pregnant, and nobody knows. It will be a while until I show, although the array of emotions and nausea just seems to hit me in full force.

Sniffling away a tear, it's hopeless, as a fresh one hits my cheek.

"Isla?" I hear Hadley's voice. Just great, ruin the host's gathering.

The door that was slightly ajar opens with a little bit of hesitation, and Hadley finds me a hot mess on the bed.

"What's wrong?" She sounds concerned.

What the hell, I need someone right now. I thought I could do this all, alone or with Vaughn as co-parents. I'm unraveling, and in ten minutes I need to be downstairs to smile at everyone while we stare in awe at April, Hadley's mom's cooking that she's bringing over.

"Hadley, I need to tell you something," I cry. "I can't keep it in anymore."

"You're scaring me," she tells me as she comes to sit next to me. Hadley touches my arm in comfort. "It's okay. If you don't like my attempt at a charcuterie board, you can tell me. Is that what it is?"

I have to smile through my tears at her statement. "It's delicious, just my stomach didn't agree."

Hadley frowns. "Oh gosh, I can't afford to poison people, not when a hockey team is relying on two of the guys at dinner tonight."

"They'll be fine. It's me. All me… I'm pregnant." Whoosh, there, I said it.

Her eyes survey my body as if she's checking that I'm not joking, then it turns to shock. "What?"

"Well, ten weeks to be exact."

"Huh?" She can't formulate words. "How?"

"A hurricane," I hiccup as I swipe another tear away.

Her eyes swim side to side as she registers my timeline. "As in…"

I blow out a long breath. "Nobody knows. Not even…" It's difficult to say Vaughn's name now, and I'm not sure if that's because I feel guilt for not telling him or sadness that he so clearly has no interest in having a family of his own anytime soon.

"Vaughn Madden," she croaks out.

I nod and grab a throw pillow to hug. "Isn't this a fun Christmas," I say sarcastically.

Hadley's hand travels up to my shoulder. "Why doesn't he know?"

"I haven't told him. First because I thought he was with someone, and then last night he said a few things that make it clear he would have no interest in this development." I glance down at my belly, still the same as ten weeks ago.

"He has a right to know, even if he doesn't want to be involved. Don't you think?"

I swallow and feel ashamed, even though that's not her intention. "You can't tell anyone, not even Connor. You promise?"

She nods. "It's not my information to share. I promise... but I think you should tell Vaughn."

"It wasn't the right moment. He said it himself that he only wants to focus on his last season without distraction."

"This is a little more than a distraction, it's a baby."

"I'm aware. I just got scared. Trust me, I wanted to tell him, but what's the point of making his life a mess?"

She massages my shoulder. "Is that what you think this is? A mess?"

Glancing to my side, a beaming smile hits me. "No, actually it's great. I think that I can really do this." I grab my phone lying by my side and swipe to show her the ultrasound photos. "Isn't he or she cute?"

"For sure." She examines the photo, and when her face goes slightly crooked, I have to laugh.

"You don't see it, do you?" I ask.

"Sorry, I'm trying."

I point with my index finger to the circle on the scan and outline the shape of a bean.

Her face brightens. "Wow, this is awesome. If you're happy, then so am I. Everyone will help you, anything you need. I know my mom will want to plan a baby shower. I would, but I rely on my mom for actual decent food."

"It's way too early for all of that. I have bigger fish to fry." I grab my dress from the bag at my feet. God, I wish I could stay like this and not dress up. I'm fairly confident that I'll need a nap in about an hour.

"Bigger fish, as in...?"

"My brother," I answer.

She offers me a sympathetic look.

———

SITTING at the counter in my brother's house, I fear the next five minutes. I decided that I wanted to wait until after New Year's to break the news. He's still in the early days with Ivy, the woman that he has spent months trying to win over. I wanted him to enjoy his victory, and they're good together. Plus, the last week, the only thing that I wanted to do was focus on work and sleep. They say it gets better once you head out of the first trimester, but that's just not happening.

Briggs offers me a glass of water and joins me at the kitchen island. He seems content and relaxed, even though he had a game on New Year's Eve.

"How is your *new girlfriend*?" I smile at him and nudge his arm with my own.

He couldn't hide his grin if he tried. "It's going well. I think she could be the one. She's good for me."

I like Ivy a lot. His interpretation of her being good for him is spot-on. I'm also fairly confident she figured out that I'm pregnant already at the team holiday party yet hasn't told him, so she automatically gets another point from me.

"Enough about me. How are you? You seemed kind of off at Christmas, well, the last few weeks really. Quieter than normal. I wanted to press, but you seemed like you need a little space." He examines me the way he always has when he feels that brother bear needs to come out of hibernation.

It's why telling him seems easier than informing Vaughn. Briggs won't leave me no matter what, I'll always be his sister. Whereas Vaughn is free to walk away.

"Yeah, that's kind of why I'm here," I reply and look down at my fingers twiddling together. When I look up, his nose is slightly flared, and he seems angry, as though he should be worried.

"What's going on? What haven't you told me?" Pure concern is apparent in his voice.

I touch the top of his hand that rests on the counter and pause for a second to gather my courage. "The thing is… I'm pregnant."

His face falls, and shock hits him at record speed. He croaks out a sound but can't gather words. Until he does. "W-what?"

I roll my eyes as I wait for him to digest the news. "A baby. You know, those little humans that cry and giggle, plus wear cute little socks. There is a baby growing inside of me."

"How?" He's in disbelief.

"Really? We need to go over a biology lesson right now?" I'm cynical.

A hardened look hits him. "Who? Who the fuck do I need to talk to? You don't have a boyfriend, so who is it?"

I rub my face in aggravation. In truth, I was kind of prepared for this. "Should we rewind and you ask how your only sister is doing?"

Briggs's face shades to a sweeter smile. "I'm sorry. How are you?"

"Healthy. Although nauseous and tired."

"Shit, that's not great… Now, who is it?" His hunt to kill returns.

I gently shake my head, annoyed. "It doesn't matter. I'm doing this on my own, so accept that. Do this one thing for me and don't push for more info. I'm happy with my choice and this surprise." I'm adamant and stern with my voice.

He takes a moment to reflect then rolls his lips in. "Okay… I don't like it, but okay. If that's what you need."

"It is. I don't want you to be disappointed in me. I really am excited for this."

Briggs gives me his signature warm smile that lights up the room. "I know you can do this. I'll be there for you. I'm just a little taken aback, but I won't leave you hanging. Anything you need, okay?"

"That's what I wanted to hear. It's still a ways to go, and I need to find a new place with a bit more room, not to mention stock up on supplies. But it just feels right."

He pulls me into a hug, exactly what I need right now. It gives me strength. It means the world to me that Briggs is on my team.

I'm not naïve, I'm aware at some point he will circle back to who the father is. But I'll hold off as long as I can, because I know there will be repercussions when he discovers the truth.

And I'm still undecided if I'll change my mind and tell Vaughn.

VAUGHN

Looking out at the sun over the Gulf, I hold a scotch in hand. That's it. The end of my career.

A AC joint injury and it's over. One injury too many and I'm out early in the season. I refuse to leave as a man sitting on the bench, unable to play. Instead, I'm going to come to an agreement on the buyout that both sides want so we can end my contract early. I would much rather retire as a man who had a good last game until the injury in the second period than a guy watching from the offside.

It's already over the sports news, the speculations of my next move.

Still, my career is setting like the sun out ahead.

My phone vibrates in my pocket, and I choose to ignore it. For the past week, I've been getting an abundance of texts, but I'm simply not in the mood to answer.

Not the one from my brother. Nor the one from Connor.

I'm allowed to wallow in this moment, right?

This time my cell rings, and I pull it out purely to hit decline and set my phone on silent. But then I see a name that I wasn't expecting in the slightest.

Isla.

And for some reason, I answer.

She's the last one I should talk to right now, considering she made it clear that we really were a one-night thing. I even got the impression that she really didn't want to speak to me anymore. Since we originally did agree on one night, then I haven't put in any effort to contact her since Christmas.

I bring the phone to my ear. "Isla." My tone is simple.

"Hey… Vaughn…" She seems to be struggling to put together a sentence.

"That's it? You called to say 'hey, Vaughn?'" It causes her to half-laugh which kind of annoys me.

I walk inside, closing the double doors behind me, listening to Isla hum a sound.

"I heard the news and watched the replay. You all right?" Huh, she sounds concerned.

"Yeah, I'm fine. Bound to happen. Is that why you're calling? To be the hundredth person to check up on me?" I sound exhausted, but I don't want to keep repeating myself.

"Yes and no."

"What's the no part?" I set my glass onto the counter and head to my sofa to kick up my feet on the coffee table.

It sounds like she is walking around. "For some reason, I felt the need to check in, like genuinely check in. See how you've been. Did you find a new cheese to like? That kind of thing."

My lips twist in an attempt to smile because it sounds like she sincerely means it. "I've discovered a Dutch cheese that's sharp and hard. I would say it's like my thrusts, but it is actually a very slow cheese that takes 10 to 14 months to ripen and must contain a fat content of 48%. But damn, it's good."

She snorts a laugh, perhaps remembering Connor's wedding weekend where we mentioned cheese during our flirty yet odd topic conversation. "You can go slow, maybe not 10-to-14-months slow, though."

"You phoned to talk cheese?"

"No, actually, I phoned to ask you to open the door."

My eyes dart to my front door down at the end of the hall. "Why would I do that?" I shoot up and begin to step down the hall.

"Uhm, the Spinners played your old team, as you know. I guess you didn't want to watch, which is understandable. I decided to come down to watch Briggs and also shadowed someone I met at that conference who works in marketing. Then I thought, hey, why not check on Vaughn."

My pace picks up as I head straight for the door. I think she is insinuating what I think she is. Opening the door, I'm faced with Isla who has her golden locks down, a bit darker than last time, framing her face. She's wearing a sort of long baggy dress that has buttons and stops short of her knees, and I wish this whole getup would show more.

I slowly bring my phone down until my arm hangs at my side.

Isla's lips lift gently. "Hi," she softly greets me.

"Hi," I rasp.

"The front gate wasn't keen on letting me in, but an old lady who lives a few floors down took pity on me and let me in."

I don't move an inch. "Why are you here? Our last encounter you kind of pushed me away slightly."

She nods in agreement. "I did. But I figured you could use a friend."

I can't think of any reason why she would show up right now. It would take too much energy, and I don't have that right now. "Are we friends? Because I'm really not in the mood to attempt to be anyone's friend right now."

"Fair enough. So, am I just going to stand here or are you going to let me in?" She gives me a humorous look.

I hesitate for a second before I step to the side so she can come inside. I watch her saunter as she slowly enters my home and examines the setting while I lazily close the door behind her.

She notices the scotch glass that I forgot on the side table; I've been nursing the glass for the last hour. "Are you somewhat sober?"

"Sober enough to wonder how you got my address." I follow her until she's by the window looking out at the near-dark sky.

"Hadley had your address from when she sent out wedding invitations last summer." Isla seems nervous, and God, I hope it's because we are alone with my bedroom not far away.

"Look, Isla, I have to be honest right now. I'm not in the best of moods. I can't be a friend, and I sure as hell can't be anything but a great fuck. So that's the boundaries for tonight."

She scoffs a sound and crosses her arms over her chest. I could swear her tits seem firmer or larger, which causes my dick to press against the zipper of my pants.

"That's clear then. You do seem like you've seen better days."

"It's fine. This time was always going to come, but it's a subdued feeling."

She takes one step in my direction then pauses. "You don't want to talk about it?"

"Nope."

"Hmm, sounds like you might see the light at the end of the tunnel after allowing a few days of misery first." She's analyzing me, and it's irritating but spot-on.

Glancing to my open kitchen, I'm tempted to pour a fresh round. "Want a drink?"

"Oh, uhm, maybe water?" Not what I had in mind, but sure, I need her hydrated if she's planning on staying any longer, because I do need her support right now. In a way that only she can offer.

Into the kitchen I go and straight to the fridge to grab a water bottle, and when I turn, she's there. We bump into one another when she reaches for the bottle, and the touch of her hand blasts a carnal need to bend her over the counter behind her.

"Thanks." She takes the bottle from my hand, causing our fingers to skim with a friction of energy crossing. I'm tempted to capture them and pull her to me tightly.

Isla twists the cap then takes a long drink. "I think you're not in the mood for conversation." She sounds near deflated.

"That's obvious? Great." My tone is mundane, and it causes her to raise her brows, not exactly pleased with my attitude. I don't care and trap my sight on her lips then slip my gaze down to examine her breasts again which only makes me harder.

"I have to be honest. I came here hoping we could talk, have a few snacks and… never mind. This was a mistake for me to come here." She begins to turn to leave, and as she walks away, I'm trailing hot on her heels until her hand is on the handle of the front door. Isla's barely been here and now she's escaping, that's just not fair. I'm quick to grab her arm, causing her to glance at me sidelong before her eyes draw down to examine my hand on her arm.

"You came here for something. In fact, I'm confident you knew the risk of what would happen when you did." My tone is serious, I'm not going to play games.

Her breath hitches slightly. "Trust me, all scenarios have crossed my mind." Why does it feel like she has her own version of tonight that I'm not familiar with? How could she not expect that it was dangerous showing up at my door?

Our gazes connect, and a wistful glaze shades across her eyes. "You're really not in the best of ways, are you?" She states it more than she asks.

"Again, I'm allowed to have a bittersweet goodbye to my career and sulk a little." I don't let go of her arm.

"Vaughn, I'm not sure what to say to make you feel better. I can only bring you complications if I open my mouth." Her sentence causes me to ponder for a mere second. "Anyway, I need to get out of here. This was a horrible idea. I'll go downstairs and order a cab."

Everything inside of me sinks to the ground with disapproval. I have whiplash over what the last few minutes were. I could pin her to the door and make her admit that she wants what I desire in this moment, but her eyes seem to plead for me to give no such attempt.

I do the next best thing.

"I barely drank… let me drive you back to your hotel." Being a gentleman, that is a turn of events I wasn't expecting.

She sighs but then nods that it's okay. I grab my key fob from the side table, and we head out in a silence, the entire elevator ride down with tension sharp between us and our gazes fixed. We're both probably thinking a dirty thought and simmering in an attraction that isn't good for me.

Heading out of the elevator, my Ferrari beeps when I unlock it, and we get in the car, where she tells me the hotel, and I type the address into the navigation. But before I start the engine, she speaks again.

"I wish I could help you right now." Her authenticity is strong, and she's looking forward, lost in a thought.

"You're a confusing woman, Isla. The queen of mixed messages. Yet still you manage to keep me on this thin tether which is fucking annoying." I'm getting aggravated.

Her eyes dart to mine. "A tether is a connection, you know." Her tone is simple.

"We have a sort of fucked-up one, don't ya think? Somehow, I have no regrets either."

Her mouth opens and a sound croaks out of her lips. "I'm not sure… maybe I might be a regret for you soon."

My eyes squint as I try to figure out what in the world is going on with her. "You're speaking in tongues. You have me at a loss."

She nibbles her bottom lip and appears to be debating with herself. "I'm sorry. I just… Forget it. You're right, I'm all over the place, but so are you currently."

"Thanks for highlighting that."

A deep breath escapes her. "I shouldn't say anything anymore, it may just send us down a hell of a night."

We stare at one another for a few beats. It's intense but somehow profound. Two people glued to an inability to end the gravity that keeps us close.

Which is why I snap.

I yank her arm. She yelps in surprise and immediately turns to me with knowing eyes. "I meant what I said Isla. I'm only good for one thing right now, and if you can't help me with that, then I now realize this drive is going to be far too excruciating."

Her breath seems to have picked up before she observes the garage where there isn't a person in sight. "Should we really be doing what I think is about to happen?" She tilts her head to the side, asking as if it's a dealbreaker, as it probably should be.

"Yes."

"Is this what you need right now to feel better?" she rasps.

I don't even answer. Instead, I crash my mouth onto hers. At first, she's taken aback, but then she melts into my kiss with a murmur. I'm not gentle. I kiss her hard as I wrap my arms around to guide her as I drag her across the middle console to have her straddling me. Instantly, she loops her arms around my neck while her legs link tighter around my hips.

Our kiss grows fervent as I bring my hand to roam the soft skin of her thighs and sneak under her dress that is now bunched at her waist. "If you want to help, then let me fuck you right now." That's my way of asking permission, and she nods once.

I jerk her panties to one side, and my fingers land on her sensitive nub. Her moan is instant, and I'm satisfied that it doesn't take long for her to experience a buildup that I'm not going to let her have yet. My fingers get soaked by her arousal pooling between her legs.

We stay connected by the mouth while she unbuckles my jeans, and I lift her enough that she can lower my boxer briefs. "Pull up your dress," I demand as I slip my finger inside of her, and she struggles to breathe normally, but a few buttons from the top of her dress snap open, and her breasts push together.

"Fuck, I shouldn't be doing this." She's scolding herself but tilts her body to use my fingers when I add another to her opening.

"Maybe you need this as much as me," I husk right before my mouth dives down to kiss her cleavage. "Bra down. Now."

Isla lowers the cups of her lace bra, and I examine her full breasts, so enticing and beautiful, with peaked tips. They definitely feel different than last time I got to bury my face and cock into them.

I drag my tongue down to latch onto a nipple and wrap my lips around to gently suck and bite, only urged on by her crooning noise.

"Don't stop," she breathes heavily, with her fingers raking through my hair.

I groan from the feeling of my length rubbing against her body. "I'm not going to sugarcoat this. I'm going to jam my fingers into your mouth so you can taste exactly how much you want me. You're fucking sweet, Isla. Then I'm going to make sure my cock is buried deep inside of you. We're not going to go slow, and you'll let me go hard as I thrust up while you ride me. Tell me you understand."

"I understand." Her throaty voice is too sexy, and it only makes the heat inside of me ignite more.

I keep true to my promise, and my fingers find a new home on her eagerly awaiting tongue, right before she sucks them off as good as when she's on her knees for me.

Aligning with her center, I nearly lose it when I feel her hand grip around my cock to guide me in, instantly feeling her tightness coat around my cock. She feels far too warm, near hot, but I don't mind in the slightest. One slow pump is all I give her before I pick up speed and ensure I fill her to the brim. We keep our bodies close due to the logistics of fucking in the front of my car and her bouncing body.

I didn't realize how much I needed this to relax until a few minutes later when I'm coming inside of her as she bites my neck because she's shaking.

We end up tangled in a mess and in silence, recovering from spontaneous sex in my driver's seat.

But then she does something peculiar and begins to straighten her clothes, now eager to slide off me and back onto the passenger seat. It's maybe a fair move since I've given no indication that this would be an all-night thing now. If she was offering then I would use her to release tension, over and over back upstairs. I don't mind sharing a bed with her one single bit, because I like her hair splayed across a pillow. However, she is creating distance between us again.

Isla gives me a look that is near remorseful. "I hope this is what you needed, but I really need you to take me to my hotel."

I blow out a breath and do as she says, the short ten-minute drive far too quiet. Before she opens the door at her destination, she pauses.

"This…" She motions between us. "It can't get complicated, and we are only maybe friends who seem to do other activities." Her tone is near flippant.

"Wow, thought I would at least get a bye. Wasn't expecting you to be so eager to run away, but fine. I'm not in a state to argue."

"Just trust me, this is for the best." She is so damn resolute.

A sound of doubt escapes me. "Right, you take care then."

"Remember, you're the guy who doesn't want anything, and we agreed on only one night then. You're most definitely not going to tell me that something has changed. Are you?" It doesn't feel like she's trying to be wise, it's almost as if she is checking.

"No. I need to focus on my next career move."

I honest to God swear I see a shade of distress fall on her face.

"Obviously." Her voice is uneven. "Take care."

Then she's out my car door, forgetting the last half-hour happened.

8

ISLA

Scarfing down the ice cream sandwich that I'm holding, Hadley comes to join me on my couch.

"Still addicted to ice cream sandwiches?"

"Yes. I moved on from those chocolate ones that have vanilla ice cream in the middle that you buy at the store. I'm now on to two chocolate chip cookies with vanilla ice cream in the middle. I think this is a craving," I explain as I capture some melting ice cream in my mouth.

Hadley gets comfortable by tucking her knees under her. "So? Did you do it?"

I swallow my last bite and then pause for a second to prepare myself. "I messed up… a lot."

Over the last few weeks, a stirring feeling chased me. I calmed down a bit and reentered the circle of wanting to tell Vaughn.

She studies me for a second. "You didn't tell him, did you?"

It all comes out of me. "It's worse, way worse."

"How? You still haven't told him you're pregnant and you're nearly halfway." She isn't impressed, as she keeps reiterating that he has a right to know, yet she doesn't judge me either.

"We had sex."

"What?" she shrieks, and her face turns confused.

I cringe. "I know, it's not what I should have let happen."

"Isla, you went to Tampa to tell him. You literally used your brother's game as an excuse to fly there to tell Vaughn in person because you feel like it isn't a conversation to have via phone or text. Yet you didn't tell him and instead had sex with him?"

I rest my head against my propped arm on the back of the sofa. "He is in no place right now to hear that he is going to be a father. I swear that I went to his home to tell him. It's just, when I got there, I could see that he wasn't in a great space in terms of moods. He also made it clear that he didn't want to talk nor be a friend, and he only wanted one thing in that moment."

"Yeah, he just wanted to fuck," she bluntly states.

I hold up my other palm to ease her. "It felt like it was what he needed to not be so down, and if I'm honest, I wanted it too. Really, you should have seen him. If I had told him then, he would have combusted. He also mentioned that he has no interest in further complications in his life. This..." I point to my belly, "is a complication."

Hadley slides her jaw side to side, clearly digesting this development. "You made this far more complex. Once he finds out, he will look back at this." I don't answer or say anything. She reaches out to hold my hand between her palms. "Can we *really* talk for a second?"

"Always."

"Not telling him after three attempts is your easy way out. It's by far harder to inform him than not. You keep having excuses why you can't tell him. They are not the real reasons, though." She stops and waits for me to pour my heart out, but again, I stay mute.

"Isla, you're scared he will be exactly like your dad and want no involvement. This is more about you than it is Vaughn," she delicately explains.

An ache hits my face as my tears come tumbling down in droplets from my eyes. Her theory didn't take much for my body to react. Simply because she's right.

"It really sucked at times not having a dad who wanted to be involved in my life. He was barely around during Briggs's first two years of life, and our dad completely took off when my mom was pregnant with me. What if this baby gets the same treatment?"

She squeezes my hand. "The only way to find out is to ask the man who is the father."

"He is in a dwelling cloud, that I'm not overreacting on."

"So, what are you going to do then?"

I sigh. "I thought about it on my flight back. I'm going to do nothing, not until he figures it out—my pregnancy, I mean. He can discover it in his own way. I can't keep attempting to tell him and then feel horrible when I don't, and I know that's selfish. I fully agree that he has every right to know, but I just don't have the strength to break the news for the reasons you mentioned. And I need my strength to ensure this baby is healthy, it should be my focus. I'm choosing my battles."

She licks her lips and sits there in contemplation. "If that's what you feel you need to do then… fine. I'll support you." I can tell she doesn't agree, but she will be on my team anyways.

"Thank you."

"Anything for you. Crap, is it me who made the pregnant lady cry?" Hadley is trying to make me smile.

"Nah, I think I managed this all on my own."

"Should I grab you another ice cream sandwich from the freezer?" She hitches her thumb over her shoulder. "I know that you stocked up."

I chortle and wipe my tears away at the same time. "Nah, I'll be big enough soon, and I want to watch my sugar intake, as it's important for the baby."

She throws a fond look my way. "You're really going to rock this mom thing."

"I hope so."

Hadley claps her hands together. "Okay, so plan of action is to give up on trying to tell Vaughn, and he will need to figure it out either by word of mouth or seeing that you're carrying prized goods?"

"Could you maybe ask Connor not to mention that I'm pregnant?" I warn. "Not sure that's the way for this all to unfold."

She points a finger in the air. "Right, check that option off the list. We are sticking to Vaughn maybe running into you and figuring it out himself."

"Exactly. I'm lucky, I guess, that I haven't really started to have a belly, especially if I wear baggy shirts. But I'll start showing soon, no way around that. My jeans barely fit. I've moved onto using an elastic band to keep them up. Which means everyone will figure out that I'm pregnant soon. At least, the people who I haven't told." I sigh and feel that pain build in my throat again. "It's really not that I'm trying to keep him out of this baby's life, I swear… it's just… he's only given me signs that I will be hurt, and I just can't bear it now," I remind her. "After I have the baby I won't feel so fragile, as if I'm about to break, and my determination to tell him will return."

She gives me a sympathetic look. "I know… it's your own fear that you need to overcome." A long silence hits us before she changes her demeanor and attempts a smile. "We should go shopping for maternity clothes. Ooh, and are we finding out the sex of the baby at your twenty-week ultrasound? A gender reveal cake is completely in order." Her excitement is overtaking her.

"Yes, to clothes, and no, I don't want to find out, so no cake, sadly."

She throws me a pretend pout. "Hmm, we'll just have to go all out at your baby shower before the baby arrives."

I look around my living room and my eyes gently gawk at the scene. "Well, at this rate I won't have much space to store anything. I need to add moving to my list. I use the second bedroom in this place as a closet."

"A closet housing dresses and your shoe collection *is* important."

I appreciate that she has detoured from our serious discussion. That's the kind of friend I need, someone who follows my cues of what to say or do.

"Ready to implement the plan of action?" I ask.

It takes only a beat before she squeezes my arm. "No telling Vaughn and Big Isla, here we come."

I laugh. "I'm hoping for a cute bump. But yes, plan confirmed."

One day, I just hope Vaughn will understand.

———

It's a few weeks later when I'm sitting at my desk going over project timelines in our Kanban boards on our project tool when my phone buzzes with an incoming message.

I finish typing my sentence when I quickly skim the screen of my phone, then my eyes shoot wide open in attention when I see Vaughn's name on top of the bubble box.

VAUGHN

Hey, I just wanted to touch base. A few weeks ago was kind of unexpected, and I'm well aware that it wasn't my finest move. Just wanted to ensure that you don't feel used or think that I'm an even bigger ass than you probably already did.

I tap my finger against my desk, taking in the fact that he's been thinking about me or that night, which is why he texted now. I'm surprised for sure, but also remind myself of my plan of action that feels more like a strong conviction.

Still, the magnetic pull of his words causes me to type back.

You didn't use me. I also offered.

Okay.

I should flip my phone over and move on, but I don't. A speck inside of me is wondering if this is a tiny door to try again or at least figure out if he is in a better place.

Hope you are feeling better?

The dots on the phone indicate that he is typing back, then he stops, then types again.

> I am actually. Maybe even partly excited for what's next. Sure as hell not in the state that I was in when you last saw me. Although I guess I'm always a little demanding in certain ways...

The corner of my mouth hitches at his attempt to lighten the conversation. I'm also happy that he seems to be in a different mood. For a second, I think about breaking the news. But then I remind myself that text isn't the way for me, but I could ask that we speak. Maybe a video call is better than nothing.

> I'm happy to hear. You mentioned what's up next, so what is that?

Maybe I'm testing the water.

> Yeah, general management for a team, and I already have a few teams interested. It's a hell of a lot more demanding schedule, but I'm at a stage in my life where I can devote my time and go all in.

My stomach sinks again, as any light that I thought might help me unlock my secret just vanished. The idea to ask that we talk is a sentiment that I now ignore. Yet again, Vaughn has no clue that he planted more doubt in my head. All indications are that our baby news is the last thing he would ever want to hear right now. And in a selfish move, I need to focus on this pregnancy and being healthy both physically and mentally. It's easier if I just leave this be.

Which is why I simply write back and brush past his innuendo.

> I need to get back to a project. Take care, Vaughn.

It's what is best right now.

9

VAUGHN

Staring up from the paper lying on the conference table, I watch the three men before me in their suits.

One is a lawyer, the other my own, and they both sit mute in their years of experience. They only interrupt when legal clarity is needed. Then there is Declan Dash, my friend's uncle and the owner of the Spinners who has been quietly pushing his case for the past year. He wears a subtle wry grin with triumph as he says all the right things.

My eyes dart down to the contract that I've already read over with my lawyer during the past few days, then back up to Declan who is patiently waiting.

He picks up a pen and wiggles it between his fingers. "What do you say? Is the offer appealing?"

I lean back in my chair, surprised that he made the effort to fly down to Florida to speak to me. Since my last season ended, I've received offers for various roles. Yet here I am with the only one that caught my interest. The wheels have been in motion since last month, but now we need to cement it all down in ink if I choose.

"Should I be thanking the GM you just fired?" I joke to lighten the mood.

Declan wobbles his head slightly. "Well, probably. I mean, I've been wanting to shake up the team for a while now. Just so happens he made that easier when the Spinners were out mid-playoffs because of a bad trade this year, so we chose not to renew his contract. And after next season, the head coach has got to go, as I don't like his methods to train the team. You made it clear that you are not eyeing any coaching position. I heard the rumors, I know Phoenix asked."

"You're right. I want a bit more of a mix, working with the scouts and coaches, getting a chance to add a little of the business side into things."

Declan splays his hands out. "And me." I chuckle softly. "You and I will have daily contact. You'll be up in my box at every game and talk to the press. I believe you are exactly who we need to shake things up. I want a man who knows hockey from the other side, and I've seen other teams hire young fresh blood, often with no hockey knowledge, and it's a success. We will need to throw you in the deep end to talk with our scouts about draft picks, and you'll play a key role in forming our new team strategy. It will take more than one season to completely reshape things, which is why a four-year contract is on the table, with every intention to extend."

A deep inhale hits me. This would be a great move. And working with Declan would be a good match. He is the type of owner who wants to be involved, as he himself used to play, and I'm the guy who wants to be the spider in the web to see through all lenses of the sport.

It's a no-brainer.

"Any way you could add Florida weather to the agreement?" My mouth tilts up, and my joke earns a chuckle from the gentlemen in the room.

"No, but you would be heading to Lake Spark during the off-season, so the next few months will feel like you never left a tropical paradise," Declan counters.

I huff a laugh. "Don't fill me up with lies. We all know summer in Illinois is not exactly predictable. Besides, the off-season is arguably just as busy for a GM, as a draft is fast approaching. Not to mention that players are at development camps. I'll need to hit the ground running."

"I can't deny that, but lucky for you, we'll get moving fast and have you in Lake Spark within two weeks. Besides, we have a great realtor that works with the team, I'm sure they can find you a not-so-humble abode that will be ideal for winter and summer."

I pause for a second as the paper is taunting me.

Lake Spark.

It does have charm. It also has Isla. The woman who made it clear back at Christmas that we absolutely will be keeping to our agreement of having only one night, only for her to let me take her again weeks later. She's hot and cold. In fact, for a split second, I could have sworn that she didn't quite want to see me again. That situation might be tricky.

However, the seven-figure salary before me is persuasive. This is a no-brainer, even if it means I'll need to forfeit my Caribbean holiday that I thought of taking next month to unwind.

Truthfully, I don't need Declan pulling out the stops. We wouldn't be here if we were still in negotiations.

Quickly I glance to my lawyer who gives me an assuring nod. There is no more stalling.

"I get to keep the pen, right?" I smile.

Ease hits Declan's face, and our lawyers even crack a smile.

Declan reaches over the table to hand me the pen. "I'll even buy you a set."

I quickly sign my initials on each page then add my signature on the last page next to where Declan already signed.

As I slam the pen down, our lawyers are already shaking hands, and Declan stands to button his suit jacket and circles around the table to shake my hand.

His other hand lands on my shoulder. "I'm excited for this. I'll be sure that someone from the team contacts you right away to sort out the logistics of the move. We need you up there as soon as possible. Of course, my wife will be expecting you over for dinner. My nephew will be thrilled, that is, if he doesn't sign with another team for next season."

"If we give him a good offer then maybe he will stay," I say. I already need to think like a manager.

Declan chuckles. "I'll stay out of that one." He leans down to look at the signed contract and then slides it to his lawyer. "We should get a bottle of champagne in here before I need to fly back. My daughter has a ballet class where the parents can watch. She's only three but watching her wobble around is the cutest."

I only nod because I can't exactly picture it.

"There is one matter that we might need to discuss. As much as I'm sure grown men can be professional, uh, Briggs Chase does absolutely hate me," I point out.

It only causes Declan to grin. "He does. But he is going to have to suck it up. Besides, I'm not sure he will be sticking around. I know contract talks might be difficult with him, as he is an unrestricted agent now, plus maybe he has gotten softer lately since his personal life has had so many changes."

That piques my interest. "Oh? Everything okay?"

"For sure, just his personal life is occupied with his girlfriend and sister. Plus, he lives in Lake Spark, and you can't not be happy when you live in Lake Spark."

I laugh because his small-town pride is a far cry from his days as bonafide bachelor, with his city penthouse.

"Be sure to send me a welcome basket," I joke.

Someone opens the door to the meeting room and brings in champagne on ice with flutes.

"That can be arranged."

It hits me that I'm going to move to Lake Spark.

———

SITTING on the private plane a few days later, I trace the button on my phone near Isla's name.

Maybe I should text or give a warning. They are announcing my new role tomorrow to the press. If she really doesn't want to see me, then she's going to have a hard time avoiding me. Plus, maybe I want to see her. She occasionally lingers in my thoughts. More than she should since that night of comfort sex in my car.

I shake off the idea of texting her and glance out the window to see corn fields, which has mostly been what I've seen for the last hour. Luckily, as we approach the private airport near Lake Spark, the view begins to change. More greenery, tall pines, winding roads amongst small hills, and an emerald lake in the far-off distance.

Tucking my phone away, I get ready for landing.

This is my new adventure.

The landing is smooth, and when I disembark from the plane, I'm instantly greeted by Declan standing on the tarmac next to Connor.

"Welcome!" he calls out while Connor grins broadly.

"Where's my fruit basket?" I tease as I step down the stairs.

When I get to the bottom, I greet him with a handshake and give Connor a side hug.

"I'm not supposed to know why you're here, but I have connections," Connor jokes.

"I would love to say I planned to stand here and wait for you, but I'm going to Detroit for a meeting and need my plane once they refuel," Declan clarifies but still grins.

"And since I'm here to drop him off, then I'll drive you into town. The Spinners are trying to go as green as possible." Connor smiles tightly while his eyes bug out and indicate the plane behind me. "So, no need to drag another car here." His sarcasm is underlying at how ridiculous this policy seems.

"Sounds like a plan." I'll get my rental car later, as they will deliver it to the Dizzy Duck Inn in town until I have a new house.

"Alright, a winning team here we come." Declan claps his hands together before he picks up his laptop bag. "Don't forget to hit up

Jolly Joe's, everyone needs their coffee with an overly-food-colored jellybean." He does a little fist pump in the air.

Connor gently nudges my arm. "Ignore him. He's hyped up on coffee from Jolly Joe's, and it has mystical powers on people." He scans the area. "Ah, I see that someone is bringing your luggage to my car. Let's get out of here. You must be hungry. We can grab some food at Catch 22 if you want."

"I guess I could eat."

We begin to walk toward his SUV, the latest model. "I would have picked you up in my Jag but figured you had luggage."

"It's cool," I promise.

Sliding into the front seat, I quickly see a message from my brother.

STONE

Enjoy small-town life with a big career. The perfect balance. What are we missing in that equation? ;) Good luck, Brother!

I'll text him back later. It will be nice having a shorter flight time and more flight options to see him. It was one of the reasons this move was more tempting. As we drive away from the airport, I feel content that it's the right choice.

"Whether I stay with the Spinners or not, I think you made a good decision." Connor must have read my mind as he focuses on the road.

"Thanks, buddy. How is married life treating ya?"

"Fucking fantastic. No complaints. Hadley is the best. Then again, we've known one another almost our whole lives. It's just now we dirtied it up a bit."

I sputter a laugh because that is something he would say. "And your good friend Briggs?"

Connor grimaces. "We told him the news earlier today to warn him. He'll get over it. Besides, he has enough happening in his private life to keep occupied from killing you."

Huh, he is the second person to say that Briggs has stuff going on.

"I guess my uncle has you jumping right in, but if the weather holds up, then we should do a ride out on the lake. My dad always has his boat out for the season."

"Nothing like Florida water, but I'll give it a go," I respond.

Looking out the window, I'm trying now to count the ridiculous signs on the road. I've now counted a sign warning for deer, another sign for ducks crossing, and a sign cautioning for, I think, raccoons. Do they even make a sign for that?

"We don't have great seafood up here. But I think we beat out Florida when it comes to hot dogs and pie season. We have some skills in that department," Connor justifies. "How is the house search going?"

"The real estate agent that the team uses is like a shark. Already had a few options sent to me last night," I explain.

"You need to give me the name of the agent. Isla has been trying to find a new place to no avail, trying to buy instead of rent. Even had a successful offer on the table for a new house the other week, but the seller pulled out. There is absolutely nothing on the market. Then again, she isn't the guy who just pocketed a solid seven figures."

Interest inflames in me. "Isla wants to move?"

"Yeah, for so many reasons. She's been looking since February," he mentions.

"In Lake Spark?" I shouldn't really care, but maybe the idea of running into her is more enticing than it should be.

"Uh-huh." Just then a call comes in on his Bluetooth, with Hadley's name appearing on the dashboard screen. "Sorry, I should take this."

"Of course, happy wife, happy life."

He sidelines his eyes to me with a smug smirk before answering. "Hey, Sprinkles." Damn, that's a little sappy.

"Connor." I hear Hadley's voice. "I need you to come right away to the hospital."

Fear hits Connor as he grips the steering wheel. "Wait, what? What's going on? Are you okay?"

"I'm fine, I just need you to come right away. Can you do that for me?" She sounds upset.

I mouth yes to Connor, assuring him that we can take a detour.

"I can be there in ten minutes, okay?"

"Hurry."

———

TEN MINUTES later we are running into the hospital and up two floors to find Hadley standing by a room, pacing the hall. She immediately runs into Connor's arms.

"Hey, it's okay. What's going on?" he asks as he holds her tight and rubs her back.

She gently pulls back. "It's Isla."

Instantly, my body tenses, and my eyes shoot to the door to Isla's room. Hadley notices me, and her face is indescribable, as if she is surprised that I'm here and equally worried.

"Oh, hey, Vaughn… didn't realize you would be here."

Connor interjects. "I mentioned this morning he will be our new GM, I picked him up from the airport."

"Right." Her T is tight.

I can't figure out why she is acting odd, but I can't focus on that. Not when I know Isla is on the other side of the door.

10

ISLA

I practice my yoga breathing while I sit up on the bed. Closing my eyes, I do my best to calm down while my hand is firmly set on my belly that has a belt of cords around it to monitor the baby, and I also have a pulse oximeter attached to my finger.

The door opens a crack, and Hadley slips through the tiny opening, careful to ensure nobody else can enter. Her face seems panicked.

"We have a problem," she states.

"What? The doctor said I'm fine and it was just a false alarm. They will just double-check everything when my doctor arrives after they notify her upstairs."

Her mouth is in a strained line as she shakes her head before her face squinches. "It's not that. I was so worried when we first arrived that I phoned Connor. I didn't say anything, so he thought it was me hurt, but that doesn't matter because…"

I stare at her blankly. "And? He's your husband. I sent a message to Briggs too because I was freaking out."

"So…" She quickly walks to my bed and perches on the end. "When I asked you to meet at my studio to go for lunch, it was actually because I wanted to talk to you about something that Connor told me about this morning at breakfast."

"Get to whatever it is faster."

"He told me that later in the week they are going to announce the new GM for the Spinners… Vaughn."

My eyes instantly widen and my nose tips up. "Come again?"

"*Yeah*… and what I didn't realize is that Connor was picking up Vaughn at the airport, and when I phoned him to come to the hospital… Vaughn was in the car."

"What!" I shriek, and the monitor that I'm attached to makes a spike on the graph. "He's here?"

She nods once. "Outside that door."

"Oh fuck." I touch my forehead, as I'm about to have a meltdown. I knew this day would come, but does it have to be right now?

Hadley touches my leg. "He doesn't know why you are here. I gave Connor a pleading look, and I think it registered in his head a connection with Vaughn, and he got the hint not to tell him about your current state. But that will only hold out for so long."

I feel as though I'm levitating away from earth. There is no way around this. Vaughn is going to find out today. I've had a thousand scenarios in my head of how this could go, but him showing up to my hospital room is not one of them.

"This is not… how today was supposed to go."

"Maybe it's for the best. You've been lucky that you only started to show after you saw him last, but with Vaughn now in Lake Spark, I'm confident that he *would* notice that your stomach is harboring a baby, and saying you ate too many cookies isn't going to fly. You're glowing during this pregnancy too, plus, well, about to push out a baby," she explains.

I rub my belly and quickly glance at the screen that's now zigzagging in lines. "Hadley, I appreciate your stellar positivity, but my baby daddy is about to find out that I haven't told him about the baby… and I'm wearing a sweatshirt with a bar of chocolate printed on it that literally says, 'I have issues.'"

She shrugs. "Helps explain your reasoning?"

I bring my hands to my face to rub as tears begin to build behind my eyes. "How do I do this? I'm attached to a machine, I can't run away."

Her lips roll in, and a sympathetic look is fixed on her face. "Maybe that's a good thing. I don't think you should escape right now… You weren't really never going to tell him, were you? You had a plan."

A long heaving sigh leaves me. "No, I don't know, yes, I mean no." I shake my head. "I'm just scared. He made his views on kids so clear and…"

"You didn't give him a chance to walk away," she highlights.

That just unlocks the quiver on my mouth to upgrade to a tear that's been begging to fall.

As much as I'm scared, she's right. He hasn't been given the chance, and I want the information on his medical history to ensure that we can get ahead of anything we might need to worry about for the baby's health.

Fuck, I'm saying "we" in my head. Maybe it is we. Since the entire town found out my current status a little while back, it's been an outpouring of support. At work, we're preparing for my maternity leave that starts in a week. Ford is even giving me extra paid leave. Hadley has attended appointments with me. Her mom, along with Brielle and Violet, is planning a baby shower coming up. And Briggs? He has slowly been stockpiling toys that are far too noisy. It takes a village to raise a baby, they say.

But Vaughn has a right to choose if he wants to be part of that village.

What the hell do I do if he doesn't want to be involved? This town is only so big, and my emotional wound already runs deep.

Blowing out another breath, I decide that maybe…

The sound of the door opening breaks my thought.

"Are you okay? What's happening?" Briggs stalks into the room and quickly lands next to me to squeeze my arm.

I wave him off. "It's nothing. An active, kicking baby scaring the hell out of me. I totally overreacted."

"Of course not. If my nephew or niece needs medical attention, then we go all out." He glances at the monitor.

"Hey, Briggs, where is Connor?" Hadley inquires.

"He's here? Didn't see him in the hall. Must have gone to the vending machine or something," Briggs answers, and my eyes shoot to Hadley.

Oh crap, Briggs is here and Vaughn.

No, no, no.

The door opens again. "Heard we can start a party here, so we're letting ourselves in," Connor announces, with Vaughn in tow.

Then it happens.

Vaughn's eyes strike mine with a hint of a smile on his lips that twitch when his sight sidelines to the machine next to me that unfairly informs everyone that my pulse is picking up. Finally, his eyes drop to my belly that I'm cradling in my hands, with his smile now dispersing into history.

He blinks a few times. Is his brain registering?

"What the fuck is he doing here?" Briggs nearly hisses.

Right, because my brother is present. Nearly forgot that, as I think there are bigger problems right now.

"You're pregnant?" The words faintly escape Vaughn's lips.

"Uhm… in my third trimester, actually." My tone is neutral as I can't tear my eyes away from him.

Is it possible that I can see inside of his mind as he counts back the months?

An unusual silence takes over the room.

"There is some odd tension happening or something," Connor comments, and Hadley instantly elbows into his ribs to shut him up, and he yelps yet gets the clue.

"Tell me now if what I'm thinking is correct?" Vaughn grits out.

Fresh tears pool in my eyes, and all I can do is nod.

Vaughn nearly falls back as though I just knocked all the air out of his lungs and scrubs a hand across his jaw.

In the corner of my eye, Briggs is whipping his vision between me and Vaughn with everything registering. "Oh no… fuck no… tell me it's not him."

"Briggs, now isn't the time." My voice is shaking during my plea.

"Whoa, him?" Connor points his thumb at Vaughn and grins like this is great news. "Wait, when did this happen?"

I give him an unimpressed look. "A hurricane. Now can we skip the specifics?"

Connor's face turns blank. "Huh… Vaughn," he reflects. "Well, now this just got really fucking awkward."

Hadley swats him and glares at him, unamused. "Now is the time to stay quiet."

Briggs stomps forward to the middle of the room and directs his attention to Vaughn. "You're the guy who knocked up my sister?" He glances over his shoulder back to me. "It's him? How the hell?"

"Jesus, calm down. She doesn't need to explain the birds and the bees to you," Hadley chides.

Vaughn remains in shock.

"I'm going to rip your head off." Briggs begins to charge at Vaughn.

Vaughn is snapped out of his daze when my brother grips his shirt.

"Briggs," I screech. He only stops for a second. "Can we stop? The baby has ears now and can hear everything."

"Fuck off, Briggs." Vaughn yanks my brother's arms away.

But my brother only pushes him, not ready to give up. "Watch the language, the baby has ears now." He isn't even mocking; he's taking his uncle duty far too seriously. "So you just get my sister pregnant and leave her to do this alone? I knew I had a reason to hate you." He pushes Vaughn again who is visibly annoyed at him.

"Connor, do something *right now*," Hadley gravels out to her husband. He is quick to tend to the scuffle happening in my hospital room.

"Just great, I have a hockey fight in my hospital room minus the skates." My shoulders slump down when I mutter to myself.

"You know I can take you down in no time, so back the fuck off," Vaughn growls.

Connor steps between them again to keep them apart by holding his arms out. "Will you two knock it off?"

Briggs looks back to me while he points at Vaughn. "I'm not going to let this go. His intentions are not honorable, and I won't forget that."

Throwing my arms up in the air, I gawk my eyes. "Briggs, we're not in Victorian times. I don't need your approval. I'm not a damsel in distress," I say, raising my voice.

"You're my sister," he defends.

"Yeah, and I'm the sister who hasn't actually told the father of my child that I'm pregnant, so leave it alone," I justify.

My brother's face falls, and it clicks in his head that Vaughn is finding out for the first time. He even flashes Vaughn a look that for the most part is neutral.

Just then the door opens again, with Dr. Forest arriving and rolling in a cart. She warily studies the room. "What a collection of hockey players here that the medical staff seemed to notice gather in the hall earlier, but the nurses' station is picking up that your heart rate is all over the place, along with the baby being more active, so you seem to be stressed."

"Understatement," I highlight.

"I think it's time that we kick out the visitors." She smiles at me.

The room goes silent as we all look at one another.

"Let's go, guys, I think Isla needs a moment." Hadley does her best to usher Connor and Briggs out. She stops short at Vaughn, maybe even gives him a cautionary look.

"I'm staying," he states firmly, with his fists clenched at his sides and his gaze still drilling into me.

The doctor notices the tension. "You can only stay if my patient agrees."

Vaughn raises his brows at me, waiting for me to answer, and it's clear there is only one answer that I can give.

Blowing out a breath, I say, "He can. He's… the father. Would it be okay if we have a minute?"

"One minute," she says sharply. Give the doctor an award for professionalism as she clearly grasps this unusual situation.

With everyone abandoning us, Vaughn steps forward.

In the background, I can hear my brother. "I swear to God, I might just commit murder."

"No, you won't. Come on, let's go for a walk. You're acting like a wild animal who needs to be tamed," Connor suggests, and they must be walking away, as the background grows silent.

Except for the sound of the machine.

"Oh, Isla, Isla, Isla," Vaughn tuts, and it's sweltering, and it would even be sexy if it weren't for the fact that I know what's about to come. "You owe me a lot of answers."

VAUGHN

Isla's chest visibly moves up and down, but my sight keeps drawing back to her swollen belly. It's visible without a doubt.

A baby.

Our baby.

I'm completely blindsided by this news. I can't even process how I feel about the fact that I created a child. Instead, fury takes over me.

"You're already in your third trimester?" I repeat what she said earlier.

"Yes, due in a few weeks."

Fucking late-season hurricanes.

I step closer to the bed, undecided what I'm doing. "So, that means you're like, what, about to birth a child?"

She takes a long breath through her pursed lips. "Seems you're great with numbers." Is she seriously attempting to make a joke right now?

"You had nine months to tell me, yet here I am after *accidentally* discovering that you're pregnant." I'm livid I think, which is why my eyes narrow in on her, and she looks kind of uncomfortable, but I believe that I have a little right to feel this way.

"First off, it's not nine months, we still have nearly a month to go."

"Cute." I flash her a contrite smile.

"I-I tried to tell you… a few times."

"So, what? You were going to wait until I saw you carrying a baby? Invite me to their high school graduation and be like, by the way, you're a dad? Were you ever going to tell me?" My voice raises slightly.

Her eyes hood closed then open, with fresh tears, and the vision of her right now has me torn, because I'm angry, but she's the woman sitting on a hospital bed.

"No, I was going to tell you… eventually."

I scoff a sound and bring my hand to my forehead to check that I'm still alive. "When? When did you try to tell me?" I want answers.

"First when I phoned you and the crazy girl answered." Shit. "Again, at Christmas when you were here for the game."

"You wanted to let me fuck you and not even tell me that you were pregnant?" I'm astonished.

"I didn't let you screw me, thank you very much," she defends.

My hands slowly clap together. "Let's give you an award for having a conscience." I'm being cynical. "That only lasted so long," I snipe.

"I freaked out because you said you didn't like kids and you didn't see yourself wanting kids anytime soon," she adds.

I shake my head. "I did say that, but it doesn't mean you had a right to withhold this critical information."

"You have a choice to walk away if you want, I know that. I tried again to tell you when I came to your place, but you were so visibly not ready to hear the news. It felt like it was the last thing that I should say."

Again, looking back, I had an inkling there was something more at the time, but I was too frustrated in my life to press her for what it may have been.

"Instead, you didn't. You let us have sex while you harbored a secret." Unbelievable. I didn't want to think less of Isla, but right now, she has crossed a major line by keeping this big of a secret. "Seriously? This is a shitty thing to do. The last thing that I would expect from you." Then another fact dawns on me, and I rub my temples. "Wait, how the hell did I not see you were pregnant when we had sex?"

She lifts a shoulder up to her ear. "I didn't really start to show until more than halfway. I mean, I had a little bump, but I wasn't wearing the right outfit to make it obvious." She lifts a finger indicating for me to wait. "And to be fair, our position of choice didn't exactly get me naked, nor could you notice my belly."

"No, instead you let your bigger boobs entice me into ramming my dick up inside of you." It scrapes out of my mouth.

Her own mouth gapes open from my harsh words.

"Incredible, you're focusing on our ability to fuck between a seat and steering wheel when you should be focusing on other aspects. I mean, really? We had sex, a few good conversations, that doesn't mean you know me inside out," she refutes.

We've had a connection from moment one when we met, which raises the scale of my disappointment.

My face falls to my hands because we may go in circles right now.

"I need to process this," I admit. Then it dawns on me that she is in a freaking hospital. "Wait, why are you here?"

She chortles to herself. "I thought something was wrong. Turns out I was a little dramatic, and it was just eating the wrong thing and had Braxton Hicks contractions, which is like my body practicing for the big day. The baby was kicking more than normal too."

"Baby? You don't know…"

"If it's a boy or girl?"

Why am I asking as though I'm already invested? I haven't figured out my feelings.

The line of her mouth slants to the side. "No. I didn't want to find out."

I nod slowly, attempting to soak this all in.

The knock on the door kind of sends a surge of dread through me, in case it's her gladiator-hyped-up brother. Luckily, the doctor peeks her head around the door.

"Ready? I need to see you now so we can get you home soon," she explains.

"Sure," Isla agrees.

The doctor walks in with a genuine smile. "I would like to do an ultrasound just to be safe, but your blood work seems good, and the baby's heart rate is strong, just spiked earlier because he or she seems to be an active one. You probably need a little rest considering your body seems under stress, and it's also preparing for him or her to come out." She begins to roll a machine to Isla's bed. "Will he be staying?"

"Yes," I blurt out. I have had enough undisclosed information for one day.

The doctor smiles at me. "That's great, but again, the patient gets to decide."

My gaze snaps to Isla to inform her that I won't be accepting no for an answer.

She grasps my demand and quickly answers. "He can stay," she assures the doctor.

"Okay, lean back and lift your shirt. You're a pro at this now. A bit of gel and then here we go." The doctor removes the contraption belt around Isla then squirts something that oozes from a bottle and places the wand-shaped thing in her hand against Isla's belly. "You should probably get closer to Isla if you want to enjoy the show."

Reluctantly, I take a few steps next to Isla's bed near her upper body. She gives me a nervous look before her head zips back to the screen attached to the portable machine.

When I can see the outline of a baby, I'm taken aback.

"Wow, the baby has grown since the last ultrasound," Isla notes with a fond smile.

"It goes really quick now. The baby is almost so big that an ultrasound won't show many new things because the baby doesn't have much room to move around." The doctor stays glued to the screen as she zooms in to different sections.

The sound of the heartbeat fills the room, similar to the sound of being underwater, but there is a rhythm. Steady and fast, a sound that I wasn't expecting to cause a twitch somewhere inside of me. For a second, I'm in awe that I played a role in creating that. It's really a baby. We're also way past the stage of debating what to do, in terms of options. I've missed the majority of her pregnancy, and this is a full-fledged baby that has a heartbeat and legs and arms... and is about to enter the world.

Isla doesn't seem fazed like I am by the image on the screen. I guess she has had ample opportunity to listen to this.

"Your file states that you didn't want to find out the sex. Still the case?" the doctor asks.

Isla shoots me a look as though I have a say. I'm not sure if I'm glaring or my face is frozen because Isla seems to try to break the air between us. "I didn't want to, but maybe..."

Is she waiting for me to answer?

"I do. I've been graced with enough shockers today." My voice is a little bitter.

Isla nods to the doctor that it's okay.

"Ooh, fun." The doctor zooms in then brings her finger to the screen. "Baby is giving us a great view today, as I can see very clearly that you're having a daughter."

"A girl?" Isla cries, but her smile indicates that they are happy tears.

I tilt my head to examine the screen, and I feel my mouth tug. *Yeah*, it's pretty visible, otherwise there would be a large line if it were a boy.

"Yep. Get ready for tea parties." The doctor keeps the wand in place so we can stare for a few seconds at the screen while she seems to be taking measurements of limbs. "Dad looks like he's already planning this girl's ice-skating career," the doctor attempts to joke.

Dad is planning nothing. I'm still in disbelief.

A daughter. Wow.

Isla seems to be searching my face for a clue to understanding where my brain is at.

"Okay, everything looks great. You're doing excellent, Isla. But really, try to be stress-free. At this point, the baby is at a good point in the pregnancy and has a better chance to live a long and happy life if born a few weeks early. The longer she stays in, closer to the due date is ideal, but any moment it can happen."

"About to go into labor." My tone is flat. "I find out when she's about to go into labor." I feel a hint of anger boiling inside of me.

The doctor stares at me with perhaps exasperation or a warning to calm the hell down. She removes the wand and turns off the machine before she begins to detach the cords connected to Isla's finger.

Isla ignores me and speaks to the doctor. "Don't worry. I'm taking my vitamins, ensuring I eat vegetables, no caffeine, not even any desserts with alcohol in the recipe, lots of sleep, and daily walks." Isla seems to be proud of her habits.

"You're doing great." She hands Isla some paper towel to wipe her stomach.

"Of course, and sorry I overreacted. I didn't expect the contractions or for her to suddenly hate Jolly Joe's cinnamon rolls," Isla apologizes.

The doctor stands. "That is a travesty. How can she ever be a true Lake Spark citizen?" she jokes. "You did the right thing. If there is anything else going forward, then call right away."

"Yep."

The doctor begins to walk out. "You're free to go. See you."

With the doctor now gone, Isla and I return to a stalemate with our eyes in a stare down.

"A girl," she whispers to herself.

An overwhelming feeling hits me, a need to assure her, but that anger keeps poking at me. I want time to process still, I'm not that type of guy who forgives so easily. She didn't tell me for months, with no plan in sight that she would have.

"How?" I state more than I ask. I'm near numb from confusion.

A sound escapes her mouth. "The low pressure in the air from a hurricane increases your chances of getting pregnant."

My head perks up in astonishment. "Really?"

"No," she deadpans. I shake my head that, of course, I'm being an idiot. "We didn't cover it up, and I forgot a pill, so this is all on me."

I debate how to answer her. "I think a man is still involved in that equation, and that just so happens to be me. I'm moving to Lake Spark. That was already happening before I discovered your little secret. We have a big discussion ahead of us, but it can't happen right now. I'm sure as hell not going to jump in as if you didn't keep this from me," I snipe.

"Are you saying that you don't want to be involved?" Disappointment floods her face. "It's fine. I can do this alone; you have an out."

I scratch the back of my head. "Isla, I'm pissed. No, furious. I need time to process. So I'm leaving and finding a strong scotch. We'll talk when I'm ready."

Then I walk away.

12

VAUGHN

I seem to be engrossed with the deep blue water next to the deck and dock of Catch 22, the restaurant in Lake Spark that has a great steak. Although, I'm not hungry.

I'm waiting for my brother, Stone. I'm thankful he lives in Chicago and just had a meeting with his publisher first thing. Go figure, a former pro athlete is writing books. I called him last night saying I really needed to see him if possible, and with no hesitation, he said he would drive out to Lake Spark this morning. He should be here any minute, which gives me time to read an email from the real estate agent. I may not have gotten much sleep last night, but I'm comfortable enough to answer back and hit send.

I toss my phone onto the menu lying on the table just as my brother arrives.

"What's up with you? That phone is getting the treatment of an empty beer can at a kegger," he observes as he takes a seat across from me, leaning across to touch my shoulder as a hello.

"Sorry, I just bought a house."

His face turns puzzled. "You only got here yesterday, and you already saw a house to buy?"

"Nope. Didn't see the house, just purchased it, all cash. I'm sure it's a great house, at least the pictures look like it." I grab my glass of water to drink.

Stone gawks at me. "You what? That doesn't sound like you."

I tip my head slightly to the side and flash my eyes. "Well, a house is a small problem right now, and I need one ASAP. And quite frankly, I don't particularly care if the walls are green or blue." Or pink if that's what Isla is going for.

Stone stares at me blankly. "Okay, what am I missing? You look like you've seen the eye of a storm."

A humorless laugh escapes me. "That's a wonderful reference considering my predicament."

"I thought you were completely excited for this move, plus your new job."

I scratch my nose before I lean into the table with my arms. "I sure as hell hope I'll be able to focus, considering I just discovered that someone I slept with is pregnant."

My brother's eyes instantly grow into saucers. "As in… you're the dad?"

"Yeah, as in I'm the dad. It's not just that… she's already about to pop, which means she never told me, with no plans to tell me."

"Shit."

The waitress arrives with a bright smile then looks between my brother and me, sensing the tension. "I'll come back in a jiffy."

"It's okay." My brother looks at his watch. "It's twelve o'clock, I'll have a beer. This guy here looks like he needs a clear mind, so bring him an iced tea."

She offers a polite smile and scurries away.

My brother snaps his gaze back to me. "What do you mean she was never going to tell you?"

I hold up three fingers. "I've seen her three times since the night we conceived a child. All of those times, she didn't mention a word, not even a clue. If it weren't for the fact that by *accident* I showed up to the hospital, then I don't think I ever would have known until I saw her on Main Street carrying a kid." I sound livid because I am.

He blows out a breath. "Holy hell, this is… big news."

I scrub a hand across my face. "I'm so furious."

My brother studies me for a few good seconds. "Do you know why she didn't tell you?"

I scoff a displeased sound. "She said she tried but every occasion there was a reason not to, not the right time."

He nods in understanding. "Now that you do know, what does she want? Wait, who is she?"

"Isla Chase."

"As in… Briggs Chase's…"

"Little sister, yep. Give me another point for making this more complicated."

He swipes his hands across his face. "Damn." It drags out.

"Again, minor detail, as we now need to figure out what's happening going forward. Stone, I don't care what she wants. She doesn't get to decide if I'm involved or not."

"She doesn't want you involved?"

I flex my jaw. "She didn't… exactly say that."

A knowing smirk appears on his face. "Jumping to conclusions then?"

Maybe he has a point. "At this rate, I don't have a lot of time to guess. You know the doctor said that the baby could actually come at any time now and still be okay. What if I wake tomorrow, and *poof*, there's a baby here?"

His eyes narrow. "You sound like you are kind of already on board. If a baby did just poof…" He makes a gesture with his hand. "Then it seems like you want to see him or her."

"It's a girl." That overpowering pull of my mouth to smile hits me again. It happened a few times during the night while I tossed and turned.

My brother smiles widely. "You're having a daughter. That's kind of cool."

"Her heartbeat is strong." A soft spot within me causes my voice to grow almost tender.

Staring at my brother, the realization hits me yet again. I'm going to be a dad.

It's a moment before Stone states the obvious. "I think... you know you're invested. Just scared."

The waitress deposits our drinks, and Stone gives her an indication to come back later.

I stew in his observation. "Yeah... I am. First it was digesting the news, I felt like someone swung a bat into my stomach. I wasn't sure that I wanted this. Then it was trying to figure out what role I would play. But the real kicker for why I didn't sleep more than an hour last night is because..." I hate saying it.

Luckily, Stone does it for me. "You're not our dad. You can be so much better than he ever was. Just believe it."

"What if I get it all wrong?" I'm throwing it all on the line because we can talk about anything.

"What if you get it all right?" he counters.

I lick my lips and glance at the lake, trying to capture some peace in my head. Then I return my gaze to my brother who's observing me without judgment.

"I don't know how to handle a girl. At least with a boy, I have hockey. A girl? I don't know what to do."

He raises his brows at me. "Now you're scared of a daughter? Nah, you're equally excited. Either way, a child of your own is a whole different territory. You'll just be seeing a lot of pink and purple."

A half-smile hits me like a wave. "I guess so."

"And just like that, we've confirmed that you're doing this. You're going to be a dad."

I nod once in agreement. "Is it bad if I thought for a millisecond last night that I should just give Isla money in a trust fund and sign away my rights?" Shame floods me that the thought even crossed my mind.

"Uh..." He scratches his chin, debating the right words to use. "I think... if it was only a millisecond then you can let it go. Because a millisecond is a speck on the spectrum of your life, not even noticeable. Hell, you can't be the first guy to think it if he discovers he is unexpectedly becoming a dad. Besides, you're here telling me all of this because you *want* to be a great dad. That's by far more important."

I think about it. "I'm not backing away from being a dad… I just don't know how to deal with Isla."

"Maybe… I don't know. She can also be scared or have some reason deep within that prevented her from telling you. You're not the only person in the world to have fears, Vaughn."

My lips quirk out, as my brain feels fried from trying to solve the mystery. "I told her I needed space and walked away."

He chuckles. "Sounds like you really don't want to make this easy."

"She never clued me in that she's about to have a baby," I reiterate.

"And? She didn't exactly say you can't be involved either. You need to talk to Isla. Sometimes we have to take the high road when we shouldn't have to. She's the one who is pregnant, so in this case, she wins."

I shake my head, aggravated, as two people approach our table. I recognize Connor and Hadley right away.

"Hey… well, this is timely," Hadley greets me, while Connor greets my brother since they know one another.

"Excuse my wife. We came for lunch and she noticed you here. Now she has a strong feeling to insert herself into situations that she should probably stay out of," Connor attempts to explain what is about to happen.

Hadley throws him a playful glare before sharply turning her head back to me. "Isla is in misery." She gets right to the point.

"And? She kept a big secret about my baby."

She stands taller. "You said your baby. Isn't it *our* baby, as in Isla and you?" She's keen to correct me.

Connor smiles tightly at me. "Hadley is concerned."

"You know, she has her reasons for why she couldn't tell you. She tried, a lot. So while you sit here debating how to punish her for that, just remember that all she's done is focus on the baby, while internally she is scared out of her mind because she *didn't* get the life that this little girl is going to have."

Fuck, it only dawns on me now that Isla and I share a similar upbringing, with absent parents playing key roles in our probably broken behaviors.

"I don't think I should be having this conversation with you," I inform her.

"You're right. You should be with Isla, planning a future whether together or not. It's eighteen years to life the way you're now bound together." Hadley is feisty but raises valid points.

Connor affectionately touches his wife's elbow to usher her away. "Come on, I think you need to give the guy some space."

She glares at me as her body turns away. "Fine. But she has a craving for ice cream sandwiches, just so you know."

Connor rolls his eyes while his wife nearly stomps away. "Sorry. She's protective of Isla who is like family to all of us. We'll get out your way and do takeout, it's safer for all of us." He begins to turn but pauses. "For what it's worth, I doubt Isla did this to be cruel or spiteful. That's just not her."

As he walks away, I do my best to take in their words, but that livid feeling of betrayal still lingers.

"See? Maybe you should put your feelings aside and hear her out, focus on the one thing that is important. Is it being angry at Isla or preparing for this little girl?" My brother is challenging me, getting my brain to rewire, that's what he is trying to do.

I sigh. "You're right. I should cool off a little more then go to see Isla."

The corners of his mouth twitch with a comforting look. "That right there is what real dads do."

A feeling of hope begins to creep inside of me near my chest. I can do this, the father thing. It's not what I have to do, it's what I *choose* to do.

"I'm doing this. I'm going to become a dad," I confirm before I blow out a breath in an attempt to chill the fuck out.

"I'm proud of you." He avoids getting too sentimental and holds up a menu. "Now, let's fuel you up."

It's a half-hour later when our food arrives, yet I only manage a few bites, instead opting for a coffee.

"Eat," my brother demands as he throws a fry into his mouth.

I take a bite of my egg salad sandwich to keep him at bay. "Sorry, my mind is still a little distracted."

"That's cool, I get it. As much as I don't want to get the wheels turning in your head again, but… could you see a future with Isla, not just as co-parents?"

Harsh. He's going for the deep questions to make my mind stir.

"I really can't say. We've only seen one another a handful of times, not talked much more than that, but somehow, I feel more linked than most." I'm being honest. As much as I felt a spark and connection with Isla, it's hard to determine what the future will bring when I've always been adamant that a future with someone wasn't for me at this moment in time.

"Do you want to find out?"

"Stone, right now, we just need to figure out the logistics of having a kid."

He takes a sip from his beer. "Right, babies need things and a roof over their head. Silly me for thinking a bowl of water and a ball would suffice."

I snort a laugh at his attempt to lighten the mood. But his mention of a roof gets me thinking about living arrangements. I vaguely remember Connor mentioning in the car that Isla has been searching for a new place; I can only imagine that she needs more space for the baby.

"Got it," I say confidently. "Isla is going to move in with me."

Yep, that's the answer for now. I may be slightly pissed still, but I'm not going to miss more moments of this pregnancy, and I'm sure as hell not missing the first weeks of a newborn.

My brother looks at me in doubt. "Surely, you need to ask her first."

"Nope. She doesn't have a choice in the matter," I say, adamant.

13

ISLA

I've barely slept, I lack coffee, and I'm doing my best to check the graphics for work, as I wanted to send a few more notes even though I'm on leave. The banana peel and crumbs on my dining room table from my toasted waffle are just a bonus in my life that is now in chaos.

The sound of the doorbell already has me dreading my wobble to the door. It's an array of options who could be on the other end, and I've done my best not to be hopeful that Vaughn would be so quick to talk.

When I reach the door and look out the side glass, I'm confused. The woman appears to be holding a sign, but she looks normal enough to avoid stranger danger.

I open the door. "Can I help you?"

The woman in her forties smiles brightly at me and seems awfully cheery. "Yes, I'm Katherine from the agency and just wanted to let you know that I'm setting up the sign now, so we should be getting some action quite soon."

"Sign?" My face must seem perplexed.

"Of course, you can't rent a house without the for-rent sign. It's an essential to get traffic to view this place."

Blinking my eyes a few times, I try to make sense of this. "Sorry, but did my landlord send you? She said she wasn't thinking of selling until next year. Did she change her timeline? Normally she's really good about talking to me directly. This is the worst possible time, right now." Now I'm internally freaking out because this is too much to add to my current state of life.

Her smile drops and she begins to look confused. "The landlord? Well, I'm here because the landlord called and said she wants to rent out this address since it will be vacated soon. The paperwork initiating the process was signed yesterday evening."

A skeptical laugh escapes me. "I assure you that I didn't hand in any notice to leave last night. Hell, I'm not even sure I left my bed last night. You must have the wrong address."

She grabs her phone from her big purse and immediately brings up a message that she quickly reads. "This most certainty is the correct place. Vaughn Madden wrote it down specifically in the email after speaking with the landlord on the phone who is down in New Mexico. He even got her to send over the paperwork via email."

"What?" My curt response has me nearly spinning.

Before she can answer, I notice a car pull up to the curb. A fancy rental, with a guy in the driver's seat that has a sharp jawline that I've enjoyed a time or two. We both watch Vaughn get out. I'm sure Katherine here is drooling and getting her panties in a twist. Vaughn is sporting a pair of jeans and a white t-shirt that is tight enough to see the outline of his muscles. His hair seems to have a little gel, as his wave is swept back, and I'm not quite sure what the small box is in his hands.

He instantly smiles a welcome to our real estate trespasser. "Hey, Katherine, you beat me here. You go on, do your thing, and keep me posted. Isla and I need to talk."

"Of course, I'll be quick, as I need to go take down a sign over on Duck Road," she greets him in passing.

I warily assess Vaughn, as I'm unsure what is happening or if I am still on planet earth. "Please explain." My sharp tone hopefully informs him that I'm not impressed.

Vaughn is unfazed by my direct tone and strides straight to me before touching my arm to guide me inside. I quickly look back to see a sign getting hammered into my lawn.

That isn't the kind of hammering I enjoy.

Vaughn kicks the door closed behind us, and I break free from his touch. "You're leaving your house and moving in with me." His tone is dismissive as we face one another.

I ogle my eyes at him as an electric shock seems to hit me. No words can express this bombshell demand, because he isn't asking, he's ordering me.

He hands me the box with a fake sweet smile. "Here."

Examining the box, I'm torn between backtracking on what he just said or being happy. "I assure you, ice cream sandwiches are not going to solve this conversation." That's the road I choose; serious discussion.

His smug appearance has me worried. "Oh, you're right on that, sweetheart." The way he says sweetheart isn't an endearing term, it's a warning. "You kept the single most important news of my life from me, and I have every intention of rectifying that little judgement error, and you may or may not like what I have in store for you."

My body straightens and again that swirl of confusion is on full flight through my body. A concern for what his decision may be, but damn, his word choice makes me hot and very bothered. I may be pregnant, but I'm ready to pounce on a little anger sex.

My glare is hopefully burning a hole through him; however, we have to put this aside. I indicate the sofa, and he nods once before going to sit down. I follow, holding the box of ice cream tightly, because despite what I said, I may need one to calm me down.

We get comfortable, and I'm waiting for him to begin. Not going to lie, I feel as though I deserve a lecture.

His head rolls to the side to look at me. "Here's the deal, Isla. I've already missed enough thanks to your doing. I'm not going to miss any more, especially if the baby will be here before we know it.

I heard you were looking for a new place to live, and I just so happen to have a house that I bought on a whim. Solution found." His firm voice is far too cocky for me right now.

My face must be turning red due to irritation. "I'm sorry, okay? I should have told you no matter what. I've thought about it every day, trying to push my fears to the side. But you can't just contact my landlord without asking. How do you even do that?" My voice cracks, because really? How *do you* do that?

"Connections, and a promise of a financial bonus on her part. I'm fairly confident you will sign what needs to be signed to make sure you vacate like the good little tenant I'm sure you are." His piercing gaze is chipping away inside of me.

"Vaughn, okay, I *have* been looking at houses because I will need more space. It's not that I can't afford a slightly bigger house to buy or with higher rent, it's simply there isn't much on the market here. People tend to rent out their three-bedroom homes for weekend and summer rentals," I explain, as I don't want him to get any ideas that I need to be saved. "Besides, I can make it work here for a bit, as the baby will sleep in my room the first few months."

He holds a finger up as if he is going to correct me. "No, the baby can sleep in her own room in *my* house where space isn't an issue."

I grumble a sound before opening the box of ice cream, not caring that it's all going to melt. Ripping open a wrapper, I stuff a bite into my mouth. "I get the memo. You want to make me move as punishment, but just throwing a sign in my yard is a step too far and far too permanent," I say with a full mouth as I chew, then I point at him with my free hand. "You know, before the baby news, I was a fun and spontaneous woman who would spend a night with hot hockey players," I begin my tangent.

"Players, plural?" he cuts in.

"Fine. You. Actually, you're the only hockey player. I've never done that before, but I am a spontaneous and fun woman. It's just when I found out I was pregnant that full-on mother bear mode kicked in. Roar." I pretend to claw him with my hand not even in fun, I've gone psychotic.

His brows arch, and his face is dead serious. "Did you just roar and try to claw me like a bear?"

I blink my eyes a few times, realizing how crazy I am acting.

His head cocks gently to the side. "Now, let's stay focused. I wouldn't say demanding you and my daughter live in my house is punishment, as you say, but it means you don't have a choice but to rely on me and my place to stay, no fucking escape. Our daughter deserves to have both her parents around her. Isn't bonding crucial the first few months? Then we can figure it out."

My head perks, and I slow down chewing my mouthful. He said *our* daughter. He isn't running away. I need to retrace my thoughts a second and break down the information that he's throwing at me through dominant demands. "Wait, you made your decision... about being involved."

Vaughn takes the ice cream sandwich out of my hand and flops it on top of the box that's now on the coffee table. Apparently, he needs me focused. "Didn't you get that clue with the whole 'you will move in with me' thing? Yeah... I'm involved." His voice is pure reverence, delicate, but in the best possible way.

I lift a shoulder. "That probably... was an obvious clue."

His nostrils flare slightly as he inhales deeply. "Isla, I'm not going to lie. Timing? Uhm, not great." His face is near cartoonish. "Although it's off-season for hockey players, it isn't really for me, and I have a lot to do to prepare for next season, especially with the draft approaching. Which is why I need you at my home, ready whenever I need."

"Ready?" I gulp.

Holy fuck, something inside of me is clinging to logic for survival while I feel a pool of wetness between my legs. I subtly shift my gaze down to double-check that he won't notice that my nipples are now tight and hard, nor hidden thanks to flimsy fabric.

His tongue darts to the corner of his mouth while his eyes stay glued to me. "I mean it's easier on my schedule. I will be traveling with the team, so I don't want to be puzzling with our calendars. When I get back from a late flight, then I better be able to simply walk in to see my daughter."

"Our daughter," I correct him, but I stay mesmerized by first the image that was in my head, followed by the emotions soaring up through my body, because as prevailing as his request is, it's because… he's invested in the baby.

The fear I had is fading away bit by bit.

"Our daughter," he repeats. "I get the keys for my place tomorrow since it was an all-cash offer and the former owners were already out. I have movers ready to pack up what you need, I have all the furniture… wait, except the baby furniture." He's making a mental note that he forgot something.

This is another side of Vaughn. I'm still in a trance.

"I really don't have a choice in this matter and guilt is taking over. Plus, I really need to nest for the baby. I was waiting for my baby shower next week to get everything in order. We were supposed to have it a few weeks ago but had to postpone due to a lot of us out with the flu," I point out blankly.

Vaughn pinches the bridge of his nose. "I'm not entirely sure what a baby shower entails, but fine. Look, we focus on the baby, but damn, Isla…" His look is now stern. "I didn't sleep, I'm still numb, and you really fucking hurt me by keeping this all a secret."

"Crap, oh no, we keep using bad word choices, and the baby can hear us."

"Really? We're still on that?" His tone is mundane.

He's right, it's silly. I comb my fingers through my hair. "I can say sorry a thousand times. I was scared, and every time it just didn't seem the right moment."

His look isn't changing, he's not impressed. "My cock inside of you while you were bouncing on my dick in my car didn't seem like the right moment? We could be as intimate as can be, yet you couldn't share the news?" he dryly highlights the replay of events.

Taking relaxing breaths, I remind myself to keep my debate from boiling up. My hands begin to rub my belly as I think of the best way to move on from this topic.

"Look, as much as I am ready to do this all on my own if needed, I still feared you wouldn't want to be involved. I'm sorry. It is what it is." I swim my eyes away from him because I can't handle seeing the disappointment on his face.

It takes a few seconds before he responds. "Like I said, that issue still needs to simmer down inside of me. We should just focus on the baby."

"I agree."

A butterfly feeling flutters underneath my ribs before a hard nudge hits me from within. It causes me to smile, as it has done every single time.

"What's wrong?" Vaughn moves to touch me, with panic appearing in his posture.

"Relax, she must be awake now and is just letting me know. Or it was the sugar kick from the ice cream." I keep my hand steady on my belly to feel her shuffling her little feet inside of me.

Vaughn seems unsure what to do.

Without thought, I grab his hand and bring it to the spot where he will feel her. "That little jab against your hand is her kicking. They say it will slow down once she is ready to rumble in her life outside of the womb. Her space is getting limited, so it restricts her from moving the way she did a few weeks ago."

The warmest of smiles begins to stretch on his mouth. "Wow, she has strength."

"Tell me about it. When she decides to kick me in the ribs at two in the morning, I'm wondering if she's trying to escape already."

I close my eyes for a moment and take in the fact that Vaughn's hand is firmly planted against my body to feel the baby we created. Something about this feels promising… and special.

"Does it hurt?" he asks while he stares at my stomach to see the little pops of a foot from inside of me.

"Nah, it's more of an ow that's quick and just makes you laugh."

"I guess we have to think of a name other than baby or she," he mentions.

Is this happening? Is Vaughn Madden really sitting next to me, touching my body and promising he will be involved?

I hate how buried emotions that aren't even his doing prevent me from fully believing him, but everything from the last few minutes gives me a little hope.

"A name, packing her hospital bag, installing the car seat, and ensuring the baby stroller is ready are all on my list. I have some stuff stored in my spare room."

Vaughn can't tear his eyes away from the spot where she kicked, even though she has stopped moving for a solid minute.

"Wow… so this is really happening." He blows out another breath.

"You said the hurricane was nothing to worry about; turns out that it was way more than that." I point to my stomach while his hand moves away to rake through his hair.

The corners of his mouth twist. "Guess so."

We stare at one another in an intense way that's filled with a lingering attraction, maybe even heightened because anger and fear tend to fuel it even more.

Vaughn clears his throat before he stands. "I need to head to the training arena."

"Sure. I'm just doing a few things on my laptop today."

"Good, you should take it easy. I guess I'll need to keep an eye on you."

My eyes bug out as I stand. "Vaughn, I'm an independent woman who won't tolerate a possessive man." It comes out a little too bouncy, and in truth, I kind of like it.

He chortles a sound before his smirk returns. "I beg to differ. You will absolutely tolerate it. You don't have a choice. I mean it, Isla. I'm not going to play a game. My mind is clear that I'm a little wounded from the secret you kept, but I'm choosing to focus on what matters. You're carrying our baby, and that's what matters right now."

I nod gently and roll my lips in response.

His eyes draw a line up and down my body for a once-over before he begins to walk away. "It's also fucking annoying that even in this situation, this attraction around us doesn't seem to fade."

A sly smile hits me. "Tell me about it," I respond softly in the same casual tone he used.

"Within three days you better be in my house," he calls out without throwing me a glance.

When he leaves, he is like the breeze that blows through a house on a summer day; chilly at first but then a welcome relief.

Let's just hope it stays that way.

14

ISLA

What in the world am I doing?

I keep thinking it to myself as I carefully rummage through the box for lighter items to take out and set in the room that most likely will be the nursery in Vaughn's beautiful modern home. It's on the side of the lake that gets great morning sun.

Fortunately, he is in his home office for a video call with a scout who is currently in Sweden. I'm kind of grateful that the last few days he has been very busy. Meeting after meeting and strategy planning, which is why we haven't spoken much. Instead, he sent me the time of when the movers would arrive. In truth, from what I have seen from afar, he seems content with his new role and maybe dare I say more relaxed than he was during his last season of playing hockey… Then he looks at me and a shade of indescribable mixed feelings hits him.

Since the movers placed my stuff upstairs, I've been wondering how this situation will all play out. I can't think clearly as my brain goes in multiple directions.

When my phone rings on the side table by the bed, I wobble over to answer because the screen flashes Briggs's name.

"I'm outside. Let me in." His curt tone has me huff a sound because I know what is about to come.

I've been lucky that Hadley and Connor have kept my brother at bay, telling him that he should give me some space and time. That was only going to last so long. "Okay," I answer and pull up the app that Vaughn sent to me for the front gate and the house door.

I manage to walk down the stairs, recognizing that I'm a tad slower than I was even a week ago.

Opening the door, I'm greeted by my brother who charges in and instantly searches the area, probably for Vaughn.

"He isn't within earshot," I inform him.

"Fine," he grits out. "I came to talk to you anyhow."

I lead him to the living room, and we each find a spot on opposite ends of the sofa.

"Get on with it." I must sound unenthused.

"What the hell, Isla? He waltzes back into town, and you just go along with moving in with him?"

I hold my hand up as if it could be an attempt to calm him. "Trust me, this wasn't part of the plan, but he makes a point. He is the dad, and when the baby comes, then he has a right to be involved, and logistically, this probably makes sense as I can't just hand over this little girl on a schedule the first few weeks, especially if I breastfeed. It was never my intention to keep him from the baby, it was only I struggled to *tell* him."

Briggs rubs his eyes as he takes in my explanation. "Not going to lie. This feels like a bit of a betrayal that of all the people you choose to hook up with… it had to be him. But this is the situation we're in."

"No, this is the situation that *I'm* in. I kind of put myself here too," I clarify.

"Admittedly, I'm relieved to hear that he didn't know and hadn't abandoned you. That is the only little speck of compassion that I'm going to give him. What happens now?"

My shoulders slacken a bit. "Truthfully, I don't know. It's kind of hard to focus when all I can think about is the fact that she can come any day now, and I have nothing ready because I wanted to wait until I knew this would be a healthy pregnancy just in case."

"That makes sense. I'm trying to wrap my head around how to handle being in the same room when that asshole is around," he nearly snarls and looks around the room to take in the décor which is quite basic yet chic, with a few boxes of baby furniture in the corner that just arrived.

It causes me to smile because I'm entertained. "Briggs." He doesn't look at me. "Briggsy Chase," I try again. "Look at me." He obeys like a child who needs to be explained why they're in timeout. "You have to find a way. He will be around. Maybe, just, I dunno, focus on your niece when you're stuck in the same room for personal gatherings. For hockey, I don't know what you'll do."

Guilt seems to hit him, and his silence plus my sibling intuition causes me to realize that there is more.

"I need to tell you something," he starts, and it doesn't feel great. "There is a rather large chance that I won't be signing with the Spinners for next season. I'll sign with another team, perhaps out in Seattle. The paperwork hasn't been completed yet, but I've been thinking about this since before Vaughn entered the picture."

"What?" I screech.

"I didn't tell you yet because I didn't want to upset you."

My throat tightens as a cry builds. "You're going to leave? You're my only family here."

He slides down the sofa to be closer to me and touches my shoulder in an attempt to comfort me. "First off, I'm keeping my house here, so every off-season, I'm here. And I'm not your only family here. Just look at everyone who is throwing you a baby shower this weekend. They love you as their own."

Tears fall. "B-but you're my brother," I stutter.

He offers me a warm smile. "You always knew this was a chance, and I'm ready for a change. I wouldn't be much use helping you with my niece in a few months since I'll be on the road. But next summer? I'm all here. Isla, you're growing your own family, whether that's alone or with..." He groans. "I can't even say his name."

"Vaughn." A firm voice causes our heads to shift to the opening between the step that leads to the living room and the open hall.

I roll my eyes, wondering what is about to transpire between my brother and the father of my baby.

"If you're going to be in my house then you can say my name," Vaughn adds.

Briggs stands. "Great, you're here. Was hoping I could avoid you, but since you're gracing us with your presence, then let's have it out."

"Geez, this isn't some battle of honor, Briggs. Please, for the sake of the heavily pregnant lady here." I hold up my hand. "Can we just calm it down a notch?"

"She's right." Vaughn steps down to be on our level. "So, what is it you want to say to me?"

"F-you." He's direct.

"Try harder," I mutter to my brother.

Briggs's jaw tenses. "Fine. My sister deserves the world, so don't be an idiot. Whether I stay in Lake Spark or not, you best believe I will be getting the full report on how you treat her and my niece. To be honest, congratulations, because having you now be the GM just makes me more eager to sign elsewhere."

"I'm not talking hockey right now with you, so let's keep the topic on Isla."

"Then answer me," Briggs volleys back.

Vaughn's piercing gaze remains on Briggs. "You have my word. Now, if we can save the lecture for another day when I actually have patience for you, then I'm sure you can find your way out without the door hitting you in the ass. I need to chat with your sister."

I stretch both of my arms out to my sides. "Both of you chill and accept that you eventually need to find neutral ground. I can't deal with this every single time."

They both glance at me then adjust their shoulders, as if they're both struggling to accept my request but will go with it.

"Fine." Briggs goes first, and I'm having a hard time believing him, but I'm choosing my battles today.

"Also fine," Vaughn adds.

I sigh in relief and stand up. "Great, let's move on."

"Sure, I'm out of here anyway. I'll text you later, Isla," my brother informs me before I nod in understanding.

He throws Vaughn one more steely glare in parting.

The moment that Briggs is out of the house, the tension in the air deflates and turns to a new kind of tension, the unknown abyss that I'm heading down with Vaughn.

Vaughn has one hand tucked into his jeans pocket and he scrubs the other across his jaw as his eyes draw a line up my body to my nervous smile.

"Settling in?" he asks.

I salute him and give a coy smile. "Yes, master."

His lips form a contrite smile. "Charming."

I turn serious. "Yeah, I am."

He indicates the boxes with a nod. "I'll have someone come to construct this stuff, just tell them where to put it."

"Oh, you don't want to have a say where it goes in the room?"

He seems kind of exhausted. "I don't care nor have the time."

"Okay, then can you have someone come to paint the walls gray?"

Lines knit together on his forehead. "Gray? That's your choice for the baby's room?"

I walk a few steps to him. "Yeah, I don't want to do pink, and gray is neutral." I continue my walk to my purse on the stool of the open kitchen and pull out samples to show him. "I think North Rain Gray is a better choice to Cloud Gray, so North Rain Gray it is."

"Cloud Gray," he counters, and it feels like he is doing it on purpose.

"You don't care," I say, calling him out on his attempt.

"Cloud Gray," he repeats.

I drop the paint samples, now aggravated. "Is this your way of saying you're still pissed at me? Because I'm positive that debating shades of gray isn't going to solve it."

Vaughn's lips roll in. "You're right… North Rain Gray it is."

"So accommodating," I say, my tone frivolous.

I begin to walk past him, but he reaches out to touch my elbow and my feet become stuck to the ground, unwilling to leave, because he has me invested in what comes next.

"I'll calm down eventually." He means it, I can tell.

"Enough to stop by the baby shower?" Maybe I sound hopeful, and I'm not sure why, considering he wasn't even in the picture a few days ago.

Now a half-smile appears, lighting the air between us. "Guys go to those?"

My shoulder rolls back. "Not particularly. I mean, some baby showers have the guys there, and they do ridiculous little games. Not this one, it's more a ladies' high tea. But the dad… normally stops by."

"I, uh, I'll see."

"Right, of course." I swallow my disappointment. Suddenly, it feels like we're not taking any steps. Besides, I was going to go to this party before he ever found out anyhow.

I begin to move again, but his hand is glued to me. "Isla…" It seems he has something profound to say. "Do you have any names in mind?" It feels like a cop out, but fine, I'll run with it.

"No, I'm struggling with that part," I admit.

"I can imagine. She'll take my last name?" His voice sounds elusive.

"Oh, I didn't really think about that yet." I'm truthful, as I just assumed she would have mine, but now that he's in the picture, I'm not sure.

"She should have it." He nods once then lets my arm go.

Feeling as though this is my opportunity for an exit, I walk away until I stop and spin on my heel. I notice that his eyes are still on me, filled with a blaze that isn't anger as his finger traces his jawline.

"Vaughn, I really am sorry," I repeat for what feels like the hundredth time.

His head tips lower before striking back up. "I think if we have any chance to make it the next few months and to raise this baby together, then you need to stop saying sorry. Eventually, I'll understand."

I appreciate that so much that a wry smile creates a line on my mouth.

"I'll send you the baby shower details."

"I'm not sure if I'll come, but maybe."

Inside something hurts a little. I recognize that it's that fear again, that he won't be fully invested in our daughter's life.

"Fine." I charge off, needing to go lock myself in my bedroom, wishing that it was his, because all is well, not only for our baby… but us.

15

VAUGHN

Staring down at the tablet in the training arena's boardroom, I'm looking over stats for the list of players that we'll hopefully manage to get in the upcoming draft next week. I'm changing windows on the screen as I compare one sheet to the other, which are contract negotiations. As much as I enjoy seeing Briggs with the other names that will probably leave, I also feel slight remorse for having that feeling. He is a great player and Isla's brother, so I better get on that bandwagon. However, I know if he goes to another team that Isla will probably be devastated.

I don't particularly want her upset, which is why I feel like a bit of a jerk lately that I've been distant and sometimes cold then warm. As much as the secret she kept is a hole somewhere within, I was right when I told her that she needs to stop apologizing if we have any hope of focusing on the future.

The future.

The one I have no clue what it will hold for us.

I've ignored every time it flashes in my mind that eventually we will need to confront the issue of us, but then it blows out of mind just as fast.

I glance to one of the guys from the management team to see that everyone is busy at work with various tasks. At least one thing is clear and it's that this career move was right, near exhilarating.

"I'll be back, just going to check in with the admin staff about travel next week," I say.

Someone in the group gives me an okay.

Sliding out of my chair, I head into the hall where I stroll until I turn a corner and instantly nearly run into Isla.

"Oh, hey, forgot you were here," she says, looking up from her phone. "Didn't see you this morning."

I've been avoiding her slightly at home, it's better that way. She was always beautiful, but right now? She's glowing, and she has my baby in her belly which just shoots the appeal to the sky.

Then it hits me. She works here, not for the team but for the facility and their training programs. And she's working today.

"Why are you here?" It comes out a little short.

"Oh, hello to you too." She's already exhausted of me.

Reaching out, I touch her arm then rub up and down. I can't not touch her. We may not be together, but I have the best claim possible.

"I mean, you should be at home resting, not here," I clarify.

Isla scoffs and her eyes widen slightly. "I'm pregnant, not incompetent. Plus, even though I'm on maternity leave, technically by law I can work until this baby arrives."

I smile tightly, a wave of protectiveness hitting me in full force. "I think not. Money isn't an issue, and you really *should* be resting. Not here."

"I enjoy my projects and want to ensure a smooth handover." She's clearly offended.

I roll my lips in to tame my temper. "That's great." Sarcasm sinks those words down. "However, as long as I can keep an eye on you while you're under my roof, then there is no escape. In a few days, I fly to Nashville for the draft picks, and then I can't ensure that you're taking it easy."

Her tongue hits her inner cheek, and it seems that she's in a similar mood and suppressing her anger. "Vaughn, as much as this alpha male behavior would be sexy in normal non-accidental-pregnancy circumstances, I can't handle this right now. You're stressing me out more than work, where I get to use fancy highlighters to write notes."

I clench my one hand, hoping it will keep me calm, reminding myself to get over my ego for a hot minute. "Okay… fair enough."

Her free hand comes to her hip, but she can barely tip her hip out because, well, she's heavily pregnant, and that area kind of merges together in a way that seems healthy and cute.

"You know, we can't keep avoiding one another considering we live together, but I get it. This is the worst time for this…" she points up and down her body, "to transpire. So, I'm letting you off the hook, as I know you want to start your job on the best possible foot. That doesn't mean that I'm enjoying this ride."

Fuck me, I was right. I'm being an ass.

She sighs one more exhausted breath. "I'll take it easy because I want to take it easy. It's not due to your demands." Isla walks past me, and I'm tempted to say something, yet I'm not sure what.

Isla beats me to the punch anyhow when she stops and turns slightly to glimpse over her shoulder at me. "Vaughn."

"Yeah?"

Her face softens and a half-smile appears on her mouth. "Thanks for leaving the new box of ice cream sandwiches in the freezer." Then she walks away.

Yup, I'm the king of unresolved feelings and actions.

My subtle act was because I have a sentimental spot for Isla. I can't deny that I've felt that way since the moment I saw her.

————

GETTING HOME LATE, I scrub my face, trying to wipe the tiredness from my eyes. It was a solid fourteen-hour day, and it will be that way again tomorrow. The house is dark, and I make my way up the stairs. Noticing the door to the nursery open, I decide to peek in, because somehow the reminder of a child entering my life feels calming in this moment, which is odd, as I was freaking out only a few days ago.

The moment that I open the slightly ajar door to the dark room, I notice Isla right away. She's leaning against the window wearing a long tight cotton nightgown, with her head resting against the glass as she cradles her stomach, completely unaware that I'm here, or maybe she is aware but chooses not to spare me a glance. The moonlight is bright tonight, which only makes this scene extra poignant. I'm tempted to take my phone out to capture a photo, but it would probably cause her to turn, and I want to soak in this scene a little longer.

I get those few seconds, and as much as I want to leave her in peace, I can't. And she seems to know that too.

"Thinking of running away?" she asks before her head turns in my direction, with her mouth sliding to the side.

I laugh under my breath and step farther into the room. "So you did notice that I'm here."

"Yeah, but I was waiting to see what you would do."

I saunter in her direction, my eyes circling the nearly complete nursery. I'm relieved that I'm in a position where I can hire people to handle this. If I had time I would do it myself, but time is sparce.

"You looked at peace, and I'm not sure how much I would ruin that." I join her at the window and lean against the edge. "Why are you not sleeping?"

"I'm restless. They say it happens as it gets more uncomfortable."

I nod in understanding. "I can imagine."

It happens yet again; our eyes get lost in one another as we take a few beats to stare.

"I'm sorry."

Her brows raise, as she seems confused. "For what?"

"I've been… well, a lot of things lately."

She hums a sound. "As much as it's whiplash, I… understand. I don't get points for doing what I did, and forgiveness isn't always fast."

Forgiveness, huh. I've just been on a train forward, focusing on this kid.

My thoughts float, and I glance to the side and stare at the crib for a hot second, then I return my gaze to Isla. "I've never been so scared in my life."

It causes her to smile. "Trust me, I can relate."

"What if, as much as I want to get it right, I just don't? The last thing I want is to be like my own father." I realize that speaking honestly with her is more of a relief than I expected.

"Sounds like we have the same fear. The last thing I ever want is for either of us to fail at this parenting thing. I want to do better than my parents, by far better. Be everything that they weren't."

Her hands stroke her belly, causing my sight to cascade down her body to land on the vision of the connection we will now forever share. "That's what I want too. Doesn't mean the anxiety vanishes."

Isla bites the corner of her lip. "Vaughn, let's just promise that we'll try our damnedest for this little girl. The parenting thing, I mean."

"I can do that."

"All I've ever wanted is to have more family, and this is my chance. Probably yours too."

I begin to smile from affection. "You seem to have become a mind reader."

"It's kind of obvious where our heads would go, considering our upbringing. Keeping it in just makes it hurt more. Saying it out loud is far too real." She doesn't blink.

Touching her arm first to comfort her, I quickly bring my hand to her navel, taking peace from this kid that somehow is the abundance of both hope and fear. Isla brings her palm over my hand. As much as this moment should be about our daughter, I can't help but enjoy Isla's touch. It makes my thoughts go haywire, because there are no warnings shooting through me, and there probably should be.

"I wish I didn't have to go away to Nashville for a few days next week, but if there is anything you need, then you'll call?"

She nods. "Of course."

I can't tear my eyes away from our binding life, yet I don't dare voice the question buzzing in my head. What about us? Partly since I don't have an answer for her. My view on relationships was thrown upside down the moment I found out I'm going to be a dad. But my attraction and wanting for her has been there from the moment we spoke about cheese all those months ago.

Easy seems to be the only solution right now. "Need anything?"

"No, it's okay. I'll just attempt to sleep again and think about what I'll wear this weekend for the baby shower." Her chin tips up, and it's obvious she's searching for an answer about whether I'll be there.

I should tell her that it's a no-brainer, but it's also a commitment. Those tend to make me indecisive.

"You mentioned."

That wasn't what she was hoping I would say. "Right, well, I should go to sleep. Night, Vaughn."

"Night," I say before she meanders out of the room.

I'm alone and look around, knowing I need to do so much better, while I admire the dreamcatcher hanging on the wall by the crib.

A moment later, I walk down the hall to my room, and Isla's door is partly open. Maybe she did that on purpose to tempt me. Either way, I watch from afar as she adjusts her body in her bed. Lying on her side, with one leg wrapping around her pregnancy pillow and her head getting comfortable on a normal pillow.

So fucking beautiful.

I realize something; she understands me on so many levels. That, mixed with a magnetism that is underlying, causes me to realize that for the first time, if I ever had a shot at something extraordinary, then maybe, just maybe, it's with her.

I just need to figure out what to do about it.

16

ISLA

Laughing, I can't help but inspect what I just unwrapped.

"This is a little… I don't know… What is it?" I look at Hadley's mom April, perplexed.

We're all sitting in a circle at Violet's house for my baby shower. She had her baby a few months ago, so it was the easiest solution of locations. The pink decorations are gorgeous, the games we played ridiculous, and of course, Hadley's mom went overboard with snacks. Also, presents…

"It's a unicorn outfit." She seems proud of her choice and starts pointing to various aspects of the clothing. "See? The little horn on the hood." I laugh again. "She'll be like a burrito wrapped up but with a special hat. Perfect for Halloween."

"That I can see, thank you." It's a cute gesture. I search for the next item from the pile of gifts. My head indicates the giant diaper cake in the corner. "Thank you, everyone, but it seems like a lot of diapers for the first few weeks, will I really need them?"

The moms in the group say *yes* in unison.

I'm not going to argue with their perspective that they calculated right. I hold my hands up. "Okay, okay. Forget I asked."

An abundance of unwrapped presents are around me, still with another pile to go. Not only do I have the usual ladies from my circle of friends who are the next best thing to family, but also a few colleagues, and of course, Ivy, my brother's girlfriend.

Hadley claps her hands. "Okay, everyone, let's take a little break before we continue to the big round."

"Great idea, I need to pee. This kiddo has been pressing against my bladder all day," I say as I stand.

By the time I'm done in the bathroom, I come out to find Hadley carrying a bag of ripped wrapping paper to the garage in one hand. "Surviving?" She grins.

"This is really a special day, thank you."

She waves me off. "It's the least I can do. You were my maid of honor, and I'm not having a kid anytime soon, so it keeps the ladies in there occupied." Hadley throws her thumb over her shoulder.

"They are *really* into this."

Hadley studies me, maybe trying to read me. I'm familiar enough to know that she is about to ask a question that I might not appreciate. "Um, should I bring up the topic?" Her face screws into a cautionary look.

I take a second. "You mean Vaughn?"

"Yeah." I hate her sympathy in trying to comfort me with her hand on my wrist.

"I invited him. If he doesn't want to come, then that's his choice."

Hadley takes a moment. "But you do want him here, right?"

I shrug my shoulders. "I do. Doesn't mean it will happen."

"What's going on between you two?"

"Nothing. Just focusing on this baby, and he's been busy with work. Not to mention, I think it's going to be a long time until he forgives me."

"So, no discussion of…" She's struggling to beat around the bush.

I shake my head. "Is there something to discuss? We are two people who gave into lust a few times."

A short laugh comes out of her mouth. "You had sex with him three times because you can't keep your hands off of one another."

"Two times. At Christmas, I was completely well-behaved, thank you very much… Besides, hurricane us were kind of at it more than once, so I'm not sure your numbers correlate." I sound far more serious than I should as I bring my arms to cross over my chest.

She tries to keep her loud laugh in but fails miserably. "I think you probably need to investigate *that*—" she circles her hand as if she is outlining a circle "—situation a little more. See if it is really just lust or a chance for something else."

I chortle a sound. "Not sure now is the time for it. Besides, I…" I lean in to ensure nobody can hear. "I'm not sure if I want to get my hopes up or if I'm already there and know I *shouldn't* get my hopes up." I stand taller. "Plus, he's been a little too possessive and broody lately. Not exactly getting points from me… Okay, it's kind of hot. But I mean, he doesn't even show up to my baby shower. Surely, a smart man would have figured out that my invite was because this means a lot to me. But no, Vaughn enjoys keeping everything in limbo, as if it's some game with my very hormonal emotions." I'm completely riled right now.

Hadley quirks her lips out, just listening, however, something feels like she won't respond to me as a sly smirk forms on her lips, her sightline over my shoulder.

The clearing of a throat instantly draws my attention behind me.

Oh shit.

Hadley doesn't say anything, because Vaughn will.

He throws me a tiny little wave. "The guy who is playing a game with your emotions is here."

My sight whips back to Hadley who smiles tightly. "Think that's my cue to leave you two alone." She walks on and spurts out a laugh.

Vaughn only steps closer. "Sorry I'm late."

I can imagine that my face must looked flushed. "Uhm… how much of that did you hear?" I ask awkwardly.

He smirks as he leans against the wall with his arm against it, and he crosses his ankles. My impression is that he enjoys making me squirm. "Enough."

I gulp and laugh nervously. "Sorry. I'm a little emotional today."

"I'll let it go. It seems like quite a spread in there." Great, he's changing the topic.

"They all went overboard, it's really sweet. Declan and Connor are in the mancave somewhere in this house… if you need an escape."

"I just got here," he states, matter of fact. "And I know. They warned me to avoid baby games like the plague, so here I am, hopefully saved from measuring your belly, although…" His head slants to the side. "Could be kind of interesting."

A smile curves on my lips. "Good choice of timing then. I still have another round of presents… the big ones. We will be needing two cars to get it all back to your house, for sure."

"You mean our house."

A sound of doubt hits my lips. "Is it, though? I'm pretty sure you dragged me there without my choice of humble abodes, and if it weren't for the fact that I'm going to be a kickass mom, then you would lock me in a tower."

He laughs. "Lock you in a tower? Nah, I'd lock you to my bed." It escapes him, and the moment he realizes, his jaw flexes.

We're flirting.

It seems we still have it in us.

Still, my eyes blaze slightly from the surprising choice of words. "I'm sure…" I try to stay calm while a painful feeling hits that nub between my legs, the kind of pain only he can relieve—or my hand, but Vaughn is so much better. "It would be an adventure." It's nearly a rasp.

His smirk pulls a tiny bit, drawing my attention to his lips.

But then he grumbles a sound, bringing us back to the present for our little offtrack distracting talk. "So, what am I supposed to do?" He straightens his posture, and his hand finds my arm. "Not that I'm not interested, it's just I really have no clue."

I giggle. "It's more that your appearance is a thank-you for all the gifts, and you sit with us for a little bit, preparing for a lot of *ahhs* and cooing. I actually have sympathy for you right now, because it's going to be a little much. Hopefully, they tame down their labor stories in your presence. They also all love to give unsolicited advice, but luckily, in a kind way. They just want to help. I'm so grateful for it."

A gleam appears to glaze his eyes. "I'm happy that you have everyone in there."

"I'm lucky. And it is great. It's just that it's… not biological, ya know?"

His head tips low. "I get it."

"Yeah… you do." An unsaid realization floats between us, an understanding. "Now come on, get ready to be sucked into an atmosphere of sickly-sweet goodness."

"Ready as ever."

Vaughn follows me, and I don't even realize until I feel a sizzle run along my spine that it causes me to glance down to see our hands holding. I'm not sure who initiated it or if it's just a natural magnetic need between us.

I like our hands interlaced, it's the type of support that needs no words. A signal that you've got one another's back. But it's also an act that only normally happens between someone holding a child's hand or between two people who are in a relationship or on their road to that.

I don't let the thought overtake me, and I can't even if I tried, because soon we are ushered by someone into the room which must feel like a pit of doom for Vaughn, but his smile seems the opposite. He must be acting polite.

The appearance of Connor and Declan in the back holding up a beer in support is also a solid vote of confidence for team Vaughn.

We sit down next to one another back in the circle and someone hands over a big box. Vaughn instantly holds it since my belly is in the way.

"Wow, this seems bigger than my body," I note as I begin to rip the paper.

A box with what seems like a highchair is soon revealed.

Violet pipes up. "It is Scandinavian design, has a few inserts so even the newborn can be table height when you're eating dinner, plus it grows with the child to the point that you can even use it as an adult as a normal stool." She claps her hands together. "We all got it for you."

I scan the circle, feeling emotions swell in me and a pool of water forming at the bottom of my eyes. Vaughn seems to notice, and his arm snakes around me to pull me into a side hug, and he speaks up. "It's just what we need, thank you. Right, Isla?" Thank goodness he can read me like a book.

"Yeah, it's… perfect. Wouldn't have thought of it," I add.

The next few gifts are far too generous. A bouncy chair, a travel cot, a few cute little onesies.

"Okay, open this one. It's the last one." Hadley hands me a bag with tissue paper, and my eyes go round with curiosity at Vaughn, who just returns the gesture.

"Hmm, I wonder what this could be." I begin to pull out the paper. When my hand dips in, I feel only softness, yarn maybe. The moment that I pull out the blanket, I'm done. Tears fall from happiness. "Oh my."

"The moms and I attempted to knit a baby blanket together. It's the most colorful, mismatched, badly knitted blanket in the history of baby blankets. We even tried to have Piper, who owns the boutique, fix it, and she said it was a lost cause. But it's still a blanket, and it's warm." She's proud with a goofy grin.

I laugh. "I-it's the best blanket," I stammer out. "So incredibly sweet. The baby will love it."

"Really?" Her face goes lopsided. "It's a weird purple mixed with a mustard yellow then gray and pink. Not even sure what the other color is." She points to a square.

"Totally sure," I swear.

"We can stich on her name once you know. Do you have any ideas?"

Vaughn and I look at one another. "Not yet," he mentions. We can add names to the list of things that we really need to discuss, but now we are showered in complete kindness.

"Good plan, see the baby first," one of my colleagues says.

"I'm sure she'll have your eyes," Vaughn nearly whispers so only I can hear.

God, why am I melting around him today. Hell, it's not even just today. It was the moment he walked back into my life.

I'm saved by Brielle, Connor's mom, announcing that we have one more surprise, and she points to the kitchen where I think Connor and Declan got roped into helping.

We all migrate over to the kitchen island, with Vaughn being instructed to cover my eyes with his hands. This isn't helping my current predicament. He covered my eyes once, with a blindfold, somewhere between taking me doggy style and missionary during a storm.

Alas, I'm unable to relive my memory because he laughs right before his hands fall away from my eyes, and instantly a wide grin hits me.

"Best baby shower ever, right?" Hadley is getting a little cocky, but she's right.

Before me lie plates of all types of cookies. Followed by chocolate chips, pink sprinkles, mini marshmallows, and anything you might want to cover the ice cream that will stuff your make-your-own ice cream sandwich.

I grip Vaughn's arm tightly because I'm not sure I can stand any more, because this feeling of gratitude is too much.

"Thank you," is all I manage to say. "Yeah… best baby shower ever."

———

THE REST of the afternoon was just spent relaxing on the sofa and snacking while Vaughn spoke with the guys and drank a beer. Occasionally our eyes would catch, and a subtle smile would form between us.

Now, we're home. It feels weird saying that but also right.

Vaughn brought all the gifts up to the nursery, and I'm now sorting through it all to find newborn clothing that needs to be washed.

"They certainly covered everything," he comments while he stuffs diapers in a drawer, even studying a few because I can imagine that he has never changed one.

I focus on my task. "It's wonderful, isn't it?"

"It is. They even sent us home with a cheese plate, what are the odds?"

I chuckle. "Does it have the Dutch cheese that's hard and sharp?"

A bashful look falls onto his face. "You remember that?"

"One of the oddest references to sex, but I'll let it go."

We have had good times together, that we can't deny.

His look doesn't fade, which is promising.

I nervously swipe my hair to my shoulder. "Actually… uhm… I got you something."

"Really?" Stunned is an understatement.

"Bottom drawer. I didn't wrap it or anything." I do my best to downplay this, I don't want it to be a big deal.

He heads straight to the bottom drawer of the dresser. It's still empty except for the gift.

A closed-mouth smirk begins to form as he holds up the tiny onesie. "My dad can fire the coach," he reads out loud.

"General manager joke," I clarify.

"Oh, I got that. This may get me into trouble, but I love it." He examines the onesie and notices the Spinners logo and can't stop smiling.

"It's a little big because I thought she could wear it during hockey season. That is if you want her to visit you at work." I'm doing my best to keep this a simple moment.

Vaughn looks at me with intensity. "For sure, I want that. Didn't really cross my mind, but since you said it, then absolutely… she'll need her mom with her." Now it feels like he is testing the waters to read me, or rather he doesn't want to say what he is really thinking. He does that a lot.

"Of course. Wouldn't miss it."

"Good, good…" He tries to focus on something else, our moment breaking, as we're both unsure of what to do with this feeling that keeps orbiting us closer.

"Vaughn… thank you for coming today."

"Truthfully, it wasn't something I thought I would enjoy, but it wasn't so bad. I got to see you completely happy, Isla."

I smile again. "I am. Well, as much as I can be." My eyes drop to my belly. "I have to push her out soon, and you… I mean we… no, I mean the situation between us is… I don't know what I'm trying to say. Can we forget this?" I ramble completely.

It only makes him more entertained. "Maybe."

I roll my eyes. Great, just great. Add this to my list of things I do to dig us deeper.

Vaughn begins to stroll out. "I need to call my brother, pack for Nashville, and take a *long* shower." Oh, now we're back to inuendo by highlighting "long."

Damn it, this isn't great for my stress levels.

"Take it easy, I'll lift the heavy stuff later."

I salute him. "Sure thing, sir."

That sexy smirk is back in full force. "Careful, Isla, I may just have to fuck our baby out of you."

My jaw drops, and he leaves me there.

17

VAUGHN

Pacing my bedroom with the phone to my ear, I wait for my brother to tell me something wise. Anything to untangle the thoughts happening in my head.

"So, you went to the baby shower? Preparing for my niece? What else are you two getting ready for? Doing one of the labor courses or something like that?" he lists his questions.

"Don't have time for any course, let alone reading a book. I'm literally winging it, all of this. Basically 95% of the presents we got from the baby shower, I have no clue what they are. Diapers?" I feign doubt in my voice. "No idea how that works."

"I bet you Isla does, and I haven't even met her," he assures me.

I pinch my nose before I sit on the edge of the bed, only to stand again due to my energy level. "I'm quite confident she's nesting or something like that, someone mentioned that's a thing. I keep catching her in the nursery doing something."

"But not doing you," he jokes.

I stop, frozen at his humor, because it brings me to my predicament. "We haven't even discussed how this lifetime as parents together is going to go."

"Ah…" I can tell he's kicking his feet up on a table while he gets comfortable for this discussion ahead. "You mean the you-and-her-together kind of thing."

My head bobs side to side in contemplation. "Again, thanks to her, I haven't had time to think about it."

"Still angry she never told you?"

My shoulders fall. "I think I've decided to bury that away so we have a chance to have some normalcy, as our focus should be on the baby."

Stone lazily claps his hands once. "Give the man an award."

"Funny. But yeah, we haven't really talked about it. I'm not sure it's even crossed her mind."

"Does it cross yours?"

Blowing out a breath, I finally flop onto the edge of the bed in defeat. "It might have appeared once or twice." Maybe I'm down-playing it. "I just can't be sure if it's the baby factor that makes me want to think it or something else."

"Hmm… well, what did you think of her before the baby equation?"

A smile jerks on my lips. "A lot of attraction, good conversation, she's funny, gorgeous, understands hockey, I think that we were both okay with our boundaries that we had set…" Damn, it's a long list.

"And do you really think those feelings just faded away? Maybe your anger and disappointment with her may have fogged those attributes, but now that you're not angry, then are they clear as day?" He's treading carefully.

"That's exactly the problem. I've never been a relationship kind of guy, but now my view might be altering, and I'm just not sure to what completely. And Isla? Well, she's as beautiful as ever, there's still good conversation, to the point I swear she can predict my thoughts, and well, she's funny yet a little feisty. All of it together is making it impossible for me to not want to kiss her. Which may surprise her, considering I've been a complete idiot lately."

The sound of something from the hall grabs my attention, but not enough for me to look.

"I don't know, Vaughn. You're nervous about becoming a dad,

but that won't always be there, and eventually you can have a little more. You may be a dad, but you're not only a dad. You get it?"

"Yes, oh wise one," I mock him, but he has valid points. Strong points. Points that make me want to begin to unbrick any walls that I have inside of me.

My eyes sideline to the clock on the table next to the bed and see that I should probably go to bed if I have any chance for making tomorrow a clear-minded day, with strong focus on work.

"I'm going to dive off this call, I really need to head to bed," I say.

"Sure thing. Keep me posted and let me know if you need anything."

We both say goodbye and hang up. Quickly, I throw on a t-shirt and strip down to my boxers, eager for my head to hit the pillow… any pillow. Yep, a pillow, it's happening, and my mind is becoming a clusterfuck, and I hear another sound. Wait, a sound in the hallway. Now, I'm drawn to investigate the sound I thought I heard, which means going into the hall and passing Isla's door.

Still, safety first, right?

With my feet on a fast trail to check on whatever it may be, I don't see anything except Isla standing in the hallway, which causes me to nearly fall forward from surprise. Her eyes seem to have been watching my door, and I swallow because I have a strong feeling of what might happen. Especially as she's wearing a barely-there tank top and shorts, with her hair still partly wet from the shower that she must have just taken.

"Were you listening?" My tone isn't accusatory; the opposite really, I'm curious.

Her sight becomes fixed on me, her eyes unable to blink while the tip of her tongue finds the corner of her mouth. She pauses for a second before a wry smile appears on her lips, and her head lowers but her eyes then peer up at me.

"So…" She's dragging this out until her smile turns to a satis-fied grin. "Tit for tat today. You heard me earlier, and now I heard you."

I have to grin to myself as my head gently lowers; I could swear that I'm near timid. I'm caught, and I don't mind one bit.

"Seems the case."

"I'm still beautiful, and I'm making it impossible for you not to kiss me?" A sultry look forms on her face.

I nod as we stare at each other, with a sweltering tension floating between us. No words needed. Which is perfect because I've never been a man to wait for what he wants.

I do what's my instinct.

I'm impulsive.

Lunging forward, I bring my hand to the back of her neck to pull her to me and kiss her. I'm not even gentle. It's deep, ensuring I leave a print on her lips. Her muffled sound into my mouth is only a sound of pleasure, which I know because her hands begin to roam up my arms to around my neck, and she tilts her mouth to give me more access so I can delve my tongue in.

My hand on her neck begins to twist her damp hair around my fingers, and I yank her gently, causing her to jolt back and catch her breath in surprise, meaning our lips part and her eyes fire with a need that's impossible to ignore.

"Should we really be…" It's a whisper from her mouth.

"Shh," I tut.

We're throwing caution to the wind, and words are not going to help our journey.

Our lips find each other again, and we begin to move. I'm walking backward, guiding her with me. She tastes sweet and eager, everything I need to drive me crazy. My thoughts leave my head because I just want to get lost in her. I can't seem to kiss her lips enough, and I'm torn to stay on her mouth or nip her neck. Her skin is extra soft, almost encouraging us to keep going, as the road is smooth. Her swollen belly currently housing our daughter between us doesn't seem to be a deterrent.

When we make it next to my bed, any hope for caution seems to be out of our heads as Isla tugs on my t-shirt, and we only slow down so I can peel her tank up and off her body, savoring every second of the slow tease.

Before the last few weeks, I've always wanted her every time I saw her. Now? I still want her but in a possessive fuck her kind of way.

"Hell, you're a vision."

Isla blushes, and I get the feeling that she might be shy as she brings up her hands to cover her breasts that appear full and heavy.

Her lips open to say something, but I instantly plant my finger against them to ensure she doesn't speak a word.

"You're more beautiful than ever," I rasp before ensuring our gaze doesn't break.

"I'm not shy, if that's what you are wondering. Not in front of you. You're the one who put a baby inside of me."

I'm about to lose it, she just unleashed a new kind of lust inside of me. A possessive and proud mood that leads my actions. "With that thought, I *need* to get on my knees for you."

That earns me a smirk from her swollen mouth.

She's standing before me like a goddess, and I'm at her mercy, but make no mistake, I'm leading us. I hook my fingers under the band of her shorts to lower them and get her naked.

I keep true to my promise and drop to my knees. I lean in to kiss a trail up her inner thighs, coasting my lips around her pussy then trailing up. I pause for a second to take in the view of her belly at my eye level.

This is very new for me. Not that I'm complaining.

I plant my hands on her sides before I kiss her gently by her navel.

"I never thought I would be taking you with my baby inside of you, but make no mistake, I want to now that I see you carrying my child. You're so fucking magnificent."

"Ours," she corrects me. The affectionate shimmer in her eyes is sentimental, and her fingers come down to rake my hair. My lips move back down, this time to her pussy where my tongue finds her soaking clit, and an instant moan releases from the back of her throat as she relaxes under me.

Why does she have to taste so subtly sweet? I want more and can't fathom stopping. I lap my tongue a few times up and down her pussy before focusing on her clit. I dip a finger inside of her then pause for a second to zip my sight back up to her.

"Does this hurt?" This is new to me, and she's heavily pregnant at that. My pregnant woman.

She half laughs. "It's fine. I'm extra sensitive in a good kind of way. It feels a little different, but I like it."

A grin begins to dance on my lips. "You've been touching yourself?"

Her mouth tightly slides side to side to hide her timidity. "How could I not with you only a few walls away."

Ditto. My shower has been my haven.

"Then let me make you feel really good."

I return to her pussy with my tongue and now two fingers. She feels extra warm, and her inner barriers are open yet welcoming. I want to bury myself in her, make her moan so loud that the only way I can quiet her is with a kiss.

"Don't stop," she whimpers, with her fingers continuing to grab my hair.

I pursue my quest until her cues imply she's close, and I stand, kissing her lips to let her tongue have a taste. My hands frame her face to ensure our stare indicates we're both on the same page before I guide her onto the bed, removing my boxer briefs before I join her.

Isla lies on her side, and I'm aware that taking her from behind will be most comfortable for her. Sliding right behind her, our bodies mold together, with my arm looping around her to cup her breasts while my cock firmly presses into her lower back. I twist her nipples, and she hums a sound that feels like sex to my ears.

Her breasts have always been my weakness, but right now, I may be an insane man. I need to take her right away and bring my hand to lead my cock inside of her, and this time we're moaning together. Breathing into her neck, I rest my hand on her belly as I take her gently yet deep. I'm constantly scared that I'm hurting her, yet I fall into a complete world of pleasure that's making me carnal.

Thrusting into her with her body in this state may become my nirvana. I'm well aware that this can't be an everyday kind of thing, as soon our child enters the world. Then it hits me that I'm not fucking her. It's on a different level, one that I'm not sure of.

Her moans become pleading, and I finally come inside of her with our mouths fused.

I quickly identify that we just confused the situation between us by far.

But I'm not going to let her leave my bed, either.

18

ISLA

Vaughn is between my legs as I sit propped up against pillows in his bed, his tongue working me into a state. It didn't take long after our unexpected evening for him to go right back at it. The man has stamina and doesn't accept recovery for my dear body. But I don't mind because he's slithering up my body, taking a detour around my giant belly until his mouth covers a nipple and his fingers play with my other one.

That's when I nearly lose it.

Actually, I'm a few seconds away from losing it.

My breasts being sensitive in the best possible way doesn't even come close to this heavenly feeling of him worshipping my body.

Then I'm gone when his finger continues to stroke my pussy. I'm crumbling into tiny pieces as my orgasm takes over my body.

"Fuck," I moan out.

Then the devil studies my facial expression with a small laugh. "The baby has ears, remember?" he teases.

"Thank goodness we don't follow the cliché swear jar, otherwise she already has a college fund based on the last few days." My breath is still heavy when he flops onto the bed beside me.

It's a minute or so before my cheek smooshes against the pillow when I turn to look at Vaughn in his glory.

"You've done the work of a superhero. I've been getting more uncomfortable by the day with this pregnancy, but you were the perfect relief to relax me."

He side-eyes me. "Except we are horrible at maintaining boundaries."

"Extremely horrible," I agree.

The back of his finger caresses my arm. "I'm completely on board with your body like this. Your tits are driving me crazy."

"I've noticed." My elusive smile can't seem to disappear.

Vaughn adjusts his body to lie on his side and look down on me. "You know, last time we did this, in my car, I swear I noticed your breasts were larger."

I breathe out a sigh. "Now you know why."

"I didn't realize I have this kink, but I'm going to struggle watching this kid suckle on your tits for weeks on end."

Now I just want to burst out laughing. "First off, I'll only breast-feed if it feels right. You don't know if you'll have enough milk, or the baby just doesn't want to do it. And secondly, many guys are into tasting milk or using it for other things." I flash him my eyes. Vaughn just looks at me, puzzled. "Like lubricant," I clarify, and his eyes bug out.

"Okay, I don't think that's actually for me. Not sure what rabbit hole of a conversation we're heading down."

I shake my head to myself, still smiling. "Think of something else. I don't dare to figure out what the hell we do now, with our spectacular ability to complicate things…" I'm not even trying to nudge him into a discussion; I really *don't* know what the hell we do now.

Thankfully he brushes past that comment and glances at the clock. "I really need to get some shuteye. My flight is tomorrow, late morning."

"Oh, I thought you said next week is the draft."

He bops the tip of my nose with his finger. "Tomorrow is Monday, that's next week," he points out.

That does make sense.

"Kind of a good thing to avoid the awkwardness that I'm sure will cloud us," I joke.

"The timing sucks, and I wish I didn't have to go, but the draft is probably one of the major points in the year for a general manager."

Vaughn brings his arms behind his head to rest on, and I can't help but follow the lines of his muscles and tattoos. I was never a tattoo kind of girl, but his are not that big and only etched in black.

Tiredness begins to take over me. Sex was great, but there's a tightness between my thighs I'm not familiar with, not in a bad way by far.

"I get it. I do. Anyhow, I should go sleep too if I can. I'm beginning to feel like an absolute whale," I note.

He touches my arm. "Stay, I'll go grab that giant pillow thing from your room." He's off before I can answer.

I guess we're sleeping together. Another point on the scoreboard for our really bad judgment to ensure we don't seem to clarify things between us. However, I want to feel a body next to me—his arms around me, to be exact. My wish wins by far right now.

Vaughn comes back and settles in behind me, and I do my best to get comfortable with multiple pillows.

"Here." Another head pillow is placed behind my lower back.

"Ugh, whale me is getting moody and frustrated. I'm not sure I will last many more days."

Vaughn rubs soothing circles on my back. "Try to relax. And did you not hear me earlier? Marine mammals did not enter my comments at any point."

I smile to myself. "Fine. I'll be cheery." I don't sound completely on the bandwagon, but then again, he's right. I've gotta go into birthing this little girl with full-on positivity and ready to party.

Vaughn's gravelly laugh feels good, and it causes me to close my eyes just before his palm finds my belly to rub circles.

It appears his hand has no plans on leaving either.

———

WAKING UP, it hits us as soon as we look at one another.

Yeah, Vaughn and I really did that last night. Had excellent sex, not worrying about repercussions.

Give us an award, because without any words and only a few good beats of searching one another's eyes, our bodies become flush and ready. He throws the pregnancy pillow to the ground right before he slides into me, and we smolder together.

This isn't fair. I'm always horny these days. He wakes up hard, and he's offering. What kind of woman would ignore all of that?

A smart one.

Nope, not me, with a college degree and motherhood on the horizon. It's me, I'm acting a fool.

But it's oh so good.

Vaughn's warm breath against my skin sends ripples through my body, and his mussed hair, with his accompanying gravelly noises in the back of his throat are just so freaking fantastic.

I would completely agree for him to tie me to the bed and take me like this whenever he wants.

He pumps into me, and it feels even more sensitive than last night. Vaughn's being tender, and our eyes connect while our hands entwine. I'm too far gone. And so is he when he's filling me up.

He collapses to his back, while I just breathe out a heavenly feeling and rest my head against the pillow.

Maybe we fall back asleep, or it's simply fatigue still circling me, but we rest for a few minutes before Vaughn vacates the bed and stands, and then I wonder if regret is now hitting him.

"Want to join me in the shower?" he asks as if this is a normal day.

I twist part of my body to look at him. "Hell no. Let's just pile up our lack of crossed lines even more."

The corners of his mouth twist. "Language, Isla," he teases.

"Oh shit… wait… no, ahh, I curse like a sailor sometimes." My eyes drop to my belly. "Sorry, little girl."

"You do that a lot? Talk to her?"

"Well, yeah, you're supposed to, so they get used to your voice," I explain.

His eyes roll. "That's just great. My daughter has heard me basically be an jackass and say really dirty things to her mom. That's how she knows my voice."

I snort a laugh. "Oops."

Then the air turns serious between us, especially when Vaughn sits on the bed next to me. "We'll talk when I'm back in a few days. Maybe my trip is a good thing, so we can both think without distraction."

"Yeah." My voice is soft. "You're right."

The back of his hooked finger glides along my cheek before Vaughn kisses my forehead then pats my belly. Then he's off to the bathroom for a shower that I choose not to join.

But I have no control of my mouth spitting out things I probably shouldn't say or ask. "Vaughn," I call out, and he stops when he is about to open the door.

He glances to me with a glint in his eyes. "Yeah?"

"Why did you insist on meeting me at the hotel?" I'm referencing Florida way back.

He tries to suppress his boyish grin, but his dimples appearing give him away. "It can be fun to follow the whirlwind path of attraction. But I think... there can be a bolt of lightning between two people, and it simply can't be ignored... so I took the initiative."

I like his answer, but I'm just not sure what to do with it. "Well... a whirlwind path of surprise obstacles we have followed."

"Obstacles, hmm." His eyes drop down then fly up. "Last night... right." His T is sharp before he gives me a faint smile and leaves me for the shower.

Inside me, fear swirls again, in case we just ruined any chance to make the co-parenting thing work. Then realization hits me that it's not that; I'm scared it won't work between us as two people in a relationship.

———

A FEW DAYS LATER, I'm sitting with my brother in the living room on the couch.

"You're really doing it then, leaving for Seattle?" I am sad about it, but Briggs is right that I'll still see him, especially during the summer.

"It's for the best. Besides, it means the dynamic between Vaughn and I can be strictly somewhat… I don't know… but you bind us." He struggles to form an explanation.

"You're not leaving because of him, right?"

Briggs waves me off. "Nah, I was already in discussions before he graced us with his presence, I told you that."

I touch his arm. "Good. If you're happy then I'm happy." It's a lie, I'll miss him.

Briggs ended up living in Lake Spark for the Spinners, and it just so happened that I found a job too. We've always been around one another, not only as siblings but also friends. Now part of my family will be away.

I begin to rub circles on my belly when a weird feeling hits me, one that I've been having all day, but it's not a cause for alarm.

He groans a sound. "Dare I ask if Vaughn is stepping up?"

I shake my head. "You have to accept all of this. Plus…" I splay my hands out to display the house. "Do you not see that he is providing?"

Briggs snickers. "It takes more than that to be a father. A good father, I mean."

"I need to give him a chance and so should you." I wince and a strained breath hits me.

My brother notices. "You okay?"

"Totally. How about a fresh round of drinks?"

He begins to stand. "I'll get it."

I grab his arm. "No, I need to keep moving, and this can be my exercise."

Briggs listens and lets me stand and walk in the direction of the kitchen. However, the moment I'm next to the kitchen island, I take hold of the counter when I feel an unusual sensation, and I swear I hear a pop.

My eyes draw a line down to my dress, and then I see water trickling down my bare leg.

"Oh no." Panic hits me.

Briggs is up on his feet and racing toward me in no time. "What is it?"

"I think my water just broke."

19

VAUGHN

Sitting on Declan's plane back to Lake Spark, the coaching and management staff study the schedule for our new players as Declan and I sit next together a good distance from everyone. The new players we drafted are very young, and we quickly need to get them settled in their new surroundings, while they also tackle development training and full-on marketing appearances.

"It feels great to have fresh blood on the team. I think our defensive players are strong," Declan mentions as he drinks from his water bottle.

I chuckle from his comment. "I've never seen an owner so involved. Normally a team is their hobby, and they only show up for games, when the board of governors need to vote, or when shit hits the fan with the general manager or coach."

He smiles proudly. "I'm not a normal owner. I played for far too many years to make me sit still. Likewise, for you. That's why we're a winning formula."

I lean into my elbow. "A good philosophy to have."

"I kind of need a break from team talk, it's been nonstop for the past few days. Ready for fatherhood?"

I chortle a sound. "Hardly, but not much I can do about that. Timing isn't on my side."

"Fate may be. You were moving to Lake Spark before you discovered the happy news. Now it just means that you get both without complication," Declan notes.

My brows raise up then down. "Uh, not exactly, but I guess it will figure itself out."

He chuckles in understanding. "That tends to happen to a lot of people. Violet and I eventually came to our senses and maybe one of you will too. There is always someone in a relationship who gets there first, yet it's not a race."

I scratch my chin, internally agreeing. An answer doesn't come to me, partly because our bedtime fun the other night may have taken us off track.

My thought is broken when a flight attendant arrives and whispers something in Declan's ear. His eyes nearly darken then he winces. When the attendant walks away, Declan looks straight at me.

He claps his hands once, as if we're about to enter a team huddle. "So, here is the thing. The pilot got a message, and it seems that Isla has gone into labor."

"What?" My voice raises an octave, and apprehension drops straight to my stomach. "She should have another week or two!"

Declan touches my arm. "The baby can also come early."

"Not while I'm on a plane she can't." I grip the armrests with full strength, trying to figure out if it's fear or worry that's the prominent emotion flooding me.

"We'll be back in an hour then get you straight to the hospital," he promises.

I shake my head. "This can't be happening… I haven't even read the baby book yet." I'm stressing now. "Not to mention, I've only known that Isla is pregnant for barely a millisecond, and now she's delivering a baby?"

Declan looks at me with a strained expression. "To be fair, nothing goes to plan like those books." He slaps my shoulder. "Besides, the first baby is normally a long labor."

Blowing out a breath, I rub my face. "I'm not sure what to do right now. I'm going to go out of my mind. Isla's in labor, and I'm not there."

"In an hour you will be. Try to relax because it could be a long day ahead. What's important is that you show up for her."

"Christ, I knew I should have listened to the daddy preparation podcast. Fuck, first I miss an entire pregnancy, and now this? Someone upstairs hates me." I tip my head to the sky, only to grumble a sound because we're already in the damn sky, as in not on the ground, more so as in I can't drive like a maniac to the hospital.

"Just stay calm."

I give Declan an unamused look because his advice is absolutely impossible.

I'm not ready for this. I thought I had a little more time to adjust. Hell, I didn't even get a gift yet for this kid. And coaching Isla through this? Holy hell, all I know is to pat her back, except she isn't some animal who gets a treat.

She's Isla.

The mother of my child.

The woman who has flipped my world upside down.

And I have an hour to switch my mind and be there for her.

————

RUNNING down the hall of the hospital, I recognize Briggs pacing, and his head whips up at my arrival. He quickly stomps in my direction before grabbing my shirt and pinning me to the wall.

I can't even process until his mouth opens. "You listen here, Vaughn Madden. In there is the biggest game of your life. I couldn't handle it. She's in pain, and they talked about needles if she wants an epidural, and I nearly fainted. You suck it right up and take one for the team."

His pep talk sounds like we're going to war.

He doesn't stop there. "Do not falter on us. It's up to you to be in there no matter what."

"Where the hell is Hadley or her mom? Is she really in there alone?" I screech.

"They're in Chicago and driving back as fast as they can. Violet can't be here because their baby has a virus, and she doesn't want to risk giving it to Isla. I've failed her, because this—" he points to the door of Isla's room "—is not meant for brothers. Now get the fuck in there, and you do not leave." He lets me go, and I immediately go to the door, already hearing Isla weeping in pain. "For the team, Vaughn. You're captain of this ship," Briggs calls out.

For fuck's sake, his speech as a sailor going to war doesn't help this situation.

Opening the door, I find Isla sitting on a yoga ball and holding onto the railing of the bed with a nurse next to her. She's trying to control her groan, nearly screaming as she's in the middle of a contraction. As I run straight to her, the nurse backs away.

"I'm here. I'm here." I touch Isla's back, and she looks at me. She seems worn out, and her hair is damp from sweat, her eyes desperate.

When her contraction passes, she cries, "It's too early. I mean, I had another week or so. This shouldn't be happening."

I cup her face. "She wants to come now. The doctor already warned us that you're pretty much ready." I do my best to ease her thoughts.

"This is our fault," she wails.

"How so?" I ask as the nurse brings a cup of ice chips and hands it to me.

Isla knocks it out of my hand with force, causing the ice to fall on the floor. "Screw the ice chips, they do fuck all. And yes, this is our fault." She breathes through pressed lips. "We had sex. They say it can induce labor." The hint of a barely-there smile graces her lips.

"Really? Why didn't you mention that to me?" I play along.

A humorous look of disapproval hits her. "Sorry if I didn't want to ruin the mood."

"Hey, you know I use these kinds of balls in my hockey training." I smile at her, but I'm met with a near sneer.

"Really?" She doesn't sound impressed. "This is the moment you want to compare labor to your training regime?"

I hold a hand up in agreement that she is right.

Another contraction hits her, and I rub her back as the pain appears to rip through her. Briggs was right, this isn't for the faint of heart. I'm hurting for Isla, but I can't show it because I need to be here for her.

"Give me the epidural," she pleads to the nurse.

The nurse looks over her shoulder, checking the monitor. "I'm sorry, Isla. You're too far dilated and so close. The best you can do is keep breathing through the pain. You're doing great."

Oh God, Briggs really was preparing me, because this is like a battle in the trenches.

Isla wails again as she abandons the ball. "Make this stop, it hurts too much." She leans her head against my shoulder.

I kiss the top of her head. "It's going to be okay. Before you know it, she'll be here."

Isla grips my shirt with both hands. "Promise me that no matter what you'll go straight to her to make sure she's okay. Focus on her, not me."

It conflicts me, because what if something happens to Isla? It didn't cross my mind until now. That thought unnerves me, but right now, she needs reassurance.

"Of course, Isla."

"Oh no, the car seat. We didn't even install it."

I offer her a simple smile. "I did. In my car before I left."

Her face brightens up with comfort.

She's delicate right now, which is why I can only be honest with her. "I think I believe that, even though I just found out about your pregnancy, it was because I am meant to be here in the moment to help you."

A lightness shades her eyes. "You're not still mad at me?"

"No, Isla, I'm not still mad," I tell her point blank.

It seems to bring relief to her, only for it to be interrupted by another wave taking over her body. I grip her arms so I can carry her weight as much as I can. I murmur encouragement until she sighs from the contraction ending.

"Okay, Isla, I think you're nearly there. I will call Dr. Forest."

Isla nods while our eyes lock. I'm not going to let her down, and I think she realizes it.

For a moment, while the nurse goes to the corner to make a call, Isla and I get a chance to have some privacy.

"I'm scared. I'm not ready," she breathes out.

Moving so she can waddle to the bed and lean against me, I hold her up, as she seems to be weak. "You can do this. I know you can. You've done everything so far because you want to give her a good life. So you'll make sure she enters this world on the right foot, and in order to make that happen, you have to get through this."

She laughs. "Easy for you to say. You don't have a baby goblin ripping through your body." Another contraction hits her, and she clasps onto me for dear life.

"You've got this. You're so close," I soothe her.

The contraction is short but seems to be stronger than what I imagined.

I smile at her and stroke her hair. "Goblin, really? That's what we're calling her now?"

It makes Isla laugh. "We don't have a name for her."

"You pick when she's here," I say to encourage her. "Well… the last name is not really up for negotiation, but you know what I mean." I try to make her smile again.

She nods again.

I kiss her forehead, reminding myself to stay calm.

By the time the doctor is here, Isla is ready to go. I believe that we're both petrified. Our lives are about to change, and we know it. The moment this girl enters the world, we'll see everything through a different lens, even I know that.

I sit on the side of the bed behind Isla to support her, with the doctor between Isla's propped knees and the nurse nearby, ready for action, and another nurse preparing things in the corner. It doesn't take long for an exhausted Isla to push, and she nearly breaks my hands when she squeezes them. Every push she amazes me with her strength that could take out any hockey player I've ever played.

Six pushes later… it happens.

A cry fills the room, and my heart grows bigger already.

"Your daughter is here," the doctor says as she holds up the red baby covered in a white coating, with a squinched face and a full head of hair to my surprise.

Isla cries happy tears then tries to peek when they cut the cord, but then they take a little longer than we expected. They hold our daughter and check her body longer than I would expect, and in a moment that now feels chaotic, terror fills Isla's eyes as she looks at me. It's only a few seconds, but it's too many for Isla. "What's happening?"

I try to get a glimpse, but I honestly don't know.

"It's okay, Isla," the doctor explains.

I try to peek again to keep my promise and attempt to study the medical staff while our baby cries. I'm not sure what is happening, but it only takes a few seconds more for a nurse to smile at me as she hands Isla our naked baby to rest against her chest then quickly covers them with a blanket.

"She's a strong one. She looks good," the nurse says.

I watch as our baby finds a home against Isla's chest. My daughter's little eyes stare straight at me, and her cry seems to soften. I'm not a crier, but tears sting my eyes at this little bundle in Isla's arms.

I guess I am a dad now, and as cliché as it sounds, my world suddenly feels like it's turning differently.

I soak in the scene of a washed-out Isla, but she seems to find renewed energy when she soaks in our daughter. "She's here," I whisper.

Isla cries as she inspects every little inch of our girl and clasps onto her tiny finger. I'm quick to lean down to get a better view and kiss Isla's cheek.

"Nora Madden is here," she whispers.

I'm taken aback by the name. It's perfect. Our daughter gets my last name and a first name of the hurricane that brought Isla and I together.

Isla glances at me with a laugh and tears drying on her face. "What? You think she will ever ask how she got that name?"

———

It was a tranquil couple days in the hospital with visitors, help from the staff, and we didn't need to stay any longer. I'm positive Nora was the best baby there too. I also got to rest her little cheek against my bare chest because apparently that's good for oxytocin and bonding. Basically, it was nothing like I expected or could imagine.

Everything is better, a fog of bliss but unreal. It's only just sinking in that we had a little baby that we took home in my car. One day Nora wasn't here, then suddenly she is.

Returning home, the house now feels different. I notice that our friends must have been here. There is a balloon on the kitchen counter next to wrapped food. A few of the baby things that are for the living area are all set up, including that Scandinavian highchair with a newborn insert that everyone raved about.

I set the car seat down at the bottom of the stairs, and Isla lets out a sigh. "Finally, back home."

"You should probably rest, you warrior you," I recommend.

Isla doesn't tear her sight away from Nora. "What if I miss something?"

I chortle a laugh. "You can't not sleep for the rest of your life."

Isla bounces her head side to side in consideration. "Maybe you're right."

"I'll carry her upstairs. You'll be okay with the stairs?"

"I'm fine."

When we reach the top of the stairs, Isla directs me to her room. "I want her to sleep with me in the co-sleeper. It will be easier to feed her at night when she wakes, and I don't like the idea of her all alone in the nursery yet. She's still so tiny and might get scared."

It feels like we are taking a step back since Isla seems to be returning to her room to sleep. It perhaps makes sense considering our circumstances.

But despite what's going on with us, I'm putting my foot down.

"She's not sleeping in your room."

"Oh yes she is, Vaughn," Isla challenges, with her hand on her hip with her sass clearly recovering well.

It causes me to smirk. "It's my decision, considering our timeline of events, or rather my lack of being on board for that timeline of events. You can both sleep in my room."

"You didn't think to bring up the sleeping arrangement topic in, let's say… the hospital, the car ride, or up these freaking stairs?" Isla seems taken aback. "Uhm…" She doesn't know what to say.

"I'm not taking no for an answer. I'll move the bassinet thing that attaches to the bed."

"A co-sleeper," she corrects me. "Or we can use the baby nest." Her palm flies up to stop me. "Wait… I don't think this is a great idea. I'm… my body is kind of, well…" Her hand outlines her breasts and heads lowers with awkwardness. "I… there are liquids coming out of my… body." She draws out the uncomfortable sentence.

I look at her, unfazed. "And? I just saw you push out a baby. I think we're good." Her eyes nearly turn into saucers from surprise or the fact that it's no big deal to me. "I don't want to miss anything, and soon I need to get back to work. Remember I said I want to come home and be able to check on her when I want. That means slipping into bed and she's nearby." *And you're nearby.*

Isla seems to be in contemplation. "It's… okay, uhm, limitations are clearly not us."

I lift the handle of the car seat, already prepared to direct this discussion straight to my room. "You're going to agree." I pretty much demand it.

Now a smirk plays on Isla's lips. "Fine. But she needs her dreamcatcher from the nursery for above the bed. I'm superstitious."

"Okay. Done."

She nods before slowly walking to my room to climb into bed to rest with our daughter nearby.

This is the only step that I know how to make right now.

Because everything between us changed the moment we became a family.

20

ISLA

S leep is a glorious thing.

If only I could enjoy a nice deep slumber. Lately, I cannot, which is why I drowsily wake up at to the sound of someone quietly clicking their tongue.

My eyes dart to the baby nest in the middle of the bed to find it empty, which causes me to shoot up in a panic, but then I ease at the sight. One that I've become accustomed to the last week since we came home.

Vaughn is bouncing Nora in his arms while he stands near the window, greeting the day. He offers her his pinky as he makes little noises. His lack of shirt isn't helping the situation.

The view warms my heart.

Vaughn must sense that I'm up, as he doesn't take his eyes off our daughter but acknowledges that I'm here. "Your mommy should go back to sleep."

I laugh. "Very unlikely." The heavy fullness with a twinge of pain across my chest informs me that something has to give. "Mommy either needs to pump or go straight to the source. Someone may be hungry soon."

It causes Vaughn to glance in my direction. "Again? Didn't you feed her like a gazillion times during the night?"

Sliding out from under the covers, I grab my robe lying on the end of the bed. "That's kind of how babies work. At first, they need a lot of milk."

A humorous smirk hits his lips. "True. She is also a strong one, this one."

"You sound like she's going to be some future queen of a kingdom."

He chuckles. "Nah, she'll just be keeping us on our toes as soon as puberty hits."

I walk to them, admiring how this is a strange yet relaxed feeling. We share a bed, all three of us, as if it was the only way to be.

I'm happy Vaughn gets his moments with Nora, especially as he has a lot of work. Having a baby in the off-season should be a hockey player's dream, but a general manager? Hell no, it's full-on preparing for the season ahead.

My hand falls onto Vaughn's arm as we look down at our daughter. "She's already getting bigger." Still her baby clothes drown her a little, and we have to roll up her sleeves.

"Everything is a blur. Fast is an understatement," he notes.

We haven't discussed even once our events prior to Nora entering the world. How could we? We're occupied with a new baby.

"I'm going to head to the training arena soon, but I'll be home early because my brother is going to stop by to meet his niece," Vaughn informs me.

It grabs my attention, as I haven't met his brother yet. I guess it's not a big deal considering he is Nora's uncle. No different than Briggs, except meeting Vaughn's brother feels a bit more confronting and serious maybe. I want to make a good impression.

"Sounds good. I'm going to see Hadley this morning, and maybe I'll stop at the general store for some things later." Our local general store is anything but, it's a gourmet supermarket.

"Sure, just take it easy." He hands me Nora. I'm fairly confident that she has his eyes.

Nora is making little faces that tell me she's hungry. "I'm just going to head downstairs to feed her." As much as I don't mind Vaughn watching me, it still causes my lips to curl into an awkward smile. It's a sort of intimacy in a different strange way.

"Okay, I'll be down in a minute."

A few minutes later, I'm sitting on the couch with Nora at my chest and my eyes taking in the morning light streaming in through the big windows. I'm chewing on some fruit since I always wake up hungry.

Random sounds in the kitchen tell me that Vaughn is about to leave and probably grabbing his protein shake for the road.

We have a routine that we easily fell into. I'm grateful for that. If he was still angry at me for not telling him about my pregnancy or insistent that everything goes his way, then I would have been walking on eggshells.

"You'll send me photos throughout the day?" He smiles at me as he's on his way to the front door.

"Always," I promise.

He pauses for a second the way he or I do on a daily basis. I'm sure we both want to say something that has no relation to our daughter, but we always stop ourselves. We just let our eyes linger instead.

"Isla, uh…"

A closed-mouth smile hits me. "I know," I acknowledge, but I really don't. It's just a confirmation that we're both in the same state.

For now, that just has to work.

———

HADLEY HANDS me a decaf coffee and a croissant as we get comfortable on the bench by the gazebo in the park, with the lake nearby. Nora is sleeping in her stroller. Getting fresh air is important for me, especially with the great summer weather we've been having.

"Sleep tight. I'm your auntie who will be your godmother and be the one you can turn to when your mom goes strict during the teenage years. I'll fill you up with sugar when you're going through the terrible twos and be the best friend your mom deserves," Hadley coos and jokes.

I hold up my coffee. "Funny. Thanks for the croissant, I'm always hungry these days. Nobody warned me how feeding a pint-sized human makes you starving. I think it's worse than labor. I just want to eat and eat," I complain.

"At least you have an excuse. Don't you burn extra calories or something?"

My head tips slightly to the side. "Good point. But I'm jealous of your caffeine-infused drink."

She slides next to me to nudge my shoulder. "One day you'll taste it again. Speaking of tasting…" Her tone changes, and she gives me playful look. "Vaughn." Her eyes nearly pop out.

I just roll my own. "It's nothing. We're so occupied and running on adrenaline still."

"I can see that. Just… won't that wear off at some point?"

I snicker a sound. "I think we both realize that."

"How are you around one another?"

My face squinches, as I know one of her signature squeals is about to hit me. "So the thing is, we're sharing a bed. Don't get excited, we have Nora between us, and her parents are grasping for straws when it comes to sleep. Except… before I went into labor, we kind of did something stupid."

"No way!" Now Hadley is fueled by the latest gossip of my life.

"Simmer down, child. It happens. I'm fairly convinced it set off my labor too." I'm only half-joking, but it's a better story.

"Are you kidding me? Don't you two ever lock it up? Every time you see one another you just go at it."

I glance blankly to my side to face her. "Attraction is attraction, but we haven't once mentioned that night since."

Hadley brings a finger to her chin. "One day it will come up, and then what?"

"I don't know. Our priority is this little princess right here. I'm also in this cloud of happiness where everything is lullabies and cute little outfits. A clear mind doesn't exist for me right now. Maybe I'm also waiting to see what the impact will be once Vaughn starts traveling with the team." I slouch because the thought isn't exactly uplifting.

She affectionately touches my shoulder. "Do you still worry that he might bail on you?"

I shrug and don't dare say the word yes.

"I really don't think he will," she encourages. "He's totally in love with Nora."

My lips quirk out. "See? With Nora. When it comes to me, then it's still confusing for both of us."

"Maybe time is what you need. But maybe you should also plant some seeds in his head of what you're thinking. Men do great when we give hints."

I yawn from tiredness while I take in her advice. "You're probably right, but that's not going to happen today. His brother is stopping by, and I want to give Nora a bath tonight, plus catch up on laundry."

"Excuses." She gives me a knowing look.

I lick my lips. "I can guarantee you that Vaughn is probably doing the same as me."

"Then it's easy. Be the one to make the first step. He did it after he found out and made you move in with him, and I think you kind of enjoy that demanding side of him." Her voice raises slightly. "It's now your turn."

A deep breath is my answer. "You're probably right."

———

STONE HAS DARKER hair than his little brother. He's also extremely kind to me, which is a surprise. I kind of expected him to be wary, considering I never informed Vaughn he was going to be a dad. Instead, Stone showed up with flowers for me and a giant stuffed monkey and a few wooden toys for when Nora is older.

He's holding her now as we sit outside on the patio with snacks on the table.

"For sure she has my brother's eyes," he states.

I smile. "Thought so." I side-eye Vaughn, confirming that I'm right.

"Geez, the jury has spoken." Vaughn grins.

"What are you going to do when Vaughn starts traveling?" Stone wonders.

Vaughn and I look at one another because we still have so much to talk about.

"I still have maternity leave for a little while, then hopefully I can find a part-time nanny or something. Daycare seems a bit too early for Nora. Plus, a friend's mother said she could watch Nora one day a week, and I trust her with my life," I explain.

"We have options. Money isn't an issue," Vaughn adds. No, it's not. Vaughn won't let me pay for anything, and it's frustrating at times.

Stone looks down at Nora as she waves her arms. "I'm not a babysitter, unless it gets me the attention of the ladies in this town," he jokes. "But I'm in the process of moving to Lake Spark soon for more inspiration."

"I still can't believe you're going to write a book," I say.

"Well, nobody is supposed to know. It's not every day you expect some retired hockey jock to write."

"A smart one at that," Vaughn adds.

"Anyway, I also have a writing retreat happening here soon. My publisher is sending some romance writer to this retreat, and I'm confident she doesn't even write her own stories. I'm not at all looking forward to it, so I may need to escape to this house."

I laugh and grab some crackers. "She's your best chance at any excitement. Pretty much all the women in this town are taken."

"I feared you would say that. It's breaking my heart," he says, playing along.

Vaughn rubs his face due to his brother's humor. "Or you could just deadbolt her in."

"Oh, like you two did." Stone glances down at Nora then back up to us.

Vaughn and I both awkwardly look at one another.

"Cheese plate?" Vaughn offers to his brother to divert the conversation.

"Nope, I'm good. What I meant to say is I'm happy to check in when my brother is out handling the attitudes of his hockey players. But what's the deal going forward? Just going to live together under one roof?" Stone isn't afraid to be bold.

Vaughn gives his brother a warning glare. "Stone, maybe focus on the kid."

"Yikes. Did I just trigger a conversation between you two later? My bad." Stone isn't the least bit sorry.

Clearing my throat, I decide to keep us moving. "You two are close. Kind of like me and my brother."

"Yep, which is why I watch out for him." For the first time since he arrived, Stone looks at me seriously.

"Christ, Stone, chill it for a bit." Vaughn's eyes shoot another caution to his brother.

I smile shyly and adjust my shirt. "I get it, I would do the same."

A silence around us breezes in.

"She's the chillest baby. Doesn't really cry much and always seems calm," Vaughn attempts to break the quiet, and his brother just smiles softly.

Taking this opportunity, I decide to escape this confronting day. "I think it's Nora's feeding time, she must be getting hungry." I stand to take her out of Stone's arms.

"Is that why her little fingers are getting grabby at my chest."

"Exactly. It'll give you some time alone with Vaughn."

"You probably won't see him when you come back down," Vaughn mentions. "Either my brother hits the road or I'll be throwing him in the lake."

I grin. "Probably go with option one."

Walking away and closing the sliding door behind me, I still manage to hear the beginning of their conversation.

"Isla seems like a great mom, I don't think you need to worry," Stone tells his brother.

"When it comes to that, I never did," Vaughn replies.

The smile forming on my lips is as natural as can be.

———

A WHILE LATER, I return down the stairs and into the kitchen where Vaughn is placing snacks back into their containers. I stop his arm so I can grab another nibble of the cheese cubes.

"Sorry, I'm like a famished monster." I hold the cube up.

His lips tilt up. "I've noticed."

He continues his quest to clean up, and then we're stuck in a long gaze.

Blowing a breath through my pursed lips, I go for it. "Look, I think we are both aware that the underlying tension—"

"Attraction," he corrects me.

Now my own grin begins to form. "Attraction," I repeat. "It's bringing a debate inside our heads. As much as I want to discuss the…" My finger twirls in the air. "What…" It drags out.

Vaughn smirks before he stands closer to me with purpose and confidence. "The not-parent part of our equation is what you're trying to say."

I suppress my laugh and instead smile tightly. "Yep, that. I just can't think clearly right now. I'm adjusting to this mother thing, and I literally get excited when she blinks."

"I get it, me too." He steps closer, and my heart rate picks up.

"Can we maybe just wait a bit to talk about everything? You know, the living situation, childcare, your traveling, my work, when to start solid foods, or should it be eggs or toaster waffles for break-fast," I ramble. "*Everything*."

Vaughn is so ridiculously amused. His finger hooks under my chin to tip my face up so I have no escape. "The thing between us is what you're trying to say." He drags his thumb across my bottom lip.

"Uh-huh." I do my best to look away, but my eyes only find his as my destination.

"You're cute when you're flustered." His eyes are lust-filled, I see it.

"For heaven's sakes, Vaughn." I'm only half annoyed. "Can you keep us on track?"

He chuckles, with zero issue that his sultry gaze is sending us down a hole. "Relax, I'm well aware that you need to recover for a few weeks, and we need to establish boundaries. But can't I enjoy looking at you?"

"No. Nope. Uh-uh," I clearly state. "We have a child sleeping between us, and she's now officially our barrier between crossing borders."

"We suck at limits." His sexy look falls to a hopeless one.

"Yeah, exactly why we should take some time to clear out our adrenaline of our life change and then address stuff." My hands pretend to shovel the air, him included.

Vaughn removes his finger from under my chin, and the excitement from his touch lessens slightly because it can now be tamed.

He kisses my forehead. "Agreed but not forgotten," he promises before he walks away.

21

VAUGHN

Isla is standing behind the boards with her jaw hanging low as she watches, unsure if this is a good idea. But Nora is now a few weeks old and loves her carrier wrap.

I'm on my skates with Nora bound tightly to me as I skate slowly around the rink. She's bundled warmly against my chest, and this is her first taste of life on the ice. I love it.

I decided my break between meetings should be this, and since we only have summer training camp happening, it's a little easy on the ice with the players. The person from the marketing team taking a video can't be helped, but the world already knows that I'm a dad. The team posted a congratulations photo on their social media channels. Naming the mom? It made a lot of fans go crazy in the good type of way. The whole "sister of the hockey player falling for another hockey player" has an angle that people seem to eat up.

Except we're not officially together, and nobody has corrected the public either. It doesn't matter, right now my focus is on being Daddy Vaughn.

I'm well aware that Nora has no clue what's going on while we skate, nor will she remember this, but her nervous mom on the other hand most definitely will.

"Just don't fall," Isla mentions when I pass.

"Relax, I'm a pro at this," I assure her.

"Yeah, and I'll beat him to a pulp if he does," Briggs pipes up as he skates by me, enjoying his time off but still hitting the ice.

I sigh because there is no escaping Isla's brother before he leaves for Seattle next season, but he has been tamer around me, and occasionally he backtracks.

"Supportive as always," I call out sarcastically.

Skating some more, I look down and notice that my daughter is slowly closing her eyes. "Uhm, you're supposed to be wide awake for this. It's your big ice debut," I tease my little girl who has no clue what I'm saying, especially as her eyes shut. I guess this is relaxing for her.

I notice that Briggs has stopped up ahead near the goal post, with his eyes skeptical as he stares at me. Approaching him, I decide to extend an olive branch, but he beats me to the punch.

"My sister seems happy. She was meant to be a mom, even if by accident."

I smile softly to myself. "Does it matter how it happened, as long as she's okay?"

Briggs swipes a hand across his jaw. "About that… as much as I hate this, I want us to have a man-to-man talk."

My posture straightens in surprise. "Probably a good idea. I was waiting for you to cool off from everything, but I also want to talk, so let's do it now."

We both glance at Isla who is far enough away that she can't hear; instead, she studies us warily.

Briggs starts. "You have to take care of her when I'm not here. She may appear to be strong, but I can guarantee that she's more scared than you can imagine when it comes to having a family. If she ever says she can do it alone, then it's a lie; she would be broken-hearted for Nora if you are not involved."

Inside I'm in complete agreement. I understand more than Briggs will ever know.

"If you're giving me a warning, then you don't need to. I

wouldn't do that to Isla or Nora. I will always be involved." More than my old man ever was.

Briggs seems to grasp my sincerity. "Good. Because I've been the one to watch her, but now I won't be here all the time. I need to know she's okay. I also don't want to break any laws if I find out she's in pain, especially if it's by you."

I pinch the bridge of my nose, trying not to get aggravated, but I could repeat myself a thousand times. "Briggs, you have my word. We can agree on one thing and that's Isla and Nora."

He scoffs a laugh. "You do realize I am only talking about the parenting factor. Whatever the hell you two do on the relationship factor, then that deserves a whole other discussion. I'm not sure what in the world you two got up to the last months before Nora entered our lives, but I sure as hell hope that my sister doesn't end up upset. It's no longer fun and games, you know."

Licking my lips, I'm not sure that I should be having this conversation with Briggs. It's far too close to home, it's a topic that I have to tread carefully around. I'm an equal partner in the Isla-and-me equation. She has the same power as me to bring disaster, as far as our non-parenting relationship is concerned.

"Again, stating the obvious. What would you like me to do to prove to you that you don't need to worry? Do I look like a man who is going to play a game with my chance at a family?"

Briggs looks at me intently, almost with a profound empathy. He even tips his nose slightly up, as if he is whiffing out my intentions in order to approve. "She no longer likes ice cream sandwiches. It's cherry cobbler, with vanilla bean ice cream."

I smile wryly at the advice he just gave me. Almost as if I should sway her. Did the world stop turning?

He begins to skate off, but I call out his name. "Briggs." His attention returns to me. "I'm also counting on you. Summer is by no means easy on the schedule for me, but it is for you. I need you to take care of her when I'm not there, be the extra support we probably need."

Briggs nods in agreement before he skates away.

I can't process fast enough what just happened as my daughter grabs my attention, sleeping peacefully without a care in the world. Completely unaware that her parents need to figure out some things.

———

ISLA and I go for a walk around the neighborhood, with me pushing the baby stroller.

"What should we do about the childcare situation?" I ask. The weeks are quickly passing.

Isla exhales with dread. "I'm trying not to think about it. I still have a little more time on maternity leave, as Ford gave me extra. They also said I can work part-time if I want going forward. It's just…"

I gently touch her back while my other hand continues to push Nora. "It doesn't excite you in the same way."

Her shoulder slants. "Exactly. Also… I don't want to feel like I'm leaving her too much. That's what…"

"Your mom did." I fill in her sentence, and we stop in our stride.

"Yeah." I hear the sadness in her voice.

I wrap my arm around her from the side from instinct. "We're not our parents."

"We'll do it better." She doesn't sound enthused. "Motto of our lives."

"It can be true."

She leans over to touch Nora's belly; our daughter is the lightness we need when things get too real. "But to answer your question, I just don't think I'm ready to head back to work, but I should."

"You don't have to rush, Isla. You don't need to work at all if that's what you want. I want to take care of you both. If you feel it's better for yourself or Nora, then we're lucky enough that it's not an issue financially." I'm offering because I mean it when I say that I want to take care of her.

"I couldn't let you do that," she's quick to protest.

I chuckle to myself and wet my lips. "Remember, I can get a little insistent. Don't be surprised if I hand in your resignation," I joke with her.

Her brows raise. "Oh, I know you would. But we're just adding to our list of things that we should establish, in parenting or with us. Because what you just offered is more than a kind gesture that doesn't necessarily involve Nora."

"And? I'm not worried about it. Nothing about you scares me," I admit. I'm drawn to her like water in a tide, unable to go in the opposite direction.

Isla seems to let my revelation sink in. "Maybe you should be. I kept a secret from you. You never once doubted my irresponsible birth control accident, or asked if she was really yours. You went in headfirst without question."

I bite the corner of my mouth. "It's because I do trust you. Even though you didn't tell me and it hurt, I slowly understand your reasoning."

"I never slept with anyone else after the hurricane or even the months before, in case you're wondering."

"Ditto for me."

Now she seems shocked. "What? You really didn't sleep with anyone else?"

I shake my head.

"We're having this conversation a little late," she one-tones.

I begin to grin. "Sounds about right."

We both look down at our daughter whose eyes are big and curious.

"I want her to know she's number one," Isla mentions.

"That's not even negotiable for either of us," I agree.

Isla leans her head against my shoulder as we continue to watch our daughter lying there with the world moving around her. "We got lucky with her."

"Yeah, we did," I nearly whisper.

I got lucky with you too.

We continue to walk slowly back to our house.

"Vaughn, I'm happy we can talk openly about this stuff. Well, the parenting stuff. It makes one aspect easier."

"Me too."

We're still avoiding the us factor like the plague, but it makes sense for now. I'm just tiptoeing us into the inevitable conversation. This is probably the tables turning. She was the one afraid to tell me about the pregnancy for all those months; now I'm the one afraid to share how I feel. More empathy hits me for the whole situation of the last months since November.

I'm going to take the easy road out right now.

"Want to go grab some cherry cobbler with vanilla bean ice cream?"

Isla's face turns appreciative, as if I uncovered the key to her soul. "Ooh, someone just gained points."

I snort a laugh. "If only this was all as easy as a hockey game."

Because I only ever do my best to win, and I'm scared that I may lose all of this.

22

ISLA

Standing at the front door, I take the cow that plays nursery rhymes in one continuous loop and throw it outside. However, the toy nearly hits Vaughn as he walks up the front path. He even ducks and looks at me preciously.

"What did the cow do to you?" His lips slant to the side, entertained.

I growl a sound as I hold a wooden spoon in my other hand as if I'm a crazed woman. "I was playing with Nora, and that stupid thing wouldn't stop playing 'Merry Had a Little Lamb.' Even the off button won't solve the problem, and the batteries won't come out."

Vaughn continues his approach to me. "And the wooden spoon?"

"I thought maybe if I hit it enough that it would stop, but it's possessed and out to give me a headache." I realize how ridiculous I must sound.

He takes the spoon from my hand before we both assess the damage of a plastic singing cow lying in the plants, although miraculously now quiet.

"Let me guess, Connor and Hadley gave us that gift," he comments.

"Or Stone. We have options. Yeah, it's all of their life's mission to give our child annoying toys." I'm still a little salty that a toy put me in a foul mood.

Following Vaughn into the house and closing the door behind me, I'm happy he's back. He came home early, as he said he would try.

The last month has been hectic. Nora grows, Vaughn has meetings, and I'm trying to keep on top of laundry.

Vaughn heads straight to our princess in her bouncy chair. "Hey, sunshine, is Mommy acting a little strange today?" He tickles her belly, and Nora's response is a bubble popping out of her mouth. Vaughn glances back at me with his eyes wide before returning his focus on our daughter. "Your mom says it's because of a poor cow, but I think it's because tonight is the night that you are getting evicted and trying out your big room."

That *is* why I'm not in the best of moods today.

I grumble a sound, as if he isn't right, even though he is. Vaughn stands and heads back in my direction, and despite being sleep deprived, he still has swagger.

"We agreed that it's for the best. If she continues to sleep near us, then she may never sleep alone for the years to come. Hell, she may even sleep better."

An upset feeling swirls inside of me. "I know, especially with her feeding schedule slightly better and also having a bit of formula. A better night of sleep for all does sound appealing." I hold my palm up. "But she's a baby, *my* baby."

Vaughn gently touches my elbows. "*Our* baby, and this is what we both agreed. Plus, you said you tried putting her in her room a few times for her naps during the day and she loved it, slept totally fine."

I stay silent and awkwardly tighten my lips.

He cocks his head to the side. "You did let her nap in there a few times, right?"

My eyes flutter. "I may have… tried… but she generally sleeps in her stroller or in the baby wrap attached to me like a koala."

He gently shakes his head, with his sexy grin staying put. "Okay, now I understand why this might be a big step. Look, it's up to you, but I think you want a little bit of routine, and this way it will be easier to have babysitters."

I sigh and growl. "You're right."

And two hours later, we find ourselves staring at Nora's closed nursery door, with her already sound asleep on the other side. Vaughn is holding the baby monitor like a walkie-talkie, and I'm checking to ensure the app is correctly installed on my phone so I can check on the video feed at any time.

Vaughn and I glance at each other, clearly more affected then either of us care to admit. "She has her dreamcatcher, she's safe."

I give him a dumbfounded look. "Oh, now you want to believe in my superstition."

My feet begin to nearly stomp away in the direction of my room, but the clearing of a throat behind me draws my attention back to Vaughn.

"Where are you going?"

"My room," I inform him like he's crazy.

"Why?"

"Why not? Nora is now in her own bed, and I need to get used to waking in the night and going to her room if she wakes," I explain, as though he has forgotten our plan.

Vaughn steps closer to me, our breaths now mingling as the tips of his fingers brush down my arm to my wrists. "You're not leaving my room."

Oh… *oh.*

I nervously chortle. "There is no longer a baby lying between us. The baby vacates your room, then that kind of means so do I. I was there because of the baby."

The pads of his fingertips draw back up my arms, causing a quiver in my body. "Do you really want to move back into your old room? In the end, you were only there a few nights," he whispers as our eyes latch onto a moment.

No words form from my side.

We've carefully treaded around the topic of Nora moving to her own room. As in, we've purposely avoided the puzzle of where I might sleep. But leave it to Vaughn to take the step.

My head retreats back slightly, attempting to wrap my thoughts around what he is trying to translate.

"Isla, you're not moving back to your old room." His voice is nearly taunting but so damn delicious and amorous.

"Am I not?" I play clueless… but really, I kind of am. What *is* happening?

Vaughn brings his finger to my cheek before skimming the line of my jaw in a tantalizing move, with his eyes firmly open. "No. You don't want to go, and you don't need to."

I snicker at this turn of events. "Vaugh, I'm not sure—"

His finger lands on my lips to shush me. "You're staying in my room." He is so damn inflexible.

I blow his finger away, determined to challenge him, except I can't. "Horrible idea." I smile.

"All the more reason to do it." He grins.

My finger points to him. "We're sleeping," I warn.

"I'm a gentleman," he counters.

I laugh once as I turn away from him to walk to the devil's den. "Hardly."

This is what continues to happen around him. He gets cocky, and a powerful force within me eagerly follows.

It's a few minutes later when I'm lying on my side in Vaughn's bed, staring at him as he is in the same position, that I know this is the beginning of a road that may lead to a destination that I'm not quite sure of.

Luckily, I'm not sure I'm ready to open business down below yet. The doctor gave the all-clear a few weeks ago, but mentally, I'm just not there. I believe Vaughn is aware, which is why it confuses me even more that his look is soft. He wants me here, in his bed, only to sleep, without our daughter present.

My head rests on my hands under my cheek. "Our wall is gone."

"Kind of the point." Vaughn brings his hand to my hair to stroke once in a comforting kind of way.

"What are we doing, Vaughn?" I hate this elatedness that must be showing on my face.

His eyes are tense yet delicate, and it feels as though he is admiring me in this moment. "Nothing. I just think it's ridiculous for you to sleep in your own room."

"Really?" I'm doubting him.

"Nah, I would have you thrown over my lap in no time to spank you if I could. However, we accidentally made a child who is amazing, which means we have to skirt the lines of caution. Which we can do in bed… to sleep."

I giggle at his word choice. "Hmm, we could end up in murky waters."

"Or it could be the start of the conversation that we've been avoiding."

I nuzzle into his palm near my ear. "It's kind of, I don't know… We're good at the physical stuff, and we have a connection, but we've never actually, you know… dated."

Vaughn sits up in a flash, as though I hit a nerve, but I'm confused why his soft look is anything but scared. "You're right. I didn't really think about it like that."

Now I join him when I slide my upper body up to lean against the headboard. "It's because you were never one to date, I think. Not for anyone. Our ability to connect so easily was also due to distance. We never had to confront the explanation of what we were doing. It was easy to just be… friends with benefits?" My voice sounds uneven, as I'm not sure my word choice is correct.

"A good way to examine it. However, all of that went out the window when you got pregnant. Kind of bound for life now."

Glancing at the monitor on the side table, I see that Nora is still sound asleep. She's also the reminder of a simple fact, which makes me whip my head right back in Vaughn's direction. "I don't think forcing something because we share a child is the right approach."

As much as I want everything for our daughter, Nora seeing her parents together because they felt an obligation isn't the best solution either.

A tickle down by fingers resting on the duvet causes my sight to take in the view of Vaughn interlacing our fingers in a way that feels far too natural.

"We agree on a lot of things, Isla. Which is why I wouldn't even be attempting to try anything if I felt it was just for Nora's sake. But it is because of her that we both get to reassess things. You're right, distance made it easier before. Now it just gives us a reason to confront it."

I can't read him right now, but my face tips up in caution. "Did you just say you're attempting something?"

Vaughn's lips roll in before popping out. "You know the thoughts in our head that we've both acknowledged yet haven't said out loud? It's something like that." The man is almost bashful, I'm not sure I've seen this side of him.

This time, I interlink our fingers. "So, I guess this is the beginning of us attempting to address the elephant in the room."

"Maybe. But the elephant is right there." He indicates with his head behind me.

Quickly I look then laugh when I see a stuffed animal on the floor.

"Smartass." I turn to Vaughn and playfully swat his arm. It only triggers us to enter a scuffle of tickling, that ends with me nearly squealing in delight, right before he pins me to the mattress, dragging my arms up over my head. Our laughter fades but our tilted smirks stay put.

It would be so easy if he leaned down to kiss me, yet the dimples on his cheeks tell me that he is about to impress me instead.

"What you said earlier, about how we never dated."

"Mmmhmm." I wait patiently for him to continue.

He looks up then back to my lips. "Let me change that. We'll go on a date."

I nearly bug out in a wonderful way. "You didn't exactly ask, you just stated." We have banter, and it's great.

"Now who's being clever? Besides, I already know your answer, so I'm saving you the consideration in your head." He doesn't let my pinned arms go.

My body curves up to him, and it's far more sensual than what I intended. We should just end our misery of feeding into our magnetism but neither one of us dares to.

"Are you going to let my wrists go so I can sleep?" I raise my brows.

He releases me. "For now, yes."

That earns him my back, because I need to roll away from him to avoid his sweltering stare, and my body feels alive in the way that's eager for me to ignore that my first time since becoming a mom will be different. Then again, it *will* be different with Vaughn, because we are on the other side of a life change.

The feeling of a warm body swooping in behind me doesn't surprise me. However, Vaughn's cuddly nature kind of does.

I've seen him with Nora, but that's fatherhood. When we all shared a bed, sure, I would tuck my body against Vaughn's while one of us held our baby. But now?

I snort a laugh. "We suck at boundaries. Our new motto."

"Totally right, but that's why we can knock them down," he confirms but only wraps his arms tighter around me.

———

A FEW DAYS LATER, I'm taking note of when Nora's next check-up is with the doctor on the shared calendar with Vaughn, when I notice that in two weeks, he will be away for pre-season games. I focus on that a little longer than I should because the thought is a little daunting.

Vaughn arrives home just as I connect my cell to my charger.

"Get dressed," he insists.

I give myself the once-over, and I'm in my usual skinny jeans and tank top. "What's wrong with this?"

He leans against the counter like a man who doesn't know anything else but swaggered stances. "Relax, it wasn't an insult. We both need to change, as we're going out."

"Oh, I should probably go pack the diaper bag." I'm about to go to my task when Vaughn grabs my wrist in record time.

He has a grimace which is slightly unnerving. "She isn't coming with."

"Huh?"

"You know, normally you don't bring kids on your first date." He watches me while everything registers. An unrecognizable sound rumbles at the back of my throat. "Remember? Date. You and me," he clarifies.

Before I can answer, the doorbell rings, and I decide answering it is the distraction I need. Only, I answer to find Connor. Now I'm confused again.

Vaughn arrives behind me to greet our guest. "Nice, the babysitter is here."

My head whizzes straight to Vaughn. "What?" I nearly spit out with great disapproval on the babysitter choice.

Connor strides in and raises his hands up. "Relax. We all know that I'm not capable of handling itty-bitty humans."

"Oh really?" I'm cynical. "Had you pegged as babysitter of the year."

"Yikes, someone is frosty today," Connor highlights to Vaughn.

He just grins at his friend before placing his hands on my shoulders from the side. "Ignore her. I caught her off guard with the date-night surprise. Perhaps now is the time to tell her the plan regarding our daughter."

Connor stands before me, casual as can be. "Yeah, sure." He throws a thumb over his shoulder. "Hadley and my mom are in my car trying to install the car seat, they're responsible tonight for your little result of procreation."

Relief hits me in whoosh. No way would I have left my little girl with Connor alone.

"Great. That's clarified." Vaughn is guiding me toward the stairs. "Now go get ready, Isla. You have twenty minutes," he calls out, slightly coaxing me up the stairs.

By the time I'm searching for clothes in my closet and settle on a black dress that will fit and do wonders, then it nearly overthrows my balance; I'm going on a real date with Vaughn.

● 23

VAUGHN

It isn't because of our daughter.

That isn't the reason why we're walking up the stairs to the roof of the Dizzy Duck Inn. I have a romantic night planned because I owe it to us to see if we have any future.

This is out of my realm, the whole dating-because-it-matters thing. Then again, so was becoming a dad, and I now believe I was always meant for that.

Maybe I'm also meant to be a better man. One that commits their life to someone.

Isla gasps when we arrive on the roof, her eyes instantly observing the scene. There is a small table with a few candles, and hanging lights border the roof. Most of all, we have the view of Lake Spark and the pines surrounding the water that are outlined by the full moon. The water has specks of a few boats with their lights on, anchored in the middle of the lake.

And we're all alone.

She pivots on her heel to face me. "You arranged this?"

I smirk as my hands rest in my jeans pockets, and my eyes lower because I've never been one to surprise a woman in this manner. "Yeah, Declan mentioned it, and I put the wheels in motion. The staff seem receptive to bribes and people who play hockey," I joke. "Figured this arrangement is a well-kept secret, and private too."

Her bright smile is pure affection. "I love it."

I tip my head in the direction of the table as I walk there. "You'll like this." I lift the cover on a tray to reveal a bunch of appetizer options, and best of all, a desserts section, with small pots of chocolate mousse, but most of all, fancy cheese with berry compote to complement. "A cheese plate for dessert is very European of us."

Isla comes to join me at the table. "It's also very us. I have to say that our periodic cheese discussion is the last thing I thought would have been the key to getting me interested in our attraction, but bravo that you did it."

We both laugh before we sit down. I hold up the wine from the ice bucket, checking if she wants a glass.

"Please. I can have a glass, it will be fine. I pumped before we left, and mama can let loose, as there is plenty of milk in the freezer. I might be a little buzzed , though, as it's been a while."

I grin as I pour her a glass. "That's okay. You might be kind of fun tipsy. Plus, I know where you live to ensure you get home safely."

Her smile widens. "Ah yes, because someone at this table put my house onto the rental market in a gutsy move."

Leaning back in my chair, I'm confident with my actions. "And? It seems to have worked out."

She playfully offers me a look of doubt. "We'll see."

I bring my glass out to clink hers. "To… a perfect daughter and a good night?" I say, questioning if that's the right toast to give.

Isla ensures our wine glasses touch. "Cheers."

It's a few seconds of silence, kind of in disbelief that this is where we find ourselves. Nearly a year ago, we were just a flirtation at a wedding brunch, with no possibility in sight. Now? We're way more than we ever imagined, our lives intertwined.

"What are you thinking?" I ask.

Her mouth twists to the side while she sets her drink down. "I think, maybe I'm a little nervous about the fact that I'm *not* nervous to be here with you."

I take one more sip then also set my wine aside. "That's encouraging for me."

She crosses her arms on the table. "Okay, so first-date questions. Let me see…"

"Work?"

"Kind of already know that. Uhm, food?"

"You change depending on mood. Currently on hummus and pretzels," I answer.

"And you love a chicken burger with a side of honey mustard sauce, but it has to be in those little dish things and never from a packet."

I chuckle. "Hmm, it seems we already know a few things about one another."

She raises her finger in the air. "I got it. Travel. Where do you want to go? It can't be any place where hockey games take place."

"Huh, that makes it kind of difficult. I love it up in Calgary and near Banff, but warm weather wins every single time. I'm kind of sad to have left Florida simply for that, but summer here is the right temperature. So I think anywhere in Mexico or the Caribbean—wait, actually, I've never been to Italy."

Excitement hits her. "Yes, the Amalfi coast or more up north near Cinque de Terre. I bet the food is amazing. I actually went to France, and that's the only place I've been in Europe. Briggs and I were planning an Iceland trip, but well… he found a girlfriend, and I became occupied with a tiny human."

I bite my bottom lip, appreciating that we align on interests, but I have to ask. "How did your brother take the news when you told him?"

Isla scoffs a laugh. "Surprisingly well. He wanted to know who to kill, but I told him not to ask, so he didn't. Instead, he supported me in every single way, no questions asked. We are kind of one another's ride-or-die, ya know?"

"Yeah, I know. Stone is the same way for me."

She grabs a piece of fresh baguette. "Your brother seems really sweet. Funny and kind too."

My eyes grow large. "Uh-oh, are you doubting if you picked the right brother?" I tease.

Isla throws a piece of bread at me. "Nah, he doesn't have dimples like you."

Bringing my long finger to slide along my chin, I point out something. "We didn't grow up in big families, in fact we lacked the essential parents in some ways. However, maybe all it takes is one person to be your family, just like we had our brothers."

Her eyes dart to the candle while she gets lost in thought. "I believe that, but it's extra special when you can create, I don't know… more family."

I nod in understanding and agreement. "We established our proven theory."

Her soft smile returns. "We have. Now tell me something else… what is your ideal Saturday? Ours have been kind of scheduled around a certain person. Wait… I already know your answer, actually."

"What? I enjoy grabbing a coffee then a walk. In the evening, go out for a drink or concert. The whole club scene is done, now that I'm past my prime. It's the same for you, no?" My fingers trace the edge of the table while I listen intently.

"Exactly. Coffee, leisurely walks. Concerts are great. We have a summer festival in Lake Spark, and they get quite a few good acts visiting."

It sounds quaint and calm. It's appealing, if I'm being honest.

"We should go."

"We missed it, but there is a big market next weekend."

"Ah, that's why I've seen signs everywhere, and Declan mentioned something about maple syrup as a sponsor or something." I grab a few fried pieces of eggplant while I hear Isla laugh.

It's a solid hearty laugh too. "Vaughn, how can you have forgotten? First…" She holds up one finger. "Everyone in town has been talking about our weekend events; didn't any of the old ladies from the knitting club stop you on the street to remind you of their bake sale? And two…" She adds a finger. "Declan's family owns Grizzly Dash, you know that maple syrup with a dancing bear on it. That's one of the reasons he has more money than we can count. His parents sponsor almost all Lake Spark events. Did you forget about his syrup connection?"

I scratch the back of my neck because I'm playing her completely as, of course, I'm familiar with my team owner's family brand. "Sorry if I've been distracted. Those coffees from Jolly Joe's, with the jellybeans, might have distracted me. Who the hell adds a jellybean to coffee?" I humorously sound frustrated.

"The wizard of happiness, that's who. It's supposed to bring luck," she states matter-of-factly before her demeanor changes to a hint of seriousness. "Admit it, Lake Spark has grown on you, even if your job wasn't in the picture."

You've grown on me.

"You completely caught me. I'm now a man who abides to signs of deer and duck crossings and patiently waits for the fresh eggs to arrive at the general store," I say in jest. Yet, I owe her an honest truth. "But you're right, I do like it here."

Isla gets comfortable on her chair, holding the wine glass close to her chest. The candlelight highlights her jubilant face and a twinkle in her eyes. "Uhm, you know, I'm kind of aware that the whole hockey-life thing means that eventually you could end up at a different location. I know you have a four-year contract, but I just want you to know that it is in my head, and that if things… flow between us." Her crooked look is priceless. "Then I'm aware that we would kind of follow you, for Nora… and me."

My jaw flexes side to side, grateful that she simply understands, and it doesn't feel like a big issue in terms of logistics, but it's colossal step when it comes to a promising future. "I guess thinking that far into the future is a bright start to this first date. You're totally going fast." I'm completely joking with her. "But I think it's a safe thought to have."

She nervously gulps a sip of wine. "Okay, I should tuck into some food. It looks delicious."

We each pile our plates with some cuisine and get settled into our meal.

"We could have had three courses, but I kind of felt that this would lead to less disruption."

Her eyes flick up at me with a sultry look. "Why? In case you want to take me here on the roof?"

"Nah, I would wait until we're in the car." I love the banter that just flows with us.

She chortles a laugh at the memory and the fact that we had an escapade in my car all those months ago.

"I'm not sure anyone has ever done something this romantic for me, this dinner and location. Sure, I've dated, but it was always simple dinners or beer at the bar. Don't get me wrong, I don't need to have fancy stuff. It's just you put a lot of thought into this."

"You deserve it, plus I only bring my A-game." I take a bite of food.

Isla sets her fork down. "It's definitely worthy of praise."

"Yeah?" I lean back, taking in the boost to my ego. "I have it in me to impress? I mean, I knew that, but you're kind of a different type of judge." *The only one who matters.*

She points her fork at me. "And I approve."

"Besides, the next two weeks are our opportunity to have these kind of nights and alone time. Game season will be sneaking in time, between games and travel… that is, if we continue on this path." I don't want to be presumptuous.

"Where is your cocky demand? You sound unsure." She's completely entertained that she's throwing me off my axis.

We need to change this up, as we keep circling back to a what-if. Action is the best step, not conversation.

I abruptly stand up and offer her my hand. "Come on?"

"Someone sounds like he has a trick up his sleeve." She accepts my hand with ease.

I pull her out of seat, and we walk a few steps until I yank her to me to ensure our bodies are close. She yelps from the surprise move but seems pleased. Clasping our hands together, my other arm snakes around her middle to lead us in a dance.

"Oh my, Vaughn Madden is dancing with me in a romantic setting underneath the stars. Violins are playing for the women in this world whose image of you as the broody playboy is broken."

I spin us around and tip her back. "Isla, they had a damn orchestra the moment the world learned on social media that you and I have a child together. The heart emoji now officially makes me sick from overuse."

"The comments did get ridiculous but in a positive kind of way. I'm just thankful that we only let them see a photo of a little hand."

"You don't mind dancing without music?"

"It kind of makes it better. You might actually hear the thumping in my chest from excitement." She squeezes my hand.

We continue to sway side to side. "I don't need to hear it, I feel it, Isla. Just like I have since you've been sleeping in my bed in my arms."

Her mouth parts open, trying not to read my eyes that are glued to hers. "I think this date is going well, don't you?"

"It's going more than alright." I tip her back.

The sound of distant thunder doesn't deter us. We continue our dance, and I inhale the scent of her hair while I bring her hand to my chest. This is nothing like I imagined a real committed date would be; it's a thousand times better.

Lightning far away, followed a few counts later by thunder only makes this more unique.

She rests her head near my shoulder, and a relaxing breath hits her. "A stormfront is coming our way. It will bring warmer temperatures this week."

I snort a laugh. "That's what's bringing the warm temperatures?" There is an underlying inappropriate meaning in my question. I swear I can hear her smile.

"Are hotels your kink?" She's witty today.

"No, it's just Lake Spark only has so many spots," I rebuff.

"This whole thing started because you showed up at my hotel during a hurricane. Here we are on a date on top of a hotel with a storm approaching."

My hand falls to her lower back to press her closer to me, which is a very dangerous move, because I just want to get lost in her. "I think this will be our start for getting it all right."

A roll of thunder is stronger than a minute ago. It breaks our moment, and we both study the clouds covering the moon and the purple-blue hue of flashes of light.

Isla backs away. "We should probably head inside."

A hand finds my heart. "I failed at my date planning and forgot to check the weather."

It causes her to grin at my humor as she saunters back to the table. "I assure you that you did great, because I'm going to say that I don't want this to end." Her head cocks to the side as I take in the news.

"Well then, I should ask them to bag this all up so we can enjoy this at home."

I stride straight to her and capture her chin between my thumb and long finger, tipping her gaze up to enable my mouth to lower. My lips mold against hers for a kiss that feels far too overwhelming because this is us kissing for all the right reasons. Everything before was attraction and sex. Now emotions are involved, and if I'm honest with myself, a big load of hopefulness too.

Isla whimpers into my mouth when she brings her tongue to mine and swirls. Her fingers find the nape of my neck and curl into my hair. We both kiss a non-respectable first-date kiss because this is far too deep, with no end in sight.

I'm so tempted to lift her up and push everything off the table to lay her down. But I'm well aware that we have to go slow, and I'm not sure she's ready, even though I know her doctor said I could worship Isla's body. Maybe not in those exact words, but I was there, as they also checked on Nora.

The point is, I can't give into lust right now. Only sink into this kiss and then angle my lips to take in another. This is long, hard then soft, and the parting of our lips is a brush of skin that zaps along my spine straight to my groin, waving to my chest in the process. It's all stirring inside of me.

Our possibilities.

Which is why when we return home and enjoy snacking on food until Hadley returns Nora—because there is no way Isla would allow an overnight—then we fall into a different kind of night.

When Isla and I climb into bed, we find one another with her leg hooking over my hip and my hand resting on her side, before our giddy looks lead us into a make-out session.

"You had to leave your shirt off? A new habit that you formed when it became only you and I in bed," she nearly pants.

A cocky grin hits my lips. "It's effective, isn't it."

She scoffs a sound before kissing me again. This is all we're going to do tonight, until she falls asleep in my arms with her head against my chest. She flicks her eyes up to study my face.

"When is the second date?" she asks.

That's promising.

24

ISLA

I watch as Vaughn speaks to the man sitting next to him at the table as we enjoy a dinner for the management team of the Spinners at Catch 22 here in Lake Spark. They rented the whole restaurant for privacy. The subtle feeling of Vaughn's fingertips on my bare thigh under the table can't be ignored, which is why a wry smile has been fixed on my mouth for the last few minutes.

My focus on the wine glass is broken when Violet touches my shoulder in passing and leans down. "Going to the ladies' room if you want to freshen up?"

"Sounds like a plan." I can use a little break and to check in.

I'm still wondering if I could be so lucky. The past week since Vaughn's and my date, a shift has happened between us. The kind of change that I welcome. We don't tiptoe around the obvious and easily enjoy our time with Nora, but we also enjoy one another through the chances of late-night dinners while she sleeps and a hell of a lot of roaming hands. But the nights that we sit outside on the patio and admire the night are my favorite. We talk about our days and things that we can plan. It was an easy yes when he asked if I would accompany him for his team dinner.

Violet and I make it to the ladies' room and are alone. We head straight to the mirror to freshen our makeup and adjust our dresses.

"This isn't too boring for you, I hope." Violet swipes on a new coat of mahogany lipstick to her lips.

I grab my blush from my bag and begin to apply. "Actually, not at all. It's kind of hot to see Vaughn in his element, plus I'm used to all of this hockey talk."

Violet lifts her brows and turns to lean against the counter next to the sink. "Let's rewind a second, the whole hot-Vaughn mention. How is that going, beyond the parenting thing?"

My cheeks raise because I am happy. "We're seeing where things go, but it feels promising. It was kind of odd doing the whole date thing, considering our past encounters, but it was just right."

She throws a knowing smirk in my direction. "Thought so. I caught wind of those occasional glances with one another and his constant need to keep his hand glued to you. Were you two whispering? Because I'm sure I saw that before you giggled like a woman possessed by a man."

I laugh and stay focused on my blush. "You and Declan are the same."

She feigns doubt with a sound. "He is my husband, but we also started as a purely physical fling. However, normally when something like that carries on, it's because there are deep underlying feelings."

I blow out a breath and turn to accompany her in leaning against the counter. "You're right. We're just both kind of scared that we might be blinded by the cloud of bliss that a new child brings. It would be the wrong reason to be together just because we felt an obligation, but then he said something…"

She pretends to clap her hands together and seems invested in my explanation. "Do tell."

I bite my inner cheek because Vaughn said something poignant, and he wasn't even trying. "He mentioned that maybe Nora is what brought us together to realize what we should be."

Violet gushes for me before she gently touches my arm. "That is more than promising, that's commitment. Sounds like he's there, you just need to accept it and decide if you're ready to jump in."

I chortle a laugh and turn my body back to the mirror to assess myself, and I feel and appear more radiant than I have in a long time. "Vaughn is a guy who won't relent, yet he has been patient. I'm beginning to see that it's me holding us back."

Violet side-glances to me. "If that's clear to you, then you just have to be the one to take action."

My head tilts as I stew in her words for a few seconds. "Maybe you're right."

"Do it in your time and be sure, but it's your turn."

I nod once in understanding, and she offers me her lipstick, and I hand her my blush. "This is a nice evening. It kind of feels as though the team is not just a team but a sort of community and family."

"For sure. Declan wanted it that way. I do my best not to get too close to the wives of the players, except Hadley, of course. Players come and go, but the management team is slightly more stable."

"That makes sense."

We both put our makeup back in our purses. "Enough relationship talk. We need to praise our kids with the latest photos."

A proud smile hits me as we both open the screens of our phones and begin our few minutes of child talk.

By the time I'm back at the table, Vaughn seems to be nearly done with his wine. I place my hand on his shoulder right before he leans in.

"You were gone for a while, I was nearly scared you ran away." He winks at me, and those damn dimples are going to cause a flood between my thighs.

"Never," I rasp, and I wonder if he heard me, as someone attempts to grab his attention.

I don't mind being his plus-one and not getting much alone time with Vaugh. It allows me the opportunity to explore my deep thoughts that have been floating in me lately. Except it's not a thought; it's truly a feeling that we can be more.

Vaughn brings his gaze back to me as the person went onto a new topic with someone else. "You okay? You seem a little out of it." His subtle smirk informs me that he must be aware that I'm contemplating.

My eyes flutter, as if I'm slipping out of a daze. "Oh yeah, totally." I reach for my wine to take a sip.

He chuckles under his breath. "Won't be much longer—"

Declan slaps a hand on Vaughn's shoulder. "This man here is who we need to keep everyone in line. Hope you're ready for me to steal him away for the season."

"I'm sure I'll behave in his absence," I retort, and both men laugh in response.

"Enjoy the last few days together before preseason games," Declan mentions.

"She will." Vaughn stares at me intensely, and I'm curious what dirty thoughts are running through his head right now.

Declan grins as he walks away, because Vaughn and I are locked into facing one another with understanding eyes.

"Come on, let's get out of your way." He stands and offers me his hand.

I gladly take it but want to double-check. "Are you sure it isn't too early?"

"I'm sure. We should get home."

Home.

I never get tired of him saying that.

―――――

THE DRIVE back to our house is quiet, as Vaughn and I sit in the back of the car since we have a driver tonight provided by the team. It's the kind of silence that heightens the tension in the best possible way. A mix of revelation and passion.

Even when we say goodbye to April, as she watched her adopted niece, and head upstairs to check on Nora sound asleep, Vaughn and I can't seem to shake the air between us, with a feeling that something is about to snap.

He quickly says he'll be right back, and I walk to our room. The moment I begin to slip off my dress, the answer feels clear.

I smile to myself before I plant myself in a spot on the middle of the bed in only a bra and black lace panties. I shake my head to loosen my hair and look down to see that my cleavage is out of control, but that doesn't matter.

Vaughn unknowingly walks into our room and stops in his tracks when he catches the view.

His brows raise from the unexpected, yet approval shades his face.

"We only have a few days left before the schedule goes haywire. Better make the most of it," I say in a sultry voice that I make an effort to speak.

He begins to unbutton his dress shirt. "Oh really? Are you sure you want to do this, considering I have about a hundred ways that I could ravish you?" He throws his shirt to the side, and it lands somewhere on the floor. Doesn't matter, as he's slowly walking toward the bed.

I move to all fours and slowly crawl toward the edge of the bed, doing my best to make it as sexy as can be. "Well, we have a problem then, as I also have a hundred ways—well, eighty, but who's counting," I tease.

Vaughn stands next to the edge, reaching out to slide his hand along my back to my ass that he squeezes, and his breath turns to a hiss. "Isla, you're so fucking beautiful."

"You've mentioned before." I push up onto my knees and peer up as I begin to work on his belt. "There is only one thing I'm craving right now."

He combs his fingers through my hair softly before they increase to a more clawing nature to keep a hold on me. "I won't deny you, that's for sure."

I feel a bashfulness take over me because something does freak me out, thanks to our daughter in the other room. "As excited as I am for this, this does kind of feel like losing my virginity again, except this time I know what I'm doing."

Vaughn chortles a sound. "Ah, yeah… I can imagine this is kind of a new realm."

I swallow. "Exactly."

"Well then, I guess I'm lucky to be the guy that you lose it for."

My mouth parts open, and I run the tip of my tongue along my bottom lip to the corner, showing him that I'm eager for a taste. The sound of his zipper that my fingers undo notifies me that I can have what I want now. Sliding his boxer briefs down, I flatten my tongue to show him right before I lean down to lick his hard cock.

He moans the moment my tongue traces his length. "Isla, you do a lot of things to me, but taking my cock like a good girl is hands down second best to being inside of you."

Taking him deeper into my watering mouth, I only want to please him. The last time we were like this was before everything changed. Still, I refuse to cement us with only vanilla transgressions. That's just not us, never has been.

My tongue continues to glide along his length while he groans a sound, with his eyes hooding closed before glancing down at my actions. I need to hold his hips as I take him deeper and don't want to lose my balance. Bobbing my head, the palm of his hand on the back of my head pushes me forward slightly to ensure he hits the back of my throat.

I make a sound from the force and breathe through my nose, as it's by no means a gentle lick of his tip. Yet I wouldn't trade this for anything else.

"Such a good girl you've always been." His hand sneaks behind to slap my ass once before he hooks his fingers under the waistband of my thong to snap once. I love his hand cascading up my spine until both his hands cradle my head. "As much as I want every last drop rolling down your throat, I need to come inside of you more. On your back."

His demanding tone has returned, but it only makes me smirk. I begin to slide backward up the mattress on my hands, purposely taking my time and letting my foot slither up his thigh as Vaughn follows me by slowly crawling to hover over me. My head raises to ensure our lips can meet for a kiss, and he takes the opportunity of space behind me to unhook my bra.

Lying back down, I get comfortable with my head on the pillow. His mouth trails down my neck by skimming his lips then ghosting around my nipple. "Your tits have been driving me crazy." His tongue darts out to lick a circle around my hard bud. I nearly whimper from the overwhelming sensitivity of it all. "I wish I could worship these more."

I sputter a laugh and bring my hand to cover my face. "Yeah, it might get a little messy if you suck. My breasts are aching, but I think this time it's all because of you, the good kind of aching."

Vaughn nuzzles his face between my breasts then gives attention to the other breast, and his journey continues down my body, tracing around my belly button.

My body is a little different than before, but for the most part, I still feel sexy. I gasp a moan when he strips off my panties.

"We might have to go slow," I whisper. Okay, I might be slightly petrified of what's about to happen. I kind of refuse to look down there, and I can't even imagine what this might all feel like.

That mouth of his, with a little evening stubble, brushes along my thighs, and he encourages my legs to open wide. He retreats his head back slightly to get a view.

"Trust me, this is nothing to be scared about. You're glistening and soaking, and I desperately need a taste," he assures me, so much that it sounds like he's being honest. It eases me a little more.

The swiping of his tongue sinks me into a moment of ecstasy. Vaughn has always been a giver, especially when licking my pussy is involved. He knows where to point his tongue and swirls in the right places until my body coils against his mouth, with my moans becoming a string of slurs.

Then my eyes shoot open the second he dips a finger inside of me. It feels different. I feel tight, but everything feels ten times better than before. I'm not sure that I've ever been this sensitive inside of me, a new kind of magic.

"Christ, Isla, you feel amazing."

A sound cracks out of me as I soak in this feeling. "I'll feel better when your cock is inside of me, please," I beg.

Vaugh kisses my thigh once more before he adjusts my legs to ensure he has space to be between them, with his cock finding home and slowly pumping in.

The instant connection causes me to gasp and Vaughn to groan in pleasure. "I'm not going to last."

"Mmhmm. Me neither."

Our mouths meet for a kiss to ride out his length driving deeper inside of me. Our breaths become one as the intensity is too over-whelming.

"You okay?" he whispers near my ear.

"Totally," I promise.

The fingers on our one hand interlink, and he draws my arm up and over my head as my pussy wraps around him, and he drags in and out until he feels comfortable enough to move faster.

I can't get enough, and I raise my thighs higher then wrap around his waist, with my toes digging into the muscles of his ass.

Our lips continue to dance around one another as we both begin to pant.

"You're heaven, you know that?" he grits out as he continues to keep us connected.

"You're just meant to live inside of me it seems."

His response is to kiss my neck with a slight nip of my skin between his teeth.

We simmer like this for a little while, and then it happens. Our eyes connect, and we slow down for a second.

The confirmation between us that we both feel this pull is by far more than we imagined. It only leads us to chase our release.

"You'll need to…" I remind him.

"Maybe a good thing, because if I come inside of you, I'll be completely gone."

A drowsy smile hits my lips. And it doesn't leave until I'm trembling around him, and he pulls out to come on my thigh.

He collapses onto his back after he cleans my thigh with his boxers and throws them to the floor, and then I tuck into him, when he kisses the top of my head and drags the duvet over us. Kissing his chest, I bring my nails to draw lazy patterns on his bare skin.

"So, was this like our second date? Because if it is, then I think I'm becoming too easy," I joke.

Vaughn ignores it and wraps me closer, tucking my head under her chin. "Nah, we always seem to be a few steps ahead."

Maybe I was, and now we can focus on our solidified relationship status.

25

VAUGHN

I shake a stuffed turtle over Nora where she's lying in her stroller while we walk along the stalls of the Saturday market in town. I'm well aware that I'm going to miss her like crazy. Every day she does something different. She's already holding her head up.

"Gosh, should we be concerned that she really doesn't cry much and just seems to be happy all the time?" I ask Isla, smiling widely at our daughter.

Isla glances sideways and throws me a humorous glare. "Don't jinx the crying part, and this all means that she is happy."

"True. We're lucky."

"I promise that I'll send you photos and videos every day," Isla mentions as she sips from her to-go cup filled with tea.

"I know you will, but it's just not the same."

"Before you know it, you'll be back. Your moments with her will be extra special."

My lips quirk out from her comment, but I have to believe she's right. "I guess we'll do an hour more here, then head home before it gets too noisy here." I have the afternoon free as everyone prepares for our first team flight tomorrow for a preseason game up in Toronto.

"We also have those noise-canceling headphones for babies that you were adamant we get so she can attend the first home game of the season." Isla twists the corners of lips, clearly finding it all amusing.

"Safety first," I defend.

She sighs as we continue our stroll. "I fear the day when Briggs will play against the Spinners. My alliance feels questioned." She's half serious.

I indicate to the free bench up near the oak tree. We both find ourselves a seat there and continue on from her statement.

I nudge her shoulder with mine. "What if I tell you that I'll let you have a pass for that game. You don't need to choose the boyfriend-slash-baby daddy over your brother."

She scoffs a laugh and brings her eyes to meet mine. "That's very kind of you. Is that what your new title is? Boyfriend-slash-baby daddy?"

My arm now rests on the back of the bench behind her in a sort of claim to the outside world that we're together. Trust me, in no part of my past was I this sweet with a woman. "We may need to work on that."

"Uh, but your offer is… I don't want you to think that I don't have loyalty to you."

I brush it off. "I know you do. But I also know how much you love your brother. So feel free to secretly support him while wearing my shirt. But only one game." I give her a sheepish look.

Her hand comes to rest on my thigh, her touch already making me untamed. Since we started upgrading our sleep time—and the shower—activities, we've both been kind of avid. Before we were orbiting around one another in a peculiar way. Now everything is on the table. We can be parents, lovers, and two people who care deeply for one another.

"Vaughn…"

I'm broken from my spell of thoughts. "Yes, Isla." I grin because her delicate tone informs me that she has a meaningful question about to hit us.

"We can be something real, you and me, right?"

My eyes widen at her. "How do you do that?"

"What?"

"Read my mind as if you knew exactly what I was thinking."

She shrugs her shoulders. "Coincidence?"

"No, it's not a coincidence." It only takes a beat to state the truth. "Yeah, Isla. We can be something real going forward. It's more than a chance too." I hear the vulnerability in my voice.

Her face lightens with that gentle smile of hers. "I was hoping you would say that."

"You shouldn't be relying on me to lead the way, although I do love it. It's just… don't be afraid to say what you want."

Isla straightens her posture and ceremoniously takes my hand in hers. "I always thought you would be the one hesitating, but I guess it's me. Except now I'm clear about what I want, and it's you."

An emotion overcomes me that feels raw, unfamiliar, but exhilarating.

It gravitates my lips straight to hers for a warm kiss. I can't get enough of this, all of this. Her.

Isla gave me a gift twice over. A daughter and a relationship with her that I never intended or expected. I'm one lucky man.

"Careful," I warn her as I murmur against her lips. "I might have to end this outing and take you right home to bed. Screw that, we can do a memory-lane session in the front seat."

Her head falls back with hysterical laughter that can't not make anyone within our radius smile. "Vaugh, please, oh please, explain how that will happen with a child in a car seat in the back."

"Solid point." Disappointment floods me. "Let's just buy a bottle of wine, and we have options. I can take you on the patio table, or we can go traditional and use a bed."

She dives in for another kiss, her finger tipping my chin. "I'm completely on board with that plan."

Which is why we walk to the general store to stock up on wine and pick up some takeout on the way home. We enjoy some tummy time with our daughter on the living room floor before I take her to the shower where I sit on the floor holding her. It's our moment that we share. She gets plenty with Isla.

"Your mom is finally being less stubborn. Seeing the light when it comes to me and her," I tell Nora, and she coos in response. "I know, right? Why the hesitation? It's me, I'm the man of her dreams, I'm sure. Her own version of Prince Charming," I lightheartedly explain to my daughter. "Go easy on her while I'm away. I'm not here to relax her in a way that she and I enjoy."

"Jesus, Vaughn, must you already traumatize our child?" Isla arrives holding a towel, ready for me to hand over the goods.

"Hey, never interrupt our serious conversations." This playfulness around our child is good for the soul. I'm not sure how anyone could turn away from this. It leaves a sour feeling in the pit of my stomach considering my upbringing, something I missed. Or how at first when I was blindsided by the news of Isla's pregnancy, I wasn't sure for a brief moment.

Isla opens the shower door, and I hand off Nora. "Be quick with the bedtime routine, we have a long night ahead of us."

"Yeah, yeah, yeah. Let me just feed her, which could be a while. She loves my chest as much as her daddy."

I grin at her. "We both know a good thing." Well, minus the milk aspect. Admittedly, I tried a little in a cup because one of the guys on the team said it's extra protein or vitamins, which is why he adds it to his coffee. *Yeah*, not going forward with that plan. Not my style.

"Don't fall asleep. I plan on coming to bed naked tonight," Isla casually mentions as she shimmies away to the nursery.

I rub my face, trying to keep myself in check, so I don't rub one out in the shower due to impatience.

I must hold out, though, because we have to make it somewhat special tonight. To reconfirm what we spoke about and to have an excellent parting before I leave. There is a lot on the line tonight.

By the time I'm lying on the bed waiting on my side, I'm nearly going out of my mind. But then my little vixen struts into the room, slowly untying the flimsy fabric of her satin robe. The robe falls in a swoosh down her skin to pool at her feet.

"I believe someone was waiting for me." Isla comes to me and is quick to push me to my back and swing one leg over to straddle me.

"This is heaven." I rest my hands behind my head.

She smirks and leans down to press a kiss on my chest then sits back up with her breasts perked out and her fingers tangling in her hair, giving me a view. I plant my hands firmly on her waist.

"I really want to watch you touch yourself before you ride me the way you want." My voice is thick with desire.

Isla takes my hands and brings them to her breasts to cup. I'm careful not to get carried away but still allow the pads of my thumbs to circle her nipples.

"I just need you in me."

I sit up and drive my thumb up to her bottom lip to drag across. "Then do it. Remember, just say what you want."

Her hips move in a wave over my cock, creating friction.

"Fill me up and show me that you meant what you said earlier." Her arms hook around my neck to ensure my lips stay close to hers.

Her pussy finds its way to welcome my shaft inside, and I slowly drive up into her.

"I meant every word," I promise and place a kiss on the curve of her shoulder. "I meant every word," I repeat and press a kiss to her collarbone. I don't stop until I'm back at her mouth.

Isla's lips grow into a satisfied smirk against my mouth. "Me too."

Then we tangle into one another, not sure where our limbs start or end. We crumble in one another's arms, forgetting that we should have been more careful, but it's a chance worth taking if it means I don't need to leave her warmth.

I stay inside, and I drop back onto the mattress, keeping Isla flush to my body.

"Shit, I wish I didn't have to leave."

She shushes my mouth with her long finger. "Stop it. Hockey is who you are, and we'll be here when you get back. Plus, Declan already said that we can join you on his plane; the perks of being an owner, I guess."

I didn't realize how much I needed her to say all of this. It's true, a lot of the times, I won't be flying with the team or coach so Declan and I can talk freely.

Inside my brain I'm figuring out what flowers to send or what our next outing will be, ignoring that our phones will become our main method of communication. A beacon of light hits me when I imagine Isla at the home games, there to support me.

It's only positive things ahead, especially since she reassures me that she'll be waiting for me.

How the hell did I miss it all those months ago that Isla was going to be more than a friend with benefits? I believe, though, that this is how it was all supposed to be.

I'm fairly confident that even though I never found the one before, I do not need to look further, as she is standing right before me. For the first time, I'm beginning to realize what this is.

She's a gamechanger.

I just don't tell her and instead kiss her with full force, catching her off guard.

But in my head, I'm beginning to be certain that this is what love is.

26

ISLA

With a baby wrapped around my middle, I'm sitting up near the owner's box where I float between the box and stands to watch the late-afternoon early-season home game. I can't control the complete contentment inside of me. Everything seems to have fallen into place in life. A far cry from a few months ago when my life seemed to have been unpredictable about what path I would end up on.

The past few weeks since Vaughn and I have made it clear that we want to do it all when it comes to us, a relief I didn't know I needed hit me. Now our days are filled with texts, occasional nights, and if he isn't in the owner's box, then I get to stare at him where he's sitting behind the team on occasion, focused on the game.

"Getting used to the new routine?" Hadley asks as she sits by my side, watching her husband like a hawk.

"Completely. So far, it's easier than I expected. Probably because I seem to subconsciously work around Vaughn's schedule."

"That's how hockey wives tend to do it. So, you've been officially upgraded to girlfriend status, but do you think one day you will get an even better title?" She casually throws that in.

I scoff a laugh. "That's probably not on our minds any time soon.

I'm thankful it never once came up during the whole pregnancy and having a baby. Vaughn never went all 'we must get married because it's the right thing to do.'"

"No, he just forced you to move out of your home and to sleep in his bed which you thoroughly enjoy, I'm sure." She gives me a straight-laced look before she flashes her eyes at me.

My head lolls to the side from her humor. "We are sticking to our pace, okay? Besides, not all happy couples see marriage as the be all and end all."

"That is also true. However, I don't know… you both seem to be bringing out this different side that I've never seen from either one of you. You both seem to be surprising all of us."

I bite my inner cheek from the remark because it's overtly true. "I can't deny it. We found our road, and now we're just enjoying the ride, no need to speed."

We both look down at our men, Connor racing down the ice and Vaughn standing near the coaching staff in a suit. I'm confident I've always enjoyed hockey because of the men in suits before and after games.

Occasionally he glances back to search for us and then winks. It's subtle and nearly a secret message. Kind of cute too.

"I'm relieved this is the last pre-season game and now we get a tiny break before the season kicks off," I mention.

Hadley gently touches the top of Nora's head who is tucked away. "I bet. Family time and alone time. We cherish these moments even more. It will be good for you and Vaughn. You're supportive of him, and right now it might feel like his needs are more important, but the sports mindset is a species in itself. He wants everything to go positively for the team."

I lean back to take a sip from my water bottle. "I completely get that, and I'm prepared as well. As much as I hate to admit it, our house is kind of turning traditional, and I don't seem to mind. You know, I keep thinking about returning to work, even though Vaughn said I don't need to. I never agreed, nor have we spoken about it since. However, I'm thinking of only helping with select projects on a freelance basis and the rest of the time being at home with Nora. I kind of get why so many wives of the hockey team run the house."

It feels that everything I worked for in life is no longer relevant when it comes to the professional world. However, I realize that the only goal in life I think I had was forming a family, and here I am. I'm not going to be shy about admitting that. Everyone can do it their own way, both in motherhood or not being a mother at all.

"You're thinking clearly, I can see it. It's great that Vaughn is supportive."

"Exactly, which is why I want to make it easier for him. Who knew laundry would be so fun," I quip.

Hadley snorts a laugh. "You're joking, right?"

"Totally. Vaughn has a dry cleaner he uses." I interlace my arm with Hadley's as we focus on the game. "Who would have thought, Hadley, that a year after your wedding this is where I would have ended up."

"You didn't even need to catch the bouquet and you still had better luck than the now ex-girlfriend of the goalie who caught it."

We both shake our heads in entertainment at this conversation then squinch our faces when we see two defensemen crash into the boards.

"I am relieved that Vaughn's new hockey career doesn't involve injuries," I note.

"Tell me about it. The only thing he has to worry about is stress and unbalanced chakras or something like that." Hadley tilts her head to study the scuffle down on the ice.

"Which is why I don't plan on causing that," I swear.

After the game, Vaughn quickly comes to see us before he heads to a team meeting. Those stolen moments are the best, even if a camera is most likely in the vicinity. He normally whispers something in my ear before looking down at our daughter with a glint in his eyes of pure cherishing. Tonight, it was murmuring into my ear how I should wait up for him. And I will.

———

HENCE, why I am standing in the kitchen barefoot and in his shirt while I load the dishwasher. It's a bit after ten when Vaughn returns home. The moment his foot steps onto the kitchen tile, we head straight to one another.

I grip his loose tie and wrap it around my hand, pulling him closer. "Every time that I see you in this outfit, I'm exceptionally wet."

His smug grin appears before his velvety raspy voice hits me. "My money is on the fact that right now you're not even wearing anything under my shirt." His brows raise.

I yank him to me for a kiss, and he brings his hands to my middle, groaning a sound in the process before he lifts me. The feeling of one hand traveling to my bare ass is heavenly but short-lived because he drops me onto the counter, parts my knees, and traps himself between my thighs.

"Did someone come home all bossy?" my voice rhapsodizes as his gleam meets my eyes.

"Isla, that's the only way I'll be coming home to you."

Letting his tie go, I opt to link my arms around his neck to play with his hair and rest my elbows against his shoulders. "Except you're kind of a softie. You sent me flowers while you were away. I wasn't expecting that."

"Then I asked you to send me a nude selfie," he deadpans, because he hates when I highlight the other side of him. The opposite of the playboy persona that used to follow him.

I hum a sound as our lips begin to dance then fuse together again, his tongue seeking entrance, which I give. Vaughn begins to guide me back, and I can hear the clink of his buckle coming undone.

I'm more than compliant to follow his lead, and I use my forearms for support as I lie back then watch him. "And you are such an excellent provider when it comes to your tongue on my pussy too," I coyly mention to maintain my list of his qualities.

He laughs sinisterly as he drags my body to the edge. "That's because I need you wet and ready so I can fuck you the way I want."

I gape my mouth open right before he dives down and licks me, my body writhing and my moan a little loud, as we are downstairs.

Time and distance do this to us. We don't hesitate, we just give into the moment when opportunity arises. Which is why he works me into a frenzy before I slide off the counter to turn over so Vaughn can take me from behind. I don't even bother taking off my shirt, and his pants are hanging around his knees. But a carnal need possesses us every single time. Slow goes out the window when we have kitchen sex.

It's becoming tradition after we've finished for him to throw me over his shoulder and walk us to the sofa where he pulls a throw blanket over us and turns on the fireplace with the flick of a button.

We should both be seeking sleep, but we can't. Our time is scarce.

Leaning against his chest, our fingers trace one another's.

"The Spinners should have a great season," I note. "They played better than last season from what I could see."

"Yeah, we managed some good trades and draft picks. The team is almost completely altered now. But I don't need to talk hockey. How was it this evening here?"

I half smile because sometimes it feels as though this homelife is his refuge. "Normal day. Bath time, milk time, white noise for sleeping, and night light. She has a good life."

Vaughn kisses my head then brings his lips near my ear, his breath hitting a sensitive spot below my lobe. "And you?" he whispers.

"Watched the highlights from Briggs's game with a bowl of soup, took a bath, then debated which shirt of yours I should wear. I'm running out of options since I seem to wear them when you're away."

"Hmm, guess that might mean you'll be sleeping naked and sending a few pics and videos." His long finger skims down my arm.

Playfully, I pinch him. "By the way, your new luggage arrived. Marketing made sure to have the team logo everywhere... Wait, sorry, no hockey talk."

"I guess it's hard. So far you're staying strong for this professional life of mine."

"It's fine. Ooh, we have the team Halloween party coming up which should be fun." I'm rambling and only stop when Vaughn captures my chin to guide my gaze up to him, as he is looking down at me.

"You're amazing, you know that?" I blush from his apparent sentimental proclamation. "I haven't decided if that makes it easier or harder when I'm away. I have a good thing happening here."

"Don't worry, all is well. Besides, you will be distracted, and I'll be distracted for different reasons, which only means our focus is there when we see one another," I promise.

Vaughn holds me closer and lets a deep breath escape as we both focus on the fire. "Tomorrow morning, I get an extra hour, so let's enjoy breakfast together before we start this routine all over again."

"Sounds perfect." I pause for a second then attempt to study his face in the glow from the fire. "You're happy with your job, right?"

"I am. Doesn't mean I can't complain about the logistics of it."

"Okay, just checking." It is a hard situation that we're in, purely from external factors. We're a new family, and throw in hockey and it's an extra layer.

"We should get some sleep." He's already dozing off, and it makes me smile.

I slip off the couch to offer him my hand. "Come on, our bed will be far more comfortable."

"As long as it has you," he laments.

"Always," I say softly, realizing I'm thinking long-term. "And that was a very cheesy line, but I'll let it go." He chuckles as he follows me along.

————

SITTING around the breakfast table with the bright morning sun flooding in through the floor-to-ceiling windows and only a few leaves on the trees beginning to change color, I watch Vaughn sip from his coffee cup in one hand while his fingers on his other hand wiggle to Nora who is in the newborn insert of the highchair so she's at our level.

My knee is propped up against my chest as I eat some cut-up fruit off my fork. This is heart-melting, all of this. The nights, the morning, him, her, us.

Everything was foggy before, but now it's clear skies for us. I breathe differently.

I smile at Vaughn who gives Nora her toy keys, and then he grabs a piece of toast for himself.

"I'm sorry about last night," he begins.

Lines form on my forehead, as I'm slightly confused. "For what? You took me in a flash on the counter. What am I missing?"

Vaughn's head lolls to the side slightly as he bites his lower lip, debating his words. "Maybe I sounded a little down or out of sorts."

"You're stressed for this season, I get it. I don't see it as a big deal."

He nods once, not quite believing me, even though he should.

But I begin to have a change inside of me, and I can't shake a peculiar instinct hitting me.

A suave smile begins to appear on his face, and he eases in his mood when he looks at Nora blowing a bubble. "I can't believe I ever doubted when you told me about the pregnancy that this maybe wasn't for me. The pregnancy and family thing. It's exactly where I should be."

It was that instinct. A strike hits somewhere near my heart, and an emotion begins to roar inside of me. "What do you mean you doubted the pregnancy?" We never really talked about this because for the most part he jumped right in, it seemed.

"You know, the first thought with the news was if I want to do this or not. There was an option to walk away." His off-the-cuff tone isn't helping this situation.

I sit up and try to wrap my head around his words, but I can't seem to do that fast enough. "You only ever said that you needed time to think and absorb the news. But really you wanted to walk away? You didn't want this pregnancy?" Now I recognize it, that fear that I thought faded is again boiling up inside of me.

"Isla, I was blindsided about the pregnancy, of course my mind went in all directions and options." Vaughn doesn't seem to get the magnitude of what he just said. Nor did I realize how an underlying fear has been lurking still.

I stand up and look at our daughter, which only sets off the tears burning my eyes, desperate to come out. "You thought she might not be something you wanted. I mean, did you think our daughter was just a mistake? I know I gave you an option to walk away, and maybe I feared it my whole pregnancy, but the moment you walked into that room, I realized I didn't mean any of that."

The gravity of my thoughts seems to hit him, and instantly his hand comes out to signal for me to calm down. "Isla, you're taking this all wrong. It's only fair to acknowledge that I was in a position where I had just discovered the truth, and for a millisecond, an absolute millisecond, I thought about an out."

The tear that I've been holding in falls down my cheek. I ignore Vaughn's gaze and begin to unbuckle the safety belt around Nora to get her out. Right now, I don't want to be here in the moment. I need to process and think, most of all shake this shudder inside of me.

"It's still a millisecond, which means eventually you can return to that thought and consider it an option," I sadly point out.

Vaughn stands up. "Isla, you're taking this out of context. I thought we were over this." I begin to walk away from the table, with aggravation filling me just as his phone sounds an alarm that he swipes off. "Shit, I have to get to the airport." He rakes his hands through his hair then drags his hand to the back of his neck to rub.

"You jumped right in or so I thought. But at first you really had doubts and thought of the out I offered?" I wonder.

His facial expression indicates *really?* "Because I see it as a non-issue, especially as this is exactly what I want."

"I never once thought of an out when it comes to her," I state blankly.

"Maybe because you knew from the start and had time to process in a normal way," he replies. But it's a scornful reminder of what I did, and remorse seems to hit us both. Him with his choice of words and me for a secret that I kept all those months. "Isla, this conversation is just sinking me into a bigger hole, when it really is a non-issue. It should be clear what I want, and I'm not going anywhere."

Vaughn walks to me, kisses Nora goodbye, then caresses my cheek with the back of his hand. "We already proved we are good parents. Sometimes we have to let go of wounds to be happy."

Then he leaves.

This is our first big disagreement since what I thought was our new reality. Or is it just an agreement? Either way, it hurts all the same.

But even I know it only takes a split second for someone's mind to change. And what happens when Vaughn does that?

27

VAUGHN

This is not good. Not in the slightest.

Isla is not in a great place now. It's been two days since I left, only because I had to go to Seattle for the team. Since then, it's been basic messages about Nora. I thought the best thing to do is give a little space.

The last thing I wanted was to upset her, but I'm not going to hide the truth either.

Which is why I'm sitting next to my brother in the hotel bar, thankful he was in Seattle for book research, whatever the hell that means.

With whiskey in hand, I sigh again. "I have to turn this around."

"You will. She's going to realize that this is something you both can move on from," Stone assures me.

I rub my forehead in frustration. "We better. This is making me lose focus and setting Isla and me back. Most of all, I can't find it in me to apologize over a thought I once had, because I can't change it. She also needs to allow some understanding to consider how this all came to be."

"Didn't you move on from the whole pregnancy secret?"

I nod to confirm that he is right.

"It's got to be different for her, and you're going to have to meet her halfway to end this lovers' tiff." He lifts his glass to me before taking a sip of his whiskey.

I give him an unamused look for his choice of words. "We are a bit more than lovers, you ass."

Stone smirks. "Yeah, which is all the more reason that you both need to accept that couples have disagreements."

"Should I feel guilty for a thought I once had?" I wonder, because I keep questioning it.

"No, like you said, it can't be changed. A lot of guys may be the same way when an accidental pregnancy happens, let alone finding out late. Even a woman can think it. But like I said, you got over that detail. Give her space. Focus on your daughter, and eventually everything will fade away."

My lips quirk out. "Nah, its more than that. I know it is."

I know a sleepless night is ahead, which isn't great, as tomorrow is game day.

"Okay, then what is your plan of action?"

I nearly groan. "I'm in Seattle. Who plays for Seattle?" I give him a hint.

Stone's voice rumbles a deep laugh. "No way, you're going to talk to *her brother*?"

"Hopefully I come out alive."

"Damn, the guy hates you."

I wince at the thought. "It eased to only dislike lately. Desperate times, desperate measures."

"When is this showdown happening?" Stone inquires.

"I asked him to come here in a little bit. Figured a public place is the best solution, plus tomorrow after the game we head off right away."

Stone grins. "Can I sit in the corner to watch the show?"

I shake my head. "Don't be an ass. Why are you here again?"

"Research," he simply states.

My face turns puzzled. "What the hell could that be?"

His head tips the side slightly. "A woman, actually."

I stifle a laugh. "Since when?"

"Since she pushed me because I threw an apple onto the ground, and she got concerned for a deer."

"Well, that's kind of weird."

He proudly grins. "*Yeah*, but here I am, because she has a book signing. She doesn't know I'm here, but I figured the element of surprise and a basketful of apples to piss her off will do the trick."

For the first time in two days, I have to smile at that ridiculous move. "I can't even process that right now."

Stone grips my shoulder. "That's good, because your murderer just arrived." He tips his head in the direction of Briggs who is standing at the other end of the bar with his shoulders puffed out.

I groan, and my jaw ticks as I prepare myself.

"Going to head to my room." Stone stands.

"No, you're not."

His grin is making me ready to push him like we did when we were kids and he stole my Ninja Turtle. "You're completely right."

By the time he is gone and Briggs fills his seat with a steely look, I feel like I might be regretting my move.

"Okay, Vaughn, you get ten minutes to tell me why I shouldn't beat your ass. Isla didn't tell me what happened, only grumbled some sounds which I feel like were not in your favor." Briggs crosses his arms.

"Hello to you too." I scratch my cheek.

"Spit it out." His tone is stern.

"Your sister is pissed because I mentioned when I found out about the pregnancy that for a split second, I wasn't sure if fatherhood was for me, but a thousand thoughts were in my head, as I was in shock." Honesty is the only way that he will give me the insight I need.

He snickers his disapproval. "Why the hell would you admit that?"

"Does nobody appreciate that I'm being open?" I sigh, slightly irritated.

He looks at me with strong discontent. "Not with Isla. You have no idea, do you?"

"Did I not immediately stay with her when I found out?"

Briggs shakes his head. "Do you know how much Isla wanted everything? The second she told me she was pregnant, she was already more than in. From moment one, she never had a single doubt. So, for her to hear that the father of her child might not have felt the same, then it only adds a hole into the fear she's always carried. She may have been petrified to tell you during her pregnancy about the baby, but she always had hope. As soon as she saw you, she realized her error and wanted only one thing. Then you hopped on the train and now it feels like false hope to her."

I stare at him, waiting for him to explain further, my eyes intent on taking in his knowledge.

"Vaughn, she holds onto the wound of our dad never playing a role. He was around the first two years of my life then completely bailed on our mom when she was pregnant and left before Isla was born. Her biggest fear is that history will repeat with her own child. So yeah, the tiniest bit of doubt will send her over the rails."

My eyes close as realization hits me. How could I not see it? Dots connect of why she may have felt panic as her first instinct.

"Why are you being this open with me?"

Briggs shakes his head. "You may have been the guy I hated on the ice, but you won't be the guy who leaves her. I fucking hate to admit that I see that. But it's also what Isla deserves."

"I'm not sure what to do to ensure she shakes that fear that seems to chase her."

"That's relationship 101. You have to prove to her that you are committed for life. Why the hell am I even pointing out the obvious to you?" He looks at me as though I'm an idiot, and maybe I am.

I roll my eyes to the side and let out a deep breath. "Because your sister isn't anyone. I haven't been in this situation before, and I want to get it right."

"Damn well you will." We stare at one another blankly, then Briggs sighs. "Look, maybe she overreacted. Hell, if I found out when a baby is about to pop that I'm going to be a dad, then yeah, a hell of a lot of thoughts would be in my head too. But just let her win this one and ease her."

Briggs stands and gives me a glare. "Do you love her?"

I think for a second with a realization sinking in. I nod. "Yeah, I do."

"Then tell her, that's a start."

"Thanks, Briggs." I mean it sincerely.

For once, he gives me a sympathetic yet agreeing look. "Fix this." He walks away but not before he stops and turns back to me. "By the way, I have every intention to crush your team tomorrow, even if it's the one I used to play on."

"Figured," I confirm.

"Oh, and our general manager is better, he at least smiles when under pressure. You look like hell."

I tighten my wry smile and hold my two fingers up in the air to wave him off. "A pleasure, as always," I call out.

It only takes a few seconds before I hear a slow clap and turn my head to find my brother casually sitting in the corner on a burgundy leather couch with drink in hand.

I shake my head, not amused. "Of course, you witnessed all of that."

Stone stands and strolls my way before sliding onto a seat at the bar. "Hell yeah, event of the year."

"Great. Add it to the memory pool for future Christmas dinners."

"He made some solid points. We also have some abandonment issues. You completely understand where Isla's mind is, and you know it."

It hurts in me that I now feel her pain. "I do, which makes this all worse."

"When is the next time you see her?"

"In two days."

"Then you have two days to figure out how you will show her that you can relate and comfort her," he reminds me.

My lips purse out with a breath. "You're right."

"And you are also better than the man who let us down. I don't need to tell you that. You love her. It's so obvious but maybe not to her."

I now look at him peculiarly. "Where the hell did you get the basis of this pep talk?"

He grins and awkwardly scratches his cheek. "Apple lady is a romance writer. Might have read a few of her books to prove her wrong and show her that her books are sappy bull that doesn't happen in real life."

"Yet here you are using her wise knowledge."

Stone's face drops. "Shit."

"I'll let you know how it goes."

"Yeah, you will. I would hate to hear that Isla kicks you to the curb or throws you into that lake."

A glimmer of subtle smile hits me. "She won't. I'm not going to let her walk away from everything I will do to assure her."

28

ISLA

Hadley walks next to me as I lead an aimless path through the grocery store. She has Nora in the carrier against her chest.

"*So,* what are we doing here exactly?" she asks with caution.

"Diapers, bananas, hope," I list with my voice, fatigued. My energy is a little low since the other day when Vaughn and I had what I wouldn't say was a fight but a discussion that caught me off guard and cracked a little bit of my heart. Disappointment flooded me, and now I'm not sure what's happening.

Hadley takes hold of the bar on the cart to stop our slow stroll. We're alone in the cereal aisle, which is kind of off course for what I needed, but that's beside the point.

"Isla, I think… you need to put yourself in his shoes."

My face floods with disbelief at the audacity of my close friend taking Vaughn's side. "What? How can you say that?"

"Because, well, given the circumstances, then maybe he deserves a little slack? Shock does a lot of things to people, and since then, he has only proven that he wants to be a dad and be there for you." She's delicate in tone but seems assertive with her theory.

"What is to say that he won't change his mind? After all, he thought once that maybe he shouldn't be involved." My reasoning has to make sense to anyone who listens.

Hadley purses her lips out then rolls them in before she tips her head to the side slightly. "Isla, do you really believe that one day he will wake up and leave? You truly believe that?"

A few ticks go by while I search within me. "Most of me believes he is fully involved for our family. I just… can't shake that tiny piece of fear."

She examines a box of bran flakes, giving us a moment to let my admission float in the air between us.

"When is he back?"

I swallow due to the logistics of time. "Tonight."

Hadley taps the cereal box with her nail. "You're not the only human to have a wound inside of them."

I sigh and look down at my daughter, feeling the crack in my throat as tears threaten to break out. "How could he even think…"

She touches my elbow to comfort me. "He doesn't think it. You know, my dad and I, we had our own issues," she begins. I've never known what they are, but I'm hoping Hadley can give insight. "Things are not always clear, and you might discover something from a time now passed. But sometimes it makes us stronger, the bond between people stronger. We also have to remember that we won't always do things the way our parents did. You have to see that. I know you do because you are the proven fact. We can be better."

Hot damn, she makes that tear fall. "I'm beginning to feel like I overreacted, and now I'm not sure what to do when I see him."

Now a warm smile slants on her mouth. "Maybe you don't need to say anything, just listen."

I nod in understanding but still take a deep breath for courage. "Am I being unreasonable?" I need to double-check.

Hadley's face turns crooked and her demeanor changes. "Okay, Isla, real talk for a second. I'm not going to sugar coat this. Yes." She throws the box of cereal into the cart. "Maybe you are overstretching, but I respect that everyone has a right to feel the way they do. I'm completely team Vaughn because he hasn't done anything wrong. He stepped up within minutes of finding out. I mean, come on, the guy literally saw you nearly about to deliver a baby and still went into action mode… one that gives you everything you've been waiting for. You get everything if you just let go a little. Now, enjoy your bran cereal," she huffs, and my daughter just coos as if she is giving her input.

As much as I'm taken aback by Hadley's abrupt disposition, I can't help but soften inside. I'm not completely ignoring what she said. It's food for thought.

I grab the box of cereal and place it back on the shelf. "Geez, Hadley, at least pick Cheerios if you're going to go on a tangent."

She scoffs a laugh and smiles at me with reassurance. For the first time in days, I feel a light beginning to brighten.

———

I'M SITTING on the living room floor while Nora lies on her back, attempting to reach for the hanging wooden toys on her baby gym while I have a video call with my brother. Pointing the camera at his niece, of course.

"She's smart."

I have to chuckle. "She's reaching for a bell, I'm not sure that's rocket science."

"And? Intelligence starts somewhere."

I shake my head and switch to selfie mode so we talk.

"You called? I saw your game. You kind of annihilated the Spinners. I feel bad saying that, but Vaughn said I'm allowed to quietly cheer you on when you play against them."

Briggs goes quiet, and it isn't often that he doesn't have anything to say. He licks his lips while he looks to his side then back at me.

"What's going on? You don't seem like a man who just won."

"Uhm, I saw Vaughn."

My shoulders slant up to my ears. "And? You were at the same game, it's kind of bound to happen."

His cheeks tighten and he scratches his chin, appearing to get comfortable with whatever he is about to say. "It wasn't at the game."

"Oh." Now I understand why he called.

"We met at his hotel bar, man to man," he explains.

I bite my bottom lip, curious yet scared about what he is about to say. A part of me is petrified that Vaughn sent my brother to deliver heartbreaking news. Even though it makes no sense.

"You should give him a chance."

Immediately, I do a double take. "Wait, what?"

Briggs grins at the camera. "You heard me. Don't make me utter the words again."

"Are you seriously defending him right now? As in, did something happen last night, aliens landing perhaps?" I'm quite frankly astonished.

"Nah, we have to communicate since he is the father of my niece. Most of all, he's the guy who is crazy about you."

A smile tugs on my lips, as it feels extra sentimental that my brother confirms what I've been feeling the last weeks when Vaughn is around. "Yeah… I may have noticed."

"He isn't going anywhere. Don't let tiny things prevent you from moving toward something better."

Now my eyes bug out. "You're giving me a pep talk? Really, is there something in the Seattle water?"

He laughs and leans back on his couch. "Isla, I'm stating the fucking obvious."

I huff yet again today and drop my shoulders. "I'm hearing that a lot lately."

"Listen, I may need to roast him in the wedding speeches if you ever get married. But Vaughn… I don't know… I hate him when it comes to hockey, but he is bearable when it comes to you and my niece. This isn't even about Nora, and you know it. You were just looking for a crack to justify that everything is within your grasp, the whole nine yards." He rolls a shoulder back and dips his eyes as if he wants to downplay his confession. "So yeah, maybe he is a little more bearable than I thought… he'll fight for you."

"Yeah, I will."

The sound of Vaughn's voice from behind me catches me off guard, and my head whips in his direction. I didn't hear him come in. But he's now leaning against the wall with his hands in his pockets and his feet crossed, his face stoic.

I quickly glance back at my phone.

"I guess that's my cue to hang up. Didn't plan this timing, but I don't particularly want to watch this go down." He drags out his words then speeds up. "Bye, Sis." And my screen shows me that the call ended.

Which means that I need to turn back to the scene of Vaughn who has returned and is ready to pick up right where he left off. This time he is calmer, poised, and making my heart thump in a new sort of way.

"I wasn't expecting you this early." I slowly manage to form a sentence.

A glimmer of a faint smirk appears on his lips. "The element of surprise is something we have experience in." Vaughn uncrosses his feet and strides toward us with a bit of swagger that just comes naturally to him.

The moment he enters my bubble, a ripple spreads across my skin. It's anticipation for what is about to come.

He leans down to greet our daughter, an instant smile appearing on both their faces. "Hey there, kiddo, you're growing a little too much for my liking. Slow it down, will ya? You're rolling over and reaching for things. Next thing I know we'll need to baby-proof the fu-… fudge out of this place."

The view of them together thaws my mixed emotions slightly.

Vaughn glances at me. "Let's get her down for a nap and then we can talk. I'll do it." He's already swooping Nora up into his arms before I can answer.

It makes sense, as the revelations that are floating around us shouldn't have little ears present, however, it doesn't help my shooting nerves. I pace a few times around the living room, debating if I should grab a glass of wine, because I need to feel a little more serene if I don't want to be an emotional mess.

By the time Vaughn re-appears, we take a moment to get lost in a gaze. I'm debating if sitting down is a good start to keep the next moments flowing. He doesn't let me decide as he walks straight to me and frames my face in the palms of his hands. His eyes stare straight into mine, ensuring I can't escape from the shackles of his fortitude in this moment.

"I'm not going anywhere, Isla," he whispers. My mouth parts open but barely a sound escapes. "I understand. Really, I do. I can't apologize for expressing the truth," he informs me.

"You kind of threw it back in my face that I never told you," I begin to rehash the other morning, but I keep my tone weak while I blink a few times.

His thumb starts to draw a circle on my cheek. "Not my intention. We can't change the facts, but we can move on from it. I promise I have. I got to see Nora born, and that's what really matters as far as your pregnancy is concerned. You get that, right?" He gently presses his palms tighter against the outline of my face.

I swallow, as this is one aspect that I believe we can both let go of. "I do. We can agree on one thing."

Vaughn steps closer which only heightens the beating in my chest. "We can agree on a lot of things. Hell, we want the same things."

"Maybe I've overreacted, okay, I probably did. But you said that once you thought—"

He cuts me right off. "Shh, Isla. I was honest, but it also takes a millisecond for things to be clear. I had a brief speck of doubt, only for extreme certainty to follow. A commitment that I'm never going to break."

Geez, can these tears stop appearing. Do I even have any left? Because water pools at the bottom of my eyes.

"I'm scared."

Vaughn presses his lips against my forehead and releases his hold on my face, only to wrap his arms around my back to pull me close to his chest. "Fear only makes us do better."

Through my tears, I snort a laugh. "Is that something from your hockey career?"

"It's the truth, though." His voice sounds eased. He holds me tighter, as if he will never let go. "This isn't about our daughter at all. Because we have something to celebrate, as we are the type of parents we hoped to be. I think you are confronted by the fact that we were probably two broken people who were missing something. But now we fit together, and it fixes everything. I believe we are one and the same. Our hope was always lingering. Now we are two people who connect on a different level than we ever expected. It's scary, but it's us."

My mouth begins to quiver. "It sounds so poetic the way you said it, even if it's the truth."

He begins to half grin, with his head tilting to the side. "I may have practiced my speech with Stone on the phone, and he gave a few tips."

I have to laugh at that.

"Stop trying to believe that it's impossible to be this happy. Just accept it."

I nod because he completely peeled away the writings inside my heart. "I don't want you to walk away one day," I whisper, a mumble against his chest where the fabric is now wet from my tears.

"You don't need to want something that you already have. I'm here to stay," he guarantees.

Peeking up to search his eyes, I only see honesty. Especially when his eyes dip down to capture my seeking plea.

With one hand wrapped around my middle, his other slides up to weave his fingers through my hair. "It's like this, Isla. My whole life I've been playing a game. But it turns out the one game that I want is the family card with a woman that I love. I've been waiting for you, and I didn't even know it. I've only ever played to win, and that's the point. Once you win, it's cemented as fact, and you can't go back to change it. Which is perfectly fitting, because this family is the win for the game I've been waiting to play."

His words touch me deep within, even reaching the dark abyss that holds every apprehension and dot of sadness. My mouth slants up slowly. "I think… I needed to hear that… Wait…" It dawns on me. "Did you say the woman that you love?" My head perks to the side as I try to digest a revelation.

That sweltering grin appears again, this time with a fixed sentiment. "You heard that right. I love you, Isla."

Now I can't help but smile through fucking tears. "Is this really happening?"

"We already happened." His voice is neutral as I soak in his words.

I raise onto the balls of my feet to wrap my arms around Vaughn's neck. "I'm sorry for the way I acted."

"Don't apologize. It's how you feel."

"We can really be something… real and raw and the dream that's now fact… especially since I love you too." I say it and realize that this proclamation has been building for months. I never wanted to let the feeling bubble up inside of me. Feeling it wouldn't be wise to assess the overpowering wave happening right now. Because I refuse to let a child be the reason for moving forward if it isn't right.

But this *is* right.

Vaughn kisses me in response, his bottom lips nuzzling my own, preparing me for the passionate kiss that ensues, then sewing in a tenderness that feels as though we are confirming we can move forward. His tongue delves into my mouth, and a dizziness hits me because suddenly my last few days of gray have been replaced with a confidence that everything has fallen into place.

I murmur, and it encourages his mouth to cover mine, ensuring our breath becomes one. I'm going weak from the overabundance of relief and his tantalizing lips. My head falls back which doesn't help, as he immediately brushes his lips down my neck, sending a ripple of sensitivity down to my toes.

"Getting you to bed will have to wait." He nips my skin then drags his bottom lip down before retracing his line back up.

We barely part, his fingers combing a few strands of my hair behind my ear. "We should talk all night. We're on the same page, but we should go over it a thousand times. If you want to have extra reassurance, then we'll put your name on this house. I can draw papers up to ensure you know that you and Nora will always be taken care of. I'm sticking around, but I'll do whatever you need."

I plant my finger over his lips to stop talking. "I trust you. Which means your word is enough."

He pecks a kiss on my fingertip before my hand drops. "Don't hide what scares you, because most likely I share it too. All the more reason we'll work hard to have the best damn family and relationship there is."

I nod and smile as I lick a tear from the corner of my mouth. "You're saying all the right things, I believe every single syllable… but I can't get these ridiculous tears to stop. It's like full-on waterfall, hormones, or the vitamin powder in my morning shake making me produce enough water for the lake," I joke.

We both let out a stunted laugh, accepting that the hard part of our conversation is over.

"It's been a crazy few months. Let it go. If you're still like this at Christmas then I'll grab a bucket so we can start a reservoir," he teases.

A quick kiss happens before we whisper again our I-love-yous.

The next hour we sit on the sofa with the fireplace on and recap our months ahead until end of season; we don't go past that in the calendar. We're both okay with going slow or fast, we're seeing where our relationship takes us.

Inside of me I'm celebrating because it's going to be everything we always wanted.

We already are.

29

ISLA

Vaughn looks at our daughter blankly. "What in the world is that?"

I give Nora an extra squeeze. "It's a snowman unicorn onesie. See? The horn has a little snowflake on it."

He blinks his eyes several times. "I'm just going to roll with this."

I chortle a sound. "Hadley's mom got her a unicorn-themed outfit for every holiday. Fear Easter with all your might," I warn.

Vaughn's face finally breaks, and he can't help but laugh.

I just arrived at the team's family holiday party. First, lunch with Santa, then ice skating—with safety because there are going to be a lot of kids around.

Vaughn takes our little girl from my arms to make our way into one of the rooms used for gatherings. It's nothing too fancy, a buffet and decorations. I'm fairly confident the two odd-looking gingerbread men were made by two rookies, and now we all have to vote who decorated which. One is missing an eye or possibly a mouth, I can't tell. It's also noisy, with a lot of aws and ohs.

It's been a few months since Vaughn and I solidified our direction, which is why everything feels like an easy breeze. We still have his hectic schedule, which means moments are sparce until the end of season, but despite our frantic lives, everything feels as stable as can be.

"Let's go take a seat over there." Vaughn indicates to Violet, Declan, and their kids. I follow, taking note that Nora is making little noises as she responds to us now, with eyes more magical.

Vaughn mutters to me when I reach his side. "We won't stay too long. I'm eager to see you in your naughty elf costume."

I shake my head, because under no circumstances am I bringing holiday characters into the bedroom… stockings and lace inspired by winter colors, sure.

We settle at the table, with a camera instantly hitting our peripheral view, which tends to happen at team events. They know they need to angle to keep Nora's face out of view; maybe we'll change our minds later. At games, she's so bundled up that I'm not sure they could even get a clear view.

"What are you two up to for the three token days off at Christmas?" Violet asks while Declan talks to someone at his side.

Vaughn brings an arm around my shoulders and, being the talented man he is, holds the baby in his other arm. "Taking it easy. My brother will join us for dinner, and my favorite brother-in-law is back in town." Vaughn smiles tightly.

I playfully turn my head to pretend to bite his arm. "He loves it. They're becoming fast friends," I say, because their relationship is nearly a 180 to a year ago. Meh, let's settle on a 90-degree angle.

"I forgot to ask. Didn't you two have an anniversary not so long ago?" Violet wonders as she hands her toddler a cucumber slice.

Vaughn and I look to one another with affection, then it twists into a goofy grin.

"You mean, do we celebrate our anniversary on the date of a hurricane?" I ask, trying to hide my smile.

"Well…" Violet shrugs. "We all kind of know the creation date of your little angel. Just assuming that's the date that you chose for your anniversary. One year is a little milestone."

"It is, which is why Isla flew out with Nora to our away game," Vaughn explains.

Violet looks at us, unamused. "Boo. Who wants to celebrate an anniversary with a baby? Albeit they are cute, but alas, a baby. Seriously, go find some alone time."

I roll my lips in, attempting to keep my tongue in check. "We do find time together, don't worry."

"Oh, I think it's our turn with Santa," Vaughn lies and stands up in record time. I play along and follow him in the direction of a dressed reindeer.

"She was a little too blunt," he states.

I wave him off. "It's okay, we're friends. Our playdates for the kids mean we don't need to hold back, plus those playdates might entail breaking out a bottle of wine around three o'clock."

"Moms who wine, sounds about right."

We approach the deer, and then it happens. At first a tiny squeak and then the quiver of Nora's little mouth before a high-pitched cry hits our ears.

Oh fudge, someone doesn't like the costumes descending upon us.

"Well, no cute first Christmas photo for us." Vaughn begins to bounce Nora in his arms.

"Was this ever going to go as planned? Last year I found out I was pregnant, this year I discover our child hates people in costumes, except when she's wearing one herself," I casually mention.

Vaughn side-eyes me before quickly kissing my cheek. "Sounds like your year only got better."

"Yeah… yeah, it did," I lament.

———

SNAP.

"There is the golden shot," Stone says as he examines his screen, as he just took a photo. It's fun having him around. He moved to Lake Spark like he said he would, which also means he stops by even when Vaughn isn't around. Believe it or not, he is a baby whisperer too.

It's Christmas Day, and we just managed to get a calm baby to comply with our photos by the tree.

"The party is here," Briggs announces, as he must have come in through the back. He's holding up a six-pack, which is kind of hilarious considering this house is anything but simple.

Briggs sets the beer on the counter then strolls right into the living area to drop onto the sofa on the other end from Stone.

"Where's your girlfriend?" I ask.

"Ivy will be here in a bit. Her casserole needed a little more time in the oven, and I wanted to be sure that I get enough time with my niece since I have to fly out tomorrow," Briggs explains.

Vaughn and I stand but leave Nora on the rug so she can admire the wrapping paper that catches her interest.

Stone tips his nose up at Briggs. "Just remember that the better uncle arrived on time."

Briggs gawks at Stone. "I'll prove to you that I can out-uncle you…" He snaps his fingers. "In a minute flat."

Vaughn shakes his head, almost annoyed. "Let's leave the Hunger Games for another day. What are the chances you can show me your teamwork skills to watch your niece for a few minutes?" Vaughn requests from both.

They both have a stiff look and raise their posture. It's utterly ridiculous, but they'll soften the moment they see Nora roll over or shriek in delight.

"On it," Briggs announces.

Vaughn and I both smile as we walk down the hall where we grab our coats and boots then walk through the garage to the back patio where a fire was already started a little while ago. Vaughn thought we should have options for where we sit today, and he wanted to deep fry a turkey with Stone, which honestly, I don't see it being a success.

He sits down then pulls me onto his lap. "We get a few minutes alone." He flashes his eyes at me.

The snow on the ground isn't light, but still the lake looks breath-taking, even with ice on the shallow water.

"Only if you keep me warm," I purr into his ear and link my arm around his.

"Are you happy?" he asks, and I notice a glint in his eyes.

My own eyes squint for a second. "Very. Are you even questioning it?"

"Not at all. It's been a great day, plus we even have a special cheese plate for snacks," he jokes.

I stifle a sound. "Remember how this all came to be? A ridiculous cheese conversation and your flirting skills."

"Ah, so I charmed you from second one."

"Absolutely."

We both sigh as we sync our breathing and stare out to the view. This is peaceful and quiet, yet completely intimate in a way, as it's us.

"We're going at the right pace? You and me?" Vaughn asks.

"Geez, what's with the interrogation? Are you okay?" Now I look at him with worry.

His smirk appearing means trouble. He has a trick up his sleeve, I feel it in my bones. "May I just throw an option out on the table?"

"Why do I feel like this isn't our usual 'catch-up and take a moment to be with one another' chat?" I lean back slightly to examine him more, as if I'm trying to solve a riddle. Then I notice Stone and Briggs standing by the window, pretending that they're not observing. It seems Briggs won the battle of who gets to hold the niece.

Vaughn grabs my attention when he breaks my daze with a kiss to draw me back to him. A long kiss, and I can feel his hand rummaging around our middle, as if he is adjusting his coat.

Our lips part, but I just want to dive in for another kiss. Yet I can't because his eyes have locked with mine.

"I'm giving us a few options for when you're ready, but I think our slow ship has sailed." His gaze lowers then pops back up.

It was a sign for me to search, and when I follow the line of his coat zipper down to his hand, I gasp.

A ring.

A big ring.

A ring that signals commitment.

A forever type of ring.

Forever.

We're not fast, we're not slow. We're exactly on track.

Bliss hits me in a swoosh, and I throw my arms around his neck again. "Yes."

"Uh, I didn't even ask. It could be a promise ring for all you know."

"Oh, shut up, you know you want to lock me in for the future."

His suave grin appears while he begins to grab my finger. "Marry me, Isla. We can wait or not, but just know that I want the longest game there is… with you."

The moment the ring slips onto my finger, my life changes yet again.

Crap, tears again. Happy tears, yet still tears.

We're going to need to start that reservoir.

6 MONTHS LATER

The sun is holding out on us, yet the dark clouds to the west should be concerning.

I'm confident Illinois June weather will hold out for us a little longer. Enough time to seal this deal, anyway.

Standing at the end of the aisle in dark jeans and a white linen shirt with the lake behind me, I wait impatiently for the next moments of this day.

I glance to my side and my face still puzzles. Who the hell knew that Briggs would go this far for his sister, that he would be the guy to marry us, since he got ordained somewhere between scoring goals.

"Remember, I'm not retired yet, which means my physical strength may be strong in the event it is ever needed," Briggs informs me in a low voice so only I can hear, but then he pats my shoulder, and a beaming smile hits him.

My eyes travel to the front row where Hadley is sitting with Connor who winks at me, and Declan and Violet smile as they wait for the big show. My brother gives me a thumbs-up from where he sits at the end of the row.

Isla and I decided that we would do simple. Casual yet elegant were her words. A buffet is waiting for us inside, with a hell of a lot of champagne, cheese, and cobbler.

My instinct has me search the aisle until the end, and there she is.

We acknowledge one another with soft smiles in a perfect image that will be imprinted in my brain and heart. Isla's in a thin-strapped white gown that looks like a second skin and has a plunging line along her breasts. She's radiant, especially as one hand holds a small bouquet, and her other arm is carrying our daughter who is in a puffy dress with a headband bow that I didn't quite agree with.

Everyone stands as Isla begins to walk down the aisle, every step feeling too slow.

Halfway down, with everyone admiring her beauty, she stops. But I don't stress. Nora is reaching her arms out for me and squeaking "Dada," which earns an *aww* from the guests. Isla laughs then decides to set Nora down who immediately starts her speeding crawl following the ribboned cloth and heading straight to me.

She steals the show, and I kneel down to pick her up.

Then we continue on with the wedding schedule.

When Isla reaches me, we can't break away from our smiles.

"Should we hand her to someone in the front row?" Isla asks, with her eyes going wide.

I turn to my future brother-in-law. "This is going to be quick, right? We requested the speedy version."

"Relax, I listened," Briggs assures us.

"Then she stays with us," I confirm.

And that's how we do it. We get married holding our daughter. The fastest ten-minute service of our lives, which is good, as storm clouds are rolling in.

I have no choice but to hand Nora to my brother because when Briggs tells me I can kiss the bride, I do just that. I tip Isla back and kiss the hell out of her. We're not going to start our life as husband and wife with a chaste kiss, uh-uh, not in my book.

The guests clap and cheer as sprinkles of rain begin to fall. Thunder in the distance breaks our kiss.

"It's going to storm," I tell my wife.

She wraps her arms around my neck. "Storms are my favorite when they're with you," she hums.

"I'm aware, which is why I paid someone up there to arrange it, assuming it makes our wedding night even better," I joke.

Isla giggles right before I pick her up and twirl her around.

"Set me down, Husband. How am I going to get inside?"

I dip my mouth down while she's in my arms and kiss her real quick. "I'll carry you, I always will."

We take a second to soak in this moment between us, with her lips gently tugging into a sentimental smile right before I carry her back down the aisle.

———

TOASTS WERE DONE, first dance complete, cake cut, bouquet thrown, and our daughter crashed from a sugar rush since we let her have two spoonfuls of cake.

Declan, Connor, and my brother are sitting outside on the terrace while they drink their whiskey. Luckily, the storm went to the south. I join them since Isla is with Hadley and Violet freshening up, which means she'll be a solid twenty minutes.

Someone offers me a glass of champagne, as they have an entire bottle sitting on the side table.

Connor tips his glass up. "A toast."

Declan reaches into his blazer's inner pocket to pull out some cigars and passes one to each of us before we all hold up our glasses.

"To locking down your wife in the most unconventional story that will be awkward as fuck to explain to your daughter one day." *Okay*, so that's Connor's speech.

It causes all of us to glance at one another.

"Listen, kid, you accidentally got married in Vegas," Declan points out to Connor. "And you really want to call Vaughn's road to marriage unconventional?"

"Says the guy who used the Dizzy Duck Inn for his secret escapades with my aunt before my dad found out," Connor counters.

Christ, we're going down a rabbit hole.

Declan points his glass to Connor. "Hey, first off, the Dizzy Duck is sacred ground in Lake Spark. I hope the new owners keep it that way. Secondly, Violet and I are married not by accident or due to a hurricane baby."

My brother looks between all of us. "Holy hell, what does this town do to people?"

Declan relaxes. "Normally hockey and finding the love of your life. Haven't you discovered that yet?" With his tone flippant, he directs his question to Stone.

"That's clear. And by the way, one of the new owners is also a retired athlete. We used to attend a few charity events together," Stone mentions, which causes me to half smile, because truthfully, he invested as a silent partner with the new owner.

"If he changes the name of this fine hotel then the town will riot," Declan points out. Stone tries to keep his face neutral as he listens.

"Aren't we supposed to be having a speech now?" I attempt to get us back on track.

My brother snickers, then his jaw ticks while his cheeks tighten.

"Something you'd care to share?" I poke.

We give up on a proper speech for a toast and all clink our glasses before taking a sip, but my focus snaps back to Stone.

He takes another gulp. "Actually, I'm kind of in a predicament with someone, a writer…"

"Apple lady?" I ask, my voice one-toned.

"Yeah, something like that… a bit more complicated, though…"